"This is in the running for favorite book of the year I've read."
—Paul Weimer, *SF Signal*

"Schafer's fantasy first novel is a welcome variation on the apprentice mage and thief fantasy adventure...grabs you from the start, with a couple of characters struggling to overcome horrible pasts, and proving surprisingly likeable despite their flaws."
—*Locus Magazine*

"*Whitefire* is one of the best novels I've read in 2011...What starts off as an adventure novel of rock climbing and trekking quickly turns into a full blown fantasy romp full of magic, ne'er-do-wells, and flawed heroes."
—*Staffer's Musings*

"*The Whitefire Crossing* is excellent, entertaining adventure fantasy."
—Stefan Raets, *Fantasy Literature*

"[Courtney Schafer's] evocative narrative makes images leap off the pages...One thing is for sure: There is more depth than meets the eye in this novel...*The Whitefire Crossing* is an original, if unusual, fantasy title that shows a lot of potential."
—*Pat's Fantasy Hotlist*

"A tense adventure fantasy, with magic, intrigue, and engaging characters in a desperate race to cross a deadly mountain range...an exciting original read."
—Martha Wells, author of *The Cloud Roads*

"Smuggling, magic, secret identities, a dark mage coming after the heroes, a grand adventure and trek over dangerous mountains...Schafer's world-building is exquisite...I can't recommend this book enough."
—*Bibliotropic*

THE
TAINTED
CITY

OTHER BOOKS BY COURTNEY SCHAFER

The Shattered Sigil
   Book I: The Whitefire Crossing

THE
TAINTED
CITY

BOOK II OF THE SHATTERED SIGIL

COURTNEY SCHAFER

NIGHT SHADE BOOKS
SAN FRANCISCO

Cover art by David Palumbo
Cover design by Martha Wade
Interior layout and design by Amy Popovich

Edited by Jeremy Lassen

First Edition

ISBN: 978-1-59780-403-5

Night Shade Books
www.nightshadebooks.com

To Kevin, who already knows the joy of adventure

CHAPTER ONE

(Dev)

I wedged my fingers higher in the crack snaking up the boulder's overhanging face. A push of a foot, a twist of my body, and the overhang's lip was nearly within reach. Good thing, since I had to finish this little warm-up climb fast, or risk a whipping if the shift bell rang before I got to the mine. Dawn's light already streaked the gorge rim far above me with gold, though it'd be mid-morning before the sun rose high enough to touch the reedy mudflats here in the gorge's depths. Beyond my boulder, clumps of men in grime-streaked coveralls trudged toward the yawning black mouth at the base of the cliffs. Lights bobbed in jerky rhythms within the tunnel as the night haulers hurried to finish sacking their quota of coal.

"Spend one instant longer crawling up that rock instead of joining your crew, boy, and I'll choke you blind."

The torc around my neck heated in warning as overseer Gedavar spoke. I jerked my fingers free of the crack and dropped to land in the mud at the boulder's base. Sudden sweat laced my palms. What in Shaikar's hells had brought Gedavar sniffing around? With the day shift soon to start, he should be relaying the minemaster's orders to the crew chiefs, not skulking about behind the prisoners' barracks. The thin copper disc of the stolen glowlight charm hidden beneath my sock cuff felt large as a wagon wheel.

"I'm on my way," I muttered, and made to dodge past him.

"Hold." Gedavar barred my path. Easy for him to do, since he dwarfed me not only in height but in bulk. All of it solid muscle, despite the gray salting his close-cropped dark hair and the lines seaming his scowling, olive-skinned face. "I heard tell from Lanedan he saw you sneaking around the quartermaster's yard yesterday. Looking to steal, were you?"

"I wasn't stealing—or sneaking, either. Jathon sent me to tell the quartermaster we only had two pallets of sacks left. I didn't touch a gods-damned thing." That was nothing but truth. The charm in my sock hadn't come from the quartermaster's stores. I'd palmed it off the corpse of a miner who'd suffocated after hitting a pocket of poisoned air. Alathian charms carried little more than glimmers of magic, but I didn't need magic for my plan to ditch this muck-infested pit of a mining camp. I just needed copper.

Gedavar smiled, not pleasantly. "I've a mind to make sure. Spread your arms."

Shit. He didn't truly believe I'd stolen anything from the quartermaster. He knew perfectly well the man kept his supply chests warded as tight as gem vaults. But Gedavar never missed a chance to scrag me. If he searched me thoroughly enough to find the charm, weeks of planning would come to ruin. I had to distract him.

I lifted my arms and sneered, "What, the camp jennies won't have you, so you've turned desperate enough to grope scut-men?"

Gedavar's broad face purpled. He twisted a ward-etched gold ring on one thick finger. The torc tightened around my throat until I choked and doubled over. A shove sent me sprawling face-first into mud black with coal grit. "Don't you mouth off to me, you piece of goat shit!"

The torc cinched tighter. Red hazed my vision. I thrashed, fear rising with the pressure in my lungs. I'd meant to provoke him into punishing me without a search, but not to strangle me outright—

A sucking squelch of footsteps announced a newcomer. "Leave him be, Gedavar. I can't get a proper day's work from him if you throttle him senseless before he so much as touches a coal sack." Jathon's raspy voice lowered to a mutter. "You want that Council mage lurking in the minemaster's office to burn your hide?"

The torc loosened. I sucked in a lungful of air and promptly set about coughing my guts out. Between coughs, I cast a wary glance at Jathon, whose weathered brown face was clean of expression, his thick-muscled arms crossed. Thank Khalmet he'd called Gedavar off—but why had he bothered? He'd never shown anything but cold disdain for me, the lone prisoner assigned to his crew of coal haulers.

Gedavar leaned over me and spat. "*That's* for Council mages and their gods-cursed orders. Daylight labor's meant for honest Alathians who've earned the right, not foreign lawbreakers. By rights this little weasel should be on scut duty with the other criminals, so deep in the tunnels he withers from lack of light."

"No argument here," Jathon said. "I'd be chewing bile if it was my nephew got shoved off to work the blacklights so a prisoner could take his place."

I froze in the act of swiping away spittle. I'd long since guessed from the muttered asides and resentful glares of Jathon's haulers that some poor bastard had gotten booted from their crew for my sake—but Gedavar's nephew? No wonder Gedavar hated me. Coal hauling might be backbreaking work, but it was as safe as picking wildflowers in a meadow compared to tending finicky, powder-fueled lights in the deeps of the mine.

Jathon shook his head and went on. "Bad enough to lose a good crewman on the orders of some sleek citified bastard of a mage. But after Halden's fuck-up with the oxen last week, we're a hundred sacks down on the quota. If you choke Dev 'til he can't haul, you leave me shorthanded with no hope of catching up before the tally tomorrow. We don't meet tally, me and every decent man on the dayside crew won't see our full pay this month. I don't doubt Dev deserves a little discipline, but for the twin gods' sake, man, do it after his shift."

Ah. Money, I understood as a motive. I kept my eyes down and prayed Gedavar would listen. Like most of the miners here, Jathon was no prisoner. He'd come to Cheltman Gorge some fifteen years ago, lured by the generous pay the Alathian Council offered skilled men willing to leave civilization behind, and he'd been crew chief over the dayside coal haulers for near half that time. Even authority-drunk pricks like Gedavar didn't care to antagonize a miner with such seniority.

"You want him breathing, teach him to rule his tongue." Gedavar aimed a vindictive glare at me that made it plain I'd only delayed further abuse, not escaped it, and stomped off toward the cook shed.

I let out a relieved breath, taking comfort from the press of the glowlight charm against my ankle. If my plan worked, I'd be free of Gedavar right along with the rest of this shithole. If it didn't…well. Gedavar would be the least of my worries.

Jathon clamped my shoulder in a meaty hand. He steered me over to join the ragged line of men plodding away from the squat wooden cabins of the camp toward the mine.

"Thanks," I told him. "I'm in your debt." Regardless of his reasons, it wouldn't hurt to show my very real gratitude.

He gave a contemptuous snort. "I didn't do it for you. I won't have my crew's pay docked because a scut-man's too dumb to keep his mouth shut. You slack even one instant today and I'll strangle you myself, no matter what that mage thinks about it. Gods only know why the Council cares for the life of a foreign charm smuggler."

Despite his harsh tone, his dark eyes held a glint of curiosity. I shrugged and took care to keep my face blank. The minemaster refused to speak on the matter, but the miners weren't fools. They'd seen me arrive in Cheltman Gorge accompanied by a mage of the Council's Watch—who instead of dumping me off to work the darkest deeps with the rest of the scut-men, had not only insisted I be assigned to the far safer role of daylight laborer, but had stayed.

For two gods-damned months, now. Not the same mage—every two weeks, they switched off. Besides lanky, curly-haired Talmaddis, who'd brought me here and had shown up again last week, I'd seen a middle-aged woman with a scarred cheek, and a short, stocky man with skin near as dark as mine. Not that the identity of the mage mattered. The snapthroat charm I wore was prison enough, but the lurking mage was the sandcat pacing beyond the bars.

The hell of it was, the Council didn't really care about me. I was merely their leverage against Kiran, the Arkennlander blood mage I'd helped sneak into Alathia. Kiran had only wanted a life free from his sadistic viper of a master. He'd meant to renounce his magic entirely rather than cast spells fueled with torture and murder.

The Council hadn't bought a word of that when they caught us. Oh, they let Kiran live, in hopes of picking his brain for knowledge of forbidden magic, but they wanted him leashed tight. And Kiran had shown the Council he'd do anything to help me, out of gratitude for my saving his skinny ass from his master Ruslan.

Which meant the Council would never let me go. I'd be stuck here as combined bait and hostage for the full ten years of my sentence—doubtless longer, if the Council had their way. But back in Arkennland, a child's life depended on me, her time fast running out. I didn't mean to fail in my promise to save her, no matter how many mages the Council sent to sit on me.

Jathon prodded me toward a veritable mountain of bulging burlap sacks beside the mine entrance. Drovers were hitching oxen into traces attached to a set of giant interlocking wheels. From the topmost wheel, a rope thick as a man's leg and studded with metal hooks carried coal sacks up the cliff to a second pullwheel at the gorge rim. There another set of haulers unloaded the sacks to pack into convoy wagons headed for Alathia's cities. Coal sacks removed, the rope snaked back down through a series of smaller guide wheels bolted to ledges on the cliff face.

The harsh clang of the shift bell sent echoes ricocheting between the gorge's sheer sandstone walls. Jathon shoved me over to a barrel-chested Alathian whose skin bore the deep pockmarks left by blacklight powder embers.

"You haul with Nessor today," Jathon told me.

Nessor's mouth curled in a brief, slight grimace. He stared over my head as if I didn't exist. As always, I stepped up as casually as if I hadn't noticed his disdain.

Jathon raised his voice. "Step lively, lads! We've still a chance for our full pay if you put your backs into hauling."

The drovers shouted to their oxen, and the wheels groaned into motion. Nessor and I heaved the first fat burlap sack up within reach of a pair of hookmen perched on a platform beside the rope. My back and arms burned with the sack's weight, though nowhere near as badly as they had when I first came. I'd been a frail shadow of myself then, my body still healing from my use of the deadly blood magic charm that had all too briefly reawakened my childhood Taint.

A bolt of bitter longing skewered me at the memory. If I were still Tainted, I could toss these coal sacks sky-high by will alone. Or better yet, smash my neck torc to gleaming shards and fly straight over the Whitefire Mountains to my home city of Ninavel in Arkennland.

Yeah, right. That charm was locked away in some Council vault now. Assuming the Alathians hadn't destroyed it. And if the Taint lasted past puberty, I wouldn't be in this fix in the first place.

Long weeks of hauling coal had restored much of my strength, though I still looked a scrawny scrap compared to the rest of Jathon's crew. As we lifted an unending stream of sacks, my gaze drifted up the cliff. Beside the second guide wheel station, purply-brown lines of kalumite streaked the craggy sandstone.

Kalumite was innocuous enough on its own, hardly worth a decet per hundredweight in Ninavel. Yet I'd learned in my Tainted days that kalumite flecks added to copper filings in a certain precise ratio, mixed in oil and smeared over a charm's surface, made the charm's magic flare up in a conflagration that burned it out within seconds of the charm triggering.

The copper from the glowlight charm in my sock would provide more than enough filings, and a flask of oil, a file, and a pot of burn salve lay hidden in a crevice on a boulder by the barracks. Better yet, I had a plan to fox the mage to stop him hunting me down once I ran. All I needed now was a fingersweight of kalumite.

The oilmen had lubricated all the guide wheels yesterday, as they did once each month. And two nights ago, I'd sneaked into the storeroom and dumped a bucket of coal grit into the cask of oil marked for the second guide wheel station. Surely it wouldn't be long now before the contaminated oil on the wheels abraded the rope enough to—

A sharp twang and an ear-rending squeal sounded above. The great wheel beside me juddered to a halt, oxen straining against taut traces.

Jathon cursed and squinted up the cliff. "Stand down, lads! A strand's snapped and snarled a guide wheel." His black brows lowered in a scowl, and I knew he was thinking of the minemaster's quota. He whistled to a drover. "Run for the laddermen, and be quick."

Beside me, Nessor thumped down a sack, his brow beetling in a frown. "Laddermen are working the Dragon's Maw today."

"Don't I know it." Jathon's scowl grew more thunderous than ever. The Dragon's Maw was another mine entrance a good mile off. The minemaster had decided a week back to string a secondary supply rope up the gorge wall there. It'd be high noon before the laddermen managed to stow their gear and hurry back, let alone set up to clear the snarled wheel.

The drover dashed off. I wiped sweaty hands on my trousers and straightened.

"You want that wheel cleared without waiting on the laddermen?" I asked Jathon. "I know a way that'll have you hauling again in no time."

Jathon cast a black look my way. "Don't think to try some scam on me, boy. A puny charm smuggler who knows nothing of minework can get us hauling again? I think not."

"I wasn't just a charm smuggler in Arkennland. Outriding was my trade, and I've guided many a convoy across the Whitefires. I've climbed cliffs that'd make your laddermen piss themselves, and I can rig ropes with my eyes closed. Give me a knife and a length of hitch line, and I'll climb up to that wheel, set a bypass, and cut the tangle free."

Jathon swung round. His dark eyes narrowed. "Never seen a scut-man so eager to get back to work."

"I didn't say I'd do it for free. Though seeing as how you pulled Gedavar off me this morning, I wouldn't ask much in return."

Jathon's suspicion shifted into hard appraisal. Plenty of scut-men tried to strike bargains for extra rations or shorter work shifts, though it was a whipping offense for miners to give us coin. Jathon tapped his ward-etched ring, twin to Gedavar's, and looked pointedly at my torc. "I could order you up that cliff."

"You could," I agreed. "But a man does his fastest work for reward, not under threat of punishment."

Jathon grunted and crossed his arms. "What kind of reward are we talking, here?"

Now came the tricky part. Ask for too little, and Jathon would get suspicious again. Ask for too much, and he'd laugh in my face and refuse. He might order me up the cliff anyway, but I didn't care to count on it. Thankfully, the morning's confrontation with Gedavar had sparked an idea.

"Make sure Gedavar stays off me. I don't fancy getting strangled every time I blink, all thanks to an order I had no hand in. But he won't cross a crew chief. He'll back off if you make it plain you'd take any further 'discipline' poorly."

Jathon stood silent, frowning. I kept my stance casual despite the churning of my stomach.

"Send him up, Jathon," Nessor said, to my surprise. "If you don't, we'll never see that coin. We've all seen him crawl up those boulders by the barracks every morning like he's got feet sticky as a blackfly's." He spoke with all the pleading I hadn't dared use. Mutters of agreement came from the hookmen on their platform above.

Jathon fixed Nessor with a disgusted look. "Lost all your pay to Temmin last night, did you?" His gaze settled on me again. "A boulder's one thing. But this cliff...wouldn't you need iron spikes like the laddermen use?"

I snorted. "Pitons wouldn't do much good without a partner to belay." As his brows lowered, I hurried to assure him, "No need for partners or pitons on something this easy. See all those cracks and ledges? Khalmet's hand, the climb's no harder than scaling a tower stair." That part was true enough. Water seeps and moss slimed the cliff in spots, but the cracks angling up toward the guide wheel station were dry.

Jathon glanced across the gorge to the minemaster's office, tucked amidst a gaggle of storehouses against the opposite cliffs.

I tapped the torc around my neck. "I can't go anywhere." Talmaddis had warned me when he brought me to Cheltman that the torc would choke me unconscious if I got more than a quarter mile from the mining camp.

"And if you fall?"

I laughed, unable to help myself. "Fall? On this?"

"Cocky little bastard, aren't you?" Jathon chopped a hand at a drover. "Get a spare hitch rope." As the drover scrambled to comply, Jathon pulled his belt knife. "Fine," he said to me. "You get that wheel unsnarled in time for us to make the quota, I'll talk to Gedavar—but only if we meet the tally, understand?"

I interlaced my fingers in the sign for a bargain sealed, then remembered he'd never been streetside in Ninavel. "Bargain's made."

He handed over the knife and the drover's coil of hempen rope. "Get to it, then."

I tucked the knife into my belt, slung the rope across my chest, and leaped for the cliff. I didn't have the spike-nailed boots I'd used for climbing in the Whitefires, but my work boots would serve well enough for rock as fissured as this. My blood sang as I wedged my fists in a slanting crack. Gods, it felt good to climb something more than a lump of a boulder, even if the cliff was a crumbling mess of sandstone instead of the clean, sharp granite of the Whitefire peaks.

A rush of memory overwhelmed me: the sun blazing down from an indigo sky, turning quartz-studded cliffs brilliant as icefields. Sharp peaks stretching to the horizon, and below my airy ledge, Cara's lithe form scaling the cliff with flowing ease, her blonde hair shining near as bright as the rock.

The stab of pain this time wasn't so easy to ignore. Cara. I missed her, desperately—and feared for her, too. Right before the Alathians dragged me off to the mines, I'd begged her to forget any ideas of rescuing me, and instead return to Ninavel to seek out the cunning bastard of a spy who represented my one last hope of saving young Melly from a life of mindburned slavery. Melly's father Sethan had been Cara's friend same as mine, though Cara didn't owe Sethan the way I did. But now I lay awake nights praying Cara wouldn't do anything too rash. Her skill in the mountains was unparalleled, but she had little experience with the darker games played by ganglords and shadow men.

Exactly why I needed to get the hell out of Alathia and sneak back to Ninavel. I stabbed fists and feet one after the other into the crack, twisting my wrists and ankles to lock each successive limb into place as I moved up the cliff. Past the first guide wheel station, the crack grew too thin for my boots. I slowed, placing my feet with care upon crumbling ledges. A shower of dirt and pebbles pattered down the cliff each time I moved.

My heart beat faster as I neared the offending wheel. The guide station was a simple scaffold of iron bars bolted over a sloping ledge. I unslung the rope from my chest, shook it out, and tied one end round my waist. Four feet into the rope, I tied a quick clover knot around the lowest scaffold bar. Dangerous to leave so much slack, since the force of even a short fall on a slack hemp rope could easily snap it, but I needed the freedom of movement if I wanted that kalumite.

I glanced down the cliff, and froze. Beyond the upturned, black-streaked faces of haulers and drovers, a lanky man in a blue and gray uniform was picking his way over the mudflats.

Talmaddis, the Council mage. Fuck! The miners didn't know the kalumite-and-copper trick, but a mage might. If he guessed my intent on the cliff, my chances of escape would vanish quick as frost on a firestone charm.

I mastered panic. He might only have glanced out the minemaster's window, seen me climbing, and decided to investigate. If I could scrape and stow the kalumite before he got close enough to spy me properly, I might still have a chance.

Hurriedly, I adjusted my stance to block my right hand from view and set the edge of Jathon's knife against a fat purple vein of kalumite. With my left hand, I picked at a dangling strand of snarled rope.

A low, grumbling roar froze my knife hand mid-scrape. Startled shouts rang from below, Jathon's gravelly voice rising over the rest.

"Earthquake! Get clear—"

The roar swelled to drown him out. The cliff shook my feet from the ledge like a horse shivering a fly from its hide. In pure, useless reflex, I tried to halt my fall with the Taint, as if I were still a snot-nosed kid rather than a good decade past my Change.

The dead spot in my mind didn't so much as twitch. I dropped like a stone. The rope attaching me to the guide wheel station snapped taut, near cutting me in two, and I slammed into the rock below the ledge. I twisted and made a desperate grab for a handhold, even as the vicious pull on my waist vanished.

I got one hand on the ledge rim, had an instant to register the rope end slithering past, the fibers sliced clean through—and lost my grip on the still-shuddering rock.

Air whistling past, the spiked teeth of the pullwheel rising to meet me, and all I could think was *Oh, fuck*—

Something yanked me sideways. The pullwheel flashed past. My plunge abruptly slowed to leave me hovering with my nose and chest not a hands-width from the ground.

For a moment I could only gasp, unbelieving. Then I looked up and saw Talmaddis on his knees in the muck, eyes shut and one hand extended toward me, the rings on his fingers glowing softly silver. Behind him huddled a group of open-mouthed haulers. The white rush of shock faded, and I laughed, shakily.

"Wouldn't want to lose your prize hostage," I said.

Talmaddis didn't answer, only lowered his hand. I splatted down into mud. The ground no longer shuddered, though the clatter of falling rocks echoed through the gorge and waterfalls of sand hissed between ledges.

A tortured shriek of metal from above made us all jerk and duck. I rolled, getting a glimpse of thrashing haul rope and a dense spiderweb of black bars, rapidly growing larger.

The pullwheel station from the clifftop—Khalmet's hand, it'd crush us all—

Talmaddis shouted a string of words, in a high, keening wail. Fiery lines streaked the onrushing iron. The fire spread, the bars crumbling to ash in its wake. I scrabbled to my feet and staggered back, still half expecting to be crushed flat.

All that reached me was a rain of embers. My heart felt like it might leap straight out of my chest. The miners cowering beside me were whey-faced, some babbling prayers.

Talmaddis's curly head was bowed, his hands braced in the mud and his shoulders trembling. His breath came in rattling gasps. Jathon was shouting, urging men away from the cliff. The smarter ones had run, dark forms scurrying to the relative safety of the reedy flats near the stream winding through the camp. Yelling men boiled out of the mine tunnel. On the opposite side of the gorge, another swarm erupted from the night shift's barracks. Several cabins had collapsed into a jackstraw of logs.

I took a step backward, then another. I should run. Now, while Talmaddis was too drained to cast another spell, and the overseers too busy to bother about a stray prisoner. I could find another band of kalumite somewhere further down the gorge, get my snapthroat charm off before anyone thought to hunt me…

"Mage!" Gedavar pushed past me. His eyes stared white from a face black with coal dust. "The quake—the main tunnel's collapsed at the Broketurn junction! Three hundred men trapped beyond, and the blacklights have gone red, means the air's turning bad—can that cursed magic of yours break through the rubble?"

Talmaddis raised his head. His olive skin had gone sickly grey, the laugh lines bracketing his mouth turned deep as chasms. "I've nothing left," he said in a raw whisper. "But my casting was more than enough to trigger the Watch's detection spells. They'll come…"

"When?" Gedavar demanded. A good question. I held my breath, waiting.

Talmaddis eased back on his heels. "For a spot so far from a city or the border, they'll need time to target a translocation spell…" He dragged a shaking, mudsmeared hand across his brow. His rings had changed from silver to dead black. "A few hours, no more."

Gedavar raised a fist, as if he'd strike Talmaddis if he dared. "Twin gods curse you, man! The blacklights are red. Those men have minutes to live, not hours."

I shuddered. Men suffocating in darkness, begging for help that wouldn't come…damn it, I couldn't let this stand. I leaned around Gedavar.

"What's this shit about waiting, Talmaddis? You need more power to cast? Then take more! There's plenty of life here." I swept an arm at the oxen, at the ferns trailing beside the cliff seeps.

Talmaddis matched my glare. "I'm no blood mage! In Alathia, our magic is fueled by our own energies. We do not steal life from others."

"You're going to let those miners die, all for your gods-damned principles? For fuck's sake, nobody's asking you to torture men to death! Who cares if you kill a tree, or an ox? Kiran could—"

"Kiran ai Ruslanov spent years training to work blood magic," Talmaddis snapped. "Do you think it's so easy? I haven't the faintest idea how to raise power as a blood mage does without either destroying myself or everyone in this gorge."

The haulers in earshot were staring at me as if I'd confessed to trafficking with demons. Rural Alathians took an even more jaundiced view of magic than the Council. They nattered on about how the use of magic poisoned a man's soul and invited the gods' anger. Even an officially sanctioned mage like Talmaddis was viewed with deep distrust. Foreigners like me who smuggled illegally powerful charms through the Alathian border were considered little better than plague-carrying vermin. As for blood mages, who even in Arkennland had reputations worse than Shaikar's devils…the miners thought the Council's policy of execution far too lenient a fate.

Jathon spoke from behind me. "No choice but to dig our men out, then." He gripped Gedavar's shoulder. "Go tell the minemaster. I'll organize a crew."

The anger leached from Gedavar's face, leaving it drawn and old. "Aye. But you haven't seen the cave-in. It'll take days to get through, even if we use blasting powder. My Rephet and the others…well." His throat bobbed in a hard swallow.

"Wait," Jathon said. "The Broketurn junction, you said? An air shaft slants in at the tunnel split. If we lower a powder charge down and blast through to the trapped side, they'll have a chance at good air until the mages come."

Gedavar pointed to a jutting prow of rock high and to the side of the mine entrance. The prow's underside was a stair-stepped series of overhangs. Water dripped from cracks green with moss. Beneath one overhang lay a round black mouth. "With the haul rope downed, not even the laddermen can reach that shaft."

Jathon turned. His dark eyes met mine. My fists clenched behind my back. Gods all damn it, I should've run.

You still can, an inner voice whispered, in the sly tone of my old partner Jylla. *Say you can't help, the climb's too hard. Accidents happen in the mines. Those men knew the risk, and you owe the Alathians nothing. You won't get another chance like this again.*

Of the two of us, Jylla had always been the clever one. Doubtless that's why she was living in luxury in Ninavel instead of slaving away in this muck pit. Yet I couldn't shake the image of Gedavar's nephew, dying by inches in darkness, all because I'd taken his place. If I hadn't climbed, if Talmaddis hadn't expended precious magic saving me…maybe Talmaddis wouldn't have been too drained to help.

"I can reach the shaft," I told Jathon. "But I'll need pitons this time." I wasn't such a fool as to think I could climb a serious overhang unaided on such rotten rock. Not to mention the risk of aftershocks after a quake so large.

Jathon clapped me on the back, hope bright in his eyes. "Gedavar, get a charge. We'll save those men yet."

Gedavar wore a dark, skeptical scowl, but he strode off, shouting to the men milling about the mine entrance. Doubtless he figured he'd nothing to lose.

"Have you any men who know ropework?" I asked Jathon. "I need a belay from the ground."

"The cartmen work with ropes and pulleys. I'll find someone and get you a set of those spikes from the supply chests." Jathon hurried away.

Talmaddis was watching me. "You surprise me, Dev," he said softly.

I barked out a laugh. "What, you thought I'd run?"

His mouth pulled in a wry, weary smile. "You considered it, I'm sure. For not doing so—I thank you. If you save the trapped men…the Council will also be grateful."

"So grateful they'll let me go?"

Talmaddis looked down. I sighed. "That's what I thought." I glanced up at the twisted spars jutting outward from the gorge rim, all that remained of the pullwheel scaffold. "If you're so grateful, tell me one thing. Are quakes this strong common in Alathia?"

I'd heard tell that the Arkennland side of the Whitefire Mountains had been plagued by earthquakes, way back before Lord Sechaveh built the city of Ninavel in the bone dry desert of the Painted Valley. When he'd offered mages the chance to work magic without law or restriction in exchange for supplying the city's water, likely he'd asked them to stabilize the ground as well. Ninavel hadn't endured a major quake since the mage war some twenty years back, when so much magic was thrown around it unbalanced all of nature. I'd only been a toddler at the time, but I'd grown up hearing the stories.

Maybe earthquakes were natural in Alathia. But if they weren't, I had a terrible suspicion I knew what—or rather, who—might've shoved the world out of balance.

"No," Talmaddis said. "Quakes so strong are not common."

His hazel eyes locked with mine. Within them I saw the echo of my own dread, and the name neither of us wanted to say.

Ruslan Khaveirin. Kiran's master, the strongest mage in Ninavel, and a vicious, clever bastard at that. Who'd want revenge not only on the Alathian Council for keeping his apprentice, but on me, personally, for crossing him. If he was casting spells in an attempt to rip apart the defensive wards that barricaded all of Alathia from foreign magic, I could well believe the earth might split and shudder in response.

And Kiran, kept under the Council's thumb in Tamanath...the chill in my blood was nothing compared to the fear he'd endure when he realized Ruslan was coming for him.

I winced and shoved aside memories of a white-faced, desperate Kiran. I couldn't afford to worry over him now. First I'd reach that air shaft, do my best to keep those miners alive. Then I'd think on Ruslan, and what I might salvage from the embers of my escape plan.

CHAPTER TWO

(Kiran)

Kiran straightened on his stool and rolled his shoulders in an attempt to relieve cramped muscles. The sky beyond the high slits of the workroom windows burned crimson with approaching sunset. The labyrinthine chalk lines of his spell diagram had already grown difficult to read; soon further work would be impossible without additional illumination.

He eyed the inert crystal sphere of the magelight perched at the table's end and set his teeth. Thanks to the binding the Alathian Council had cast on him, he could no longer cast even the simplest of spells. He'd grown accustomed to the constant gnawing rasp of the binding against his *ikilhia*—his soul's fire, the source of his power—but not to the bitter ache of yearning every memory of magic brought.

The charm gleaming beside his slate seemed to mock him, mutely. A burnished vambrace of silver long enough to cover a man's arm from wrist to elbow, the metal was encrusted with gemstones and etched with sigils. Even with his inner senses dulled by the Council's binding, Kiran could feel the vast reservoir of magic bound within, a deep, soundless thrum that shivered his bones. The charm's dizzyingly complex spellwork had allowed the blood mage Simon Levanian to walk through Alathia's supposedly impassable border wards. Not just once, but on multiple occasions, with the Alathians none the wiser.

The Alathian Council had spared Kiran's life on his promise he could decipher Simon's spell and explain how he'd breached their defenses. More, they'd promised if Kiran could provide the knowledge quickly enough, they'd hear a plea for Dev's release from the mines.

Frustration tightened Kiran's throat. He laid a hand on the charm, once more seeing Simon's magic in a dense, fiery scrawl across his inner sight. He was so close now to a full sketch of Simon's pattern, but the last piece was by far the most difficult. How had Simon managed to stabilize the flow of the charm's immense energies without distorting his spell into uselessness? All week, Kiran had sketched diagram upon diagram, struggling to find the solution. Yet his every attempt contained some fatal flaw.

After all he owed Dev, he'd sketch diagrams until his fingers fell off, if that was what it took. But if he wanted light to work after sunset, he'd have to ask Stevannes.

Kiran glanced at the far side of the workroom, where Stevannes sat before another broad table of polished cinnabar wood. The arcanist's auburn head was bent over an array of slender malachite and jasper rods set within a charcoal sigil sketched on the table. Above the rods, the air rippled as if seen through heat haze. Occasional hints of viridian and indigo tinged the shifting air, reminiscent of the way Simon's charm had stained the air with color as it revealed and penetrated the border wards.

Alathia's foremost expert on defensive magic, Stevannes had made it all too clear he bitterly resented any interruptions by the Council's pet blood mage to his own investigation into the breach of Alathia's wards. He had a savagely sharp tongue at the best of times; and today his mood had been black from the start.

Yet success was so nearly within Kiran's grasp. He squared his shoulders, resolving to hold his calm no matter what Stevannes said.

"Pardon the interruption, but—"

A staccato series of raps on the workroom door silenced him mid-sentence. Surely Kiran's guard hadn't come to collect him yet? Usually he was allowed to keep working so long as Stevannes remained, and Stevannes's dedication was so fierce as to be disturbing. He worked hours that would put a blood-bound slave's to shame, and rarely left before midnight.

Stevannes twisted on his stool to aim a swift, vicious glare at Kiran, and flicked a ringed hand at the door. The black lines scribed around the doorframe glowed briefly silver as the workroom's wards released.

The door creaked open to reveal a slender, straight-backed young woman whose blue and gray uniform bore the copper braid of a lieutenant of the Council's Watch.

"First Lieutenant Lenarimanas." Stevannes's glare vanished. He stood and bowed with formal precision. A wash of cerulean shot through the shimmering air above his table. "You've come to remove the blood mage?" He sounded hopeful.

Kiran gripped his slate. "Lena. It's early yet, and I'm so close to completing this pattern. If I could just have a few more hours…"

Lena nodded to him, her brown face grave under its crown of dark braids. "You needn't leave, Kiran. I bring a message for Stevannes from Captain Martennan." She handed a sealed letter to Stevannes and came to peer at the diagram on Kiran's slate. "You've made progress, then? The captain will be pleased to hear it."

Stevannes snorted as he broke the letter's seal. "Progress? Hardly. His spell diagram hasn't changed a whit all week. All he does is dally over his slate and waste my time."

Silence was always the better option with Stevannes, but Kiran couldn't let the remark go unchallenged. Lena might be the closest thing he had to a friend in Alathia, even allowing him to call her by the short form of her family name, but she reported every scrap of information on his work to her superior, Captain Martennan, and through him, the Council.

"Deciphering these last power pathways is more difficult than I'd hoped," Kiran said, carefully mild in tone. "Simon used a technique for them I'm not familiar with."

Stevannes's iron-gray eyes lifted from the letter. "You're a blood mage, same as he was. Either you're stalling, or you're incompetent."

"I'm working as fast as I can," Kiran protested. "You can't fault me for not instantly grasping Simon's methodology. He wasn't my master. His mind follows different paths than Ruslan's. It's not an easy task, to think like him—"

"Easy enough for you, I'd imagine," Stevannes snapped. "All you blood mages think alike, seeking power without the least shred of morality. The Council should never have agreed to this farce of yours. Better to put down a rabid dog before it bites—"

"Stevannes." Lena spoke with cool authority. Though she was only in her mid-twenties and a full decade younger than Stevannes, as Martennan's first lieutenant she outranked even a master arcanist. "You know how important this work is, and you cannot think your insults are helping."

Stevannes's shoulders stiffened. "Why do you defend him? You know what he is."

"I judge men by their actions, not hearsay," Lena said.

"Hearsay!" Stevannes looked incredulous. "He raises power by murdering innocents. Not even he denies it." He jabbed a finger at Kiran. "I saw the report Pevennar and Alyashen wrote after they examined him. Even with his power bound, he still steals life from everything around him. He's not a man, he's a parasite."

"What?" Kiran's slate dropped from nerveless fingers to clatter on the table. Six weeks ago he'd agreed to spend a day being poked and prodded by the healers in the Sanitorium in exchange for a scry-vision to confirm Dev's fair treatment at the mine, but the healers had barely spoken to him. They certainly hadn't mentioned anything like Stevannes's claim.

"Don't pretend you didn't know," Stevannes said. "You may have fooled Lenarimanas with your meek lamb act, but you don't fool me."

Kiran ignored him, looking to Lena. "Is what he says true?"

Lena sighed. "Yes."

Kiran could only stare at Lena, mutely. The dissonant discomfort of the binding heightened until pain clawed along his nerves.

Lena's brows drew together. "Kiran, you're not harming anyone. The power draw is minuscule. Alyashen and Pevennar think it's completely out of your control, like your heart beating. They have a theory it's meant to prevent you from aging."

Kiran put his head in his hands. He'd known the *akhelashva* ritual Ruslan had performed when Kiran came of age involved more than anchoring the mark-bond that permanently linked their minds and souls. He'd even known Ruslan had created a connection between Kiran's body and *ikilhia* to allow magical repair of physical injury. But he'd thought that connection internal to himself, and under conscious control.

What else had Ruslan done to him without his knowledge?

"Did they find anything else?" His voice sounded tinny and faint in his own ears.

"Nothing conclusive," Lena said. "The healers say your blood reacts strangely when exposed to the substances they use for healing diagnoses, but they don't know the cause. Pevennar believes that when Ruslan mark-bound you, he altered your body in a variety of subtle ways to make it more congruent with a blood mage's style of magic."

Stevannes issued a derisive grunt. "More congruent with slaughter and torture, you mean. Let me guess," he said to Kiran. "It feels *good* when you kill someone, doesn't it?"

Power rushing in, sweet and burning, like sunlight after endless dark—Kiran couldn't get enough air. "I don't kill people."

Stevannes's mouth curled, his eyes horribly knowing. "Simon Levanian is dead, isn't he? He tried to use you in a spell, and you destroyed him. And what about the convoy men you killed in the mountains?"

"The drovers' deaths were an accident! I tried to take only from animals when I cast to divert the avalanche from our convoy. And I had to cast—if I hadn't, the slide would have killed hundreds." Yet Kiran couldn't meet Stevannes's gaze. Harken's gentle, weathered face still haunted his dreams, accompanied by the shadowed figures of the drovers Kiran hadn't known.

"So you claim," Stevannes said. "Do you think a handful of feeble excuses for your murders are enough to make us forget who you truly are?"

Kiran flinched. Ever since the Council had spared his life, he'd cherished the hope that one day the Alathians' distrust of him would soften. That they'd stop seeing him as a threat, and allow him the time and materials he'd need to discover some means of dissolving his mark-bond. Yet if Stevannes's attitude was any indication, that day would be years in coming—if it ever did.

"*Enough*, Stevannes." Lena's voice was colder than he'd ever heard it. "I will not warn you again."

Stevannes drew himself up. "Forgive me, First Lieutenant. I merely wished to clarify the point." He thrust the opened letter at her. "Tell Captain Martennan I will indeed search the Parvyi treatises for—" He stopped, his head tilting.

The floorboards under Kiran's feet shivered. Chalk rolled along the tabletop to fetch up against his slate as the tremor subsided.

Stevannes dropped the letter and knelt to place his hands on the floor. Lena mirrored the movement, frowning. Kiran put his own hand on the table and strained his inner senses, but felt nothing beyond the dissonant throb of the block on his power.

"Another tremor." The disdain had vanished from Stevannes' voice.

"Go," Lena said. "I'll check."

"Be certain." Stevannes stood and left without a backward glance.

"Lena? Another tremor—there've been others?" Kiran hadn't noticed any, but the quake had been so swift and subtle. Locked in concentration on his spell diagram, he might easily have missed it.

Lena approached, close enough he could have counted the smattering of dark freckles that marked her nose and cheeks. She reached for his temples. He shied away.

"What are you—"

"Kiran. This is necessary." She reached again.

Reluctantly, Kiran held his ground. Her hands settled lightly on his skin. A slender thread of power snaked through his head, swift and shining as quicksilver.

"My apologies." Lena stepped back. "I needed to examine your binding."

"You think the tremor was my doing?" The words came out sharper than Kiran had intended, but the notion was so ridiculous. From the moment the Council had bound him, he'd been unable to use his magic for anything but passive reading of charms, living day and night with the constriction of their spell flaying his inner senses raw.

A faint frown creased her forehead. "I do not."

"But others do, and not just Stevannes." Kiran's hands clenched. "Isn't it enough that you keep me bound like this? That I've done everything the Council has asked?"

"The Council is entrusted with the safety of Alathia," Lena said coolly. "Do you truly think their caution with you is unreasonable?"

Kiran didn't answer, his attention caught by Stevannes's still-active spell. The shimmer above the sigil had taken on a sickly gray tinge, mottled by holes with dark, crackling edges. Dread coalesced in Kiran's chest. He pointed at the spell.

"If that represents your border wards…it's Ruslan, isn't it? He's casting against Alathia, and your wards are failing." He'd known this day would come. But so soon—he'd thought Ruslan would need more time to analyze the ward patterns. For all Ruslan's hot temper, he was far too clever to cast against an enemy in haste. He'd waited twenty years to strike down Simon Levanian, until Kiran had unwittingly presented him with the perfect opportunity. Kiran hadn't dared hope for nearly that length of time before Ruslan moved against the Council, but he had thought he'd gained a few seasons' grace.

"Our wards hold." Lena passed a hand over the sigil on Stevannes's table. The gray shimmer vanished. "Stevannes's spell showed…merely a warning." But her eyes slid aside from his, her motions abrupt as she collected Stevannes's carved stone rods.

"You don't deny Ruslan is casting against you." *Return him to me, or I will tear down your country stone by stone,* Ruslan had said; and the Alathians had refused him.

Lena surveyed him, a sharp line between her brows. "There is no direct evidence of Ruslan's involvement."

Kiran blinked. "What? But—"

"I cannot say more." Lena turned away. She thrust Simon's charm into the warded copper chest sitting beside Stevannes's neatly ordered stacks of treatises. "Put away your things. You're finished here for today; I'll escort you back to your quarters."

Her clipped tone said he'd learn nothing further. She must have been ordered to keep silence; and while Lena might treat him with calm kindness, she'd never disobey an order.

Kiran's mind raced as he picked up chalk shards with cold, fumbling fingers. No direct evidence…given the cunning Ruslan had displayed against Simon, the Alathians had to realize Ruslan's capacity for subtlety. Yet if Ruslan cast against Alathia, why should he conceal it? The Council would suspect him regardless. Far better for Ruslan to strike openly, counting on his dark reputation to instill further fear and division within the Council.

It didn't make sense. Yet Kiran couldn't shake the bleak certainty within. His reprieve from his master, brief as it had been, was over.

✳

(Dev)

I knelt amidst bedraggled reeds and thrust my hands into the chill shallows of the stream. Weariness dragged at my eyes and turned my muscles to lead. The sun had long since set; stars spattered the strip of sky visible between the black bulwarks of the cliffs. The peeping of mossfrogs echoed from the seeps, punctuated by clanks and shouted orders from the mine as crews worked to shore up the main tunnel. In the dim silver glow of Talmaddis's magelight, the blood crusted on my hands and forearms was as dark as the grime coating my clothes. Talmaddis stood silent beside me, his shoulders slumped, as I scrubbed gore from my skin.

Jathon's idea had worked. The powder charges I'd eased down the airshaft had blasted through the back side of the cave-in. The shaft wasn't large enough for a man to pass, but it allowed enough good air through to keep the miners who'd survived the initial collapse alive until a crew of mages from the Watch finally showed up.

I'd hoped for another chance to slip away, but Jathon kept me dangling from pitons beside the airshaft to relay messages to the trapped men until the mages managed to create a narrow passageway through the cave-in. The effort of keeping the tunnel stable and the air breathable apparently took all their concentration; they left it to the rest of us to evacuate the injured. I'd spent the rest of the day climbing through rubble under Talmaddis's supervision, seeking those survivors too badly hurt to make their own way out.

I grimaced and scraped harder at my fingers. Talmaddis had given me bloodfreeze and skinseal charms, but even so, I'd lost count of the men who died before I could lever them free.

I'd seen my dead mentor Sethan in every gray, pain-wracked face. *Splintered bone gleaming in the pitiless glare of high altitude sun, blood pouring from Sethan's nose and mouth as I screamed curses and shoved at the boulder pinning him...* I yanked my hands from the river.

"That scut-man, the one whose crushed leg I had to sever—will he live?" The miner had looked as young as Kiran, somewhere in his late teens. His screams had dwindled into ragged croaks as I'd sawed through the flesh of his pulped leg. Thank Khalmet, he'd fainted before I had to drag him out the crack I'd slithered through to reach him.

"He may." Talmaddis sounded as tired as I felt, though he no longer looked so haggard as he had in the immediate aftermath of the quake. His rings were still black, but he'd sparked the magelight easily enough. I took that as a warning. He might not have the full strength of his magic back yet, but he'd need only a trickle to deal with an untalented man like me. "Captain Jevarrdanos brought a full supply of herbs and elixirs, and several among his Watch have made extensive study of healing spells. If anyone can save a man from wound fever, they can."

I swiped my hands dry on my pants, uncaring of the grimy cloth. Coal muck I could live with, now I'd consigned the dead men's blood to the river. "If he's not dead by the time they bother with a mere scut-man."

"This isn't Ninavel." Talmaddis's voice gained an edge. "Those worst injured will be treated first, regardless of their status."

"Yeah? If the Watch is so concerned for the injured, how come you're still breathing down my neck instead of helping cast healing spells?" I pointed at the distant lantern-lit bulk of the camp's mess hall, which now served as a makeshift infirmary.

"Because I'm not an idiot." A brief, sardonic smile touched Talmaddis's mouth. "You think I haven't sensed that glowlight charm you've got stuffed down your sock? Admit it: you have some ill-conceived plan to run."

My heart jolted. I stood, carefully casual. "No harm in carrying a perfectly legal charm in case I get sent on an errand in the tunnels. I just don't want it stolen off me. I share barracks with criminals, you know."

"Ah." Talmaddis's tone made it clear he didn't buy that for an instant. "Well, consider my presence as an appeal to your better judgment. A clever man like yourself must realize the dangers of venturing outside our protection. Ruslan Khaveirin bears you no love, and you well know the torment a blood mage can inflict."

Yeah, Ruslan was a vengeful, sadistic bastard. Yet Kiran had once said, *He thinks of untalented men as tools to be used or cast aside, not enemies worthy of attention.* It was Kiran he'd shatter the world to reclaim, not me. With all Ruslan's attention focused on tearing down Alathia's wards, I figured I'd stand a fair chance of surviving a return to Arkennland, so long as I was quiet about it. Hell, I'd probably be safer there than here, if the day's quake was any indication.

"After today, I'm not overly impressed with your protection," I told Talmaddis.

"Even after I saved your life twice? You're a hard man to please," Talmaddis said dryly.

I winced, remembering my fall, and the plummeting pullwheel station. "Right. Uh. Thanks for that."

"You can thank me by refraining from anything foolish." Talmaddis passed his hands over his face. "Especially tonight. I warn you, I won't be in a forgiving mood if I'm roused from my bed to drag you back to camp."

"Don't worry," I told him, truthfully. "I'm not even sure I can make it back to the barracks." Better anyway to wait until the latest crew of mages returned to Tamanath before I tried again for some kalumite, no matter how frustrated the delay left me. Far easier to fox one mage than a horde of them.

"Nevertheless, you'll understand if I insist you hand over that glowlight charm." Talmaddis stuck out a hand.

"You want it, it's yours." Copper wasn't hard to come by, not with half the chipping crews wearing the weak little glowlight and sharpening charms considered legal here. I slapped the charm into his waiting palm. "Trust me, all I want right now is sleep. Stand over my cot all night if you like, so long as you don't wake me 'til the day bell rings."

I moved for the barracks, but Talmaddis gripped my shoulder. "Hold a moment."

A magelight bobbed toward us over the mudflats. As it got closer, the holder proved to be the scar-faced female mage I'd seen before. Mud smeared her uniform and her graying hair was fraying loose from its braid, but her walk remained as rigidly precise as a soldier on a parade ground. She dipped in a perfunctory bow.

"Talmaddis, we've received orders from the Council." She brandished the jeweled gold band of a message charm at him. "Captain Jevardanos and the others are to remain and assist in returning the mine to normal operations, but you and I are to take him"—she jerked her head at me—"back to

Tamanath, without delay." She shifted to face me, and rattled off, "Devan *na soliin*, the Council wishes to review your sentence in the light of your assistance in the rescue effort."

"Oh, for fuck's sake," I snarled. I wasn't so dumb as to believe that little campfire tale. With Ruslan clawing at their door, the Council surely wanted both me and Kiran right to hand. Shaikar take the Council! Planning a getaway from the mine had been tricky enough, but in Tamanath I'd be buried up to my ears in mages and wards. Though in Tamanath I might get to see Kiran. Maybe I could help him, find some way to ensure the Council didn't throw him to Ruslan to save their asses...I squelched the thought. Best thing I could do for Kiran was to escape the Council's clutches so they couldn't use me as leverage anymore.

I rounded on Talmaddis. "Can't I get a few hours sleep before you two spell me off to Tamanath?" I needed a chance to think. My brain felt like cold sludge. My only certainty was that I'd never escape the Watch in the heart of their power.

"Unfortunately, we won't be returning via translocation spell." Talmaddis sounded wearier than ever. "A spell of that magnitude requires far too much power to be cast here. We'll have to travel overland. So yes, I think it wise to get some sleep before leaping on a horse."

I perked up as I recalled the maps I'd seen of Alathia. Tamanath was some ten days' ride from the Cheltman mines, along a road that traveled a maze of sandstone gorges and verdant forest, and passed within a few miles of the border gate at Loras. Maybe I wasn't so screwed as I'd thought. Even mages had to sleep sometime, and where there was sandstone, there was kalumite.

Talmaddis turned to the scar-faced mage. "We'll leave at dawn. Aiyadaren, please inform the minemaster we'll require three horses and a pack mule; and tell Captain Jevardanos I'd take it as a great favor if he could spare someone to sit watch on the barracks for me until morning. I'd prefer not to trust solely in Dev's collaring charm tonight." He cast a jaundiced glance at me.

"Oh, I'm not going anywhere," I assured him. Not yet. But once we rode out into the wild, I sure as hell didn't mean to let them get me within spitting distance of Tamanath.

※

"Welcome to Tamanath," Talmaddis announced, in a voice so bright I wanted to hit him. My fists clenched as our carriage passed under a freestanding stone arch patterned by crystalline swirls that reminded me all too well of the wards on Alathia's border gates. Behind us, unadorned black carriages waited in a patient, orderly line to undergo inspections just as thoroughly nosy as those at the border. We'd bypassed the line and gotten waved through after a quick exchange between Talmaddis and an officious young mage. Aiyadaren had slept through the whole thing, propped against the carriage window with her mouth slack and her breathing heavy. She hadn't so much as twitched since we exchanged our horses for the carriage at a guard outpost a mile back.

Shaikar take her, and Talmaddis too. For ten days they'd stuck closer than river leeches, traded off shifts watching me day and night, and worst of all, they'd done something to my snapthroat charm so it strangled me unconscious the moment I got more than ten feet from the one on duty. Bruises still ringed my throat from the last time I'd tried.

Beyond the arch, rolling fields changed over to whitewashed houses half-hidden by trees and neatly trimmed hedges. I slumped in my seat and fixed my gaze on the shining, jagged line of peaks barely visible above the eastern hills. Longing and frustration twisted my heart. The Whitefires had never felt further away.

"No need to look so sour," Talmaddis said. "Tonight, not only do you get to sleep in a real bed, but you'll be spared the pleasure of our company while you do it." He flicked a hand at himself and Aiyadaren with a wry little grin.

"Khalmet's hand, you mean you'll actually let me alone for two heartbeats? You're not worried I'll slink through your border the moment your back's turned?"

"Not from a properly warded room, you won't," Talmaddis said. "Preferably one far from me. You snore like a rock bear."

"You've got me confused with her." I jerked my chin at Aiyadaren, who chose that moment to let out a bench-rattling snore. Talmaddis laughed.

My mouth twitched, despite myself. Aiyadaren's glacial reserve would've fit right in among Jathon's coal haulers—the whole trip, she'd spoken to me only in terse orders—but Talmaddis was different. His dry, easygoing humor seemed completely unfeigned, and he had a repertoire of outrageous campfire stories that rivaled a convoy man's. He'd said he spent some years with the Alathian embassy in Ninavel before ending up as Captain Martennan's second lieutenant. His time in Ninavel might explain both the stories and the lack of a stick up his ass.

Friendly or no, I never forgot he was my jailer—and neither did he, damn him. I scowled out the window as hedges gave way to tidy storefronts with flowers trailing from windowboxes. If I couldn't slip my leash to cross the border, I needed a new plan to get myself free of this mess.

We'd had three more quakes on the journey here. None of them as strong as the one in Cheltman Gorge—the last tremor had been hardly enough to rattle a cup—but I'd seen the grim glances Talmaddis and Aiyadaren exchanged afterward. They were worried.

So was I. If the Alathians got desperate enough, I figured all the Council's sanctimonious talk about refusing to bow to demands from foreign mages was worth less than mule piss. Bargains or no bargains, they'd toss Kiran and me to Ruslan in an eyeblink if they believed the alternative was Ruslan raining magefire down on Tamanath. I thought of Ruslan's cold, cruel smile, and shuddered.

Our carriage turned into a broad square with a central fountain carved of golden stone. Beyond loomed a forbidding gray hulk of a building. No flowers brightened its rows of tall, narrow windows. Instead, the stone surrounding each slit bore the black whorls and spirals of inset wards.

"Ah! The Arcanum, at last." Talmaddis leaned to look out the window with the eager relief of a man delighted to see home. He elbowed Aiyadaren, who twitched and straightened mid-snore. Her stern face softened when she caught sight of our destination.

I eyed the Arcanum with a lot less cheer as our carriage pulled up to the arched entryway. Talmaddis had told me it served as both a military barracks for the mages on active duty in the seven Watch companies, and a scholars' institution for those charged with maintaining Alathia's defensive magic.

A single mage waited to one side of the heavy wooden doors. Instead of holding himself piton-straight, he slouched against the wall with his thumbs hooked in his belt. His face was hidden in shadow, but the braided silver cord signifying a Watch captain encircled the gold seal of the Council on his uniformed chest.

I recognized that deceptively casual stance. Our greeter was Captain Martennan of the Seventh Watch, who'd first arrested Kiran and me. Not that I remembered it, having been unconscious at the time. I'd had my fill of Martennan in the days afterward. He played the sympathetic advisor, but I'd seen the cool calculation lurking behind his show of good humor. I'd bet a thousand kenets he'd been the one to suggest me as the Council's lever to make sure Kiran did whatever they asked.

Talmaddis bounded out of the carriage the moment it stopped. He bowed, hands crossed over his chest, as Martennan emerged from the archway. Martennan's dark hair was longer than I'd last seen it, standing up in soft spikes instead of cropped close to his head in typical Alathian style, but the bright smile on his round face was as irritatingly cheerful as I remembered.

Martennan made a bow of his own and pulled Talmaddis into a brief, laughing embrace, saying something I couldn't hear.

"Out. Now." Impatience tinged Aiyadaren's voice. No doubt she couldn't wait to wash her hands of me.

"I'm going," I muttered, and climbed out into the courtyard, Aiyadaren close on my heels.

Martennan turned to me, all warm courtesy. "Dev. I'm delighted to see you safely back in Tamanath. I hear we've many lives to thank you for."

He spoke with a drawling accent far different than the usual clipped speech of city Alathians; I'd learned in the mines the drawl was common to those born in the rugged hills lining Alathia's distant coast. As ever, the sharp intelligence in his black eyes set my stomach jumping. If the Alathians meant a word of all this gratitude, they'd be aiming it at Jathon, not me. Jathon's idea had saved those men; I'd only been the pack mule.

"You want to thank me, Martennan? Then let me talk to Kiran." *Let me make sure he's not so naïve as to trust you,* I added silently. Last I'd seen, Kiran had been lapping up Martennan's helpful act.

"Of course," Martennan said. "I've arranged for you to stay with Kiran while the Council reviews your case." His smile brightened. "Kiran's quite eager to see you. I'll take you straight to him."

Easy as that, huh? My nerves buzzed all the louder.

Martennan stepped in close, ignoring my flinch, and ran a finger over my snapthroat charm. He glanced at Talmaddis and Aiyadaren. "Clever work. But, here…" The metal tingled against my skin. "He's in my charge, now. Go on, you two—get some rest. I'll hear your reports later."

He urged me toward the carriage, not even waiting for Talmaddis and Aiyadaren to finish their bows. Before I could climb in, the Arcanum door thudded open and a young mage scampered out.

"Captain Martennan, wait!" She waved a folded square of paper as she panted up to us. I caught a glimpse of a thick wax seal marked with a familiar design of interlocking circles.

My gut went cold. A missive from the Council? This couldn't mean anything good.

Martennan broke the seal and scanned the paper's contents. His eyes widened before his expression smoothed back into its usual cheerful mask. The cold hole in my gut grew larger.

Martennan balanced the letter on his flattened palm. His rings flared silver, and the letter vanished in a rush of pale flame.

Damn. No chance of sneaking a look. "Show-off," I muttered.

The flame winked out, leaving not even ash behind. Martennan let his hand fall. "Thank you, adept. Tell Councilor Varellian I shall call upon her within the hour."

The little mage bowed so deeply her knot of braids brushed the flagstones before she dashed back into the Arcanum. After a brief, low-voiced exchange with the driver, Martennan herded me into the carriage and settled himself on the seat opposite.

"Want to share what that was about?" I asked Martennan, as we rattled off.

He slanted me an amused glance. "No. Though I have another letter I'd like to share with you." He pulled another folded paper, this one unsealed, from within the front flap of his uniform and offered it to me.

I took it warily. But when I opened the letter, my heart leaped. Cara's bold handwriting sprawled over the page.

To Captain Martennan of the Seventh Watch:

You said you owed me a debt for warning you of Simon Levanian. If you've any shred of honor, you'll see Dev gets this letter. He's the one you truly owe, and he deserves news of home.

A brief blank space, and then:

Dev, you needn't worry for me—I'm safe and sound in Ninavel. I'm writing this from the Blackstrike, listening to a bunch of drunk Varkevians try and outdo each other on tabis drums. They're not very good. Reminds me of that stonemason two years back who thought it'd be fun to learn to play a shrike whistle while crossing the Whitefires. Thank Khalmet old Nuli saved our ears by tossing the damn thing off a cliff.

Yeah, I remembered that trip. This truly was from Cara, then, and not some trick of Martennan's. She must've sent it by one of the hard-riding merchant house couriers that traveled the Whitefire route in summer.

I looked up your cousin. She and the kids are all fine. The oldest is growing fast. Your cousin thinks she might be ready to apprentice out by the end of the season. I'll give them what coin I can, in your stead.

So Red Dal's den minder Liana thought Melly would reach her Change by summer's end. I'd known her time was running out, but the confirmation still hit like a fist to the gut. Six weeks, maybe less, until Red Dal sold Melly off to men who'd force taphtha down her throat until she was nothing more than a compliant, empty-eyed jenny, her mind gone forever.

Speaking of, I'd thought to find your drover friend, the one you'd said might buy your Whitefire maps, but he hasn't yet returned from his convoy job. I tried to talk with his boss, but he's apparently too busy a man to see a simple outrider like me.

I'll check with some of your other streetside friends, see if they're interested.

Oh, shit. I struggled to keep my face blank, my breathing even. Cara hadn't found Pello, the shadow man who might've arranged Melly's freedom in exchange for the full tale of Simon Levanian's destruction. She'd tried to go direct to Lord Sechaveh, the ruler of Ninavel and the man Pello claimed as master. But without Pello to smooth the way, she'd likely been turned away by guardsmen who knew nothing of Sechaveh's interest in our convoy trip.

Now in desperation she meant to try and find someone in the employ of one of Ninavel's streetside ganglords to act as a shadow broker. Ganglords dealt in information same as any other commodity. But while a ganglord would gladly sell Cara's tale to Sechaveh, they'd also sell her out to Ruslan for the chance of profit on the side.

I miss you, Dev. Remember what you said to me after I fixed up your head in Kost? I feel the same. So keep your head down, and don't do anything stupid. Things'll come right in the end.

A lump in my throat joined the lead weight in my stomach. *I won't ever abandon you again,* I'd said, while her fingers traced lazy circles on my skin. And then, we'd—

No. If I thought too long on that one glorious night, I'd crack like hammerstruck granite. Instead I meticulously refolded the letter, aware of Martennan's gaze on me. He was too clever not to realize Cara's talk of cousins and drovers held a deeper meaning. I just prayed he knew too little of my past to understand it.

"Can I keep this?" I asked. Thank Khalmet, my voice came out steady.

"By all means," Martennan said. "You have a good friend in Cara. It should set your mind at ease to know she's looking after your interests in Ninavel."

Damn his eyes, he'd seen my dismay, despite my attempt to cover it. I shrugged, carefully noncommittal. "I'd feel better yet if I could join her there." A truth that was no secret.

Martennan was the very picture of sympathy. "You may yet. The Council will need some weeks to review your case, but when they finish, the outcome may be a happy one. It's hard to wait, I know, but give it time."

"Right." I didn't even try to keep the sarcasm from my tone. A happy outcome, sure—but for whom? And time was one thing I didn't have.

CHAPTER THREE

(Kiran)

Kiran shoved aside the leather-bound book, tempted to cast it straight into the slate fireplace on the study's far side. The text contained yet another overly dramatic, maddeningly vague account of Alathia's founding. Pages upon pages of praise for Denarell of Parthus's vision in convincing a few hundred families of Harsian descent to leave the decadent cities of eastern Arkennland, cross thousands of miles of wilderness, and carve out a new country; and not a word about what supplies they'd brought or artifacts they'd discovered. So much for his hope of finding clues to what materials Alathia's mages had used when they first cast the spells powering their border wards.

In her chair beside the fireplace, Lena lifted her gaze from a slim volume. The title proclaimed it a naturalist's discussion of the deserts of Sulania.

"It's lovely outside today." She indicated the arched window behind her. Late morning sunlight streamed through the patterned glass, turning the polished wood of the study's bookshelves to cinnamon and amber. "Have you considered a walk in the back garden? You've been huddled in here for days."

"If I'm forbidden from useful work, I'd prefer to read." Kiran struggled to keep his tone civil. Since the day he'd felt the tremor in Stevannes's workroom, he hadn't been permitted to return to the Arcanum. He'd been kept cloistered in the lavishly appointed guest house that had been his quarters since his trial. For all its expansive library and beautifully manicured garden, the wards lurking within the property's walls were powerful enough to make it a perfect prison.

"Have you any news of Dev?" he asked Lena. Ten days ago, Captain Martennan—or Marten, as he'd asked Kiran to call him—had told Kiran of the disaster at Cheltman. He'd assured Kiran of Dev's survival and claimed the Council would bring Dev back from the mines for safety's sake. Yet since that visit, Marten had been conspicuous in his absence. Kiran feared it meant the Council had changed their minds about Dev's recall—or worse.

Lena shook her head. "If Talmaddis left the mine with Dev right after the order was relayed, they should arrive any day now."

Kiran sighed, hoping she was right and his fears unfounded. He moved to the shelf and pulled free a compilation of tales from early Alathian trading expeditions.

"I didn't realize you had such an interest in history."

Though Lena's words were mild, Kiran's nerves tightened. "Ruslan didn't teach us much of Alathia. I'd like to remedy that, to learn more of your culture and history. I thought it best to start with the earliest texts I could find and read onward."

It wasn't a lie. Yet his true urgency ran far deeper. He had to find something he could offer the Alathians to prove his value to them. After hearing about the loss of life at Cheltman, a completed design for Simon's charm no longer felt nearly enough to ensure both his and Dev's safety. Far better if he could offer the Council methods to counter attacks on their wards from blood magic. But to predict spell interactions and develop countering patterns, he needed to know the materials used to bind and direct the spells in question.

He'd asked if he might help shore up their wards, and been flatly refused. But he couldn't simply sit around hoping the Council held to their promises. If he could just develop some definitive spellwork to offer…

Lena regarded him steadily. "Us…I assume you're speaking of Ruslan's other apprentice. Did you and Mikail always have lessons together?"

She sounded honestly curious. Kiran looked away. "Yes." Longing pierced him, swift and poisonous as a viper's tooth. All those hours he'd spent learning with Mikail, magic unfolding before them like a neverending chamber of wonders, their only concern to earn Ruslan's approval…and even when they suffered Ruslan's darker moods, it was together, their bond as mage-brothers as solid and unchanging as Ninavel's stone…

Nausea twisted Kiran's stomach. Mikail was as much a monster as Ruslan. He'd betrayed Kiran's trust, given Kiran's beloved Alisa into Ruslan's hands— had been *glad* of her death, afterward. How could he be so traitorous to Alisa's memory as to miss Mikail?

"My apologies," Lena said softly. "I didn't mean to cause you pain."

"No, it's just..." Kiran stared at the sun-dappled tree branches outside the window. "Have you ever wished you were *nathahlen*—born without mage talent, I mean?" He regretted the foolishness of the question the moment he asked it. Calm, reasonable Lena, with her place assured in Alathia's hierarchy...what cause could she ever have had to regret her magic?

Yet when he stole a sidelong glance at her, he found Lena's eyes had gone distant, her straight brows drawn together. She said slowly, "Most mageborn children in Alathia are identified and brought to the Arcanum quite young, two or three years old, but my family lived deep in the Kilshasa Hills, two days' ride from the nearest town. I was six before a Council magefinder came through the area. I'd shown no sign of talent, so when she proclaimed me mageborn it was a shock to everyone. My parents asked if she could burn out my magic rather than take me away to Tamanath. I begged for that as well, but the magefinder said such a thing isn't possible without damaging the mind beyond repair."

Lena smoothed a hand over the cover of her book. "The first months at the Arcanum were hard. I missed my parents and sisters terribly. I thought I hated magic, because it had taken me from them. Yet the first time I cast a spell..." She held out her hand. A whisper of magic brushed Kiran's senses. A shining ball of palest rose appeared, floating in her cupped fingers. "The joy of it, the *rightness* that I felt, was—"

"Incredible," Kiran finished softly, remembering his own first spell, a simple illusion of the little copper wagon that had been his favorite toy. His own excitement, Ruslan's pride, Mikail's delight, all of it secondary to the soul-deep satisfaction the trickle of power had left behind.

"Yes." Lena snapped her fingers shut and the ball of light vanished. "Do you truly wish you'd never experienced magic?"

"If I'd been born *nathahlen*, I wouldn't know what I was missing." Unlike now, when his soul cried out for it like a desert traveler deprived of water. "Did you ever see your parents again?" Kiran couldn't keep the wistfulness from his voice. He'd never known his parents, hadn't even a single memory of a time before Ruslan.

"Yes, though not until I was inducted into the Watch. The journey to Tamanath is long, and they couldn't afford to leave their steading. We wrote letters through the years, but by the time I went back to visit..." She shrugged. "My sisters had married, had children of their own, and I was no longer the little girl my parents remembered. We had little left in common."

"I'm sorry," Kiran said awkwardly.

"Don't be." Lena raised her eyes to meet his. "I don't regret my talent now. You may feel differently about your own in years to come."

Kiran released a bitter chuckle. "Oh, certainly. The day Ruslan miraculously relinquishes his claim and the Council decides I'm not a demon in disguise, I'll delight in magic once more. Yet to hope for that feels as foolish as wishing for snow in Ninavel."

"Even Ninavel has…" Lena stood, her head tilting, as a muffled sound of feet and voices filtered through the study door. Kiran straightened, torn between curiosity and worry. If Marten had returned at last, his visit would be welcome if he brought news of Dev. Yet Kiran couldn't shake the fear the tidings might be darker.

A smile lit Lena's face. "Ah, Kiran, this should help your troubles fade. Look: you have a visitor."

The study door swung open. Marten strode in, beaming. Behind him trailed a wiry young man wearing dirt-streaked leathers, a thin gold torc gleaming around his neck.

"Dev!" Kiran hurried forward, delight banishing fear. "You're here, and safe—I'm so glad, I wasn't sure—" He stopped, not wanting to admit he'd doubted Marten's promises, and abruptly struck by worry that Dev's friendship might have faded into resentment during his time in the mines.

Dev grinned. He looked thinner than Kiran remembered. His bones were sharp under skin the rich brown of seasoned mahogany, his vivid green eyes as startling as ever in contrast. "Good to see you, too." He caught Kiran up in a quick, rough hug.

A knot loosened in Kiran's chest. He ducked his head, embarrassed at the force of his relief.

"I'll leave you two to catch up," Marten said. "I have a few matters that need discussing with Lena, and then I'm afraid I must dash back to the Arcanum for a meeting. I'll return afterward—at which time, Kiran, I hope I can be more forthcoming in response to your questions about these recent tremors."

Dev cast Marten a sharp glance. Kiran nodded, an uneasy mix of nerves and hope churning in his gut.

"One last thing…" Marten laid a finger on Dev's torc. The faint mutter of quiescent magic in the study's walls abruptly heightened, then resettled.

"Dev, I've keyed your collaring charm to the wards here," Marten said. "You'll have the freedom of the house and back garden, but one step past the walls, and—"

"Your gods-damned charm strangles me into submission, yeah, I know." Dev rubbed a hand over his throat.

The darker shading of skin there—not dirt, but old bruises. Guilt stabbed Kiran.

With a bow and a last genial wave, Marten exited, Lena following. The moment the door shut, Kiran spoke.

"Dev, I'm sorry. For the mines, and for—for everything…" He couldn't take his gaze from the black shadows ringing Dev's throat. "I worked every waking moment on Simon's spell. I was so close to finishing before all this. If only I'd deciphered the pattern faster—"

"Hey." Dev cuffed his shoulder. "Don't tie yourself in knots. Who's to say the Council would've kept their end of the deal, even if you'd finished? Never mind me…" His green eyes searched Kiran's face. "I'd ask how you're holding up in the face of these quakes, but the answer's written all over you. When was the last time you slept, huh?"

"Sleep has…been a little difficult." He hadn't managed more than scant moments of rest in between the nightmares that woke him, shuddering and sweating, the remembered taste of blood gagging his throat.

"I'll bet." Dev studied him, frowning. "Look, the quakes…you're certain they're, uh, unnatural?"

From his hesitant phrasing, he must think Kiran would dissolve into a whimpering heap if he mentioned Ruslan's name. Kiran said dryly, "You mean, are they caused by overspill from Ruslan attacking Alathia's wards?"

Dev spread his hands in silent, self-mocking apology. "Yeah."

Kiran sighed. "With my power bound, I can barely sense spells cast in the same room, let alone what might be happening a hundred miles distant at the border. But I'm certain it's Ruslan. Who else would have the strength and desire to damage the wards?" He told Dev of the diseased-looking holes he'd seen in Stevannes's spell, and his banishment thereafter from the Arcanum. Dev's expression turned grim as he listened.

Kiran finished off with, "The Alathians won't tell me a thing, or listen to my offers of help. Marten says to be patient, but—"

"*Marten*, is it now?" Dev cast a dark glance at the door.

"I know you're wary of him," Kiran said. "But he and Lena have been kind to me. The others, well…" He trailed off, embarrassed. Even Stevannes at his most acerbic couldn't compare to what Dev must have endured at the mine.

"The others, what?" Dev demanded.

Kiran shrugged. "They never forget I'm a blood mage." Stevannes was the most vocal about it, but Kiran had seen the wary revulsion in the other Alathians' eyes.

"You're not a blood mage," Dev said flatly. "Not anymore. Fuck the Alathians, if they can't get that through their heads. But…I know what you're afraid of, because I am too. Question is, how do we stop the Council from tossing us back to Ruslan?"

Kiran's chest tightened at the thought. "I don't know," he admitted. "I thought if I could devise some defensive spellwork to offer…but it's difficult, without access to proper materials and information."

"Access." Dev's fingers rose to tap on his torc, and his gaze drifted to the wards bracketing the study window.

Kiran sucked in a breath of sudden surmise. Dev had spent his childhood as a thief. As an adult he no longer had the Taint to help him slip past wards, but he'd proved on their trip through the Whitefires that his cleverness could make up for the lack. Perhaps Dev thought he could sneak into the Arcanum and find the information Kiran needed? Between Dev's collaring charm and the mages guarding them, it seemed an impossible task. But then, Dev's specialty seemed to be succeeding at impossible tasks.

Dev raked a hand through his coarse dark hair. He darted another glance at the door and slid a folded letter from his shirt.

"I've news from Cara. Thought you might like to read it, know she's okay." He brushed a finger over his lips, a warning clear in the intensity of his gaze.

The wards in the study walls were fully quiescent to Kiran's inner senses, with no hint of scry-magic tinging the aether. But if Dev was so concerned over eavesdroppers from the Watch, Kiran would be cautious. He gave Dev a slight nod and took the letter, curiosity rising.

As he scanned the scrawled text, Kiran's breath caught, his fingers whitening on the paper. Before Marten had escorted Cara to the border, she'd pulled Kiran aside and told him in a sharp, hurried whisper of her intent to sell information to the spy Pello in exchange for his help freeing Melly. Kiran had been so relieved; Cara seemed so competent, so assured, he'd thought she'd surely succeed in fulfilling the promise Dev had forsaken to help Kiran. But if this letter referred to Pello, and she couldn't find him, or some other way to rescue Melly in time…"Your drover friend…the one from the convoy, with the patchwork cap?"

Dev nodded, his mouth a tight line.

"Dev…" Kiran felt sick. He leaned close and whispered, "I know it's my fault you're trapped here. Truly, I'd almost finished the spell. Perhaps I can bargain with Marten—"

"*Don't* bargain with Martennan," Dev whispered harshly. "Not yet. If you can help me get this Shaikar-cursed snapthroat charm off and cross the wards, I've an idea—"

The door creaked, and Dev hastily sat back. Lena poked her head into the study. "Dev, the housekeeper says your room is prepared. After your journey, I thought you might like the chance for a hot bath and some clean clothes."

Dev stood. "Sure. Khalmet knows I've got a minecart's worth of coal grit to scrub off."

"Perhaps afterward I can show you the garden," Kiran said. "It's really quite beautiful." Unlike the wards in the study, those on the garden walls held no element of scrying, and the splashing of the central fountain would cover the sound of conversation. If he could touch Dev's torc, see the spell pattern Marten had set within...spells could be disrupted if a charm was physically damaged or altered in a spot critical to the pattern's flow. Then again, even if Kiran could circumvent the charm so Dev could safely cross the wards, he didn't know what Dev might do to help Melly after that. Sneaking into the Arcanum had seemed difficult enough. Dev would never make it to the border before Marten and the others noticed his absence.

"The garden sounds good," Dev agreed. The glint of wary hope in his eyes brought an answering thread of warmth to Kiran's chest. Whatever Dev's plan, Kiran wouldn't fail him. Not after Dev had given up so much for Kiran's sake.

✳

"Khalmet's hand, I can't get over how green it is here." Dev surveyed the garden, looking bemused. Kiran knew the feeling. The garden's high stone walls enclosed flowerbeds and vine-covered arbors whose lush vibrancy far outmatched any he'd seen in Ninavel. But then, water was no jealously rationed resource here. Kiran still marveled at the mildness of Alathia's climate. In Ninavel, summer's searing heat kept even the lowest of servants from venturing outside while the sun was high. Yet here in Tamanath, he stood with Dev in full sun on a midsummer afternoon and felt no more than pleasant warmth.

Dev's gaze settled on the walls. "Damn," he muttered. "They know how to place wards. And no trees or anything nearby high enough to let me jump clear. Can't even get close enough for a good look, thanks to those rosebushes." Roses in shades of deepest red and violet lined the base of the walls, their canes bristling with thorns. Fifteen feet above the blooms, black whorls and loops marked the gray stone, warding every inch of the wall's top.

"Come see the fountain," Kiran said. At the garden's center, low wooden benches bracketed an obsidian sculpture of four rearing swans. Water arced from the swans' beaks to splash in a pond dotted with floating, jewel-toned flowers. Kiran led Dev around the fountain's back side. When he was sure the swans blocked the view from the house windows, he halted.

"I'll try and read your collaring charm's pattern," he told Dev. "Hold still." Kiran reached for Dev's torc—and jerked his fingers back, hissing, as fire seared his nerves.

"What's wrong?" Dev demanded.

"Marten warded your charm against me." Of course; the healers had taken several vials of blood from Kiran during their examination of him. Marten must have used one to design and key a warding spell. Remembering that casual brush of Marten's finger over Dev's torc, Kiran felt a twinge of admiration for the man's skill.

"Shit." Dev aimed a fierce glare at the house. "Should've known. Don't suppose you have any kalumite?"

"Kalumite?" Kiran had never heard of it.

"It's a mineral found in sandstone. Glassblowers and mosaicists use it for color. But if you mix it with copper and oil in the right ratios, you can burn out a charm. The cliffs in Cheltman had veins of it, but I didn't get a chance to get any before I got dragged back here."

"Burn out a charm…" Kiran dropped to sit on a bench, thoughts racing. The kalumite and copper mix must provide an alternate conduit for the charm's magic, diverting it from its intended paths in an uncontrolled release of power. "There are geological texts in the study. If I can identify kalumite's properties, perhaps I can devise another way to produce the same effect."

Dev thumped a fist on the slate rim of the fountain bowl. "Good. Once past the house wards, I'll go find the nearest merchant house that deals in exports to Ninavel. In high summer, merchanters send dispatches out by courier every few days. I'll sneak in and slip a message for Cara into the next batch marked for delivery to Ninavel. I know a few secrets that can get her audience with a ganglord capable of brokering a deal with Sechaveh, and even keep her from getting stabbed in the back, if she plays it right."

Hesitantly, Kiran said, "But it'll take some time for us to circumvent the wards, and then weeks for a message to reach Ninavel. Won't it arrive too late?"

Dev's shoulders slumped. "Probably." When he turned, his stark desperation hit Kiran like a blow. "That's the best I can think of for now. I also mean to scout the Arcanum, try and find if they've got a stash of confiscated illegal charms. If we could get hold of that old amulet of yours, the one that blocks magic—"

"Ah! There you two are." Marten strode around the fountain, his smile as cheerful as ever. Dev shut his mouth and leaned against a bench as casually as if he and Kiran had merely been discussing the garden's splendor. Kiran tried not to look guilty.

Marten's round face settled into serious lines. "Kiran, I have an important matter to discuss with you."

Kiran's stomach curdled. Was the Council reconsidering their decision to give him asylum from Ruslan? "What is it?"

"I know you understand the ramifications of the recent earth tremors," Marten said. "I'm sure you've guessed the tremors are not the sole source of our concern."

Kiran nodded. The lump in his stomach grew heavier yet.

"In short, we've seen some alarming fluctuations in the border wards, of late."

Kiran shut his eyes. He'd suspected since the moment he'd seen those dismaying voids in Stevannes's spell. Yet to hear it confirmed…the icy ball of fear within grew razor-sharp claws. "How much longer will your wards hold against Ruslan?"

"I fear I can't discuss the wards' specific state," Marten said. "I can say this: Ruslan may not be the cause of the damage." At Kiran's incredulous look, he gave a mirthless chuckle. "Oh, we'd certainly assumed his involvement. Yet today we received a dispatch from our ambassador in Ninavel that throws the issue into serious doubt."

Kiran exchanged a wary, disbelieving glance with Dev. Ruslan was subtle and clever enough to have found a way to cover his spellcasting, but Kiran wouldn't be fooled. From the skeptical scowl on Dev's face, he felt much the same.

"What did the dispatch say?" Kiran asked.

Marten trailed a hand in the fountain bowl and flicked water from his fingers. "Our ambassador believes the quakes are related to a series of magical disturbances in Ninavel that have killed several mages and appear to be aimed at disrupting the city's supply of water."

"What?" Dev straightened, his eyes narrowing. Kiran knew his concern. The Painted Valley held no natural sources of water. If the magic that kept Ninavel's cisterns replenished were to fail, the lives of thousands of untalented residents would be at risk.

Marten said to Dev, "There have been no serious shortages as yet, and Lord Sechaveh has been keeping the matter quiet. So far as the city's populace knows, a few mages are dead, nothing more. Even our ambassador hasn't succeeded in learning much else. But she believes Ninavel is the real target, and not Alathia."

Could Marten be right? No. This had to be some ploy of Ruslan's meant to distract the Council until it was too late. Kiran rubbed his head, where an ache was building.

Dev slouched against the bench with a sharp, sarcastic grin. "Now you think it's Ninavel in trouble and not your precious border, the Council's gonna just sit back and watch Sechaveh scramble, is that it?"

"You don't understand," Marten said. "It doesn't matter if the damage to our wards is merely a byproduct of someone's spellcasting against Ninavel. We can't afford to let anything disrupt them."

He turned to Kiran, grave and intent. "The Council has authorized me to take a team to Ninavel to investigate. Kiran, I'd like to bring you with us."

Shock set Kiran's heart hammering. He shook his head in mute, stunned denial. Return to the city Ruslan called home? How could Marten even think to ask it of him?

Marten said, "Kiran, I will not force you to go. But if you help us stop this disruption to our wards, then upon your return, the Council will release Dev from his sentence."

Kiran wanted so badly to earn Dev's freedom. But to face Ruslan again… no. He couldn't. The very idea congealed his blood and left him trembling. Yet shame squeezed his heart at his cowardice. Dev had taken on both Simon Levanian and Ruslan without a single glimmer of mage talent to help him, all for Kiran's sake.

"So I'm your gods-damned carrot again?" Dev snapped. "Tell me you're joking, Martennan. Take him to Ninavel? In what taphtha vision does that make sense? Ruslan'll show up in a heartbeat, and I may not know much about magic, but I'm pretty sure he can kick your ass."

Marten said, "It's true that blood magic is the most powerful way for a single mage to cast a spell." Kiran started a protest, and Marten held up a hand. "Yes, Kiran, I know your channeled spells involve two mages, but only the focus mage is actively casting. The channeler's role is essentially passive. In any case, my point is that Alathian magic is not designed to be cast by a single mage. Even blood magic can be countered by more subtle methods if enough mages are working in tandem."

"Even if you could counter channeled spells, what of my mark-bond?" Kiran demanded. "The moment I pass your border wards, Ruslan can control me. Unless…wait, you've found a way to dissolve the bond?" Kiran leaped to his feet, hope a fire in his veins.

Marten hastened to shake his head, his expression regretful. "I'm sorry, Kiran, but no. We haven't found a way to break the binding, not without killing you."

Kiran sank back onto the bench. Of course the Alathians hadn't found a way. Foolish of him to imagine they could discover a method so quickly, when every scholar agreed the mark-bond was unbreakable while both mages lived.

"We can't break it, but we can prevent him from using it," Marten said.

Against his will, interest sparked. "Truly, you can block the bond? How?" The *kizhenvya* amulet Kiran had worn to flee Ninavel had protected him for a few days, but Ruslan had come terribly close to worming his way past the amulet's spellwork before Kiran crossed the Alathian border. If the Alathians knew some more permanent method, perhaps he wouldn't have to be so dependent on their border wards for protection.

"Let me show you." Marten drew out an amulet on a thin silver chain.

Kiran leaned forward. The amulet was made entirely of twisted strands of metal, with no gemstones or crystals set amidst them. Even more strange, the individual strands appeared to be of different metals, which Kiran would have thought impractical for proper pattern matching. He thought he recognized silver, copper, and gold, but several strands had a dull greenish striation that was completely unfamiliar.

Marten held out the amulet. "Go ahead, take a look."

Kiran touched a metal strand. A rippling veil of fire washed over his inner sight, so blindingly bright he gasped and yanked his finger back.

Dev tensed. "What's wrong?"

"Nothing. Just..." Kiran touched the amulet again, gingerly. "There's a lot of power stored here." It reminded him of the vast, sleeping magic lurking in Simon's border charm, but Simon's charm used gemstones as reservoirs, not mere metal, and the energies flowed in a traditional—albeit horribly complicated— set of contained pathways, unlike the chaotic rush of the amulet's magic.

"Without a pattern, how can you direct the magic?" Kiran asked.

Marten grinned. "I'll demonstrate. I know your binding interferes with your senses, but you can feel my soul's energy, correct?"

'Yes." Even through his inner barriers, beyond the binding's dissonance Marten's *ikilhia* burned bright as a watchfire. Even Dev's *ikilhia*, the barest of flickers in comparison, was detectable if he concentrated.

Marten put on the amulet and chanted something quick and soft.

His *ikilhia* vanished. He remained standing before Kiran, calm and smiling, but no hint of his life tinged the aether, as if he were merely a scry-image. Kiran reached out before he thought, half expecting his hand to pass through Marten.

Marten offered his wrist. His flesh was warm and solid under Kiran's hand, and beyond...Surprise filled Kiran anew, as he came up against an ever-shifting wall that changed so rapidly and hypnotically he couldn't identify even a single glimpse of a pattern.

"That's amazing," Kiran said, and meant it. The utter absence of Marten's *ikilhia* from his senses meant the warding was powerful enough to block even the mark-bond, and the constant mutability of the pattern would make it extremely difficult to target a spell to break the warding. Yet, the distant look to Marten's eyes…

"You're casting, aren't you? Constantly, to keep the pattern changing."

"Yes," Marten said. "The one downside. For you, one of the Watch would need to remain at your side to cast in your stead. We'd take the duty in shifts. That way, even while you sleep you'll be fully protected."

So not only was the amulet far from the long-term answer he'd hoped for, it would keep him wholly dependent on the Alathians. Disappointment flooded Kiran.

"I know it's not a permanent solution." Marten removed the amulet and slipped it back into his uniform. "Even so, for a short stay in Ninavel, I believe it would suffice. Especially since I don't intend to depend solely on the amulet for your protection. If you agree to come, I'll be happy to explain my plans in more detail."

"Why are you so hot to bring Kiran with you?" The stiffness of Dev's posture still spoke of anger, but his lean brown face had turned impassive, his eyes hard with calculation.

"Same reason as the one that convinced the Council to commute his death sentence." Marten hadn't taken his gaze from Kiran. "Kiran, if we find the cause of the disruption to our wards is a working done with blood magic, or another type of magic outlawed in Alathia, you could decipher the spell pattern and figure out how to counter or disrupt it much faster than one of our mages. A few weeks, that's all I ask. When you return, not only would Dev be free, but your efforts would go far toward convincing the Council you can be trusted."

Kiran stared down at his hands. The amulet would block the mark-bond, yes, but Ruslan would never allow that to stop him. And it wouldn't just be Ruslan. Lizaveta and Mikail would be in Ninavel too, helping Ruslan cast.

Marten said, "Consider this: without your help in Ninavel, we may not be able to stop the deterioration of our wards. If they fail…even if Ruslan is not the architect of that failure, he will certainly seize the opportunity to reclaim you."

That, Kiran could well believe. But if he went to Ninavel, Ruslan would have a chance at him far sooner.

"If you let fear control you, you'll never be free of him," Marten said softly.

Dev slapped the bench, making Kiran jump. "Khalmet's bloodsoaked hand, Martennan! You want your wards fixed up fast, then I've got a better proposition:

bring me, not Kiran. You say Sechaveh's keeping things quiet. Maybe from foreigners and highside idiots, but trust me, ganglords can sniff out the deepest of secrets. They'd never deal with you; too risky, if Sechaveh finds out. But me…I know how to play their game. You mages are smart, you don't need Kiran to break a spell. Leave him safe here, and I'll get you information you'd never find otherwise and save you far more time."

Kiran willed Marten to agree. He had every faith Dev spoke truth, and once in Ninavel, Dev could work with Cara to save Melly. While Kiran would be left safe behind Alathia's wards…his shame swelled, but it didn't lessen his relief at the idea.

Marten raised his brows. "An interesting offer, but I think you underestimate how difficult it is for us to interpret magic that differs so sharply from our own. I have far more confidence in our ability to discover the truth of what's happening, than our chances of stopping it without Kiran's help in time to prevent our wards from failing. That said, Dev…if Kiran were to agree to go, I believe I could convince the Council to authorize your inclusion on the trip. With both of you working to help, we'd have all the more chance of success."

Kiran's relief died. He should have known the answer wouldn't be so easy. He passed a shaking hand over his eyes, remembering Dev's desperation when he'd spoken of Melly. Kiran owed Dev his life, his very soul. How could he refuse Dev the chance to gain both Melly's and his own freedom?

Especially when—in sudden, searing insight—Kiran knew just how easy saving Melly would be. He'd vowed in the Whitefires to make choices worthy of his lover Alisa's memory. To embrace her bright courage, and not give in to cowardice. Twice before, he'd lived up to that ideal and risked capture by Ruslan for the sake of others. Still, summoning his courage was the hardest thing he'd done since first leaving Ninavel. He opened his mouth.

"No," Dev said sharply. He shoved past Marten to grip Kiran's shoulder, his green eyes blazing. "*Kiran.* Don't fall for this."

Kiran looked past him at Marten. "Before I answer, might I have a moment alone with Dev?"

Marten didn't hesitate. "By all means, discuss this with him. I know this is no easy decision for you. I'll wait in the study."

Dev's wary scowl as he watched Marten retreat to the house didn't bode well, but Dev was no stranger to risk, and Kiran knew how deep his loyalty to his dead mentor ran. Dev had put Melly's life over Kiran's before. When he heard Kiran's plan, he'd do it again.

CHAPTER FOUR

(Dev)

"Did you get brain-burned while I was gone?" I snapped at Kiran, the instant Martennan disappeared into the house. "I didn't save your ass from Ruslan just to have him get his hands on you again before the season's out! Keep on telling Martennan you won't go. Trust me, once he sees you mean it, he'll give in and take me instead."

Kiran spoke in a fierce, intent whisper barely audible over the splashing of the fountain. "Dev, listen. I've thought of a way you can save Melly, and you won't need a fortune in money, or to find Pello. If Marten takes us both to Ninavel—"

"Yeah, perfect. That way Ruslan can cut out my heart, right after he burns out your will and makes you his drooling slave. If I go to Ninavel while you sit tight here in Alathia, there's a chance he'll stay so focused on breaking the border wards he won't bother with me—and more importantly, no chance he'll get hold of you!"

"I know the risk would be high for both of us. But if Marten can protect us from him, even if only for a short while...think! If we're both in Ninavel, and you arrange a meeting for me with your old handler, what was his name—"

"Red Dal," I muttered.

"Tell me, what do you imagine Red Dal would do if a blood mage walked in and demanded he hand over one of his Taint thieves?"

I stared at him, then breathed, "Suliyya, mother of maidens. That could actually work." No streetsider in Ninavel would dare refuse a blood mage. We'd all heard the spine-freezing tales of the power of their magic, and the depth of their cruelty. Red Dal's instinct for self-preservation was the only thing more highly developed than his love of profit. He'd hand Melly over in a heartbeat…so long as he was convinced he truly risked a blood mage's wrath. I eyed Kiran's earnest, determined face, and frowned.

"Oh, I can act the part." Kiran's teeth flashed white in a bitter smile. "I've had an excellent teacher." He shut his eyes and drew himself up, tossing his black hair back over his shoulders. When he opened his eyes again, they burned with predatory arrogance. He turned that fiery gaze on me, and despite myself, I backed a step.

"Khalmet's bloodsoaked bony hand," I said, forgetting to whisper. "Impressive, but still…Red Dal's a canny bastard. He'll need more than sigil-marked clothes and a good job of acting. Besides, if I understood that business with the amulet right, you'll have an Alathian dogging your heels every damn minute of the day, and you can't risk ditching them."

"If I could spellcast, I could convince Red Dal. Not to mention protect myself with the amulet." A brief, sharp smile twisted Kiran's mouth. "Marten bringing you along to Ninavel isn't the only condition I intend to put on my acceptance."

Ah. He meant to demand the removal of his binding. He hadn't said the Council's spell still pained him, but I'd seen it in the abruptness of his movements, the strain that never left his face. More than that, I could guess how badly he missed his magic. If I had a chance at having the Taint back, I'd take it, no matter the cost.

Slowly, I nodded. "All right, yeah. With a suitably showy spellcasting, I think Red Dal would buy it."

"I thought so," Kiran said, with soft satisfaction.

My heart lifted as I allowed myself to imagine it: Melly free, and my old promise to her father Sethan fulfilled at last. Easy enough in Ninavel to get my hands on enough kalumite and copper to burn out the snapthroat charm, and then ditch the Alathians and slip out of the city with Melly. Take her somewhere far from mages and ganglords and Alathians…after all, Arkennland was a big country, Ninavel a mere speck in the wildlands of its western territory. I'd heard the far north had some decent mountains. I doubted another range could match the beauty of the Whitefires, but settlements up there must hold opportunities for men skilled in ropework and snow travel. I could get Melly set in a proper apprenticeship and carve out a new life safely distant from Ruslan. Maybe Cara would come with us…my breath quickened, thinking of Cara's bright laugh, her tanned skin beneath my hands…

My gaze lit on Kiran. Resolve firmed his jaw and straightened his spine. Yet his blue eyes were shadowed, the circles beneath them as inky black as his hair, and even the rich golden wash of afternoon sunlight couldn't soften the pallor of his skin. My happy little fantasy crumbled.

"Kiran. Look. I know you want to help me, but after everything you've gone through to get away from Ruslan, are you sure about this?"

He sighed. "Honestly? No. But Marten is right. If I stay to cower behind the wards and they fail, then Ruslan will have me anyway. I'd prefer to go where I might do something to prevent it."

Well, that I could understand. The gods knew I hated to sit around on my hands praying somebody else could stave off disaster. "Fair enough. But before you commit to going, make Marten explain the rest of how he means to counter Ruslan. If you're not completely convinced he can do it, for Khalmet's sake, don't agree to this."

Kiran jerked his head in a nod and strode for the house. I followed, more slowly. Gods, if this worked…and yet, I couldn't shake the sick feeling I might've just agreed to trade Kiran's freedom for Melly's.

In the study, Martennan uncoiled from a high-backed chair before the fireplace. "Have you made a decision, Kiran?"

"If you will take us both to Ninavel, I will agree to go—on one other condition." Behind his back, Kiran's hands clenched around each other so tightly I thought his fingers might break. "I want the binding on my magic removed."

Martennan went still. "That will be a far harder case to make to the Council."

"I refuse to go within Ruslan's reach without the ability to defend myself." Kiran's voice was thin. "Even if you can block the mark-bond, you know that won't stop him from casting against me."

"Unless we stop him otherwise," Martennan said. "Our ambassador in Ninavel has been working to convince Lord Sechaveh to sanction our investigation. If Sechaveh issues an edict of protection for us—"

Surprise made me blurt, "You want to go openly to the city? Are you crazy? Might as well march up and pound on Ruslan's door. I thought you meant to sneak in!"

Martennan said, "Concealing our presence from Lord Sechaveh would be an impossible task. He keeps a far closer eye on events in Ninavel than most people realize, and his hands-off policy on magic doesn't extend to representatives of foreign powers. But with official sanction, we'll gain not only access to information and the freedom to cast as we please, but far better protection from Ruslan than any wards could provide."

"Sechaveh's a mage, then?" I couldn't help but be curious. Nobody knew the truth, streetside. Sechaveh had to be some two hundred years old, but I'd always leaned toward believing those who claimed he was so rich he could pay mages to keep him alive. Pello had talked about him like he was untalented, but then again, Pello was a professional liar. If Sechaveh was a mage as powerful as Ruslan, no wonder he'd managed to kick out Simon.

"He's not a mage," Kiran said flatly. "No edict of his will stop Ruslan."

I turned to look at him, surprised all over again. Martennan's head tilted, and he said, "Have you met Lord Sechaveh before, Kiran?"

"Not directly, but I've seen him. He came to visit Ruslan, sometimes." Kiran's eyes took on the stricken darkness they always got when he spoke of life before he ran. "Trust me, he's untalented."

"Oh, I know it," Martennan said. "I haven't met Sechaveh myself, but the older mages here in Alathia remember him well. Before he founded Ninavel, he spent seventeen years as the Arkennlander ambassador to Alathia."

"Well, that explains a lot," I muttered. Sechaveh must've gotten really sick of all the Council's rules.

Marten went on. "But while Sechaveh is no mage, his sister was, and a powerful one. Perhaps even a blood mage—we're not certain. But unlike most Arkennlander mages, she didn't sever ties to her birth family. When Sechaveh decided to build a city over the largest confluence of magic yet discovered, he asked her to cast a spell that bound him to that confluence. We haven't yet discovered all the details of that binding, but we know two things: it makes him effectively immortal so long as he remains within the Painted Valley's confines, and it allows him to deny mages the use of the confluence to fuel their spells, should they anger him. It's one of the ways he maintains his rule."

I said, "So if Ruslan breaks Sechaveh's edict of protection, no more confluence for Ruslan. But he can cast spells without it, right?" The lack of the confluence certainly hadn't stopped him from casting against us in the Whitefires.

"True," Martennan said. "But much of blood magic's power lies in its ability to harness the forces of the confluence. Without its aid in his spellcasting, and with a group of us working together to counter him, we have every chance of defending against Ruslan."

"How many mages are you bringing on this little mission?" I asked.

"Not so many from Tamanath," Martennan said. "Only myself, my two lieutenants—Lenarimanas and Talmaddis, you know them both—and an arcanist. But once in Ninavel, we'll have assistance in spellwork from the mages already stationed at the embassy."

"I've never understood how so many of you can mesh minds so closely." A hint of wistfulness lurked in Kiran's tone.

Martennan didn't miss it. "If we succeed in Ninavel, I hope to sway the Council to ease their restrictions on you. The moment they do, I'll be happy to teach you our style of magic."

Kiran looked like a man dying of thirst who'd been offered a waterskin. My hands twitched with the urge to strangle Martennan. It'd be a bright day in Shaikar's hells before the Council decided to trust a former blood mage, if the way they treated him now was anything to go by. But arguing that point wouldn't help anything.

Kiran's spine straightened, and stubborn determination replaced the yearning. "Even if you can counter Ruslan, my condition stands: either remove my binding, or I won't go."

I raised a silent cheer for him, even as I bit back the words that wanted to burst free: *I'll go even if Kiran doesn't*. Time enough to try again for a solo deal with Martennan if the Council refused to take their spell off Kiran.

Martennan tapped his fingers on the chair back, his black eyes gone as opaque as onyx. At last he said, "I fear the Council would refuse any request to release your binding before we leave Alathia, but I may be able to persuade them to authorize our embassy in Ninavel to perform the ritual."

I grunted in disgust. "So you'd leave Kiran helpless for weeks while we cross the Whitefires? Come on, Martennan. Ruslan's not going to wait for us to reach Ninavel before he casts."

"We won't be crossing the Whitefires," Martennan said. "The situation is too urgent to waste weeks traveling through the mountains."

I stared. "Then, how…?"

"You intend to cast a translocation spell? For a distance of that magnitude?" Kiran was goggling at Martennan like that was as crazy as us growing wings and flying to Ninavel.

"Yes." Martennan didn't so much as blink.

"But…the power required would be incredible! And the border wards! How could your spell penetrate a barrier so strong—" Shock flared in Kiran's eyes, his head rocking back. "The wards…you're going to release them, and draw on their source to cast the translocation spell?"

"You'll understand if I can't discuss the particulars of our spellcasting." The sudden impassivity of Martennan's face was an answer in itself. My own jaw dropped.

"*Release* the wards?" I demanded. "Did the entire Council eat staggerweed by mistake? How is that a good idea?"

Kiran added, "Even if you intend to rebuild the wards immediately after casting your spell, you must realize a few moments of opportunity are all Ruslan needs to destroy your defenses beyond repair. How do you know this isn't what he's been waiting for all along?"

Martennan said, "Whatever the risks involved in our methods, be assured they've been carefully weighed, and steps taken to ensure Alathia's safety."

I chewed my lip. If the border was unwarded for only a few moments, then yeah, I could think of a host of ways the Alathians could use their people in Ninavel to make sure Ruslan was too busy to spellcast at a specific time. What worried me more were the implications of the ultra-cautious Council taking such a drastic step merely to save a few weeks' travel time.

"How close *are* your wards to failing?" If the Council was truly desperate, Kiran and I might have a hell of a lot more leverage than I'd thought.

The ironic glint in Martennan's eyes said he knew perfectly well why I'd asked. "The situation is not dire. Merely urgent. But the Council would prefer I complete my investigation in Ninavel within weeks, not months."

He turned to Kiran. "If the Council should agree your binding may be removed in Ninavel, would that satisfy you? Once in the city, we'd need a little time to prepare the casting, but no more than a day. I promise you, you'd be safe until then. And afterward, for that matter, though I can understand your desire to mount your own defenses."

Kiran stood silent, his head bowed. When he spoke, his voice was so low I could barely hear him. "If the Council agrees, and you show me their authorization and give me your personal word you'll remove the binding in Ninavel—then yes, I'll go. But Marten, if you lie to me in this…" His voice cracked and he stopped, his hands fisting at his sides.

"Kiran." Martennan's voice was soft. "I have never lied to you."

"There's always a first time," I snapped. Yeah, men like Martennan didn't lie. They didn't need to. Play on a mark's emotions, earn his trust, and he'll fill in any omissions with his own assumptions and walk placid as a lamb to his own funeral. "Tell me, Martennan, if you want Kiran to go so badly, why the song and dance? You and I both know the Council could've ordered him there. Told him either he goes, or they hand him straight over to Ruslan."

From Kiran's dark glance at me, he wished I hadn't suggested that idea. But if he thought Martennan hadn't considered it, he wasn't nearly as wary of the man as he should be. Personally, I suspected Martennan didn't have the Council's full support in this little plan to take along his own personal blood mage. But I wanted to hear what Martennan would say in answer.

Martennan spoke with cool confidence. "This investigation is my responsibility, and as such, I choose what methods to use, not the Council. Our task in Ninavel will be challenging—and yes, dangerous, I don't deny it. I want people at my side whose efforts are wholehearted, not grudgingly given under duress."

Kiran looked reassured. I wasn't. Martennan certainly had an interesting definition of duress. Despite my distrust, I'd play his game so long as I thought we had the slightest chance of survival. Crazy as this venture was, no question it was my best hope for Melly's freedom, and my own.

❋

I spidered sideways along the garden wall, my fingers cramping from clinging to tiny imperfections on the stone. Beneath me lurked the thorny sea of rosebushes, and above, the wards that prevented me from touching the wall's lip. Between roses and wards, the traverse was as challenging as an overhanging ascent up chossy sandstone. My forearms burned by the time I reached the wall's end, and I nearly impaled myself on a set of thorns as long as my thumb when I jumped down to the flagstone path.

Lena sat on one of the benches beside the fountain, the vivid red of the cinnabar wood contrasting with the muted fabric of her uniform. After Martennan had left, she'd agreed readily enough when I asked if I might traverse the wall for a bit of exercise, though she'd watched me keen as a banehawk the whole while.

I dodged around flowerbeds to cross to her bench. The sun had set only moments ago, and the thin clouds streaking the sky glowed in a brilliant display of carmine and orange. Fireflies sparked green in the shadows, and the splashing of the fountain's water mixed with a growing chorus of nightbugs in the trees. Beyond Lena, the door to the house stood open, a warm golden glow from the oil lanterns spilling out onto the lawn.

"Where's Kiran?" I asked. Last I'd seen, he'd been pacing between the redbud trees behind the fountain, his shoulders up around his ears, but he wasn't there now. If he'd gone inside, I thought it odd Lena hadn't followed. I'd never seen a mage on guard duty let him get more than a room away.

"When Talmaddis came out to relieve me, Kiran said he was tired and went in. I thought I'd stay and enjoy the sunset." Her smile involved her eyes more than her mouth. "I also enjoyed the climbing demonstration. You make it look so easy."

"Ha. That's because you don't have anything hard, here." I flexed my hands backward, one after the other. Coal hauling had helped me regain the strength in my back and biceps, but the small muscles of my wrists and forearms were sorely out of shape after two months without serious climbing. I had a feeling I'd need all my skills in Ninavel.

"And Ninavel does."

"Ninavel has buildings more than three stories tall. And towers." Not that I'd ever climbed one of the slender, soaring spires that formed Ninavel's highest districts, though I'd given them more than a few longing looks. But the high towers were the province of mages, and every streetsider in Ninavel knew better than to piss off a mage.

Hard to believe I'd soon see Ninavel's familiar skyline again. Martennan had said the Watch would have the translocation spell ready by tomorrow night. Kiran had tried to hide his dismay, but it was clear he felt that was horribly soon.

For me, the trip couldn't come soon enough. I prayed the Council didn't balk at releasing Kiran's binding. The more I thought on Kiran's plan for Melly, the more badly I wanted the chance to try it. Besides, anybody could see Kiran wanted his magic back as bad as a Tainter just past their Change.

If only getting the Taint back was so easy. I arched over in a stretch and asked Lena, casual as I could, "Hey, whatever happened to that Taint charm of Simon's, the one that fucked me up so bad?"

Her face had grown indistinct in the twilight, and I couldn't tell if the question surprised her. She said, "The charm was destroyed on the Council's orders not long after Kiran's trial, along with all the other charms of Simon's that were determined to have deadly effects."

Her answer hit me like a crossbow bolt to the gut. Damn it, *damn* it...I turned aside to stare at the shadowed bulk of the fountain, struggling to weather a black wave of loss. Stupid, to think I could ever have the Taint back. To have that dead void in my mind alive again, to feel whole, even if only for a few moments at a time...that was all I could have dared to wear the charm lest it rip my insides to shreds again, but to have even that chance vanish...

"I'm surprised Kiran didn't tell you," Lena said. "He asked about Simon's other charms some weeks ago. He was...quite upset, to hear the answer. It's the only time I've ever seen him shout at Marten. He said we should have waited to destroy them; that studying them might have given him more insight into Simon's methods of design, and helped him to decipher the border charm faster. I believed that at the time, but now...he wanted that charm for your sake, didn't he?"

Damn. She might not have Martennan's skill at manipulation, but clearly she shared his cleverness. I shrugged. "Not likely. Kiran said I'd be a fool to even touch the charm again." But I had to wonder. Maybe he'd thought he could find a way to make it safe to use—I stomped that thought flat, as pain lanced my heart. The charm was gone. No point in mooning over it.

"He was right. You couldn't possibly use that charm safely without an entire group of mages casting continuously to heal you." Lena shifted forward on the bench. "You miss the Taint so badly, then? Even though it meant you lived in slavery as a child?"

"Slavery?" I laughed. "Is that what Martennan told you?"

"Isn't it true that you were sold to a criminal as a child, and forced to work for him?"

I stopped laughing. Yeah, she had the basic facts right. I'd been sold to Red Dal when I was too young to remember it, and I'd used my powerful Taint to steal for him for years. Until puberty hit, my Taint vanished, and he sold me off to someone far worse. I gritted my teeth, glad that the growing darkness obscured my face. I had no intention of explaining to Lena that my years as a Taint thief hadn't felt like slavery at all.

"So? Don't sit there and tell me how different things are in Alathia. Kiran told me how mageborn kids here get taken from their parents and dragged off to live in some soldiers' barracks as soon as they're old enough to talk. It sure didn't sound to me like there was a choice involved."

"That's different." Lena's voice gained an edge to match mine. "Mages are vital to Alathia's security, and with mage talent so rare, the Council can't afford not to have every talented child inducted into the service."

"A strong dose of the Taint is rare, too," I said. "But in Ninavel, the parents have a choice." True, the choice might be between their entire family dying of thirst versus selling a strongly Tainted kid to a handler for a lifetime of water rations, but no need to get bogged down in details. I frowned as something occurred to me.

"How does Martennan know that I—"

A harsh, ragged shriek drowned out my words. I leaped to my feet and sprinted for the house, not waiting for Lena. I knew Kiran's voice when I heard it, though I'd only heard him scream that way once before.

CHAPTER FIVE

(Kiran)

Blood everywhere, pooled within darkened channel lines and clotted on the workroom's anchor stone, the gaping wounds in Alisa's limp, manacled body black with it. Kiran couldn't move, his body frozen as Alisa's head turned toward him with a terrible, wet sound, dark fluid oozing from the flayed muscles of her neck. Her remaining amber eye fixed on him.

"You did this," she whispered, the words an airless croak. "You, and no other."

No, Kiran tried to say, though no sound came. Ruslan had been the one who savaged Alisa's flesh as Kiran battered against the magic holding him helpless. Yet when Kiran reached for Alisa, in his hand was a silver knife, the blade streaked with gore. A scream hung trapped in Kiran's chest as Ruslan spoke soft as a lover in his ear, "Did I not tell you, akhelysh? Our natures are the same."

A hand gripped Kiran's arm. He flung himself blindly away. "No, don't—!"

He choked and stopped. The room before him held bookshelves gleaming in the mellow light of oil lamps rather than bloodied stone in magelight. And instead of Alisa's mutilated body, he faced Lieutenant Talmaddis, whose hand was still outstretched, his mouth open in shock.

"I told you touching him was a bad idea," Dev said from the open door of the study. Behind him stood Lena, her brows angled in concern.

"My apologies." Talmaddis bent to Kiran in a little half-bow. "I only meant to wake you. You seemed, ah…distressed."

Kiran winced. The scream he hadn't been able to voice in the dream must have escaped his throat after all. His head swam. The colors in the room seemed too garish, the whole scene unreal, as if any moment it would fray into the bloody twilight of Ruslan's workroom. He bent to brace his hands on his knees.

"You okay?" Dev dodged around Talmaddis to offer a steadying arm.

"I…" Kiran struggled to calm his breathing. His thoughts felt as tattered and insubstantial as mist. "Yes. Only a nightmare. I'm sorry for…for alarming you." He let Dev steer him to one of the chairs before the fireplace. The other had been knocked over, presumably a casualty of his panic upon waking. The shattered pieces of a mug lay about the chair, the dregs of his tea puddled on the polished wood of the floor. Embarassment heated Kiran's face as he sat.

Lena said, "I'll get some water for you, Kiran. Talmaddis, perhaps you could get a towel or two; I think we can clean the floor without the housekeeper's assistance."

As the door shut behind them, Kiran blessed Lena's tact. She and Talmaddis wouldn't go far, but a little privacy was better than none. Almost, he wished Dev had gone with them. He shut his eyes and took slow, even breaths. Gradually, his stomach settled, the lingering sense of unreality fading.

Dev righted the toppled chair and leaned against one of the arms. "That must've been one hell of a nightmare. You didn't make half so much noise in the Whitefires."

Kiran strove for a light tone. "I have to say I'm not much impressed with the housekeeper's calming tea." He'd hoped the tea combined with reading the most boring treatise he could find might ease his nerves before sleep. He should have known nothing would suffice for that.

"Calming tea?" Dev bent to touch a finger to the liquid on the floor. He sniffed his finger, then tasted it. His brows shot up. "There's vallis root in this."

"That's not meant to calm?" Kiran had no idea what vallis root might be.

Dev spat into the fireplace. "Oh, it calms all right. For most people. For some, it works the opposite, brings on nightmares. One time out on a convoy trip we had a stonemason who drank some and near brought an avalanche on our heads with all his yelling afterward." He prodded the remains of the cup with a foot. "Who made the tea for you?"

"The housekeeper," Kiran said. "I asked if she had any blackmallow tea like I used to drink in Ninavel. When she said no, Talmaddis suggested I try one of her calming teas instead."

"Did he." Dev's eyes narrowed.

"You think…what? He wanted to induce a nightmare? What would it profit him?" Kiran could imagine Stevannes stooping to that kind of petty malice, but not Talmaddis. Kiran hadn't seen as much of him as Lena, but in their few interactions Talmaddis had treated him with a measured friendliness that lacked any hint of disgust or disdain. "In any case, it's not like I need the aid of herbs to suffer nightmares."

"True." Dev sighed. "You know, if the thought of going to Ninavel makes you wake up screaming like you're being gutted, maybe we should rethink this."

Kiran looked away. "It's not that."

Dev made an exasperated noise. "Go on, tell me you weren't dreaming about Ruslan."

"I wasn't. That is...not entirely." Kiran stared at the slate lip of the fireplace and took a deep breath. "Tomorrow is...was...Alisa's Naming day."

"Alisa." Dev's voice had turned careful.

"You heard...in Simon's cave, when Ruslan came..." He'd never spoken of Alisa to Dev, but Dev had been hiding in the wreckage left by the cataclysmic backlash of Simon's disrupted spell. Dev must have heard what he and Ruslan said to each other in the aftermath.

"I heard," Dev said quietly. "You loved her, and Ruslan killed her. Right?"

Kiran's eyes felt hot. "Yes, but..." He picked up a cup shard, turned it over in his hands, traced the ridged patterns on the glazed ceramic. "I never warned her," he admitted. "I never told her the truth of what I was." She'd known he was a mage, but he'd never had the courage to explain what kind.

"Khalmet's bloodsoaked hand," Dev snapped, so fiercely that Kiran dropped the shard. "You think it's your fault?"

"Isn't it?" Words spilled from him in a hot, searing rush. "I knew Ruslan had forbidden us contact with *nathahlen*. I knew he'd be furious if he discovered I'd defied him. I thought he'd only punish me, the way he had before...I was such a fool, I should have listened to his warnings! But I disobeyed, too selfish to think of consequences, and because of that, she died!"

Dev's glare grew all the more ferocious. "So now you're buying into Ruslan's head games? Fuck that. There's only one person at fault here: that manipulative demonspawn you called master, and don't you forget it."

"It's easier to blame Ruslan," Kiran said, his voice low.

"Yeah, because he's the one that *actually fucking killed her.*" Dev flung his arms wide. "I can't believe we're arguing about this." He grabbed Kiran's wrist. "Get up."

"Why?" Kiran resisted, but Dev tugged until he stood.

"You said tomorrow's Alisa's Naming day, right? Well, I know a better way for you to honor her memory than screaming nightmares." Dev stomped over to the door and threw it open. "Hey! Lena, are you lurking out there?"

Lena appeared, a glass of water in her hand and her brows arched in inquiry.

"Forget the water. Where's the wine?" Dev asked. "I need that, and some fire stones. Or wait, you Alathians aren't much on charms. Firewood, then." He turned to Kiran. "Trust me, this is a fine outrider tradition. We'll go out in the garden, make a nice big fire, get drunk, and tell stories about the people we want to remember. Only about the good times, mind you. No bad memories allowed."

For a moment, his eyes were shadowed. Kiran remembered a comment Cara had once made about the number of outriders that died young. Melly's father Sethan couldn't be the only friend Dev mourned.

"All right," he said reluctantly.

Dev glanced at Lena. "This'd work better without a minder."

She surveyed him, then Kiran. "I think Talmaddis's duty is still satisfied so long as he can see you through a window. Try not to set any plants on fire, though, unless you want to explain yourself to the groundskeeper—he may be retired from active duty on the Watch, but he can still spellcast, and he's got quite the temper. Oh, and blackberry wine will have to do. That's all we keep in the cellar."

"I've drunk worse," Dev said. "Come on, Kiran. Let's go find something safe to burn."

✳

(Dev)

I dumped Kiran unceremoniously onto his bed and stepped back with a satisfied grunt. He was well and truly out of it, his body slack in the moonlight striping the quilt. He'd probably have a nasty hangover in the morning, but if he had another nightmare tonight, I'd eat one of the damn rosebushes.

I weaved a bit as I headed for the door. I'd made sure Kiran did the lion's share of the drinking, but the blackberry wine had been stronger than I expected. Hell, it had only taken a couple drinks before Kiran got some color back in his face and stopped flinching at the sound of Alisa's name. After a few more, he even managed to tell stories about her.

He'd sounded just like any other lovestruck young idiot, starry-eyed and utterly convinced that his beloved was without flaw. The moonbrained delirium of first love had lasted longer for Kiran than most; turned out he'd been sneaking off to meet Alisa in scant, stolen hours spread over nearly three years. I'd been surprised he could hide it from Ruslan that long. I hadn't said so, not wanting to get onto dangerous ground, but Kiran read it in my face. He said tersely that he'd taken care only to slip away during times when Ruslan was busy with other matters, and he'd had Mikail's help in covering his absences—until the end, when Mikail betrayed him. Seeing the growing anguish in his eyes, I'd changed the subject in a hurry, coaxing him into yet more dreamy-voiced memories of the beautiful, clever, oh-so-wonderful Alisa.

No woman could be that perfect, not once the blinders of infatuation wore off. But Kiran would never get to know the reality of her, thanks to Ruslan. I rubbed a hand over my face, wearily. Mother of maidens, what a mess.

As I negotiated the doorway, I heard a low mutter of voices drifting up the stairway at the hallway's end. One of them had Martennan's drawling accent. What was he doing back here? I slid along the wall with all the stealth I could muster.

"...grant you permission to take both of the Arkennlanders?" That was Talmaddis's light tenor, shaded with concern.

"I believe so," Martennan said. "Though some in the Council think me either a madman or a fool. But Varellian supports me, and I think she will carry the day in the end. I fear by now my debt to her is so great I'll never repay it."

He sounded like that debt was a real concern. After a considering pause, Talmaddis said, "Well. When she calls in a favor, it can't be as bad as that mess with the ships we handled for Orenntavis. I still have nightmares about those sea monsters."

Sea monsters, huh? Maybe life in Alathia wasn't quite so boring as I'd assumed.

Martennan chuckled ruefully. But when he spoke, the words were dead serious. "I think our task in Ninavel will make poisonous tentacled horrors seem a pleasant diversion."

So. Not quite as blasé over the risk as he'd been in front of Kiran. He might just mean Ruslan, but I had a dark suspicion there was something he hadn't told us.

"Oh, I believe you," said Talmaddis. "I spent three whole years stationed there, remember? Human monsters are the worst by far. But enough of that...you look like the Council dragged you through a herd of angry pronghorns. Come relax a moment. Have a glass of wine, assuming the Arkennlanders haven't guzzled every drop in the house."

"Your company will be relaxation enough." The depth of warmth in Martennan's words made me blink. I risked a glance around the corner, down through the staircase's iron railings. In the foyer below, Martennan and Talmaddis stood facing each other, mere inches apart. Even as I watched, Martennan put his palm flat on Talmaddis's chest, right above the Council seal on Talmaddis's uniform. Talmaddis covered Martennan's hand with his own in a motion just short of a caress. A smile both fond and wicked spread on Talmaddis's lean face before the two men moved off toward the study.

Lovers, then. Interesting. I'd heard that in Alathia's common guard, officers were forbidden to pair with soldiers under their command, to prevent favoritism. It'd be nice to think what I'd seen might provide a lever against Martennan—but then, he and Talmaddis hadn't exactly seemed furtive about their affection. Maybe the Council gave the mages of the Watch more leeway in personal matters to make up for all the other restrictions piled on them.

"Do you need something, Dev?" Lena spoke from behind me.

I turned a little too fast and had to steady myself on the wall. "Uh. No. That is, I wanted to get some water from the kitchen." At least I managed to speak without slurring. Much. How long had she been standing there? She couldn't blame me for listening to Talmaddis and Martennan when they were standing right out in plain view.

Lena took in my death grip on the corner, and her mouth twitched. "I take it your efforts with Kiran were successful?"

"Yeah," I said. "No more screaming, tonight at least." I peered at her. "Martennan had better bring some yeleran extract along to Ninavel. Hell, I don't know why Kiran's not using it here. He wouldn't need any calming teas then." I'd learned on our trip across the Whitefires that yeleran sent Kiran into a heavy, dreamless sleep, the same way it did for everyone else.

"When the healers at the Sanitorium examined him a few weeks ago, they told us not to allow him any more doses," Lena said. "They said Kiran had been using yeleran too often, and they were worried about an imbalance of the body humours."

"Well, shit. In that case, bring some earplugs." Getting Kiran drunk had worked tonight, but I didn't think that was such a good idea in Ninavel, not with Ruslan lying in wait.

"I know the trip won't be easy for him." Lena glanced back towards Kiran's room. Her expression softened subtly. With pity, or something more? I remembered Cara watching Kiran walk past the campfire one night early in our crossing of the Whitefires, and saying *Damn, Dev, sometimes the kid's too pretty to be human. If I were young and dumb like you, I'd have him in my bed so fast your head would spin, apprentice or no.* I'd laughed myself sick and called her an old crone the rest of the night. But Khalmet knew she was right about Kiran's looks. I'd thought the Alathians so ice-blooded as to be immune, but if not, good. Kiran needed all the advantage he could get.

Lena herself was nicely easy on the eyes, especially after two months spent with miners as ugly and bad-tempered as rock bears. Her slim curves reminded me of Cara, though she lacked Cara's sure, easy strength, not to mention her quick tongue and bright, carefree laugh. But if she had Cara's courage, that'd be far more important for Kiran.

"The trip not easy? Hell," I said. "Would you have the guts to walk into a rabid sandcat's den on the say-so of a man you can't trust?"

She laid a light hand on my arm. "I know you're wary of Marten. I'm sure I'd feel the same in your place. But you didn't see how hard he fought to save Kiran's life after the trial. The Council was convinced execution was the safest course. They feared Kiran's rejection of blood magic wouldn't last; that Ruslan's influence had been too strong. Marten called in every favor he had, staked his reputation and his commission as Captain on his belief that Kiran deserved the chance to prove them wrong."

I pulled my arm free. "Sure, he fought—you were the one who told me at the trial Martennan wants to convince the Council to back off their restrictions on magic. He saw the chance to use Kiran as a lever and a resource, and he took it. Am I grateful Kiran's alive? Hell yeah. Just don't expect me to believe Martennan cares one whit for him, or anyone else. I know his kind—all smiles and warm words until you'd fucking turn your soul inside out for them, and then the minute they've had their use of you, they cast you into Shaikar's hells without even *pretending* to feel sorry for it—!"

I checked my shout, as my brain finally caught up with my tongue. Gods all damn that blackberry wine, anyway! The startled pity on Lena's face made me want to strangle her. Or myself.

"You're wrong about Marten," she said quietly. "He has faults, I admit it. But they lie in…other areas." From the sudden shuttering of her expression, she'd thought better of elaborating on those faults to me.

"Like bedding his second lieutenant?" She must know about Talmaddis and Martennan. Maybe she wasn't too happy about it, especially if it meant he favored the lower-ranked Talmaddis over her.

Lena's gaze sharpened. But she shrugged and said, "That's no fault. Marten and Talm have shared a bed for years. He's never let it affect his command decisions."

Damn. I should've gotten her drunk along with Kiran. Maybe then I could've found out something I could use. Then again, maybe with a little prodding…

"You think I've got Martennan all wrong, then fine. Tell me what he's really like."

"He keeps his promises, no matter the cost. And he'd swim through a lake of magefire for his friends." Lena's mouth curved. "Rather like you, from what Kiran tells me."

Yeah, that wasn't exactly a comforting thought. I knew the depths to which I'd sink to keep a vow, and I sure didn't believe Martennan counted us among his friends.

"Good to know," I said, bright as I could. I started down the staircase, gripping the railing for stability.

"Dev."

"What?" I glanced back. The intensity of her gaze made me uncomfortable. She said only, "You and Kiran should have news of the Council's decision by noon. If your head aches when you wake, tell Talmaddis—he can aid you."

Practical as a quartermaster. It reminded me once again of Cara—though Cara would've mocked me 'til the sun came up for getting drunk on something mild as blackberry wine. I nodded to Lena, and even managed a smile before I staggered off to the kitchen to gulp down water that tasted faintly of roseships. Once back in my room, I flung myself on my bed and tried to think of nothing but Cara, and how in Ninavel I'd see her again. But the memories that chased me down into sleep weren't of Cara's lithe body and flashing smile, but of Simon's Taint charm glittering on my wrist, and a rock hanging high in the air as I laughed in wild exultation, uncaring of the pain savaging my gut.

✳

(Kiran)

"You know the worst part of this translocation business?" Dev said, as he and Kiran trailed Lena through the gray stone corridors of the Arcanum. "I could've really used some time in the Whitefires."

He said it lightly, but Kiran caught the flash of longing in Dev's eyes. He remembered Dev dangling from pitons on an improbably steep cliff, his head thrown back in a laugh of purest joy, and a pang squeezed Kiran's chest.

"If all goes well in Ninavel, maybe you won't have to wait long to climb in the mountains again." Perhaps not long at all. Kiran knew Dev had no intention of returning to Alathia once beyond the border, regardless of what happened in Ninavel. A thought that brought equal parts relief and regret.

Marten and Lena were kind enough, but the shadow of the Council hung over every interaction. It felt so good to have a friend whose loyalty was unconstrained.

"Maybe." Dev looked wistful again. His stride held a simmering energy Kiran hadn't seen in him since the Whitefires.

Kiran's footsteps were far heavier. Ever since Lena had brought the news the Council had agreed to his conditions, he felt as if he stood in the path of an onrushing avalanche, helpless to cast against it. He tried to think only of the removal of his binding in Ninavel. No more cramped, gnawing confinement of his senses, his *ikilhia* freed to spark spells once more...oh, how he yearned for it! Yet the specter of Ruslan shadowed his heart.

Lena halted before the door of Marten's personal workroom. A thicket of black ward lines covered the frame, so dense hardly any wood showed. Lena laid a palm flat on the wards.

Marten called something encouraging but indistinct from within, and the wards glowed silver. Lena pushed open the door and led them inside.

No matter how many times Kiran visited Marten's workroom, the disarray within never ceased to startle him. Ruslan had always been adamant in his insistence upon order, with all spell materials, diagrams, and treatises catalogued and neatly stored. Stevannes and the other arcanists seemed similar in outlook, but Marten worked in a kind of floating chaos. Scribbled diagrams covered the walls, while random assortments of gems and metal rods lay scattered over shelves. Marten himself stood behind a desk half buried under teetering piles of papers and books.

"Good news, you two." Marten skirted a stray pile and waved Dev and Kiran to a pair of empty chairs amid the clutter. Lena remained standing by the door, her hands behind her back and her spine as straight as any soldier's. "The preparations are almost complete for the translocation spell. The Watch will cast at moonrise."

Moonrise was little more than an hour away. Kiran nodded, his mouth gone dry.

Marten said, "I told you my team would include an arcanist. I'm pleased to say my top choice agreed to come to Ninavel with us." He glanced at Lena. "Did you send Talm to find—"

A rap came on the door. Martennan brightened. "Ah, excellent. There's Stevan now. Come in!"

Kiran stiffened. Stevan—did Marten mean...?

Stevannes strode into the workroom, accompanied by Talmaddis. Chalk smudged the sleeves of the arcanist's uniform, his wiry auburn hair in disarray. He carried a rosewood box covered in gold sigils of an odd, angular style Kiran never seen.

"Stevan." Marten's greeting was as warm as if he and Stevannes were mage-brothers. "I'm delighted to have a man of your expertise on this mission."

"*Captain* Martennan." Stevannes bowed, icily formal. "I know my duty."

Kiran ducked his head to hide a dismayed grimace. It made sense Marten would want to bring an expert in defensive magic, but couldn't he have found someone less virulent in his prejudice?

Marten hitched a hip onto his desk and aimed a genial smile at Stevannes. "I'll introduce you to the rest of the team, then. You know my lieutenants, and you've worked with Kiran, but I don't think you've met Dev. He'll be accompanying us to Ninavel."

Stevannes's fingers whitened on his rosewood box. "I knew you intended to bring the blood mage—a decision questionable enough!—but now you intend to bring his criminal accomplice?" His mask of formality cracked. The frustrated fury revealed beneath blazed as hot as Ruslan's had in the days after Kiran's *akhelashva* ritual. "Marten, I don't understand you. Pandering to the blood mage this way, championing him to the Council! How you, of all people, can stomach that—"

"Stevan." Marten laid a hand on Stevannes's shoulder. The two men stared at each other in silence, though Kiran had the sense of something wordless passing between them. Stevannes shook his head sharply and backed away. His expression froze into formality once more.

"It is, of course, your decision. Captain."

Dev's eyes had narrowed to green slits. "Oh, what fun this trip will be," he muttered.

Kiran burned with the desire to quiz Marten on what Stevannes had meant. *You, of all people...* He'd have to wait, ask Marten in private. As well as ask what had possessed Marten to include Stevannes on the trip. For all Stevannes's skill, he'd surely provoke every Ninavel mage he met into a blood-feud.

Marten said, "Dev's connections in the city should prove quite useful to us, Stevan. And Dev, Stevan's skill with defensive magic is unrivaled in the Arcanum. It's thanks to his efforts that we can block Kiran's mark-bond." He surveyed them, sternly. "If we're to work together as closely as we must in Ninavel, I think it best to apply the rules I've set for the officers in my own Watch. If you have a complaint of anyone's behavior, you bring it to me first; and we'll use informal names. All of us." He directed a pointed look at Stevannes, whose mouth pinched like he'd eaten a rotten thornapple.

Marten went on. "Speaking of your mark-bond, Kiran, there's one issue we must discuss further. You recall the amulet requires active casting to protect you properly. To ensure your safety, Stevan recommends not just one, but a team of mages work together in shifts for the casting. Three of us should be sufficient. The mages stationed at the embassy can help out as shift members, but the shifts must be led by either me or Stevan, and it's vital that you stay close to the shift leader. I can't stress that enough. Do not get more than a few feet away."

"That's the craziest thing I've yet heard," Dev said sharply. "He'll have to drag an entire gang of you around wherever he goes?"

"Until we are certain of Sechaveh's protection, yes," Marten said. "Perhaps even afterward, during times Kiran travels outside the embassy's wards. I want to be assured of his safety."

Kiran exchanged a worried glance with Dev, whose frown had deepened. Kiran knew Dev's fear: how would they carry out their plan for Melly with a constant entourage of Alathians in tow? Kiran's concern ran deeper. He trusted Marten, but Stevannes was another matter. If all it took was one moment of inattention on Stevannes's part, deliberate or otherwise, to leave him exposed to Ruslan…

"Must the other shift leader be Stevannes—Stevan, I mean?" he asked Marten.

Stevan turned a look of cold disgust on him. Marten sighed. "Stevan and I are the only ones qualified for this type of spellwork. Kiran, I vow to you on my honor as Watch captain that Stevan will execute his duty regardless of his personal feelings."

Stevan said, "As a blood mage, doubtless you can't conceive of loyalty to anything beyond your own selfish desires. But you may rest assured: I obey the Council's orders. Always."

It was difficult to feel reassured when Stevan's tone was more reminiscent of a threat than a promise.

Dev leaned toward Kiran and muttered, "You can still change your mind."

Cowardice whispered that Kiran should seize the excuse. Yet if he wanted the chance to seek true freedom from Ruslan, he had to earn the Council's trust. More, during that long night after his trial, he'd promised Dev: *should you ever need my help, you'll have it.* The restriction on Kiran's movements needn't stop them from helping Melly, particularly if he could convince Dev to explain the problem to Marten. Working with Marten as closely as they must, surely Dev would see that his distrust of Marten was unfounded.

Fear is the most insidious of weaknesses, Ruslan had once said. *You must learn to raze it from your soul, or risk defeat in all you do.*

"I understand," Kiran said to Marten. The words felt heavy as stones. Once said, they left his chest hollow.

Marten awarded him a smile as warm as the midsummer sun. "Excellent. We've set aside some supplies for you and Dev, clothes and the like—Talm can show you, while Stevan, Lena, and I make a few last preparations."

Kiran nodded, not trusting himself to speak again. The closer their departure came, the more impossible mastering his fear seemed.

※

Kiran followed Marten and Dev into the cavernous space of the Council chamber on legs that felt like a stranger's. Moonrise was mere moments away. He risked a glance upward at the stacked circular galleries rising above the chamber floor. A chill prickled his skin at the sight of the ranks of uniformed mages lining the rails.

He'd stood on this sigil-marked floor once before, locked within wards as the Watch dug through his memories and forced a binding onto his magic. His chest cramped with remembered agony, but he forced himself to walk steadily after Marten.

A scattering of sigils had been incised outside a set of four interlocking circles at the floor's center. The sigils must help the Alathians direct the power into their desired spell pattern, in place of the channel lines Kiran was accustomed to working with. But the Alathians' techniques were so different from those he'd been taught, he couldn't tell a thing about the spell. The sigils' complex black scrawls held no meaning he could read, and their sparse, seemingly random placement looked nothing like the dense channel diagram Ruslan had once shown him for a translocation spell.

"Khalmet's bones," Dev said, as they halted within the circles. He dropped his pack and eyed the surrounding sigils uneasily. "What happens if they screw this up?"

"Then our worries will be over," Kiran said. Even with an anchor point ready and waiting in Ninavel, the amount of power needed for the translocation would be massive enough to make any mistakes fatal.

"What a comforting thought." Dev glanced at Marten, who stood conferring with two other captains. "I wish they'd hurry up."

The chamber's side door opened, and the other members of their little group entered. Stevan still clutched the rosewood box, which Kiran had learned contained the link-blocking amulet. Talm lugged a much larger sigil-marked chest, and Lena carried a satchel stamped with the green tree of the Sanitorium.

Kiran couldn't take his eyes from Stevan's box. Marten had warned him no charms could be worn during the translocation spell's casting, lest spell patterns interfere with each other to catastrophic effect. *We'll put the amulet on you the instant we reach Ninavel,* he'd assured Kiran. At the time, that had sounded reasonable. Now Kiran's nerves screamed otherwise. The defenses he'd woven from his own *ikilhia* felt horribly frail, limited as he'd been by the Council's binding.

"Hey. You'll be fine." Dev's voice was low but firm. His neck was bare, his snapthroat charm removed by Marten before they'd entered the chamber.

Kiran realized he'd been rubbing at the left side of his chest, where Ruslan's *akhelsya* sigil lay hidden beneath his shirt. He dropped his hand. "I hope so," he said, and tried to smile at Dev. It felt more like a rictus.

The two Watch captains bowed to Marten and backed away as Councilor Varellian descended the stairway from the galleries above. Varellian's face was as stern as Kiran remembered it from his trial, the folds of her blue and gray uniform starched to knife-blade sharpness.

Marten bowed, arms crossed over his chest. "We are ready. Have you word from Ambassador Halassian?"

Varellian nodded. "Lord Sechaveh is open to granting sanction and protection, but he insists on seeing you first. Ambassador Halassian has arranged an audience for you upon your arrival." She paused, studying Marten with piercing intensity. "The future of our country depends on your team's efforts, Captain. I pray our faith in your talents is justified."

For once, Marten's expression was perfectly grave. "We will not fail you."

Kiran's nerves shrieked louder yet. He'd hoped Sechaveh's edict would be in place before they left Alathia. His muscles trembled with the urge to flee from the sigils, to tell Marten, *I cannot do this, the risk is too great.* The awareness of Dev at his side steadied him. Dev must have felt this same fear when he came to Simon's valley to seek Kiran, yet he hadn't let it stop him. Kiran wouldn't either.

Varellian strode for the gallery stairway, the two captains at her heels. Marten turned to Kiran and Dev. "You two, stand here…" He positioned them in the precise center of the pattern, as Lena, Talm, and Stevan moved to stand within the surrounding circles. "I'd suggest closing your eyes," Marten added, as he backed to the final circle. "When the spell takes effect, the transition will be a bit disorienting."

The chamber doors boomed shut. Kiran wiped sweat from his palms and concentrated on breathing through a throat that felt as tight as a reed. No turning back now. The mages in the galleries started a low, droning chant, first in unison, then diverging into interweaving harmonies. The sigils on the floor lit with the strange, soft glow so different than the harsh fire of activated channel lines. Power rose with the slow inevitability of water trickling into a cistern.

The mages' song patterned the magic into a fascinatingly elegant structure formed of shifting pulses and currents. The power peaked, held. The song took on a subtle dissonance, like the muttering of thunder before a storm. A trio of voices called out in a wild, keening descant, and Kiran gasped, hands flying up in an involuntary warding gesture, as a soundless concussion slammed against his inner barriers.

An immense rush of magic howled through the Alathians' pattern. The sigils' glow heightened to blinding intensity. Kiran shut his eyes against the glare and felt a sudden dizzying wrench in his stomach, as if he'd stepped off a cliff. Power crashed over him, and he bit back a cry, his senses reeling.

Deep in his mind, a shock of connection. An echo of surprise shifted into fierce triumph, and Ruslan's voice whispered with dark, delighted promise:

Welcome home, Kiran.

CHAPTER SIX

(Dev)

Glaring afterimages blocked my vision, my ears ringing as if they'd been boxed. Retching, I doubled over, lost my balance and fell to my knees. I planted my hands on cold stone and cursed Marten. A *little* disorienting? Khalmet's bloodsoaked hand! My stomach was trying to crawl out my throat.

Dimly, I registered shouting, tinny through the whine in my ears.

"Hurry, get it on him!"

"Stevan, *now—*"

Oh gods, Kiran and the amulet! I dragged an arm across my eyes and squinted through fading swathes of green.

Kiran was hunched on his knees with his fists pressed to his temples. Marten knelt before him, one palm braced against the amulet glinting on Kiran's chest, his other hand gripping Kiran's shoulder so tightly his fingers showed white. Stevan, Talm and Lena stood rigid behind Marten. Concentration hazed their eyes, Stevan's teeth bared in a grimace of effort. Beyond was a wall of white stone streaked with silver ward lines, the room far smaller than the high-ceilinged expanse of the Council chamber. Sigils glowed on the floor, their light slowly fading. On the far side of the sigil pattern, a pair of uniformed mages watched us with wary intensity.

I staggered to my feet, careful to avoid the sigils. Mother of maidens, if the amulet didn't work, and Ruslan got hold of Kiran...my legs twitched with the urge to run.

Kiran shuddered. His hands fell from his temples to clutch at Marten's arms. "He knows. Marten, he knows I'm here…"

"The link," Marten said, voice urgent. "Can you feel him, Kiran?"

Kiran let out a long, wavering breath. "No. Not now."

Oh, thank Khalmet. Though if Ruslan knew Kiran had come, he'd already be scheming another way to get at him. I eyed the ward patterns on the wall. Ninavel-made, not Alathian, and deadly as any I'd ever seen. Somebody in the embassy wasn't so dumb as to hold to the Alathian legal standard. I took another look at the silent mages watching us. Both had the olive skin and straight dark hair so common to Alathians, but that was where their similarities ended. One was a muscled plug of a man who looked more suited to ore hauling than spellcasting. The other was a rail-thin, hawk-nosed woman in her forties.

"Have a care, Marten." The slow, cold precision of Stevan's speech signaled the effort he continued to make with Kiran's amulet. "I don't know how deeply Ruslan might have read the boy before I blocked the link. He may know far more than the mere fact of our arrival."

"Kiran?" Marten helped Kiran to his feet. "What did you sense?"

Kiran's face was as white as the stone surrounding us, his blue eyes distant and dark.

Haltingly, he said, "I felt Ruslan's thoughts. He was surprised. Then… pleased." The last word snagged in his throat like it'd been caught on a thorn. "He would have felt mine. But I'd woven defenses—they still stand, I don't think he penetrated deeper than the surface." His fingers clawed into Marten's shirt. "Marten, the binding—please, you must release it, if he's coming for me I have to *fight*—"

My fists clenched in sympathy. Nothing worse than facing a threat helpless.

"Soon as we can prepare the ritual, I promise you." Gently, Marten disengaged Kiran's grip. "Stevan is leading this first shift. Remember to stay close to him." He looked past me and bent in a deep, formal bow. "Ambassador Halassian. Forgive my delay in greeting you, but this matter was too important to wait."

I turned. Standing in an archway was a short, plump woman whose granite-gray hair was bound up in a knotwork of braids even more complex than Councilor Varellian's. She wore a long, billowing Sulanian-style dress, but the fabric was in subtle shades of blue and gray, the Council seal plain on her left shoulder.

"Yes, yes." She flapped a hand at Marten. "Welcome to Ninavel, Captain. Good to see the translocation spell didn't turn you to jelly. Better yet to see that trinket of yours actually managed to keep a snake like Ruslan

Khaveirin at bay." She glanced at the mismatched pair of uniformed mages. "Jenoviann, Kessaravil, go recheck the main wards. Tell me if you feel the slightest hint of that sly bastard testing them."

They bowed and hurried out. Marten said to her, "You'll remember Talmaddis from his time stationed here, but let me introduce the rest of my team…" He pointed out Lena and Stevan, and introduced me as "Devan *na soliin*, of Ninavel," using the old Arkennlander form that politely indicated I lacked a family name. Halassian studied me with keen interest; an interest that sharpened further when Marten got to Kiran.

"So this is Khaveirin's wayward apprentice," she said. "Well, he's pretty enough, but aside from that I don't see what all the fuss is about."

She said it in just the right tone of dry irony. Kiran blinked, a hint of color staining his cheeks, and lost some of his snared-roundtail look. Nice to know the Council had better sense than to send a typical Alathian prig as their ambassador to Ninavel. Halassian was the first Alathian I'd met who spoke direct as any streetsider, and thank Khalmet for that. I'd take bluntness any day over evasions and polite lies.

Marten's grin held only a shadow of his usual cheer. "You wouldn't dismiss Kiran so readily if you'd helped bind his power. Speaking of which, I need supplies and assistance in incising the sigils for the release of that binding… but first, I must know: how soon may I speak with Sechaveh?"

Good question. I didn't hold much confidence even the strongest of wards would stop Ruslan for long. As for the amulet, it might be working, but from the strain on Stevan, Talm, and Lena's faces, keeping Kiran safe was no easy task.

"Sechaveh's granted you audience in Kelante Tower at dawn," Halassian said. "It's not just you he wants to see, Captain. He insists on meeting everyone for whom you want sanction and protection. No exceptions." She glanced at me and Kiran.

Dawn was a mere two hours away. That part sounded good, but the rest… "We have to leave the wards to see him? That's an ambush waiting to happen."

Halassian chuckled, a surprisingly hearty sound for such a short woman. "Direct as a magefire strike, aren't you? And from Acaltar district, unless I miss my guess." She turned to Marten. "Good thinking bringing him. Ninavel's not like Tamanath. Important business here is all backroom deals and viper's games, and if you want to track down the source of these deaths and disturbances to Alathia's wards, you'll need eyes and ears streetside."

She sobered and met my gaze. "It's a risk to leave the wards, young Devan, but not so high as you fear. Even a mage as powerful as Ruslan will be hard-pressed to cast against you with so short a time to prepare."

"It's Dev, not Devan." Only the Alathian Council used my full name, and hearing it made me think of trials and sentencings. "Don't be so sure Ruslan hasn't time to cast. Kiran thought that in the Whitefires, right before Ruslan hammered us with a spell-made snowstorm that almost did us in."

Kiran nodded. "It's a terrible mistake to underestimate him," he said softly.

"We all know it," Marten said. "Yet we need the protection against Ruslan's casting that Sechaveh can provide. The embassy's wards won't hold forever against him if he chooses to launch a sustained assault. Ambassador, how far to Kelante Tower?"

"A half hour's brisk walk to Kelante's warded gate if you use the Tourmaline Bridge and climb the Blackstar Stair," Halassian said. "I can send Kessaravil with you if you'd like an extra mage on hand who's not tied up pouring power into that amulet. I'd send Jenoviann too, but I want her here on the wards."

"The help would be appreciated," Marten agreed.

From Halassian's description of the route, the embassy must be high in the spires of Seltonis District. I grimaced, thinking of half an hour spent walking the steep, airy causeways that spiraled around highside towers and spanned the gaps between them. Maybe the mages could survive the fall if Ruslan shattered a bridge from under us, but I wouldn't.

Kiran lifted his chin, his jaw set. "When will you unbind my magic?"

"I'll start the sigils as soon as I may," Marten said. "If Halassian can spare someone to help me complete them after our audience with Sechaveh, we should be ready to perform the ritual by evening."

"You can't work faster and do it before dawn?" I asked. If I were Kiran, hell if I'd want to waltz over to Kelante Tower without the means to defend myself.

Behind Kiran, Stevan said, "Magic isn't as simple as scratching a few sigils on the floor." Despite the labored pace of his words, the contempt came through plain as day.

Halassian said sternly to me, "One mistake in lifting this binding and your friend could be mentally crippled or even killed. Any casting that happens in this embassy is my responsibility, and I say it's done right, with full precautions, or not at all."

Hard to argue with that. I glanced at Kiran. He nodded, though I could tell he thought tonight distant as the eastern sea.

A sharp voice called from outside the room, "Ambassador! We've sighted wardfire."

We all stampeded after Halassian through the archway. Kiran shadowed
Stevan close enough to trip on his heels, Talm and Lena right behind him.
My heart hung in my throat. I'd told them Ruslan wouldn't dally. How long
could the Alathians hold him off?

In a wide room full of silk hangings and sleek, cushioned couches,
Halassian's two lieutenants stood beside a great arched window. Copper
panels inscribed with wards bracketed the window on all sides, the shutters
open to admit the night breeze. To my surprise, the ward panels were dark
and silent, without even a warning glimmer.

"Wardfire, where?" Halassian demanded.

"The Aiyalen Spire." Hawk-nosed Jenoviann pointed a skinny arm out
into the night, where nearby towers glittered with colored magelights like
a jeweler's showcase. Aiyalen was the tallest of them, a soaring pinnacle
capped by five stone crescents as sharp and thin as nightstar blades. Beyond,
the jagged wall of the Whitefire Mountains blocked out half the night sky,
the rest dusted by stars brilliant in the dry desert air.

The sight of that familiar skyline struck a pang into my heart. Gods, I'd
missed the Whitefires—and Ninavel too, for all it was a nest of vipers. I
squinted at the Aiyalen Spire. I didn't see any wardfire. What did—

The entire top third of the tower flared a lurid violet. Silent lightning
wreathed the stone and clawed at the air above, flickering through indigo
and blue to a bruised, poisonous green.

I gasped right along with the mages. Mother of maidens, I'd never seen
wards trigger on such a scale. But… "Why's Ruslan attacking Aiyalen and
not here?" It had to be Ruslan; nobody but a blood mage could cast a spell
strong enough to spark such a display.

Marten stretched a splayed hand out the window into the night air. "I
sense no blood magic—no hint of any spellwork cast against the tower, in
fact. How can this be?"

Halassian said, "I have no answer for you. Yet I don't believe this wardfire
is Ruslan's doing. In recent weeks, we've seen wards trigger on the Aiyalen
Spire and other towers, though not to quite such a spectacular level. Each
time, as now, we can't sense even a single offensive spell. The caster is using
a type of magic completely unknown to us—and believe me, we know the
feel of blood magic."

I looked to Kiran. His eyes were squeezed shut, his head tilted as if he
strained to listen for some faint sound. "The confluence—the currents feel
odd, unsettled…but between the amulet and my binding, I can't sense

anything more."

The wardfire vanished as abruptly as it had appeared. I stared at the spire, not sure whether to feel relieved Ruslan wasn't yet casting against us, or more worried. Ruslan might be scary as shit, but at least the Alathians knew how to counter him. If they couldn't even sense the casting of whoever was striking at the towers, how could they stop it?

The first step in scouting a mark was to find out what they wanted. "What's up there in Aiyalen, Sechaveh's personal gem vaults? I didn't even know wards came that strong." Red Dal hadn't let his Tainters dream of trying to sneak into Aiyalen. A policy I understood after seeing that little fireworks show.

Kiran said, "That section of the spire is where mages cast water spells for Lord Sechaveh."

Oh, hell. Ninavel had storage cisterns, one in each district, but they'd be drained in days if Ninavel's mages didn't continuously refill them. The closest natural sources of water were the glacial lakes west of the Whitefires' fanged crest. Reaching those lakes required several days' climb up a trail that'd kill waterless travelers long before they reached the pass. Scarce water would mean riots, deaths...and I'd no doubt those in the poorer districts would suffer first and most. Streetsiders, like me and my city friends.

Marten and Halassian had both turned to stare at Kiran. "You've worked in the tower, then?" Halassian sounded eager. "We know that's where the water magic is cast, but Sechaveh's never allowed foreigners inside."

"No." Kiran's shoulders hunched. "Ruslan wouldn't let us work real magic until we came of age." He looked like he was praying Marten would change the subject.

Stevan said, "You told the Council you went through the ritual two months before you left Ninavel. In all that time, you never helped your master with water duty?"

"I said no," Kiran snapped. He wrapped his arms tight around himself like a man cold to the bone, though the day's heat lingered in the air.

I'd never asked him what had gone on during the time between Alisa's death and the day he showed up in Bren's office seeking my help to cross the Whitefires. Now, I wondered. He couldn't have fought Ruslan the whole time. He must have pretended compliance at some point to be allowed the freedom to go down streetside to meet Bren. How far had that compliance gone?

"Too bad." Halassian pursed her lips. "It would certainly be helpful to know the exact nature of the wards within the tower."

"When Sechaveh gives us sanction, perhaps we can find out." Marten ran a finger along the wards on the windowsill. "Your dispatches spoke of mages dying. Did the deaths happen in the towers during wardfire events? The energies in the aether must be horrifically dangerous to any mage nearby."

"No, and that's the oddest part," Halassian said. "According to our informants, the mages died in their own homes."

Kiran said, "I know Alathian laws restrict what wards mages may use, but here, the wards on a workroom might be equally as powerful as any Sechaveh has on the Aiyalen Spire. If the mages' personal wards triggered in the way we just saw, the overspill could easily be fatal."

Halassian grunted. "True, but we've heard no reports of wardfire like that in the residential sections."

"What else have you learned?" Marten asked.

"Very little." Halassian's scowl spoke of frustration. "Sechaveh hasn't let anyone not in his employ set foot in the dead mages' houses. He's got a Seranthine scholar, a sand mage, in charge of the investigation. Weedy little fellow, but clever as a kitfox and tightlipped as they come. Our usual informants claim not to know anything else, and ordinary Arkennlanders all clam up the instant they realize one of us is nearby. I dare not use any listening spells, not with every mage and highsider covered in defensive charms."

She looked at me, her expression lightening. "That's why Dev here will come in handy. I'll wager he can find out more in one night streetside than we could learn in weeks up here. We'll have our work cut out for us sifting fact from embellishment, but I'd far rather worry about that than have no information at all."

"I'll do what I can," I said. "Assuming I can step outside your wards without Ruslan leaping on me."

Marten said, "That's why it's vital our audience with Sechaveh goes well. Those of you coming to Kelante Tower, listen to me..." He beckoned to Kessaravil, who approached with a fluid grace surprising in a man so muscle-bound. Stevan, Lena, and Talm lost some of their distant air, focusing with sober attention on Marten.

"The meeting will be a delicate diplomatic situation," Marten said. "As such, I must insist that no one but me speaks to Sechaveh unless I explicitly give you permission. I'll enforce silence if I have to." He gave me a particularly pointed look.

I scowled. Yeah, I got the message. He'd shut me up with magic the minute I dared to open my streetsider mouth.

"I must also ask that you trust my judgment and follow my lead, whatever Sechaveh may say." This time his gaze swept across the mages of the Watch.

"Of course, Captain." Lena's words were as slow as Stevan's had been, but full of calm assurance. The others murmured assent.

"Good," Marten said. "I have a few Council matters to discuss with Halassian before we leave for the audience—Halassian, perhaps your lieutenants can show my team their quarters, and where our supplies may be stowed?"

Halassian waved a hand. "Jenoviann, Kessaravil, if you would?"

Jenoviann had none of Kessaravil's grace. She stalked along beside him as stiff as a bone puppet as they led us back to the sigil-marked room to retrieve our packs. Though her gaunt face remained impassive, I caught her darting repeated glances at Kiran, and I didn't think she was admiring his looks.

Packs in hand, we followed her down another short hallway to a set of interconnecting rooms furnished with simple but sturdy beds and a few chairs. From the scuff marks on the bare walls and the rumpled look of the rugs, I suspected the rooms had been hurriedly converted to bedrooms from storage space.

Kiran and I dumped our packs in a room that held two narrow beds and a round window. The window was far smaller than the one in the embassy's receiving room, but the view of magelit spires against the sawtoothed bulk of the Whitefires was equally magnificent.

I peered out, careful not to touch the wards on the sill. Beyond was an eight-story drop to the nearest bridge. Highside towers always had enough carved friezes and depressions between blocks to make a climb possible, if tricky. But the window's wards were powerful and well-placed. They were designed to prevent intruders from getting in, not leaving; if I could climb out without touching the frame, they wouldn't fully trigger. They'd flare enough to warn Marten I'd crossed them, though, and once outside I wouldn't be able to climb back in. Not that I had any intention of leaving the embassy's wards on my own while Rulsan was salivating for any means he could use to get at Kiran. But if we gained the protection Marten hoped for from Sechaveh, I wanted to find Cara, preferably without any Alathian watchdogs in tow.

The thought drew my gaze down to the dark, winding maze of streets far below. No magelights down there. Only the sparks of lanterns, and the ruddy glow of smelters' fires. The outer districts would be more lively, as pack trains prepared to head out to the mines of the Whitefires' lower slopes before the summer sun turned the Painted Valley into a furnace.

Somewhere down streetside, Melly would be returning from a night spent looting highside spires with the rest of Red Dal's crew of Tainters. Thinking of it, a fire grew in my blood. I was truly in Ninavel! What with all the worry over Ruslan and wardfire after our arrival, I hadn't had time to consider what that meant. Melly within reach, and Cara here to help me...a crazy, heady confidence bubbled up inside. Hell with Ruslan—I'd outplayed him once before. I'd outwit him, Marten, every last mage in this city, whatever it took.

Kiran joined me at the window. I ignored Stevan, who hovered like a sour-faced vulture a scant foot behind him, and asked, "How are you holding up?" I could see the answer in the white set of Kiran's face, but it wouldn't hurt for him to hear my concern.

"It feels so strange to be back in the city. I keep thinking perhaps this is all a dream, and I'll awake...somewhere else."

Not somewhere good, if the look in his eyes was anything to go by. I wished I could give him a fraction of the fierce confidence that filled me.

"Sometimes before tackling a challenging climb, outriders get this sense like you can feel the touch of Khalmet's good hand. No matter what the mountain might throw at you, you know you'll stand on the summit and come home alive."

"You feel this now." He was staring at me like he thought I'd gone mad.

"I do," I admitted. "Maybe it's just seeing Ninavel again, when I feared I never would. But when I've felt this way before a climb, I've never failed. Like Kinslayer crag. Remember when we got the carcabon stones to peek Pello's wards?"

"You nearly died on Kinslayer." Memory darkened his eyes; if anything, he looked more upset.

True. I'd leapt to clear a sheer, holdless stretch of rock, and one hand had missed its grip. Thank Khalmet, I'd gotten a heel hooked on the ledge above before my other hand failed and sent me tumbling to splatter on sharp-edged talus. How my blood had sung afterward! I couldn't stop a wistful sigh.

"I didn't die, and that's the point," I told Kiran. "Doesn't matter how close you come if you walk away whole. Hell, it just makes for a better story to savor."

"Savor." He passed a hand over his eyes. "Sometimes I don't understand you at all."

"No?" I looked out at the sharp black outline of the Whitefires, each peak and notch so gloriously familiar. "Think about your magic being unbound tonight. Then tell me if that's worth all you're enduring now." I knew what I'd feel, if I could have the Taint back again.

He stilled. "It is," he said softly. "But perhaps that frightens me most of all."

CHAPTER SEVEN

(Dev)

Sechaveh's audience chamber looked a lot different than I expected. I'd assumed someone rich as him would want to show it off. Khalmet knew every inch of the highsider houses I'd sneaked into as a kid had been covered in jade statues, gem-studded mosaics, and exotic wood and bone carvings.

But when Kiran and I filed into the chamber with Marten and his little crew, the walls and high dome of the ceiling showed nothing but creamy marble polished smooth as glass. Then again, Sechaveh didn't need any fancy statues. The audience chamber sat in the very summit of Kelante Tower, and the view out the broad windows spaced around the room was breathtaking. To the west, city spires linked by a delicate lacework of bridges stood silhouetted against the Whitefires, whose jagged summits glowed crimson with dawn. Eastward across the sagebrush and alkali flats of the Painted Valley, shadow still softened the arid brown ridgelines of the lower, less rugged Bolthole Mountains.

Sechaveh himself sat on the room's north side in a hulking stone chair, his clothes all creams and tans except for a deep purple cloth tied loosely around his throat. At first glance you might mistake him for somebody's kindly old uncle, with his long silver hair tied back in a simple tail and his brown face seamed with laugh lines. But the eyes glinting under his half-closed lids were as flat and yellow as those of a nightclaw lizard.

On the floor before the chair, three concentric rings of obsidian marked with silver runes were set in the floor. A sea of flame roiled and heaved within the innermost ring, in colors shading from deepest violet through blue to a molten white. I'd have thought it some highside version of a firestone charm if not for the way Kiran checked when he saw it, his blue eyes going wide.

"What is it?" I whispered to him, as Marten halted some ten paces from the ring.

"The energies, so strong—I think the rings must form a...a type of window, onto the confluence..." Kiran fell silent as we came up behind Marten. The other Alathians ranged themselves behind us, Stevan near breathing down Kiran's neck.

Marten bowed deeply. "Lord Sechaveh, thank you for granting us audience. I am Captain Martennan of the Seventh Watch. You'll see in my credentials that I am authorized by the Alathian Council to represent their interests with full diplomatic powers..." He skirted the obsidian rings to hand a set of papers embossed with the Council's seal to Sechaveh. "The Council is most concerned over the recent magical disturbances originating in Ninavel. I offer you the expertise of myself and the other members of my team, to assist you in finding the source of these disturbances and preventing damage to your city."

Sechaveh flicked a desultory glance over the papers. His laugh lines creased, though his lizard's eyes never changed. "Ah, yes. I had wondered how long it would take the Council to send someone begging at my door. Desperate to fix up your border wards, are you?"

Marten didn't let the hit show, only smiled and said, "No more than you are eager to prevent any disruption of Ninavel's water supply. I saw the wardfire on the Aiyalen Spire last night. A spectacular sight, though perhaps a trifle worrying to the merchant houses."

Well, that was putting it mildly. The highsiders we'd passed on our way to the tower had been skittish as kicked cats, giving us wide berth accompanied by a host of wary, sidelong glances. Those living in the districts near Aiyalen who remembered the casualties and destruction of the mage wars were likely packing up to hightail it out of the city.

Sechaveh chuckled, a dry, crackling sound like pinewood burning. "Ninavel is not a city for the faint of heart, Captain. I assure you, these... disturbances, as you call them...will not affect the city's trade."

"Then you have discovered their source, and know how to stop them?" Marten stepped forward, his shopkeeper's face going earnest. "If so, by all means, turn me away. If not—consider, Lord Sechaveh: we share a common problem, and you know how motivated we are to solve it. Any information my team and I discover would be shared without reservation. As proof of the Council's goodwill, they offer a ten percent reduction on import taxes for the Ninavel merchant houses of your choice for five years, if you will give my team your sanction and protection."

Clever. Sechaveh was so rich that more coin for his own vaults wouldn't be much of an incentive, but he still played plenty of power games. A carrot to dangle in front of the greedy merchant houses vying for ascendancy in Ninavel had to be attractive.

"An interesting offer." Sechaveh surveyed us. His gaze passed over the Alathians quickly, but lingered a moment on me, and far longer on Kiran. Unease crept through me. If Pello had reported to Sechaveh the tale of our convoy trip, Sechaveh might suspect just how useful a bargaining token Kiran could be.

Sechaveh straightened in his chair. "Shall I share some information with you now, Captain? The magical fluctuations that trouble your border wards are caused by brief-lived but explosive upheavals in the confluence of earth-power beneath this city."

Marten's face didn't change, but beside me, Kiran drew in a sharp breath. Yeah, explosive sure didn't sound good to me.

"Do you know the cause of these upheavals?" Marten asked.

Sechaveh smiled thinly. "The cause remains to be determined. Captain, I am no mage, but I understand something of Alathian magic. You are not experts in the use of confluence energies. In a situation as delicate as this, I cannot afford to have well-intentioned but inexpert mages meddling with the great forces of the Well of the World."

Marten said, "I understand your concern, Lord Sechaveh. But unlike many mages in Ninavel, our magic does not depend on the confluence. We need not disturb its forces when we cast. Consider further: how well do you trust the mages you rule? These disturbances might well be caused by one of them seeking to depose you. You know our motive in this matter, and it has nothing to do with your rule of the city. You can trust we cannot be suborned, and will report to you the whole of all we find."

Sechaveh tapped his ringed fingers one after the other against the stone of his chair. "You make a good argument, Captain. Yet I must be cautious with the confluence, and have not the expertise to fully judge your claim that your magic does not disturb it. Here is my offer: you may make your case to my lead investigator. If he agrees to accept your help and you are willing to work under his direction, then I will gladly take your Council's terms. I'll give you and your team sanction to perform magic without restriction, and such protection as I can provide."

Marten smiled brightly, but I could tell from the rigidity of his posture he wasn't happy. I wasn't either. Every moment we stood here gave Ruslan more time to plan his spellwork, and now we'd have to wait for yet another meeting?

"Call in a mage to verify our methods of casting if you must, but would it not be better for us to act independently?" Marten asked. "Especially if one among your inner circle is a traitor."

Sechaveh leaned back in his chair, his lizard's eyes half-lidding again. "I repeat: in this situation, I must be cautious. You have only two choices, Captain. Work under my lead investigator, or run along home to Alathia and wait for me to sort this out. And I assure you, it will be sorted out." This time his smile showed his teeth.

Kiran was looking more worried by the moment. I willed Marten to agree already. The sooner he did, the sooner we could get the fuck on with this. Halassian might think Sechaveh's lead investigator clever, but I didn't doubt Marten could manipulate the man in his sleep, scholar or no.

Marten's shoulders slumped a fraction. "When may we meet with your lead investigator?"

"No need to wait, Captain," Sechaveh said. "I arranged in advance for him to join us." He nodded to the guardsmen standing against the back wall. They swung the chamber doors wide.

Ruslan swept into the room. I recognized the arrogant confidence of his walk even before I saw the unmistakable red and black sigils patterning his clothes, the sigils every resident of Ninavel learns to fear. Shock turned my body to stone, a prayer to Suliyya yammering in my head.

Kiran went the color of old snow. Stevan, Lena, and Talm drew closer to him, their eyes slitted and their lips shaping rapid, silent syllables.

Three mages tied up with Kiran's amulet, leaving Marten and Kessaravil to fight Ruslan if he cast against us...I had the terrible feeling that wasn't enough. I tensed, ready to run. Only thing I could do if it came to a magical fight was get the hell out of the way.

"It's my understanding that you and Ruslan Khaveirin have already met, Captain," Sechaveh said, his voice bland.

I spared a moment to curse Halassian's incompetence. Did the Alathians know nothing of shadow work? Surely she could've found out her damn Seranthine wasn't the one in charge if she'd tried.

Marten didn't blink, but the muscles under his mage's uniform were as tight as guy ropes. "Then you well know this man is no friend to Alathia."

Ruslan never took his eyes off Kiran. "A matter that can be easily remedied."

His voice was clear, but full of that odd accent I'd never been able to place, much stronger than Kiran's barely noticeable one. His coloring was odd, too. He had the golden skin and almond-shaped eyes of a Korassian, but his eyes were hazel in color, his hair auburn instead of shining black. Even so, it always surprised me Ruslan looked so damn normal. You'd think a blood mage should have red teeth and clawed nails, or a silver, triply forked tongue like the demons in the southerners' tales. If not for the sigils' warning, you could almost mistake Ruslan for a highsider, his arrogance that of wealth rather than power. Almost, until you saw his eyes, or his smile.

"Kiran remains under Alathia's protection," Marten said, his tone a warning.

Ruslan laughed, a smooth, dark chuckle. "Does he?" He turned to Sechaveh. "You asked me to consider allowing these foreigners to investigate under my direction. I doubt their efforts will prove helpful, but as a favor to you I will agree…*if* they return my apprentice, Kiran ai Ruslanov, whom they have stolen from me and even now stands in their midst."

I ground my teeth and glared at Marten's profile. He should have seen this coming, damn him. Kiran was staring at Ruslan with glassy, terrified gaze of a roundtail cornered by a direwolf.

"Kiran came to Alathia of his own free will and requested our protection," Marten said to Sechaveh. "When we gave it, this man threatened to destroy us. Yet we are still willing to work with him if he revokes this unreasonable demand."

Willing to work with Ruslan? What the fuck was Marten thinking? We ought to be leaving. Now. I backed a step and bumped into Kessaravil's solid, unmoving bulk. He clamped my arm in an iron grip.

Sechaveh regarded Marten. His rings chimed against stone in slow, maddening cadence. "Ruslan's request seems perfectly reasonable to me. The boy is his property, after all, and not Alathian. If you return him to Ruslan, it would go far toward showing us your good will."

There were times when I could understand the Alathians' disgust toward Ninavel. I burned to protest, but held my tongue. I wasn't so dumb as to think Sechaveh would listen to a streetsider like me, assuming Kessaravil let me get a word out. Marten would have to talk us out of this, and by Khalmet, he'd better pull it off.

Marten laughed, without humor. "Forgive me, Lord Sechaveh, but even if we handed Kiran over, I do not believe Ruslan Khaveirin would soften his attitude towards us. Have we not all heard tales of the lengths he will go to satisfy a grudge? Giving him Kiran would only make him the more eager to seek revenge, which would distract us all from more important matters."

Sechaveh steepled his fingers in front of his chin. "The captain has a point, Ruslan. I know your temper of old, my friend, and it has already cost me the city's best source of knowledge on confluence energies."

Ruslan moved his broad shoulders in a graceful shrug. "It was your decision to exile Simon Levanian from Ninavel. I merely enforced your desires."

Sechaveh's weathered face twisted in irritation. "I ordered him exiled, not killed. Now his knowledge is lost to us."

When Pello told me of Sechaveh and Simon, he'd made it sound like Sechaveh simply hadn't been able to break the protections warding a blood mage to kill Simon. If Sechaveh had made a deliberate choice to let Simon live, then I thought him an overconfident idiot. But if he was annoyed over Simon's death, that was a lever Marten could use. Sure enough, Marten had the air of a hunting cat that had scented prey.

"Simon lived for twenty years in exile safe and sound," Ruslan said. "Had he stayed there, he would yet live. His own choices led to his destruction."

"Choices provided by you," Marten said. "Lord Sechaveh, perhaps you have not heard the full tale of Simon's destruction. Ruslan used his apprentice as bait to draw Simon out of Alathia, and gambled your life and the fate of Ninavel on the slim chance Kiran could disrupt Simon's spellwork enough to destroy him. All this, to satisfy his own desire for vengeance."

This was the story I'd hoped to sell to Pello, both for Melly's sake and in hope of drawing Sechaveh's anger toward Ruslan. I held my breath, watching Sechaveh.

Instead of angry, the old bastard looked amused. "A gamble that paid off for him, it would seem. I always admire a man who can play a clever game."

Shit. Marten had better have another line of attack in mind.

"Gamble with Ninavel all you like, but keep your games confined to Arkennland." Marten's face set in stern lines. "The next time you exile a dangerous mage like Simon Levanian who threatens the security of Alathia's borders, provide us warning—or the terms Ninavel's merchants receive will become unfavorable indeed."

For the first time, Ruslan looked directly at Marten. "Ah yes, it all comes down to your precious border. I imagine your Council is quite upset over the threat I pose, are they not?" He smiled, sharp and predatory. "I meant what I said to you two months ago, Captain. You keep my apprentice at your peril. But in light of these recent disturbances…I am willing to set aside my enmity, if you return him to me. Think of it, Captain! You can return to your Council with the news that your beloved border wards are safe not only from confluence fluctuations, but from me."

His smile widened into something that flooded my body with the deep, animal instinct to run. Kiran jerked as if flame-touched. He lifted his chin, desperate defiance printed on his face.

Marten only raised a disbelieving brow and said dryly to Ruslan, "I am not so gullible as to take your word for it." I had to give him points for not flinching in the face of that smile.

"Would you take mine?" Sechaveh sat back, looking down his nose at them both. "Return Ruslan's apprentice, Captain, and I will ensure that he works no magic against you or Alathia."

Marten's air of skepticism grew deeper yet. "I know something of your methods, Lord Sechaveh. You can deny Ruslan the confluence, true. That would not stop his casting, only restrict him to the use of lesser spells."

Khalmet's hand, why was Marten even talking about this? He ought to tell Sechaveh to dive straight into Shaikar's deepest hell. We weren't getting the protection we'd come for. Better to leave and figure out an alternate plan, fast.

Kiran was balanced on the balls of his feet like he wanted to bolt. But he met my gaze with mute frustration and cut his eyes toward Stevan, who stood statue-still, his features twisted with effort.

My own frustration burned just as hot. Kiran was chained to Stevan by the amulet, and Kessaravil's grip hadn't left my arm...I glared at Marten, praying he'd hurry up and see sense.

"Oh, I can do more than forbid Ruslan the confluence," Sechaveh said. "You know the binding nature of a blood vow, yes? If Ruslan gives me such a vow and consigns his blood to the confluence..." He pointed at the fiery sea within the obsidian rings. "Should he break the vow, the confluence will burn him to ash."

"I would gladly forswear my vengeance," Ruslan added smoothly. "All I want is my apprentice back, Captain. Once I have him, Alathia is no concern of mine."

Suliyya grant Marten wasn't buying into this pile of goat shit. To my relief, his dubious expression didn't change.

"Perhaps you doubt me," Sechaveh said. "How do you imagine I've reigned here this last century, over men and women with more magic in their least breath than exists in all the charms I own? Every mage who wishes to reside here must swear such a vow, never to cast against me."

Marten frowned. "Simon Levanian cast against you before you exiled him."

"He cast against the mages I employ, thinking if he removed those who protect me, a knife might suffice where his magic could not."

Marten shook his head, slowly. "Perhaps there's truth in what you say. But I need time to think on this…there may be another way we can come to accord."

Finally, talk of leaving. And yeah, if Marten left the option open of handing Kiran over, he might buy us more time before Ruslan started spellcasting.

Sechaveh's face hardened. "I have no patience for men who dally. You've heard my offer. Fair and reasonable terms, Captain. Either take them and begin your investigation, or leave my city this day. The decision is yours, but you must make it now."

Oh, shit. I willed Marten to say no. We'd have to leave the city, yeah—the embassy's wards wouldn't hold if Sechaveh sent a host of mages against us along with Ruslan—but I knew a couple places we could hole up in the lower reaches of the Whitefires. There must be a way we could sneak back, investigate covertly instead. Marten couldn't be considering agreeing to give Kiran over. Not even he could be such a gutless weasel.

"Marten," Kiran said, low and urgent. Marten was staring at Ruslan with his boyish face clean of expression. Ruslan wore a tiny smile.

Marten's mouth drew into a thin line. "Very well. We'll take your offer."

Mother of maidens, *no!* My shout died unvoiced in my throat, as Kessaravil's grip tightened and magic turned my muscles to stone. I strained against his spell that locked me in place. I might as well have tried to move a mountain.

Kiran stumbled backward, abject horror on his face. "Marten, *please*—!" His cry cut off as Stevan grabbed his wrist. I cast a desperate glance at Lena. *Don't let Marten do this,* I begged her silently.

Lena's freckles stood out dark against skin gone sallow, but she refused to meet my gaze. It was Talm who spoke. "Captain, this can't be the way—"

"*Lieutenant.*" Marten transfixed him with a look as cold and forbidding as an ice cliff in midwinter. He held Talm's gaze until Talm shut his mouth and bent his head.

I cursed Talm for a coward. As for Lena, hatred was too kind a word for what choked me. I'd known Marten's cheerful benevolence was an act. But Lena…I'd thought she was honest. Had they known from the start Ruslan was in charge? Was that the true reason Marten had wanted Kiran to come? Cold descended over me.

Marten said to Sechaveh, "If—if!—Ruslan Khaveirin gives a blood vow he will cast no spells with intent to harm me, my team members, or the country of Alathia, not only for the duration of this investigation but as long as he lives…then we will return Kiran to his custody and work with him in our investigation."

Ruslan's eyes burned with eager triumph. "I will vow. Though in the interest of clarity...I do not count Kiran among your team."

My stomach rolled over. Of course Ruslan wouldn't risk the slightest chance a vow might prevent him from ripping Kiran's mind apart and doing gods knew what else to him in the bargain.

Marten spoke with the cool lack of emotion he might've used haggling over a bag of beans. "So long as you include myself, Lieutenants Talmaddis and Lenarimanas, the arcanist Stevannes, the Arkennlander Devan *na soliin*, and Ambassador Halassian and her two lieutenants, Jenoviann and Kessaravil."

If Marten thought by including me in his little list I'd forgive him for this and play the helpful spy for him down streetside, he could fucking well think again.

"Acceptable," Ruslan said.

"The vow's terms must bind your apprentices as well," Marten added sharply.

"Of course." Ruslan made a dismissive gesture.

Mother of maidens, the sick terror on Kiran's face...I still had dreams about the expression he'd had when I'd betrayed him in Kost. This was worse. I fought to move, to speak, to do *something*. I budged not an inch.

Sechaveh clapped his hands once. "Done, then. Captain, while you work under Ruslan, you are free to remain in Ninavel and investigate as you please. Ruslan..." Sechaveh slipped off a braided silver ring bearing a fat ruby and held it up. "You know what I require."

Ruslan inclined his head, his expression ironic. He drew a wickedly curved dagger from his belt. Blood welled dark on the palm of his left hand as he cut a sigil into his skin.

I had the same awful, nightmarish sense of inevitability I'd had in Simon's cave, when I'd been forced to watch as Kiran got sliced open. The memory of my idiotic confidence of a few hours ago brought bile to my throat. Why, *why*, had I ever thought this trip a good idea?

Sechaveh tossed the ring to Ruslan, who caught it with his bloodied hand.

"Make your vow," Sechaveh said, his voice stern.

Ruslan shut his eyes and clenched his hand around the ring. The blood that dripped through his fingers glowed unnaturally crimson, the drops sizzling and vanishing before they reached the floor. "I vow that neither I nor my apprentices will ever knowingly cast a spell with intent to harm Captain Martennan and his team members"—he rattled off the list of names Marten had given him—"or the country of Alathia." He moved the knife in several quick passes through the air. A fiery sigil appeared before him and cast a sullen glow over the planes of his cheekbones.

"This I vow, Ruslan Khaveirin of the tenth lineage of the *akheli*, bound by my blood and *ikilhia*." Ruslan cast the ring into the flames in the warded ring at Sechaveh's feet. The fire leapt high, colors merging and shifting to a deep, vicious red.

Kiran and the Alathians all flinched like miners caught too close to a powder blast. Even Ruslan twitched as the sigil flared and vanished. Sechaveh only watched, satisfaction plain in the curl of his mouth.

The flames within the ring settled, the red bleeding back into cool blues and violets.

"Does that satisfy you, Captain?" Ruslan's rich voice was full of scornful amusement.

Slowly, Marten nodded.

"Then it's your turn." Ruslan looked past Marten at Kiran, his eyes hot and eager. Nausea choked me so strongly that black spots bloomed in my vision.

Sweat stood out on Kiran's skin, his breath coming in sharp pants. His eyes darted between Marten and the other Alathians, full of frantic pleading, as Marten moved to stand behind him. If Marten felt even a shred of guilt over betraying Kiran so thoroughly, I saw no hint of it.

No, no, no, oh you lying, demon-tongued bastard, may Shaikar eat your black heart—

"Stevan," Marten said quietly. He lifted the amulet out from under Kiran's shirt and over his head. Ruslan gave the amulet one swift, penetrating glance. Stevan let out a breath, all the lines in his face relaxing.

Kiran tore his arm free of Stevan's grip and threw himself sideways, only to stop short again with an awful, choked cry. He swayed on his feet as if he might faint, his face gray.

"You've bound his power," Ruslan said to Marten, his eyes locked on Kiran. "I should thank you. It wouldn't have mattered, but it does spare us all a scene." His voice lowered, became gentle. "Kiran. Come here."

Kiran took a dragging step forward. The utter despair in his eyes turned my fury so hot I thought I might burst into flame. Mage or not, I'd make Marten pay for this. The Alathians couldn't leave me a frozen statue forever, and by Khalmet, when I got loose I'd make them all regret this day.

Kiran kept walking with those horrible, jerky steps until he finished up in front of Ruslan. His muscles were trembling; even without his magic he must be trying to fight Ruslan's hold.

Ruslan put a hand on Kiran's forehead, his eyes closing briefly. The tension drained out of Kiran's body like water spilling from a broken jar. Ruslan took Kiran's shoulders and turned him around. Kiran's eyes were blank, his features slack. Horror filled me as Ruslan smiled at Marten over Kiran's head.

"Captain, now that we've concluded our agreement, you must excuse me. I have…a family matter to attend to."

"As long as you are not distracted from your duties for too long," Sechaveh said.

"I will send papers to the embassy describing our findings to date," Ruslan said. "Captain Martennan and his people may review them and begin what investigations they see fit. I suggest we meet in…oh, a day's time." He looked down at Kiran, with that terrible, gentle smile. "Yes, I think a day would be quite satisfactory."

"Very well," Sechaveh said. "One day, Ruslan."

Without a second glance at the rest of us, Ruslan took Kiran's arm and led him from the room. Kiran moved with the dreamy slowness of a sleepwalker. A scream of rage burned trapped in my chest as the audience chamber door closed behind them.

※

"Tell me you have a plan to get him back!" Lena shoved past me, heading straight for Marten with Talm hot on her heels. Marten didn't pause in his descent of the marble stairs leading to Kelante Tower's gate. Kessaravil still had hold of my arm. His Shaikar-cursed magic kept me plodding at his side, mute and docile as a taphtha addict. All I could do was glare holes in Marten's back as Lena caught up to him.

"*Marten!* I trusted you as you asked, but twin gods above—!"

"Not here," Marten snapped. "Wait for the embassy." He picked up his pace.

Talm muttered something to Lena, who shook her head. She and Talm hurried after Marten in silence, their spines as rigid as the stairway's iron railings.

My hatred only grew more bitter. *Now* she protested, too late to do Kiran a damn bit of good? I sure didn't believe Marten had some miraculous plan in mind. He'd got the protection and sanction he wanted, and now he'd do his best to use that clever tongue of his to convince us all that Kiran was an acceptable sacrifice.

Nobody else spoke while we retraced our route. The morning sun turned the pale stone of bridges and stairs eye-wateringly bright, which only worsened the throb of fury in my head. When we reached the embassy,

Marten led us straight through the main receiving room to reach a small antechamber that held only two cushioned chairs and a circular, warded window. The window's shutters hadn't yet been closed against the day's heat, and the faint, wavering calls of a waterseller from the causeway below drifted in along with scents of orangeblossom and baking spicebread.

"Release him," Marten ordered Kessaravil. "Then leave us. All of you."

Stevan retreated straight off, but Lena and Talm hesitated, and Kessaravil didn't let go of my arm. He cleared his throat and said, "Perhaps I should—"

"I'll handle this." When nobody moved, Marten's shoulders stiffened further. "Out. Now. You heard me." His drawling accent had vanished, leaving his words as clipped as any city-born Alathian.

"As you wish, Captain." Kessaravil released my arm. A tingling rush swept over my skin. My muscles were my own to control again. Finally. I jerked away from him.

"You goatfucking spawn of Shaikar! I knew you were a liar, right from the start!" I kept on shouting curses and made a few accompanying rude gestures with my left hand, turning my body to hide the slow movement of my right hand toward the slit in my belt. The blade hidden within was only that of a boning knife I'd stolen from the kitchen back in Tamanath, but it might serve. I was no fighter, but I was quick on my feet.

Marten's black eyes stayed steady on my face. I took the risk of moving a little closer.

The door snicked closed behind the others. I shut my mouth mid-curse and slashed at Marten's thigh, aiming for the artery.

My little blade stopped short a hair's breadth above the fabric of his trousers, the air there flaring briefly silver. The shock numbed my hand as if I'd struck stone. The blade dropped ringing to the floor from my nerveless fingers.

"Nice try," Marten said. "If it were that easy to kill a mage, life in Ninavel would be quite different."

I spat at him between forked fingers in the old streetside gesture of ultimate contempt. And then I vaulted straight out the window.

That, he didn't expect. The wards flared in warning as my body passed the gap, but didn't burn or stop me. Eight stories below, the sunbleached stone of the nearest bridge glared bright enough to blind. I twisted as I fell and snatched at a frieze of snarling beasts.

My fingers caught on a sandcat's jaw. Pain shot through my tendons as my arms jerked taut, but my grip held. I thrust the toes of my boots into a shallow, mortared depression between stone blocks and stretched for a second handhold. If I could get out of sight around the corner in time, I might have a chance—

Fingers touched mine where they clutched the sandcat. A wave of prickles raced up my arm. Fuck! I looked up. Marten was straddling the windowsill, leaning down at a precarious angle to reach me. The wards around the window glowed faintly silver.

"Come back inside," he said.

My body obeyed him without a thought, for all I screamed at my muscles to do otherwise. I scrambled back up to the window, hating the overwhelming advantage Marten's Shaikar-cursed magic gave him. He must've released the window wards; they didn't trigger as I climbed over the frame.

Marten swung himself back into the room. "Twin gods preserve us," he said, with some force. "Lena told me how skilled you were at climbing, but that seemed a little extreme." His drawling accent had returned, although without any of the usual cheerful tone.

He hadn't prevented me from speaking, but I didn't bother to answer. I watched him with the cold, intent gaze I'd use on a snake blocking my path, and waited. I'd missed this chance, but if I saw another, I wouldn't let it pass.

Marten pointed at one of the chairs. "Sit."

I sat, unable to so much as delay my obedience.

Marten sank into the opposite chair. He studied his hands, white-knuckled in his lap. When he raised his head, he looked tired, his cheeks sunken. "My first responsibility is to my country, regardless of my personal feelings. The last thing I wanted to do was to give Kiran to Ruslan. But my orders from the Council were clear—the investigation must be my top priority. If it was the only way Sechaveh would allow us to remain and investigate, I had no choice."

I couldn't keep silent any longer. "Fuck you, Marten. You Alathian mages make like you're so fucking pure compared to Arkennlanders, but you know what? I don't see a shred of difference between you and Ruslan. Hell, you're worse—at least blood mages don't pretend they're honorable men."

"Ruslan acts out of sheer self-interest," Marten said evenly. "I act for the good of my country."

Lena had as much as warned me: *He keeps his promises, no matter the cost.* I should've heeded her, and convinced Kiran that Marten's loyalty to the Council made him far too dangerous to trust.

I bared my teeth at Marten. "You think it matters why you betrayed Kiran? You saw his face in there. Khalmet's bloodsoaked hand, how can you live with yourself after that?"

Marten gave me a bitter, knowing smile. "The same way you did, I imagine, after you handed him to Simon in Kost."

"I didn't—!" I choked on my words, too furious to speak. If I could have, I would have thrown myself at Marten again, hell with the consequences. I clenched my teeth, breathing hard, and managed to get myself back under control. "I didn't know about Simon when I brought him to Gerran," I said, my voice still rough with anger. "And when I found out, I fucking did something about it. I didn't leave him there, with that sadistic devil's spawn, like—"

"Neither will I." Marten's hands fisted on his thighs. "I have no intention of abandoning Kiran. When we finish this investigation, I promise you, I will free him from Ruslan."

"When you *finish*? He'll be mindburned by then, good as dead—hell, Ruslan's probably destroying his will right now!"

"No," Marten interrupted, sharp and insistent. "I saw Kiran's memories at his trial. What I saw of Ruslan in those—he will not take such a drastic, irreversible step. Not without first trying some other method of breaking Kiran to his will. He spent long years training Kiran to act as a focus for channeled spellcasting, a role a mindburned mage cannot play. He won't readily abandon all that effort. There is time yet to get Kiran away with his mind intact."

Oh gods, I wanted to believe him. Yet I knew his skill with manipulation and lies. "Even if you're right about Ruslan, it'll be a bright day in Shaikar's hells before I believe you'll do a damn thing to help Kiran. 'When the investigation's done'...what kind of idiot do you take me for?"

Marten sighed. "Though the investigation must remain my top priority, that doesn't mean I'll set aside Kiran entirely." He leaned forward, his black eyes holding mine. "I know what you risked when you tried to save Kiran from Simon. Are you willing to accept that risk again? He needs you now, more than ever."

"Don't pull that shit with me, Marten," I snarled. "Just spit it out: what the fuck do you want?"

"Ruslan believes he has won," Marten said. "Even so, he's no fool. I'm sure he suspects my intentions. He'll be watching my every move, and he'll do everything in his power to keep me from Kiran. But you..." Marten turned one hand over, palm up. "Ruslan knows you aren't a mage. In his mind, that makes you insignificant. He won't keep nearly as close an eye on you."

"What makes you think I'd have any better chance at helping Kiran? Ruslan didn't even let him talk to the servants, for Khalmet's sake. And that was before he ran."

"Before Kiran underwent the *akhelashva* ritual, yes, Ruslan took every precaution to keep Kiran isolated and dependent on him," Marten said. "Now with the mark-bond in place, he no longer needs to be so careful. He believes his control over Kiran is absolute. Think about it—when he sought revenge on Simon, he didn't care it meant Kiran would spend weeks traveling the mountains with you and the other convoy members."

I wasn't convinced Ruslan would let me anywhere near Kiran. He'd already underestimated my presence once, and Ruslan didn't strike me as the sort of guy who made the same mistake twice. "What the hell do you expect me to do? Ruslan's right, I'm no threat to him." I'd caught him by surprise once thanks to Simon's Taint charm, but even that had been a temporary thing.

"If you can find out Kiran's exact situation—perhaps even speak to him, learn what you can of Ruslan's intentions, it would be extremely helpful."

"You mean, you're hoping Kiran can play shadow man for you against Ruslan, the same way you wanted me streetside." I'd give anything to have Simon's Taint charm back, to be able to smash Marten's face in regardless of his magic.

"I can't hope to help Kiran without information," Marten said. "But in the end, all I ask is that you be Kiran's friend." He looked down, his fingers tugging at the edge of his uniform sleeves. "He'll need one."

Another memory of Kiran's fear and despair sliced through me. "Then let me go, damn you. I can do that part just fine on my own."

"Can you?" Marten shook his head. "How will you gain access to Ruslan's house? Climbing skills won't help you there."

He was right, damn it. I clenched my teeth, hating to admit it.

"If you let us, we can help you, Dev. Keep working with us, and I'll make sure you get access to Kiran…and any other help you need to keep older promises."

"I don't need any help from you, you—!" My protest died mid-sentence. I stared at him, feeling gut-punched, as a whole bunch of pieces slotted together in my head.

He knew about Melly. He'd been so careful to hand me Cara's letter before bringing me to Kiran, and give us the time alone so I could show it to him…he'd wanted Kiran to know time was running out, to let my own urgency put that much more pressure on Kiran to agree to go to Ninavel. If I hadn't been so fucking stupid, maybe I would have realized it earlier. Lena had shown that night in the garden she knew more than she should about my past, and she'd even implied she learned it from Marten.

"Oh, you blacksouled bastard!" I remembered the horrible thought I'd had during the audience with Sechaveh. "You knew all along about Ruslan being in charge, didn't you? That's why you were so keen to use me to make sure Kiran would come."

Marten had that weary, resigned look again. "I suspected," he said, his voice low. "Especially after Kiran spoke of Sechaveh visiting Ruslan. Stevan told me the earthquakes implied Ninavel's confluence was involved somehow, and blood mages are the uncontested experts in confluence magic. If Ruslan and Sechaveh were friendly, it made sense Sechaveh would turn to him for help. Even so…" He bowed his head. "I hoped it wouldn't come to this."

I couldn't believe he had the balls to admit his deceit. "Khalmet's bony bloodsoaked hand! You *are* worse than Ruslan!"

"Maybe so." Marten rubbed his hands over his face and up through the soft spikes of his hair. "It doesn't change what I said before. Kiran needs you. I think you're a good enough friend to him that your anger with me won't prevent you from helping him. If I'm wrong…you're free to go. This time I won't stop you."

I'd never in my life wanted so badly to hurt someone. I trembled on the verge of leaving without another word—to hell with Marten, and Lena, and all of it. I wanted to disappear into the lower city, find a tavern, and drink enough to erase the memory of this entire summer. Ruslan had vowed not to cast against me; I could walk the city's streets freely again.

But Kiran's white, stricken face hung in my mind's eye, and I knew it was no good. He'd gotten into this mess trying to help me, and I couldn't let him pay the price for my own stupidity.

"You win," I said bitterly to Marten. *For now*, I added silently. "For Kiran's sake, I'll work with you. But I won't lift a damn finger for you outside of what's necessary to help him."

"Fair enough." Marten didn't show so much as a hint of triumph. Still, I turned aside, unable to bear looking at the lying bastard one second longer. To work with him…fuck! I'd be lucky if my head didn't explode out of sheer, frustrated rage.

CHAPTER EIGHT

(Dev)

Ihammered on a metal door painted with brightly colored snakes twining around a pair of crossed ice axes. Even after the long walk from the embassy into the depths of Acaltar district, fury still burned like magefire in my veins. I kept seeing Kiran's despairing eyes, hearing the agonized terror in his shriek while caught in his nightmare back in Tamanath. Was he screaming like that now?

"Samis, you in there? Open the damn door!" I needed to find Cara, near as bad as I needed breath. Samis was a metalworker by trade, who crafted pitons, ice axes, boot spikes, and other specialized gear for mountain travel. He rented out spare rooms on the cheap to outriders in between convoy jobs. Cara had often bunked with him during her brief stays in the city, and his back courtyard was something of an informal gathering spot. Even if Cara wasn't here, Samis might know where she was.

I pounded harder and scowled at a serpent painted in particularly eye-straining shades of orange and green. Samis fancied himself skilled with paint as well as metal, and all suggestions to the contrary bounced right off him. I'd never known what Cara saw in the man. Yeah, he was a genius with iron, but I found his scatterbrained self-absorption annoying beyond belief.

After what felt an eternity, the bronze wards on the plaque nailed to the doorframe glimmered violet. Samis swung the door open, bleary-eyed and wearing only a rumpled pair of pants that threatened to slip off his narrow hips.

"What the fuck's all this racket?" he demanded.

All right, so I did know what Cara saw in him. He was tall like her, with

90

muscles strong as any outrider's from pounding out pitons on his forge, and he had a face handsome enough for a jenny-boy. His coarse dark hair was tied up in a series of knots spiked with charms, one free-hanging lock dyed the color of honey. I tried not to glare.

"Samis, is Cara here? I've news she needs to hear."

Samis squinted at me. "Dev. Huh. Thought you always told anybody who'd listen that you'd rather be tied to a fire ant mound than set foot in Ninavel in midsummer. Yeah, Cara's bunking here—you want to find her, she's in back."

Bunking here…just in the house, or in his bed, like she'd done in the past? Damn it, so what if she was? We'd made no promises of partnership. I started forward. Samis barred me with an arm across the open doorway.

"Next time, don't wake me 'til a civilized hour, or I'll double the price for your next set of pitons. You outriders cavort about at all hours, but I'm an *artist*. I need sleep, or the vision doesn't come."

"Sorry," I muttered, mastering the urge to throttle him. He sniffed in satisfaction and dropped his arm. I brushed past and hurried through darkened rooms piled with metalworking tools and mountain gear. The house's back door stood open, sunlight leaking in through a beaded hanging made of quartz chips strung on hemp strands. I ducked through, and stopped.

Half the courtyard was taken up by a web of ropes knotted to pitons jutting from cracks in the walls. Cara balanced barefoot along one swaying hemp line. She wore threadbare trousers hacked off at the knees and a long sleeveless overshirt belted with a green sash. The smooth, strong muscles of her calves flexed, her hips shifting with easy grace as the rope moved. She'd pinned her long blonde braid up on her head so it wouldn't affect her balance. A fierce grin split her tawny face, her pale eyes fixed on a wiry, balding male outrider who edged toward her along a second strand of the web. High above, a tarp stitched out of gossamer-thin prayer banners filtered the harsh summer sun into a hazy golden glow.

It wasn't just the sight of Cara, lean and lovely as a sandcat, that closed my throat so tight I couldn't speak. It was the memory of all the winter days I'd spent in this very courtyard, challenging friends to crazy feats of balance, laughing and planning future climbs, utterly free of the fear and anger that weighed my heart now.

A female voice called, "Twenty kenets says you can knock Vanik off before he touches a single piton, Cara!" I recognized the two other outriders who lay sprawled on their elbows beside a stack of scrap iron. Gevia, with skin dark as night and her beaded braids bound into a single thick tail; and Ikkio, who was Korassian-born and deceptively thin, his raven-black hair hanging past narrow shoulders that were pure corded muscle.

Cara balanced on one foot and stretched a leg out to kick Vanik's strand of rope. He broke at the waist, arms windmilling, but arched backward in an improbable curve and kept his balance. Gevia hissed, while Ikkio whistled in approval.

I finally managed to summon my voice. "Cara."

Cara twisted so fast she lost her balance. She leaped down to the flagstones, her blue eyes gone wide. "Dev?"

She sprinted across the courtyard and pulled me straight into a kiss whose passion and force left me feeling a hell of a lot better about Samis. Ah gods, the press of her slim, muscled body against mine, the spiced-honey scent of her hair...I held her tight with my throat choked all over again. At the mines, I'd dreamed of this reunion. But not like this, not with Kiran sacrificed to achieve it.

"Khalmet's hand," Vanik said, still swaying on his rope. He and the others were staring at us with their jaws hanging open. "Thought you had a rule, Cara. No outriders or convoy folk in your bed." He sounded more than a little disgruntled.

"Didn't you hear?" Gevia's grin held an edge. She and Cara had been close ever since their apprentice days, but she'd never much liked me. "Dev's no outrider, not anymore. Got blacklisted for life. Though, damn...looks a fair trade, doesn't it? Cara, if I ditch an avalanche-struck convoy before they can even dig out, will you tumble me?"

I'd abandoned that convoy for Melly's sake, and in doing so, saved Kiran from Ruslan. Yet even now, the reminder of the cost of my choice sliced deep. Insults crowded my tongue, but Cara spoke first, cheerfully mocking.

"Not likely, Gevia. Didn't you bail off the east face of Vanadys Peak because you got too tired to hammer pitons? I like my lovers with a little more stamina."

Gevia slapped a hand to her heart and groaned in theatrical anguish, as Ikkio and Vanik snickered. Cara dragged me back through the quartz-chip hanging into the cool semi-darkness of the house.

"Ignore her," she said, and kissed me again, deep and slow. "I can't believe you're really here. I should've known you'd get yourself free."

The mix of exultation and relief in her words twisted my gut. "I didn't," I admitted. "The Alathians brought us to Ninavel."

"Us?" Cara peered at me. "You mean, Kiran too? But...I thought he couldn't return, not with Ruslan..."

Gods only know what showed on my face. She sucked in a breath, her grip on my arms tightening. "Dev. What's happened?"

"It's that fucking Marten," I snarled. "Didn't I tell you he had a viper's soul—" I checked, looking from the open door to the darkened hall. Cara, I trusted; Samis and the rest were another story. "I'll tell you the lot, but not here. I know a spot nearby that's safe to talk, but you'll want some boots to climb in." This time of morning, in full sun the city walls would already be hot enough to blister unprotected skin.

Cara glanced down at her bare feet. "Yeah, give me a minute." She retreated down the shadowed hall. Voices drifted back. Samis's started off sharp, then faded into plaintive grumbling. Cara reappeared wearing a longer pair of pale cotton trousers, a thin, long-sleeved shirt, and her leather outrider boots, firmly laced.

She followed me out Samis's door and down the narrow street past warded doors and shuttered windows. Both of us stuck to the shadows beneath balconies where we could to avoid the glare of the sun. Sweat soaked my shirt and shone on Cara's brow. The street was empty of all but little gold-speckled whiptail lizards splayed unblinking on the pavestones. The emptiness was deceptive. As we passed the mouths of alleys I heard the occasional rustle of movement from behind makeshift shelters built of tile fragments and tattered cloth. Streetsiders too poor to pay for both water rations and living quarters wouldn't venture out in midday heat, but they'd listen eagerly enough to any conversations in hopes of catching some scrap of information worth a coin or two from the local ganglord's shadow men.

I ducked around the corner of a charmseller's shop into a slit of an alley, so deep and narrow the sun didn't penetrate. The heat remained smothering in intensity, but the walls wouldn't burn our fingers off when we climbed. Ten stories above, one wall ended in a crumbling line of stone silhouetted against a sky seared white by the sun. This area of Acaltar district had sustained some serious damage in the mage war twenty years back, and unlike similar spots highside, nobody'd ever bothered to repair it.

"Up here," I told Cara, and scrambled up the wall. Enough cracks marred the stone the climb was easy as breathing. Beyond the walltop, a sea of blinding white rooftops rose toward the thin spires of Kulori district. Overhead, the stone supports of a bridge that had once spanned the gap up to the lower terraces of Kulori's towers arched to end in mid-air. The underside of one support had a dark gap where stone blocks were missing. I pulled myself into the gap and squeezed up through a crevice in the floor of an open-air cupola that'd been the province of the bridge's tollkeeper. Broken mosaic tiles lay scattered over the cupola's floor, the waist-high walls slimed by the droppings of rock swallows, but the roof was intact, providing blessed shade.

Cara grunted up through the hole in the floor; her height made the crevice more awkward than it'd been for me. She mopped sweat from her face with a sleeve and took in the excellent view the cupola afforded of Kulori's towers. "Let me guess. This is one of your haunts from your Tainted days."

"Yeah." I'd spent many a night here with my Tainter crew, taking turns watching the highside dwelling Red Dal wanted us to hit, playing skipstone with colored bits of glass or making racecourses for roaches to pass the time. Until our minder gave the signal, and we'd swoop like bats through the cool night air up to Kulori, ready to pit our Taint against highsider wards. I kicked aside a broken tile with more force than necessary.

Cara dropped to sit cross-legged against a wall. "All right, Dev. Nobody but the damn swallows can hear us now. What's going on?"

I slid down the wall next to her and drew my knees up to my chest, gripping them as if I could brace myself against the tale I had to share.

"I figured a way free of the mines, but then came an earthquake…" I told her of the disaster at the mine, my return to Tamanath, and how Marten had convinced Kiran and me to come to Ninavel, adding plenty of side commentary about Marten's ancestry and character along the way. When I got to our audience with Sechaveh, I stared at the cupola wall's ragged lip of stone and forced myself to keep going, though the memory of Kiran's horror and the possessive lust in Ruslan's eyes brought nausea so strong I could barely speak.

After that, it wasn't as hard as I'd feared to tell her of my last conversation with Marten. To admit the way he'd used me despite my caution, was still using me, and I had no choice but to let him. I told her everything—well, everything except the part where I tried to kill Marten. The thought of his dry amusement afterward was too infuriating.

Cara listened to it all in silence. When I finished, she slumped against the wall. "Shaikar's innermost hell, Dev. This isn't a nightmare? You're truly here, telling me this?"

I huffed out a short, unamused laugh. "Believe me, I wish this were a nightmare."

The white sun-lines around Cara's mouth and eyes deepened. "Martennan…I liked him. When you were wary, I thought you were jumping at shadows, because of—well, because of your childhood. But to give Kiran to Ruslan like that…" She looked down. "I can't believe I misread him so badly."

The stricken note to her voice made me glance at her, surprised. I hadn't thought she'd seen much of Marten. But then, Cara prided herself on her keen eye for character. Her skill at assessing people was what made her head outrider on convoys when she was only six years my senior. She'd seen straight through Jylla, who fooled me blind right up until the day she stole every kenet I owned and cast me to the winds.

I scowled at my knees. "The only thing I can't figure is how Marten knew about Melly. If he hadn't realized how to use your letter as leverage, I'm not sure Kiran would've come." I'd certainly have made a hell of a lot stronger effort to talk him out of it. Instead, I'd let myself get all caught up in the idea of Kiran saving Melly for me, and ignored my instincts. "Maybe Kiran told Marten while I was stuck at the mine. If he was that stupid after I told him not to speak of her—once I get him free of Ruslan I'll kick his skinny highside ass from here to the Whitefires!"

"Dev." Cara's voice was oddly choked. "It wasn't Kiran. It was me."

"What? No. You were careful in your letter," I assured her.

She drew in a slow breath, her shoulders set as if braced for a blow. A cold hollowness spread within me like a crevasse yawning open.

"That wasn't the only letter I sent," she said.

I waited, the crevasse growing deeper.

"The week after I sent the first letter to you…I found people here in Ninavel who claimed to work as shadow men, but they all laughed at me when I said I wouldn't spill my tale to them, only to a ganglord. One even tried to force it out of me. I sparked a bane charm and got free, but it made me think twice about trying again. I kept thinking, if only I had a mage's help to find Pello, or get me in to see Sechaveh…so I sent Martennan another letter, asking if he could arrange any help from the Alathian embassy. He told me when he escorted me through the border that he regretted the Council's decision about you. He said if I ever needed his help, he'd give it. I thought if I explained we were trying to save an innocent child, he'd be sympathetic. I was sure he'd see that if Melly ended up a brain-burned taphtha addict, it was the Council's fault for taking your money and sending you to the mines."

Pain stabbed my palm as my hand clenched on a broken tile. "You told him about Melly. After you promised your silence. When you knew I'd rather throw myself off a cliff than give him that kind of leverage over me." All that time in the mines, I'd been so certain I could trust her. That unlike Jylla, she kept her promises.

"I'm sorry, Dev! With you stuck in the mines and Melly's Change coming so soon, I had to do something. You're not the only one who cared for Sethan. Hell, I was friends with him years before you! You think I could have lived with myself if I didn't try everything I could to save his daughter?"

I knew her desperation. How could I not, when I felt it beating in my own blood every damn instant of the day? Yet the hurt still went as deep as if she'd cut the rope between us while belaying me on a climb. "I *warned* you Marten couldn't be trusted."

Cara raised her chin, her pale eyes fierce. "Telling him was a bad move. I admit it. But gods, Dev—you should understand how it's possible to misjudge someone despite warnings."

The breath left me as if from a blow. How dare she compare this to Jylla? I'd had years' worth of reasons to believe Jylla sincere, not one brief conversation at the border. Besides, even for Jylla, I'd never broken my word.

I wanted to tear into Cara, spit out a vicious stream of words that might vent some of the darkness boiling within. Instead, I squeezed the shard in my hand all the harder, struggling for control. I'd given in to anger time and again this season, and what good had it done me?

Better to take the lesson I should've learned from Jylla's betrayal, and shut out all but cold practicality. She'd always said feelings had no place on a job. I wouldn't be feeling half so gut-stabbed if I'd had the sense to stick to the easy, uncomplicated friendship Cara and I had shared until that one night in Kost. I sought out the dark, frozen crevasse inside and sank into its emptiness until I could speak without shouting.

"Oh, I know all about mistaken trust." I couldn't stop an acid smile. "So. Marten fooled you the same as he did Kiran. No help for it but to deal with the consequences."

Cara looked all the more unhappy. "Like Melly. What now, since your original plan won't work? I talked to Liana just this morning. She says Melly's Taint remains strong, but she warned me Red Dal's already got a bid in from Karonys House for her."

I winced. Karonys was just what I'd feared. They catered to highsiders with nasty kinks, and used taphtha to turn their jennies into empty-eyed, compliant dolls. "How much is the bid?"

Cara shook her head. "Liana doesn't know, but she says Red Dal's been looking awfully happy, so it must be high. She doesn't think he's taken it yet, says he always likes to wait 'til the Change to sign a contract."

Yeah, Red Dal wouldn't sign early and lose the chance to hear competing offers. If only the Council hadn't taken the fortune I'd earned smuggling Kiran across their border, I could have given him a bid Karonys could never match. Weariness washed over me.

"Maybe if I can get Kiran free quickly enough, he could still help," I said. "If I can't…" I dropped my head to my knees and mumbled into them, "No doubt Marten will help. For a price." One far steeper than coin, if today was any guide.

Cara said, "I know how you must hate him. But even if he took Melly hostage, that's a far better fate than she faces now." She laid a tentative hand on my shoulder.

I twisted away and shoved to my feet to stare out at the damaged bridge. "I know."

Tiles rattled behind me as Cara stood. The erratic tock-tock-tock of a drillbird hunting spar beetles on the cupola roof was loud in the silence. At last Cara sighed and said, "And Kiran? What will we do about him?"

"We?" I laughed sharply. "*We* aren't going to do anything. No point in letting Marten get his claws into you, too. You've seen how good he is at it. You want to help me, fine. Keep your eye on Melly for me, make sure Liana tells you the instant her Taint weakens. It's safer if Red Dal doesn't catch me sniffing around Melly before I try and get her free, whether that's with Marten or without him."

"While you do...what? I'm guessing you think Marten was lying when he said he'd get Kiran away from Ruslan."

A spike of anger threatened to fracture my tenuous calm. I snapped, "Of course he's lying! He wants me to play shadow man for him, so he dangles a nice fat carrot. 'Oh, I'll help Kiran, once you've danced to my tune'...yeah, right. Besides, I'm not going to wait around for weeks. Suliyya knows what Ruslan might do to Kiran in the meantime."

"You mean to go against Ruslan without another mage's help?" Cara's hands twitched like she wanted to shake me. "I know you survived Ruslan and Simon before. But the way you told it, that was thanks to Kiran and that Taint charm his mage-brother gave you."

True. Simon had been scary enough, but Ruslan? Might as well take on Shaikar himself. If I thought too long on my chances, I'd break and run. But I'd learned long ago in the mountains how to deal with insane levels of risk. Narrow the focus, take the ascent one step at a time, and it's amazing what odds a man can beat.

I said, "This time I've actually got a hope of killing Ruslan. If I can make him break his vow, he'll get blasted to a cinder." Better yet if Ruslan broke the vow by killing Marten. "No question I'll need Kiran's help, though. That's why I've got to play along with Marten, so I can get the chance to talk with him. Kiran knows Ruslan better than anyone. If there's a way to trick Ruslan into casting, he can help me find it."

Cara frowned. "Wait. Kiran's bound to Ruslan, right? If you make Ruslan break his vow, and the confluence destroys him...might Kiran die too?"

Fuck. Now that was a complication I hadn't considered. "I don't know. So yeah, all the more reason I've got to talk to Kiran. I might know wards, but I don't know shit about active casting."

Cara's frown remained. "When are you going back highside?"

"I told Marten I'd go back to the embassy tonight." A prospect I wasn't looking forward to. Maybe I could keep calm talking with Cara, but I doubted that'd last with Marten. The thought of his infuriating smile already brought bitterness to choke me. "Marten claims he'll have a plan to reach Kiran ready by then. I have a few things I want to get beforehand. Right now I haven't so much as a warding charm."

"If you need coin, I've some at Samis's place," Cara said.

"Keep your money for water rations. I've a feeling they're gonna get expensive soon." I didn't have a single kenet to my name, but that was easily solved once the night markets opened. I hadn't spent years as a Taint thief for nothing.

"I'll keep on meeting with Liana. But this mess with Kiran..." Cara hesitated, watching me. "I know you're angry. But damn it, Dev, you don't have to face this alone."

"Alone is better," I said. "Ruslan didn't vow not to cast against you." Alone, I wouldn't have to worry for her safety. Or deal with the hurt that still clawed at me.

Cara's hands fisted. "Neither did Simon, but you took my help just fine in Alathia. For Khalmet's sake, Dev, you're going against a blood mage! You can't afford to turn help aside just because you're too mad to see straight. You want to shout at me? Fine. Whatever it takes to clear that stubborn head of yours. I can take it, trust me."

"*Trust* you—!" I clamped my mouth shut on the words. Took a breath, and said carefully, "Some things aren't helped by talking. I just...need time, Cara. It's been a hell of a day."

"I can imagine," she said. "Just don't run off and pull some crazy solo stunt like you did at the end with Simon. You nearly died—would have died, if not for the Alathians' skill with healing—and if you do something stupidly rash and get killed after I've only just seen you again, I'll—" Her voice failed, and she turned aside.

I clung to the shreds of my reserve. "Cara..."

"Look," she said tightly. "You need every advantage you can get. So don't rule out my help, hear?"

"I won't." She was right, I'd be a fool to let emotion handicap me. Yet the words stuck in my throat, for a whole host of reasons.

She let out a relieved breath. "I hope you can get to Kiran tomorrow," she said quietly, as I moved for the hole in the floor. "I've seen the fear in his eyes when he says Ruslan's name. He'll need the hope you bring."

Hope. I sent a swift, fervent prayer to Suliyya that Ruslan would leave Kiran in good enough shape I could provide it.

✳

(Kiran)

Soft voices spoke at the edge of Kiran's hearing, awareness stealing closer. He struggled to sink back into dark oblivion. Pain was all that waited for him on waking.

A hand stroked his forehead, and a deep voice called his name in a tone impossible to deny. "Kiran, open your eyes. Come, Kiranushka, wake for us now..."

Kiran's eyes opened. The sight of Ruslan leaning over him froze his breath—but Ruslan smiled gently at him, his hand warm on Kiran's brow, and fear slipped away, replaced by confusion. He'd been certain Ruslan would be angry, but why? He couldn't think past the ache in his head.

He lay in his bed, surrounded by the familiar warded walls of his room, the inset shelves piled with books, charms, and stacks of slate and chalk. Beyond Ruslan, Mikail sat in the ironwood chair from Kiran's writing desk. The tightening of the skin around his slanted gray eyes spoke of worry, and his sandy hair hung disheveled on his shoulders. Beside Mikail stood Ruslan's mage-sister Lizaveta, her beautiful face grave and her bare arms crossed over her crimson robe. The sunlight slanting through the bedroom window sparked fire from the jeweled amulet at her throat, silver gleaming against rich umber skin.

The pain in Kiran's head was an unfamiliar, deep throb, quite unlike the sharp agony of overload from pushing his magic too far.

"What—what happened?" His throat was raw as if scraped by knives.

Ruslan helped him upright against the bed pillows and handed him a jade cup containing rosewater. "Tell me, Kiran, what do you remember?"

The rosewater eased Kiran's throat. He sought to ignore pain and concentrate. He remembered making an error in a channel design—but no, that was years ago, and Mikail had been the one badly injured. The last thing he remembered was...

Flashing, blurred glimpses came, of Mikail bent over his slate in their shared workroom, Lizaveta laughing as she ate cloudberries, Ruslan tracing a spell diagram...but the memories slipped away as quickly as he tried to grasp them. Kiran focused deeper, turned his mage-sight inward.

Fear lanced through him. Rather than a smooth unbroken ribbon of experiences, the portion of his mind where his memories lay was a lacework of gaping holes. The memories weren't disordered or blocked—they were *gone*, as if eaten away by acid. His barriers were in a shambles, and at his core, his *ikilhia* pulsed in a raw, bruised knot, frighteningly dim.

"My mind—Ruslan, what's done this to me? I can't remember, I can't—"

"Hush, hush…" Ruslan pressed Kiran back down on the pillows. "You were caught in the backlash of a disrupted spell. Damage is to be expected. In truth, you're fortunate to have survived. As it was, we feared you might never wake; or that if you did, your mind might be destroyed beyond hope of repair. To hear you speak, and see your *ikilhia* intact…ah, Kiran, you don't know what a weight off my heart that is."

Indeed, relief was plain not only on Ruslan's face, but Mikail's and Lizaveta's. Kiran isolated the last strand of his damaged memories, and got a quicksilver flash of fire and agony.

"A spell backlash? But…what spell? Was I the one casting? What *happened?*"

Ruslan said, "You and Mikail cast a spell to create a tenth-level *voshanoi* charm, but your channel pattern was not designed properly and could not contain the energies. As the focus, you took the brunt of the backlash."

Kiran felt the blood drain from his face. *Voshanoi* charms were meant to shield a mage from the great forces of the confluence while casting, and as such, required equally immense amounts of power to create. Truly, he was lucky to be alive. "I'm sorry," he whispered. "I must have been too eager to cast. I should have asked you to check the pattern first…"

Ruslan stopped his words with a finger. "Do not trouble yourself; the error was not yours." He flicked a glance over his shoulder at Mikail, his expression darkening. "Mikail has already paid the price for his mistake."

Mikail bowed his head. Kiran swallowed. He didn't even want to imagine the punishment Ruslan would have inflicted for an error of that magnitude. The ache in his head increased. Kiran rubbed at his brow, wishing the pain would fade so he could think properly.

"Does your head hurt, *akhelysh?* Let me see…" Ruslan set his hands to Kiran's temples. His presence filled Kiran's head, red fire in a banked glow rather than a blaze. Soothing warmth spread through Kiran's mind. He sighed in relief as the ache dwindled to a faint soreness.

"That's better, is it not?" Ruslan withdrew his hands. "Now you are awake and I can properly assess the damage, I can speed your healing further." He turned to Mikail. "Bring me a *zhivnoi* crystal."

"Yes, Ruslan." Mikail hurried from the room.

"I will heal, then? This damage to my mind and memories…it isn't permanent?" Kiran couldn't help the desperate note to his voice. His *ikilhia*, so bruised and faint…what if the backlash had crippled him? He could dimly sense the deep, swirling pulse of confluence energy beyond the room's wards, but little else.

Ruslan chuckled, soft and knowing. "You fear for your magic, do you? You needn't. Your *ikilhia* will regain its strength soon enough."

"What about my memories?"

Regret shadowed Ruslan's eyes. "I fear the missing ones are lost forever. *Ikilhia* may be resilient, but the mind is a strangely fragile thing, sometimes."

"But so many are gone…" Kiran concentrated again. Frayed threads were all he had of recent years, though further back the holes diminished, until at last the ribbon of memory ran smooth again through his childhood, all the way back to the old wall that had always blocked him from his earliest days. "If I can't remember what Mikail and I learned of spellcasting—if I have to study it all again, it'll take years to recover!"

"You may not need to relearn as much as you fear, little one." Lizaveta padded forward to stand beside Ruslan. "I have seen mages endure this type of damage before. Knowledge that is internalized and regularly used will often remain when memories are lost. Even if not…time is one gift we *akheli* have in abundance."

Ruslan nodded. "Mikail will gladly help you. The moment your *ikilhia* recovers, he can take you through the progression of exercises you learned together, and we will soon see what gaps in your learning must be remedied."

"How long must I wait before casting?" Even if he found he had to relearn all his spellcraft, knowing the long path ahead would be better than the horrible uncertainty he felt now.

Ruslan smiled at him in fond approval. "Not long at all. If your recovery proceeds as I hope, you'll be casting again within days."

"Though a further delay might be wise." Lizaveta laid a ringed hand on Ruslan's shoulder. "Go gently with him, mage-brother, if you do not wish to risk losing him. We came too close, as it was."

Ruslan's hazel eyes gained a hint of frost. "He is my *akhelysh*, Liza, not yours. It is my decision to make, and I will do what is best for him."

Lizaveta's kohl-lined eyes lowered, and her red lips curved. "I know it, brother mine." She bent, her shining black hair spilling over one crimson-clad shoulder to pool on Kiran's bedsheet, and kissed him softly. "Welcome back to us, little one. I am glad to see you well."

Her jasmine scent and the honey-sweet taste of her lips left him pleasantly light-headed. "Thank you, khanum Liza," Kiran said, and smiled at her.

"Ah, Kiran." She traced a finger down his cheek. "I feared I might never again see your smile."

He'd assumed the accident with the spell had been mere days ago, but Lizaveta's tone suggested it had been longer. "How long have I been unconscious?"

"Only a day," Ruslan said. "Our fear for you made it feel an eternity." He turned to Lizaveta and spoke words full of harsh consonants and liquid vowels. Kiran recognized the language as that of Ruslan and Lizaveta's long-ago childhood, a tongue Kiran and Mikail knew only in scattered words and phrases. Ruslan had never taught them more, saying he preferred to keep some things private between himself and his mage-sister.

Lizaveta answered in kind, her head tilting. Ruslan's eyes softened. He brought her hands to his lips and kissed them. "Perhaps," he said. "As you said, we must take care."

Mikail strode back into the room bearing a faceted black crystal. The red gleam at the stone's center made Kiran uneasy without knowing why. *Zhivnoi* crystals held stored life energies, ready for a mage's use in minor spellcasting. Kiran had used them countless times throughout his childhood. Perhaps the shiver along his nerves was some lingering memory of the spell that had injured him.

Ruslan took the stone. "Relax now, Kiran, and let us see if we cannot heal you faster..." He folded the sheet down to bare Kiran's chest.

Kiran started at the sight of the red and black sigil etched into the skin over his heart. Ruslan's *akhelsya* sigil...Kiran had already been through the *akhelashva* ritual, then? He knew Mikail bore the mark-bond, could even summon a brief image of the pride shining in Mikail's gray eyes as he showed Kiran the sigil on his chest...but of his own ritual, nothing.

Ruslan traced the sigil with one long finger. "You don't remember. A shame, to lose a memory so sublime. But never fear, *akhelysh*, time will bring new ones." He held the stone over Kiran's heart.

Magic poured into Kiran in a smooth rush, shot through with the fire of Ruslan's will. Kiran lay unresisting as Ruslan flowed through his body and mind, healing, adjusting, smoothing over the raw places. His eyes slipped shut, and he floated in red light for an indeterminate length of time. When the light faded, he felt too sleepy to open his eyes again.

"Rest, Kiran. Sleep, and let your mind heal," Ruslan said softly. Kiran obeyed and sank into darkness.

CHAPTER NINE

(Dev)

I clung in the inky shadows beneath a balcony, my back braced against stone and my toes and fingers dug into a worn pattern of vines carved into the supports. Across the dark void of the alleyway, the arched window of Red Dal's Tainter den glowed warm with lanternlight through a linen curtain. Enough light spilled through to show the wards surrounding the window. They were carefully placed, extremely nasty, and new. Looked like Red Dal had gotten just as twitchy as everyone else in the city.

My right calf muscle spasmed. I eased my foot free, flexed the ankle a few times, and stabbed my toes into a new hold that at least taxed my thigh muscle instead of the calf. Khalmet's hand, and here I'd thought scouting Simon's house from that damn drainhole in Kost was uncomfortable.

Hopefully I wouldn't have to stay braced under the balcony much longer. Full dark had arrived, the stars a diamond spray above the ragged lines of the rooftops. Magelights sparkled in the distant highside towers, and a chaotic babble of streetsellers' calls underlaid by the thump of tabis drums echoed from the alley's mouth. If Red Dal's Tainters were working a job tonight, they'd be leaving any minute.

His den minder Liana was too wary of Cara to let her see Melly in person. Me, she would've welcomed; we'd been Tainters together, and I'd dropped by the den often enough in the past. But I didn't fool myself those visits had been kept secret from Red Dal. I didn't think Liana would lie to Cara about Melly, but today, trust came hard. I had to see Melly for myself. Make sure of the one whisper of hope in this whole disaster, that I'd reached Ninavel in time to save her.

Even if I couldn't save Kiran. Fear still ate at me that within Ruslan's house I'd find only an empty-eyed puppet with Kiran's body. I sent a quick, fervent prayer to Khalmet, begging him to favor Kiran with the touch of his good hand. Kiran would need god-given luck to survive Ruslan intact, let alone escape him again.

The curtain twitched, and my breath quickened. A hand drew the curtain aside to reveal Red Dal himself. A bitter pang shot through me at the sight of his dark curls and wiry shoulders. I was too far away to see his face clearly, but I knew just what it'd show: the laughing eyes, the mischievous grin that invited you to share the joke. Kids loved him. Other handlers kept their Tainters leashed with drugs or painbender charms, but Red Dal prided himself on doing it through sheer force of personality. It might've been better if he'd used fear to keep us motivated. Maybe then the fall wouldn't have been so hard.

Red Dal opened the window and leaned out to touch each ward in turn. The sly bastard probably hadn't keyed the wards to anyone but himself.

He backed away, replaced by the eager faces of children, Melly's foremost among them. My heart twisted in my chest. Mother of maidens, but she looked like Sethan! It wasn't just her hair, the deep, vivid red of magefire flame. She had his long-limbed, graceful build, too, and a certain way of tilting her head, so familiar it made my breath catch.

Her long-lashed almond eyes and caramel skin must have come from her dead Arkennlander mother. The combination of traits was striking; where Sethan had been merely handsome in a foreign sort of way, Melly looked to match Kiran for jaw-dropping beauty when she grew up. Easy enough to see why Karonys House was panting after her. Red Dal could make more on her sale than he had on all his previous Tainters combined.

Melly said something to little dark-haired Jomi beside her and slid an arm around the boy to squeeze his shoulders. The mature confidence of the gesture cramped my gut. Even in the few months since I'd last seen her, she'd grown several inches. How much longer before her Change? Weeks, or mere days?

The light went out. Silently, small bodies swarmed out the window and up the wall to crouch on the roof's edge. Melly was easy to recognize even with her red hair hidden by darkness, thanks to her relative height compared to the younger Tainters. An adult crawled from the window up to the roof, moving far more awkwardly. From the build, it wasn't Red Dal, only one of his minders. Most of them treated climbing as an irritating necessity rather than a passion. We'd mocked them behind their backs in my day, safe in our assumed superiority.

Once the minder reached the roof, they were off, flitting across the stone like shadows. I watched them go, and only after they were out of sight realized my teeth were clenched so hard my jaw ached.

I'd hoped seeing Melly would reassure me. Instead, the drumbeat of urgency that haunted me had increased. Nobody could predict the Change exactly, but when it came, it happened quick. I remembered my own all too well. One day I'd been boss Tainter of the gang, able to fly faster and lift more weight than any other kid. Next night, I'd had to ask for help wafting loot down a tower. Red Dal had come the next morning and tested me; gods, the awful pit in my stomach when I'd found I could barely lift myself head-high. The other kids had been wide-eyed and solemn when Red Dal told them I had to leave for my new family. I'd joked and pretended not to care, though inside it felt like I'd swallowed ground glass.

I should've listened to that feeling. I sheered off from the memories of what came after, when I found all Red Dal's breezy talk of a new family was a lie. The black hell I'd endured in Tavian's gang was a paradise compared to what waited for Melly.

Red Dal's dark shape reappeared in the window. Faint blue flashes lit the darkness as he reactivated the wards. Once he shut the window and the curtain glowed with light again, I slithered sideways around a section of carved stonework and scrambled down to street level.

The evening crowds were out in full force. People choked streets lit by colored lanterns and firestone charms. Shops hawking everything from spice-infused liquors to sun shrouds had their shutters thrown wide, their wares displayed on tables edged with crude copper thief-wards. The pungent scents of curried meats and spicebread clogged the night air, and the ululating wails of demon singers soared over the cheers and catcalls of spectators ringing illusionists, acrobats, and storytellers.

The crowd's babble had a nervous edge. Laughter sounded forced, and wrists gleamed with warding charms. But it was peak convoy season; enough wide-eyed, wardless foreigners wandered the night markets that I safely lifted enough coin to buy some low-grade but useful charms, along with a heaping bowl of rasheil-nut curry.

Another time I might have reveled in the spices exploding over my tongue, so welcome after months of bland Alathian mush. I might've sought out friends at the Blackstrike, joined them in drinking cinnamon-laced firewine and gambling with bloodstone tiles while we heckled our favorite performers. Or lost myself in the shifting rhythms pounded out by groups of tabis drummers, and spent long hours stamping and whirling in the knot of dancers surrounding them.

Tonight not even the insistent pulse of the drums could cut through the tangle in my head. Without Kiran's help, stealing Melly away from a handler as wary and clever as Red Dal would be a hell of a trick. Especially since Melly herself wouldn't want to go. No, she'd still be loving life as a Tainter, fiercely loyal to Red Dal and convinced of every lie he'd ever told her. Red Dal trained his Tainters well. He drilled into them from their earliest days in the den never to go anywhere with an adult unless he ordered it, not even someone as familiar as Liana. And Melly was Tainted enough to kick my ass ten times over if I tried using physical force.

If I could only get Kiran free first, then we could work our old scheme, or use his magic in some other way. But even if I didn't find Kiran mindburned, I doubted freeing him from Ruslan would be easy, or quick. After seeing Melly again, I couldn't bear to wait any longer to ensure her safety. Not when she might Change any day.

Which left me one last horribly bitter option: Marten. Reason said that Cara was right, Melly was better off as his hostage. Yet after seeing how terribly he'd used Kiran, every instinct in me screamed against the idea of placing her life in his hands. Then again, if Marten truly wanted me to play shadow man, maybe I could bargain cleverly enough to avoid giving Melly to him outright.

It was well after midnight when I trudged up the causeway that circled up the Dawnfire Tower to face the interlocking gold circles of the Alathian seal on the embassy door, shining bright in a pool of pale magelight. I stood there for long moments, fighting to armor myself against a furious boil of emotion. My body ached to run straight back down streetside so I'd never have to endure the sight of Marten's hypocritical face again.

Instead, I laid a hand flat on a blank copper plaque set amidst the door's ward lines. The copper warmed under my palm. The mage on watch would know I'd come.

Lena swung the door open mere instants after I touched the ward. Relief flashed in her dark eyes before they fell from mine. "Marten told me to expect you, but I wasn't certain you'd return."

Of course it would be Lena. Hatred ate at my resolve. I fixed her with a cold stare. "I'm here for Kiran's sake, and Kiran's alone. Somebody's got to help him after you high-minded Alathians screwed him so thoroughly."

"Dev, I…" She stopped; swallowed. "I regret Kiran's situation. You don't know how deeply. But Marten had no choice—"

"Of course he had a choice! So did you. And you stood there and did *nothing*." Unbidden, I heard an echo of Marten's voice: *just like you did, when you handed him to Simon in Kost.* The cramp of guilt only made my anger burn hotter. It wasn't the same, damn it. I hadn't known the consequences. Lena had.

Lena said in a low, fierce voice, "Marten won't leave Kiran with Ruslan. I told you before: he does not make empty promises."

"Then tell me his brilliant plan, the one that'll outsmart Ruslan." When she didn't say anything, I laughed, the sound as cutting as I could make it. "Yeah, I didn't think so."

Lena shook her head. "Dev. He can't tell you what he intends because you're not a mage."

"What fucking difference does that make?"

"Ruslan can't breach a mage's inner defenses without harm, and therefore breaking his vow. But you...you have no defenses. Without power of your own, even the best charms we have might not prevent a mage as strong as Ruslan from plucking information from your mind, should he touch you. Kiran's best hope is for Ruslan to have no hint of what Marten plans, and so Marten can't risk sharing such plans with you."

Well, I'd take one part of that to heart: never get within touching distance of Ruslan. As for the rest... "Did Marten share his plan with you?"

"Not...all of it." Her gaze dropped again. She twisted at the rune-marked rings on her fingers. "He thinks it better to be too cautious than not enough."

The faint glimmer of hope within died. I should've known better. Marten was playing on her faith in him, telling her just what she wanted to hear. Lies, all of it. *Oh, I'd tell you my plan if I could...*right.

More furious words boiled up in my throat, and I locked my jaw shut. Yeah, this was going well. I hadn't even passed the embassy's door and already I was near blind with anger. If I kept this up, Marten would manipulate me as easy as a bone puppet. Cold, damn it; I had to stay cold. Find that crevasse inside again, and let nothing shake me from it.

"Come inside." Lena was watching me with an anxious frown. "Please. Marten's waiting for you."

I sucked down a slow, steadying breath and let her lead me down a dimly lit hallway. A faint glow of magelight fanned out from under the curtain blocking the archway to the receiving room. I heard a mutter of voices in the room beyond, low and sharp.

The voices fell silent as I pushed through the curtain. The receiving room was shadowed, with only a single magelight glowing in a copper bracket at the room's far end. A cool wash of silver illuminated Marten and Talm, glaring at each other before the window with the expansive view of the city's magelit spires. Marten's posture was as rigidly formal as I'd ever seen it. Talm's arms were crossed, his ringed fingers biting deep into his biceps.

I allowed myself a vicious little grin. Nice to see Marten's smooth tongue wasn't working so well tonight. If Talm remained angry, maybe I could use that somehow. Marten might not have shared his plans with Lena, but maybe he'd told his lover.

Marten turned to me. "Dev. Thank you for returning."

Talm shot me a glance as dark as if I were the source of his anger, not Marten. "Stay your course, then," he said to Marten, his voice clipped. "Just remember: our task is to restore Alathia's wards, not protect this city's monsters." He dipped in a stiff bow and stalked past Lena.

She exchanged a silent, meaningful look with Marten, who shrugged in weary dismissal. Lena hurried out after Talm, doubtless to play the good lieutenant and smooth over the rift.

"Dissension in the ranks, is there?" I asked Marten, poisonously bright.

Marten sank into a chair. "It's been a difficult day for all of us."

"Especially Kiran." I remained standing. "So let's not fuck around, Marten. If you've got a plan, I want to hear it."

Marten nodded. Thank Khalmet, he didn't try any false cheer or sympathy. The tired, serious look to his face was probably another mask, but at least it was one that didn't set my teeth grinding. "We're to meet with Ruslan in Sechaveh's audience chamber, two hours after dawn. During that time, Lena will take you to Ruslan's house in Reytani district. Stevan believes he's devised a spell to let you cross the house wards."

"Why send Lena and not Stevan, if he's the one so clever with warding magic?" Stevan might be an asshole, but I'd take his company any day over Lena's. At least Stevan hadn't ever pretended to be Kiran's friend.

"Lena has the deftest touch of us all with spellwork," Marten said. "You'll need that to cross Ruslan's wards without leaving traces of your passing. Though I should specify: only you will be able to cross them. A mage's innate energies are simply too difficult to conceal from warding spells. Lena will cast to get you through, but she must remain outside."

"Ruslan's not likely to leave him unguarded," I pointed out.

"Lena should be able to sense the presence of any other mages in the house. She can create a diversion for you, and provide you at least a short window of time to safely seek Kiran."

"What guarantee do I have that I'm not the diversion? That you're not sending me inside intending my capture?"

Marten sighed. "I'm sure nothing I say will assuage your fears entirely. Remember, I want information, on both Kiran and Ruslan. That can't happen without your safe return."

I'd bet the real reason Lena would remain outside Ruslan's wards was that unlike me, Marten didn't consider her expendable. Still, he'd given me the opening I wanted to bargain for Melly's sake.

"If you want me to sneak alone into Ruslan's house and play shadow man for you, then I need something more solid in return than vague talk of helping Kiran."

Marten only watched me steadily. "Such as?"

"The money the Council confiscated from my accounts in Kost. I want it back. All of it." With that much coin in hand again, I could outbid Karonys House, easy.

Marten raised his brows. "That's a bit steep of a reward for a single morning's effort."

"You know damn well it's your fault I need the money. Give it to me, and I'll play your game just like you want. If you don't…Kiran's my friend, yeah, but it's like you said: I've got other, older promises to keep."

"If you want the child safe, the embassy can negotiate with Sechaveh to have him claim her as our ward," Marten said.

"So you can leash me tighter? Fuck no, Marten. You think after today I want you anywhere near someone I want to protect? You so much as *look* at her, and you can forget any shadow work from me."

"I understand your fear," Marten said quietly. "I want to help you. But I cannot simply hand over that much money, not without justifying it to Halassian and the Council. Go streetside for me, get me information that leads directly to the success of our mission, and I can make a case to convince them."

I'd known he'd balk at the full amount. "You're awfully quick with promises, Marten, and I haven't seen you keep one yet. But, fine. You show me a sign of good faith—a thousand kenets, say—and I'll do some hunting down streetside." A thousand kenets would be more than enough earnest money to convince Red Dal a bid for a far larger amount was real. I could put in the bid now, and before payment came due, either squeeze more money out of Marten or use my access to the embassy to steal it.

Marten's smile was dry. "I'll talk to Halassian, but I'll need my own show of good faith from you tomorrow. Get me something I can use, whether it's from Ruslan's house or elsewhere."

Yeah, I much preferred dealing with this version of Marten, who offered blunt bargains without trying to honeycoat them. No doubt he knew it, and had changed tactics accordingly. It hadn't escaped me that my agreement meant I'd end up playing exactly the role he'd wanted. I just prayed one day I'd get to see all his masks fall to ruin. I wanted to see him be the one to suffer.

"Fine," I said. "If the meeting with Ruslan is soon after dawn, better if I stay here until then. I'd hate to oversleep, and the least you can do is pay for my water rations." Much as the thought of spending more time in the Alathians' company revolted me, I needed to stick close, especially if I wanted the chance to scout the embassy's vaults.

"I was going to suggest that you sleep here." Marten stood. "Come, I'll take you to your room."

He didn't want me walking around unescorted, knowing otherwise I'd seize the chance to snoop. No doubt he'd keep me guarded all night, damn him. At least he stayed silent as he showed me to the little room I'd shared with Kiran, and retreated to the hall the moment he sparked the magelight.

I shut the door and reached for the lock-hold charm I'd bought streetside, only to snort in disgust at myself. Something as simple as a lock-hold wouldn't stop mages. Instead, I sat down on a bed and took off my boots. The empty bed against the other wall loomed large in my vision. Fuck; the Alathians had even left Kiran's pack sitting right where he'd left it beside mine, as if they thought he'd come back any minute.

On sudden impulse, I hauled his pack up onto the bed, unlaced the top flap, and started digging through its contents. Wouldn't hurt to see if I could find a comb or something with a few hairs that could be used to key a find-me charm, even if right now I had a pretty damn good idea of Kiran's location.

Hidden behind a flap of torn fabric at the pack's bottom, my fingers touched something that crackled. I pulled out a folded parchment, far heavier than ordinary paper. When I turned it over, I blinked in surprise. My name was inked in Kiran's handwriting on an upper corner.

Maybe it was a letter, but why would he have written one to me? I glanced at the closed door. No sounds came from the hallway. I unfolded the parchment.

It wasn't a letter. Drawn on the parchment were a host of lines coiling about each other in a pattern so complex my eyes crossed trying to follow it. Scattered sets of incomprehensible symbols were marked in random places. I stared at the drawing, frowning. I'd seen something similar before, but it hadn't been on paper.

Kiran, sprawled on his back among tangled spirals of scorched and blackened silver in Simon's cave… Shit, I knew what this was: a spell diagram, for what Kiran called a channeled spell. Blood magic. I dropped the parchment as fast as if I held a sand adder.

Khalmet's bony hand, no need to act like a superstitious southerner. This was a piece of paper, not a charm or a ward. From things Kiran had said, I'd gathered that blood mages worked out complex spells ahead of time before they cast them, the way a convoy boss might plan out his schedule and supplies for a mountain crossing.

The Alathians had wanted Kiran to figure out Simon's border charm. Maybe the diagram had something to do with that. But if he'd worried about Marten's sincerity and brought this as some kind of insurance, why hadn't he told me of it? I peered at the diagram again, as if I could figure it out if I just looked closer. Part of the pattern seemed sparse compared to the rest, lines stopping in mid-swirl like they weren't finished.

I studied the diagram until my eyes felt full of sand, but got no closer to answers. At last I folded it back up and tucked it into my own clothing. The only conclusion I'd reached was that I didn't want Marten or any of the other Alathians to see it. I'd bring the diagram with me tomorrow. If Khalmet favored me—and how I prayed he did—maybe I'd get an answer direct from Kiran.

✳

(Kiran)

Kiran woke with a start, jerking upright in his bed. He was panting like he'd run up a tower stair, a miasma of unease thick in his mind. Sibilant, incomprehensible whispers played about the edges of his hearing. When he strained to listen, the whispers faded into the rapid thump of his heart. Perhaps they'd only been a product of nightmare, though he couldn't remember any dreams.

The window in the far wall showed only darkness outside. The dim rosy glow of a magelight perched on his writing desk illuminated Mikail's sleeping form slumped in a chair a few feet away. Kiran blew out a rueful breath. For all Ruslan's earlier assurances, he must still be worried for Kiran's health if he had left Mikail on watch.

Thanks to Ruslan's healing, Kiran's inner senses had recovered enough to pick out the energies of the wards in the walls, even through his repaired mental barriers. In fact, the sensations felt painfully sharp, though the energies were quiescent. Kiran winced away from concentrating on them. He felt oddly on edge despite the weariness that weighted his eyelids. Almost, he imagined he could still hear those maddeningly faint, disturbing whispers, sliding along his senses like snakes through sand.

Beyond the wards, the familiar slow swirl of confluence energy abruptly shifted. Power spiked violently upward in a soundless explosion to hammer against his barriers.

Mikail surged out of the chair, gray eyes wide. On walls and ceiling, protective wards blazed into fiery red scrawls of light. Energies roiled and twisted as the wards fought to channel the wild magic safely back into the earth through the stones of the building. Kiran struggled to reinforce his barriers, his *ikilhia* frighteningly slow to respond.

"Mikail! Is someone attacking us?" He found it hard to imagine anyone would dare strike at Ruslan, but he'd never felt the confluence behave like this before.

"No," Mikail said shortly, without taking his eyes from the wards.

"Then what's happening?"

Mikail held up a hand, his gaze still intent. A few sparks sizzled off the wards by the window, but the patterns held. Quickly as it had come, the wave of confluence energy ebbed away. Kiran frowned, his head tilting. The magnitude of the energies beyond the wards felt normal again, but the currents coiled and heaved now in a strangely irregular way. Mikail had said this was no attack. If Kiran released his barriers, then painful as it might be to his damaged senses, he could get a better view...

Mikail's hand closed hard on his arm. "*Don't* drop your barriers." He held Kiran's gaze, his pale eyes tinged scarlet by magelight, until Kiran nodded his assent. Mikail sat back, blowing out a breath. "Ruslan's orders," he said in response to Kiran's puzzled stare. "The confluence has become unstable. After a spike like we just felt, there'll be aftershocks, and no warning. If your barriers were down when one hit, you could be hurt badly."

"The confluence, unstable?" Disorientation washed over Kiran. The shifting tides of the confluence were as much a part of the city as the stone that formed its spires. Dangerous to touch directly, yes, but predictable in their flow, and as eternal as the stars. Or so he'd thought. He rubbed at his temples. His lacerated memories held nothing helpful. "When did this happen?"

"It started a few weeks ago. You don't remember, I know." Mikail shifted in his chair, a shadow crossing his broad face.

"I don't blame you for the accident with the spell," Kiran said softly. "You know that, don't you?"

Mikail shut his eyes. "Brother…" He left the chair to settle on Kiran's bed. Pulling Kiran close, he rested his forehead against Kiran's, the way he'd always done when Kiran needed comforting as a child. "I wish you hadn't had to suffer."

Kiran returned Mikail's grip, his throat choked. He and Mikail weren't brothers in the usual sense, but Ruslan had always insisted that the bond between them as *akheli* apprentices went far deeper than that of ordinary family. *You put your life in your mage-brother's hands every time you cast a channeled spell,* Ruslan had said. *You will learn to trust each other without reservation, as Lizaveta and I do.*

Kiran might only recall scattered threads of recent years, but he still possessed a wealth of earlier memories that proved the truth of Ruslan's words. Mikail's steadfast patience, his fierce protectiveness, his dry, deadpan humor, the rare brilliance of his smile—even now, Kiran's knowledge of his mage-brother ran heart-deep.

"I'm just glad I didn't lose all my memories." To forget Mikail entirely would be a loss so terrible Kiran could scarcely bear to imagine it.

Mikail swatted Kiran's head. "We're all grateful you didn't lose more. It's hard enough to tell you have a brain in there as it is."

Kiran shoved Mikail away in mock indignation, but couldn't suppress a smile. Mikail had always teased him for being too excitable and emotional, unlike his coolly logical mage-brother. "I like to keep your life interesting."

"There's such a thing as too interesting." Mikail said it lightly, but his eyes were grave. Kiran sighed, one hand drifting back up to his temple. Memory loss certainly was far more frightening and disturbing in reality than it had ever seemed in the tales of magic and adventure he'd loved as a child.

Better to change the subject, lest Kiran make his mage-brother feel worse over the accident than he did already. "I'd say this confluence instability qualifies as worrisome more than interesting. What's causing it?"

"An excellent question," Ruslan said from the doorway. Kiran and Mikail jumped and straightened as one. Ruslan waved his hand, and the magelight brightened until the furniture cast sharp-edged shadows across the flagstones.

"Lord Sechaveh is quite anxious for us to discover the answer, in fact." Ruslan paced to the window, brushing a finger across each ward in turn as he went. "Mikail. You instructed Kiran not to drop his barriers?"

"Yes, Ruslan." Mikail backed to stand beside the chair. "The change in the confluence energies woke us, but the wards held, and afterward I made sure he kept his barriers up."

Kiran shifted in the bed. The spike wasn't why he'd woken, but he hesitated to bring up what was likely only a lingering remnant of some forgotten nightmare.

Ruslan turned. "Kiran, you wish to speak?"

His voice had softened, but Kiran still felt strangely tongue-tied. "I…right before the confluence spiked, I woke and thought I heard…whispers. Too faint to make out, and unsettling, somehow…but probably it was just a dream."

"Interesting." Ruslan tapped a finger against a ward, his eyes on Kiran. "When a mage's mind has undergone trauma like yours, it sometimes results in a heightened energetic sensitivity that can manifest in odd ways. If there is a change in the confluence energies prior to an upheaval that can be detected, this could be quite useful." He nodded to Kiran. "You'll tell me if you hear these whispers again, yes?"

"Yes, Ruslan," Kiran said. "Then—we don't know yet what's causing this?"

"Not yet, but I have confidence we soon will." Ruslan left the window to stand by Kiran's bed. "However, there is one complication we must discuss. For diplomatic reasons, Lord Sechaveh requested that we allow a team of Alathians to aid our investigation." His tone made it clear that aid was the last thing he expected from Alathians.

"Alathians? Why would they concern themselves with Ninavel?" What little Kiran knew of Alathia said their ruling Council had as little to do with Ninavel as possible, despising Sechaveh for the freedom he allowed mages.

Ruslan shrugged. "The instability in the confluence causes corresponding fluctuations in the veins of earth-power that extend throughout this entire region. The wards the Alathians cower behind are too poorly designed to handle the fluctuations, and are near failure. Sechaveh wishes to gain trade concessions, so he asked me to humor the Alathians when they begged to participate in our search for answers."

He spread his hands. "Lord Sechaveh might be *nathahlen*, but his sister was not, and she once provided a great service to Lizaveta and me. For the sake of that debt, I've granted Sechaveh's request…but be warned, the Alathians are not to be trusted. They hate and fear the *akheli*, jealous of our power, and continually seek ways to undermine us. I have experience with them of old." His deep voice was stern, and sorrowful. He laid a hand on Kiran's shoulder. "As the youngest of us, Kiran, they will believe you to be the most vulnerable, and will concentrate their efforts on you. You must be on your guard. Although they have little real power, they are experts in the use of lies. They will try to make you distrust us, distrust yourself; and by any means they can, try to turn you against us."

"I won't listen to them," Kiran assured Ruslan. If the Alathians mistook his youth for weakness, he'd prove them wrong. His ties to Ruslan and Mikail ran deeper than any outsider could understand. Unthinkable, to turn against them.

Ruslan's smile was warm. "Good, *akhelysh*. I have faith in you. Should you ever be troubled, you have only to come to me, or even Lizaveta, and we will help you."

Kiran nodded, and Ruslan squeezed his shoulder. "There is one last matter…I promised Lord Sechaveh we would refrain from casting any spells with intent to harm the Alathians, regardless of provocation. I know you and Mikail would not knowingly disobey me, but I must ensure no mistakes happen. I set the stricture in Mikail already, but you…"

Red fire cascaded through Kiran's head. He cried out, arching backward, as a binding pattern seared deep into his *ikilhia*. Strong hands caught him, lowered him to the pillows. Through a haze of pain and dizziness, he heard Ruslan's voice.

"There, I am sorry for the discomfort, Kiranushka…I know you are sore yet." Fingers stroked disordered hair back from Kiran's brow, as Kiran shuddered and twitched in helpless aftermath. "I would have waited longer to cast the will-binding, but we are to meet the Alathians this morning."

"You intend to take Kiran with us?" Mikail sounded startled. "But…" His gaze flicked to Kiran before it returned to Ruslan. "He's still recovering. Wouldn't it be better to leave him in Lizaveta's care rather than expose him to the foreigners' attention?"

Kiran struggled back upright, steeling himself not to wince away from Ruslan's touch. His master hadn't wanted to cause him pain; it wasn't Ruslan's fault the accident had left Kiran's mind so horribly raw. Kiran should act as an adult, not a whimpering child.

"I don't need coddling," he announced. "I've lain in bed long enough! My barriers are repaired. I'll show no weakness in front of the Alathians."

Ruslan gave him an approving look. "Exactly. Best to show the foreigners our unity from the start. Besides…" He held Mikail's gaze. "With Kiran not fully recovered, I prefer not to chance any mishaps while I am away."

With a last pat to Kiran's shoulder, he stood. "Back to sleep, *akhelyshen*. I will reinforce the wards to keep aftershocks from disturbing you. Mikail, you may return to your room, if you choose. I think we need not fear another major disturbance in the confluence this night."

Mikail's gray eyes faded back into colorlessness as Ruslan dimmed the magelight. "I'll stay. I don't mind." He looked at Kiran, the skin seeming to tighten over the flat planes of his cheekbones. "I'd rather make certain he's all right, with no aftereffects from the accident."

Mikail's voice hitched on the final word. Kiran swallowed the exasperated protest he'd intended to make. His mage-brother's guilt over Kiran's injuries wouldn't be assuaged by simple words. If it made him feel better to hover at Kiran's bedside, so be it.

"Stay if you like," he told Mikail. "Though you don't have to. I'm telling you, I'm fine." The fire in his mind had faded, though the will-binding lurking deep in his *ikilhia* nagged at him with a faint, phantom itch.

Mikail only shook his head and settled back into the chair.

"As you wish, Misha." Ruslan ran a hand over Mikail's hair in a swift, light caress. Kiran was glad to see the tightness in Mikail's face ease at the touch.

Kiran lay back down and watched as Ruslan moved around the room, wards flaring at his touch. Ruslan worked so deftly that Kiran could barely sense his casting, only the resulting shift in energies.

Unlike when Ruslan had bound him. Kiran shivered. The ease with which Ruslan had cast the will-binding, without any blood-to-blood contact, as if Kiran were *nathahlen* and utterly lacking in mental barriers...he must have used the mark-bond to bypass them. Kiran trusted Ruslan, of course he did, but he couldn't help but feel uneasy at the demonstration of the depth of power Ruslan now had over him. He resisted the urge to rub at the *akhelsya* sigil on his chest. No; he was proud to bear Ruslan's mark-bond, to be *akheli* in truth as Mikail was. Anything else was mere childish nerves on his part.

(Dev)

"Dev."

I woke to see Lena standing in the doorway holding a magelight. I sat up, bleary-eyed. "Early, aren't you?" The window was shuttered, but I was pretty damn sure it wasn't dawn yet.

"We just received a message from Lord Sechaveh. Another mage has been killed, and he's requested that we come at once. Marten wants you with us so that if Ruslan also comes, you and I can take the opportunity to seek Kiran."

Cobwebs cleared from my head as thoroughly as if she'd thrown a bucket of glacial meltwater over me. I threw off the sheet and reached for my shirt and boots. The plain but sturdy set of clothes I'd brought from Tamanath, not the delicate highsider silk crap somebody had left folded on a chair. If Marten didn't like it, too bad. I wanted clothes I could climb in, not something that'd rip if I brushed against a wall wrong.

Lena lingered in the doorway. She didn't look like she'd slept well—or at all, maybe. Shadows dark as coal smudges lay beneath her eyes. As I dressed, once or twice she drew breath like she wanted to speak, but no words escaped her.

I ought to try and draw her out, seek some advantage. Yet anger still coiled in my gut every time I looked at her. Oddly, I'd found it easier to rein in my tongue speaking with Marten. Maybe it was because I'd never seen him as anything but a cold-blooded viper. With Lena, after two sentences I feared I'd break and start shouting. I concentrated on donning my boots and tried not to look as unfriendly as I felt.

When I joined her in the hall, I paused, surprised. Two male voices raised in song drifted from the receiving room at the hallway's end. A deep, rich baritone and a warm tenor, both sliding and diving around each other in a wordless, oddly compelling pattern.

Lena said, "Marten and Stevan are casting to map out Ruslan's wards before we leave."

Curiosity drove me to ask, "Sometimes you sing when you cast, sometimes you mumble, sometimes you don't say a damn thing…why the difference?"

Lena looked relieved to hear me ask an ordinary question. "We use sound when we build a complex spell without the aid of pre-existing patterns like those bound in charms or amulets. The more complex the spell and the more mages involved in casting, the more variety and precision of sound is needed. If a spell is simple enough, it can be patterned by will alone—though even then, we often use chants as aids to concentration."

Magic always sounded so damn complicated. "The full-on singing is your version of channeled magic, then."

"In a way," Lena said. "Though we use our own soulfire to fuel the spell, never that of an unwilling victim."

It sure didn't stop them from fucking people over. I managed to keep that behind my teeth, barely; but Lena surely saw it in my face. She led me into the receiving room without speaking again.

Marten and Stevan stood before the great arched window, their eyes closed and their rings glowing bright as they sang. Marten was the tenor, Stevan the baritone; flickers of colored light chased over the window's wards every time their voices met on a note. The sky outside was growing pale with the approach of dawn, the towers ghostly in the low light.

Talm leaned against a table laden with glazed ceramic cups and a tray of fruit and flatbread. His expression was odd as he watched Marten and Stevan: wistful admiration, but a hint of something darker lay in his eyes. I hoped it meant his anger with Marten hadn't faded.

I stalked over to the table. The cups proved to contain mint-scented water. I downed one and snatched up a handful of food.

Talm said to me, "They've almost finished." He looked at Lena as she reached for a slice of rockmelon. "Impressive how smoothly they cast together, isn't it? I'm not sure I could manage that with my old training partner from the Arcanum."

Or maybe all I'd seen was simple jealousy. Maybe Marten and Stevan had been something more than training partners, back in the day.

Lena said softly to Talm, "It's my hope this mission will revive their friendship. For Stevan's sake, if not Marten's. I remember Stevan in his adept days...in the final year before his commissioning, he used to demonstrate spells for my year-class. He was so different then; as quick to laugh as to criticize, passionate about all manner of things along with magic..."

Talm nudged Lena, grinning at her with the casual, teasing ease of long-held friendship. "Had a crush on him, did you?"

The corner of her mouth lifted. "Plenty of us did. To see him now..." She shook her head, her amusement vanishing. "He's been so angry since Reshannis's trial."

"I can imagine." Talm's eyes went back to Marten. For an instant I caught a flash of sadness so deep it startled me, before his expression settled into his usual wry humor.

"What trial?" I asked.

Lena looked away. Talm shrugged and said lightly, "Sorry. Nothing more boring than hearing other people reminisce, is there?"

Marten and Stevan stopped singing. Marten turned with an air of satisfaction. "We have a good idea of Ruslan's outer wards. Enough for Stevan to key a spell for Lena's use—yes, Stevan?"

Stevan nodded, as icily impassive as ever. He pulled a jeweled golden disc from a pocket and shut his eyes again, his lips moving soundlessly.

Ambassador Halassian stumped into the room, her gray hair pinned up in a loose bun instead of intricate braids. "Haven't you left yet, Captain? Sechaveh will expect a prompt response in this."

"We're nearly ready," Marten said, glancing at Stevan. "We'll hurry, the moment Stevan completes his spell."

Talm asked, "Did Sechaveh's message say the manner of death, or any information about the victim?"

"No," Marten said. "It was rather carefully phrased. I suspect Lord Sechaveh didn't want the messenger to know the details. We were simply requested to go to a certain residence in Vaishala district as soon as possible, in regard to a fatality related to our purpose in Ninavel."

I swallowed a lump of flatbread, frowning. Vaishala district was highside, the next district over from Seltonis. The residents were wealthy families high up in the hierarchies of mining guilds and banking houses, with a sprinkling of mages to boot. As a Taint thief, I'd been sent there on jobs by Red Dal a couple times, but not often. The residents of Vaishala could afford seriously powerful wards, and many families were what counted as old wealth in Ninavel. From Red Dal's perspective, that meant they weren't as apt to brag over their possessions, making it tricky to know which houses were worth the risk. Not that any family was truly old wealth in Ninavel, since Sechaveh had only built the city a little more than a hundred years ago. But the families who'd lived in Ninavel a few generations were a bit more wise to the ways of Taint thieves than those who'd come more recently.

"Jenoviann can guide you," Halassian said. "Before she came to Ninavel, she spent several years working with the healers of the Sanitorium. You'll want her expertise in anatomy if you have the chance to examine the body. You'll want to walk, not take a carriage; if you climb the Ramhorn stair as a shortcut to Vaishala, that'll get you there far faster than traveling the causeways."

"Stairs." Talm sighed. "Of course it would be stairs. You'd think this city was built by mountain goats."

Marten chuckled. "The exercise will help us all shake off sleep."

I noted with contempt that he and the rest wore their usual uniforms. They'd regret all that heavy blue and gray fabric fast if we had to spend any time out in the sun. Unless they could use magic to keep themselves cool? Out of reflex, I looked around for Kiran to ask him; and then I remembered. I thumped my cup down on the table hard enough to make the tray rattle.

Marten and Lena both glanced my way, but neither said anything. Stevan opened his eyes and pocketed his charm. "The spell is complete."

Marten didn't waste any time heading for the door. I slid up close to him as Jenoviann released the wards. "You'd better have gotten authorization for that little show of good faith."

Marten said quietly, "A thousand kenets, yes. The money's yours, the moment you give me something of use."

Thank Khalmet for that. I'd get that money in my hands by tonight, and put in a bid straight off with Red Dal.

Two bridges and one hell of a lot of stairs later, we reached the steep stone causeways of Vaishala, spiraling up past courtyard walls glittering with elaborate mosaics of agate, amethyst, and quartz. The rising sun tipped the spires above us with gold, the air clear and already warm. Scattered groups of people moved along the causeway, most of them servants heading for the morning markets before the midday heat took hold.

A few watercarts creaked past, bearing fat storage barrels with merchant house crests emblazoned on the sides. A small horde of scowling, wary-eyed guards accompanied each cart, deadly charms glinting on their wrists and palms. Highsiders had house cisterns they refilled with water purchased from the main district cistern. Sechaveh's men guarded the district cisterns and took payment for water rations, but once beyond the cistern gate, protection from theft was up to the buyer. Highside, merchant houses rented out their private armies to guard water in transit. Down streetside, anyone who dared to leave a cistern with so much as a jug's worth of water rations had to pay a ganglord's protection fee. Either that, or fight off the ganglord's entire crew, and thirsty opportunists besides.

When we reached the residence described in Sechaveh's message, the courtyard's iron gate was blocked by a line of guardsmen wearing Sechaveh's scorpion crest. One stepped forward, a man whose shirt above his golden sash bore the flowing blue sigils of a wind mage. Marten showed him Sechaveh's message, and after a quick exchange, the wind mage let us through the cordon.

The courtyard beyond was plain by highside standards, holding only a set of hardy citrus trees in marble planters spaced around a central mosaic worked in tiles of onyx and silver. The door to the house was closed and barred. Another two guardsmen stood before it, accompanied by a second wind mage, this one a woman.

"Sechaveh told me to expect you," the wind mage said in a reedy voice. "But our orders are to bar entry to the house until his lead investigator arrives."

So. Ruslan was coming. Funny to think that was actually good news. Behind Marten, Lena's freckled face stiffened with resolve. Marten said genially to the wind mage, "We'll gladly await Ruslan Khaveirin's arrival to enter. But could you tell us a little of what to expect inside? Sechaveh's message said the victim was another mage...the owner of this house, perhaps?"

The wind mage shot him a narrow-eyed look. "Yes. A cloud mage named

Jadin Sovarias. I haven't been inside myself, and know nothing more." *So don't bother to ask*, her scowl said.

Marten gestured in rueful acceptance and ambled over to examine the orange tree next to me. I muttered, "Quit dallying, Marten. Pretend you forgot something and send Lena and me for it." My nerves buzzed with a mixture of excitement and worry. The thought of crossing wards as powerful as Ruslan's made my palms sweat, even knowing he wouldn't be lurking inside them.

"Not yet," Marten said softly. "When Ruslan arrives, I want to see who's with him. If he brings Mikail, that'll mean one less possibility for a guard on Kiran…ah. Ruslan's arrived—twin gods, the man's soulfire glares bright enough to blind even through the gate wards."

Marten straightened and strode to the courtyard's center, Lena and the others falling into formation behind him. I edged up behind them, just enough to one side that I could still see the gate. I wanted to stay as much out of Ruslan's notice as possible.

The outer gate swung open. Ruslan swept into the courtyard, resplendent in finely tailored clothes of bronze silk marked by jagged sigils. Trailing him, one on each side, were Mikail and Kiran.

Surprise hit me with the force of an avalanche. Kiran! I'd never thought Ruslan would be so arrogant as to parade him right in front of us. Ruslan must mean to force his obedience with the mark-bond, knowing it would upset and distract us. He could torment Kiran further in the bargain by making him face the man who'd betrayed him so thoroughly. I winced just thinking of the bitter rage Kiran would endure in seeing Marten.

Unlike Ruslan, Kiran and Mikail wore unrelieved black, their crimson sigils standing out in sharp relief on their shirts. I recognized the largest of the sigils; I'd seen it etched into the skin over Kiran's heart. He'd told me it was Ruslan's personal mark.

I dragged my gaze up from the sigils, dreading what I'd see in Kiran's face.

My surprise deepened into shock. He looked…relaxed. His blue eyes were clear, his head held high, and though his skin remained startlingly pale, his face showed no hint of strain. I'd never realized just how much stress and unhappiness had always been visible in his demeanor, all the way from the first time I'd met him. Until now, when for the first time I saw him without it.

My first thought was the mark-bond. But Kiran walked with easy confidence, not the dragging jerkiness or the slow, dreamy movements I'd seen from him when Ruslan used their link.

Stevan hissed at Marten, "See? He's been Ruslan's creature from the first.

He acted the lost waif only to spy on us."

Marten's black eyes narrowed, watching Kiran.

"That's not true." My whisper was equally harsh. Stevan was wrong. He had to be. I knew Kiran, damn it. Nobody could be that good an actor. Ruslan had to be controlling him somehow. Or maybe Ruslan had threatened him, forced him to put on a show? But he didn't look under duress, or even drugged.

"*Quiet.*" Marten stepped forward to meet Ruslan, his expression settling into its usual good-natured mask.

"Captain Martennan. Good to see you are prompt," Ruslan said. "You know of my apprentices, Mikail and Kiran ai Ruslanov." He laid his hands on Kiran and Mikail's shoulders. Kiran didn't flinch from the touch. He looked straight at Marten and showed nothing more than a faint wariness.

"Of course," Marten said, irony shading his voice. He bowed, carefully formal. The other Alathians didn't. Stevan and Jenoviann had assumed expressions of cold, stone-faced politeness, but Lena and Talm were staring at Kiran, identical sharp lines between their brows.

Ruslan smiled, and I had to look away, unable to bear the mocking satisfaction in it. He'd seen our dismay over Kiran and he was enjoying the hell out of our surprise and unease. I did my best to imitate Mikail's stolid calm. Fuck if I'd give Ruslan the pleasure of realizing just how thrown I was.

Kiran glanced at me—and blinked, his eyes twitching back to mine, then away.

Oh, mother of maidens! I knew that reaction. Most people did something similar when they first met me, thanks to my eyes seeming so out of place with my dark Arkennlander coloring. It was like they couldn't believe they'd seen the color of my eyes right, and had to check again.

If Kiran didn't recognize me…had Ruslan fucked with his memories? I got a flash of Kiran, white-faced from the pain of his broken arm on the Whitefires' western slopes, saying, *I don't remember anything before Ruslan. He always said it was because my life only truly started when I came to him.* But erasing the past of a kid too little to question it was one thing. Ruslan would've had to destroy Kiran's memories going as far back as Alisa's death last winter, maybe further. With that long of a gap, Kiran would realize his loss and be curious, even suspicious. Unless Ruslan had replaced his memories with false ones, somehow?

Maybe I was reading far too much into a brief instant's reaction. I couldn't afford to make a mistake in this. I refused to believe Stevan's accusation, but there might be another explanation than lost memory. I prayed there was another explanation. If Kiran truly thought me a stranger, I was in serious trouble. I'd counted on his help, both for himself and to pry that coin out of Marten. I had to talk to him, discover the truth.

Marten was too far away for me to speak without Ruslan hearing. I eased toward Lena, who stood closest.

"Captain, you are welcome to engage in whatever investigative methods you see fit, provided you do not interfere with mine." Ruslan spoke with the indulgent condescension of a den minder telling her youngest Taint thief he could help make dinner.

Marten awarded Ruslan one of his disarmingly bright smiles. I hoped Ruslan found all that casual cheerfulness as annoying as I always had.

"For our part, we ask only that you share your findings," Marten said.

"Of course," Ruslan said, in a tone that precisely matched Marten's earlier irony. He strode for the house, Mikail and Kiran right behind him. The guardsmen hastily unbarred the door and backed away, as did the wind mage. Their bodies were tense and their eyes firmly fixed on the ground. Not even Sechaveh's handpicked guards were immune to all the terrible stories about blood mages.

I gripped Lena's wrist and spoke low and fast. "Stevan's wrong. I've a theory, but I need proof. Tell Marten he's got to distract Ruslan somehow so I can talk to Kiran."

Lena's frown deepened, but she nodded. At the door, Ruslan swept a hand through the air. Silver scrawls of wards blazed bright and then dulled. Mikail said something to Kiran as they followed him inside, and Kiran's teeth flashed white in a smile.

I'd thought the task of freeing Kiran hard enough before. But how did you free someone who didn't even know he was in bondage?

CHAPTER TEN

(Dev)

The foyer of the dead mage's house fit right in with what I expected of a highsider. Jeweled tiles in the pattern of sigils decorated the polished, rose-streaked marble of the walls and floor. Brilliantly colored stained glass skylights were spaced along the graceful arch of the ceiling. Magelights sat perched on intricate Sulanian bone carvings. Despite the knots in my stomach, curiosity pricked at me. I'd never been inside a mage's house in Ninavel. No Taint thief handler with any kind of smarts would risk sending his kids into one. Wards were one thing; those could be shattered or fooled with the Taint, if a Tainter was clever enough. Active casting was something else, and everyone in Ninavel knew it.

A short, scrawny man wearing Sechaveh's scorpion crest waited for us at the end of the foyer. The blocky golden sigils of a sand mage marked his drab clothing. He had the brown skin of an Arkennlander, with a hooked nose and a kink to his dark hair that suggested he had some Sulanian blood. He looked older than usual for a Ninavel mage, appearing to be in his forties, and his skin had a jaundiced tinge in the unwavering glow of the magelights, as if he didn't go out in the sun much.

"Good, good, you're here," he said to Ruslan. He had an abrupt way of speaking, half-swallowing the end of each word as if anxious to get to the next one. Glancing at Marten, he bobbed his head. "You must be Captain Martennan."

Marten bowed, deep and formal. "Whom do I have the honor of addressing?"

"I'm Edon," the mage said. "Seranthine High Scholar."

So this was the man Ambassador Halassian had thought was in charge. Despite his awkward manner, his dark eyes were sharp as they skipped between us. Maybe he played the graceless scholar the way Marten acted the cheerful shopkeeper, to set people off their guard.

Ruslan made an irritated noise. "Enough pleasantries. Report, Seranthine, and quickly."

Like the guardsmen, Edon wouldn't meet Ruslan's gaze. "When the mage Jadin Sovarias failed to appear for his scheduled water duty, guardsmen were sent to investigate. They inquired here at the house and woke Jadin's servant, an untalented man by the name of Torain ap Vedak. Torain searched the house for his master and found him dead in his workroom. The manner of the death appears...ah, violent. Not at all like the earlier deaths, you understand, which seemed clearly due to mishandled confluence overspill during upheaval events. But this...well. This is different. You'll understand what I mean when you see the body."

"The servant. You've kept him here?" Ruslan's tone implied that Edon was in serious trouble if he hadn't.

"Yes. Of course. He's in the receiving room." Edon pointed through the archway. "He seems, er...quite distraught. Obtaining a coherent report from him has proved difficult."

"Perhaps I will have more success," Ruslan said, with a glimmer of dark amusement. Beside him, Mikail's stolid expression remained unchanged. Kiran, who had been watching Edon with wary curiosity, dropped his gaze. His shoulders gained a hint of tension.

His discomfort brought me a thread of hope. Whatever had happened to him, he knew Ruslan wasn't all sunshine and roses, and he didn't much like it.

Edon ducked his head to Ruslan and led us through the archway into a broad circular room chock full of statues and wrought-metal furniture. A heavyset man in a pale robe sat in one of the chairs, his head down and his hands twisting around each other in his lap.

"Torain," Edon said. The man didn't look up. Edon grimaced in annoyance and made a sharp gesture. Torain jumped, his head flying up.

He was terrified. His eyes were so wide the whites showed top and bottom, and his breathing was fast and ragged. At first I assumed it was Edon and Ruslan he feared. But his gaze skated right past Ruslan's sigils to dart about the room as if he expected some hidden enemy to leap out and attack him.

"He keeps babbling about Jadin's death being the work of demons, even under truth spell." Edon's expression turned clinical. "The only remotely useful information I've had from him is that he claims to have heard and seen nothing unusual prior to finding his master, and none of the wards on the workroom door were activated."

Demons. Not a total surprise; Torain's dark curls and coppery skin marked him as Varkevian in ancestry, and all the southern countries were big on demons. Varkevians in particular had a whole vast pantheon of them, all beautiful as the morning and vicious as rabid sandcats, if you believed the stories. Which I didn't. I half believed in Khalmet, Suliyya, and some of the other southern gods worshipped in Ninavel—but gods were one thing. I'd never bought the idea that demons lurked around amusing themselves by poisoning souls and savaging men. I'd seen plenty of men die, but never in ways that couldn't be accounted for by god-touched bad luck or simple human evil.

Like Ruslan's. He was studying Torain, arms akimbo. Torain still seemed oblivious to his regard. Probably it was a completely new experience for Ruslan to find himself considered the lesser of two evils. It was certainly beginning to make me more than a little uneasy about what we'd find in the dead mage's workroom. Some of the demon tales I'd heard around convoy campfires outdid the stories of blood mages.

"Show me the body. I'll question the *nathahlen* afterward," Ruslan said.

"Whatever you prefer," Edon said. "I'll remain here and, ah, finish my own interrogation. You'll find the body in the workroom. The wards remain inactive." He pointed at a metal door bracketed by heavy curtains on the room's far side. A filigree of copper ward lines covered the door, which in my mind had begun to take on a distinctly sinister aspect. Especially with Edon's clear reluctance to go back in himself.

Ruslan only looked thoughtful. He moved to the door and pulled it open. He paused, silhouetted against a cool glow of magelight; and then he continued inside.

A sharp, coppery stench of blood rolled out through the open door, chokingly strong. I gagged and hastily turned it into a muffled cough, fighting down the terrible memories the smell triggered. I refused to show weakness in front of a whole roomful of mages.

Kiran and Mikail glanced at each other, one quick unreadable look, and followed Ruslan into the workroom. Kiran's shoulders still held that slight tension, but he walked in with the same easy confidence he'd shown outside.

A sign that he didn't remember Alisa's death? Surely if he did, he wouldn't be able to waltz right into what smelled like an abbatoir.

The Alathians didn't look too happy. Marten's face had closed up into a careful blankness, Lena's freckles stood out stark against her skin, and Talm looked near as haggard as he had at the mine. Even Stevan's mouth thinned. But we all moved forward until we could see into the room beyond.

Yeah, there was a dead guy inside. Very dead. Jadin Sovarias lay face up, sprawled naked in a black pool of blood. Clotted gouts of gore streaked the table behind him and spattered the walls. Ragged slashes like giant clawmarks ran the length of his torso, exposing raw, glistening things I didn't want to look at too closely. His mouth was open in a silent scream, his lips flayed away so his teeth showed grotesquely white. And his eyes… his eyes were gone. Charred holes backed by the sickly gray of brain matter were all that remained.

My gorge heaved. I swallowed, hard, and yanked my gaze from the mutilated mess on the floor. No wonder Torain was out of his head with fear. The burned eyes, the slashes…the scene could've come straight from the tales of the Ghorshaba, the supposed nastiest demons of the bunch.

When the Ghorshaba decided to play, they never killed only one person. No, they always killed everyone in the household, drawing it out over a couple days to make it more fun. Torain hadn't blinked when faced with a blood mage because he believed he was a dead man regardless.

In the stories, we would be too, for entering before the demon was done. A cold trickle of fear curled down my spine. Damn it, I didn't believe in demons. Surely spells could produce injuries every bit as horrible in the hands of a mage like Ruslan. But if some mage really wanted to imitate the worst tales of demonkind, we'd made ourselves targets the moment we stepped in the door.

✳

(Kiran)

Kiran surveyed the blood-smeared workroom, fighting not to betray the rebellion of his stomach. He and Mikail had used both fresh and preserved blood in childhood spell exercises. More, he knew real magic involved death—and presumably, since he'd been through the *akhelashva* ritual and come of age, he'd cast spells that were more than exercises. Hadn't he? The gaping voids in his memories refused to answer. The sight of the horribly damaged body on the floor continued to nauseate him, his chest so tight he could barely breathe.

He pulled his gaze from the corpse and focused on the energies that swirled through the room. With his barriers up, it was like looking at a blurred charcoal sketch instead of a detailed color painting, but he could sense enough to make him frown in confusion. The thick, sullen power of violent death filled the room, ebbing slowly. Underneath, the deep pulse of the confluence permeated the house just as it did the rest of the city. But he sensed no residue of any other magic, defensive or otherwise, aside from the faint, fading traces common to a room where spells were regularly cast. If not for the corpse on the floor, he would have sworn no significant magic had been performed within the room for the past several days.

"His personal wards are untouched," said the Alathian with the wiry ginger hair and hard gray eyes. *Stevannes*; the name floated up to his consciousness from Ruslan's binding deep within, accompanied by a twinge of inhibition. *Cast no spells to harm him.*

Kiran forced himself to look at the body again. Powerful defensive charms glittered on the man's wrists, their silver clear and the gems sparkling and whole. If the mage had used them and been overpowered, the metal would be blackened and the gems shattered.

Ruslan flicked a contemptuous glance at the dark-haired leader of the Alathians. "None of the wards or charms in this room have been used."

Kiran knew that tone well. Ruslan had little patience with those he considered fools. Kiran hesitated, then nerved himself up to speak, his curiosity too great for him to remain silent.

"How is that possible?" He kept his voice low, but the Alathians all turned to look at him.

To his relief, Ruslan's answer was calm. "You feel no magical residue, and this confuses you, yes?"

Kiran nodded. He glanced at the Alathians. Ruslan made a slight encouraging gesture, and Kiran went on. "Why would his defensive wards not trigger, with an attacker casting such lethal magic against him? And why do we not feel traces of the attacker's spellwork? Wouldn't such a powerful spell leave residue?"

"Ordinarily, yes. But there are ways…" Ruslan turned a hand palm up. Feeling the Alathians' eyes on him, Kiran knew why Ruslan wouldn't elaborate. "While speculation might be interesting, it is unnecessary. We can find out easily enough what happened here." He waited expectantly, as if Kiran and Mikail were in a lesson.

"By casting a *zhaveynikh* spell," Mikail said.

"Exactly," Ruslan said, the word warm with approval.

Dismay seized Kiran. He didn't recognize the spell name, didn't know how Ruslan might discover the truth of the man's death—proof of all he'd lost.

Ruslan caught his gaze. Kiran twitched in surprise as Ruslan's mind touched his, deep at the core of his *ikilhia* where the mark-binding link lay. *Death gives power, Kiran. While that power remains, it can be manipulated to produce a scry-vision of the originating event. In design, the spell is similar to those you cast in childhood to create simulacrums.*

Simulacra spells, Kiran remembered. They required more delicacy than power, fine control of the spell essential to its success. Yet even so, to shape a scry-vision from the miasma of energies in the room, Ruslan must require the assistance of channels.

"You intend to cast a channeled spell," Captain Martennan said, echoing Kiran's thoughts. His voice was flat, his round-cheeked face gone hard.

Mocking amusement gleamed in Ruslan's eyes. "Have no fear for your delicate sensibilities, Captain. This death is yet recent enough to taste. I have all the power I need, right here." He flicked a hand at the savaged corpse.

They are afraid of real power, Ruslan had said. If Martennan was afraid, he hid it well. His black eyes showed only distaste. Ruslan had warned Kiran to be wary of Martennan in particular, and now Kiran had seen the man, he understood why. Despite Martennan's polite speech and apparently sunny disposition, something about him made Kiran profoundly uncomfortable.

Equally discomforting was the way the *nathahlen* with the startlingly green eyes kept staring at him. No name had come to Kiran from Ruslan's binding, though he felt the same warning inhibition against casting as he did for the Alathian mages. Ruslan had mentioned in passing that the Alathians had hired a local man as a guide and informant. Still, Kiran was surprised Ruslan's binding included a mere servant. Strange, too, that the Alathians hadn't hired someone older, with more experience. The green-eyed guide looked only a few years Kiran's elder, and his callused hands and rough clothing seemed more suited to menial labor than Ninavel's embassies. Kiran thought it odder yet that the Alathians had brought a *nathahlen* with them into the dead mage's workroom. Still, what did he know of Alathian customs?

"We don't have enough silver, or even copper, to lay proper channels." Mikail eyed the workroom shelves with a dubious expression. Kiran shared his mage-brother's concern. Lesser mages like the dead man lacked the talent to channel power properly with blood and precious metals. The workroom shelves contained only stone chips, crystals, and glass cases of vividly colored liquids. A few bloodspattered bars of silver lay on the table behind the corpse, enough to make charms with, but nowhere near enough to lay channels.

"For a spell of this nature, blood alone will suffice as the conduit if care is taken in the casting." Ruslan skirted the body to scan the workroom floor. He nodded in satisfaction. "We have enough space here to set the pattern."

The Alathians were whispering to each other. Watching them, Ruslan's expression darkened. His head lowered as if he weighed some decision. Silent words echoed once more in Kiran's mind. *Mikail will channel. Kiran, I want you well outside the pattern. You are still healing, and I do not wish to risk disrupting that process. Wait outside the workroom's wards and keep your barriers firm.*

Kiran couldn't hide his disappointment. True, his senses remained raw, and proximity to channeled magic was certain to bring pain. Yet he badly wanted to see Ruslan cast. The theory of the spell might have been torn from him by his accident, but he could deduce much of it simply from observation.

A faint smile lifted Ruslan's mouth. *You may watch,* akhelysh. *I would never deprive you of a learning opportunity. Leave the workroom door open and you should have a fine view.*

Gratitude leaped in Kiran's heart. Ruslan's smile grew. He stepped close and slid out a set of silver bracelets from a pocket. The sigils incised in the silver proclaimed them simple damping wards; wearing them would further muffle Kiran's senses. Ruslan handed the bracelets to Kiran, and said, "Go, then," his voice soft. He turned away, his expression settling into mocking condescension.

"I suggest you and your people remain and observe, Captain," he said to Martennan. "Do not touch the pattern, and look to your defenses. Your safety is your own concern."

Martennan inclined his head, brightly cheerful once more. "I believe we can handle ourselves."

Ruslan began pacing out a pattern, his face intent with concentration. Kiran started toward the door, only to stop short as Mikail caught his arm.

"Watch yourself, little brother." Mikail cut his eyes in the direction of the Alathians, who had ranged themselves in a line against the wall. Even as Kiran looked, Martennan glanced their way, his black eyes assessing.

"I will." Kiran's unease returned. He pushed it away. With blood as the medium, preparing and casting the spell shouldn't take long. He could handle the Alathians if any of them chose to leave the room. He'd be happy to prove that Ruslan's faith in him was justified.

✳

(Dev)

I sent a swift prayer of thanks to Khalmet as Kiran walked out of the workroom. I had no clue why Ruslan had sent him outside, but the reason didn't matter. I sure as hell meant to seize the opportunity. I caught Marten's eye.

He didn't miss a beat. "The energies during this casting will be dangerous, Dev. We'll cast our own protection, but as you are untalented, I think it safest if you wait outside the workroom's wards."

"Sounds good to me." I headed along the wall for the door. Marten and the others took up a chant that swelled and ebbed in a sighing rhythm like wind through pines, their eyes shut and their rings glowing.

Mikail blocked my path. The murdered mage's blood darkened his hands; to my disgust, he and Ruslan had started using it to paint spiraling patterns about the man's body. I stopped myself from looking back for help from the Alathians. Mikail couldn't touch me, bound by Ruslan's vow. Or so I prayed. Besides, Mikail might be as good a source of information as Kiran. He'd been talkative enough the previous time we'd met—hell, he'd been the one to give me the Taint charm that'd let us escape Ruslan.

"What has Ruslan done to Kiran?" I kept my voice low, hoping the Alathians' chanting would mask it. The last thing I wanted was to attract Ruslan's attention. He was kneeling beside the body, his back to us. One hand was sunk deep within the dead man's gutted stomach.

Mikail gave me a small, ironic smile. "Far less than could have been his fate, if Ruslan's love for him did not temper his anger." His words were as quiet as mine, as if he were equally eager to avoid Ruslan's notice.

So Ruslan had done something to Kiran, then. Good to get confirmation Stevan was wrong.

"If you think Ruslan loves Kiran, you've no fucking idea what love is." That wouldn't surprise me, given what I'd heard from Kiran of their childhood. "But you…I know you care about Kiran. Otherwise you'd have let him die fighting Ruslan in Simon's meadow. Are you going to help him now, when he needs it most?"

Mikail's gray eyes grew hooded. "Help? Kiran needs none. He's home where he belongs. If you call yourself Kiran's friend, you'll accept that and leave him alone."

Fuck that. If Mikail was too much of a coward to help on his own, I'd happily give him some incentive. "Tell me exactly what Ruslan did to Kiran, or I'll tell him who gave me that Taint charm."

Mikail huffed out a nearly silent laugh. "Oh, he knows it was me."

I felt as if a seemingly solid ledge had broken off beneath my feet. "He does?"

"You know nothing if you believe I could have hidden it from him." Mikail's hand rose to touch his heart, in an unconscious gesture I recognized all too well.

"Khalmet's bony hand," I muttered. My eyes went to Ruslan, whose hands were black with blood. I couldn't even imagine how pissed off he must've been at that little revelation.

Mikail's expression turned ironic again. "Ruslan was angry, but not for the reason you imagine. When he questioned me, he saw in my mind my intentions and understood. His anger was for my miscalculation."

I frowned, thinking back to how I'd knocked Ruslan unconscious with the Taint in Simon's meadow, and my desperate run to the border with Kiran afterward. My stomach hurt at the memory, for more reasons than one. I'd been so exultant to have the Taint back, even as the charm tore my innards apart...oh, shit. Of course.

"You sadistic little fuck! You knew exactly what that charm would do. You never intended for us to reach the border."

Mikail shrugged. "I knew if I could prevent Kiran from killing himself in the fight, then given enough time his mark-binding link would restabilize. With the link in place, Ruslan could bring him home safely." He inclined his head to me. "I thought the charm would kill you faster. I underestimated your strength."

He sounded wistful about it. I bared my teeth at him in a smile. "I hope Ruslan expressed his anger properly."

Mikail's eyes slid away from mine. "Yes." A fine shudder, barely noticeable, ran over him. "I won't underestimate you again."

A threat if I'd ever heard one. A shiver prickled along my nerves. The Alathians were still chanting, but Ruslan had pulled his hand from the body and looked about to stand. His back remained to us, but he might turn any moment. I wanted the conversation over before then.

"I'll keep that in mind." I fixed Mikail with what I hoped was a look of cold dismissal. "Now get out of my way."

I thought he wouldn't move, and I'd have to call on Marten for help after all. But he stepped aside, with a mocking little flip of his hand. "Have a care for your safety when we perform the spell. Magic can be so dangerous to the untalented."

He couldn't cast against me. I repeated that all the way out of the room, but it didn't stop my skin from crawling at the feel of his eyes on my back.

※

(Kiran)

Kiran watched through the open door as Ruslan cut a sigil into the skin of the corpse's forehead. Mikail wasn't in view. He must be finishing the outermost channel lines, meant to safely contain the spell's power. The Alathians were also out of Kiran's sightline, though he could hear soft chanting and sense a thin veil of protective magic building within the room's wards.

Dark lines of blood laced the stone around the dead man like a great black web. Kiran had been afraid he wouldn't be able to read the channel pattern, too much of his knowledge lost. But no; he could visualize the spell structure, a construct fascinating in its elegance. He couldn't immediately follow all its intricacies, but he could see well enough how the spell would take the death energies and trace them back through time, like reversing the ripples from a stone thrown into a cistern.

He was glad to analyze the spell's design. Thinking of it, he could look at the corpse as an abstract component of that structure rather than a hideously mangled remnant of a living, breathing man.

The Alathians' guide walked out of the workroom. His arms were crossed, a sharp line between his dark brows.

Kiran straightened, nervous. Yet none of the Alathian mages followed, and their song continued apace. They must intend to watch Ruslan cast from within the wards, and had only sent this man out because he was *nathahlen* and lacking in innate protection.

The guide leaned a shoulder against the doorframe. "What exactly is this spell supposed to do?"

Kiran blinked in surprise. As a child, he'd grown resigned to the way most *nathahlen* in Ninavel were too afraid to speak to a blood mage, even an apprentice one. Ruslan's servants refused to meet his eyes and spent as little time in his and Mikail's company as they could. He'd never liked it, but Mikail always said it was for the best. Ruslan had warned them countless times that associating with the untalented was a mistake.

The guide met Kiran's gaze without a shred of fear, his expression expectant. Kiran hesitated. The man was *nathahlen*, yes. Yet Ruslan had said they would need to share information relating to the investigation with the Alathians, and the question was relevant.

"It'll show us the victim's death," Kiran said. "Like a scry-vision, except of the past. The vision will appear in the center of the pattern." He pointed at the air over the body.

The guide's brows lifted. "You mean you can use this spell to see anything that's ever happened?" He sounded quite eager over the idea. Probably he imagined it could provide some form of monetary gain. Ruslan had told Kiran that *nathahlen* lusted after coin, in pale substitute for the magic they could never have.

"No, not at all." Kiran couldn't stop a wistful sigh. If spells could so easily reveal the past, he wouldn't need to worry over his missing memories. "Events that create power leave traces. The more the power, the stronger the trace. It fades with time, but in this case the death was so violent and recent that a spell can use the trace to recreate the original event."

"Huh." The guide looked disappointed. His green eyes stayed on Kiran's face. "My name's Dev, by the way. In case you didn't know."

Kiran looked away, feeling oddly guilty for not having known the name. "Oh," he said. And after another moment, "I'm Kiran."

"I know." The dryness of Dev's tone made Kiran flush. Of course Dev knew his name. Ruslan had introduced both him and Mikail to the Alathians in the courtyard.

"Nice to meet you, Kiran." Dev wore a wry little half-grin. "So how come you're not in there, working magic with the others?"

He asked the question casually enough, but Kiran tensed, suspicion rising. Did the Alathians suspect his handicap? They might have ordered Dev to speak with him in hopes of learning the extent of his weakness.

"Only two mages are needed to cast a channeled spell," he said shortly.

Dev cocked his head, studying Kiran. "Yeah, but how come you're standing out here? Wouldn't you get a better view from inside?"

Kiran had never been good at lies. Instead of attempting one, he shrugged dismissively.

"Hey, if you want to stand out here, I don't care," Dev said, with a shrug of his own. He grinned at Kiran, his eyes lighting. "More fun with company, anyway. Otherwise I'd have no clue what was going on. I don't know shit about spellwork."

Dev's grin was infectious. Kiran's suspicion ebbed, despite himself. Dev wasn't an Alathian, or even a mage. Kiran got none of that deep sense of unease that the leader of the Alathians inspired; on the contrary, he felt oddly comfortable in the guide's presence. Dev's coarse language and clothing suggested he didn't ordinarily spend time in the upper city. If he knew so little of magic, that might explain his unusual friendliness—perhaps he simply didn't know to fear blood mages as *nathahlen* in the wealthier districts did. The Alathians might have deliberately sought out such a guide, thinking his ignorance would keep fear from clouding his loyalty to them.

Inside the workroom, Ruslan and Mikail paced around the pattern, surveying it with focused concentration. Ruslan flicked a hand at the workroom walls, and wards sparked to life. Magic shrouded the room in a protective cocoon.

"They're about to cast," Kiran said to Dev.

"Finally." Dev glanced through the doorway. "Are they going to, uh... clean their hands?"

Ruslan and Mikail's hands remained black and crusted with the blood they'd used to create the pattern. "No," Kiran said. As Dev grimaced in disgust, he tried to explain. "The blood gives them a physical connection to the pattern. It makes the spell easier."

Dev slanted him a glance, but didn't speak. Kiran ran a finger over the warding bracelets on his wrists, sending a thin thread of power from his own *ikilhia* into them to spark their spells. The world dimmed as if a veil had been drawn over his eyes, his inner senses fading.

Mikail and Ruslan stopped on the opposite side of the workroom. Lacking an anchor stone, Ruslan knelt and placed his bloody hands on the outermost pattern line. Mikail backed a few paces. He shut his eyes and extended his hands.

Even through mental barriers, workroom wards, and damping bracelets, the surge of power hit Kiran with a force that left him dizzy.

The lines of blood blazed into crimson life. Unlike the smooth glow of properly conductive channels, they flickered with ghostly flames, energy bleeding off into open air. Kiran held his breath, watching Mikail's intent face. His mage-brother would have a difficult task to control the magic with makeshift channels like these.

Ruslan held perfectly still, his gaze focused on infinity. Translucent flames leaped higher, power cresting. Over the corpse, air shimmered and blurred into a pale wash of shifting colors. The colors spread to the inner boundary of the pattern, obscuring Kiran's view of Ruslan and Mikail. Slowly, they cohered into an image of the workroom.

The dead mage, now hale and unbloodied, stood beside the table, bent over an open book. He had the abstract look of a man deeply involved in research. He flipped to a different section, frowning. Abruptly he straightened and turned, a mixture of irritation and surprise on his face. He stepped forward, his mouth moving in silent question.

A dark blotch, man-high, appeared at the edge of the spell's boundary. To Kiran's surprise, the spot stayed blurred and dim, the edges wavering and flickering in a way that obscured all detail. The dark blur advanced. The mage catapulted backward, his back slamming against the table's edge.

The mage's mouth gaped in a scream. Blood sprayed as the great slashes appeared on his torso. Kiran forced himself to keep watching, to think analytically—what was causing the wounds? No blade touched the man, no glimmer of magic. The dark blur stood stationary a few feet from the mage's contorting body. A blinding flash made Kiran squint and blink, shielding his eyes with a hand. When the flash subsided, the mage lay naked and dead, his eyes burned out. The dark blur remained.

The power pouring through the spell rose further. Colors within the image grew sharp, the light glaring in intensity. Energies writhed as Ruslan sought to force the dark figure into focus. Pain sparked along Kiran's nerves. He winced and backed a step.

"You okay?" Dev's voice was a distant mutter beneath the assault on Kiran's senses.

Kiran nodded, not taking his eyes from the image. Colors bled and ran, flames arcing between the lines of blood beneath them. Ruslan was dangerously close to the limit of power the makeshift channels could contain. The dark spot remained a shadowed blur as it moved backward to disappear beyond the spell's limit.

The air wavered, colors fraying, and the vision disappeared. Ruslan's kneeling figure was once more visible on the pattern's far side, his hands still planted on the floor. Ghostly flames guttered and subsided as Ruslan guided power safely back into stone.

Ruslan's head bent. The channel lines crackled and vanished, leaving only faint dark stains behind. Blood crisped into ash on Mikail's and Ruslan's hands.

Mikail lowered his hands. Sweat streaked his face and darkened his sandy hair. Ruslan stood, his face impassive. He brushed ash off his fingers, the motions sharp.

"How very interesting." Martennan strolled into Kiran's field of view. "It would seem our mystery assassin is powerful indeed if he can block even the best effort of a blood mage."

Kiran drew in a sharp breath. Ruslan would be in no good mood after the spell's failure to reveal either the attacker's identity or methods. The Alathian was a fool to bait him. He braced himself for a display of his master's quick temper.

Ruslan ignored Martennan completely. He stood staring at the corpse, his eyes narrowed in thought.

"So…all that, and for nothing?" Dev watched Ruslan with a distinctly sardonic expression.

"Not entirely," Kiran said slowly. He released his bracelets' wards, his senses growing sharp again. "The spell confirmed that the killer's magic is linked in some way to the confluence disturbances."

Dev frowned. "It did? How?"

"The length of time for the energies to coalesce in the spell—it tells us the exact moment of death. That man died at the same time as a major upheaval in the confluence last night." Kiran rubbed his hands over his wrists. A sudden sense-memory of magic crashing against his barriers as he sat startled in his bed washed over him. Disturbing, to realize at that very instant this man had died in agony.

"But then, what—" Dev stopped short as Ruslan broke from his stance and strode for the door. Kiran hurriedly backed from Dev, guilt flashing through him. Had he been too open with the *nathahlen*? Perhaps he should have refused to speak at all.

Ruslan swept past without a single glance, Mikail in his wake. Kiran hurried after them, across the circular receiving room and into a study lined with bookshelves. Inside, Edon stood watching the servant Torain, who sat in a chair clutching a charm in a white-knuckled grip and mumbling to himself.

"Move," Ruslan snapped. Edon nearly fell over a chair in his haste to obey.

"What are you doing?" Martennan spoke from the doorway. Behind him, Kiran caught a glimpse of Dev, his eyes green slits and his mouth tight.

"Questioning him," Ruslan said, and smiled, sharp as a blade. He laid a hand on the servant's forehead.

Torain spasmed in the chair. A hoarse, ragged howl of pain erupted from him. The scream spiraled upward, agony building in it until Kiran desperately wanted to block his ears. *Stop,* he wanted to beg Ruslan; but he knew from experience such pleas would only anger Ruslan further. *Mikail, screaming and convulsing, while Kiran shook with silent sobs, his tongue and body bound by magic sharp as thorns…*His damaged memory yet retained plenty of childhood punishments.

Torain's shrieks died away into a rattling gasp. Kiran risked a glance up and saw Torain slump forward, his skin gray and blood drooling from mouth and nose. Kiran hastily looked away, hoping his dismay didn't show.

"As I suspected, useless," Ruslan said. "He knows nothing of value." He met Martennan's eyes, still smiling. "However, I like to be thorough."

Martennan's face could have been carved from stone. "Will he survive?"

Anger lanced through Kiran. If Torain died, it was Martennan's fault. Ruslan wouldn't have been so vicious if Martennan hadn't provoked him in the workroom.

Ruslan shrugged. "Doubtful. If he does, you're welcome to question him yourself."

Edon cleared his throat. "If I may suggest…if he does live, Sechaveh's guardsmen should take him into custody. It would be, er, inadvisable for him to spread hysterical tales of demons among the lower districts of the city. The laborers can be so superstitious."

"I suspect our assassin hoped to induce exactly that hysteria," Ruslan said. "Whether he lives or dies, take the servant into custody. Inform the guardsmen that if any of them spread tales, they will answer to me." He glanced at Martennan. "Stay if you wish; Edon will supervise. I see nothing more to be gained here without further research. Our meeting with Lord Sechaveh has been moved to tomorrow morning. Use the time until then in whatever way you see fit."

With that, he stalked out, brushing past Martennan and Dev as if they didn't exist.

As Kiran followed, Dev watched him pass. The guide's eyes were hard, his expression dark. He wouldn't be so friendly with Kiran any longer, not after he'd seen what an *akheli* like Ruslan could do. Regret welled up in Kiran. He struggled to stifle it. Why should the opinion of a *nathahlen* matter? Next time, Kiran would heed Ruslan's warnings and keep his distance.

CHAPTER ELEVEN

(Dev)

The moment Ruslan left, Marten knelt by Torain's slumped form. He gripped the man's slack wrist and called for Jenoviann in a voice as brittle as frost-coated glass.

I dodged aside as Jenoviann rushed past. She stooped over Torain, her bony frame all sharp angles, and laid a hand on his bowed neck. I held my breath, remembering Halassian's mention of Jenoviann's years at the Sanitorium. I was proof of the Alathians' skill with healing. Maybe Jenoviann could work a similar miracle with Torain.

My stomach sank when she shook her head. "Captain, the damage—I've never seen the like. Even if I can keep him breathing, I doubt I can repair his mind."

"Try," Marten ordered her. Jenoviann splayed her hands over Torain's temples, her rings glowing silver. She began singing a soft, repetitive chant, her voice thin but surprisingly sweet.

Edon gave Marten a quizzical look. "You wish him to recover so you may question him? I searched his memories myself prior to Ruslan's interrogation, and I made note of every visitor Torain admitted to the house in the last few months. Beyond that, I assure you that Ruslan was right: the man knew nothing of interest. Jadin Sovarias was not such a fool as to share his affairs with a mere servant."

Marten rounded on Edon with a fire in his eyes that near matched Ruslan's. "Be that as it may, I trust you will not interfere with Lieutenant Jenoviann's efforts. Lord Sechaveh gave me the freedom to investigate as I see fit."

Almost, I cheered for Marten. Torain's screams still echoed in my ears. He must've figured out pretty fucking quick he should've been more scared of the live blood mage in the room than some lurking demon. Yet foolish as he might've been, I prayed Jenoviann could save him.

Edon shrugged. "So long as the guards take him—or his body—into custody when we leave the house, do what you like with the man."

Marten bowed, rigidly precise. "You say you made note of Jadin's visitors. Perhaps you would share their names with my first lieutenant, along with any other knowledge you have of Jadin's enemies and associates? I doubt the killer chose his victim at random." He beckoned Lena inside the study.

"Of course," Edon said. "While you, ah…?"

"The rest of my team and I will continue examining the workroom," Marten said. "Our methods may yet succeed where Ruslan's failed to uncover the killer's identity."

Edon bobbed his head and gave Lena a twitch of a smile. Yet as Marten left the room, Edon's dark eyes followed him with a cool, measuring curiosity that made me all the more certain he wasn't the incompetent he seemed.

Marten gestured for me to follow him, along with Talm and Stevan. Reluctantly, I trailed after them back into the gore-streaked workroom. The stench was less after Ruslan had used up so much blood in his spell, but the mangled corpse still made my stomach heave. I wished we could talk in the clean air of the courtyard, but Marten clearly meant to capitalize on Edon's apparent squeamishness to hold a private conversation.

Once inside, Marten shut the door and faced me. "You spoke to Kiran. What did you learn?"

"Ruslan's messed with his memories somehow. Kiran doesn't remember us. Not me, not you…my guess is he doesn't remember a damn thing from these last months."

Marten closed his eyes briefly, the lines in his face deepening. "Only these last months? Or do you believe the gap extends longer?" The urgency of his tone surprised me. Made sense Marten would be upset over losing Kiran as a willing source of information, but I didn't see why he'd care about the length of time Kiran had lost. I sure didn't believe it was out of concern for Kiran.

"No way to know, not without talking to him further. Why?"

Marten only shook his head, his expression grim. "You must find out how much he's missing."

"Get me another chance to talk to him, and I will." I already itched to speak with Kiran again. He'd talked to me readily enough of magic. If I could just think of the right questions to ask without raising suspicion, I might learn what I so desperately needed to know: the truth of his bond with Ruslan. If Ruslan broke his vow and burned to ash, would Kiran burn too?

"Don't leap to conclusions, Marten," Stevan said sharply. "Kiran seemed perfectly capable, not at all lost or confused. To destroy memories so selectively would require incredible finesse on Ruslan's part. It's far more likely his flight from Ruslan was entirely a sham. He pretended to reject blood magic to insinuate himself into Alathia and learn what he could of our defenses. Now he merely pretends a loss of memory to cover the truth of his deception."

"Oh, for Khalmet's sake!" I'd had enough of ignoring the boulder-sized chip on Stevan's shoulder. "If Kiran's the demon you think him, why should he pretend now, rather than gloat over how he fooled us all? *I* think it more likely that you're a prejudiced idiot too blind to see the truth when it's plain as day."

Stevan's face darkened. He drew breath to speak, but Marten put out a staying hand and said to me, "I'd like to hear what evidence you have of his memory loss."

I recounted my conversation with Mikail, who'd as much as admitted Ruslan had altered Kiran's mind. Then related how after his first wariness, Kiran had been friendly enough, but treated me as a stranger. Stevan listened with a sour, skeptical expression that made me want to kick him where it hurt, but Marten and Talm both listened with grave attention. When I told them of Kiran's clear reluctance to explain why he'd been sent from the room, and the warding bracelets on his wrists, Marten nodded, looking thoughtful.

He said to Stevan, "Ruslan could not have removed memories without damage, leaving Kiran dangerously sensitive to magical energies. Besides, I think it far more plausible that Ruslan used the mark-bond to alter Kiran's memories, than to believe one young apprentice could deceive all of us who searched his mind at his trial."

Stevan crossed his arms. "Perhaps. Or perhaps you saw in his mind what you wanted to see. You know the cost of willful blindness, Marten. You saw with Reshannis that corruption of the soul cannot be reversed, no matter how badly you want to believe otherwise."

"Twin gods, Stevan," Talm interrupted, with exasperation that held a lurking edge. "After seven years, don't you think it's time you stopped taking your guilt out on Marten? He wasn't the one who—"

"Talm. I prefer that we focus on more relevant matters." Marten wore the air of cold, implacable authority that had cowed Talm so effectively in Sechaveh's audience chamber. It worked just as well now. Talm promptly shut up, looking abashed.

Stevan had gone pale, his breathing rapid. Anger glittered in his eyes, but he, too, held his tongue. A shame. Any topic that riled Stevan so deeply and made Marten so eager to change the subject was one I wanted to know more about. I needed every weapon I could get.

Marten turned back to me. "When you spoke to Kiran, you didn't try to hint at the truth?"

"Didn't you see how wary he was, particularly of you?" I'd seen the nervous looks Kiran had given the Alathians, and his obvious relief when I exited the workroom alone. "Ruslan's told him some kind of lie. He won't believe an accusation, not without proof." His skittishness had made me decide not to try showing him the spell diagram I'd found in his pack. Not yet, anyway. "He said one thing I think you'll find interesting…"

Sure enough, even Stevan leaned forward with sudden, focused attention as I explained how Kiran had said the time of death lined up exactly with a confluence disturbance.

"Interesting, indeed." Marten rubbed his chin. "That makes me wonder if the confluence disturbances are deliberate on the part of the killer, or merely a side effect of his or her method of spellcasting. Regardless, knowing the precise time of death will certainly aid in any spellwork we cast to trace the murderer."

That ought to earn me my thousand kenets. For good measure, I said, "There's something else you should know, if you don't already. The way this guy died, the burned eyes and the clawmarks…it's just like the tales of the Ghorshaba. That's what had Torain so upset."

"Ghorshaba…" Martennan's head tilted. "I've heard the name—demons out of southern myths, aren't they? I'm not entirely familiar with the legend."

Yeah, I'd learned in the mines that most Alathians didn't believe in either demons or the myriad southern gods worshipped in Ninavel. They held to some old religion from across the eastern sea that claimed only two gods existed: twins, neither male nor female, their true names unknowable by mere mortals, their purpose to hold the world in balance. A balance the Alathians believed the twins maintained only on a grand scale, through plagues, droughts, floods, and the like. No favors granted, no prayers for leniency answered, all joyless, impersonal austerity…much like the Alathian Council.

I told Marten, "The Varkevians say Shaikar created the Ghorshaba to guard his innermost hell, but a few got loose when Noshet broke in to rescue his guardians. They wander the world, and every now and then decide to descend on some poor bastard and recreate a little of their old fun. The stories differ on what draws their attention, but the result is…well, this." I glanced at the corpse, then quickly away again, my stomach churning.

"They're thorough bastards, too. Insist on killing everyone who enters the house before the blood of their first victim is cleansed."

"You actually believe this is the work of some demon from a story?" Stevan couldn't have sounded more condescending if he'd tried. I indulged a brief fantasy of shoving him off the Aiyalen Spire.

"No." Though damn, I had to wonder, after all this talk of intangible magic and the way Ruslan's spell couldn't show the killer. "Someone's sure trying to make it look like a demon's work, though. That means everyone who's entered this house today could be a target. Maybe you mages aren't worried, but by Khalmet, either give me some serious warding charms, or enough additional coin to get my own." I made sure to emphasize the *additional* part. Warding charms hadn't done the dead man any good, but coin or charms, either would serve as currency streetside, and I meant to squeeze as much of that from Marten as I could.

Marten said smoothly, "We'll be happy to ensure you have protection, Dev. As for the imitation of demons...I think Ruslan is likely right. Our killer wants to incite fear in the city populace."

Stevan was frowning. "These demon tales...do the demons drink blood?" He aimed the question somewhere above my head, like he couldn't bring himself to look a streetside smuggler in the eye. Fine with me, since I didn't much care to lock gazes with condescending, narrow-minded assholes.

"No," I said. "Some stories say they eat their victims' hearts, but no story I've heard says they do anything special with blood other than make a mess. Why?"

Stevan said to Marten, "Before you called Jenoviann in to heal the servant, she told me she didn't think there was enough blood spilled given the man's severe injuries."

Not enough blood? Jenoviann had to be joking. Even after Ruslan's casting, half the room was black with it. Talm grimaced like he was thinking the same thing, while Marten peered at Stevan like he wasn't sure he'd heard him right.

"I know," Stevan said, with a rueful glance at Marten that was the most human expression I'd yet seen from him. "I find it hard to imagine, myself, but Jenoviann said it's suprising how much blood a human body contains. Given that Ruslan's spell showed the slashes on Jadin's body happened while he yet lived, Jenoviann thinks he should have bled in far greater quantity before his heart stopped beating. I find myself wondering if the attacker stored some portion of the blood and took it with him."

As if the mutilated corpse wasn't disturbing enough. I asked, "What, you mean the killer might want to use it later in a spell, like a blood mage would?"

Stevan looked down his nose at me. "Perhaps." He turned to Marten.

"One thing is certain. If Jenoviann is right, Ruslan would have realized this as well."

I didn't doubt Ruslan knew to the last drop how much blood a victim contained. He might've kept silence about the missing blood merely to gain advantage. Or maybe he had a darker reason.

Talm said slowly, "I know Halassian believes the attacks aren't Ruslan's doing. What if she's wrong?"

Marten's gaze rested on the corpse. "When we first entered, we felt no taint of blood magic."

"We didn't get the chance to search properly with a linked harmonic spell, not before Ruslan cast his own spellwork—which conveniently didn't show the killer," Talm said. "Now the whole room reeks of blood magic. We'll never untangle the traces, and Ruslan's mindburned the only possible witness. It strikes me as more than a little suspicious. I say either Ruslan murdered this man, or he's allied with the mage who did."

Yeah, Ruslan was as sly as they came, and while he might be friendly with Sechaveh, I didn't think he cared a whit for anyone's interests but his own. I could imagine him arranging the attacks in hopes they'd bring the Alathians running, and he'd get his hands on Kiran. Only one part of that didn't quite fit.

"If Ruslan's behind the attacks, why would he bother to continue them now?" I asked. "He's already got what he wanted. Thanks to you." I aimed the last straight at Marten, but if the bolt struck, he didn't show it.

"Maybe Kiran isn't all Ruslan wants," Talm said. "Maybe he intends to bring Sechaveh down, in hopes he can gain release from the vow he made not to take revenge on us."

Now there was an unsettling thought. Though if Talm was right, and we proved it to Sechaveh—maybe he could turn the confluence on Ruslan, without the need to trick Ruslan into vow-breaking. Hell, even if Talm's theory wasn't true, if Sechaveh thought it was—my mind whirled with new possibilities.

Marten said, "I'd swear Ruslan was as startled as any of us that his spell failed to show the killer. Yet if the killer were another blood mage, it might explain his or her ability to block Ruslan's spellwork. Talm, the embassy keeps track of the powerful mages in the city, correct? Do you recall the number of blood mages residing in Ninavel from your time stationed here?"

Talm raked his hands through his curls. "It's been five years since I was here last, so you'll want to check with the Ambassador. But let's see…besides Ruslan's little group, there was Simon Levanian. But we all know what happened to him, and his apprentices were killed back when he first defied

Sechaveh. He and Ruslan were always the flashy ones, and you know how blood mages are, they don't share territory very easily. I know of only a few others…a female pair who only shows up every few decades, a solo woman who's said to be positively ancient and live off somewhere in the Bolthole Mountains, and another man whose partner mage died some years back when a spell they cast went spectacularly wrong; he hasn't cast channeled magic since. None of them have even close to Ruslan's reputation."

Thank Khalmet for that. One Ruslan was more than enough in my book.

Marten glanced at me. "Have you any knowledge to add?"

After a moment's thought, I reluctantly admitted, "Not this time. People tell plenty of blood mage stories down streetside, but the stories never give names, and descriptions are no good—from the tales, you'd think every blood mage was a deformed monster. It's like demon stories. You tell 'em for a good scare, and embellishment is half the fun." Every streetsider knew blood mages were real, unlike demons. But it was pretty damn rare for mages so powerful to come streetside, and most of us hoped never to cross paths with one.

"I'll set you the task of researching these other blood mages," Marten said to Talm, who nodded.

"What of Ruslan's partner mage?" Stevan asked. "Lizaveta, I believe the name is?"

Talm shrugged. "We know she came to Ninavel with Ruslan, and she's never taken any apprentices of her own. She spends time on water duty as all resident mages do, but I've never heard of her casting powerful spells aside from that."

Marten said, "I saw her in Kiran's memories at his trial. It seems she and Ruslan were apprentices together under Ruslan's master, the way Kiran and Mikail are Ruslan's now. She apparently took a considerable interest in Kiran and Mikail, though Ruslan handled all their training." He looked at me again. "Has Kiran ever spoken of her to you?"

"Not really." Most of this talk of Lizaveta was news to me. The only time I remembered Kiran mentioning her was in the terrible conversation with Ruslan I'd overheard in Simon's cave. *I thought she cared,* he'd said to Ruslan, bitter anguish in each word. *I should have known she'd be just as soulless as you.*

Stevan said, "It's obvious Ruslan chose his apprentices for more than their magical potential. Perhaps he learned to prioritize sexual appeal from his own master. In which case, this Lizaveta may be a blood mage, but her talents may lie more in the bedroom than the workroom."

And here I'd thought Stevan had nothing but icy brine in his veins. Had he talked this way around Kiran, who flinched and blushed at even friendly teasing over his looks? No wonder Kiran had disliked him so much. I suspected Stevan wasn't wrong about Ruslan, though. Which put Kiran's discomfort in a whole new disturbing light.

"I doubt any master who chose and taught Ruslan would be satisfied with an apprentice of less than extraordinary ability," Marten said. "Just because we haven't heard of Lizaveta's exploits the way we have Ruslan's doesn't mean we can safely discount her. Kiran believed she, not Ruslan, was the one who cast the binding he used to disrupt Simon's spell and destroy him."

A horrible thought struck me. "Wait. Ruslan's vow bound himself and his apprentices, not this Lizaveta. She can cast whatever she likes against us—you threw Kiran to him, and for *nothing*—"

"Not for nothing," Marten said sharply. "Channeled magic cannot be cast without two mages. Lizaveta can cast minor spells against us, yes—but those we have every hope of successfully defending against."

"Ruslan's vow means she can't cast with him, Mikail, or Kiran, but what if she joins up with another blood mage?" I demanded.

"It's no simple task for blood mages to cast together," Marten said. "Their style of magic requires mental linkage at so deep a level they must train together for years to achieve it. Even if Lizaveta were to take apprentices of her own and mark-bond them as Ruslan has done, she cannot cast channeled magic against us any time soon."

Fury took my tongue before I could stop it. "So you bought yourself, what, a few years? In exchange for a lifetime of hell for Kiran. Great bargain."

Stevan snorted. "Hell? Hardly. I saw no suffering in him today. If anything, the opposite."

My fists clenched. "You don't know him," I snarled at Stevan. "If you did, you'd know how desperate he was to escape, how terrified he was Ruslan would do exactly this to him—rip his mind apart, make him into someone else, someone he'd rather have died than be—"

"There's hope for him yet, Dev." Marten's words were quiet but insistent. "From what you said of him, it appears his will is intact even if his memories aren't. He can still choose to leave Ruslan. I will make that choice possible, but you must help him remember that Ruslan's path isn't one he wants to travel."

I crossed my arms tight over my chest and choked back angry words. I didn't buy Marten would *make the choice possible*. He just wanted me to turn Kiran back into a willing informant. But I still needed the access Marten could give me, now more than ever.

"Oh, I'll help him," I said. "But if Ruslan's going to drag Kiran everywhere he goes, then you've got to bring me whenever you meet Ruslan, and do what you can to distract him."

"Gladly," Marten said. "But to call a meeting with Ruslan, we need a reason. I'd like to send you streetside today to find out what you can on these attacks. If magic won't suffice to reveal the killer's identity, perhaps more ordinary means will."

"Sure. So long as you agree I've already given you something useful, and keep your end of our deal first." I wasn't doing any more work for him for free.

Marten gave me a weary smile. "Yes, of course. Take this back to the embassy and show it to Ambassador Halassian." He slipped a thin gold disc inscribed with the Council's seal from a pocket and handed it to me. "Talm, go with Dev, first to the embassy and then down streetside. If the killer decides to hunt us, he might believe an untalented man the easiest target. Your company will be better protection for Dev than any warding charms we could provide."

Shit. I'd walked right into that one. But so long I had those thousand kenets in hand, I'd tolerate a watchdog. I could work around Talm's presence, and I had to admit I wasn't too keen on ending up slashed to shreds like the dead man on the floor.

I said to Talm, "Tell me you've got some different clothes. I'm not going anywhere streetside with you in that uniform."

"Don't worry." A fleeting, sardonic grin touched Talm's mouth. "The embassy has a few sets of streetside-style clothes and charms. Granted, when I was stationed here I didn't go streetside often, but I know enough to play the part."

"Well, that's a relief." I headed straight for the door. The sooner I put in that bid for Melly, the better.

❋

(Kiran)

Kiran studied the channel pattern inscribed in the workroom floor. The spiraling lines were clean, shining silver, the air sunlit and scented with honeysuckle—a far cry from the stench of blood and death filling the murdered mage's workroom that morning. Yet Kiran's stomach fluttered with nerves. Ruslan had refused all their questions on the way back from Vaishala district, his expression dark and his manner distant. The moment they arrived home, he disappeared into his study, ordering Mikail to take

Kiran through a progression of spellcasting exercises. Until now, Kiran had successfully shaken off thoughts of mangled corpses and mindburned servants. He'd performed each exercise without flaw under Mikail's patient supervision.

But exercises were one thing, requiring only trickles of power from his own *ikilhia*. Now the time had come to attempt true spellcasting, in which he would release his barriers and draw on channeled power for the first time since the accident. The power would merely be stored *ikilhia* from a *zhivnoi* crystal, just as Kiran had done countless times before...and yet, the red gleam in the crystal Mikail held unsettled Kiran as deeply as if it were the eye of some slumbering beast, ready to wake and devour him. He scanned the delicate spirals of silver yet again, searching for the merest flaw in their placement. Even a relatively simple illusion spell such as he meant to cast would be dangerous if the pattern wasn't perfect.

Or if Kiran lost his focus. He shut his eyes, seeking calm.

"You'll be fine," said Mikail. "You were still waist-high when we first cast this."

"I know." He could recall his own childish excitement, Mikail's solemn eagerness, the shock of delight when they'd succeeded in linking minds deeply enough to cast together. "I'm ready."

Mikail handed him the crystal and stepped back into the channeler's position, coolly confident. Kiran bent and placed the *zhivnoi* crystal at the pattern's anchor point. The red glow heightened, the *ikilhia* within ready and waiting to flow at Kiran's direction.

His unease surged. He blocked it out. He'd cast a thousand times before without harm; this would be no different.

Kiran released his barriers, opening his senses wide. The life energy stored within the stone snapped into sharp focus as an orb of contained light. Mikail's *ikilhia* blazed as bright as a signal fire. Beyond was the glowing shroud of the workroom wards, a steady thrum of energy keeping the raw, wild currents of the confluence at bay.

Unlike the snarl of violent power Ruslan had forced through makeshift channels that morning, the *ikilhia* within the crystal didn't hurt when it lapped against his mind. Far from it. The stored power sang to him, sweet and seductive. His soul ached for it as strongly as if he'd gone *years* without tasting magic. All hesitation forgotten, Kiran reached out.

Energy poured into him. Magic swelled in his blood, joy rising with it. He gloried in the sensations for a timeless interval, letting magic eddy through body and mind.

"Kiran," Mikail said, chiding but amused.

Recalled to his purpose, Kiran stretched his senses for his mage-brother. Their minds meshed with smooth ease, far more easily than in his childhood memories. With Mikail's strength as his anchor, Kiran sent power coursing out into the channels. As he layered the spell into shape, Mikail shadowed his every move, smoothing and adjusting the channels' flow to support Kiran's efforts. When the intricate latticework was complete, Kiran narrowed his focus and brought his will to bear. Nothing else existed but his desired result; he commanded the spell to supply it.

Magic leapt to obey. In the center of the room, the air flared bright, and a shining pillar formed. Gradually, the pillar resolved into a peach tree, the trunk rooted in the stone floor, the branches laden with rosy-gold fruit and the leaves thick and green.

Kiran called back the remaining power and funneled it safely away into the crystal's spelled reservoir. As the magic dancing in his blood faded, his link with Mikail thinned and dissolved. Reluctantly, Kiran rebuilt his barriers. His ordinary senses felt muffled, the world leached of beauty and color.

"Nicely done, Kiran," Ruslan said from the doorway. A spark of pride warmed Kiran's chest as Ruslan studied the peach tree. The illusory leaves appeared to quiver in the gentle breeze wafting through the open window. "Ah, snow peaches. Lizaveta's favorite kind. Shame they're only illusion."

"We could make her some real ones if we cast a higher level spell," Mikail said.

Ruslan shook his head. "Enough for today, I think. Kiran, did you feel any discomfort while casting?"

"No." Kiran's inner senses tingled, but in a good way, as if he'd stretched muscles that hadn't been used in too long. "It felt…" Words couldn't suffice to explain the glory; he settled on, "Wonderful. Can't I cast another?"

Ruslan chuckled. "Patience, *akhelysh*. Better to do less than you can than too much. You were not so comfortable this morning even with the damping charms, yes?"

"It only hurt when you neared the limit of what the channels could hold," Kiran said. "Even then, the pain wasn't bad."

"Still, any pain means you have not yet fully recovered." Ruslan's face grew stern. "I have another question about this morning, Kiran."

Kiran's delight withered. Had Ruslan seen how his questioning of the servant had upset Kiran? Or was this about the *nathahlen* guide? Kiran swallowed and met Ruslan's eyes, waiting.

"The Alathians' guide stood with you while you watched my casting. Did you speak to him?"

Kiran nodded, his stomach sinking. Surely Ruslan couldn't be angry over such a brief conversation? "He asked what the *zhaveynikh* spell would do. I only answered because you said we need to share information with the Alathians."

Ruslan leaned against the wall. His hazel eyes bored into Kiran's. "Was that all you spoke of?"

"No," Kiran admitted. "I told him the spell had showed us the time of death. If that was a mistake, I'm sorry—but I said nothing else of consequence, I swear it!"

"I'll be the judge of that." Ruslan's casual stance didn't change, but magic slammed into Kiran through the mark-binding link. Kiran choked and fell to his knees, his vision darkening as Ruslan scoured his mind with the implacable, brutal force of a sandstorm. Ruslan found and examined the memory of his conversation with Dev, brushing away Kiran's instinctive attempts to block him with casual strength.

When Ruslan released him at last, Kiran found himself splayed face-down on the workroom floor, sweat soaking his shirt and stinging his eyes. His muscles trembled and his head throbbed with renewed pain.

"I'm sorry!" he gasped. "I didn't mean to disobey—I wouldn't have—"

"Enough," Ruslan said.

Kiran shut his mouth so fast he nearly bit his tongue. He stared at the stone beneath his nose, trying not to think of the agony in Torain's cries. He could only hope that Ruslan wouldn't decide to punish him in earnest.

"I did not intend you to share information with a mere servant," Ruslan said. "In the future, I suggest you remember that speaking to *nathahlen* is a waste of time."

"Yes, Ruslan." Kiran rolled to sit up, shaky with relief. He struggled to silence the voice within that insisted Ruslan's rules on talking to the untalented were both unreasonable and unfair. Ruslan was never so strict with Mikail.

"I must leave you for a time," Ruslan said. "If Lizaveta seeks me, tell her I had to depart on an errand in the lower city, and will return as soon as I may. Kiran, no more exercises. Instead, review the theory behind the *zhaveynikh* spell you saw cast this morning—Mikail can show you the appropriate volume of the Dyadi codices. Mikail, you may return to working on the spell designs you began last week."

"Yes, Ruslan," Kiran said in concert with Mikail. He couldn't help wondering what Ruslan sought in the lower districts, but he kept silent, fearful of rekindling Ruslan's ire.

Mikail was braver. "Do you seek the killer? I would come, and help you—"

"No, *akhelysh*," Ruslan said. "Finding our quarry will require more than a morning's research. Have no fear, I'll call upon your assistance soon enough. For now, continue your studies as usual."

He stretched out a hand to the illusory peach tree. A tendril of power sliced through the spell's pattern. The tree blurred and dissolved into nothing, the remaining mist of energies easily absorbed by the workroom wards. Ruslan left, after a last, satisfied nod.

Kiran climbed to his feet, waving off Mikail's offered hand.

"I'm fine," he mumbled. It was mostly the truth. The ache in his head had diminished to a dull throb.

Mikail sighed. "Why do you always test him? You know it never ends well."

"I wasn't trying to test him—I thought I was doing the right thing!" Kiran blotted sweat from his forehead, glaring. "His rules on *nathahlen* are ridiculous. Why can't I talk to them if I please? What difference does it make?"

"That guide is working for our enemies." Mikail's voice was flat. "Ruslan had every right to rebuke you."

"Ruslan was the one who said we had to share information! Besides, you speak with *nathahlen* sometimes and Ruslan doesn't care. If it bothers him so much, why doesn't he ever punish you for it?"

"Because I remember my place, and theirs." Mikail's eyes held a hint of the same anger Kiran had seen countless times in Ruslan's. "I don't make the mistake of treating them as equals." The final word came out in a sneer.

"Just because they lack mage talent doesn't mean they can't be interesting," Kiran said, thinking of Dev's easy, friendly grin.

Mikail turned his eyes to the warded ceiling, his jaw clenching. "Little brother, sometimes you're a complete fool." He gripped Kiran's shoulders and shook him, hard. "Look around you! Ruslan's given us everything. Most men only dream of the lives we have, and the power we wield. How can any *nathahlen* possibly compare?"

Rare, to see his placid mage-brother so visibly upset. Kiran blinked at him in puzzlement. "All I did was converse for a few moments. Ruslan wasn't that angry. Why are you?"

"You were lucky." Mikail's grip tightened. "Next time, you may not be. Risking his anger is never worth it. Never. I don't understand why that's such a hard concept for you to grasp."

"Look who's talking," Kiran said. "What about that time you broke into his vault to steal a *zhivnoi* crystal because you wanted to try and make it snow in Ninavel? You thought it was worth it then."

"That was years ago! We're not children anymore, Kiran." But Mikail's gray eyes softened, one corner of his mouth lifting. He released Kiran with a shove, sending him staggering. "Go clean yourself up. I can't concentrate on designing channels with you stinking of sweat like some *nathahlen* brute."

Kiran went. In his room, he changed his shirt, and absently splashed citrus-infused water on his face from the full ewer at his washbasin. Regardless of the years he'd lost, he knew his mage-brother. Mikail's cool composure wasn't easily shaken. This business about *nathahlen*…something must have happened during the time Kiran couldn't remember, to upset Mikail so deeply. But what? It was so maddening to have the past such a void. Kiran turned away from the washbasin, determination filling him. He might not be able to recover everything he'd lost, but this—this, he would find out.

CHAPTER TWELVE

(Dev)

I slipped into an alley barely wide enough to walk in, glad to escape the fierce blaze of the afternoon sun. Talm trailed after me. He wore the loose, flowing clothes Sulanian drovers favored, complete with a headwrap that left little more than his eyes showing, and cheap copper warding bracelets circling his wrists. So far he was good as his word about fitting in streetside, mostly because he was smart enough to keep his mouth firmly shut around others.

We'd already visited the few Acaltar taverns open at this hour, populated by sunburned, sweating foreigners too dumb to realize they should be sleeping off the day's heat instead of drinking. I'd heard all kinds of rumors about the wardfire on the Aiyalen Spire. Each rumor was crazier than the last, none of them of any obvious use. But at the Blackstrike tavern, I'd left a message for Cara: a ward-sealed envelope containing a hastily snipped lock of my hair and the words *find me*. She could use the hair to key a charm to track me down, regardless of where Talm and I wandered to hunt information.

The banking scrip Halassian had given me was tucked firmly in my inner shirt pocket. I wanted to keep my bid for Melly anonymous, lest Red Dal rightly suspect I didn't own the coin to pay up. Red Dal's runner boys and minders all knew me, but they didn't know Cara. I'd send her as my courier as soon as she met up with me.

"How do you stand living here?"

I turned, surprised. Talm was squinting up at the strip of searingly bright sky showing between the alley's high walls. He said, "I'd forgotten how the lower city makes me feel like a rat in a well. All that weight of stone above us…doesn't it bother you, to see so little of the sky?"

"When I want a view, I climb up onto a roof. At least Ninavel's not buried in woodsmoke and river fog, and no man could be bored in the night markets." That said, I desperately missed the expansive vistas and crisp, cool air of the Whitefires' high cirques. This was the first summer in nine years that I hadn't spent in the mountains.

Talm slowed, staring at me. "You actually like this city. But…you were Tainted. You've experienced firsthand how viciously men misuse power here! Children enslaved by criminals, the untalented killed or ruined on mere whims, with no recourse to any authority—how can you possibly think Ninavel anything but a plague den?"

I shrugged uncomfortably. "Some of it is, yeah. But it's not all bad." I thought of lazy afternoons full of laughter in Samis's courtyard, of listening rapt to storytellers from every country under the sun, of friends like Sethan who'd fled the harsh laws of their home cities and cherished the chance to begin anew.

"Marten told me why you agreed to come," Talm said. "Of the Tainted child you hope to save. Have you never thought of trying to change this… system of abuse? Stopping the enslavement of children entirely?"

Khalmet's bloodsoaked hand, did he think it would be so easy? Gods all damn mages and their arrogance. I laughed bitterly. "If I were a mage, maybe. Maybe then I could take on every ganglord in the city. Even so… have *you* ever thought about stopping Alathia's forced conscription of mageborn kids? I'd bet you'd have just as much luck."

"Some of us do hope to change the conscription laws," Talm said. "Marten, in particular. It's one of the reasons I requested to be transferred from Ninavel to join his Watch. He sees beyond the fear that keeps the Council so militant. He's worked tirelessly to convince the Council that giving mages a little more choice in their lives and their magic would help and not harm our country. I only wish more in the Watch shared his strength of vision."

He spoke with all the fervor of some sun-touched temple cultist. It pissed me off. As I dodged left into an even narrower slit of an alley, I said, "You want to talk about abuses of power? What Marten did to Kiran was as bad as anything I've seen from a ganglord. Pretend all you like, but I know the truth: Alathia's no different than here. Men with power sacrifice those without to get what they want. It's just that in Ninavel nobody bothers to lie about it."

Talm blew out a sharp, exasperated breath. I thought he'd argue, but instead he said, "What's down here, anyway?"

"A place you can't go." I halted well short of the alley's end, where a deceptively battered-looking door lurked in a grimy recess.

Talm had already stopped dead, his gaze riveted to the door. "Those are kill-strength wards."

The ward lines lay hidden beneath the grime, but of course a mage didn't need to see lines to peek a ward. "Yeah," I said. "That's only the half of it. That door leads to Acaltar's best charm dealer. She commissions charms direct from highside mages, supplies ganglords and shadow men, and hears every last rumor in the city—but she doesn't like strangers. At all. So you're gonna wait out here while I go have a chat."

"A little hard to protect you from out here," Talm said. "Especially with those wards swamping my senses."

I'd hoped the wards might stop him using magic to spy on me. I meant this chat to be a private one. "A necessary risk, if you want information. A half hour, that's all I ask."

Talm sighed. "Any longer, and I'll break those wards to come for you. I won't be happy about it, either."

"If I don't return by then, I'll need you to come after me." I eased up to the door and scratched on a battered copper plate at head height, then stood still, my hands raised and open.

After a moment's silence, the wards flickered and the door cracked open. I slid inside, pushing through tattered prayer shrouds into a room whose walls glittered with charms, most of them deadly. Blood-boil, boneshatter, heartrot, poisonteeth, and more hung beside esoteric amulets whose runes I didn't recognize. The acrid pall of belthis-root incense fogged the air, making my eyes water.

"Hadn't thought to see you darken my door in high summer, boy." Behind a table cluttered with jeweler's tools stood a stocky woman perhaps fifty years in age, whose coarse thatch of dark hair and coppery skin spoke of mixed Arkennlander and Varkevian blood. She wore clothes as black as her eyes, a jeweled scorpion amulet on a silver chain around her neck, and owned no name but *Avakra-dan*, the Varkevian word for the deadly brown-furred spiders that lurked in crevices in the dry canyons of the Bolthole Mountains. Not a mage, but as dangerous as her namesake just the same. "Shouldn't you be off playing the fool in the mountains?"

How I wished I was. "I thought I'd branch out from courier jobs this year," I said. "Now that I'm working solo."

Avakra-dan grinned, displaying teeth stained indigo from chewing gavis beetles. Some streetsiders swore by the beetles, said they made the mind work faster. I'd tried one once, back in my days as a runner boy for Tavian's gang. If my thoughts moved quicker, I sure hadn't noticed, occupied as I was in scrubbing my tongue raw to clear the rank taste from my mouth.

"Ah, yes." Avakra-dan's eyes took on a cruel gleam. "I heard how that sly little partner of yours robbed you blind so she could play jenny-toy to a mage."

Even after all these months, the memory of Jylla's betrayal still stung like scorpion venom. I shrugged, carefully nonchalant. "Good riddance."

"That's the spirit," Avakra-dan agreed. "A clever boy like you only needs the lesson once: love is for fools and marks. About time you started playing proper shadow games instead of mucking about with courier work. But tell me, if you're working solo—who's that skulking in my alley?"

"Client representative," I said. "One I'd prefer to keep clear of streetsider business."

"Clever and cautious, good." Avakra-dan awarded me another indigo grin. "Come, tell Avakra-dan what you seek."

I slid a paper from my shirt. On it was a sketch I'd made of the magic-blocking amulet Kiran had worn when he'd first fled Ninavel. I'd done my best to replicate the complex, whorled pattern of the silver, and written in the type and color of each gem.

"My client wants to find a charm to match this one," I told her. Simon Levanian had said of Kiran's amulet: *I have seen its like before.* Hopefully that meant the amulet now locked in an Alathian vault wasn't the only one in existence. Kiran had told me the charm blocked his bond with Ruslan; and more, it had saved me from dying in the inferno of magic released in Simon's backfired spell. If I could find an equivalent charm, I hoped it could prevent Kiran from dying along with Ruslan if their bond went as deep as I feared. Even if it couldn't, I'd have plenty of other uses for a charm powerful enough to hide me from both Marten and Ruslan.

"Hah." Avakra-dan's brows rose as she studied the drawing. "A seven-stone charm?" She darted me a sharp glance. "I'd guess your old lover's not the only one cozying up to a mage."

I'd known she'd suspect a mage's involvement. Most Ninavel-made charms were designed so an untalented owner could spark them with the right trigger word and a few drops of blood, but that trick only worked for lesser spells. Nobody but a mage could spark a charm as powerful as Kiran's amulet, though once sparked, I knew from experience the amulet would work even if worn by someone untalented.

"Guess all you like," I said. "I'm not gonna mouth off about my client's business. Except to say he'll know if the charm's a fake, and he won't be pleased. Can you get one?"

Avakra-dan smirked. "There's no charm Avakra-dan can't procure, boy. Only question is how long the search takes. The more coin you pay, the faster it goes. For a charm as unusual as this one…at least five hundred kenets deposit. Fee is refundable less ten percent if I fail."

"Three hundred kenets, five percent, and a two-week time limit," I countered. I didn't need to devote the full thousand I'd gotten from Marten to my bid for Melly, but the more I had to offer Red Dal, the better.

"Two weeks!" Avakra-dan spat. "Perhaps you mistake me for one of Noshet's guardians, able to call down miracles from the mountaintops…"

We settled down to bargaining in earnest. I got her to agree to a four-week time limit with a bonus if she found the charm sooner, but she demanded a fifteen percent failsafe. I didn't much like that—she might decide to simply take the failsafe and forget the rest—but in the end I agreed, on the condition she throw in a boneshatter and a linked pair of twin-seek charms.

"Skimming off your client, eh?" Avakra-dan laughed, a gurgling chortle. "Knew you were clever. All right, boy, you have a deal. Long as you're willing to sign a blood-mark contract. I don't take procuring jobs without one. No exceptions."

I'd known it when I walked in her door, but it didn't help me like the idea any better. Blood-mark contracts were simple: we'd each stain a copy of the terms with a few drops of our blood. If either of us reneged on the contract, the offended party would have a blood sample in hand to key a deathdealing charm with. I didn't intend to back out, but I sure as hell wasn't comfortable with Avakra-dan holding a sample of my blood. Ruslan might not be able to use it, but his partner mage Lizaveta could. Still, what choice did I have? No serious procurer in the city did jobs without blood-marks.

"I'll sign, if we return contracts the moment the job's complete," I said.

"Wouldn't have it any other way." She rooted around in the piles on her desk to produce two blank sheets of paper, a silver writing stylus, a pot of ink, and a copper needle.

As she wrote out the terms, I said, "With all this wardfire, and mages dying…you must be doing quite the business in defensive charms."

"Best summer I've had in years." Avakra-dan paused in her writing to open a jar full of squirming beetles and flick one into her mouth. I winced at the hard grind of her teeth on the shell. "So you needn't fear I'll turn tail and run from the city, like these weak-minded fools moaning over signs and omens."

"What, have people seen more than just wardfire?" I kept my eyes on the contract, my tone mildly curious.

Avakra-dan finished one copy and started the second. "Wardfire's enough to panic some. You know how southerners are, they wring their hands and yap about demons the instant anything unusual happens. But now word's come that Benno's best deathdealer got found in a pool of blood on a rooftop, gutted like a rock bear clawed him open. That'll scare them proper, watch and see."

Every nerve sprang to attention. "Shit," I said. "Hadn't heard that one. When?" Benno was top ganglord over in Julisi, the next district over from Acaltar.

Avakra-dan shrugged. "Couple days ago. Benno's tried to keep it quiet, but no secret's safe in this city. The rumors have half his men spook-eyed and slinking for the city gates. Can't say I blame them, but here's another lesson for you, boy: profit's always best when times are worst. You can't handle a little risk, you don't deserve to get ahead."

"Why get spooked over someone taking a knife to a deathdealer? That's not exactly unheard of." I wished I dared ask direct if the wounds matched the tales of the Ghorshaba, but I didn't want to reveal anything that hadn't yet come streetside. If she realized I was involved in the investigation, that might lead her straight down the path to selling my blood to Lizaveta.

"Rumors don't stick to truth." Avakra-dan slid the completed copies over to me. "I've heard ten different versions of the tale, each wilder than the last, until you'd think Shaikar himself had crawled out of his hells to slay the man."

Oh yeah, Talm would salivate over this when I passed it on. "Where'd they find him?" The body wouldn't remain, but I could maybe find someone who'd seen it firsthand.

Avakra-dan offered me a sly smirk. "Have a ghoulish streak, do you? Or perhaps you're playing other games. For twenty kenets, I'll tell you the very spot."

I didn't much like the hard glint of calculation in her eyes. I'd originally thought to show her the spell diagram I'd found in Kiran's pack and ask for a consult, but now I shelved that idea. Risky enough to show her the drawing of his amulet. I didn't want her seeing any further association between me and blood magic if I could help it.

"Curiosity's not worth coin," I said, scrutinizing the contracts. If rumors were spreading as fast as she said, I'd find out easily enough where the death had happened by listening to tavern talk in Julisi.

"Your loss." Avakra-dan crunched another beetle.

I handed one copy back to her. She pricked a finger and let five fat drops of blood fall on the paper. I did the same with the second copy. As I watched the red stains spread, I prayed to Khalmet I wouldn't regret it.

※

(Kiran)

Kiran slipped into the study, easing the door shut so as not to disturb Ruslan. His master sat frowning over a host of books spread open on his desk. Further piles of books balanced precariously around the desk's edge alongside papers dark with notes and diagrams. Ruslan's chestnut hair was tied back in a careless tail, and ink and charcoal smudged his fingers. Kiran had seen him like this before; when researching some esoteric area of magic or developing a new spell, Ruslan's focus was intense, bordering on obsessive. His apprentices disrupted it at their peril.

But Ruslan had never forbidden them access to the plenitude of books housed in the study's ordered ranks of bookshelves; he only demanded they be quiet about it. Kiran tiptoed across the patterned rug to a set of shelves containing treatises on the mental aspects of magic. Sharp silver light from magelights set in iron sconces illuminated even their deepest recesses. He traced a finger over the spines, scanning titles.

"Try the Lernis."

Kiran winced and turned. Ruslan was watching him, half-twisted in his chair. To Kiran's relief, no hint of anger showed in his eyes.

"The fourth section of the treatise contains a discussion of the effects of backlash energies upon the mind of a mage," Ruslan said, with a little, knowing smile. "Though I fear you'll find it confirms that when damage is severe, memories cannot be recovered."

Kiran flushed. "I know I ought to take your word for it. But...I've lost so much. I can't just accept those memories are gone, not without even trying to find if there's some spell that might recover them."

"I would be disappointed in any apprentice of mine who gave up before researching a problem," Ruslan said. "A mage should never assume a solution is beyond reach. Though a mage must also have the wisdom to move on if a problem proves intractable."

Kiran nodded, though his determination didn't falter. There had to be some hint, some suggestion lurking in a book that would show him the path to regaining his memories. Ruslan's talk of patience and moving on was all very well, but he couldn't know the frustration of having years of life and knowledge vanish.

Ruslan bent back over his books. Kiran pulled the Lernis volume free and retreated to one of the padded chairs near the study door. He settled into comfortable pillows and opened the book to the section Ruslan had mentioned.

Lost in a dry but chilling analysis of mages whose minds had been shattered, he barely registered the sound of the study door opening. Lizaveta's voice broke his concentration.

"I brought the Valsadd codices from my library." She padded over to Ruslan's desk, bearing an armful of thin, yellowed parchments. She set them down as gently as if they were spun glass. "Your description of the blurring of the *zhaveynikh* energies reminded me of a description one of their sages wrote of a Jularian adept at work."

Ruslan eyed the parchments with keen interest. "Which sage?"

Lizaveta lifted one bare brown shoulder in a shrug. The motion rippled the floor-length folds of her violet and black dress, held clasped at her neck by a ring of silver. The dress's open back exposed the curve of her spine from neck to waist, and the soft fabric clung to the swell of hip and breast in a way that left Kiran short of breath. A fragment of memory slipped past, of fingers gliding over his chest, a woman's low, delighted laugh in his ear. His face heated. Had he and Lizaveta…? He remembered seeing her caress a teenage Mikail with possessive languor while Ruslan looked on, but Kiran had been too young then to think it much different than the affection she'd lavished on them both throughout their childhood. Perhaps he was only imagining the implications in hindsight. Though if he wasn't… he swallowed, his gaze caught by the smooth perfection of her skin.

"It might have been Keldar Severius," Lizaveta said to Ruslan. "He went to Jularia, I believe. Or perhaps Mordan of Ishelhaut. It has been a long time since I last read the codices."

Ruslan's mouth twitched in amusement. "Some hundred years, I would think. You never liked the Valsaddi formal court style."

"So longwinded and so boring," Lizaveta agreed, with a delicate little shudder. Ruslan reached for the top parchment, and she caught his hand in hers.

"You've been working for hours, my brother. Will you not join me in a glass of wine, and relax for a few moments?" Her kohl-lined eyes were limpid in entreaty. Kiran didn't know how Ruslan could resist agreeing.

Indeed, Ruslan looked tempted. But he shook his head, sighing. "You know the stakes in this, Liza."

"I know what you fear," she said. "I think you are being overly pessimistic. Have we not weathered greater storms than this?"

Curiosity pricked Kiran. He'd have to seek out Lizaveta later and beg her to tell him what she meant. Ruslan didn't often speak of the past, but in the right mood, Lizaveta could be persuaded to share tales of their travels. As children, Kiran and Mikail had listened entranced to many a story of long-lost cities both wondrous and strange in their customs.

"Best to stamp out small problems before they grow into large ones." Ruslan brought her hand to his lips and kissed it. "This, I learned from you."

Lizaveta laughed and withdrew her hand. "As long as you remember that the tired mind often misses what it seeks. But if you insist, I will leave you in peace."

"Thank you," Ruslan said, his voice dry.

Lizaveta turned, her gaze lighting on Kiran. He hastily bent over his book, embarrassed at being caught listening instead of reading. He stared at the words without seeing them, aware of Lizaveta's approach in his peripheral vision.

"Ah, Kiranushka. Studying so hard already?" Her voice was barely audible, but even so, rich with teasing warmth. She settled on the arm of his chair and leaned over him to examine the page.

"You worry too much, little one." She trailed her fingers through his hair and pulled it away from his neck. He shivered, as much from her touch as the cool air on his bared skin. Warm hands settled on his shoulders to knead tight muscles with expert precision. Tension leaked away even as his heart sped up. He let his head fall forward, the book sliding closed in his lap.

"That's better, is it not?" Her scent surrounded him, jasmine with a hint of spice. She drew the neck of his shirt open, her fingers tracing slow patterns on his skin. Kiran shifted in the chair, torn between the warmth coalescing in his groin and a nagging sense that somehow her touch felt wrong, as if his body expected different hands.

Lips touched the nape of his neck, feather-light but hot as a brand. Kiran twitched and gasped. A tug deep in his *ikilhia* made his head fly up. Ruslan was looking straight at him, his palms laid flat on the open book in front of him.

But Ruslan didn't look angry this time, either. Instead, his eyes held a heat that made Kiran's stomach jump and his heart race for another reason entirely. Another flash of childhood memory came: Mikail, wide-eyed and serious, asking Ruslan, *When we come of age, we'll be your partners, just like Lizaveta?* And Ruslan, smiling benevolently at them both: *Just like Lizaveta, yes—though our bond will be deeper yet.*

Was it Ruslan's touch his body remembered? His unease didn't fade at the idea; indeed, it increased, even as he grew painfully, achingly hard.

Ruslan stood, his eyes holding Kiran's. He moved around the desk with predatory grace, and Lizaveta smiled against Kiran's skin. She slid off the chair as Ruslan approached, her fingers trailing upward through Kiran's hair.

"Do you always get what you want?" Ruslan murmured to Lizaveta.

"Always." Her pearly teeth showed in a sharp smile. "Think of it as a gift, my brother. I know how difficult these last months have been for you."

Difficult…how, and why? Kiran opened his mouth to ask, only to halt, all thought arrested, as Ruslan slid his hands into the black coils of Lizaveta's hair and drew her into a deep, passionate kiss.

Kiran could imagine the lush warmth of Lizaveta's mouth, taste the sweetness of the lira berries she loved to eat, feel her body soft and pliant beneath his hands. Was it memory? The sensations grew in strength, drowning his disquiet. His hands clamped on the chair's arms, his breath coming fast. It was almost as if he were the one kissing Lizaveta, not Ruslan.

Ruslan pulled back from the kiss, his hazel eyes locking with Kiran's again. All at once, Kiran understood. Ruslan was using the mark-bond, channeling all that he felt straight into Kiran.

The link has many advantages, Ruslan agreed in Kiran's head. He smiled, slow and sensual. Answering heat bloomed in Kiran's body, his mouth gone dry as ash.

As if she'd heard the silent communication, Lizaveta twisted to look at Kiran. Her dark eyes widened, and she laughed.

"Hardly fair, my brother, when I have no such advantage. Don't worry, little one. I have another way." She slipped from Ruslan's hands to straddle Kiran, twitching the folds of her dress aside as she settled onto his lap. The warm weight of her on his groin destroyed the last fading vestige of unease. He gripped her hips, pulling her hard against him, his mouth seeking hers.

She kissed him hungrily. To his surprise, the salt taste of blood mixed with sweetness. She nipped at his lower lip, brief sharp pain, and he rocked backward with the shock of power as his blood met hers within the kiss.

Lizaveta slid into his consciousness with the blood contact, deep violet tendrils spreading through his mind. Ruslan joined her there, voracious flames coiling over the tendrils until Kiran arched in the chair, a strangled moan torn from his throat. Lizaveta's mouth left his, only to be replaced by Ruslan's, fierce and demanding, as hands pulled his clothes open. Their power rose to enfold Kiran, spiraling upward until his vision was all sparks and light. Bodies pressed against his, one all soft heat, the other hard strength. He yielded to the hands that moved him, gripped him, stroked over him as he writhed, pierced by pleasure so sharp it shattered his innermost defenses. His mind and *ikilhia* bled into theirs, all boundaries gone, the pleasure building until it caught Kiran up in an inferno that burned through the deepest well of his soul.

When the world reformed around him, he found himself lying on the floor before the chair. His head lay pillowed in Lizaveta's lap, the silk of her dress smooth against his cheek. Ruslan sat beside her with his shirt hanging open and his trousers half-laced. Ruslan's fingers carded through Kiran's hair, the motion soothingly repetitive. Kiran's mind felt white and empty, his body near boneless.

"He's well on the way to recovery, don't you think?" Ruslan said to Lizaveta, with a lazy, satisfied smile.

"What did I tell you, brother?" Lizaveta leaned her head on Ruslan's shoulder. "Sometimes patience yields the best results."

"Hmmm." With a last caress of Kiran's hair, Ruslan stood and refastened his clothing. "Now that you've had your way, I really must return to my work."

"By all means." Lizaveta helped Kiran sit up, her dark eyes gleaming with amusement. "No more distractions this night. I give you my word."

Kiran fumbled his way back into his own disheveled clothes. His fingers felt slow and clumsy on his shirt laces, his muscles full of a deep languor. He staggered to his feet and let Lizaveta guide him out of the study and down the hallway to his room.

Halfway there, they met Mikail leaning against his own open door. Kiran hung back, a spike of nervousness piercing the fog in his head. His mage-brother had surely felt all that raw magic, and Kiran's rumpled clothes told their own tale. Would Mikail be jealous? Or was this commonplace for the both of them, and Kiran just didn't recall it?

Mikail's mouth quirked. "Magic's not the only thing he's ready for, I see," he said to Lizaveta.

Kiran ducked his head, embarrassment rising. Lizaveta laughed. "Oh, yes. An invalid no more."

"Good." The fervent tone of Mikail's answer snapped Kiran's head up. His mage-brother's amusement had disappeared, replaced by an intensity of joyful relief as rare to see as his earlier anger.

Kiran peered at him, wishing his thoughts didn't feel as sluggish as sun-warmed honey. Had Mikail truly been so concerned for his health after the accident, or did this have something to do with whatever had prompted his anger in the workroom?

"Next time, you'll not be left out." Lizaveta bestowed a kiss on Mikail and murmured something too soft for Kiran to hear. His gray eyes alight, Mikail nodded and withdrew into his room.

Next time. Kiran shivered, conflicted once more. The pleasure had been staggering, and yet…now that the tide of desire had ebbed, an icy core of unease remained, accompanied by something that felt strangely like shame.

Lizaveta drew him gently onward. She opened his door, and said softly, "Sleep well, Kiranushka."

He wanted nothing more than to fall into his bed, but instead he braced a hand on the doorframe and faced her. "Khanum Liza, does your library contain any books that discuss ways a mage might see the past?" He couldn't be the only mage who wanted to see more than a *zhaveynikh* spell could show.

She looked taken aback. He tried to explain. "If my memories are truly gone, I thought…perhaps there's another way I could at least glimpse what they contained. I know you say I can relearn all my spellcraft, but that's not all I've lost. Besides, I don't want to wait years, and waste Mikail's time, and Ruslan's…I want to be all that I was. *Akheli*, not a half-trained apprentice."

Lizaveta stroked his cheek. "So impatient," she said. "Ah, Kiran, sometimes you are so much like Ruslan it steals my breath. As if you were the child of his body, not just his heart."

He began a protest; *child* was not his relationship to Ruslan, not after tonight. But Lizaveta put a finger to his lips. "Never mind, *ardeshka mayei*. I only ramble because I, too, am tired. I do not know of a specific book that may help you, but you are welcome to come to my home and use my library any time you choose. I will also speak to Ruslan…he knows my library as his own, and will know best how to guide you." Her dark eyes lingered on his face, her expression unaccountably solemn.

"Thank you." Kiran kissed her hand in imitation of Ruslan, and was rewarded with the flash of her smile. She inclined her head to him and left. He shut the door and threw himself onto his bed, sinking gratefully into down pillows. He'd intended to consider further the oddity of Mikail's reactions and his own curious reluctance, but sleep claimed him before he could form a single thought.

✳

(Dev)

I perched on the edge of a rounded cupola. All around me, terraced roofs glimmered pale in the light of the horned moon rising over the eastern mountains. According to the hushed tales of multiple Julisi residents, the flat roof before me was the spot where an eggseller seeking swallow nests had found Benno's deathdealer in a mutilated heap. The roof's stone certainly had a shadowed look to it darker than could be accounted for by mere grime, though maybe the stain was my imagination. Talm was crawling around with his nose nearly pressed to the roof and his rings glowing silver. Every now and then he stopped to stroke the stone, or chant a soft set of incomprehensible words.

"Haven't you found anything yet?" Impatience drove the question from me. Talm had announced he was seeking spell traces and insisted in a tone just short of an order that I wait and not wander off. But dawn wasn't more than an hour away, and I still hadn't seen Cara. Damn it, where was she? I'd thought she might have trouble narrowing in on us with a find-me charm as we navigated Julisi's maze of alleys, but I'd been sitting still on this roof a good hour now.

"Not so far," Talm said, without looking up. "Nor will I, unless I can properly concentrate."

I sighed. I'd hoped the spot would provide a lead significant enough for me to pry another payment out of Marten. I'd have to cajole more of Benno's men into talking. The murder couldn't be random. The deathdealer must've seen or heard something, or maybe he'd been sent after someone the killer wanted to protect. I'd already spent much of the night haunting taverns in hopes of finding out those details, but so far all I had was a bunch of conflicting stories about the identity of the deathdealer's target.

Maybe Cara had thought better of helping me. The gods knew I hadn't exactly been appreciative at our last meeting. The sawtoothed black outline of the Whitefires drew my eye. Cara must miss them as badly as I did. Maybe even more. She disliked cities and crowds, to the point that when winter's snows turned the Whitefires impassable, she signed on with convoys traveling the desert routes. She'd never understood how I could stand to live in Ninavel all winter. After two months stuck in the city hunting Pello, followed by me insisting I wanted to work alone, maybe she'd decided to wash her hands of this entire mess in favor of returning to the Whitefires before season's end.

If so, I should feel relieved, even though it'd complicate my plan to bid for Melly. After all, it was what I'd wanted: Cara safe, and me free to bury the dismaying tangle of hurt and regret that afflicted me every time I thought of her. Instead, I felt as tense and twitchy as a lionclaw addict deprived of a dose. When a soft scrape sounded at the roof's edge, I twisted so fast I nearly fell off the cupola.

A dark figure levered itself onto the roof with familiar, long-limbed grace. Talm jerked upright, one ringed hand rising.

"Talm! Wait." I hastily vaulted down off the cupola. "You remember Cara, right? I asked her to check around for me streetside. No need to stop your search. She and I can talk behind the cupola and keep it quiet."

Cara had frozen on the roof's edge in a wary crouch. Talm sat back on his heels and lowered his hand. "Very well," he said. "So long as talking is all you do." His teeth showed white in a grin.

"Wouldn't dream of disturbing you," I said dryly. "Still nothing?"

"No." He sounded far more sanguine about it than I felt.

I led Cara around the cupola's back side. The sky was lightening already, the triplet of stars known as Noshet's Tears bracketing the Aiyalen Spire's five-pointed summit.

"Marten set you a watchdog, I see," Cara said, in a voice pitched to carry to my ears and no further. "But what's he looking for?"

"I'll explain," I replied, equally quietly. "But first..." I shifted on my feet, hating how awkward I felt. I missed the uncomplicated ease of our old friendship. "Thanks for coming."

She folded her arms. "Did you think I wouldn't?"

"Crossed my mind," I admitted.

She said in a fierce, outraged whisper, "Khalmet's hand, Dev, what do you take me for? You think I'd run out on you, or any friend who needed help?"

"No, I..." I stopped, certain anything I said would only anger her more. "Look, never mind. I've got good news for once. But let me catch you up..." I launched into a rapid, much-abridged tale of the past day's events, from Kiran staring at me like a stranger over Jadin's mutilated corpse, to my search with Talm for the scene of the deathdealer's murder. I left out my deal with Avakra-dan, all too aware that Talm might cast a scry-spell to listen in on us.

"Mother of maidens." Cara leaned against the wall of the cupola like she wasn't sure her legs would hold her. "You said you had good news. I sure hope so, after hearing all that."

In answer, I handed her my remaining banking scrip and the carefully worded letter of bid I'd drawn up for Red Dal, then sparked the glowlight charm I wore on a neckchain. I shielded the glow with my hand and held the charm out so she could read the letter.

Her eyes went wide. "Dev, this...oh, thank Khalmet!" She caught me up in one of her rib-crushing hugs, papers still clutched in her hands. I returned her hold, awkwardness ebbing under the force of my own relief over Melly. For one blessed moment I was conscious only of the warmth of her body against mine, the sure strength in her arms.

"I need you to place the bid," I whispered in her ear. "I don't want him to know it's me. I wrote out what you need to do." She'd have to exchange the scrip at a banking house for a contracting writ, so Red Dal couldn't just simply take the earnest money. He'd have to accept the bid first, by returning a signed contract to a blind account at the banking house.

I pressed one of the twin-seek charms I'd gotten from Avakra-dan into her hand. "Spark this if anything goes wrong, or if Liana warns you the Change has started." I wore the braided copper band that matched her charm on my bicep. If she sparked hers, mine would heat to warn me, and lead me to her good as any find-me.

"I'll do it straight off. But, Dev…" She drew back to peer at my face. "So much coin. You got it from Marten, didn't you? What did he want in return?"

"Just that I play shadow man." I flicked the glowlight charm with a finger to darken it and leaned in close again to whisper, "I don't have all the money for the bid yet, but I'll get it before payment comes due."

"Assuming you survive until then," Cara said, low and strained. "A killer who can rip apart mages and leave not a trace of his spellwork…" She looked down at the letter and scrip in her hands. "I hope you're demanding protection as well as coin."

"Why d'you think I let Marten saddle me with Talm? I'm safer than most are streetside."

Cara tucked away the letter and scrip, her head still bent. "I know you don't mind risk, and I understand you've got to keep working for Marten. But listen, about Kiran…maybe you should rethink this idea of taking on Ruslan."

"What?" I stared, sure I couldn't have heard her right. "What about, 'I'd never run out on a friend who needed help?'"

"Kiran's not being tortured or imprisoned, right? You said he even looked happy." As I started an outraged protest, she held up her hands. "I know, I know. He'd never have wanted this. But why not back off and wait, see if Marten follows through on freeing him before you risk bringing Ruslan down on your head? Don't you think you've got enough to worry about already?"

"Oh yeah, let's sit back and trust Marten," I hissed. "That worked so well before. Damn it, Cara, Marten will vanish back to Alathia the moment he's sure their wards are safe, and then how the hell am I supposed to get near Kiran to help him? Kiran came here for me, even though he was fucking terrified over it. If you tell me that in my place you'd shrug and walk away while Ruslan molds him into some obedient lapdog, then you're a hell of a lot more like Jylla than I thought."

Cara went rigid. "Damn you, Dev, that's not what I—"

The roof shuddered under our feet, hard enough to send us sprawling in a tangle of limbs against the cupola wall.

"Dev!" Cara rolled off me and pointed, her voice urgent. "The towers!"

Wardfire cascaded off all the spires in Reytani district, Aiyalen among them. Colored lightning stabbed between towers as ghostly flames licked along the bridges. All across the city's rooftops, lines of silver burst to life along the stone of edges and walls in a great, shimmering web.

Quake wards! I'd heard of them in stories of the mage war. Supposedly the city's stone was laced with them, though I'd never seen them trigger before. The stories said they kept stone standing, but only if the quake wasn't too large. They'd failed many a time in the mage war.

The roof stilled beneath me. The shining web of the quake wards faded, though the wardfire on Reytani's spires remained. I scrambled around the cupola to see Talm standing rigid at the roof's center, his gaze locked on Reytani's fiery display.

"Can you sense anything? Will Aiyalen's wards hold?" I demanded.

He didn't answer. A cacophony of shouts echoed from the streets below. Shutters rattled, and doors thumped. Half the city was probably taking shelter, the rest—those too dumb, or too new to the city to properly fear a mage war—sprinting for a view of the commotion.

The wardfire flickered out, leaving the spires unmarred in the moonlight. Talm rounded on me. "We go to the Aiyalen Spire by the fastest route you know. Now."

Cara caught my arm. "Watch yourself, Dev. Whatever caused that wardfire, you're no mage to survive it."

"I know." Risk be damned, I couldn't miss the chance to speak with Kiran again. Whatever waited for us in Aiyalen, Ruslan was sure to come. "You'll handle the other matter?"

"You can trust me." She said it with bitter emphasis. I hesitated, words of apology piling up on my tongue, but Talm was already slithering down to the next lower roof. I sprinted after him, regret fading into nervous anticipation.

CHAPTER THIRTEEN

(Dev)

It took Talm and me a solid hour to reach Aiyalen's gate, even at a pace that had us both panting and dripping with sweat by the time we climbed the final steps. The sun was slipping over the undulating ridgeline of the Bolthole Mountains, the Whitefires glowing molten gold. We found Marten, Lena, and Stevan already at the gate, arguing with a huddle of Sechaveh's guardsmen and several skittish-looking mages. The mages wanted to refuse entry, claiming no foreigners could enter Aiyalen, but Marten corralled one of them and talked her into finding Edon.

When the mage hurried off, Talm gave Marten a swift report of the news I'd had from Avakra-dan and our search for the murder scene. He admitted unhappily his failure to find traces of blood magic. "But the confluence is so powerful here. At any location unprotected by wards, the currents erode away traces quite rapidly. I think my failure proves only that the death was too old for me to read properly, not that blood magic wasn't involved."

"Maybe magic can't help, but I still can," I said. "If I nose around more, maybe I can figure out why the killer wanted Benno's man dead. But first, take me with you into Aiyalen and give me that chance at Kiran you promised."

Marten nodded. "Get him to speak of Ruslan's reaction to the wardfire, if you can. And remember, I need to know how far his memory loss extends."

Again, I wondered why. Before I could ask, Edon emerged from the spire. His pinched face was sallow, his speech even more abrupt than before. "Four mages dead in the upper tower," he announced. "You may visit the scene of the murders—the mages died in an outer waiting room, not where water spells are cast—but you may not cross the wards to the interior chamber."

"Did the killer cross those wards?" Marten asked. I waited nervously for the answer, praying all that wardfire didn't mean Ninavel's water supply was fucked.

Edon shook his head, looking grimmer yet. "We're not yet certain. Ruslan is checking now."

Gods. I hoped Cara would urge our city friends to get out while they still could. Unfortunately, for far too many folk leaving wouldn't be an option. In high summer the desert routes were furnaces, the cost of the water needed to traverse them prohibitive for all but the largest of merchant houses. The route over the Whitefires to Alathia was kinder in climate but far worse in terrain, the cost of supplies to survive the passage still higher than most streetside families could pay. I resolved with new determination to find something that would let Marten and Sechaveh stop the asshole responsible for all this.

Edon passed us through the gate wards and sent us onward, claiming he would follow after speaking with the guards. About a million stairs later, we reached an antechamber with a few chairs and a warded copper door, guarded by a pair of men who looked pale around the mouth. Though the door was shut, the rusting-metal stench of fresh blood filled the air. At least this time I was prepared. I pricked a finger and touched it to the rune-inscribed copper disc hanging on my neckchain beside the glowlight charm. The deadnose charm worked just as the shop dealer had promised: the stink immediately faded. I couldn't smell anything else either, but I thought that a small price to pay.

The guards swung open the door. Despite the deadnose charm, my gorge heaved. Four dead mages—three male, one female—lay sprawled on the floor of the room beyond. The bodies were mutilated in similar fasion to Jadin's, slashes, burned eyes, and all. Blood coated the floor, reddened the walls, and soaked the lavishly cushioned couches lining the room. If any was missing, it sure didn't look like it.

Ruslan entered through a tiled archway on the far side of the room, Kiran and Mikail behind him. He ignored us and crossed to where the guardsmen stood.

"Inform Lord Sechaveh the spell chamber was not breached, and I have personally seen to the repair and reinforcing of the wards."

My initial trickle of relief dried up. Repaired the wards himself, had he? If he was behind the attacks, talk about the perfect opportunity to leave some nice big gaping flaw in the new wards. Sechaveh had better be smart enough to have another mage check Ruslan's work. He might not allow foreigners like the Alathians to do it, but Marten could insist Edon bring in another Ninavel mage.

Marten said, "I take it the killer did not succeed in disrupting the water supply?"

Ruslan gave Marten an unfriendly look. "Not directly, but these mages were preparing to take the next shift."

Marten cocked his head. "Forgive the question, but I'm not completely familiar with the ways of Ninavel…from what I understand, all mages living here must contribute in some way to the water magic. Yet I assume that not all mages are capable of working the actual spells?"

I listened with interest. Everyone in Ninavel knew mages had to spend time on water duty, but nobody streetside knew exactly what that meant.

"Lesser mages contribute stored power in whatever form they are able," Ruslan said. "But a certain threshold of ability is necessary to cast a spell powerful enough to provide a useful amount of water."

"Ah," said Marten. "With the wide variety of magical methods in evidence among mages here, I assume the spells used must also differ widely. But I believe the relevant question is this: how many mages now living in Ninavel are capable of useful water magic?"

Ruslan's eyes narrowed. "More than enough."

I drew in a breath, seeing where Marten was going. Sure enough, he said, "Then our mystery assassin cannot hope to disrupt the city simply by killing all the mages capable of water magic?"

Ruslan laughed. "If that is his plan, he is a fool. Lesser mages may die easily. *Akheli* do not." Mikail's expression mirrored Ruslan's, full of confident amusement at the idea of someone killing a blood mage. Kiran didn't look amused, but he didn't look like he disagreed, either.

Was Ruslan really so arrogant as to think himself invincible, even with the evidence lying at our feet that magic wasn't much good against the killer? Or did he laugh because he knew perfectly well the killer's identity, and knew himself safe? I entertained a brief fantasy of the assassin showing up at Ruslan's house and kicking his arrogant ass straight into Shaikar's innermost hell. If only I could guarantee Ruslan's death wouldn't result in Kiran's, that'd save me a hell of a lot of trouble.

"What if this is the work of a blood mage?"

It was Stevan who spoke, in his most freezing tone. Marten flicked a sharp glance his way before turning a gaze of patient interest upon Ruslan. For once, I cheered Stevan on. Marten might want to pussyfoot around our suspicions, but I thought it high time someone took the initiative to poke Ruslan and see how he jumped.

Ruslan laughed again, derisively. "It is not."

"You sound very certain," Marten said. "Has your research produced some information on the killer's methods?"

"My research is not yet completed," Ruslan said. "But I assure you, this was not done with blood magic." His voice was flat.

"Why do you say so?" Marten asked.

Ruslan hesitated for a fraction of an instant before his expression settled into amused condescension. He drew a hand over a bloodstain on the wall, slowly as a man savoring a fine fabric. "For one thing, killing so quickly and crudely displays a lack of both talent and imagination. Slow death provides far greater power, as well as…satisfaction."

I looked to Kiran, hoping to see disgust, dismay, or even fear. Something, anything, that showed he realized what a sick bastard Ruslan was. He was solemnly watching Ruslan, but I saw nothing of the kind in his face. A cold lump weighted my stomach, as I remembered how uncomfortable he'd been when Stevan pushed him on whether or not he'd cast blood magic before leaving Ninavel. I'd always thought Kiran rejected blood magic out of principle, once he understood what casting it really meant. What if that wasn't true? What if he'd been fine with the idea of killing and torturing people, until Ruslan did it to his lover and it hit a little too close to home?

Damn it, he'd looked plenty upset back when Ruslan questioned Torain. Maybe he'd just gotten better at schooling his face, out of sheer necessity. Surely the Kiran I'd gotten to know as we fled through the Whitefires wasn't solely a result of Alisa's death. He had to be the same person, even without his memories. Right? I stared at him harder, wishing a charm existed that could show me his thoughts.

Ruslan was still talking. "If the attacker had raised power properly and cast true blood magic, he would have easily broken through to the spell chamber. Yet he only managed to pierce the outer wards, and was unable to breach the inner defenses. I believe the conclusion is obvious." *Even to you*, his contemptuous look at Stevan said.

"Yet certain wards were affected." Marten eyed the corpses. "Between that and the rather extensive display of wardfire on this district's towers, it must be possible to trace the killer's spellwork."

"The tower wards triggered to safely transmute dangerous confluence energies, not protect against a specific offensive spell," Ruslan said. "Surely you've realized that upheavals in the confluence spill over into the physical realm, and if large enough, cause earthquakes."

"We're aware," Marten said dryly. I grimaced, remembering the roof shuddering beneath my feet as lightning lanced the towers. If these so-called upheavals got much stronger, I had a nasty feeling the quake wards wouldn't be enough to prevent a Cheltman-style catastrophe.

Marten continued. "From the timing, it seems clear the killer is causing these upheavals. Have you any insight yet on how?"

"As I said, my research is not finished," Ruslan said. "I fear sharing half-formed theories would only waste time better spent seeking knowledge to confirm or contradict them."

"I see," Marten said mildly. He turned to the guardsmen at the door. "Did anyone else in Aiyalen witness anything? Surely there were other people present in the tower."

After a nervous glance at Ruslan, one of the guards said, "Several people were present in the antechamber when the attack happened, none of them mages. They've told us they heard screams and tried to enter the room, but couldn't get the door open, and saw nothing."

"I will question them, of course." Ruslan's dismissive tone made it clear he didn't expect much.

"We'd be glad to conduct the questioning for you," Marten said. "That way your valuable time need not be wasted." Remembering Torain's screams, I held my breath.

Ruslan's eyes lit with gloating amusement, and I bit back a curse. "No, Captain," he said. "I insist on handling that myself."

"As you prefer." Marten said it as readily as if they spoke of ordering tea, but his hands locked white behind his back. "May we examine the bodies?"

Ruslan made a dismissive gesture. Marten and the others huddled around the nearest body and started waving ringed hands over it while exchanging muttered, cryptic comments. I eyed Kiran, but he was standing far too close to Ruslan to risk speaking to him.

Something else caught my attention. Black streaks like scorchmarks marred the walls in spots, half obscured by blood. There'd been nothing of the kind in Jadin's workroom. Did it mean these mages had tried to defend themselves? I glanced at the nearest body. His face was a ruined mess of blood and bone, but an amulet in the shape of a rayed sun set with rubies shone untarnished on his chest. The fat silver bracelets on his wrists were likewise intact.

I crossed the room to examine a streak. Definitely a scorch mark. I opened my mouth to call to the Alathians, then hesitated again. From here, I had a view through the archway leading to the inner spell chamber. A short, straight set of steps led to double doors covered in ward lines so thick I could barely glimpse the iron behind them.

The ward lines were gleaming, intact silver. Some of them looked so bright as to be freshly laid. Those must be the ones Ruslan had replaced. But on the lintel of the highest stair, a few scattered bits of metal caught the light.

I eased into the stairwell and gingerly ascended to examine the lintel. The metal bits proved to be fingernail-thin, sharp-edged scraps of silver.

Wards breached by magic didn't show physical damage. But I'd seen ward lines shatter into shards like that many a time in my days as a Tainter. I picked up the closest shard.

"Watch your step, *nathahlen.*"

I turned, hastily sliding the shard into a pocket. Mikail blocked the base of the stair, his gray eyes cold and his arms crossed.

"Changed your mind on helping Kiran, have you?" Not that I believed it. That glare certainly didn't look friendly.

"I will not let you incite him to rebel again." Mikail's near-whisper was as venomous as a sand adder's hiss.

Even as I tensed at the threat, its implications brought a spark of wary hope. "Incite him? For fuck's sake, I've barely spoken five words to him. If he's balking at Ruslan's yoke, it's none of my doing."

Mikail's hands fisted. "If you care at all for Kiran, then *listen,* you fool. If Kiran rebels again, Ruslan will not stay his hand. He would rather have Kiran mindlessly adoring at his side than gone forever from us. This is Kiran's last chance—do not destroy it, and him."

"Oh, I believe you," I assured Mikail. "But don't you get it? Kiran will rebel again regardless. He's not a murderer like you and Ruslan! If he stays, Ruslan will mindburn him. You want him to live, mind intact, then you've got to help him leave." I stopped short of saying, *you've got to help me.* I didn't want to confirm that I planned to get Kiran free. Not unless I thought Mikail truly willing to help.

Mikail's mouth curled in derision. "You think you know him so well after scant weeks in his company? I've spent my life with my mage-brother. He may have acted the weak *nathahlen* for you, but make no mistake, he is *akheli* at the core."

The intensity of his conviction brought my earlier worry flooding back. No, damn it. He was wrong. I refused to believe otherwise.

"Mikail." Kiran appeared in the archway.

In a heartbeat, Mikail's derision vanished, his face once more impassive before he turned. Kiran darted a quick, curious glance at me, and said to Mikail,

"Ruslan's set us a task."

Mikail nodded and strode back into the bloodied room, drawing Kiran with him. I descended the steps in time to see Kiran cast another glance at me over his shoulder. His expression was odd, puzzlement mixed with something I couldn't identify. Had he heard any of my conversation with Mikail? If so, I hoped it would set that curiosity of his afire. It'd sure be easier to get him aside if he was as eager to seek me out as I was to speak to him.

I grinned at him, friendly as I could, as I sauntered out the archway. He looked all the more confused before he and Mikail knelt beside one of the bodies.

Talm intercepted me. "Come. We have to leave."

"Not yet," I protested, in a fierce whisper. "I haven't talked to Kiran, and Marten promised—"

"Ruslan insists." Talm sounded as annoyed as I felt. "He says he and Lizaveta will complete the water magic in place of the dead mages, and no foreigners—or those in their employ—are permitted in the Spire while water magic is cast."

Marten and the others were already filing out into the antechamber under Ruslan's stern gaze. I looked back at Kiran and Mikail, huddled over one of the corpses. A glass vial glinted in Mikail's hand, a silver knife in Kiran's. "They're not doing water magic, I'd wager."

"Ruslan claims he's got some idea for a spell that'll provide information on the killer." Talm shook his head. "Another stalling tactic, I think. Don't worry, we have a few ideas for spellwork of our own."

I fingered the shard in my pocket. Had the killer brought a Tainter to Aiyalen in his attempt to break the wards? I winced at the thought of a kid like Melly forced to watch such gruesome murders. Yet if so, I could ask around for word of a missing Tainter, maybe get another lead to chase. I'd show the shard to Marten, but only after deciding how best to use it as bargaining token. I wanted the killer caught, yeah, but I didn't dare let any chance for advantage pass me by.

As Talm ushered me out the door, I strained for one last glimpse of Kiran. So much for today's chance to speak with him. Suliyya grant I'd get another.

✳

(Kiran)

Kiran bent over the murdered mage. The man's head was black with blood, his braid embedded in a sticky, half-dried puddle. Ruslan had asked him to obtain unstained locks of hair from each body, but finding one from this victim would be a challenge. At least the intensity of Kiran's curiosity over both Mikail and Dev's behavior helped keep his revulsion at bay. Even so, bile soured his throat every time he had to touch blood-matted hair, or look at the raw, empty holes where the man's eyes had been.

On the corpse's other side, Mikail finished scraping a sludge of blood and brain matter into a vial. Kiran cast a furtive glance at the doorway. Ruslan had finished herding the Alathians out and was speaking to the Seranthine scholar in the antechamber. Almost, Kiran wished that he could have found some chance to speak with Dev again unobserved—but then, questioning Mikail over their interaction was far safer.

He leaned closer to Mikail. "Who's the one disobeying Ruslan and talking with *nathahlen* now? What happened to, 'that guide is working for our enemies?'"

Mikail didn't look up from capping the vial. "I wanted to know why the guide was nosing around the spell chamber, that's all."

Kiran sat back on his heels and regarded his mage-brother. The conversation with Dev might have started that way, but Kiran knew that wasn't all the truth. "I heard you," he said quietly. "You said, 'He may have acted the weak *nathahlen* for you, but he is *akheli* at the core'…you were talking of me, weren't you?"

Mikail's hands stilled. "All right, yes. I was talking of you. I warned the guide to keep his distance—that you were *akheli*, and not some fellow *nathahlen* to chat with in a tavern. Do you think I enjoy watching Ruslan punish you? I know you, little brother—you forget yourself too easily. I don't intend to let it happen again."

Forget yourself…that was the trouble, wasn't it? Kiran finally isolated a tuft of dry hair. He sliced the lock of hair free with a jerk of his knife and slid it into a vial of his own. Mikail's answer made sense on the surface, yet something still didn't fit. He'd only heard that last, hissed line from Mikail… but as he'd approached, he'd had a view past Mikail of Dev, crouched on the stairs. Dev hadn't watched Mikail with the fear of a *nathahlen* faced with an angry blood mage. Instead, he'd shown an odd, frustrated urgency. And then his smile at Kiran afterward, as friendly as if he'd never seen Ruslan tear the servant's mind apart…

The thump of the chamber door closing disrupted his thoughts. Ruslan barred the door and strode to stand over Kiran and Mikail.

"Do you have the spell materials as I asked?"

"Yes, Ruslan." Kiran held up four glass vials with unstained hair inside, one from each mage. Mikail showed his own vials of blood and brain matter.

"Good. Blood and body will not be enough for the spell I intend, however." Ruslan surveyed the dead mages, arms crossed. "Proper samples of each mage's power will also be required. You will go to each mage's house and search their workrooms for items imbued with their magic. A recently created charm is preferable to a ward."

"Can't we just use their defensive charms?" Mikail pointed to the ornate bracelet on the outflung wrist of the dead man before them. Just as with Jadin, the silver shone untarnished, the gemstones clear.

Ruslan shook his head. "Any charms within this room must be considered tainted by their proximity not only to the attacker's magic, but to the unleashed magic of the other victims. I need pure samples."

"I don't understand why their charms show no outward damage," Kiran said, frowning. "The dead mage in Vaishala district was caught by surprise, but here, we find magefire burns, the residue of defensive magics—these mages tried to defend themselves. Why didn't it work?"

"Tell me, if I wanted to send a thought into your mind using the mark-bond, would it matter if a stone wall stood between us?" Ruslan asked.

"No," Kiran said, still frowning.

"Would the wall be damaged by the thought's passing?"

"No…" Kiran straightened, as understanding fell into place. "Oh! You mean that the killer's magic somehow operated on a different plane than theirs, the way thoughts are on a different plane than the physical?"

Ruslan smiled at him approvingly. "Exactly. I believe the energetic traces are also on that different plane, which why we cannot sense or focus them properly."

"It's like the Taint," Mikail said abruptly. "We can't sense that either." He gave the barred doors a dark look. Kiran followed his gaze, but saw nothing there to warrant the expression.

"The idea is similar," Ruslan agreed. "The Taint operates purely on the physical plane, allowing the manipulation of simple physical forces. Magic operates on the higher energetic plane, which is why even the most strongly Tainted *nathahlen* is no match for a mage." He smiled again, sharply this time, as if at some private joke.

"So…the killer's magic was on a higher plane than that of the dead mages, the same way normal magic is above the Taint?" Kiran asked.

"Possibly." Ruslan's eyes lit, his expression softening. "Imagine it! If we can access such a plane, the magic of the *akheli* might be enhanced further yet."

Mikail frowned down at the corpse. "If his magic operates on a higher plane, are you saying he is more powerful than us?"

Ruslan laughed. "You need not fear, *akhelysh*. He may work magic in a way new to us, but I have seen no evidence that his raw power can match ours. Remember, he could not breach the wards on the spell chamber, a task well within an *akheli*'s abilities. No, I believe his method is unique, but his talent is mediocre." He traced a finger over the dried blood coating the dead man's brow. "A man of such mediocre talent likely does not realize that it is possible with enough finesse and power to read lingering mental traces instead of energetic residue."

Kiran said, "That's what this spell we're preparing will do? Allow us to know his thoughts during the moments he killed these mages?" The idea was fascinating—thoughts and strong emotions changed *ikilhia*, yes, so Kiran could see how the shifting patterns of a person's life energy might leave traces that could be read. But he couldn't even imagine the complexity of a spell that could successfully isolate and enhance something so minuscule in effect.

Ruslan nodded. Mikail rolled a vial between his fingers. "If we're focusing on the killer's thoughts, why do we need samples from the other mages?"

Ruslan said, "Mental traces are faint, overlapping, and easily confused. But with samples of blood, body, and power from the dead mages, I can form enough of a template for their minds to exclude their traces from consideration, leaving only the thoughts of our quarry."

He rested a hand on Mikail's shoulder. "Go, now, the both of you. Lizaveta is on her way to help me complete the water duty. I want to see you back at home, your task completed, when I return. I am eager to work this *altavish* spell and see what information we can gain about our quarry."

"Yes, Ruslan." Kiran stood along with Mikail. Ruslan gave them a last nod and disappeared through the archway toward the spell chamber.

"We can split up," Kiran suggested to Mikail. "I'll search two of the houses, and you take the other two."

"No." Mikail glanced again at the barred door. "We should stay together. It'll be faster to locate the right kind of charm in a workroom with both of us working as a team."

Kiran smiled at him ruefully. "You mean, you're a lot better at reading charms than I am."

Mikail shrugged. "I didn't say that, did I? Come on, little brother. Let's get this done."

✳

(Dev)

I hurried down the causeway that spiraled through Reytani district's lesser towers. It felt strange to walk alone after Talm dogging my heels for so long. When we left the Aiyalen Spire, Marten had wrangled permission from Edon to hang around in the courtyard outside the gate and cast some kind of spell, something to do with trying to track the killer through ripples in confluence currents. I'd balked when Marten told me the casting should only take a few hours. Hell if I'd sit around on my ass that long when I could be doing something useful, like hunting news of any missing Tainters at the dawn markets.

Marten had been reluctant to let me go, claiming he feared for my safety. Apparently all the Alathians were needed to cast the spell—in fact, Stevan and Talm had argued over whether or not all of them together were enough to pull it off—so Marten couldn't spare one as a watchdog. All the better in my view, though I had to admit I felt a touch jumpy without a mage's protection. I'd escaped Aiyalen's courtyard by promising to return by midmorning and agreeing to wear a signaling charm that I suspected would let Marten track me far more easily than any find-me.

Sunlight spilled in a golden river along the towers, but the causeway was still in shadow. The gated courtyards I passed were full of desert roses whose profusion of pin-sized blooms hadn't yet closed for the day, their sweet scent strong in the air.

A flash of blue caught my eye. I looked sideways into a narrow, gated archway, and stopped dead.

Jylla stood in the shadows, her back to me. She looked every inch the wealthy highsider, her dress made of layers of rich indigo fabric, her midnight black hair caught up in a gold clasp and jewels winking on the straps of her sandals, but I knew it was her. How could I not, when I'd spent long nights memorizing every curve and hollow of the lush body displayed to such advantage by that dress?

A black, bitter wave crashed over me. She'd betrayed me and stolen every kenet I'd earned in four years of mountain trips. If not for her, I never would have taken the smuggling job that had gotten me into this mess. Never crossed any Shaikar-damned blood mages, never gotten barred from outriding and courier work...yet that wasn't what hurt the most. It was the other, older memories that cut so deep I thought my heart might fail in my chest. She'd dragged me out of despair after my Change, comforted me when I'd lain bruised and bloodied in Tavian's cellar, schemed with me and laughed with me and shared her very soul with me…how could all that have been a lie?

Jylla's back was tight with tension, one hand white-knuckled on the gate's iron bars, the other hidden by her body. Even as I watched, the gate cracked open and she slipped through into the courtyard beyond. I glimpsed an amulet in the shape of a rayed sun clutched in one hand, before she moved out of my sightline.

I'd seen that amulet's like before, and recently. Around the neck of a bloodied corpse in Aiyalen. How had Jylla gotten hold of it? And what was she doing, sneaking into some highsider's house instead of lounging around in her lover's garden?

The gate was still open, the wards dark. I fingered the signaling charm on my wrist. I could summon the Alathians. But if I did, I'd interrupt their spellwork. Stevan had warned Marten that the longer they waited to cast, the less chance the spell would have of tracing the killer. I wasn't sure yet that Jylla's amulet truly linked her to the deaths in Aiyalen. Maybe amulets like that were commonplace among highside mages.

Besides, Jylla wasn't a mage. My boneshatter charm would work just fine for protection. And if I ended up confronting her, I'd far rather that conversation didn't take place in front of Marten. The last thing I needed was for him to get yet more insight into how best to fuck me over.

I edged into the archway and peered through the gate. The courtyard beyond was empty of all but flowering karva vines and slender, ghost-pale ashblossom trees. In the far stone wall, a door stood slightly ajar, the wards as dark and silent as the gate's.

I eased through the gate and cat-footed my way up to the door. Listening at the crack, I heard only silence. When I peeked through, I saw only stone walls cluttered with bone masks, knotwork tapestries, and jade sculptures. I slipped around the door, the rune-marked oval of the boneshatter charm gripped tight in my right palm.

"Thought you'd never come in." Jylla stepped from the corner behind the door.

Oh, hell. I lunged for Jylla with the boneshatter charm. She skipped aside.

"Easy, Dev! I just want to talk."

I halted, but kept my right hand raised and ready. "Why the game, then? You could've hailed me in the street."

Her cheekbones and temples were painted with subtle, shimmering colors that made her pointed face look somehow softer, younger. Yet her sloe eyes still held the old, familiar glint of sardonic amusement. "Would you have stopped if I had?"

"Fuck, no," I said. "I'm not staying, either. Not unless you tell me how you got that amulet you were waving around at the gate, and whose house you've lured me into."

"Both amulet and house are mine," she said. "Or rather, Naidar's. My patron."

Patron. Ha. Naidar was a swaggering asshole of a crystal mage who drooled over women of Korassian descent like Jylla. She'd hooked him good, and promptly stolen all my earnings so she could pull off the role of highside courtesan and keep him dancing to her tune.

An image of the mutilated corpse bearing the rayed amulet sprang into my mind's eye. I'd only ever seen Naidar from afar, and the corpse's face was ruined beyond recognition, the hair so matted with blood I wasn't certain of the color. But damn, the height was right.

Best to be sure. "Where's Naidar now?" I asked Jylla.

"Dead in the Aiyalen Spire," Jylla said flatly. "As you well know. I saw you strolling in and out of the Spire with those foreign mages."

"How did you know he's dead? They haven't let anyone else inside the..." My stomach sank. "Oh, shit. You were there? In the tower?"

Jylla nodded. "Naidar and his friends liked to take their lovers with them to the Spire when they took a water magic shift." She gave a little, wry shrug at my incredulous look. "He liked to show off how important he was. Only mages are allowed in the inner spell chamber, but we'd gamble and talk a while in the waiting room, until it was time for their shift and they'd send us out to wait in the antechamber. When the screaming started, Alia went to pieces, but Lisel and Jory tried to get the doors open." She shook her head, looking disgusted. "Suliyya knows what they thought they could do if they did. As for me—well, I'm not stupid."

"You ran," I said, bitterly amused. Of course she had. Jylla's sense of self preservation was even better honed than Red Dal's. "I bet you were down those stairs faster than a red-eared hare."

She shrugged without a trace of regret. "Like I said, I'm not stupid. I'd heard the rumors—and if a mage can't protect himself, well, I sure as hell won't be able to help. I waited 'til the wardfire vanished, then found a spot to hide in the outer courtyard. I saw Sechaveh's mages and the guardsmen come running, and heard them talking, after. That's how I knew Naidar and his friends were dead."

Her hands had locked tight around the sun amulet she still carried, though I saw no hint of grief in her eyes. She said, "I also saw the blood mage come, and tell the guards he wanted to question any witnesses."

"Yeah, and by questioning them, Ruslan means mindburning them while they shriek their lungs out." I had a moment of black satisfaction when she flinched.

Her painted eyes widened, imploring. "I feared as much. Then I saw you, talking with those mages like a born highsider. I knew you could help me."

"*Help* you?" I spat at her feet. "Fuck, Jylla. After what you did, I ought to hand you straight to Ruslan and laugh. Why in Shaikar's hells would I help?"

"Because I've got information related to Naidar's death," Jylla said. "You're working for those foreigners, right? Don't you want to get a jump on them, learn something you can use to bargain? Trust me, Dev, ordinary folk like us need every advantage we can get when playing games with mages."

A dark voice within urged, *Give her to Ruslan. Let him mindburn her, make her pay.* I got a vivid image of Jylla, slumped and drooling blood like Torain—and winced, feeling sick. The gods knew I'd wanted her to suffer for her betrayal of me, but that...no. For all my harsh words to her, I wasn't so vicious. Marten, I'd gladly watch die screaming, but Jylla...if she'd known about Melly when she took my earnings, then maybe. But I'd never told her, too intent on keeping the silence I'd promised Sethan.

Besides, she was right. I needed more to offer Marten. "Fine. You give me something worthwhile, I'll see you don't get mindburned."

Jylla glanced down the corridor. "The servants will be back from the dawn markets soon, and I'd rather talk where they can't overhear. My room's warded, and I've got a quiet-shroud charm there, strong enough no one can listen in."

I hesitated. She might still mean to set me up somehow, but I could understand wanting to keep this private. At the first sign of any trouble, I'd use my boneshatter charm on her and run. Warily, I followed her.

The inner rooms were almost a parody of my expectations of a highsider. Ornamentation everywhere, the walls covered in jewels and carvings, expensive cinnabar wood furniture from Alathia crowding every room. Jylla halted in front of an arched wooden door carved with elaborate geometric patterns. I winced as I eyed the garishly painted statues of leaping pronghorns framing the doorway. Samis probably would've pronounced them the height of art.

"Let me guess, Naidar wasn't born a highsider," I said to Jylla.

She pressed the rayed amulet against the tangle of ward lines circling the door handle. The ward flashed blue.

"Of course not." Jylla pushed the door open. "None of the mages in Ninavel were born here."

I paused in the doorway, surprised. "Mages can't have kids, yeah, but some of them must get born here, right? To ordinary parents?" Everyone knew spellcasting made mages sterile, but I'd never heard Jylla's claim before.

"I heard Naidar and one of his mage friends talking once about how all Ninavel mages are immigrants. Kids birthed here are never mageborn, only Tainted. Naidar said there's some big natural reservoir of magic here, so powerful it burns out the minds of untrained mages—he thinks exposure to so much wild magic kills any potentially mageborn babies in the womb. He said that even older mageborn kids brought here from elsewhere can't survive without special protective bindings until they're past puberty."

"Huh." I'd known Kiran hadn't been born in Ninavel, since he'd told me he'd never had even a hint of the Taint. I hadn't realized that applied to every mage in the city.

Jylla's room was huge by streetside standards, but relatively plainly decorated compared to the eye-searing circus outside. Silk drapes in soft shades of rose and lavender hid the stone of the walls and formed a canopy over the enormous bed. I sucked in a breath as I recognized the collection of little animals cut from quartz, amethyst, and malachite sitting on the inset stone shelf at the head of the bed. I'd given her most of those either as Naming day gifts or to celebrate our reunions after my mountain trips.

She probably kept them as a trophy of how skillfully she'd manipulated me. Or maybe I'd meant so little to her she'd never even thought to ditch them. My fists clenched, but I held my tongue. She was as clever as Marten; she'd seize any opening I gave her.

Jylla shut the door, reactivated the wards, and rooted around in a carved wooden chest beside the bed. After a moment, she made a small, pleased noise and stood up, dangling a jewel-studded silver amulet on a delicate chain from one finger. "Quiet-shroud charm," she said, and slipped it on over her head, careful not to snag the chain on her hairclasp.

She approached to stand mere inches away. I backed, but she held up a warning hand. "It's a powerful charm, but we need to stand close for it to cover you as well as me."

I gritted my teeth and stared over her head as she slinked up to me again. "You seriously think we need a shroud charm? I saw those wards on the door." Naidar might have been a gullible, insecure show-off, but he knew how to make wards. Even in my Tainted days, I would've had a hard time slipping past wards that strong.

"If anything, I'm not being cautious enough. Naidar's magic didn't save him in the Aiyalen Spire, and I've heard the rumors. Mages dying, Tainters vanishing…"

Startled, I looked her full in the face. "What do you know about missing Tainters?"

She shrugged. "A streetside friend came to me last week wanting names of mages who might be willing to make highside-strength protective wards sized small enough to be worn by kids. I was curious, so I did some asking around. The handlers have been keeping it quiet, but a bunch of Tainters have disappeared recently while they're out on jobs, enough so handlers are demanding their ganglords do something about it."

Melly. My gut twisted with new worry. I'd thought the killer might've snatched one kid to test Aiyalen's wards, but I hadn't imagined anything near so widespread. Why would he want so many?

"I assume you mean the kids aren't just failing against wards." One mistake Tainting a powerful ward meant death for a Taint thief. Any bodies found by the wards' owners were usually dumped along with the rest of the house's garbage. The muckboys who carted highside trash off to be burned in magefire kilns were happy to earn extra coin by showing handlers the corpses.

Jylla nodded. "No bodies, no activated wards…the kids go into a mark's house and never come back."

"How many have disappeared, and in which districts?" My feet itched to run go check Red Dal's den right now, make sure Melly wasn't among the missing. But if Melly hadn't returned to the den after last night's job, Cara would've heard about it from Liana by now, and signaled me. The twin-seek charm on my bicep remained cold and inert, just as it had been all morning.

Jylla shrugged again. "I don't know exactly how many. I heard the handlers in Julisi are complaining the loudest, but it's happened in Gitailan and Baroi districts as well."

Julisi district again. Thank Suliyya she hadn't said Acaltar, but my worry didn't lessen.

Jylla said, "My point is, whoever's out there is grabbing kids and murdering mages like their defensive charms are as useless as devil-wards. I'd say that justifies a healthy dose of caution."

"Yeah," I muttered. Disturbing as this was, apparently it wasn't even Jylla's real bit of news. "All right, Jylla. I came here like you wanted. What do you know related to Naidar's death?"

She took a deep breath, and let it out, slowly. If I looked down, I'd have a great view of the honey-smooth swell of her breasts, held high and tight by that damn dress. Resolutely, I kept my eyes on her face and tried not to think of all the countless times we'd talked like this, planning out a job—and what had come after, when the talking was done.

Jylla said, "Over the last two days, someone was watching this house, and even shadowing Naidar. I don't think it's a coincidence that now Naidar is dead."

"He didn't notice someone stalking him? He was a mage, for Khalmet's sake!"

She gave a small snort. "He was a mage, sure, but he was blind to his surroundings like any ordinary highsider. More so, maybe, because he didn't think harm could touch him. When the wardfire started, he scoffed at the rumors. He said the mages who died were just too weak or dumb to protect themselves properly."

Yeah, that sounded like the arrogant asshole I remembered. His arrogance wasn't all hot air. We'd all heard the tales streetside of the ugly deaths suffered by those who crossed mages. A shadow man would have to be either desperate or cocky as hell to take a job scouting a mage. Unless…

"Was Naidar's shadow a mage, too?"

Jylla shook her head. "No sigils on his clothes, but more than that, he didn't move like a mage. Not even a hint of arrogance. I'm pretty sure he was streetside. Oh, he blended in highside well enough, dressed the part and all…but he had quick eyes."

"Yeah, and maybe he had nothing to do with Naidar's death," I said skeptically.

Jylla's mouth quirked. "Because mages get shadowed every day in Ninavel. Besides, I'm betting your mage friends could use a lead."

True. If Marten's spell didn't work, the Alathians would be desperate for something to go on. "What did he look like?"

Jylla's eyes took on a cunning gleam. "Ah, now that's a good question. Tell me, Dev, what would your mage friends give in return for that information?"

I'd been waiting all along for something like this. Jylla never gave anything away for free. "Protection from Ruslan isn't enough for you? Blood mages don't need to barter, Jylla, they just take. Ruslan will rip the shadow man's image straight out of your head."

She changed tactics without even blinking. "What about you? What would you give?"

"Fuck if I'll give you a single kenet after all you stole from me." Pain surged, sudden and vicious, sending words pouring from me like blood from a wound. "Besides, nobody can give you what you really want. Not me, not even whatever Khalmet-touched fool of a mage you get your claws into next."

"You think so? Then tell me, what do I really want?" Jylla's smile was kitfox-sharp.

I bared my teeth in a knowing grin. "Nothing ever replaces the Taint, does it? You think it matters that you're highside now, acting the jenny-slave to a bunch of puffed up mages? You're still a cripple with that fucking hole inside where the Taint used to be, dead as the southern blight. How does it feel, watching them cast magic when you'll never taste it again?"

Her smile vanished as if I'd slapped her. For an instant her eyes went wide and unguarded, the pain in them an echo of my own.

"We know each other too well, don't we, Dev?" Her voice was lightly mocking, but I recognized the bitter undertone and knew the mockery wasn't all directed at me. She slid closer until her lithe body pressed right up against mine. I didn't back away. She was trying to get control of the conversation again, and I didn't mean to let her.

"Tell you what, Tainter," she said. "I'll describe that shadow man for you, down to the length of his eyelashes—in exchange for one, simple thing."

"Yeah? And what is this 'one, simple thing?'" I sneered.

"Something I've missed this summer," she said, the bitter undertone still in her voice. Quick as an adder's strike, she wound her hands in my hair and tugged my mouth down to hers.

She wanted to unsettle me? I'd show her it wasn't so easy. I returned her kiss. Deepened it into something hard and hungry, and skimmed my fingers along the exposed skin of her back where her dress dipped low.

She made a small, low sound that jolted straight to my groin. Her hands slid down over my arms to slip beneath my shirt. I caught her wrists, pulled them behind her back—damn it, I wasn't such a fool as to let her search me. She gasped and rocked her hips against mine, her tongue doing truly wicked things in my mouth, and I found myself backing her toward the bed. I should shove her away, laugh in her face, but it had been so long, her body still a perfect fit against mine, and I knew just where a touch would make her shiver...

The creak of the door opening broke through the haze in my head. I leaped away from Jylla, one hand snatching for the boneshatter charm in my belt. She'd set me up after all, Shaikar take her, and I'd fallen right into her honey-trap—

I checked so hard I nearly fell flat on my face. The intruder wasn't some streetside thug or sneering highsider. It was Kiran.

CHAPTER FOURTEEN

(Kiran)

"What are you doing here?" Kiran blurted, one hand still raised and his mind entangled with the energies of the door wards he'd just broken.

Dev's mouth opened, but nothing came out. He cleared his throat. "Marten—Captain Martennan, I mean—asked me to interview Naidar's associates."

Kiran damped out the last of the ward energies and focused more closely on Dev and his companion. Amusement displaced confusion as he registered the flush on the woman's cheeks and the abnormally rapid flicker of both her and Dev's *ikilhia*. Clearly Dev's method of questioning was far kinder than Ruslan's. "She's one of his...associates, I take it?"

A courtesan, more specifically, if the enormous bed and the elegant artifice of the woman's appearance were any guide. Kiran had read in books that some lesser mages took *nathahlen* as lovers. Ruslan viewed the practice with utter contempt. Kiran had to admit he didn't see how a mere physical encounter could compare to the depth of union he'd experienced with Ruslan and Lizaveta.

"Associate, yeah. Unfortunately, she doesn't know anything." Dev peered warily at the open door behind Kiran. "Is Ruslan here too?"

He must hope to avoid subjecting the courtesan to Ruslan's version of interrogation. Kiran couldn't blame him.

"No," Kiran said. "He sent me and Mikail to...examine the dead mages' workrooms." If Dev asked for specifics beyond that, he would refuse to give them. Kiran knew Ruslan's dismissal of the Alathians before explaining the spell he hoped to cast was no coincidence. Kiran already risked Ruslan's anger in speaking to Dev again—but so far, he thought the conversation easily defensible. Ruslan would want to know what a representative of the Alathians sought in the murdered mage's house, after all.

"This isn't the workroom," Dev said, with a lift of a brow.

"Mikail's there already," Kiran said. "I sensed the active wards here, so I came to check…" He trailed off, not wanting to reveal he'd been looking for newly-made charms. He'd thought perhaps the wards protected a secondary workroom. Some mages preferred to keep a separate area devoted solely to charm creation.

Instead, he now had an excellent opportunity to speak to Dev unobserved by either Mikail or Ruslan. He badly wanted to discover the truth behind the oddity of Dev's reactions to him and Mikail. Yet fear of Ruslan's wrath and the presence of the *nathahlen* courtesan combined to leave him tongue-tied, unable to think of a properly innocuous question that would coax Dev into revealing what Kiran wanted to know.

He settled for a foray on a lesser matter. "How do you know her?" he asked Dev, indicating the courtesan. Even aside from what Kiran's entry had obviously interrupted, Dev's repeated glances at her, and the way he'd edged in front of her, as if to block Kiran's view, had Kiran convinced she was more than some newly-met witness. He wanted to know what tie a lower-city man could have to a wealthy mage's courtesan—and if Dev lied and claimed they'd only just met, that would be instructive, too.

"We used to work for the same man. A long time ago." Dev said it casually enough, but this time his glance at the courtesan was dark. The courtesan kept her eyes downcast, as she had ever since her first sight of the sigils on Kiran's clothes, and stayed silent.

If Dev spoke the truth about a shared employer, it couldn't be that long ago. Both Dev and the courtesan looked to be close in age to Mikail, only a few years older than Kiran. But if Dev had once worked for someone in the upper city, another mage perhaps…that might explain some of his unusual ease around mages.

Before Kiran could press for more details, Dev went on. "If you're looking for something here in the house, maybe I can help."

Kiran hesitated, torn once more between curiosity and worry. He couldn't risk revealing what he and Mikail sought here. But how could he squander the chance to question Dev further?

"Have you learned anything of interest?" If Dev had even a hint of relevant information, Ruslan couldn't fault Kiran for continuing the conversation.

"Actually, yeah. I've something to share. Why don't you and I head toward that workroom?" Dev gave Kiran a pointed look, tilting his head toward the courtesan. She raised her eyes to give Dev a sharp, quizzical glance.

Kiran's curiosity burned hotter yet. "Very well," he said coolly, as if he weren't equally eager to speak in private. He turned to the door, and heard Dev mutter something swift and fierce to the courtesan. He wondered with a flash of dark amusement if Dev's motive in wanting a private conversation was simply to get Kiran away from her. A sudden, irrational urge to assure Dev he wouldn't hurt the woman swept him. Kiran shook it off, as Ruslan spoke sternly in his memory: *A mage cannot afford to show weakness, especially in front of* nathahlen.

Once out in the hallway, he waited as Dev shut the bedroom door. The hinges creaked, and at the far end of the hall, an older woman in the dress of a house servant peeked around the corner of the kitchen archway. Her face paled at the sight of Kiran's sigils, and she hurriedly ducked back within.

"What have you learned?" Kiran asked Dev.

Dev didn't speak, only jerked his head in the direction of the hallway. Bemused, Kiran followed him as he strode past the kitchen. It wasn't until they rounded a corner that Dev stopped. He glanced around, as if checking for witnesses.

"I want to show you something." He unfolded a piece of parchment and handed it to Kiran.

Surprise stopped Kiran's breath. The parchment held the inked lines of a channel diagram, and one for an incredibly complex spell at that. "This... where did you get this?"

"It's a spell diagram, right? For what you call a channeled spell?"

Kiran couldn't take his eyes from the diagram. He didn't know the pattern, and yet something about it nagged at him. "In a way. It's for a charm," he said absently. He leaned forward to study the diagram more closely. The inward-spiraling channels would focus the magic back upon the wearer, but not in the manner of a protective charm...He frowned, as the lines he followed ended abruptly.

"It's unfinished," he said, startled into looking up at Dev.

"Yeah, I figured," Dev said. "What does it do?" He sounded frustrated. Kiran could appreciate the feeling. Mikail could probably divine the charm's purpose from a brief look at the diagram, unfinished or not. Whereas Kiran always had to work through the entire pattern, and read all the notations. Thinking of that, he focused on the symbols inked beside the charm's outermost pattern layer.

Shock rippled through him. "Where did you get this?" Kiran demanded, harshly enough that Dev backed a pace.

"Someone gave it to me. Look, my name's on it, in the same ink." Dev turned the parchment over. Sure enough, his name was written in small letters below one of the creases. Kiran rubbed at his eyes in disbelief.

"What is it? What do you see?" Dev asked.

"This—it's mine." Kiran reached for the diagram, but Dev pulled it away, his hands tightening on the parchment.

"How do you know?" Despite his white-knuckled grip on the diagram, Dev didn't sound defensive, or disbelieving. Instead, he almost sounded eager.

Kiran didn't need to look at the shorthand symbols denoting the channel layerings again; they were burned into his mind's eye. Especially the third symbol, the *zalephka*, with its hook drawn slanted instead of properly curved. How many times had Mikail teased him for drawing it that way? And Dev's name…that was in his handwriting as well. The memory of Dev facing Mikail in the Aiyalen Spire leaped into his mind, accompanied by sudden conviction.

Sometime, somewhere, he and Dev had met before, the details gone in the void of his lost memories. And something related to that meeting had inspired Mikail's unusual display of anger—anger directed not at *nathahlen* in general as Kiran had assumed, but at Dev in specific.

"Dev, was I the one who—" Deep unease rolled over Kiran, harsh whispers clawing at his inner senses. He hurriedly reinforced his barriers, only to stagger back with a cry as the confluence exploded, wild energy crashing all around him.

"Kiran! What the hell?" Dev reached for him, green eyes gone wide.

Under the wild roar of the confluence battering against Kiran, a sharp flare of energy collapsed in on itself, turning into a voraciously strong current that tugged at him even through his barriers. Horror froze Kiran's blood. Ruslan had told him, *Once you are* akheli *in truth, you need never fear physical violence. Should you suffer a mortal wound, your body will reach instinctively for the* ikilhia *needed to heal.*

"Mikail!" Kiran's voice cracked with the force of his shout. Almost, he dropped his barriers, despite the danger posed by the roiling confluence energy. Beside him, Dev gasped and fell to his knees. The dim pulse of his *ikilhia* guttered as the current of Mikail's need pulled at it. New horror lanced through Kiran.

Dev had no barriers, no protection—that sucking, hungry current would rip his life away. Mikail must be unconscious, the power draw wholly without volition, bypassing Ruslan's will-binding. Kiran couldn't cast to harm Dev, but perhaps he could cast to save him.

He snatched at Dev's wrist. Between one heartbeat and the next, he cast a protective binding fueled by his own *ikilhia*, weaving a barrier tight around Dev.

Stymied, the current swirled around Dev and flowed onward, still seeking. Kiran felt the shock when Mikail connected with another source of *ikilhia*. Raw power surged past him in a flood.

Kiran released Dev's arm and ran. Dev would be safe enough now, but Mikail needed help. He skidded around a corner and pounded up the stairs leading to the workroom, digging frantically in his pocket. With the confluence so wild, he didn't dare drop his barriers to call power. But he and Mikail both carried *vidya* charms, meant to reinforce their defenses. The power stored within could be safely drawn by touch and used to fuel magic.

The copper workroom doors were shut, their wards silent and still. Kiran didn't slow. He threw out his free hand, releasing a swift, pure pulse of power. The doors slammed open.

Mikail lay crumpled against a stone wall beneath shelves glittering with charms, his clothing sodden with blood. A dark figure bent over him.

Kiran yanked power from the *vidya* charm and struck. A tornado of azure fire lanced at his enemy. A brilliant flash seared the room white, the shock of energies sending Kiran staggering to one side. A howl of pain and rage echoed throughout the room. Fierce triumph filled Kiran as he raised his hands to strike again.

A blow drove the breath from his body, throwing him hard against the wall.

Kiran! Ruslan's silent shout filled his mind, his master's presence suddenly with him as strongly as if he knelt at Kiran's side. *Strike again!* Through the mark-bond, power flooded into Kiran, humming and sparking in his blood. Kiran's vision doubled, the room wavering in his sight, but he sent the borrowed power blazing in a firestorm at the dark figure advancing toward him.

The dark shape shimmered and disappeared just before the magefire hit. The subsequent explosion shook the room and blinded Kiran once more. He gasped for air, feeling as if a giant sat astride his chest. When his vision cleared, only a charred jumble of rubble remained where the table and far wall of the workroom had been. The dark figure was nowhere to be seen. The seething roil of the confluence ebbed.

Mikail lay still and silent in a pool of blood. Kiran pushed himself upright, desperate to reach his mage-brother. Pain seared his torso, and he sank back with a strangled cry. He reached a shaking hand to his side.

Blood soaked his shirt and pattered to the floor from deep slashes in his stomach and side. Underneath the stabbing physical pain, a different ache gnawed at his senses, a throbbing pulse of wrongness yearning for power and held in check only by his defensive barriers.

Kiran reached for power again, but the *vidya* charm was dark and empty, its magic drained. Pain swamped his concentration, his barriers growing ever more difficult to hold. If he released them, his body would draw power instinctively as Mikail had—but from living things. People.

One *nathahlen*—perhaps more—had died already for Mikail's sake. Kiran shut his eyes, nauseated, thinking of the blood leaking from Torain's mouth, Dev's choked gasp when he'd fallen. He couldn't steal a man's life, not deliberately, couldn't kill some innocent servant whose only fault was to be in the wrong place at the wrong time.

He could seek power in the charms on the workroom's shelves. But many were melted and misshapen, their magic burned out by proximity to his magefire strike. When he strained his senses, he felt only faint flickers of magic in those that remained intact. Not enough, not nearly enough to stave off his body's insistent cry for power.

The unsettled, sullen throb of the confluence caught his attention. The only way to safely tap confluence energies was with a channeled spell, or so Ruslan had always said. Yet an attempt to use confluence power directly had to be better than killing blindly. He focused on the confluence, readying himself to try.

No, Kiran. I forbid this. Ruslan's will pressed down on Kiran through the link, building an impenetrable wall between Kiran and confluence.

Ruslan, please! Kiran knew Ruslan felt his desperation, but the wall remained.

"Kiran!"

Kiran opened his eyes. Dev squatted beside him, his green eyes full of concern.

"Fuck, that looks bad." Dev reached for Kiran's stomach, then snatched his hand back, clenching it into a fist. "I know, I shouldn't touch you."

"You're safe," Kiran said, the act of speech sending new agony stabbing through his gut. A faint glimmer of power still shielded Dev's *ikilhia*. The binding he'd worked should hold for a few hours yet. Questions welled up through the red weight of pain. How Dev had known the danger in touching him while Kiran was injured? Did the Alathians understand blood mages so well? Or was it another clue about the past?

Dev's eyes narrowed, holding his. "You did something to me, back in the hallway. I felt it." He rubbed at his wrist.

Kiran gave him a tiny nod, trying not to jar his side.

"Two of the women in the kitchen are dead, though. The others were screaming…" Dev's jaw clenched. He eyed Mikail's slumped form. "Was that because of him? Did he kill them?"

"Not…on purpose," Kiran said softly. "Instinct. Unconscious." He stopped; talking hurt so much.

Dev's face darkened further. "I'd have been the one dead, if not for you, huh? 'I vow never to *knowingly* cast'…should've known there was a fucking boulder-sized loophole in that." He shook his head. "Your wounds—we've got to halt the bleeding. Here—" he shucked off his shirt. "Press this against your side."

Kiran obeyed, with cold, fumbling hands. Dev glanced up at the mangled charms on the workroom's remaining shelves.

"There's gotta be something here we can use as a bloodfreeze—"

"Mother of maidens protect us!" The black-haired courtesan appeared in the doorway, her black eyes wide as she surveyed the destruction in the workroom.

Dev jerked as if touched by magefire. He jumped to his feet and spat, "Jylla, what the fuck are you doing? I told you to get out of here!"

She approached, her gamine features set in stubborn lines. "I heard Callie screaming, and found Jesa and Loris dead. I came to see if you were all right." She eyed Kiran with cool interest, showing no sign of being upset by his gaping wounds. "A mage survived an attack? That's new, isn't it?"

Kiran gathered himself to speak, fighting the pain. He had to tell Dev to make his friend leave. She had no binding to protect her. When his barriers failed, as they would all too soon from pain and blood loss, if she were the closest source she would meet the same fate as the kitchen servants.

The pounding thump of footsteps broke his concentration. Ruslan burst into the room at a near run, his face grim. Kiran swallowed his words, his heart thudding painfully in his chest. Too late now for a warning.

※

(Dev)

When Ruslan charged into the room, I swear I felt the touch of Khalmet's bony hand on my shoulder. What the fuck had possessed Jylla to poke her nose in here instead of running like she had from the Aiyalen Spire? And how had Ruslan beaten the Alathians here? I'd signaled them before I even reached the workroom—where were they? I stared at Jylla, wishing I could make her disappear by force of will alone. She'd frozen in place like a hopmouse in the shadow of a desert hawk.

Ruslan took in the half-destroyed workroom in one quick glance. "Mikail," he said, the name a command.

Across the room, Mikail stirred. He pushed himself up to his hands and knees, his head hanging low.

At my feet, Kiran let out a shaky breath. Relief softened the strain etched in his face. Personally, I was pretty fucking disappointed that Mikail had survived. Especially given the means he'd used to do it.

"I'm all right," Mikail croaked. He staggered to his feet. Blood dripped from his sodden shirt, but the skin I glimpsed beneath was unmarked. He shook his head, as if to clear it. "Where's the mage who attacked me? I couldn't—" His gray eyes went wide as he caught sight of Kiran crumpled on the floor. "Kiran! Is he—"

"Do not concern yourself," Ruslan said. "Our enemy escaped, though not unscathed, I suspect. As for your mage-brother…" He bent over Kiran, his expression growing stern.

"Kiran, why have you not obeyed me?" He sounded sorrowful rather than angry, but Kiran's hands whitened on the bloodsoaked wad of my shirt. His blue eyes flicked between me and Jylla. The desperation in them chilled my spine. I took a slow step toward Jylla and willed her to look at me instead of the blood mages.

"Ruslan, please," Kiran said, in a choked whisper. "Give me a *zhivnoi* crystal, I need…" He coughed, blood showing on his teeth.

Jylla finally looked my way. Low down at my side, I twisted a hand in one of our old signals, the one we'd used to abort a job if the risk was greater than we'd thought. Her mouth tightened, and she darted a glance at Ruslan. Thank Khalmet, his whole attention was focused on Kiran. She eased backward toward the door, and I prayed to all the gods that he wouldn't notice.

"I see no reason to waste a *zhivnoi* crystal." Ruslan folded his arms. "All you need is within your reach, Kiran."

Shit. He meant me and Jylla. I stood closest. But Kiran had said I was safe. I remembered the needling rush that had raced over my skin when he grabbed my wrist in the hallway, the abrupt end to the horrible, draining weakness that had assaulted me. Whatever he'd done to protect me from Mikail might save me again—but it wouldn't help Jylla. *Move faster*, I willed her. She was still ten paces from the door.

Mikail shuffled along the wall to block her path. He looked straight at me

with a little, malicious smile, and his eyes said, *I don't think so.* I suppressed
a snarl of fury, wishing that the killer had ripped him to screaming shreds.

All at once, Mikail's broad face lost its smile. He said reluctantly to Ruslan,
"Your promise to Lord Sechaveh…"

Ruslan pointed one long finger at me without taking his eyes from Kiran.
"He's protected," he said, his voice edged with irritation.

Surprise flashed in Mikail's eyes. He scowled past me at Kiran.

"I did it to keep your promise," Kiran said to Ruslan, still in that raw-throated
whisper. He sounded earnest, but his eyes fell away from Ruslan's as he spoke.

Ruslan surely guessed that wasn't all of the truth. But he only said
smoothly, "You see, you need not fear. Drop your barriers, Kiran, and all
will be well."

Kiran swallowed, hard. His blue eyes were dark with pain, the pupils
huge, and he looked at Jylla the way a man stranded in the desert might
look at the snowcapped summits of the Whitefires.

Oh, fuck. Kiran had told me once that not taking life to heal an injury
was like deliberately holding your breath: impossible to do forever. If I told
Ruslan Jylla knew something important to the investigation, that might
save her—for the five minutes it'd take him to tear her mind apart and leave
her as good as a corpse. For all the pain she'd caused me, every fiber of me
rebelled at the thought of those clever black eyes gone blank and dead.

I was lucky she wasn't dead already—from what I knew of the mark-bond,
Ruslan could easily force Kiran into killing Jylla. Instead, he stood watching
Kiran with cold, unflagging patience.

Yet Ruslan's stance didn't match the patience on his face. His body held
the eager, checked energy of a man anticipating some long-awaited event.

My throat locked. Shaikar take the soulless viper, he wanted Kiran to
choose to kill someone.

"Drop your barriers," Ruslan said to Kiran, his voice gone dangerously
soft. Kiran shut his eyes and didn't answer, sweat standing out on his brow.

Where was Marten, curse him? I pointed at Jylla and said, fast and urgent,
"Captain Martennan asked me to bring this woman to him. He needs her
for some spell he's going to cast, important to the investigation—Sechaveh
won't be happy if you mess that up." After what'd happened to Mikail and
Kiran, I no longer believed Ruslan responsible for the attacks. He must
want the bastard caught, if only so he could take revenge for the assault on
his apprentices.

Ruslan ignored me as completely as if I'd never spoken. He knelt at
Kiran's side, unheeding of the blood, and tugged my shirt from Kiran's grip

to reveal his wounds. One hand settled over the worst gash, the one running from Kiran's stomach all the way across his side. Ruslan pressed down in one swift, vicious movement. Kiran jerked and keened, his already pale face going the color of dirty chalk.

"Don't pretend you didn't hear, you bastard," I snarled at Ruslan. "If she dies, Sechaveh will make you regret it—"

"Drop your barriers," Ruslan said again, and stroked Kiran's sweat-dampened hair off his forehead with his free hand, the motion horribly gentle. He dug his fingers into Kiran's wound and clenched them until his knuckles showed pale. Kiran screamed, his eyes rolling up to the whites.

Desperate, I faced Mikail. He couldn't cast against me—if I could shove him clear of the door and distract him long enough, maybe Jylla could get past. She might not understand exactly what was happening, but from the fear in her eyes, she'd have the sense to run if she got the chance. I tried not to think about how if she did get away, someone else would die in her place, the way the kitchen woman had died instead of me.

"What's going on here?"

I'd never been so happy to see an Alathian uniform, or hear the icy disdain coloring Stevan's voice. He pushed his way past Mikail into the room, followed by Lena. About fucking time! I raced to Lena's side.

"You've got to save her!" I hissed in her ear, pointing at Jylla. "Ruslan will make Kiran kill her, and she knows something we need—I told him Marten needs her for a spell, but he won't listen to me. You're a mage—*make* him listen!"

Lena looked from Jylla to Kiran, lying curled in a spreading pool of blood with his eyes squeezed shut and his breath coming in ragged pants. She gripped Stevan's arm and said something in a curt, commanding whisper.

Stevan's shoulders went rigid. He nodded, one tight jerk of his chin, and opened the belt pouch at his waist. Lena put her hands on Jylla's shoulders and whispered in her ear.

Ruslan rose to his feet, simmering anger visible in every line of his body. "This is none of your affair, Alathian. Do not think to interfere."

"I have no intention of interfering with your investigation," Lena said quietly. "But we have need of this woman, and your apprentice needs healing. As compensation, we offer a source of power for his use."

Stevan pulled out the twisted-metal amulet Marten had used to block Kiran's mark-bond. Ruslan checked, his anger altering to intent appraisal.

Stevan's lips moved in a barely audible song, and the amulet's metal strands glowed softly white.

Kiran made a startled noise, his eyes flying open. Stunned relief spread over his face as he stared at the amulet. Ruslan glanced down at him, with a sudden, ironic smile.

"Go ahead, *akhelysh.* But we will speak of this later." His voice was soft and level, but the banked-coal look to his eyes made me wince on Kiran's behalf.

Kiran sighed, his eyes fluttering shut, and slumped in a boneless heap. The amulet in Stevan's hand flared up bright enough to make my eyes water. The bloody gashes in Kiran's torso knit together to leave clean, whole skin in their place.

The light from the amulet went out like a snuffed candle. Instead of a graceful series of interlaced twists, the amulet's shape was now melted and misshapen. Stevan looked nearly as furious as Ruslan had moments before. He clenched his hand into a fist around the destroyed amulet.

Kiran lay in a limp huddle, eyes still shut. Ruslan bent and put a hand to his forehead. Once again I glimpsed the strange, terrible tenderness he'd shown in Simon's cave.

"Kiran will recover?" Lena asked.

Ruslan slid his arms under Kiran's knees and shoulders and lifted him as easily as if Kiran were a child. His face when he turned to the Alathians displayed only his usual mocking contempt.

"Of course he will." He glanced at Stevan's clenched fist. "What a pity you had to waste such a valuable item."

Stevan's gray eyes might have been chips of granite. "A shame," he said, enunciating each word with cold precision. "I trust you intend to share with us your knowledge of what happened here?"

"I prefer to wait until I may speak to your captain directly," Ruslan said, all benign condescension. "Tell him he may call upon me this evening. I must first attend to my apprentices to ensure their full recovery, and then return to the Aiyalen Spire."

"You didn't complete the water magic," Lena said.

Ruslan glanced at the pile of blackened rubble. "The power we raised was needed elsewhere." His gaze slid to the bloodstained stones at his feet. He drew in a deep breath, and all the blood in the room sizzled and burned away in a flare of red light. Including that on my shirt, leaving it a ruined mess of cloth scraps.

"I'll be most interested to hear if you learn anything useful from the woman," Ruslan said to Lena. "Let me know the moment you finish with her."

Jylla tensed under Lena's hands. Ruslan smiled, predatory and cruel. For the first time, he looked straight at me. The depth of burning malice in his gaze sent me stumbling backward before I could stop myself. My mind knew he couldn't cast against me, but my body had other ideas, every instinct shrieking in panic.

He didn't speak; he didn't need to. The message was clear enough: *vow or no, I'll make you pay.* He knew Kiran hadn't saved my life merely to keep his vow; looked like I'd just gotten promoted from inconsequential tool to enemy worthy of revenge.

I didn't try to hide my fear. Let him think me cowed. Fear had never kept me from a goal before, and it wouldn't this time, either. I stared at the stone beneath my feet and promised silently, *I'll beat you. When you burn, I'll be the one laughing.* Yet even in my head the words sounded hollow.

Ruslan and Mikail strode out, with Kiran still cradled limp in Ruslan's arms.

I released a huge, pent-up breath. My muscles felt as shaky as if I'd just climbed the Kanyalin Spire. "Where were you?" I demanded of Lena. "I signaled you when the killer first showed up—if you were in Aiyalen's courtyard and Ruslan at the summit, how the hell did he get here first?"

She looked apologetic. "We didn't stay in Aiyalen's courtyard. The aether around the tower was terribly muddied, and Talm suggested we might have better success casting instead from a location where the confluence currents were not so wild. We left the courtyard to seek such a spot—and then came the confluence upheaval, followed by your signal. We saw more wardfire on Aiyalen and feared the killer might have returned there. Marten and Talm went to investigate, while Stevan and I sought you."

"Thank Khalmet you came when you did." I'd thought Jylla was dead for sure. And gods all damn the killer for showing up when he did! Kiran had been about to ask me if we'd met before, I knew it. He'd been ready to hear at least some of the truth, maybe even be coaxed into working more directly with me. But now, after he'd betrayed his interest in me to Ruslan, defied him to save Jylla's life...I remembered Mikail saying, *If Kiran rebels again, Ruslan will not stay his hand,* and my gut went cold. Suliyya grant I hadn't gotten him mindburned by showing him that diagram!

Jylla bowed to Lena and Stevan, her arms extended and crossed at the wrist, the way Arkennlanders from the great cities of the east showed respect. "I owe you a great debt."

It was a nice performance, but I knew better than to believe her sincere. Already, that cunning mind of hers would be seeking a new path for advantage.

"Greater than you know." Stevan opened his hand to display the remains of the amulet. "An irreplaceable artifact destroyed, all to preserve a blood mage." He threw the words at Lena like blows.

"To spare the life of an innocent bystander," Lena corrected him, her voice as unyielding as her stance. "No artifact is worth that price."

To my surprise, Stevan flushed as red as his hair. He looked aside and said, "Forgive my lapse. It is...not easy, to watch mages here go unpunished for their crimes."

Lena said, "No. But take care you do not let the past blind you, Stevan. Kiran is not Reshannis. He resists casting predatory magic rather than embracing it."

Pain spread over Stevan's face, sharp and unmistakable. "I once believed Reshannis would rather die than cause harm. I was wrong. So are you. Every mage has a breaking point in the face of temptation, Lena. And unlike Reshannis, Kiran was not trained to be moral." He turned his back and stalked over to examine the melted charms on the workroom shelves.

I protested to Lena, "Doesn't matter a damn bit how Kiran was trained. He spared Jylla's life even though he knew he'd catch hell for it." Yet I couldn't help wondering how much longer Kiran would've held out if Lena and Stevan hadn't come.

Some dark emotion flared in Lena's eyes, there and gone before I could identify it. "I know."

Jylla spoke up, in soft, earnest apology. "I'm sorry your charm got destroyed. I have information I would be glad to give you to repay you for your help."

I stared. I'd never seen Jylla give something away without even trying a bargain first.

She added, "Couldn't we go to some safer place, first? What if the killer returns?"

Ah. Killer, hell. Jylla wanted protection from Ruslan, and she knew the Alathians were her best hope of it. Play the doe-eyed, helpless waif, get them to take her to their embassy, and find a way to stay there safe and sound—yeah, that was Jylla all over.

Sure enough, Lena said to her, "We will take you to our embassy. The Ambassador will be eager to hear all you and Dev can tell us of this attack." She looked to Stevan, who was pacing beside the workroom shelves, waving his hands over the charms. "Come, Stevan. Once we've seen Dev and his friend—Jylla, is it?—safe and heard their tale, we can return in force to seek traces."

Jylla, staying at the embassy...great. That was just what I needed. A sudden memory of her lithe body pressed against mine as I backed her toward her bed assaulted me. Shame heated my face. Fuck, what was wrong with me? Two months in the mines left me so desperate that one kiss blinded me like some drunken fool of a highsider? If I had to lose my head to lust, far better to do it with Cara. For all the hurt I'd felt over her letter to Marten, I didn't doubt the depth of her concern. Whereas Jylla…I might not want her dead, but that didn't mean I was dumb enough to think she saw me as anything but a mark to manipulate.

Stevan said curtly, "We should ward-seal the room to prevent entry in our absence."

"I'll do it," Lena said. "Go on ahead, and guard Jylla well. I'll soon join you."

Stevan took Jylla's arm in a firm grip. She gave him a tremulous smile; he ignored it and hustled her straight out the door.

Forget the embassy, what I wanted was to run straight to Liana and demand a look at Melly, make absolutely sure she was safe. When I refused Marten's offer to claim her as the embassy's ward, I hadn't known leaving her with Red Dal until her Change might get her snatched by a murderer. Maybe I should ignore my instincts and beg Marten for help, but I still didn't trust him an inch. There had to be another way…

I'd hesitated a little too long. Lena touched my bare shoulder. "Are you all right?"

"Terrific." I scowled down at the remains of my shirt. I could get a replacement from Naidar's rooms, but likely he only owned silk so delicate it'd rip if you looked at it twice. In some hideously bright shade, no less.

Lena said, "I'm sorry we didn't come sooner. It's a terrible thing to see someone you care for threatened while you are helpless to protect them."

Her bleak certainty suggested she spoke from experience. I wondered who she cared for, and how they'd been hurt.

An idea burst to life in my head, drowning out curiosity. I knew how I might get Melly safe without involving Marten. But could I pull it off? I wasn't good with people. Setting a plan, foxing a ward, climbing a cliff…all those things I could do, no problem. But sweet-talking marks, manipulating their emotions to nudge them into line—that had been Jylla's skill, not mine.

Well. High time I learned. I glanced at the door. Stevan and Jylla had already moved off down the hall.

"You're right," I said to Lena, and let the weight of my fear for Melly show. "If you understand that…can I ask you something?"

Lena looked surprised, even a little wary, but she made an encouraging gesture.

I shut the workroom door. A risk to talk here, but I didn't want to wait for another chance to speak with Lena alone.

"Has Marten told you about…" Even knowing the excellent reasons for it, I found it hard to speak of Melly to an Alathian. "About why Kiran and

I agreed to come to Ninavel?"

"He told me you wished to help a child, one living in slavery as you once did."

"It's not slavery," I protested, before I could think. I softened my tone and tried again. "Slavery is what'll come afterward, for Melly. When her Taint fails and her handler sells her. She's too pretty for her own good." I explained about Karonys House.

Lena shook her head, her expression dark. "Talm warned me that Ninavel has no limits on depravity; I see he was right. Marten told me of the arrangement he made with you. This is why you want the money? So you can buy Melly's freedom?"

"Yeah. But now I'm worried Melly won't make it to her Change." I told her of the missing Tainters.

Lena's mouth tightened as I spoke. She said, "I understand your fear. But why tell me? If you go to Marten—"

"I can't trust him! Not after what he did to Kiran. You think I can't see that he'd sacrifice anyone and anything to gain the slightest advantage on this mission?"

She flinched. I said, "I want Melly free of this. Wholly free of this—not someone's pawn, not trapped in a city that might collapse into anarchy. Before, you said you were sorry for what Marten did to Kiran. Did you mean it, or was that just empty words? Because you could free Melly tonight."

Her face turned austere. "I will not give you money behind Marten's back."

I barked out a laugh. "No, you don't understand. I'd have to offer the entire contents of Sechaveh's richest gem vault for Red Dal to sell a Tainter before her Change. But I don't need money, not with a mage to help me. See, back in Tamanath, Kiran…Kiran had this idea." I stumbled over the words, remembering his quiet courage, his certainty he could help me. What fools we'd both been. "In case you haven't noticed how it works here in Ninavel, whatever a blood mage wants, he gets. Kiran thought he could walk into Red Dal's place, flash Ruslan's mark on his chest, maybe do a little magic in the bargain, and demand Melly be given over to him. Red Dal wouldn't like it, but he sure as hell wouldn't risk crossing a blood mage."

"You're asking me to pretend to be a blood mage?" She looked at me like I'd asked her to climb an icefall barehanded. I didn't blame her.

"No. Not a blood mage, Red Dal would never buy that." I certainly couldn't picture calm, poised Lena pulling off the predatory arrogance that came as easy as breathing to Ruslan. Red Dal would see through her in ten seconds flat, even if she faked a sigil like Kiran's, and she had no history in the city to back up her claim.

"Then..." Her brow creased in confusion.

"Look, if you live here, you learn to stay on the good side of all mages, not just the nastiest of the bunch. You march in there wearing something with mage sigils on it—some suitably obscure type of sigils—cast a spell or two to show off, and Red Dal will give you what you ask for. He won't want to piss off a mage, no matter what kind." He wouldn't roll over quite as automatically as he might have for Kiran, and we'd have to sweeten the deal with at least a token payment, but I thought it could work. Especially if Lena was willing to make a few appropriately ominous threats.

Her frown deepened. "Then I'd give you Melly, and you'd vanish from the city with her—depriving us of our best source of information streetside."

"No," I said. "I'd send Melly away with Cara, get them both clear. Then I'd be free to concentrate on helping you stop this killer—and to help Kiran. He needs me just as badly. I won't leave, Lena. Aside from Kiran, I've too many other friends in the city who stand to suffer if this bastard fucks up Ninavel's water."

Her dark eyes searched mine. I said, "You want to ask me under truth spell? Go ahead. I swear to you, I'll do anything you ask, if only you'll get her free."

Lena stood silent. I waited, my breathing harsh. When I couldn't stand it any longer, I said, "Lena...you want me to beg? *Please.* I'll give you my blood, bear any binding you like—"

"If I consider this, then you must vow to me," she said. "You will keep working with us. You will give your best effort, and you will not hold back information you find related to these attacks."

"Yes," I said, without hesitation. I'd give a lot more than that for Melly's freedom.

"Also...I warn you, I cannot lie to a superior."

I wondered if it was duty or magic that would compel her tongue. "You wouldn't have to lie to Marten," I said. "Just...don't mention it to him, until Melly's safely gone from the city. It'd be simple, I swear. I'd tell you what to say. The whole thing would take maybe an hour of your time, and you wouldn't have to act different than normal." I paused. "Well, okay, if you could imitate Stevan a little, that'd help." In a mage, Red Dal would mistake Stevan's type of cold formality for another style of arrogance.

"Very well," Lena said. "Give me your oath, and I'll do as you ask."

"Thank you," I said, my voice husky with relief. "Do you want a blood-mark, or...?"

"I will not bind you," she said. "I would cast a truth spell, but Stevan would feel it and want an explanation. There is another way...I ask to enter your mind and read the truth of your oath as you speak it. You must give me permission, though; the Council forbids us from entering the minds of the untalented, else."

Let her into my head? I bit back my instinctive, horrified refusal. I'd said I'd do anything. "I'll permit you, but...just this once. No more. And only to see the truth, not...dig around."

"I assure you, I will not abuse your trust." Her eyes were earnest.

I could never do this with Marten. But Lena...could I trust her? I'd never yet seen her lie. But as I'd warned Kiran in Tamanath, there was always a first time.

For Melly's sake, I'd take the risk. I nodded reluctantly.

"Take my hand." She held hers out. I took it, not without a spike of nervousness.

A faint pressure spread behind my eyes. Thank Khalmet, it was nothing like the icy, crushing force I'd endured from Simon Levanian. I hurriedly said, "I promise I'll do all in my power to help you seek this killer, and give you everything I learn." And added, more slowly, "I already have plenty to tell." The silver shard in my pocket felt as heavy as an ingot.

A faint smile touched her mouth. "I thought you might." She released my hand, and the pressure in my head vanished. I prayed she hadn't left any lurking spellwork behind.

I said, "I'll set up a meet with Red Dal. I'll say I'm acting as middleman for an employer—you—and word the message so he'll think you're looking to hire his Tainters for a job. Once at the meet, you'll demand Melly. I'll coach you on what to say. I'll even come with you; Red Dal won't think it unusual, middlemen often help with negotiations." Red Dal wouldn't have believed a solo bid from me, but he'd accept me as a middleman, if I played it right. If he got suspicious, easy enough to convince him Lena had forced me into her employ.

"First, we go to the embassy," Lena said. "Marten needs to hear what you know."

New energy sped my stride as I followed her out of the workroom. *I won't fail you,* I told the Sethan living in my memories. *A few hours more, and Melly will be safe at last.*

CHAPTER FIFTEEN

(Dev)

Watching Jylla and Marten dance around each other at the embassy was better than watching a streetside illusionist's shadow tale. Jylla clearly wasn't sure how much I might've told Marten about her, and just as obviously, Marten wasn't certain what she knew of him or the investigation. For my part, I kept a close eye on Marten, trying to figure out if he knew the full tale of my shared past with Jylla. Thank Khalmet, Cara had refrained from explaining the whole sordid mess in her letter to Marten, saying only that I'd lost all my earnings thanks to a business partner's betrayal. Still, I wouldn't put it past Marten to have somehow winkled out every last detail.

If he didn't already know, he would soon. A prospect that killed all my amusement over their dance.

But oh, Jylla was good. She agreed readily enough to speak under truth spell, and showed not a flicker of nerves when Marten had her stand in a hastily-drawn sigil in the receiving room, or when Stevan, Lena, and Kessaravil started chanting in soft, shifting harmony. When the spell was in force she answered Marten's questions without any tell-tale hesitations and in enough detail to keep the Alathians satisfied. Yet without ever telling an actual lie, she managed to downplay our mutual past and imply she'd sought me out because she felt too nervous about approaching a foreign mage directly. To my surprise, she completely avoided mentioning the disappearance of Tainted kids, and to my great relief, she implied that all we'd done in her bedroom was talk about Naidar's streetside shadow until

Kiran interrupted us.

When she told them of the streetside shadow man, the tense, eager silence of those Alathians not spellcasting betrayed their interest, and Jylla's mouth curved in a tiny, satisfied smile. She described the man all the way down to the charms he wore on his wrists, and both Marten and Halassian looked as pleased as jennies who'd spotted a rich mark.

At last, Marten nodded to Stevan, Lena, and Kessaravil, and the sigil on the floor stopped glowing. He bowed to Jylla and said, "I'm sure you'd like the chance for some rest and food after such a difficult experience. If you'll follow Lieutenant Jenoviann, she'll arrange a meal and show you to a room."

"You'll keep me safe?" Jylla asked, all winsome entreaty. "Between Naidar's death and the blood mage this morning, I feel so frightened. But you've been so kind—if I could stay here for a time, then when you catch that shadow man, I can confirm his identity for you."

Marten patted her shoulder. "An excellent thought. You are welcome to stay at the embassy until this entire unpleasant affair is over."

She smiled at him, shy and grateful, and it took an effort not to roll my eyes. But my nerves surged again when she left the room with Jenoviann and they all turned to me.

"Your turn, Dev." Marten beckoned me over to the couch he and Halassian shared. A sun-shroud of palest green covered the receiving room's great window, filtering the midday sun into a soft glow like light seen through lakewater. Frostflower charms dangled from wall brackets; their bone-cold silver spirals weren't enough to entirely vanquish the day's fierce heat, but at least the room didn't feel like a smelter's oven.

"What, under truth spell?" I said it with weary sarcasm, as if I didn't much care. Though I certainly did. I'd follow through on my vow to Lena and not hold back anything directly related to the investigation, but I had plenty else I didn't want to share with Marten, and I wasn't sure I could answer quite as cleverly as Jylla.

Marten chuckled, lightly as if we actually trusted each other. "I don't think that's necessary. But please, we'd like to hear your version of events."

"Before that, I've got news you should know—however the mystery assassin is killing mages and crossing wards, it's got something to do with the Taint."

Marten straightened out of his slouch against the couch pillows. "Why do you say so?"

"For one thing, I found bits of silver in Aiyalen, right in front of the spell chamber doors." I slipped the shard free of my pocket and held it up. "Ward lines can't be shattered by physical force—assuming the ward was designed properly, anyway—but magic can't block the Taint. Pick the right spot, strike it hard enough, and wham, you've got a pile of metal shards and a disrupted ward. The shards aren't my only evidence, though. This morning, I saw part of the attack on Kiran."

"You claim you were in the workroom during the fight?" Stevan eyed me like he was convinced every word out of my mouth without a truth spell in force was a lie.

"I'm not an idiot, to waltz whistling into a magical battle. But the workroom doors were wide open, and I had a pretty damn good view from the hallway. I got there just when the killer struck at Kiran." I frowned, searching for words to explain the certainty that had gripped me. "The way Kiran was thrown through the air, like he got swatted by some huge invisible hand, with no fire or flashing or sparking to be seen…that's exactly what it looks like when somebody gets hit with the Taint." I thought back to how I'd slammed Ruslan into the tree in Simon's meadow, and felt my mouth stretch in a hard grin. "Trust me, I know."

Talm shifted forward on the couch opposite Marten's, his expression abruptly intent. "Adults can't be Tainted. Did you see a child with him?"

"No," I said, and looked at Marten and Lena. "You know it's not impossible for an adult to use the Taint."

"Only with the assistance of a powerful blood magic charm, and even then, only for a short while," Lena said, her dark brows drawn together. "Even wearing Simon Levanian's charm for such a brief interval nearly killed you. Would have killed you, in fact, if not for long days of effort afterward by our best healers."

"The killer might not have to wear such a charm for long, though." Marten took the silver shard from me and peered at it. "The attack Ruslan's spell showed us lasted mere minutes. If the killer used the Taint, it would certainly explain why none of the wards activated, and why the mages' defensive charms did them no good."

"If we're talking about charms made by blood magic, then we're right back to Ruslan," Talm said. "Makes perfect sense, doesn't it? He creates a charm, gives it to someone else to carry out the attacks, and then pretends to hunt them."

After a brief, silent struggle with myself, I said reluctantly, "I don't know. When Ruslan showed up, he looked plenty upset to see Mikail and Kiran hurt." The gods knew I'd prefer it if Ruslan was behind the attacks. But if he wasn't, and we chased after him instead of the true killer, the city might pay a horribly steep price.

Talm looked sour. Halassian rubbed her square jaw, thoughtfully. The complex knot of her gray braids had not a hair out of place, but she still wore a loose, subtly patterned dress instead of a uniform, and leaned against the couch arm with a casual ease that matched Marten's.

She said, "The slashes and other physical mutilation seen in the victims… granted, I'm no expert, but you can't live in Ninavel as long as I have without getting to know something about the Taint. I've never heard of a Tainted child being able to cut with it like a knife."

They all looked at me. I spread my hands with a shrug. "That's true. I was Tainted as strong as they come, and I couldn't do that." I shoved down the memories of all the fun things I *had* been able to do. "Some kids have better fine control than others, but it's still more like…like using a sledgehammer rather than a dagger."

Stevan said, "If the wounds can't be made with the Taint, then we've no reason to suspect a charm like Simon Levanian's is being used. The killer could have brought a Tainted child to Aiyalen as part of his attempt to breach the wards. I hardly think a brief glimpse of a magical fight by an untalented man is enough to base a theory on. Unless you have more to support your claim?" He gave me a cold stare.

Here came the tricky part; I had to play this right if I wanted sanction from Marten for Lena to come streetside, without arousing his suspicion over my motives. "Yeah, I do. Taint thieves have been going missing recently, like somebody's snatching them, and none of the handlers know why. If it'd been only one kid taken, then I'd say the killer snatched a Tainter just to test Aiyalen's wards. But to grab multiple kids, from multiple districts…something else is going on."

"When did you hear that?" Talm's hazel eyes had turned awfully sharp. I knew why. He'd been with me all last night as I'd hunted rumors in taverns, and I hadn't mentioned anything like this to him. He thought I'd been holding out on them—or maybe, like Stevan obviously assumed, that I was lying as part of some scheme of my own.

I didn't want to admit that I'd gotten the news from Jylla, since then they'd wonder what else she hadn't told them. But Lena was watching me with steady intensity; when I'd told her in Naidar's house of the missing Tainters, I hadn't mentioned my source by name, but she must suspect it was Jylla. This might be a test on Lena's part, to see if I'd keep my vow or if I'd lie.

"Jylla told me," I said. "She didn't realize the full significance, though. Otherwise she'd have told you." I still wasn't sure why she hadn't. In the old days, I'd have said she meant to help me, by ensuring I had a bargaining token that'd let me gain advantage with the Alathians. Now, I knew with dead certainty that the only advantage she cared about was her own.

Talm's gaze grew all the more piercing, but Marten only turned the shard over in his fingers. "Do you know when this began, or the number of children missing?"

"Not sure," I said. "I can find out, if I poke my nose around further. But the streetsiders I need to speak with don't take kindly to visitors, and have serious wards. I'll need a mage's help. Only this time I want Lena with me, not Talm."

Marten's brows lifted. "Why?"

"You said she's the best of you at sneaking people through wards. If you don't want half the district to know what we're hunting and where we've been, I'll need that."

Talm no longer looked suspicious, only amused. He gave me a theatrically soulful look. "I'm hurt. Admit it, Dev. You just want someone prettier than I am at your side."

I grinned at him. "Not hard, is it?"

He laughed. Lena said with her usual calm gravity, "I would be happy to assist you, Dev." Thank Khalmet, she didn't betray by so much as a hairsbreadth twitch that we'd spoken of this in advance.

I felt the weight of Marten's gaze like a boulder pressing down. But all he said was, "Very well. Dev, I'm certainly in favor of you continuing to have more protection than charms can provide."

I was glad of that myself. I hadn't forgotten Ruslan's unspoken threat. Maybe his partner Lizaveta couldn't cast channeled magic against me, but I had a terrible feeling the so-called minor spells Marten had dismissed so readily would be more than enough to leave me a bleeding ruin.

Talm grew serious again. "Regardless of the assassin's methods, I'm still convinced Ruslan is the mind behind these attacks. So far he or his apprentices have contaminated every site we've been allowed to visit, or chased us out before we could properly search for traces of blood magic."

That started everyone arguing about how best to seek traces, and whether blood magic could enhance or even mimic the Taint. I leaned my head on my hand, wishing they'd either shut up and move on, or let me leave the room. All this hunting rumors at night and wardfire by day meant I was running awfully short on sleep. I'd need at least a few hours before I faced Red Dal tonight, or I'd regret it.

Marten gave me a sympathetic look when I yawned wide enough to make my jaw crack.

"Dev, if you'll give us a quick recounting of the rest of your time in Naidar's house, then I promise we'll let you get some rest."

I smiled inwardly. Perfect. Now if they ever found out I'd skipped over a few things—like my moment of idiocy with Jylla—I could always say I'd forgotten to mention it out of sheer exhaustion. I rattled off a brief account, sticking to bare facts. I didn't mention the spell diagram or Kiran's reaction to it, though I did explain how he'd saved my life with his magic.

What a mistake that was. Khalmet's hand, you'd think Ruslan had been the one to work the spell, the way Stevan carried on about the dangers of lingering bindings. He insisted on all of them checking me over with magic, which took forever, involved a lot of chanting, and made me feel as if ants were crawling all over my skin. I bore it with gritted teeth and a lot of murderous looks at Stevan, who pretended not to notice. Fucking asshole.

Finally, Marten said I could go, though he stood and dogged my heels as I made for the archway. Just outside the receiving room, he put out a hand to halt me.

"Dev, I can't tell you how relieved I am to hear of Kiran's concern for you, and his refusal to hurt Jylla. I had feared…"

"Feared what?" I demanded. "That Stevan is right about him? You know better than that, Marten."

Marten said, "I'm well aware of Stevan's prejudice. Yet that prejudice is not without a grain of truth. I've told you I saw Kiran's memories at his trial. Even as a child, Kiran had a certain empathy for others…yet before he met Alisa, Ruslan was well on his way to training Kiran into restricting that empathy to Ruslan's little coterie and burying all qualms beneath his love for magic. Alisa was the one to open Kiran's eyes to the worth of untalented lives and plant the seeds that would grow into rebellion. Without her influence, I fear Kiran would have readily become a blood mage, fiercely loyal to Ruslan just as Ruslan desired him to be."

I remembered Marten's insistence I find out how much time Kiran had lost. "You thought that if Ruslan took all Kiran's memories of Alisa, that'd…what? Erase Kiran's conscience, leave him happy to murder and torture people?" Thank Khalmet, Kiran had proved that theory wrong.

"Let us say that I think it leaves Kiran dangerously susceptible to Ruslan's influence," Marten said. "Which makes yours all the more important. Kiran's memories may be gone, but I believe some remnant of the emotional responses built by those memories remains. Ruslan will try to change that in Kiran. You must do what you can to counter Ruslan in this, stop him from coaxing Kiran down a path that would make it impossible for him to seek refuge again in Alathia."

I saw Marten's game now. This would be his excuse for ditching Kiran once the investigation was over. He'd claim Kiran had become too much of a blood mage, and shuffle off the blame onto my shoulders for not "countering" Ruslan as he'd asked. For fuck's sake, how did he expect me to influence Kiran when I could barely get near him?

Familiar fury bubbled up inside. But I only smiled—a thin, tight smile—and said, "I'll do all I can." *All I can to free him despite you, you lying weasel.*

Marten beamed at me. "Good. Sleep well, Dev."

Instead of stabbing him, I headed straight for my room. Only to find Jylla perched demurely on one of the two beds and Jenoviann nowhere in sight.

"You are *not* sleeping in that bed," I snarled, ready to march back to demand other quarters.

"Oh, they gave me a bed elsewhere," Jylla said. "I told Jenoviann I wanted the chance to thank you privately. Besides, Dev, why so stingy with your space? You certainly didn't mind getting close earlier." Her eyes traveled my body, her lips curving in a teasing grin.

"Sure, when I thought you had something useful to offer." I said it with all the casual contempt I could muster.

"Hmmm." Jylla toyed with one of her opal earrings, watching me through long, black lashes. "I saw your face when you thought the blood mage would kill me."

"Just because I didn't want him to kill you doesn't mean I want you in my bed. Or anywhere else near me." I aimed a pointed look at the door.

"What about my help?" Jylla said. "I also saw how you look at the Alathians, especially Martennan. He's got something over you to make you dance to his tune, doesn't he? You want off his leash, you know that's the kind of game I'm good at."

I'd tried not to betray my hatred of Marten in front of her, but I should've known she'd see it anyway. She'd always been able to read me as easily as if I shouted every thought aloud. Horribly, I was tempted to take her up on her offer—because if anyone could outwit Marten, she could. But no, no, *no.*

"I've already got a partner in this. Someone I trust. Unlike you."

Surprise widened Jylla's eyes. "A partner? You do move quickly. Who?"

I shook my head, unwilling to say Cara's name. But Jylla's head tilted, her expression gone thoughtful. "No, wait, let me guess...I heard that outrider friend of yours, Cara, came back alone from Alathia and then turned down a bunch of convoy jobs to hang around the city all summer instead. Suliyya knows she always eyed you like she wanted to drag you off and tie you up as her jenny-slave. How long did it take her once she heard you and I split to ditch her silly rule? Two heartbeats, three?"

"She hasn't broken her rule," I snapped. "Know why? I'm no longer an outrider. Thanks to you."

"Funny, I don't recall asking anyone to blacklist you," Jylla said. "I thought you'd keep right on playing in the mountains, not decide to throw yourself hip deep in mages. But now that you are…sure, I bet Cara's great on a climb. Maybe even between the sheets—Suliyya knows she's got enough experience there with all those traders she's bedded. But playing against mages? Look me in the eye and tell me I'm not the better choice."

I shut my eyes. "Jylla. You're clever, yeah. But right now, what I need most is someone who won't stab me in the back the moment it's turned. That's not you."

"What if I said I regretted it?" The teasing vanished from her voice, leaving it rough. "You were right, what you said about the Taint. I thought maybe Naidar's magic could make me forget the dead spot inside, the way the mountains do for you. Oh gods, Dev, you don't know how jealous I was of you for that! But it didn't. When I realized it…every moment since, I've wished I'd chosen a different path."

I'd swear the pain lacing her words was unfeigned. But then, every mark Jylla had ever fooled would swear the same. My laugh came out as jagged as splintered ice. "Not enough to actually take one. Not enough to return the money you stole, or even apologize for it. Words don't mean shit where there isn't trust, Jylla. And there'll never be trust between us again."

Her mouth twisted. "Maybe not. But you were the one who taught me nothing's impossible." She stood and smoothed her hands down the gauzy layers of her dress. "If this game of yours turns sour on you…my offer will stand. Help, free and clear…well, maybe not completely free." As she slid past, she trailed a hand across my groin, too quick for me to slap her fingers away.

I slammed the door shut the instant she was outside it, not caring if the Alathians heard. I cursed my traitorous body for responding to her touch, and fought to blot out the memories of her golden curves and cunning tongue with those of Cara's steadfast support and honest passion until sleep claimed me at last.

✳

(Kiran)

Kiran floated in red-tinged darkness, dimly aware of the sound of voices.

"You know I do not tolerate defiance." One voice was deep and male, harsh with heat like the fierce winds of late summer.

"As is proper, my brother. Only think—will not patience serve your purpose better than acting in haste?" The second voice was female, dark yet cajoling, as smooth as blended acacia honey.

"I have been patient," the first voice insisted.

"Then be patient for yet a little longer. Think of a thoroughbred colt compared to a drayhorse. The drayhorse responds well enough to the lash, and no further care is needed because he is easily replaced. But a racehorse must be treated with delicacy, lest he be ruined. For such a prized and sensitive animal, far better to lead him down the path with sugared fruit than drive him with a whip."

After a little silence, the deep voice said, "What sugared fruit would you suggest?"

"The kind that sings in the blood of all the *akheli*." The honeyed voice was now streaked with teasing laughter.

"You were always the temptress," said the deep voice, harshness fading into fond warmth. "Very well. We will see if sugar can dissolve stubbornness."

The honeyed voice turned serious. "Best if we ensure the *nathahlen* cannot whisper more poison."

"I've already taken steps to that end." The dark promise in the words stripped away some of Kiran's dreamy disconnection. He struggled to surface from the void.

"Shhh—he stirs…" Red warmth enveloped him, drawing him deeper into darkness, dissolving both disquiet and memory.

When he woke at last, the rich red-gold light of sunset warmed the warded stone of his bedroom walls. Kiran rubbed at his eyes, confused. Why was he asleep so late in the day?

Memory jolted him upright: the attack, his injuries. He ripped the sheet away from his stomach. His skin was unbroken, and his muscles moved easily, without even a twinge of pain. The only ache within was from simple hunger.

Kiran ran his hand over the healed skin of his side. Remembered agony shortened his breath. The desperate struggle to hold his barriers, even as Ruslan demanded he drop them—he cringed and glanced around, a little wildly. The bedroom was empty, his master nowhere in sight. Kiran sighed, unable to feel much relief. Punishment would come, of that he was certain.

Fear whispered at him to hide, to run. Yet Kiran had learned long ago that attempts at evasion only brought worse punishment. Better to accept and endure the consequences for his disobedience, however painful. Ruslan's hand was heavy, but he'd never tasked Kiran with more than he could bear.

So long as punishment wasn't immediately forthcoming, he might as well find something to eat. His stomach was a growling void. He hadn't eaten since the morning, assuming this was even the same day. He got up and pulled on the black trousers and sigil-marked shirt that someone, likely one of the silent house servants, had left folded on his writing desk.

Stepping outside his door required a few steadying breaths; he half-expected Ruslan to descend on him like some vengeful god of legend. But the corridor outside was as empty as his room, the sky beyond the unshuttered skylights a soft, fading rose. Kiran padded down the hall and ducked into the sunroom, relieved to see that a tray containing dates, spiced flatbread, and soft cheese remained on the lacquered table set before windows shaded by vine-covered trellises. Rather than eating a heavy meal before resting in the noonday heat as was usual in Ninavel, Ruslan preferred to eat more frequent, smaller meals whenever the mood struck him as he worked. But since he insisted on always having a formal evening meal, the servants often cleared the sunroom's table by afternoon's end.

"There you are." Mikail uncurled from a pile of cushions on a long divan, a book in his hands. "I thought you'd never wake up."

Kiran made a show of wrapping dates and cheese in a slice of flatbread, remembering the spell diagram Dev had shown him, and his own startled conviction that Dev was no stranger to either him or Mikail. He was sorely tempted to demand answers from Mikail, particularly on the point of how Dev had come into possession of a spell diagram drawn in Kiran's hand. But if by chance Ruslan didn't know of Kiran's conversation with Dev before the attacks, Kiran certainly didn't want to bring it up anywhere Ruslan might overhear.

"How long was I asleep?" he asked, settling on the divan beside Mikail with flatbread in hand.

"For half the day," Mikail said. "I was worried something was wrong, but Ruslan said not. He says you're still not wholly recovered from your accident, so your body and *ikilhia* take longer to come back into balance after a healing."

The mention of Ruslan soured his mouthful of date-studded cheese. "How angry is he?"

"Angry enough." Mikail shut his book with a thump. "What were you thinking? Why didn't you drop your barriers and let your body heal itself?"

Kiran swallowed a final lump of bread with some difficulty and picked at the gilded edge of a cushion. How could he explain to Mikail what he hardly understood himself?

"It didn't seem right," he finally said.

"Why not?" Mikail's voice was tight with frustration. "You were hurt and you needed to heal. When that happens, you take whatever power you need; it's that simple. Or do you like pain?"

"Of course not," Kiran said, stung. "But...that courtesan had done nothing wrong. She didn't deserve to die."

"Who said anything about deserving it? When you eat meat, does that mean the animal deserved to die? No! It means you were hungry, and you took what you needed to survive. There's no difference," Mikail insisted.

"It's not the same," Kiran muttered, thinking of the fear haunting the courtesan's painted face, and Dev's desperate anger.

Mikail shook his head, grimly. "Ruslan's not going to accept that."

Kiran dropped his head into his hands. "I know." He shivered as anticipatory pain ghosted along his nerves. "What can I say to him? I didn't want to disobey him. But I couldn't do it, not with her standing right there."

Mikail huffed out an exasperated breath. "You've got to get over this bizarre squeamishness of yours. You're *akheli*, Kiran, not some lesser mage—and you're certainly not *nathahlen*. Trying to pretend otherwise will only bring you pain, and not just from Ruslan."

Kiran stared at the stone beneath his feet. What was wrong with him? Why couldn't he treat killing as Mikail did, with dispassionate reserve? "I think Ruslan will bring me pain enough."

Mikail rubbed gently at Kiran's hunched shoulders. "Relax, little brother. Once again, you're luckier than you have any right to be. The Alathians were so anxious to spare the woman that they let you destroy some special charm of theirs, which pleased Ruslan greatly. That will temper his anger."

Temper it, perhaps, but not erase it entirely. Kiran's muscles stayed knotted despite Mikail's coaxing touch. "What of the spell we gathered materials for? Has Ruslan cast already?"

"Not yet. I helped him lay channels all afternoon, until he sent me out for rest and food. I'm to channel for him tonight." Mikail said it with grave pride. "The spell—oh, you should see it, Kiran! So complex, and yet so elegant; I could have studied the problem for years and never designed a solution so brilliant."

A sigh of wistful envy escaped Kiran. "Perhaps if Ruslan's not too angry, he'll allow me to at least view the pattern. I'll certainly be curious to know if the spell succeeds in reading our enemy's thoughts." He straightened and rolled his shoulders, thinking back to the dark figure leaning over Mikail. "Did you see him when he attacked you? I never saw his face."

Mikail shrugged. "I didn't see a cursed thing. I was sorting through charms deciding on the best one to take, and then the confluence spiked. I was so busy disengaging from the charms and reinforcing my barriers that the mage caught me totally by surprise. He struck, and then I woke up on the floor with my shirt slashed to ribbons, the room in ruins, and you acting like a complete idiot." He cuffed Kiran's shoulder before he could dodge away. "At least before you lost your head you cast a decent strike. Ruslan says he thinks you hurt our enemy, even if you didn't kill him."

"The first time I struck, the mage yelled, like he was in pain. The second time—he vanished, completely as if by translocation spell, before my strike reached him." Kiran struggled to remember every detail. It had all happened so fast. "Translocation is so difficult to cast, and he certainly wasn't using channels. I don't see how he managed it."

"Still, I hope you gave him a nice deep magefire burn to remember us by." A fierce grin spread on Mikail's face. "Don't you see? Even if he healed himself afterward, this means he's not immune to our magic. If we make the right preparations, we can destroy him." His almond eyes lit with the same cruel, cold light that Kiran had seen many times in Ruslan's.

Newly uncomfortable, Kiran looked aside. "Why did he come to the workroom in the first place? The mage who owned it was already dead."

"For us, of course," Mikail said, in a tone that said he thought Kiran was being slow. "He must know that we're hunting him. He's trying to kill us before we can stop him."

"Stop him doing what? What does he want?"

Mikail shrugged again. "What does any mage want? Power."

"That doesn't make sense," Kiran protested. "The confluence already provides immense power to us all, for anyone with the talent to use it."

Ruslan strode into the sunroom. Kiran froze, his scant meal congealing in his stomach, but Ruslan only leaned a hip against the table and plucked a date from a jade bowl. His chestnut hair was straggling free of its tail, his sleeves rolled up to the elbows like a laborer's, but his face showed no hint of strain from his long afternoon's work laying channels.

"Some men confuse magical power with the more mundane sort," Ruslan said, as mildly as if Kiran had never disobeyed him. "Lesser mages are particularly prone to this error. When they reach the limits of their talent, they often turn to the accumulation of wealth, or seek to reign over *nathahlen*, as if that makes up for their lack." He tossed the date once in his hand before extracting the seed and popping the rest into his mouth.

"You mean he wants to...to rule the city? Instead of Lord Sechaveh?" Kiran couldn't fathom why a mage would want to concern himself with taxes, and guardsmen, and the operations of the mines. None of that had anything to do with magic. Ruslan had often said that what he liked best about living in Ninavel was the opportunity for uninterrupted study, and

Kiran had to agree.

Ruslan lifted one shoulder. "It's possible. His actions thus far certainly seem designed to disrupt Lord Sechaveh's rule here. But his ultimate motive is still in question."

He paced behind the divan. Strong hands settled on Kiran's shoulders. "I am pleased to see you well, Kiran...but your conduct earlier this day did not please me."

For all Kiran had known this was coming, it didn't lessen the abrupt renewal of fear. "Forgive me, Ruslan," he said, through a throat gone tight with hopeless dread.

Ruslan's fingers dug painfully into Kiran's collarbones. Kiran flinched, caught in a welter of conflicting memories: those fingers clawing agony into his gut, and the very same hands gliding over his hips as he writhed in pleasure. Love and cruelty, neither a sham—but oh, how he wished he could find the path to earn only the former.

Ruslan asked, "Do you regret this gift I have given you? Do you wish to die as easily as a *nathahlen* might, your *ikilhia* snuffed out, your flesh decaying and devoured?"

Darkness descended over Kiran. He no longer sat on the couch beside Mikail. Instead, he lay naked on cold stone, his limbs dead weights. Out of the blackness around him came a soft, horrible chittering, as of a thousand insects...

Carrion beetles, the dead-eaters. As a child he'd heard Lizaveta speak of this, the death rites of her and Ruslan's ancient birthplace—he'd had screaming nightmares for days afterward. He struggled to move, but his body was mere meat, unresponsive to his commands. His magic—he couldn't feel it, his inner senses as dead as his limbs—

It wasn't real. It wasn't *real*. Yet the air was cool and dank on his skin, the stone solid beneath his body, the scent of decay strong in his nostrils. He struggled to move, his body unresponsive, his magic gone as if it had never been. Panic rose, drowning reason.

The chittering grew louder, a scuttling tide sweeping toward him in the dark. Squirming, crawling things spread over his feet, followed by needling pain, countless voracious, tiny mouths gnawing at his flesh. The tide swept higher, up his legs to his genitals, pain swallowing him in a red, terrible wave, his voiceless shrieks unheard. Beetles in his mouth now, eating his tongue, his eyes, *please, Ruslan, no more, please—!*

Pain and beetles vanished. Light seared Kiran's eyes. Ruslan's hands still gripped his shoulders, the couch soft and yielding beneath his back and legs. Kiran tried to claw at his skin, still feeling the phantom touch of skittering legs, but he was shaking so hard he succeeded only in weak, twitching motions. A keening whine assaulted his ears; he realized it was coming from his own throat.

"Hush, *akhelysh.*" Ruslan caught his hands to still them. "Lizaveta tells me I should be lenient with you, that your recent trauma has left you unsettled in mind as well as body. This once I will listen, and refrain from more than this brief taste of correction."

Kiran slumped, his relief so huge he couldn't summon speech. The next time he saw Lizaveta, he would prostrate himself before her in gratitude. Awful as the carrion beetle vision had been, it was a mere love-tap compared to what he might have endured for his disobedience.

Ruslan continued. "But hear this, Kiran: if you care so much for lives beside your own, then think on your mage-brother, not worthless *nathahlen.* Should you defy me again, Mikail will share your punishment, magnified ten-fold."

A brief spike of agony pierced Kiran, like a dagger plunged into his skull and as swiftly withdrawn. He gasped and stiffened; but beside him, Mikail doubled over with a hoarse, anguished cry.

"Ruslan, no!" Kiran twisted to catch at Ruslan's hand in supplication. "I was at fault, not him—he's done nothing to earn your anger—"

"Then remember that, next time you're tempted to disobey." Ruslan freed his hand and reached to stroke Mikail's still-shuddering back. "Forgive me, *akhelysh,*" he murmured, in a lover's tender tones. "Your mage-brother needs the lesson: his refusal to accept his own nature not only harms himself, but all of us who love him."

Mikail pushed himself upright and rubbed at his temples with hands that shook. "I'll see he learns it."

Kiran gave him a stricken, apologetic look, but the tight set of his face didn't change.

"Good." Ruslan patted Mikail's shoulder. "Rest a while longer. We'll cast at midnight. Kiran…" He turned, his expression growing stern once more. "Go to the training workroom and begin a study of the Akalic sages' hundred spells of wounding—I've left the relevant treatise on your writing desk. Tomorrow you will cast the first three of them, and you have only four hours to study before midnight."

Implications crowded Kiran's mind. Casting spells of wounding…he had a terrible suspicion Ruslan meant him to cast on *nathahlen* for practice—and if he refused, Mikail would be the one to suffer. And then there was Ruslan's mention of midnight…

"Do you intend me to watch while you cast tonight?" Beneath his unease, curiosity over the spell still glimmered. But if Ruslan meant to cast a fully channeled spell, he wouldn't be using *zhivnoi* crystals to harness the power of the confluence. A *nathahlen* would die tonight. A condemned criminal, most likely, sold off by merchant house guardsmen to save the effort of execution by noose or sword. Someone who deserved death, unlike the courtesan...but Kiran felt cold thinking of it, just the same.

Ruslan smiled at him. "Oh, more than watch, *akhelysh*."

"But...if Mikail is channeling and you're casting, then what...?"

"You'll see," Ruslan said. "Now go."

Ruslan couldn't ask him to take the life needed for the spell—the power had to be raised by the mage casting. Or did it? The mark-bond might very well allow Ruslan to siphon off and use any *ikilhia* that Kiran took.

Kiran left the sunroom on leaden feet. If he believed in any of the gods revered by *nathahlen*, he would abase himself and pray in desperation. *Let Ruslan not ask me to kill...*

Even if he was spared the choice tonight, he knew it would come, inevitable as the burning heat of highest summer. Better to pray for the easing of his strange reluctance, so obedience would be as simple as Mikail found it.

❋

"Enough studying, little one. The time has come for a more interesting lesson."

Kiran looked up from a diagram of the channels needed for the third Akalic spell—an inventively nasty piece of magic meant to infest an enemy's lungs with ravenous mites—to see Lizaveta standing in the workroom doorway. Her black hair was bound back by silver clasps fashioned in the likeness of star jasmine, her dress a clinging sheath the deep red of heart's blood overlaid by a delicate lacework of black sigils. The silk was slit from one braceleted ankle to the curve of her hip, revealing an expanse of smooth brown leg.

For once, Kiran wasn't stirred by her beauty. His throat was as dry as the sand on his parchment, his mind a fevered tangle. He'd barely been able to concentrate on his spell diagram, too caught up in imagining one distressing scenario after another. Yet the sight of Lizaveta brought a welcome glimmer of hope.

"Khanum Liza..." He abandoned his stool to kneel at her feet. "Thank you for swaying Ruslan to leniency. I haven't the right to ask more, but can you not convince him to confine his punishments to me if I should... displease him again? It's not fair for him to hurt Mikail..."

Lizaveta drew him upright. She took his face in her hands, her dark eyes piercing his. "Do you plan on displeasing him, Kiran?"

"I...I don't want to, but..." He looked away, sick with the memory of the courtesan's fear. "I don't know if I can...can cast as an *akheli* should." *I don't know if I can kill.*

Lizaveta gently but firmly turned his face back to hers. "You need not fear, Kiranushka. We all have our weaknesses; none are impossible to conquer. As your master, Ruslan will do whatever is required to ensure you prevail. It is perhaps a touch more challenging for him to help you overcome a flaw he does not share, but I think tonight will do much to help you. I promise you, he will not ask anything you cannot give."

The tide of Kiran's worry didn't retreat. "But if he did...please, khanum Liza! Mikail shouldn't have to suffer because of me." The horror of the carrion-beetle vision returned to tighten his chest. To think of his pain and panic magnified ten-fold...Kiran cringed.

"He will not suffer, because you will obey Ruslan as you should, yes?" Lizaveta laid a soft finger on Kiran's lips to halt another anguished plea. "You know I do not interfere with Ruslan's decisions for you and Mikail once he has made them. You are his *akhelyshen*, not mine." A little, rueful smile curved her lips. "I have not the patience to teach, or the strength to choose what is best for an *akhelysh* when they beg otherwise, as you do now. This is why I take none of my own. Instead, I get the far better bargain...I can enjoy you and Mikail as I please, without need to worry over discipline."

She kissed him, a deep, coaxing kiss that left him dizzied anew, though it didn't soothe the roil of his stomach. She didn't understand the depth of his dismay over harming *nathahlen*; none of them did. Otherwise, they wouldn't assume he could so easily shrug it aside.

"Come," Lizaveta said softly. "Ruslan and Mikail await you."

He will not ask anything that you cannot give. Kiran had to trust that Lizaveta spoke truth. What other option did he have?

She led him up the spiraling marble stairs that led to Ruslan's primary workroom. With each step, his fearful anticipation crested higher. The spells he remembered casting had always been performed in lesser chambers, bounded by powerful shielding wards that muted the confluence energies to tame levels. Ruslan cast his spells in a chamber whose wards permitted full access to the immense forces of the confluence. Kiran had rarely been allowed to enter. He must have had more frequent access after the *akhelashva* ritual, perhaps even participated in Ruslan's spellcasting...but the voids lacing his memories remained stubbornly empty.

Ruslan waited before the chamber doors, Mikail at his side, the scarlet sigils embroidered on their black clothing a reverse image of Lizaveta's gown. Kiran climbed the last steps, his heart thudding so hard he thought his chest might split open.

Ruslan took Kiran's shoulders. "Tonight we work the true magic, *akhelysh*, the greatest endeavor to which a man may aspire. All else is shadows and ashes." He pressed a kiss to Kiran's brow; not passionate, but firm in benediction. "Lizaveta will help you observe."

Observe…perhaps Ruslan did not intend him to do anything more. Yet Mikail's posture radiated tension, though his expression was as impassive as ever. Was he nervous merely because he hadn't channeled for a spell of this difficulty since the one that had gone so badly wrong, or did he fear that Kiran might disobey an order?

Ruslan put his palms flat on the doors. The ward lines coating the iron flared red, and the doors opened.

Mikail and Ruslan had indeed been busy. A silver labyrinth of knots and spirals covered nearly the entire extent of the workroom's stone floor. Kiran struggled to follow the pattern, but kept losing the spell's shape in the intricacies of individual lines.

Captivated by the spell, it wasn't until Lizaveta tugged him gently forward that he thought to look at the anchor stone.

A man lay spread-eagled on the waist-high chunk of onyx, his ankles and wrists bound with warded silver manacles tight enough to leave bleeding runnels in his flesh. A black hood inscribed with crimson sigils covered his face, but Kiran could hear the harsh, ragged sound of his panicked breathing. His naked body was thick-muscled and heavily scarred. A set of recent raw brands on his chest marked him a condemned man, sentenced to death by the merchants of Goranant House.

Kiran's stomach seized. A bloody haze stole across his vision, and he wavered on his feet, the room lurching around him. Deep in his mind, something stirred, black dread stealing up his spine.

Across the room, Ruslan turned to look at him, sharply. In an instant his presence filled Kiran's mind. Red light burned away the spreading darkness, layering calm over him like sand burying a ruin. Kiran's vision cleared, his stomach settling, and Ruslan withdrew. Yet Kiran couldn't look away from the man on the stone. What had he done to deserve Goranant House's judgment? Had he stolen money from them? Killed one of their merchants? Whatever his crime, he couldn't have anticipated this fate.

Lizaveta interposed herself between Kiran and the anchor stone. "Don't think on it, little one. In the end, death is death, whether it comes from a hangman's noose or a warded blade. At least this way, his death serves a purpose."

Ruslan had said as much, many times before. Kiran took a shallow, shaky breath and allowed Lizaveta to lead him along the curve of the outermost channel line, heading for a clear space of floor encircled by the looping helix of a protective ward. She positioned him within the ward with his back to the anchor stone, and pulled a needle-thin silver blade from her sash.

Kiran fought the urge to look over his shoulder at the bound man. He let Lizaveta take his hand and slice a thin, burning line down his palm. She cut a matching line down her own palm and clasped his bloodied hand tight in hers.

The world faded around him, a subtle, lacy network growing to surround his mind and senses. *Drop your barriers, little one, and wait for Ruslan...*

He did as she asked. His inner senses opened wide, the channel lines behind him burning bright and sharp in his head. Lizaveta, Ruslan and Mikail's distinctive *ikilhias* stood out like tightly contained pillars of colored fire. The bound man's life energy was duller, chaotic and uncontained, the space around him stained with a dark, flickering energy that Kiran realized came from his fear. Underneath it all, the confluence heaved in a vast lake of fire. Great currents swirled in dizzying spirals, already sluggishly mimicking the channel line pattern in spots.

Disorientingly, his perception shifted, as if he now stood beside the anchor stone as well as before Lizaveta. Startled, he resisted, only to feel soothing reassurance from both Ruslan and Lizaveta.

The mark-bond—Ruslan was once again projecting his own perceptions into Kiran's mind. The understanding helped Kiran adjust to the odd, doubled sense of the world. As Kiran's resistance faded, Ruslan pressed deeper yet, until Kiran's sense of self blurred.

The knife hilt warm and familiar in his hand; the bound body on the stone before him merely a canvas to be viewed with concentrated, clinical attention. A cut here, a slow twist there, pain the instrument to spark the body's dim ikilhia *into a blaze powerful enough to harness the confluence's currents...*

Faintly, Kiran heard screaming, but the sound seemed thin and distant, nearly lost under the power swelling to overwhelm his senses.

If the power from the *zhivnoi* crystal had sung in his blood like a fine wine, the power Ruslan raised brought a dark joy nearly soul-shattering in its intensity. Kiran was dimly aware of falling to his knees, his head thrown back; he would have collapsed completely if not for Lizaveta's grip. The yearning to taste that power firsthand rather than at a remove was so strong he might have lost all control and reached blindly for it, heedless of the dire consequences of disrupting the carefully channeled energies, if not for

Lizaveta's presence surrounding his mind. She held him within her magic the way she might hold carved crystal in her cupped hands, supporting and restraining at the same time.

The power built, spiraling upward, filling the containment channels nearest the anchor stone until they seared Kiran's senses raw, pleasure sliding over into pain. Again, Lizaveta was there, dimming the sensation, gently pulling him back.

Blood slick on his hands, noticed only in caution lest the knife slip; the body's ikilhia stoked to the highest level possible, about to collapse back in on itself and vanish: now.

Ruslan's blade descended one final time. The shock of the man's death ignited the containment channels into a raging inferno, even as Ruslan released their wards. Power raced outward through the pattern, shaped and directed by Mikail, and pulled the fiery currents of the confluence into alignment, the energies enhanced a thousandfold. The spell blazed into shape, a construct of searing beauty and sure, inexorable power.

Ruslan paused, gathering his concentration. And then he cast, exerting the full force of his will through the pattern, his entire being *demanding* his desired result; and the confluence bent the world to his desire.

The sensation was intoxicating in a different, deeper way than the touch of power had been. Kiran felt with Ruslan the certainty that in this moment nothing was beyond his grasp, that no god imagined by man could match his absolute control over the world.

As the spell took effect, it was as if Ruslan stood within the bloodied room in Aiyalen, a dark mist of mental energies swirling sluggishly around him. Delicately, carefully, Ruslan manipulated the mist, drawing out and rejecting everything that matched the mental patterns of the dead mages, all four patterns held simultaneously in his mind. The strain was immense, but Ruslan's will and focus never faltered. Slowly, he molded the mist into a smooth, clouded chain. Ruslan released the dead mages' patterns and gathered his concentration once more, focusing on the thought-chain.

Wrenching transition; anticipation. Surprise is on my side, and these vipers cannot stand against me. Hatred; exultation. How shocked they look, when their bodies are torn apart. All their cursed magic made useless; a taste of the triumph to come. Soon all the vipers will burn and the old ghoul with them, the great wound in the mother-vein cauterized at last. I care not for the stains on my soul if I can free the world of their poison... But first, the destruction of the ghoul's water source. Frustration; anger. Vaz-Kavash curse him and his soulless servants! Perhaps with enough of the vipers' blood, I can devise a better method… Nervousness; tension. I have tarried long enough; already, the stone's glow fades. Wrenching transition…

The chain ended, the energies controlling the confluence currents fading, nearly used up. Ruslan's concentration did not waver. Methodically, he fed the remnants of power back down into the confluence, smoothing its currents until no trace of the spell pattern remained.

Kiran's doubled perception vanished. The absence of Ruslan's fiery strength left him disoriented once more, his body's rhythms strangely disordered. He bent over his knees, sucking down harsh breaths and fighting to slow the runaway gallop of his heart.

A steadying wash of shimmering violet slid through his body. Kiran climbed to his feet with Lizaveta's aid and wiped sweat from his temples with his shirt sleeve. His heart might have slowed, but his mind remained fogged with confusion, thoughts jittering into vapor before he could complete them.

A last tingle of magic made Kiran's palm itch, as Lizaveta fed his body enough energy to heal the cut she'd made. She smiled knowingly at him, her eyes as dark and deep as the night sky.

"You enjoyed your taste of real power, did you not?"

Kiran flushed. Linked as they had been, she'd felt every bit of his desperate yearning and joy. He nodded, looking down.

Lizaveta put her palm to his cheek, her touch cool against the heat of his skin. "There is no shame in it, Kiran. This is what we are. Ruslan speaks truly when he says there is nothing greater."

Kiran turned to look at the anchor stone. The condemned man's body had vanished, burned away to nothing in the blaze of power his death had generated. But dark stains dulled the stone's glossy surface, and Ruslan's great silver knife lay on top, the blade black and clotted with blood. A fever-chill passed over Kiran. He wanted with an ache so deep it left him breathless to stand in Ruslan's place, to have all that glorious power at his own command. Yet to slice a helpless man open, to deliberately cause and prolong pain…*the knife firm in his hand, blood welling from flayed muscle…* Kiran choked and wrapped his arms around himself.

"Are you all right?"

Kiran dragged his gaze from the anchor stone to meet his mage-brother's worried gaze. Strain still pulled at Mikail's face, his sandy hair lank and sweat darkening the collar of his shirt.

"I'm fine," Kiran said, hating the weak, thin sound of his voice. Mikail didn't look convinced. He said something quick and low to Lizaveta, who picked her way over darkened channel lines to where Ruslan stood, his head bent and his chestnut brows drawn in a deep, thoughtful frown.

When she touched his shoulder, Ruslan started. He took her hand and glanced at Kiran. "Forgive me, *akhelysh*. Thinking on what we learned, I forgot how unsettled your mind yet is, after your accident. A problem easily solved…"

Blessed, cool calm filled Kiran to smother both yearning and revulsion. He sighed in relief, and Ruslan smiled.

"What did you learn?" Mikail looked between Ruslan and Lizaveta in eager inquiry. A channeler needed to devote all his concentration to maintaining the spell pattern. Mikail had probably only gotten a vague impression of the thoughts revealed by the spell.

Ruslan looked at Kiran. "Well, *akhelysh?* What information did we glean from our quarry?"

Kiran struggled to order his mind. Though his emotions had calmed, his thoughts still felt dismayingly scattered, the flame of his *ikilhia* oddly erratic. "He uses the blood of his victims in some fashion, though I don't see how blood from the dead can support any significant spellwork…" Even old blood could hold power, true, but far less than metals or gems. "Whatever his method of magic, it cannot be sustained for long; he was concerned about it running out. He cursed with the name Vaz-Kavash, like it was a god's name, but I've never read of that god in the southern or eastern pantheons. That implies he's not Varkevian, Sulanian, or Arkennlander by heritage."

"Vaz-Kavash is the name certain Kaithan tribes give the lord of dust and bone, the carrier of dead souls," Lizaveta said thoughtfully.

Ruslan nodded. "That combined with their myths about ghouls makes me think our quarry is Kaithan by birth. But his heritage is far less important than the implication of his attitude toward mages. Hard as it may be to believe, I suspect our quarry is *nathahlen*."

"Not a mage?" Mikail sounded stunned. "But…how can that be? Mere charms can't provide such thorough protection against defensive magic. Even the Tainted cannot stand against mages as this man has done."

Kiran had to agree with Mikail. "I don't see how an untalented man could have survived the strike I cast against him in the workroom this morning, let alone disappear as if by will."

Ruslan shook his head, slowly. "I share your confusion, *akhelyshen*. If he is merely a mage's catspaw, then that mage is far cleverer than I had imagined to cover his participation so well. The man whose thoughts we heard believes himself the architect of these attacks."

"How interesting." Lizaveta traced a finger along her slender silver blade. "A *nathahlen* enemy…we have not been threatened by such a one in countless long years."

"A threat we must remove soon." Ruslan's tone was far heavier than Kiran would have expected. "Sister mine, I fear my pessimism is confirmed. The deaths and attempted disruption of water magic are secondary to our enemy's main aim: the destruction of the confluence."

"The confluence?" Kiran stared, shock piercing layers of calm. "'The great wound in the mother-vein, cauterized at last'…that's what you think he means? How could he possibly hope to do it?" That incredible sea of magic, so wild and deep that even the spells of the *akheli* left no more than ripples on its surface…Kiran couldn't imagine how any mage could seriously affect it, let alone a *nathahlen*.

"It has happened before," Ruslan said. "Far from here, and with a confluence much smaller in size…but I have seen it done." His eyes held Lizaveta's, sharing some memory that turned their faces strange and ancient, a brief glimpse of the centuries that lay beneath their unchanging vitality. "A confluence exists because a balance of forces within the earth restricts the usual flow of magic, instead causing it to pool like water in a cistern. Disrupt those forces enough, and the magic will burst free to seek new paths, in similar fashion to spell energies when a channel pattern is too weak to control their flow."

"But a backlash of forces as powerful as the confluence's…" Kiran went cold. *Soon, all the vipers will burn…* "That would kill every mage in the entire Painted Valley." Along with any *nathahlen* bound to them; and the *nathahlen* who survived the initial magical conflagration would find themselves without water.

"Yes," Ruslan said simply. "And distance will not save any mages who might flee. All of us who reside here have made blood vows to Sechaveh that link us irrevocably to the confluence."

Kiran swallowed. He didn't remember making any such vows, though it could well have happened in the days he'd lost. Not that it mattered—the mark-bond he and Mikail shared with Ruslan meant any vows Ruslan had made linked them just as tightly to the confluence.

"Isn't there some way we might dissolve that link?" Mikail asked. "If the binding could be released, we could seek safety elsewhere, and return afterward—"

Ruslan snorted. "To what? Should our enemy succeed, this valley will be left as barren of magic as the mountains. I will not run away like some sniveling charm-maker. Lizaveta and I searched for long decades to find a source of magic plentiful as this one. No one, mage or *nathahlen*, will take it from me."

"If you know how this disruption of forces is done—how do we counter him?" Kiran asked.

"By destroying him," Ruslan said. "We have not the time to counter him otherwise. To hold the balance of forces, we would first have to map their every detail; whereas our enemy needs no such knowledge. Think of a spinning top: easy for a child to flick it over with a finger. Far more difficult to use that same finger to keep the top in continuous motion. Thankfully, our enemy's mediocre level of talent once again works in our favor. If he had the strength to alter confluence currents as we *akheli* can, he could have pulled the earth-forces out of balance long since. But instead of altering the currents to his design, I believe he waits for the confluence's natural pattern to be in a propitious alignment, and then causes upheavals large enough to send the currents battering against the forces that contain them. A crude, brute-force method, and one that will need time and repetition to succeed. I think we have a week, perhaps even two, before he can increase the stability of the confluence beyond recovery."

A week didn't sound very long to Kiran at all. He exchanged a troubled glance with Mikail, who asked, "Do you know the alignment he seeks, and can we predict its next occurrence? If we knew when he would next strike…"

"Prediction is always challenging with currents as complex as those of the confluence, but yes, I intend to anticipate him," Ruslan said. "Then we will see how he fares when facing not one *akheli*, but four." The smile he swept over Kiran, Mikail and Lizaveta shone with savage anticipation.

No wonder Ruslan had wanted him to study wounding spells. Kiran would have no hesitation whatsoever casting against the man who'd so badly injured both him and Mikail.

Lizaveta stretched, slow and languid. "A shame we'll have to kill him swiftly. Death seems so meager a payment for the trouble he's caused us. But here, brother…your *akhelyshen* are wavering on their feet. Show them some kindness and let them rest while I help you analyze the confluence currents."

It was true, Mikail looked exhausted, and Kiran felt little better. Even without his active participation, the spellcasting had left him drained and weary, especially coming so soon upon his body's healing.

"Your advice is as excellent as ever." Ruslan kissed her hand and nodded to Kiran and Mikail. "Rest while you can. The hunt will come soon, and I need you both ready to cast."

Kiran followed his mage-brother out of the workroom, the stained anchor stone looming large in his mind. Ready to cast…he had to get over his reluctance over blood magic, and soon. With the life of every mage in Ninavel resting on their spellwork, he couldn't afford to balk. If he could only understand why he struggled so with the idea of harming *nathahlen*…

He stopped short near the base of the staircase. "Mikail."

Mikail swung around. His gaze flicked to Kiran's white-knuckled grip on the iron banister. "What's wrong?"

"Something happened, didn't it? In the time I can't remember. Something to do with a *nathahlen*, that caused the…squeamishness I feel now. You have to tell me what it was."

Mikail's mouth set in a hard line. "Nothing happened."

Kiran descended to take his shoulders. "Don't lie. Not to me. Please, Mikail…" He bent his forehead against Mikail's. "Something changed me, left me weak. I know it in my bones. How can I overcome the weakness if I don't know the cause?"

Mikail's breathing faltered. His hands slid up to tangle in Kiran's hair. "You're not weak, Kiran. You're just…recovering. Believe me, remembering the past wouldn't help that recovery one jot."

"You don't know that," Kiran insisted.

Mikail let out a laugh that was halfway to a sob. He drew back, enough so he could hold Kiran's gaze. "Little brother, *trust* me. You know I'd give my life for you. The past has nothing you need. If you've any love for me…then promise me you'll leave this be."

He waited, eyes fierce. Kiran pulled him close again, so Mikail couldn't see his face, and said quietly, "I promise."

A pang of guilt stabbed him when Mikail relaxed. But it was love that had driven him to lie; if he didn't want Mikail punished for his sake, he had to find the key to remove his own reluctance. Besides, he'd meant part of the promise: he wouldn't task Mikail with any more questions.

Mikail wasn't the only person he could ask. Once Mikail had fallen into exhausted sleep, and Ruslan and Lizaveta were barricaded behind wards to study the confluence, Kiran would have a precious window of time in which he could leave the house unhindered and unobserved. A chance he didn't intend to waste.

CHAPTER SIXTEEN

(Dev)

"Here we go," I muttered to Lena, and pushed open the door of the Silvermule tavern's back room. Inside waited Red Dal, lounging in a battered old chair with his legs kicked out before him and a drink in his hand. His collar was open, the wide crimson birthmark that'd inspired his name showing like a splash of blood at the hollow of his throat. The warm glow of the oil lamp overhead revealed signs of age the darkness had hidden during my vigil outside his Tainter den. Gray threaded his dark curls, and the lines graven in his mahogany skin were far deeper and more numerous than I remembered. He still bore the glint of mischief in his eyes that'd charmed me blind as a kid.

I hadn't been in the same room with him in years. Even after all this time, seeing him up close burned like I'd swallowed magefire. Yet at the same time, a near-manic anticipation bubbled through me, strong as any I'd felt upon climbing the final pitch up a mountain summit. After all these months, I'd walk out of this room with Melly's freedom assured at last.

Red Dal raised his glass in greeting. Ward charms glinted on his wrists, though his real protection was his arrangement with Acaltar's top ganglord. Anyone who touched him would answer to her deathdealers. Word was she even employed a mage or two to take care of particularly tough targets.

Red Dal said, "It's been a long time, Dev, hasn't it? Nice to see you've turned your hand to brokering. I always like to see one of my kids do well for himself, and you were one of my best."

His words were warm, his expression fond with a wistful hint of nostalgia.

Bitterness scalded me. "I see you've the same smooth tongue."

Red Dal's dimples deepened. "Sit, and let's discuss what I can do for you…and your employer." His laughing brown eyes raked over the silver sigils patterning Lena's overtunic. If he was surprised to see me working for a mage, he was too canny to show it.

Two equally hard-used chairs sat facing his. The windowless room was barren of all else. Red Dal didn't bother with an office. Enough streetside taverns had private rooms and owners willing to keep their mouths shut that he didn't lack in spots to meet potential clients.

Lena stalked over to the nearest chair and lowered herself to sit piton-straight on the very edge of the seat, doing a fair imitation of Stevan at his most icily impassive. I followed, but didn't sit, instead standing behind and to her left like a sulaikh-servant.

Red Dal sipped from his cup, watching her over the rim. "I must say I'm a trifle puzzled, now you're here. Dev's message implied we might do business…but what can a humble man like myself do for a mage?"

"I require a certain commodity I was told you could provide." Lena's tone was as coldly polite as her face.

Red Dal's eyes took on a gleam of interest. "And this commodity would be?" Plenty of scholars and highside collectors hired Taint thieves to steal items out of a rival's house. Mages didn't usually do the same, since the Taint wasn't much good against active casting, but it happened on rare occasion.

"I am researching the interaction of the Taint and magic, and I need a strongly Tainted subject for study," Lena said.

Red Dal lost a little of his smile. "Oh my. I'm afraid that could be difficult. Unless…" The smile returned, full force. "How old would the subject need to be?"

I knew what the rat bastard was thinking. He wouldn't want to lose an experienced Tainter at the height of his or her power, but a toddler just old enough to show real talent would be a different story. It's not easy to find strongly Tainted kids, but certainly not impossible.

"The best subject for my research would be a child close to their Change. I'm told you have a girl nearing that age." Lena didn't look at me, but Red Dal did, his eyes sharp.

"You surprise me, Dev. I thought you had a fond spot for my kids."

I kept my body relaxed and my expression sardonic. "So? Fondness doesn't mean shit when it comes to a payday. Learned that from you, in fact." I gave him a sandcat's razored grin. "You know the one law in Ninavel."

"Profit over all," Red Dal agreed, with a sly, conspiratorial wink that made my hand ache for my boneshatter charm.

Lena allowed a hint of irritation to cross her face. "Is the child available, or isn't she?"

Red Dal set his cup down on the floor, his expression shifting to one of pained regret. "Unfortunately, she's already spoken for, and my next oldest is still a good few years shy of his Change. I could make inquiries for you in other districts…"

He was far too cagey to have signed a contract yet. He just didn't want to lose the nice fat windfall the bids for Melly had promised him. I bit my tongue and didn't look at Lena. I'd warned her he might not cooperate at first. Now she'd have to get creative.

"I've made my own inquires," Lena said, colder than ever. "Your oldest child is the closest match for my needs. Are you saying you refuse me?" She lifted a hand, silver light sparking on her rings. Red Dal's tin cup glowed cherry red and melted into a sludge of metal.

I cheered silently as Red Dal's throat bobbed in a hard swallow. He edged his feet away from the smoking remains of his cup.

"Believe me, I'd love to do a deal, but it really is impossible." Real fear lay in his eyes, and I frowned. Something wasn't right, here.

"Explain," Lena commanded him.

"The girl is already promised to another mage. A blood mage." Red Dal spoke in an urgent, pleading rush. "Surely you can see my position. I signed a sigil-sealed contract with the girl's blood on it as surety—the deal's been made, and I can't go back on it, not for any price you offer. Look, I've even got a message from him—just got it this evening, says I should show it to anyone who disputes his claim…" He dug in a pocket.

My first crazy thought when he said "blood mage" was that somehow Kiran had gotten his memory back. But Red Dal's fear was all too damn familiar. Horror seeped through me.

"This blood mage," I said tightly. "Was he a tall, broad-shouldered man with long red-brown hair and a strange accent? Ruslan, by name?"

"He didn't give a name. But yes, that's him." Red Dal sounded surprised. "You know him?"

I shut my eyes, fighting the urge to scream, or stab someone. Ruslan! How the fuck had he found her? Kiran's memories were gone, and I hadn't once let Ruslan touch me. He had Melly's blood…shit, *shit!* Even if I snatched her away, it wouldn't matter how far we ran. With a blood sample to target his spells, Ruslan could kill her as easy as crushing an ant, whenever he chose.

"Oh yes," Lena told Red Dal grimly. "He is known to me. Show me his message."

Red Dal handed her a paper with a single red sigil on it. Lena frowned and traced a finger over the sigil. Nothing happened. She looked all the more grim, and held the paper out to me. "Take this, but don't touch the sigil."

I tweezed the paper between wary fingers. The sigil promptly flared and spread into a line of dark, spiky writing.

One word to him of his past, and I'll make the girl-child eat her own flesh.

The paper dropped from my nerveless fingers. "You said you got this tonight. When did you sign the contract?"

"Yesterday." Red Dal shifted in his chair, his eyes darting between us. "Heard two days ago a stranger had been asking after me, but nobody would say who, or what he looked like. Next thing I know, a blood mage stalks in through my door."

Yesterday. Ruslan must have started looking for Red Dal right after I'd spoken to Kiran the first time. Kiran and Marten had both thought Ruslan too dismissive of the untalented to treat me as an enemy—and even today, when I realized they were wrong, I'd thought he go after me directly. That with Kiran's memories wiped away, Ruslan would have no insight into my past.

What a fool I'd been! He must've interrogated Kiran about me before he blotted out Kiran's memories. Kiran wouldn't have told him of Melly willingly. Nausea twisted my gut as I imagined Kiran screaming like Torain had. What else had Kiran told him? Oh shit, I had to assume he knew about Cara. I had to warn her, tell her to run. Ruslan meant to use Melly as hostage to keep me clear of Kiran, but he wouldn't stop there. Not after today. I thought of Kiran's shadowed eyes and screaming nightmares, and my chest constricted like I'd fallen into an ice-melt lake.

"The child is still in your possession?" Lena asked Red Dal.

He nodded, watching her warily. "The blood mage said I could use her while her Taint holds, though she's his by contract. Said if she's handed off to another's care, though, he'll know, and would take it, ah…badly."

So not only was Ruslan ready to savage her in an eyeblink, she'd still be going out on jobs that could get her snatched by the mystery assassin. Sick, desperate fear weakened my knees. Ruslan could do whatever he wanted to Melly and I couldn't stop him, couldn't—

Wait. The embassy's wards were among the strongest I'd ever seen. If I could get Melly there before Ruslan realized it, maybe the Alathians could stop him casting against her.

I clamped Lena's shoulder and whispered in her ear, "I want her out of there. Make him give her to you, hurt him if you have to, I don't care what it takes—"

Lena gripped my wrist and my voice locked. Furious, I jerked against her hold, even as she ordered Red Dal, "Leave this room, but do not wander far. I shall call you back momentarily, and if you are nowhere to be found, I will be the one to take it badly."

He nodded, his face gone sallow, and darted out the door as fast as if a direwolf chased him.

Lena raised her free hand and chanted a quick phrase. She held the pose a moment longer, then nodded in satisfaction.

The block on my voice released. "Why the fuck did you let him leave?" I snarled, tearing free of her grip.

"You and I need to talk. I cast a silencing spell so we can speak freely." Lena stood, casting her chair aside in one sharp movement. "I will *not* hurt him to get Melly for you. Ruslan is the problem now, not Red Dal. We must tell Marten—"

"No more waiting! Get her to the embassy. Halassian said your wards were strong enough to hold off Ruslan, right? If Marten doesn't like it, tough. Every damn lead you've had in this has come from streetside. You tell him he won't get a single thing more unless I see Melly safe." Even if safe meant Marten's hostage. Gods all damn me! I'd been so sure I could navigate a middle course, avoid handing her to him entirely. But now, if ever, I had to choke down hatred, for all it helped me ignore the black weight of self-recrimination. Marten would use Melly to keep me leashed, yeah, but he wouldn't skin her alive.

Lena said, urgent and frustrated, "No. Think. This is why Ruslan left her with Red Dal. He wants you to panic and run off with her to the embassy. Then he can go to Sechaveh and complain we've stolen his property, claim we are hindering his investigation, and insist that Sechaveh revoke our sanction."

I turned aside to brace my hands on the wall, breathing hard. Damn it! I could see Ruslan trying something like that. And Marten would hand Melly and me both over to Ruslan in an eyeblink before he'd risk getting evicted from the city.

How I wished Ruslan would find a way to hurt Marten, too; that I wouldn't be the only one to feel this agony of helplessness. I struggled to think past fear and fury.

"Does Marten have a way to stop Ruslan using the blood-mark? Some ward to protect Melly, or charm she could wear?"

Lena said reluctantly, "I'm not certain. The amulet Kiran wore would have been sufficient, but…"

The amulet Kiran had destroyed today to spare Jylla's life. Pain clawed at me. "Can you make another one?"

Lena shook her head. "Stevan modified an existing artifact to create that amulet. We have nothing of the kind here in Ninavel to work with."

"Gods all damn it!" I slammed a hand against the wall.

Anxiety tightened Lena's face. "It doesn't mean we can't help Melly. If there's a way to protect her, Stevan can find it. Truly, Dev, there's no man alive who's more skilled with defensive magic."

I knew a charm that might be powerful enough to protect Melly. The one I'd asked Avakra-dan to find, in hopes it could save Kiran. The Alathians had one, back in Tamanath—but even if Marten requested the Council send it, it'd take too long to reach Ninavel by courier, and the Council would never agree to release the border wards and cast another translocation spell for my sake.

I'd have to go to Avakra-dan again. Check on her progress, and offer her more coin—offer the moon, if necessary!—to get another one of those charms. In the meantime...

I said to Lena, "Go tell Marten, and be sure he's clear on this: either he gets Melly safe, or I'm done helping him. But first, call Red Dal back. Tell him you mean to bargain with Ruslan for the use of Melly in your research, and until then, you want to be sure she stays undamaged. No more jobs for her or you'll fry his ass. Give me that comfort, at least."

"You should return to the embassy with me and speak with Marten yourself." Lena's brows were drawn, her arms folded.

"I need to go warn Cara, and I'm not waiting one more instant to do it." I headed for the door, reaching for the copper band of the twin-seek charm on my bicep.

Lena blocked my path. "If Ruslan is moving against you, you shouldn't go alone."

I gave an acid laugh. "He's not moving against me, is he? Just my friends. I know Ruslan's kind. He'll want to see me suffer. No fun in torturing a dead man."

"Ruslan is not the only enemy we have to fear," Lena said.

"You mean the killer? Seems to me that if two blood mages got their asses kicked fighting him, you wouldn't fare much better. Hell, I'm probably safer solo than with one of you by my side. The bastard could've killed me easy as breathing in Naidar's house, but it was Kiran and Mikail he went for."

Her worried frown didn't change. I said, "Look. You've still got to question Red Dal about what he knows of missing Tainters. But this blood-mark is bad enough. If Ruslan finds Cara before I do, I'll—I'll—" The very thought was enough to stop my tongue, another wave of panic rolling over me.

Lena reached as if to offer comfort, her eyes soft with sympathy. I backed, and she dropped her hand, her fingers clenching. "All right. But don't wait to spark your signaling charm, should you notice anything odd. The last time you left to walk the streets alone, we found you in a bloodsoaked, ruined workroom about to attack a blood mage with your bare hands. I'd greatly prefer to avoid a repeat performance."

"Me too." Though in honesty I'd embrace any risk, no matter how insane, if it meant I could get Cara and Melly safe.

✳

I'd never had a more welcome sight than Cara hurrying toward me through a group of drunken miners staggering between taverns on Vasalis Street. The miners whistled as she dodged past. Some turned to watch with sloppy, appreciative grins, but none accosted her, warned by her scuffed outrider leathers and the charms glinting on her lean, muscled forearms that she was no easy slip. The crimson light from the taverns' burning firestone charms gave her pale hair a bloody cast. Her jaw was set, her face shadowed, yet she looked as beautiful to me as a mountain morning.

I caught her up in a hug, an avalanche of relief burying all else. "Cara, thank Khalmet. You've got to leave the city, right away. You've got to run—"

"Wait, what?" Cara twisted free of my grip. Her eyes widened, searching my face. "Oh, fuck. What's gone wrong now?"

I poured out the latest litany of disaster in a low-voiced rush, even as I drew her onward. I didn't mean to stop until we reached the stableyards just inside the city's sandstorm wall. This late at night, most would be barred and warded until the hour before dawn, but I knew a few whose owners would rouse readily enough for a bit of extra pay. I wanted Cara on a horse galloping out the Whitefire Gate as soon as we could arrange it. But it near killed me to see the depth of horror in her eyes when I explained what Ruslan had done, and why.

"It's my fault, I know it." I side-stepped around a charmseller's cart. Old childhood habit had me checking blurred, dim images of the market crowd behind us in the polished metal of dangling amulets. "I should've gotten Melly clear before I said one word to Kiran. He and Marten were so damn sure Ruslan wouldn't think me a threat, but I should've known better. I'll fix this—I'll get Melly safe if I have to sign my soul over to Marten to do it!—but you need to run for Alathia." Ruslan didn't have Cara's blood, and Kiran had once told me untalented souls were so dim they were nearly impossible for a mage to distinguish without something to key on. If she rode hard, she'd have a good chance of crossing Alathia's wards before Ruslan could find her.

A bare-chested Sulanian teenager with beaded braids hanging to his waist slid up to us. "You two look in need of relaxation. Bad times like these, you want Tanit's pleasure house! Jennies for a bargain price, trained in all the arts of love, glad to teach a lovely pair like you a few new tricks—"

Cara turned a glare on him that set him scampering backward. "Dev, I can't just run for Alathia! Bad enough to abandon you with Melly in such danger. But I've been working on finding passage for Gevia's cousin Keni, and Brant's widow Salvys with her twins, and Jasso—you didn't hear, but he broke a leg a month back climbing for carcabon stones—hell, all our friends who haven't the coin right now to leave the city. If I run, they'll be stuck here. Water rations went up to fifty kenets a liter today, did you know? People say there was a near riot at the Gitailan cistern. A bunch of streetsiders too poor to pay tried to force their way past the guardsmen at the cisternhouse gate. The guardsmen triggered the defensive wards, and thirty people died. Things'll only get worse, and you know it."

I'd heard the dark edge to the crowd's mutter, the absence of laughter. People stood in tight clumps, their eyes wary and their hands clutching charms. "If you stay and Ruslan slices you into screaming ribbons, that doesn't help them either." I angled for another look at the shifting eddies of people behind us, this time in the murky glass of an ironmonger's shop.

Cara pinched the bridge of her nose. "What if I go to the embassy? You said their wards are strong. Hell, you said Jylla's hiding out there. If I stay there, not only could I still help Keni and the rest, but I can keep an eye on that backstabbing bitch for you in the bargain." I opened my mouth, and she held up a hand. "Don't give me shit about Marten. He's already got enough to leash you ten times over. One more hostage won't matter."

I slowed. "Fine, the embassy. Run to the Dawnfire Tower, fast as you can. Go by the roofs, not the streets."

"You're not coming with me?" Cara stopped dead.

"Keep walking," I said, in a sharp whisper. "No, I'm not. We've got a shadow man trailing us, and he matches the description Jylla gave. I'm going to draw him off while you run." It'd taken me longer than it should have to notice, between talking to Cara and the dim light of firestone charms and shop lanterns, but now I was certain. A man whose night-dark skin spoke of Sulanian blood, who had muscular arms, a topknot of tightly curled hair, and a narrow, cleft-chinned face...he wore the copper-stained coveralls of a miner and moved casually, sometimes appearing to stop and talk, other times ducking into market stalls as if making purchases. But he'd stayed with us the whole length of the street, and as Jylla had said, his eyes were quick.

Cara didn't try to gawp around for him, thank Khalmet. She strode on, though her hands fisted tight. "What if Jylla's right, and he's working for the killer?"

The thought of Naidar's shadow marking him out for a bloody death in the Aiyalen Spire had the skin of my neck crawling. Wouldn't be long before the markets started shutting down until dawn. He might be waiting 'til the crowds thinned to make some move. But I had one advantage Naidar didn't, for all his magic.

"No shadow man can follow me if I take to the walls," I said. "If he does work for the killer, this could be the best chance for a lead yet. I'm signaling the Alathians now." I tapped my fingers in the pattern Marten had taught me on the gold band circling my wrist, and felt the metal warm. "Once you're clear, I'll scramble up and lose him, then turn the tables and do a little shadowing of my own."

"Dev…" Reluctance was all over Cara's face.

"*Please,* Cara. Best thing you can do is to get to the embassy and tell Ambassador Halassian what's happening here."

Cara grimaced, but she jerked her head in a nod.

"When we cross behind that spice cart, split off down that alley," I told her. We passed behind battered shelves redolent with cinnamon, cardamom, and anise. Cara cast me one stricken, burning glance, and disappeared into the alley's darkness.

I strode on, heart pounding. Thank Khalmet, the shadow man did too. Two streets down, I ducked down a slit between two wineshops. The walls loomed above me, ten stories tall, the stars glittering high above.

I didn't dare wait for my eyes to adjust to the darkness. I brushed my fingers over the wall and found a mortared crack. Right as I pulled up, a voice spoke from behind me.

"*Assilia kora meit,*" it said, in heavily accented Varkevian. A rush of wind as hot and violent as a sandstorm tore me from the wall. I hit the rough stone of the alley floor hard enough to knock every wisp of air from my lungs.

Dazed, my head ringing, I tried to roll to my feet. Nothing happened. My muscles burned and tingled as if pierced by a thousand tailor's needles, and wouldn't respond to a single one of my desperate mental commands.

Hands gripped my shirt and yanked me up. My back slammed against the wall. Magelight flared to paint the walls with sickly green. The cleft-chinned miner loomed over me. Behind him stood a woman whose belted gray dress was marked with purple sigils of a style I didn't know. The magelight gleamed from a thick triangular crystal held in her upraised hand.

Oh, fuck. None of the charms I carried would do much good against active casting, even if I could move to reach them. How long until the Alathians came? If I'd ever needed their help, it was now. At least Cara was clear. I squinted at the light of the alley's mouth. A steady trickle of people passed beyond. None of them looked our way. Every streetsider in Ninavel learns fast and early to keep clear of shadow business.

"Now here's a sight to gladden a man's heart," said a male voice whose mocking familiarity stopped my breath. Pello slid into the magelight. His mop of curls was hidden beneath a woven cap, but his sharp-chinned, coppery face was as sly as I remembered. "The resourceful outrider, helpless as a newborn kitten."

I tried to speak and managed only an airless wheeze. Pello grinned at me, his dark eyes glinting. Khalmet's hand, what was he doing mixed up in this? Back in Alathia, he'd claimed to work for Sechaveh. That must've been another lie.

"Well?" Pello asked the mage. "Did he signal anyone before you struck?"

The mage said, "He carries an active signaling charm, but I dissipated its magic the moment he triggered it."

Shit. Cara would tell the Alathians, but it'd take her a good hour to reach the embassy. Far too long, if Pello and his pet mage had anything truly nasty in mind.

The mage had spoken with all the bored impatience of someone stuck doing a distasteful but necessary job. She must've been paid to help Pello ambush me. But paid by whom?

"What of his other charms?" Pello asked. "Shaikar only knows what he's carrying."

Irritation twisted the mage's round face. "Don't concern yourself, shadow man." She leaned around the miner to clamp a hand on my shoulder. I braced myself for some awful manifestation of magic. Instead, in clipped tones, she proceeded to tell Pello exactly what charms I carried and where I'd hidden them. The thick-muscled miner kept me pinned to the wall as Pello dug every one of my charms out of their hiding places and dropped them into a sigil-marked cloth bag.

When he had them all, he handed the bag to the mage. She intoned something else in Varkevian. The sigils on the bag burst into violet flames. When the flames faded, the mage turned the bag over. A powdery cloud of ash drifted out to mix with the sand and grime coating the alley's stone.

"No mage can trace the charms now," she said.

I glared, fear and fury rising together. No chance of trying again to bring the Alathians, let alone using my boneshatter charm on Pello or the miner.

"Turn him around," the mage said.

My muscles still wouldn't obey me, nor would my voice. The miner yanked me around and shoved me face-first against the wall. A hand pulled the neck of my shirt down to expose my upper back.

Something cold and metal touched the base of my neck, right over my spine. Needling pain pierced my skin, like myriad fangs digging deep. The metal warmed to pulse unpleasantly.

Shit! They'd put a painbender charm on me. I couldn't pull the thing off. It had legs like a spider's that'd driven deep around my spine.

The miner swung me back around. Pello held out his hand to the mage. She dropped two thin gold rings into his waiting palm.

"It's ready to be keyed."

He pricked a finger and touched it to one of the rings before slipping the ring on. The metal at the back of my neck pulsed again. I took as deep a breath as my tingling muscles would allow, guessing what was coming next.

Sure enough, Pello held up a hand as the mage turned away. "Wait. I want to be sure this works." He whispered a word and clenched his fingers.

Knives of fire ripped through every organ in my body. A scream tried to escape me, though all that emerged was a hoarse croak. Agony blurred my thoughts, my vision going dark.

Abruptly, the pain ended. I hung limp in the miner's grip, my eyes burning and my chest heaving.

Pello watched me with a sharp, avid smile. "That's for the crossbow bolt you put in my shoulder."

It'd been Cara that shot him, not me. But she'd done it on my order. I mouthed a silent curse and spat.

He laughed and nodded to the mage. "Your part's done."

Her hands flexed like she wanted to cast something unpleasant on him. "Tell your employer my debt is paid."

I sure wished somebody would mention just who that employer was. This all felt a little too streetside for Ruslan. Besides, whoever wanted me, clearly wanted me alive. That mage could've killed me on the spot with her strike. Maybe the killer thought I could provide him information that'd let him ambush Kiran and Mikail again and win this time.

The miner let go of me. I stumbled and fell, my legs still useless. The miner scowled down in disgust. "How long before he recovers from your strike?

Look at him. We'll have to drag him the whole damn way to the meet."

"Not my concern." The mage strode out of the alley, taking the magelight with her.

The miner sighed and knotted a fist in my shirt to heave me back up to my feet. "Mages," he grumbled to Pello. "Raving assholes, every one."

"You have no idea," Pello said, with a depth of bitterness that set me wondering all over again. Whoever his employer was, he didn't seem thrilled about it. "Quit whining and start hauling."

The miner half-dragged, half-carried me toward the street, Pello pacing at his side. The tingling in my muscles slowly faded, but I let my feet drag. While I wore the painbender charm, I couldn't run, not unless I could get the control ring away from Pello first. If he thought me too weak to do anything, maybe he'd get careless.

At the alley's mouth, Pello edged out ahead to survey the street beyond. I let my hand swing out and scrape against the corner, hard enough to rip a shred of skin from my knuckles and leave a barely-visible smear of blood. Maybe nobody would see a stain so small, even the Alathians, if they ever came hunting. Still, it might be enough for a mage to use in a tracking spell.

As the miner hauled me along progressively darker and emptier streets, I couldn't help thinking of the horribly mutilated corpses in Aiyalen. Every spine-chilling tale I'd ever heard of demons ran through my head.

But when we finally ducked down another dark alleyway and they pulled me through a warped and stained metal door into a lantern-lit room, it wasn't some aloof mage who waited there amidst the crumbling stonework.

"About time," my former employer Bren snapped. "What, did you decide to go drinking along the way?"

He was a tubby Arkennlander in his late fifties, with a moon-round face and a generous mouth. Tonight he showed no trace of the jovial amiability he pretended with his clients. His stance was unyielding, his dark eyes cold and deadly, betraying the ruthlessness that made him Acaltar's best and longest-lived smuggling boss. The miner dumped me onto the cracked stones at his feet.

"The snatch needed to be quiet." Pello fished the second painbender ring from his pocket and handed it to Bren. "We had to wait until he slipped off and tried to lose Jasin. Besides, you're not the one paying me in this. You don't call the game."

Bren spat something guttural in Varkevian. It sounded like an insult rather than a protest. I wondered who was calling the game—the killer?

Pello ignored Bren and bent over me. "Shame you never learned to play any part but a token's. But you're not the first man to be crippled by his loyalties." His tone was mocking, but his eyes were dead serious.

My voice was finally working again. "Thought you worked for Sechaveh," I husked out.

"Not anymore." He said it flat and hard. Before I could frame another question, he said to Bren, "He's all yours," and slipped out, the miner on his heels.

"Bren? What the hell is this?" I shoved up, but only made it as far as my knees before Bren kicked me back down.

"Did you think you could cross me and get away with it?"

"Cross you? Other way around, wasn't it? Who tricked me into trying to smuggle a blood mage across the border, without so much as a hint of the true risk? I finished your Shaikar-cursed job in spite of all you left out, and earned my pay as fair as you could ask for." I'd nearly died about ten times over on that Khalmet-touched trip, and my survival was no thanks to him or his partner Gerran.

Bren clenched his ringed hand. Pain savaged me, blotting out thought. When it finally ebbed, I found myself lying curled at his feet, every muscle aching and my breath coming in hitching gasps.

Bren said, "You left out the part where you sold out Gerran and his entire operation."

"Oh shit, the Council—" I blurted, before I could stop myself. "They arrested Gerran, didn't they." Marten hadn't told me, damn him. Though I should have guessed it. At Kiran's trial, the Council had questioned me under truth spell about my smuggling. They must've followed up on what I'd told them and ferreted out Gerran and his holdings. I hadn't spared Gerran a thought until now, being more than a little preoccupied with other matters.

"Arrested him, confiscated the contents of his warehouses and all his accounts, and executed him," Bren agreed. "He and I built our business over more years than you've been alive, you little shit. You have no concept of how much your big mouth has cost me."

My stomach sank. I'd worked for Bren because he never went back on a deal, but that went two ways. Men who broke faith with him didn't live long. The ominously dark stains on the room's stone loomed large in my eyes.

"When a bunch of Alathian mages grab you and question you under truth spell because they're all riled up over a blood mage crossing their precious border, you don't have too much say in what comes out of your mouth. Look, I'm sorry about Gerran. But for Khalmet's sake, I didn't do it deliberately! I didn't even know they'd grabbed him."

Bren laughed, a grating chuckle. "Right. That's why the first news I hear of you back in Ninavel says you're errand boy to a gang of Alathian mages."

"Did Pello tell you that? You know he lies like other men breathe." News traveled fast in the city, but this was a little too fast. I'd taken care not to be seen streetside with anyone in an Alathian uniform. If I'd been recognized with them highside, that pointed to surveillance of either the Alathians themselves, or the specific sites where the killer had struck.

"Didn't need a shadow man for that. Seems at least one of your foreign friends doesn't like you much. Can't imagine why." Bren's smile displayed far too many teeth. "Got a nice sigil-sealed letter telling me all about how you dance to the Council's tune now. Before you try and deny it, I'll have you know I did my own checking. You're the cause of my woes, sure enough."

"That letter wasn't from any Alathian." I wasn't sure yet how Pello played into this, but I'd been wrong again about Ruslan. Practicality must have won out over sadism. He'd use Bren for the killing thrust, and never once break his vow. "Fuck with me, Bren, and you're fucking with not just one, but an entire crew of mages."

Bren snorted. "You think those Alathians will care if you vanish? They'll find a new informant without blinking twice."

"Oh, they'll care," I assured him. "Because they'll assume I got snatched by the mage-killer they're hunting with Lord Sechaveh. When they find the trail leads only to a streetside smuggling boss, you think they'll just let you walk away whistling? They'll be pissed at all that wasted effort and take it out on your hide." Not that I believed Marten would bother to take revenge, but Bren wouldn't know that.

"Luckily, you're not the only one who can make deals with mages," Bren said. "The trail won't lead here."

He spoke with complete certainty. Maybe Ruslan had promised him safety from retribution. Or perhaps he meant Pello's mystery employer. Sweat slicked my palms. "Trusting a mage is like asking a scorpion not to sting, and you know it. Otherwise, we wouldn't be talking. You'd have had your pet mage kill me in that alley."

"Didn't I say I wanted a chat?" Bren leaned down. "You're going to tell me every word you blabbed to the Council about my methods and couriers. Hell, by the time I'm done with you, you'll sell out your dearest friend if I ask it. And then, when you beg me nicely—*that's* when I'll kill you. Or maybe I won't. Did you know that if a painbender charm's triggered for too long, it can burn away a man's nerves entirely, leave his limbs forever useless?" The painbender ring glittered as he clenched his fist, slowly.

Every nerve screamed. I convulsed, clawing at the back of my neck, as if that'd make a difference. The pain went on and on, a red wave drowning me. Some part of me laughed, outraged and ironic: to think I'd survived blood mages and years of dangerous climbs, only to be crippled by a streetside smuggling boss. Until the wave crested higher, and all thought shredded away.

CHAPTER SEVENTEEN

(Dev)

Someone shouted. A blaze of azure light pierced the crushing weight of agony, and the pain vanished. The relief was so great that for a moment all I could do was lie quivering face-down on stone, my mind still a cringing blank.

Slowly, sense returned. Bren lay sprawled right in front of my nose, his eyes shut and his body slack. Oh thank Khalmet, the Alathians had come. I'd kiss even Marten's feet for saving me this time. My limbs—could I still move them? My toes and fingers wiggled at my command, and I rested my forehead briefly on the stone, my eyes damp with relief. I rolled over, graceless as a drunk, and froze in surprise.

A dark figure stood in the shadowed alley beyond the open door. The jagged red and black sigils on his clothes seemed to writhe like serpents in the flickering light of Bren's candle lantern.

"K—Kiran?" My voice was rough, my throat raw. I'd probably been screaming, though I didn't recall it. Only the pain, huge and terrible.

Kiran emerged from the shadows. I squinted at the darkness behind him, fearing to see Mikail—or worse, Ruslan. "What are you doing here? Are you—?"

"Alone? Yes." Kiran looked down at Bren's limp body, his face every bit as cold and severe as Ruslan's. A chill slid down my spine.

"Did you kill him?" I couldn't tell if Bren was breathing.

Kiran turned to me. His black brows drew together. "No. Do you wish me to?"

Yes. The word trembled on my tongue in pure vindictive reaction. But I wanted answers about Pello. Besides, Kiran was watching me with a strange intensity. I thought of Marten saying, *You must show him Ruslan's path isn't the one he wants to travel.*

"No." I kicked Bren's side, not gently. "He may know something useful."

"What did he want from you, and what might he know?" Kiran asked.

"He was just pissed because he thought I'd sold his smuggling operation out to the Alathians," I said. "But to get hold of me, he dealt with someone who might work for the killer." I reached for the painbender charm that still hugged my spine. "Can you get this damn thing off me?" I could take the control ring from Bren, but the ring was still keyed to him and wouldn't respond to another.

Kiran brushed a hand over the charm. Metal claws retracted from my flesh, the thin, needling pain a lover's kiss compared to what had come before. Kiran caught the charm as it fell. He held it up a moment, studying it; then tossed it aside with a contemptuous flick of his wrist.

"Thanks." I put the full weight of my relief into the word. "For this, and for...what you did earlier, in Naidar's house. I hope Ruslan wasn't too hard on you for it."

He looked away, the skin seeming to draw tighter over his high cheekbones. "No. He was lenient."

I wasn't certain I believed him—and he still hadn't answered my first question. "What brings you down streetside to save my ass this time?" I sure didn't think this little rescue was any part of Ruslan's plan.

Kiran shifted, minutely. "I came seeking you. I...have certain questions I need answered."

A startled laugh escaped me. I'd been touched by Khalmet's bony hand tonight, and no mistake. How badly had I wanted this chance? Here Kiran was, ready at last to hear the truth about his past. A truth I no longer dared tell him. Unless...if I could walk a clever enough line, reveal just enough to make him desperate for further answers, maybe I could turn this into a chance of a different kind.

※

(Kiran)

"Why do you laugh?" Kiran demanded. A voice within whispered, *You want answers from him? Then take them.* One touch, and he could slide straight into Dev's unprotected mind and hunt through his memories. That wasn't the same as a spellcasting; if he took care not to cause damage, Ruslan's will-binding would not prevent him. But even so, Dev would know the violation of his mind.

Why did that idea disturb him so deeply? Mikail would curse him for a fool.

"Your timing's both terrific and terrible." Dev looked exhausted, his eyes bruised and dark. Not surprising, given that mere moments ago he'd been contorted in agony, his hoarse, ragged howls audible long before Kiran reached the room. A surge of reluctant sympathy swept Kiran. He'd come within a heartbeat of killing Dev's *nathahlen* tormentor, and felt not a qualm. Part of him still wished the man dead, regardless of what he might know.

"Terrible, how?" Kiran certainly didn't see why Dev would be anything but grateful for his intervention.

Dev circled the unconscious *nathahlen* to peer out into the alleyway, as if he feared Kiran might have lied about being alone. "Before we talk further, I have to know—does Ruslan know you're here?"

"No." Kiran locked his hands behind his back. He didn't have to use Ruslan's methods with Dev. Besides, the Alathians would surely be watching for any signs of mental tampering in their guide. If they found evidence of it, they'd complain to Sechaveh, and then Ruslan would know his disobedience.

"He didn't feel you using magic just now?" Dev nudged his downed tormentor with a foot, then looked pointedly at the charm glittering in a grimy corner.

Kiran blinked, caught once more by surprise. How could a *nathahlen* know the mark-bond let Ruslan feel Kiran's magic as his own? "Only a small casting was needed, and Ruslan is currently...otherwise occupied." Behind the powerful wards of his workroom, with his attention fully focused on the confluence currents, the risk was small that Ruslan would realize Kiran wasn't merely casting a spell exercise. As long as Kiran kept any spells suitably minor.

"But once he's not 'occupied?'" Dev asked. "Will he see this conversation through that mark-bond of yours?"

Dev's knowledge had limits, then. Kiran said, "Only if he has reason to look for the memory." A scenario he certainly intended to prevent.

Wary relief showed on Dev's face. "Ask your questions, then."

Kiran took a steadying breath. Ever since he'd cast the seeking spell that had led him to Dev, he'd worried over how to phrase questions so he wouldn't reveal the full extent of his weakness. He feared there was no hope of avoiding it entirely. But he had to be cautious. Mikail was right in his warning that Dev worked for their enemies.

"The charm diagram you showed me in the murdered mage's house… where did you get it?"

Dev stepped over the *nathahlen* to lean against the scarred, stained stone of the wall. Despite the casual pose, Kiran sensed tension emanating from him. "From a friend."

The careful way he spoke the words brought sudden surmise. Dev was under constraint of some kind. Perhaps the Alathians didn't want him and Kiran talking any more than Ruslan did.

"A friend," Kiran repeated. "An Alathian?"

Dev shook his head. Still in that careful tone, he said, "You recognized the drawing, said it was yours. If you drew it, you know what the charm's for, right?"

"Yes." Dev didn't need to know how long he'd puzzled over the pattern frozen in his memory. In truth, he still didn't understand the charm's utility, but he had at least deciphered the spell's direct effects. "The charm would—"

The sudden, sharp interest in Dev's eyes made Kiran realize the question wasn't some type of test; that he held a bargaining token.

"I'll tell you what it would do," he said to Dev. "But you must answer one question first."

"Yeah?" Dev's expression grew guarded again.

"How long have you known Mikail?" *How long have you known me,* he wished he dared ask. But that would make his memory loss horribly plain. By coming at it slantwise, he might avoid revealing just how far that loss extended.

Dev stared at Kiran for a long moment. Then he grinned, sardonic and one-sided. "You should know. You were there when we met."

Frustration set Kiran's hands trembling. It would be so terribly easy to rip the knowledge he sought from Dev. "Don't play games," he snapped. *You don't understand how important this is,* he wanted to shout. But he wasn't such a fool as to explain to Dev that he needed to know the past to overcome his reluctance to harm *nathahlen*. "That morning in the dead mage's courtyard wasn't your first meeting with Mikail."

"You're right about that," Dev said, in a voice as dry as the desert. "But you don't remember." It wasn't a question.

Oh, Kiran would pay, and Mikail with him, if Ruslan ever found this memory. Yet a reckless defiance rose within him. He might as well ensure he learned something worth the risk. "Perhaps I don't. So why don't you tell me of it?"

Dev squeezed his eyes shut, as if in pain. "Mother of maidens, wouldn't I love to."

"You're afraid of the Alathians?" Kiran made a dismissive gesture. "Don't be. I can—"

Dev laughed sharply. "The Alathians? Hell, no. Marten would jump at the chance to answer your question."

Kiran rocked back on his heels as understanding flooded in. "You fear Ruslan's anger." Why would Ruslan want to prevent Kiran from discovering what Dev knew?

Dev said, bitter and mocking, "Don't sound so surprised. Everyone in Ninavel knows what it means to cross a mage. I'm no different."

Kiran frowned, struggling to understand. "But you're under Lord Sechaveh's protection. Ruslan vowed not to harm you."

"Oh, come on!" Dev snapped. "You know Ruslan better than that. Yeah, fine, so he won't burn me to ash on sight. Believe me, there are plenty of ways to fuck someone over without touching a hair on their head."

Kiran got a flash of the frantic, guilty horror he'd felt upon hearing Mikail's cry of pain. "He's threatened someone you care for."

"Exactly." Dev's eyes burned. "A helpless little kid, to be specific. He said if I told you of your past, he'd make her 'eat her own flesh.' Your master is one sick son of a bitch."

Kiran looked down. Part of him wanted to protest, to defend Ruslan. *You don't know him*, he wanted to say. *He's not always cruel.* But Ruslan only showed his gentler moods with fellow *akheli*. He might well have threatened a *nathahlen* child and meant every word of it. The thought made Kiran's stomach twist. "If you fear for the child, why are you even talking to me?"

"Because you're my best chance at saving her," Dev said. "Ruslan holds a blood-mark contract for the Tainted child Melly *na soliin*, signed by her handler Red Dal. Get me that blood-mark, and I'll tell you what Ruslan's so desperate to keep you from remembering, under any truth spell you care to cast."

Kiran was silent, torn. He wanted answers, yes. But sneaking out to question Dev was one thing. To defy Ruslan so directly would risk punishment on a scale his heart quailed to imagine.

Dev was watching him, fierce and intent. "How much have you lost? Months, years? How can you stand not knowing what he took from you?"

Kiran's chest went cold. "*Took* from me? It was an accident. A spell backlash."

"Is that what he told you?" A terrible, unmistakable pity shone in Dev's eyes.

"I…" A shiver ran over Kiran. Could Ruslan have…? No. Ruslan was harsh in his punishments, but they never came without cause, or resulted in lasting damage. He would never cripple Kiran so deeply. *Unless he believed it necessary,* a small voice whispered. But what could drive Ruslan to that extreme? And to believe that not just Ruslan, but Mikail and Lizaveta would all lie to him so thoroughly? No, it wasn't possible. Ruslan had warned him of the Alathians. *They are experts in the use of lies… They will try to make you distrust us, distrust yourself.*

Shame seared him to realize how readily he'd been thrown into confusion. "Tell your masters they cannot so easily turn me against Ruslan. The bonds among *akheli* run far too deep to be weakened by your lies."

Dev's face tightened with frustration. "You don't want to believe me about Ruslan, fine. But I *know* you, Kiran. I know how this…this hole in your mind must drive you crazy. I want to give you answers—you don't know how badly! But I won't sacrifice Melly to do it. Help her, and let me help you."

I know you. Against all caution, the words tugged at him. While Dev might lie about Ruslan, either deliberately or as a dupe of his Alathian masters, Kiran's gut insisted Dev wasn't lying about that. Dev's knowledge might yet be the key Kiran needed to remove his hesitation over blood magic. But if he stole the contract from Ruslan as Dev asked…what if Dev was lying about the child? This could be some scheme of the Alathians, meant to entrap Kiran.

At Kiran's feet, the *nathahlen* man stirred and groaned. Kiran glanced down, ready to siphon away more of the man's *ikilhia* to send him unconscious again. Only to abort the power draw when he found the man staring up at him in stunned recognition.

"You!" The man croaked.

Kiran met Dev's startled gaze, saw Dev's green eyes go wider yet.

"Kiran, *wait*—!"

Kiran knelt and snatched at the man's bare wrist. Slipping into the *nathahlen*'s mind was simple, the man's instinctive resistance destroyed as easily as ripping away a gauze curtain. He sought his own image in the man's memories, chasing down linkages still bright with the man's surprise at seeing him.

He found a memory of himself, looking strained but imperious, standing in a dingy room with crudely warded walls. *I wish to leave Ninavel and cross the Alathian border in secret. No one must know my identity as a mage.* The *nathahlen*—Bren, his name was—had nodded, readily agreeing…because earlier, Ruslan had stood in that same office. *My apprentice will come to you*

seeking passage to Alathia. You will arrange it—but beforehand, you will see that news of his intended crossing reaches an exiled Arkennlander mage living hidden in the Alathian city of Kost. Whatever bargain the exile wishes to make with you, you will take, and you will ensure my apprentice does not learn of it.
And then, a later memory: himself in the office again, silently watching as Bren hired a reluctant, sharp-eyed Dev to guide him across the border.

Shock threatened to shatter his concentration. Kiran clung to his focus. He searched further, found memories of Bren reading messages from his business partner Gerran in Alathia, messages that had been couriered across the border and then charm-sent. First a message saying Kiran was to be handed unwitting to the exiled mage in Kost; later, another claiming the handover had gone successfully, all payments made. Then, silence. Bren's increasingly worried messages gone unanswered, the news eventually coming by courier: Gerran executed, all his holdings gone. Later yet, a letter sealed with an Alathian sigil, telling of the courier Dev's testimony against Gerran at the blood mage Kiran ai Ruslanov's trial—

His focus broke, the weight of surprise too great. He dropped Bren's wrist, leaving the man twitching, only semi-conscious. "I was *captured and tried by the Alathian Council?*"

Dev's body was as taut as a bowstring. "How much did Bren know? Do you remember why you went to Alathia?" The question held a strange mix of dread and hope.

Kiran clawed for Bren's wrist again, dug through memories with wild abandon. Nothing, the man knew nothing, curse him! Bren had been too afraid of Ruslan to risk digging into his affairs in Ninavel, and the news he'd had of events in Alathia was maddeningly sparse. The letter he'd received said Dev had exposed Gerran and agreed to work for the Council to avoid execution, but said nothing of Kiran beyond the mere fact of his trial.

"I don't." Kiran cast Bren's wrist aside and stood. "But you know, don't you? You guided me there, were captured with me..." He advanced on Dev, power rising to strain against the inhibition of Ruslan's will-binding. But he didn't need power. All he needed was to touch Dev. He had to know the truth. Nothing else mattered, not with answers so tantalizingly close.

Dev hastily backed, his eyes flicking from Kiran to the doorway beyond. "Kiran, don't. If you learn all that I know—trust me, you won't be able to hide it from Ruslan! I've nothing that can block your mark-bond, not yet—"

Kiran reached. Dev ducked aside, leaped over Bren and darted for the door. Kiran snapped out a tendril of power to seal it shut. Dev yanked at the door, muscles straining. When Kiran approached, he turned, his eyes wild.

"No! He'll find out, and it's not just Melly that'll suffer—he'll mindburn you, Kiran! You're at risk enough already! One hint to Ruslan of what you got from Bren, and you and Melly are both fucked..." He threw himself sideways, as Kiran reached again. "Mother of maidens, Kiran, *please!*"

The naked anguish in the word hit Kiran like a lash of spellcast ice. He halted, abruptly uncertain, reminded of his fear the Alathians would complain to Ruslan if he searched Dev's mind. He didn't believe Dev's claim of mindburning, but any realization by Ruslan of his disobedience would mean agony for Mikail. And if Dev wasn't lying about the child—Kiran winced, struck by a sudden image of Ruslan raising his knife over a small, screaming figure.

"The blood-mark," Dev said. "Get me the blood-mark, let me get Melly safe, and I swear to you, I *swear* it in Suliyya's name, I'll tell you everything, let you turn my mind inside out if you like!"

A new sensation snapped Kiran's head up. Power brushed at the edge of his senses, the taste of it both foreign and familiar...the Alathians were coming. Now he truly dared not touch Dev. The realization brought both disappointment and a strange, shaky relief.

"Your masters are coming for you," he said to Dev. "I must go."

Dev let out a ragged breath. He didn't shift from his tense half-crouch. "Will you help Melly?"

"I..." Kiran pressed the heels of his hands to his eyes. "I cannot promise anything. I need to think."

"Don't take too long," Dev said, strained and urgent. "If you find the blood-mark—how can we arrange another meeting?"

He should refuse to even consider this. Yet Kiran knelt by the barely conscious Bren and pulled free the thin silver band of a warding charm from the man's wrist. The spell bound within was crude, the metal impure, but the charm held enough power to work with. He reached for the spell pattern, twisted and reshaped it to match the one in his mind's eye.

He tossed the charm to Dev. "Take this. If it grows warm, spark it with your blood and the word *ashantya*, and then concentrate. You'll hear me speak in your mind and can reply likewise."

Dev's eyes narrowed. "This would let you into my mind?"

"It doesn't create a true link," Kiran said. "The charm allows for a brief communication of surface thoughts, one time only. The metal is too impure for anything more."

"So you say," Dev muttered, turning the charm over in his hands. When Kiran moved for the door, he backed along the wall to keep distance between them, watching Kiran with the wary intensity of a man guarding against a predator.

Guilt itched at Kiran. An apology rose to his tongue; he swallowed it down. He shouldn't show weakness. But his inner discomfort halted him in the doorway. He said in a low rush, "The charm diagram you asked about, before…a charm made with such a pattern would severely alter the body's functioning. It would compress and simplify the wearer's life energies, to the point they resemble a child's rather than an adult's…though why anyone would—"

"Khalmet's bloodsoaked bony hand," Dev said, in a tone that made Kiran turn, startled. "It's for a Taint charm." Dev slid down the wall as if his legs had given way. His upturned face had a strangely defenseless look.

"A Taint charm?" Kiran knew next to nothing about the Taint. New frustration burned in him. Why and how would he have designed such a pattern?

Dev sounded dazed. "It lets an adult use the Taint again. If you used to be Tainted." He stared at Kiran, his eyes wide. "That's what you—oh, mother of maidens." He covered his face.

A host of new questions boiled up in Kiran. But the Alathians were mere moments away. If he wished to leave without confronting them, it must be now. With a last, frustrated glance at Dev's bowed head, he hurried off. Alathia, the Taint, the exiled mage, Kiran's trial, Ruslan's supposed threat to the *nathahlen* child…how would he ever unsnarl the tangle? Perhaps… perhaps he should at least try to discover where Ruslan might keep the child's contract.

✳

(Dev)

I leaned my head onto my knees. I should get up, but now Kiran had gone, I couldn't bring myself to move. My body felt as heavy as stone, my eyes hot and swollen. A Taint charm. Gods. Thinking of Kiran tracing that spell out from memory for my sake made my chest hurt. Especially after seeing him act so dismayingly like Ruslan. The cold, predatory look in his eyes as he'd stalked me had chilled my soul.

What if he could complete that diagram and make another charm for me? Maybe even fix it so the spell didn't hurt me… Craving as strong as any addict's set my hands trembling. Next time I saw him, I could ask him, find a reason to demand it…

The charm was blood magic. It'd take murder to fuel the casting. Part of me recoiled at the thought. Another part of me—a deeper, savagely selfish part—didn't care.

"Dev?"

I looked up to see Marten hurry into the room, his round face full of concern. Stevan, Lena, and Talm piled through right behind him and fanned out with all the precision of a ganglord's crew. Talm knelt beside Bren's limp form, Stevan angled over to pick up the painbender charm gleaming in the corner, and Lena came to crouch at my side.

"I knew I shouldn't have let you leave alone. You look terrible." She put a cool hand on my brow, ignoring my reflexive flinch. A swift tingle swept over my skin. Her jaw tightened. She said to Marten, "Someone's used a pain inducer on him."

I leaned away from her hand. "Is Cara safe?" Suliyya grant she'd made it to the embassy.

"Yes," Marten said. "Though when she realized no signal from your charm had reached us, we nearly had to cast a binding on her to ensure she stayed at the embassy. We cast to seek you, at first without success. I feared you dead—or that if some mage had veiled you, that our spellwork wasn't strong enough to tear through...but then, all at once, the spell took."

"Here's the source." Stevan approached, painbender charm in hand. "This charm has a shrouding spell within it. Not blood magic, though the room reeks of it."

"Kiran was here," I said. "He took that painbender charm off me. He—"

"Did he kill this man?" Talm took his hands from Bren, looking more upset than I'd ever seen him.

"Kill? No! Bren's not dead—or at least, he wasn't when Kiran left..." I scrambled forward to stare at Bren's slack body. His skin was gray, his eyes open and staring.

"He died just now." Talm's hands were shaking, his face nearly as gray as Bren's. "I'm sorry, Marten. I haven't Jenoviann's skill with healing, and the man's mind was ruined as badly as the servant Ruslan questioned."

I sank back on my heels, cold once again, remembering the white intensity of Kiran's face, the ferocity of his grip on Bren's wrist. Easy to dismiss the price of blood magic when it wasn't right in front of me. Lena looked like she'd been kicked in the gut, and dismay showed plain on Marten's face.

Stevan said to them in bitter vindication, "You keep telling me Kiran is nothing like Reshannis. Yet he destroyed this man's mind, with no more care than Reshannis showed Vinalyn—" His voice broke, and he stopped, gripping the painbender charm like he wanted to hurl it at Marten. "He is no innocent! You must see that now!"

I said sharply, "Kiran saved me. If Bren's dead, he deserved it." I ran through a quick account of the snatch and its aftermath. I didn't mention the charm diagram, not wanting Marten and Lena to realize I'd been less than wholly honest on prior occasions. Or for them to realize just how tempted I was to ignore the cost and beg Kiran to make one. I also downplayed Kiran's near-assault on me. Hell if I'd give the Alathians more reason to condemn him. Kiran had been desperate, that's all. I'd done plenty of things in that state I'd regretted later.

"Twin gods above." Marten began pacing, his black eyes sharp with calculation. "The spy, Pello...Lena, Talm, you two led the hunt for him before Kiran's trial. I know we haven't any more of his blood here to key a seeking spell, but do you remember the pattern well enough to cast again?"

"I believe so." Lena glanced at Talm, who'd recovered his composure, though his hazel eyes remained bleak. He nodded in agreement. Lena said, "However, if Pello is veiled as thoroughly as Dev was, even a keyed spell may fail."

"Kiran didn't seem to have a problem finding me despite this veil you talk about," I said.

Stevan's mouth twisted. "He cast with blood magic. It's not so difficult to fashion spells powerful enough to rip through any amount of veiling, when you steal the lives of others to fuel them."

I stared, shocked. "You think he *killed* someone to find me?"

"Ruslan would have felt that, no matter the wards between them," Marten said. "I suspect Kiran used one of the warded reservoirs Ruslan keeps to fuel practice spells."

"The source of those energies is still murder," Stevan said harshly. "Kiran may not have killed the victims himself, but he uses their lives without regard for the cost."

I flinched, thinking of the Taint charm. Marten rubbed at his temples. "A discussion for another time. Stevan, I want you to study the shrouding spell in the painbender charm, in case we encounter its like again. Perhaps you can identify a weakness. Lena, Talm—go cast to seek Pello. You'll have a better chance of success if you cast from a spot where confluence currents are at an ebb and won't muddy your senses. Contact me if you feel the spell take. Lena, I'll also task you to send to Halassian. Ask her to contact Sechaveh immediately and ask what he knows of Pello."

Stevan bent over the painbender charm, not without a final dark glance at Marten. Talm and Lena bowed and hurried out. Marten started pacing again, with short, jerky strides. "I can hardly imagine a worse time for Kiran to learn of his past," he said. "Without the amulet, I cannot protect him."

"Don't I know it," I muttered. Shaikar take that mark-bond of Kiran's! If not for that, I'd have let Kiran see everything. He'd have turned against Ruslan then, no question, and I could've risked making a grab for Melly with his help. But without a way to block the mark-bond, Kiran couldn't hide, or run. If he returned to Ruslan's house knowing of Alisa's murder and tried to play the obedient apprentice, I gave him all of five words before Ruslan saw through the deception.

Marten said, "If he comes to you again, if he brings this blood-mark—you must stall him, until—" He stopped, his mouth compressing to a thin line.

"Until what?" I'd gambled everything that if Kiran found Melly's blood-mark and came back demanding answers, by then I'd have a way to save him too.

"Until Stevan can devise another means of protection," Marten said, so smoothly that I knew it wasn't what he'd originally meant to say. For the first time, I wondered if he truly had some plan in mind to take down Ruslan. Not that I could afford to trust him if he did.

Marten asked, "As it is, do you think Kiran can keep what he knows from Ruslan?"

"I'm not sure," I admitted bleakly. "I warned him, best I could. I know he can hide things—he kept Ruslan ignorant of Alisa for three years!—but if he doesn't heed my warning…gods, Marten, say you've a way to protect Melly."

Marten raked his hands up through his hair. "I wish you'd asked my help earlier. Ensuring her safety now will be challenging, at a time we can least afford distraction. Sechaveh sent us word: Ruslan believes the killer's aim is to destroy the confluence, in a conflagration that will kill every mage in this city, leave the untalented waterless—and destroy Alathia's wards beyond hope of rebuilding, for that matter. Ruslan thinks we have only scant days remaining to prevent disaster."

My mouth fell open. "Shit. Do you believe him?"

"In this, yes," Marten said. "Neither Sechaveh nor Ruslan would have revealed such weakness to foreigners if they didn't believe the situation dire."

Dire. No kidding. When this news spread, the city would dissolve into chaos, merchant houses fighting each other for the water and supplies needed to flee.

Unless the news didn't spread. "Sechaveh's not going to tell anyone, is he?"

"No," Marten said. "He warned that if any one of us spreads the word, he'll revoke our sanction and kill us all. He says, 'The best course is to find and stop the city's enemy, not make futile attempts to mitigate failure.'"

Fuck. It wouldn't keep me from trying to warn my friends, even if I had to be circumspect about the reason. But if time was so short, Marten wouldn't want to bother with any spellcasting that didn't help him catch the killer.

"So you won't help Melly, then." Especially not when I'd already given them another lead to chase, in the form of Pello. I'd have to pray I could get that magic-blocking charm from Avakra-dan. If Kiran came through with the blood-mark, then I'd need it for him, once I told him the truth. If he didn't, it'd be my last hope for Melly.

"I didn't say that." Marten looked wearier than ever. "But..."

Stevan looked up from the painbender charm. "Of course we will," he snapped. "Or does your sympathy only extend to blood mages and not their victims, Marten? You talk of protection for a murderer like Kiran, knowing it will take a miracle to devise it. The child is far more deserving of my effort."

"Stevan's right," I said, though the words near choked me. "Melly needs it more."

"Very well," Marten said heavily. "Stevan, if you will—"

The ground shook and sent us all staggering. Pale dust sifted down from the ceiling, accompanied by an ominous grinding. I lunged for the doorway. Silver limned the alley walls. High above, red and violet wardfire flickered across the stars.

Abrupt pain twisted in my chest, like a hook setting deep, and the world went black.

Hands were on me, my skin prickling with a warning of magic—I fought, frantic to get clear.

"Dev, hold! It's only us." Marten spoke in my ear. I was lying on unmoving stone. The walls were dark again, the night sky above clear of lightning. Marten was gripping my shoulders, and Stevan's hand pressed on the bare skin of my chest where my shirt had been pulled open.

"What the fuck?" I tried to push Stevan's hand away. I might as well have tried to move a stone pillar.

"You're right, he's been bound," Stevan said to Marten. "I don't recognize the type of magic, and I can't discern its caster. Yet I doubt the timing with the quake is coincidence. I think it the killer's work."

Marten asked me, "Did anyone tonight take a sample of your blood? Pello, or even Kiran?"

"What? No! I mean, I left a trace on a wall when Pello snatched me, but—

what the hell do you mean, bound? The killer can force me to obey him, like Ruslan with Kiran?"

"Impossible to say for certain, not without detailed study." Stevan spoke with clinical dispassion. Another prickling of magic chased over my skin. "The link is strange…almost, it reminds me of the blood vow Ruslan made Sechaveh. It ties to your body, not your will, and appears to terminate in the confluence."

"The confluence that's about to burn out in some magical explosion?" I demanded. "Tell me you can break this…link, binding, whatever the fuck it is!"

A tinge of his usual contempt crept into Stevan's voice. "Did I not say the magic is unknown to me? It's highly dangerous to try and break a binding without understanding it first. But a binding so strong can't be cast without either willing participation of the subject, or blood to key the spell, and a trace amount wouldn't be enough. If you want the binding broken, be honest: who in this city holds your blood?"

"Oh, hell." I struggled upright. "Avakra-dan."

CHAPTER EIGHTEEN

(Dev)

Avakra-dan's alley was as dark and silent as the depths of a crevasse. "A little help?" I asked Marten and Stevan. "Pello took my glowlight charm." I sure didn't want to risk touching the wrong spot on her warded door in the darkness.

I'd reluctantly explained my bargain with her to Marten and Stevan while we fought our way through shouting, frightened crowds in Acaltar's streets. Marten had listened in silence, but Stevan made enough acid comments about my idiocy and deceitfulness for both of them.

Marten's rings glowed softly silver, enough for me to see the copper plate amidst the grime on Avakra-dan's door. I scratched gently and stood back. Nothing.

"I say we break the wards, Marten." Stevan's face was all hard angles and shadows.

"Just be ready for trouble," I said. "Avakra-dan's untalented, but still. If anyone can fight a mage, it's her."

Marten flashed a grin at Stevan. "See what fun you've been missing, cooped up in the Arcanum? Come, then. Under my lead…" He and Stevan stood shoulder to shoulder before the door, their hands hovering over the surface. Marten started a low, sonorous chant. Ward lines burst to life beneath the dirt, glowing a lurid purple.

Stevan joined Marten, at first in perfect unison. Then his rich baritone diverged, sliding over and under Marten's voice in a pattern that diverged further with each repetition. The wards flared brighter, until I had to shield my eyes. A final searing flash made me hiss and duck, even as the wards went dark.

Marten and Stevan fell silent. They exchanged a swift, grim glance.

"You sense it?" Marten asked. Stevan nodded.

"Sense what?" I asked.

"Death," Marten said, and opened the door.

The light of his rings illuminated three eyeless, mutilated bodies dangling upside down from the ceiling. Their feet were impaled on hooks meant to hold charm amulets, their mouths gaping in lipless screams. Blood still dripped from their wounds to pool deep on the floor.

I choked and put my arm over my nose. No matter how many times I saw the killer's handiwork, I couldn't help but feel sick to the core. Marten and Stevan slid into the room, their rings glowing and their eyes intent. I jerked my gaze from the corpses, half fearing to see the killer lurking in some shadowed corner. If these deaths happened during the quake, he'd been here not a half hour ago.

The charms on the walls had all melted and fused into lumpy, gleaming runnels of metal that coated the stone like an icefall. On the bloodstained, blackened desk sat two copper strongboxes, their lids open wide, their wards shattered. One still held a minor fortune in coin and gems. The other was empty but for a few scraps of paper.

Didn't take a scholar to realize the empty strongbox had held her blood-marks. I grimaced, thinking of mine in the hands of the killer. Best case, he'd used up all my blood in casting the mystery binding. Worst case…what other spells might he cast on me?

That wasn't all I had to fear. From the looks of this, I'd lost all chance of finding a charm strong enough to protect Melly. Then again…I peered at the corpses. Two men and a woman, their ruined features obscured by gore, their bloodsoaked clothes coarsely woven and lacking in sigils. Yet the woman was too lean of build to be Avakra-dan.

"Avakra-dan's not here," I said. "But she'd never have left her den with clients inside it. She had to have been here when the killer came. Maybe he took her somewhere, along with her blood-marks." I pointed at the empty strongbox. "But if he's the one who cast the binding on me…why? And how the hell did he know my blood was here?" Bren's voice came whispering in my head. *Seems one of your foreign friends doesn't like you much…*

Stevan circled the corpses to examine the back wall. The stone there was adorned by tattered, reddened hangings instead of melted charms. "Look." He pulled aside a hanging to reveal a second door, scribed with both concealment and protective wards. "These wards are undamaged but inactive. Someone released them, and not long ago."

Marten opened the door and disappeared into the dark passageway beyond. He soon returned. "This leads to another alley. I saw no other bodies, and sensed no traces."

"Either she left with the killer...or perhaps she escaped him." Stevan heaved Avakra-dan's worktable aside, grimacing as his feet skidded in blood. Revealed on the floor were a series of copper rings set with clouded emeralds. The innermost ring's gems had splintered to shards, dark streaks radiating outward from the holes where they'd been. "Power was stored here, quite a lot of it, but none remains now. Released from its reservoir without control, the raw magic would have reacted against the magic stored within her charms and destroyed them in quite spectacular fashion." He waved a hand at the slagged metal on the walls.

"So you think she breached the reservoir as a distraction, and ran." That sounded like Avakra-dan, all right. I prayed she'd made it. Aside from any information she could give on the killer, or even my damn binding, I had to know if she'd found the charm I needed.

"Perhaps a more thorough examination of that alley is in order." Marten moved for the back door again, beckoning Stevan to follow.

"Wait." An old memory teased at me. Tavian's office had held an escape route much like this one. You never knew when lionclaw addicts would get violent, and some of his clients had been highsiders, with access to seriously nasty charms. Yet Jylla had once told me his setup held a dual purpose. "Do you sense any active hide-me wards remaining in the room?"

Marten frowned. "Hmm. It's a touch difficult to untangle traces with the confluence still so unsettled, but..." He paced along the back wall, past more shredded hangings. "Something here, quite subtle." He knelt and passed his hand over one of the broad stone blocks at the wall's base, humming.

The block shimmered. Hinges appeared, and a tracery of ward lines.

Ha. She did have a bolthole. Set off a nice big distraction, open the escape route as a decoy, then duck into the bolthole, leaving your enemy to chase down the wrong direction—classic.

"Someone's inside." Marten laid his palm flat on the false block. "Come out. Now. Or I will cast against you, and that paltry defensive charm I sense will not stop me."

Hinges creaked. Avakra-dan slithered out of the dark, cramped space behind the block, a heart-rot charm clutched in one hand. Her coarse mop of hair was singed half away, the skin of her face and arms a patchwork of raw, oozing burns and dried blood.

"So kind of you to ask nicely." Her black eyes settled on me, bright with anger. "Clever boy, to guess my bolthole. A bit too clever, yes? Shame about your blood-mark."

Did she mean something more than the binding the killer had already cast? I burned to demand answers, but I'd be a fool to show her how badly I wanted them. I'd make sure Marten and Stevan squeezed every last drop of information from her. But Alathian truth spells could be dodged, as Jylla had demonstated so well. Better to offer incentive first.

"Bigger shame your business got destroyed, isn't it? We're hunting the viper responsible. Tell us what happened here, and you'll have the chance for some revenge. But don't think to bargain. Either you speak, or my employers will cast." I tilted my head toward Marten and Stevan.

"No need for casting." Avakra-dan spread her hands palm-up, though she didn't drop the heart-rot charm. "I'll gladly speak if it hurts that *adesh-toi* demonspawn. I was the middle of negotiating a deal with Jevis, here"— she grimaced at the mutilated woman—"and her guardsmen, when the air shimmers, and *kaz!* The demonspawn is standing there. One after the other, Jevis and her men are screaming and bleeding like slaughtered pigs, and the ground's shaking like it'll split open. I didn't wait. I sparked my failsafe— better a fortune lost than my life. Khalmet's hand, you've never seen such fireworks. A thousand charms burning out, molten metal raining down…"

She heaved a bitter sigh, surveying the mess on her walls. I could practically see her tallying the lost coin. "The bastard didn't like it much, I tell you. He may have a demon's power, but he curses like any man. By the time the charms' magic faded, I'd set my decoy and was tight in my bolthole, praying to Khalmet the quake wouldn't crush me. I've a peephole in there. Not a great view, but enough. The demonspawn didn't even try chasing after me. He just ripped out my strongboxes, shattered their wards, and grabbed my contracts. He took a flask from his robe, poured something red all over them—blood, it looked like, though I've no idea why he'd carry extra, when he was already wading in it. He spat and said, 'All those who feed on the innocent will burn.' The blood-marks flared up in blue flames like wardfire, and the contracts burned away, didn't even leave ash behind."

If Khalmet was kind, maybe that meant I didn't have to fear further spellcasting…but I knew better than to count on it. Marten and Stevan both wore deep, thoughtful frowns.

Avakra-dan continued. "After that, the room went black and the ground stilled. I couldn't see a cursed thing, so I waited, in case the demonspawn remained. Just when I'd scrounged up the guts to crawl out, my door wards flared. I stayed put, and you broke in."

"You call him demonspawn," Marten said. "What did he look like?"

Avakra-dan shrugged. "Male, around your height, not heavy, amber eyes...hard to say more. He wore a Kaithan tribesman's *gabeshal* robe, near every inch of skin was covered. I've no idea of his ancestry or age. I did spot metal on the back of his left hand, extending up into his sleeve. The metal was set with an opal and filigreed like some kind of charm, but it looked dark like iron, and iron can't hold power."

"Interesting." Marten drew Stevan and me aside, and said softly, "Dev, perhaps your binding isn't intended as a strike against us directly, but happened as a mere side-effect of our enemy's apparent crusade against Ninavel. He may hate ganglords as much as he does mages. If he binds the clients of dealers in deadly charms to the confluence, in similar manner to the vows that bind Ninavel's mages..."

He trailed off with a glance at Avakra-dan. I heard the rest just fine: when the killer destroyed the confluence, it wasn't just mages who'd burn. My hands clenched in frustrated fury. *All those who feed on the innocent*...what a pile of goat shit! Yeah, ganglords and their crews dealt with Avakra-dan. But so did plenty of others—streetsiders desperate for protection, or healing charms, or any manner of magical assistance.

"Twin gods, Marten!" Talm appeared in the main doorway, Lena at his side. They stared at the corpses in dismay. "What did the killer want here?"

"Your seeking spell failed." Briefly, Marten's face blazed with a strained, desperate frustration that matched my own.

"Pello is indeed veiled," Lena said. "We could tell he's in the city, but not where. Also, Ambassador Halassian passed on a message: Sechaveh claims he's had no word from Pello since prior to Simon Levanian's death. He assumed Pello dead or taken captive by us."

Avakra-dan had hunched in on herself like a spider ready to squeeze back in a crevice, but her eyes glittered with interest. I turned to her. "You know every shadow man in this city. We're looking for Pello: Varkevian-born, used to work out of Gitailan district. Any recent news of him?"

"Pello." Avakra-dan smiled, sharp and sly. "I know him. Sechaveh's man, is he? I always suspected he had a highside master."

"The killer might've turned him," I said. "So if you've news, tell."

Avakra-dan shook her head, her smile gone. "Pello would slit his own throat before he'd work for anyone responsible for Nayyis's death."

I knew that name. "Benno's murdered deathdealer?"

She nodded. "Nayyis and Pello were as close as oath-brothers. They came to Ninavel on the same caravan from Prosul Varkevia, back when they were a couple of scrawny teens. Or Pello was scrawny. Nayyis was already a fighter, whipcord tough and deadly as they come."

A nice tale, but I wasn't sure I believed Pello cared for anyone's hide but his own. "You heard anything recent of Pello?"

"No." But she said it awfully quickly, and her eyes had gone as hard as obsidian.

"She knows something," I told Marten. "Ask under truth spell."

Avakra-dan's hand clenched on the heart-rot charm. I took a cautious step back. But she surrendered the charm when Marten demanded it, and stood in the sigil Stevan sketched on a hastily cleaned patch of floor. Over the sound of Stevan, Lena, and Talm's soft chanting, Marten asked again about Pello.

Her mouth worked, and words spilled out in a faltering tumble. "Saw him two days ago. He came in, bought a painbender and two dragonclaws, and asked if I knew any charms that could protect against the Taint."

I tried not to betray any reaction. Marten said, cool and clinical, "What did you reply?"

She spat. "Told him no, of course. No magic can do that."

"What else passed between you?" Marten asked.

"I asked him if he knew who'd done for Nayyis, and if he was out for revenge. He wouldn't answer, but I saw the hate in his eyes. He wants revenge, all right. Bad enough he'd eat his own soul for a chance."

"Why did you wish to keep this from us?"

Avakra-dan sighed. "He paid me to keep silence about his visit, and said if I broke that silence, he'd see me in Shaikar's hells if it was the last thing he did. With some men that'd be bluster, but not Pello."

Before Marten could ask another question, I met Avakra-dan's gaze and said, "The charm I asked you to seek—did you have any success in finding one?"

Every fiber of me prayed for a positive answer, but her teeth showed in a malicious, indigo grin. "No. Only a bone mage or blood mage could make so strong a charm, and they don't deal with the likes of me. I'd thought a highsider collector might have one, but Khalmet wasn't so kind. Given a long enough timeframe, I could've sent to my contacts down in Varkevia, but four weeks? I knew it a gamble from the start. Why do you think I wanted so high a failsafe?"

I stared at her, my throat closing tight. I hadn't realized just how much hope I'd pinned on her finding a charm. Not until now, when it was crushed. The nightmarish corpses seemed to leer at me, the stench from them so thick I couldn't breathe. Avakra-dan was watching me, and so was Marten. Vipers, both of them, cold and calculating, marking my weakness, figuring how best to use it…fuck. Fuck this, all of it.

I turned and shoved past dripping corpses. At the door, Lena broke her chant to say something, and Talm put out a hand. I elbowed them aside with a snarl. Let them cast against me. I wasn't staying in that room drowning in blood and death one instant longer.

The alley outside Avakra-dan's door was blessedly cool and dark. I leaned my back against stone and stared up at the stars. Anger ebbed to leave a black, dragging despair deeper than any I'd felt since the Change. Why had I ever thought an untalented man like me could take on Ruslan, or do a damn thing against the killer? Melly and Kiran both were one slip of Kiran's tongue away from disaster, the city about to implode in death and chaos, and I felt so fucking *helpless*. What I wouldn't give to be wandering the Whitefires, blissfully ignorant of all this!

The door scraped open. Probably Lena, come to offer more empty words of sympathy. I slid to a crouch, resting my throbbing head on folded arms. Maybe she'd take the hint and go away.

"Forgive the intrusion," Marten said, quiet and serious. "We must talk."

"Yeah?" I was so damn tired. "You here to tell me you're cutting me loose?" That's what I would do in his place. Between the killer's binding and Ruslan holding Melly's blood-mark, I was far too compromised now to be anything but a liability in his eyes. He'd bar me from the embassy, toss Cara out too, leave her and Melly at Ruslan's mercy, and claim he was merely giving us freedom.

"No," Marten said.

"Why not?" I asked warily.

He leaned against the wall. "Shall I tell you the answer you'll believe, or the deeper truth you won't?"

"Whichever," I muttered.

"If I have a man whom an enemy might suborn, I prefer to keep him close under my eye, not send him forth where I'll have no idea of his actions. But more than that…I brought you and Kiran to Ninavel. What befalls you here is my responsibility, and I do not take that lightly. I told you I would not abandon Kiran. The same is true of you."

"You're right, Marten. I don't believe a word of that last."

"I don't expect you to," he said, with a glimmer of his old cheerful humor. "I must know…you told Lena you wouldn't help us further without Melly's safety assured, but you didn't know then of the confluence's imminent destruction. Stevan will do his utmost to devise a solution for Melly, but in the meantime…will you help us hunt Pello? Regardless of his employer's identity, it seems clear Pello knows something of the killer. Far more lives than Melly's are at stake here—yours as well, if we cannot break your binding—and we have so little time."

I wasn't so callous as to ignore the cost if Marten failed. Faces flashed through my head. Liana, the other kids in Red Dal's den, all my outrider and streetsider friends…They wouldn't burn right off if the killer succeeded, but how many would die in the aftermath?

"I'll help," I said. "Though I've one thing I'll ask in return."

Marten shifted like he meant to protest. I said, "Don't worry, it's nothing that'll cost you in either coin or magic. Just tell me this: what the fuck happened with this Reshannis to make Stevan so set against Kiran? I'm getting a little tired of watching you all dance around the topic every time Stevan drags it up."

Marten stood silent long enough I thought he wouldn't answer. But in the end, he said, "Reshannis was…a friend of mine and Stevan's, from our days at the Arcanum. She had the strongest talent of us—ah, how her soulfire burned!—but the very strength of her magic made it difficult for her to mesh minds properly with a larger group, as we are taught to cast. Her frustration over the problem drove her to seek out other magical methods in secret. First in hope she might find something to help her…but when she saw what feats she could perform alone with forbidden techniques, she began pursuing the knowledge for its own sake."

He sighed. "Stevan caught her casting. When he confronted her, she was agonized, remorseful…she vowed that if the Council would only give her a second chance, she would never again break Alathia's laws. Stevan believed her. He reported the infraction, as we must, but he enlisted my help to testify on her behalf. Together, we argued for her…and the Council agreed to a probationary period rather than immediate sentencing. She was forbidden from the archives, restricted in her duties, and Stevan was to supervise her and report any signs of illegal casting. He thought he had won such a victory…"

"She didn't stop casting, I take it," I said.

"No." Marten's voice was devoid of emotion. "Later, she was caught again, this time by one of Stevan's fellow arcanists, a woman Stevan cared for deeply. Reshannis tried to remove Vinalyn's memory of what she had seen—she claimed, later, she never meant harm—but mind magic is terribly dangerous, and the casting went wrong. In the days afterward, Vinalyn's mind crumbled, her personality and intelligence falling to ruin, and our best healers couldn't stop the deterioration. Stevan was devastated. And furious, even after—after we saw Reshannis executed."

The cool dispassion of his words cracked at the end, revealing pain as strong as any I'd ever wanted to hear from him. I couldn't help a vicious little twist of satisfaction, even as I wondered exactly how close a friend Reshannis had been.

"I can get why Stevan would hate Reshannis, or even himself," I said. "Why's he mad at you?"

Marten's teeth gleamed white in a sharp, swift grimace. "Because on me, Reshannis's casting worked."

That was so far from anything I'd expected to hear that all I could do was boggle at him. "She...she fucked with your mind?"

Marten shrugged, deliberately casual. "Only a tiny casting. Apparently I'd seen far less than Vinalyn. Or so the arcanists said when they examined me. But oh, I was furious, just like Stevan..."

He shook his head and sighed. "Reshannis ran. I was the one to hunt her down. But when I brought her to face the Council's justice, the things she said...they haunted me, long after my anger had died to ashes. I believe now that if she'd been allowed to explore other methods of magic openly rather than in secrecy and shame, she could have found a more innocent path. She could have ended as a powerful asset to Alathia instead of costing us not only Vinalyn but herself. Stevan...disagrees with me."

Well, that certainly explained a lot about Stevan. Maybe even about Marten, though it hadn't escaped me how he spoke of even this Reshannis as a tool for Alathia's use. I shoved to my feet.

"You want me to start looking for Pello now?" The question came out with about as much enthusiasm as if Marten wanted me to crawl through a viper pit. For all he was right about time being short, I felt more than half dead already, my body an aching weight and my head full of sand.

Marten said in wry sympathy, "I think we can give you the chance for a few hours' rest at the embassy. I intend to first try a linked harmonic casting using every mage at the embassy, to see if we can pierce Pello's veiling. You can sleep while we cast."

I said slowly, "You realize blood magic might find him where yours can't."

Marten sighed. "I know it. If we haven't found Pello by tomorrow evening, I will ask Ruslan's help. But asking him to cast is the same as asking him to kill. I prefer not to do it unless I have no other option."

Marten's talk of casting brought another jittery spike of fear for Melly. Suliyya grant Kiran kept his mouth shut! And I'd pray to Shaikar himself if it meant Kiran came through with Melly's blood-mark. For all Marten's talk, I suspected Stevan would be far too busy casting in search of the killer to come up with anything useful on Melly's behalf. No, Kiran was my last hope, now Avakra-dan had failed.

✳

(Kiran)

Kiran hurried across the shadowed expanse of Ruslan's courtyard, past trellises laden with fat white moonflowers and night-blooming jasmine. The house wards glimmered scarlet, their tracery of fading fire a remnant of the confluence's most recent upheaval. Kiran could only hope that the disturbance hadn't drawn Ruslan and Lizaveta out of Ruslan's workroom. If Ruslan had realized his absence…his breath came short, the miasma of unease and confusion in his head growing so thick he could barely think.

He touched the door, threaded his senses through the outer wards—and nearly collapsed in relief. High under the house's domed roof, Ruslan's primary workroom remained wholly encased within a sun-bright blaze of shielding magic, the barrier intact and uncrossed.

Kiran dampened the door wards and eased inside the house. The foyer was dark and silent. If he were truly lucky, perhaps Mikail's exhaustion had kept him asleep during the confluence upheaval, and he, too, might remain unaware of Kiran's clandestine excursion. Kiran shut the door, getting a last glimpse of star-dusted sky around Reytani's spires. Far distant across the Painted Valley, heat lightning flickered in silent staccato over the Bolthole Mountains, from a dark bank of clouds that were another sign of the confluence's growing instability.

Kiran's mind felt as unsettled as the choppy, heaving roil of the confluence. All the way home, he'd struggled to make sense of his supposed journey to Alathia, to no avail. He kept circling back to the same question: *why* had Ruslan and Mikail not told him of it?

He restored the door wards and tiptoed through darkened halls to halt outside Mikail's door. Silence within, and he could sense Mikail's *ikilhia*, a subdued, banked glow consistent with slumber.

He trembled on the edge of bursting into Mikail's room and demanding answers. *You know I'd give my life for you,* Mikail had said. Never before had Kiran doubted the depth of their bond as mage-brothers. But how could Mikail have concealed something so enormous in its impact?

Mikail hadn't done it lightly. The memory of his distress at Kiran's questions spawned a new thought, chilling in its implications. Dev had claimed the damage to Kiran's mind was deliberate. What if his memories had indeed been torn from him—not by Ruslan, as Dev had insisted, but the Alathians? If they had infiltrated his mind so deeply, Ruslan might well fear Kiran still bore some lurking binding. That would explain his determination to prevent contact between Kiran and anyone in the Alathians' employ. But again, why would Ruslan lie to Kiran about the nature of his injury? Did he and Mikail trust Kiran so little now?

Kiran rested his brow against Mikail's doorframe. He couldn't bear this. Mikail had made it plain earlier he wouldn't—or couldn't—give answers. But Kiran had to know.

He pushed away from Mikail's door and hurried to Ruslan's study. The wards passed him through as they always had; Kiran sparked a magelight and surveyed the ranks of bookshelves, the carved ironwood of Ruslan's desk. The desktop was clean but for a neatly ordered stack of treatises. Ruslan never left his notes or spell diagrams out, saying he detested carelessness and clutter. At the end of a session of study, he filed everything away in the warded vault set into the marble of the study's back wall.

The sigil-scribed vault door drew Kiran with irresistible force. If he could read Ruslan's notes, see what spells he'd researched and what purchases he'd made in recent months, surely he could piece together more of the truth.

And if not…the vault was the most likely location for the child Melly's contract.

Kiran laid a hand on the vault door. A labyrinth of fire printed itself across his inner sight. He could never slip through these wards undetected, not without long study of their pattern. But where Mikail's greatest talent lay in pattern analysis, Kiran's lay in the raw strength of his magic. He could destroy the ward. If he damaged the outer house wards as well, made it seem as if the confluence spike had overwhelmed them and leaked through to cause the destruction…

"What are you doing?"

Kiran yanked his hand from the vault and turned. Mikail stood in the doorway. His sandy hair was disordered from sleep, his only garment a creased, rumpled pair of black silken trousers. But his gray eyes were all too sharp and awake.

Kiran's fevered determination abruptly cooled. He groped for the wall, his legs unsteady. Perhaps Ruslan and Mikail were right not to trust him. How could he be certain his actions were all his own and not influenced by some remnant of a binding?

He couldn't bring himself to speak to Mikail of his fears and admit he'd broken his promise. "I was…checking the wards. Another confluence upheaval happened a short time ago—did you feel it? I was afraid spillover from the outer wards might have weakened others in the house."

"You," said Mikail flatly, "are a terrible liar. I felt you come back in the house wards just now. Where did you go, Kiran?"

"You were pretending to sleep?" Kiran should have remembered that Mikail's skill with deception far outstripped his. He stared at the flat planes of his mage-brother's face, so difficult to read, fearing guilt blazed from his own features.

"The confluence spike woke me," Mikail said. "I found you gone. I cast to seek you and found you climbing the Cloudfall Stair. So don't tell me you were merely taking a stroll in the garden, or checking the house wards."

Mikail must have seen Kiran was returning to the house, and waited to see what Kiran would do once back inside. Kiran shut his eyes, cursing himself for an idiot. "You didn't tell Ruslan?"

"Have you gone mad?" Mikail snapped. "I don't wish either of us punished. But if you don't give me the truth, I *will* summon him."

"No! I…I'll tell you." Kiran braced his back against the wall, fearing otherwise his legs might give way. He desperately wanted to tell Mikail everything, to pour forth the entire terrible cloud of fear and anger and confusion that fogged his thoughts. Yet if Mikail should tell Ruslan, and the *nathahlen* child suffered because of it—his heart cried out against the idea.

Perhaps he could take a middle course. Tell Mikail as much truth as he dared, yet not all.

"I know I promised you I'd leave the past alone. But I couldn't sleep, and I couldn't stop worrying over this…difficulty I have, with hurting *nathahlen*. I went out, thinking if I walked among them, I might find some clarity. But—in the lower city, there was a *nathahlen* man, a criminal—he *recognized* me, Mikail! I couldn't let it go. I searched his mind, saw his memories…"

Mikail was looking more horrified by the moment. Despite himself, Kiran's voice rose. "He arranged passage for me into Alathia on Ruslan's orders, and it was the Alathians' guide, Dev, he hired to take me across the border. I went, and Dev and I were captured by the Council—I don't know how I got free, but…*how* could you keep this from me? You and Ruslan…I thought us closer than family. What did I do, for you to distrust me so much?"

"Kiran..." Mikail's eyes were bright with anguish. He came forward to grip Kiran's arms. "Oh, my brother. We love you, never doubt it."

"Prove it, then! I've given you truth. If you love me as you say, give me the same." Kiran held Mikail's gaze. "My memories...they weren't lost in an accidental backlash, were they?"

Mikail shut his eyes. "No."

The answer staggered him. Kiran clutched at Mikail's shoulders. "What happened, Mikail? You must tell me. This will drive me mad, otherwise."

Mikail was silent, his breathing uneven. At last he spoke in a ragged whisper. "Ruslan had an enemy in Alathia, a rival he had long hoped to kill. He saw a chance to draw his enemy out of hiding, using you as the bait. You agreed, though Ruslan could not tell you his entire plan, lest his enemy be warned of it. You went to Alathia, and played your part perfectly—Ruslan's enemy was destroyed, and he was well pleased. But afterward—the guide, Dev, betrayed you and gave you over into Alathian hands. Ruslan was desperate to get you back. We all were! Ruslan thought he would have to break their cursed border wards to do it—but then came this problem with the confluence. Ruslan bargained with the Alathians: they would return you, and he would let them join our investigation."

Mikail's tale sounded plausible, if disturbing, and yet... "If it was the Alathians who took my memories—why did you not tell me?"

"Because it wasn't the Alathians." Mikail's voice cracked. "Oh gods, Kiran, it was us."

"*What?*" Dev had been right? Kiran couldn't grasp it—there must be some mistake, some misunderstanding. "Why?"

"It was the only way to save you." Mikail spoke with desperate, impassioned intensity. "What the Alathians did to you...they bound your magic, corrupted your mind, forced you to become their creature, their willing tool. Their spellwork went so deep Ruslan could not remove it without damage. He did his best to spare you, but..." Mikail bowed his head. "I channeled for him, and I still have nightmares of you screaming..."

He choked and went on, his voice thick. "Afterward, Ruslan couldn't bear to tell you he'd caused you such harm, and—and neither could I. He also feared if you knew how terribly the Alathians had used you, your desire for revenge would blind you to all else. It's hard enough for me to work with them, knowing how they hurt you." Mikail raised his head. Tears stood in his eyes, something Kiran hadn't seen since his earliest childhood. "I'm so sorry, Kiran. But you must believe me—Ruslan had no other way to restore you to yourself."

Kiran slumped to sit against the wall. He felt battered, his *ikilhia* seared and raw as if from a magefire strike. If the Alathians had indeed altered his mind so deeply, his lingering aversion to blood magic made a horrible kind of sense. As did the depth of his nervousness around Captain Martennan. But if Dev had betrayed him to the Alathians, why did Kiran feel so easy in his presence?

"You're certain it was Dev who betrayed me?" Kiran asked. "Martennan and the others, I feel wary of...but not him."

"Yes," Mikail said fiercely. "Trust me, Kiran, he's no friend to you. He seeks only his own profit."

That, and the child Melly's safety—assuming that wasn't a lie. If Dev had betrayed him as Mikail insisted, no wonder Dev hadn't wanted Kiran to see his memories. Cold fury trickled in, slowly at first, then ever faster. Power rose with the fury, roiling within Kiran until he feared his barriers might fail under the pressure. He jerked to his feet.

"I do want revenge." Despite his attempt at control, the air around him sizzled and sparked, the wards flaring in answer.

"On the Alathians, or on Ruslan and me as well?" Mikail's eyes were anxious.

In truth, Kiran's fury wasn't only for Dev and the Alathians. A helpless, betrayed anger throbbed in him at the thought of Ruslan, a child's cry of *How could you let this happen to me?* Knowing the emotion was childish didn't reduce its strength. But Mikail...

"I'm not angry with you," Kiran said, and it was almost true. "Sending me to Alathia was Ruslan's choice, not yours."

Mikail reached for Kiran's hands. Kiran allowed the contact, let Mikail siphon away the wild power seething within until his *ikilhia* reached a tenuous balance.

Mikail said, "If you're angry with Ruslan, little brother, I understand it. But please...don't show that anger. Not until we've found and killed this enemy who seeks to destroy us. If you reveal that you know the truth, Ruslan will be deeply upset and angry in turn with me, just when he needs to hunt undistracted."

The last thing Kiran wanted was for Mikail to suffer Ruslan's anger, and their enemy could not be allowed to succeed. "That...will be difficult. You know I'm no good at hiding things."

Mikail released a brief, sharp laugh. "Oh, you can do it when you've a mind to." He paused, and said more softly, "I hope you find your anger with him fades when you've had time to consider. He loves you, Kiran. You don't know how terribly he regrets your suffering."

"Regret never stops him from hurting us," Kiran muttered. Yet it was true that the clean heat of his fury was far preferable to the morass of confusion it had replaced. At least now he knew the truth. He no longer needed to agonize over the choice between defying Ruslan to steal the child's contract and remaining in ignorance. He didn't even need to struggle with his dismay over the child's possible fate; he would avoid Dev, and Ruslan would have no reason to hurt her. Besides, now he understood his reluctance over hurting *nathahlen* was some remnant of a malign binding, he had the will to fight it. He would cast at Ruslan's side no matter how sick it made him and prove to the Alathians they had not crippled him.

"I still have questions," he said to Mikail. "Who was this enemy of Ruslan's, and what was my part in Ruslan's plan?"

Kiran listened as Mikail told him of Simon Levanian's exile from Ninavel, and how Ruslan had asked Kiran to pretend to flee to Alathia, so Simon might think to use him against Ruslan, and in doing so, provide the chance for Kiran to strike him down. It all sounded so improbable, like something out of the most fanciful of adventure tales. Yet the memories he'd taken from the *nathahlen* bore silent witness that Mikail spoke truth. And the gaping voids in his own memories proved that in real life, unlike tales, adventures came at a cost.

He hadn't yet exhausted all his questions for Mikail when the blaze of magic around Ruslan's workroom vanished. Ruslan spoke through the mark-bond. *Mikail, Kiran: come.*

Kiran exchanged a glance with Mikail, who said, "Remember, no anger."

"I know." Kiran hurried after Mikail, out of the study and up the spiral staircase to Ruslan's workroom. But oh, it was hard to stamp down the blaze of outraged hurt he felt the moment he sighted Ruslan waiting for them at the door. He did his best not to stiffen when Ruslan took his shoulder. He even managed to return Ruslan's welcoming smile. Mikail gave him a quick, approving look as Ruslan led them inside.

Lizaveta leaned against the anchor stone, her eyes smudged and dark with exhaustion. Ruslan looked little better, his face drawn and his broad shoulders slumped. Yet his expression held more triumph than weariness.

"Success, *akhelyshen*. We've identified the pattern of currents our enemy seeks, and know the hour when it should next occur. Better yet, during his recent attempt, we discovered a mark of his presence."

A sense-image welled up from the mark-bond: the confluence, vast and wild, its currents boiling forth in a welter of disturbed energies—but in one spot lurked a dark vortex nearly too small to see. Magic swirled around it in odd, irregular surges not at all like the confluence's natural flow.

"I believe the vortex to be a manifestation of our enemy's unique method of magic, and the very act of wielding that magic to be what agitates the confluence into an upheaval," Ruslan said. "The death-born power he releases by killing mages only enhances the effect."

Lizaveta nodded in weary agreement. She swept her long fall of hair off her neck and twisted the shining black mass into a rough knot. "I would dearly love to know his method. I've never seen the like of that vortex."

"Nor have I," Ruslan said. "Regardless, it should suffice to target channeled spellwork."

Mikail said, "If the vortex is only present during the brief moments of an upheaval, how can you prepare the spell and cast in time before it vanishes?"

Ruslan said, "Kiran, you still hear these…whispers…in advance of an upheaval, do you not? That will provide us warning."

"Not much warning," Kiran said. "I only hear them right beforehand." Though the mental whispers had been growing harsher and more unsettling with each new disturbance.

Ruslan said, "A precisely targeted spell cannot be cast in time, it's true. I intend something a touch more crude, yet still effective. Kiran was able to hurt our enemy with a simple magefire strike when more elaborate defensive spells had failed. Therefore…Lizaveta and I will raise channeled power, as much as we can, and hold it in waiting. You two will observe the confluence from outside the wards. When Kiran warns me our enemy's arrival is imminent, I will link minds with you through the mark-bond. The instant one of you spots the vortex, I will cast the channeled power at its location as simple magefire."

Surely Kiran had misheard Ruslan. "You'll cast with the full power of the confluence in a raw strike? You'll reduce an entire district to rubble!"

Ruslan shrugged. "I'll contain the magefire, though not too tightly—I do not wish our enemy to escape. Buildings and bridges can be rebuilt. The confluence cannot. Sechaveh will consider the losses acceptable given the stakes."

How many lives would that loss include? A dozen, a hundred…more? Kiran choked back a protest, alarmed at the strength of his dismay. He had to remember the feeling was false in origin, the product of the Alathians' attempt to chain him. Yet the only thing that stopped his tongue was the knowledge that far more lives would be lost if Ruslan did not cast.

"Will you tell the Alathians of your plan?" Mikail asked.

"No." Ruslan's smile was savage. "I vowed never to knowingly cast to harm them. I think it best if I have no contact with them before we strike, and know nothing of their whereabouts. I would hate to be prevented from casting, should they happen to be in proximity to our enemy when he appears again."

The fire in Ruslan's eyes said how fervently he hoped the Alathians would happen to be in range of his strike. For once, Kiran was in complete agreement. He might be angry with Ruslan, but the Alathians...the Alathians, he hated. He wanted them to burn.

"You said you could predict when that next appearance might be," Mikail said. "When must we be ready to cast?"

"The confluence will reach the proper alignment during the hour before noon," Ruslan said. "Now, Lizaveta and I will eat and take an hour's rest. Then all four of us will lay channels, to ensure we are ready in time." He slung his arms around Kiran and Mikail's shoulders and pulled them close. "Our victory will come soon, *akhelyshen*, and then we can rest in truth."

Lizaveta laughed, low and full of promise. "Or celebrate otherwise."

"Just so." Ruslan kissed first Mikail, then Kiran. It was easier than Kiran expected to submit to the kiss; with his blood still blazing with the desire for revenge on the Alathians, his anger with Ruslan felt of no more consequence than a thorn-scratch. Yet when Ruslan released him, he shivered in relief, and hoped Ruslan wouldn't realize the reason.

CHAPTER NINETEEN

(Dev)

I woke to sun shining on my face, hot enough to be uncomfortable. I squinted up at the unshuttered window over the bed in bleary confusion. The embassy. Right. I'd been only half-conscious by the time we arrived before dawn, so exhausted I remembered only a blur of faces and voices, Cara's loud and relieved among them.

From the angle of the sun, it was already midmorning. Muffled singing drifted into the room, the rhythm hypnotically repetitive. The Alathians must be casting. High time I dragged myself out of bed and thought up some alternatives in case their spell failed to find Pello. Half a morning's sleep wasn't enough to clear my head entirely, but at least the ache in my muscles had diminished to a nagging soreness. I rubbed at my chest uneasily. I couldn't feel the killer's binding, wouldn't even know it was there if Marten and Stevan hadn't told me—and that just made my skin crawl worse.

I sat up, and paused at the sight of Cara asleep on the other bed. She had her face buried in the pillow, one bare arm dangling off the mattress. Her hair was loose of its braid, snarled and knotted from sleep, pale as ashblossom honey against her amber skin. The sheet had slid down to pool around her narrow hips, and the thin cotton of her sleeveless undertunic was tight as a second skin over the curve of her back.

Memory stole my breath: the jahla-spice taste of her mouth, her body arching under mine on a makeshift bed of furs. We'd only had the one night in Kost, but gods, how I wanted more. The fear I'd endured for her last night made the hurt I'd felt over her letter to Marten seem stupidly petty. I ached to lie beside her and draw her close, slide off her undertunic and kiss every inch of her skin…

No. This was as dangerous as anger; more so, because I wanted it so badly. Now, if ever, I needed a clear head. If we survived this, time enough then to see if Cara still wanted anything more than friendship. It wouldn't surprise me if she didn't, after all I'd already done to shove her away.

I reached for my boots. She stirred and sat up, yawning. I strove for a grin as cheerful and easy as any I'd greeted her with on a convoy trip. "Morning."

She appraised me with a keen, critical gaze, every bit the head outrider. "You look a shade better than last night."

"I feel a lot better," I assured her.

"Good. Then you can tell me what the hell happened, in proper detail this time instead of barely intelligible grunts. I got some of the story from Lena after you collapsed, but I want to hear your version."

If we hadn't been sitting in the embassy, I'd have told her the full tale without any omissions. As it was, I kept to the same version I'd given the Alathians. Cara listened in silence, worrying out the tangles in her hair and rebraiding it with swift, neat fingers. When she pulled on trousers and shirt and I lost my view of all that tanned skin, I sighed in regret. Thank Khalmet, she didn't notice. When I finished talking, she sprang off her bed to pace.

"Painbenders and blood mages and bindings…I swear, Dev, sometimes I don't know if Khalmet's touched you with his good hand or his bad one. It drives me wild that I'm stuck behind these wards like some hapless sulaikh-maiden. The very least, I'll make sure the Alathians break that binding of yours. I talked to them last night. No question Stevan's got prejudices deep as the Blackstar Chasm, and I won't argue with you about Marten, but the rest—Lena, Talm, Halassian and her people—they may be more help than you think. They're not vipers."

"How wrong you are." The voice was Jylla's. The door creaked open and she slid through. She wore a gauzy dress just as fancy and revealing as the one she'd worn in Naidar's house, though her feet were bare, and she hadn't bothered to paint her face. Her quiet-shroud amulet dangled from one hand.

I jumped up and glared. "Nobody invited you to join the conversation." How long had she been lurking out there listening to us? Thank Khalmet I hadn't mentioned the Taint charm diagram. If Jylla ever realized a mage like Ruslan could give her some semblance of the Taint back, she'd stop at nothing to make it happen. The gods knew I still burned to beg Kiran to make one, despite all conscience.

Jylla said, "You should invite me, since clearly there's not a brain to spare between you." She turned to Cara. "Weren't you listening to his little tale? Or were you too busy thinking about yanking him into your bed?"

Cara gave Jylla a look as cold as glacial snowmelt. "Outriders make a living by skill and teamwork, not by bleeding men dry in bedroom schemes. I should've guessed you'd be sneaking about spying. If anyone in this embassy's a viper, it's you."

"If you don't want to be overheard, use a silencing charm," Jylla said. "Speaking of..." She shut the door and put on the quiet-shroud amulet. "There. Now, let's talk vipers."

"Thought you said the charm wouldn't work without standing close," I said.

She grinned at me, merry and mocking. "I lied."

Of course she had. I repressed a snarl, aware of Cara's sharp glance my way. If Jylla mentioned my moment of weakness in Naidar's house, I'd throttle her bare-handed.

The wicked glint in her eyes said she knew my fear. But she fingered her amulet, and her expression sobered. "For Khalmet's sake, Dev. Bren as much as tells you an Alathian sold you out, and you ignore it?"

"It was Ruslan who sent Bren the letter." But I wasn't so sure, not anymore. Why had the killer struck Avakra-dan's den, out of all the charm dealers who supplied ganglords? Ruslan hadn't known of my initial visit to her—but all of the Alathians had, even if they hadn't known of my bargain. If the killer meant to destroy Ninavel's mages and as many ganglords as he could manage, maybe somebody here had decided that was a goal worth the destruction of Alathia's wards. They could've leaked the location of Avakra-dan's den to the killer, in hopes Marten would ditch me after finding me bound, and lose me as a source of information.

"Ah," Jylla said, watching me. "I see you've been thinking on it; good to know you haven't lost all your wits." She perched on the foot of my bed and drew her knees up to sit in a tidy curl like a cat on a sill. The familiarity of the pose brought a sharp pang. How often had she sat like that, listening with amused interest as I told her of mountain adventures?

She added, "My money's on the woman. Lena. She's guilty as hell over something—don't tell me you haven't noticed it."

I'd seen the shadowed sleeplessness in Lena's eyes and thought it regret over Kiran. Hell, I'd counted on that guilt when I asked her to help me free Melly...but what if I'd been the one played for a mark? I'd let her touch me, read my thoughts—she could've learned about Avakra-dan's stash of blood-marks, and a lot more besides. Maybe when she saw I meant my promise to keep helping Marten, she'd decided to get rid of me. Pello and his crew had latched onto me right after I left Lena's side, and she'd been the only Alathian to know my whereabouts that night.

But what proof did I have? Nothing Marten would believe, that was sure. And I couldn't rule out the others…after all, if anyone's hatred of Ninavel was strong enough to drive them to sabotage Marten's mission, it was Stevan. Even easygoing Talm saw Ninavel as a plague den, and his years stationed here meant he would've known how to contact a smuggling boss like Bren.

Cara crossed her arms and eyed Jylla with disdain. "Maybe you just assume Lena's a liar because you can't conceive of a woman being anything else."

Jylla only smiled condescendingly. "Not at all. Take you—I know you've not a shred of skill with deceit. Maybe that's fine in the mountains. Here in the city, it'll get you killed. I wouldn't care, except you're dragging Dev to the grave with you."

My laugh was harsh. "Come on, Jylla. You won't shed a single tear if I burn."

She ignored me, her eyes fixed on Cara. "You and that idiot Sethan! Turning Dev soft, blinding him with all these idiotic notions of honor! Highsiders can afford to keep promises. Streetsiders have to know better."

She knew about my vow to Sethan? Of course she did. She'd seen that Marten had some hold over me. She must've been panting to know what could keep me leashed so well. No doubt she'd weaseled the whole damn story out of the Alathians within hours of first setting foot in the embassy.

Cara shook her head, disgusted and pitying. "Maybe if you'd ever set foot outside a ganglord's cesspit, you'd realize that loyalty's the best quality a man can have."

"I prefer a live oathbreaker to a loyal corpse," Jylla said. "If you cared for Dev, you'd help him see that his life's worth more than a vow made to a man four years dead." She looked at me. "Tell me you haven't wished you'd never gotten involved in this."

I couldn't meet her gaze. Instead, I snapped, "I wouldn't be involved, if not for you."

"Didn't I say I regret it?" She leaned toward me, her eyes wide and earnest. "It's not too late, Dev. Make the Alathians break your binding. Once they do…run with me. Seems to me your precious little Melly would be safest if you weren't here to make her a target. Better if you leave the city with me and forget this entire briar tangle. Hell, bring Cara with us, if she's hooked you so well. You know she's not safe in this embassy. None of us are."

Cara made a strangled, incredulous noise. I stared at Jylla, then laughed again. "Admit it, Jylla. You think the city's going to fall, you want to save your own sweet ass, and you figure your best shot is to get a pair of experienced outriders to take you across the mountains." Plus, she needed me to sneak her out of the embassy. Without the Taint, she couldn't slip past the powerful wards on the embassy's door, and unlike me, she couldn't climb well enough to negotiate the drop beyond the windows.

"Of course I want to survive," Jylla said, with an exasperated sigh. "Doesn't mean I'm not anxious you should too. Use your head, Dev! Lena—or someone—has tried to get rid of you once already. You think she'll stop now?"

"No," I said. "But I think any traitor here doesn't dare cast against me directly, for fear of getting caught. That means if I'm cautious, I've got a chance at exposing the viper before she or he can try again." Ironically, being cautious meant sticking close to Marten. He was the only one I was certain didn't want me dead—because otherwise, why go through all the effort to bring me to Ninavel and keep me leashed?

Cara's scowl had turned thoughtful. She asked me, "Are you going to talk to Marten about this?"

"Not until I've got something more than mere suspicion," I said. "Marten won't want to believe one of his people's a traitor—especially not if it's his first lieutenant. So, look…" I turned to Jylla. "You want to survive? Then put your shadow talents to use. Work with Cara, see if you can find any evidence here at the embassy that someone's scheming against Marten."

Cara and Jylla both looked at me like I'd said they should go dance in a magefire. Jylla said, "Work with a sanctimonious idiot, who hasn't the least idea of shadow games? Why in Khalmet's name would I do that?"

"Because if you do, and you find evidence—real evidence, Jylla, not invented—I'll get you through the embassy's wards, and give you enough coin to pay passage over the mountains." I'd make damn sure I had some of Jylla's blood as insurance first, to prevent her from turning around to sell me or the Alathians out to the killer.

Jylla studied me. Abruptly, she chuckled. "Why not? I'll work the job for you. I haven't had a challenge in a while…not since you and I tracked down that illusionist who ran off with a ganglord's entire charm stash."

That had been the job we worked right before she cast me aside for Naidar. I refused to show how deep the memory cut. "So long as you understand: I don't trust you in this, not one fucking bit. So the deal's only on if Cara's your watchdog." I looked to Cara.

She said to Jylla, "Dev and I need a moment alone. And by alone, I mean without you lurking outside the door."

"Of course," Jylla said, with another of her sly grins. "Hope you take advantage of it. The gods know I've missed him in my bed. Especially after the taste of it I had the other day."

Shaikar take her! "Out. Now," I snapped, and herded her through the door. Once in the corridor, I said in a venomous mutter, "Don't think you can rile Cara into avoiding you. She'll watch you keen as a banehawk no matter what you say. Try any schemes that harm her, and I'll have Marten bind *you* to the confluence."

"Hooked deep, I see." Her black eyes weren't mocking like I expected, but serious, even sad. "It won't last, Dev. You can pretend for a while, but she's not crippled like you and I are. We know how to help each other survive because we share the same scars. But her...when she realizes that dead spot in your soul can't ever heal, she'll tire of trying. In the end, she'll seek someone whole."

"Scars can fade," I said tightly. "I'm not like you, Jylla. Not anymore. Sethan taught me better."

Jylla laughed. "Oh, Dev. You always did like to fool yourself. When your illusion crumbles...remember, I warned you." She sauntered off down the hallway.

I stared after her, jaw clenched. She was wrong. I was nothing like her. I stalked back into the room to find Cara watching me with narrowed eyes, her arms folded.

"Jylla just wanted to make you angry," I said. "She doesn't want you agreeing to shadow her, in case she decides to try some scheme against us."

Cara's gimlet-eyed gaze didn't soften. "Dev, if you let her get her claws into you again, I'll kick your ass so hard you'll never sit a saddle."

She looked ready to start right now. I lifted my hands. "Don't worry, I know she's poison. She's also brilliant at shadow work. She can sniff out any traitors here and figure out how to prove their guilt to Marten. But I don't trust her not to lie or make up evidence. That's why I'm asking you: stick close to her, and check over anything she claims to find. You're smart, and you've a good eye for lies. More importantly..." I held her gaze, hoping she'd hear the depth of apology in my next words. "I trust you. Completely."

"Do you?" Cara shook her head. "You think I haven't noticed how whenever you want something, you draw me close—and the minute you think you can do without my help, you push me away?"

I winced, hearing the echo of Jylla's warning. "Sometimes...sometimes partnership isn't easy for me. But I mean it, Cara...there's no one I trust more than you."

"That's not saying much," she said with a snort. I took a breath, hunting for words, but she said, "Listen. I'll play watchdog over Jylla, even though I say we'd be safer chucking her out the window. But, Dev…I know you have reason for this dance of yours. Yet there are things I'll tolerate in a friend that I won't in someone who's more. Assuming you want more."

"I do," I said, my throat suddenly tight. "Gods, Cara, you've no idea how much."

Her mouth quirked. "I think I've some idea." Her gaze traveled my body, slow as a caress, and I found myself short of breath. She took a slow step closer. Desire spiked through me like summer lightning. If she wanted me, I'd let myself burn—

The distant singing stopped. A mutter of voices sounded in the hall, and Cara halted. The vivid frustration on her face matched mine. But she gave a rueful chuckle and said, "Wonder if their spell worked?"

I tried to steady my breathing. Damn the Alathians! You'd think mages would have a better sense of timing. "They don't exactly sound excited." I cracked the door open, quiet as I could. Cara eased up behind me to listen at my shoulder.

The voices came clearer: Talm and Marten.

"…even if we find Pello, who's to say he can lead us to the killer?" Talm sounded as weary as I'd felt last night. "Marten, if the worst should come, and we can't stop the confluence's destruction…I know you intend to send Ambassador Halassian to safety. Won't you consider going with her?"

Right. The Alathians weren't bound to the confluence like Marten had said Ninavel mages were. They could escape death if they ran before it burned. I felt a twinge of sympathy for Talm. If it were Cara in Marten's place, I'd be down on my knees begging her to leave.

"How can you think I would flee?" Marten sounded half-chiding, half-sorrowful. "My duty is here. So long as there is an instant left to prevent this disaster, I will use it."

Talm sighed. "I know. You wouldn't hold my admiration so deeply if you said otherwise. Yet, Marten…"

I peered through the crack, saw Talm bow his head, his hands white-knuckled on his belt. He said in a low, ragged voice, "My life and death are the Council's to spend, and I have no regret for it. But when I think of your soulfire extinguished, the yoke is hard to bear."

Tenderness blazed from Marten's face. He cupped Talm's neck, drew him close. "It's no easier for me, knowing the risk to you. Have faith in me a little longer. We can still stop this, and no one need die."

Talm didn't reply, though one hand rose to clutch at Marten's shoulder. Marten bent his head to Talm's and said something too soft for me to hear. I eased the door shut, unable to bear the stark intimacy of their pose any longer.

Cara said quietly, "I don't think it's Talm. He loves Marten, no question."

"Love doesn't always mean loyalty. Mikail thinks he loves Kiran, yet it didn't stop him from telling Ruslan about Alisa." Yet I knew I was grasping at thin holds. The simple truth was that I'd rather believe the traitor was anyone other than Lena. I didn't want to admit I could've made another error so terrible in giving my trust.

Footsteps approached in the hallway. A knock came on the door, and Marten poked his head in. His cheerful mask was firmly back in place. "Good to see you're awake, Dev. If you'd join me for a moment?"

Cara said, "Go on. I'll talk to Jylla."

She said it nice and bland, and Marten didn't blink. I nodded to her and followed Marten out. Talm was nowhere in sight. Neither was Lena, thank Khalmet.

"Your spell failed?" I asked Marten.

"We couldn't pierce the veiling entirely, no. But while we couldn't find Pello directly, we believe we've identified a location Pello has frequented often in recent days. A room, sealed by wards, in Julisi district. I'd like you to come with us; you know Pello, as we do not. If he isn't in that room now, perhaps something there might give you insight into where he is or what he's doing."

"You're coming on this little jaunt?"

He nodded. "Talm, Lena, and I will go. Stevan will remain here to work with Ambassador Halassian and her people on Melly's situation, among other tasks."

Good. If either Lena or Talm wanted me dead, I didn't think they'd try anything right under Marten's nose; and the same went for Stevan, with Halassian. "What about my binding?"

"Stevan and I don't believe the spell allows for more than a simple link of your life to the confluence. As such, you're in no more danger than any mage in this city. Stevan might be able to break the binding if he studies it further—but I told him you'd see Melly as the higher priority."

"You're right about that." Though I thought it more probable that Marten had told Stevan, *Leave him bound. He'll work all the harder for us if he's desperate not to die.*

We'd reached the receiving room. I headed straight for the tray of spice bread and rockmelon on the side table. Damn, I was hungry. "Well, nothing like a walk in the heat to…" I stopped, spice bread forgotten, as I glimpsed the sky outside the unshuttered window.

The jagged peaks of the Whitefires were dim and gray beneath a great boil of cloud black as Shaikar's heart. Lightning stabbed distant summits, too far away to hear thunder. That'd soon change, as the storm moved eastward into the Painted Valley.

Summer thunderstorms were common enough in the Whitefires, and the larger ones occasinally made it out of the mountains to give the city a fireworks show, albeit without any rain. But they never came so early in the day—except in the tales of the mage war.

"If that storm is because of the killer messing with the confluence, I'm guessing that's not a good sign," I said to Marten.

He was staring out the window, his jaw tight. "Not a good sign, no." He turned, calling for Lena and Talm. I eyed the storm again and tried to ignore the conviction that Jylla had the right of it: the city would fall, and I'd die with it.

※

"This is it," Marten said, pointing to a battered door with a few tarnished ward plaques nailed around the handle. Talm and Lena crowded forward to peer at the wards. All three Alathians were dressed in rough streeside-style clothes, Lena's dark hair swinging in a single thick plait instead of her usual complicated crown of braids.

I couldn't help staring at her freckled face, so intent and serious. Before today, I'd have sworn she was as fiercely loyal to Marten as one of Noshet's legendary spell-sealed guardians. Was she so good an actress? And if she was, how would I prove it to Marten?

"Shouldn't take much to break those wards," I said. The door didn't look any different than the rest we'd passed on the narrow, chipped stair that wound up the outer wall of the smelters' warren. Most of those living here worked as rakemen and haulers, and barely had enough coin to buy their families' water rations. At this hour of the day, the warren was still and silent. The day workers were on shift in the smelting houses, everyone else sleeping away the heat. We'd passed only starveling-thin kids huddled over rat traps and a few wizened oldsters whose skin was shiny with burn scars from years tending charm-fueled furnaces.

Talm chuckled. "Think again." He swept his hand over the door. The surface shimmered and ward lines appeared, as clean and powerful as anything I'd seen highside.

"Clever," I said. "Pello must keep this as one of his boltholes. Think he's inside?"

Marten glanced at Lena. "You're the best of us at threading through veiling spells."

She splayed a ringed hand on the door. "I sense nothing within, and this is the room's only entrance."

Yeah, and maybe she'd long since warned Pello we were coming. Marten rubbed his hands together. "Let's break these wards, then."

They started chanting. I fingered my belt. I'd cajoled Marten into stopping past a highside charm dealer and paying for a replacement boneshatter charm. The charm wasn't as strong as the one I'd had from Avakra-dan, but it'd still serve as protection against an untalented man like Pello.

A few minutes of chanting later, I followed the Alathians through the door. The room beyond was scarcely larger than one of the embassy's closets. A pallet with a single cotton blanket lay against one wall. A shrike whistle sat on a crooked shelf, along with a handful of the cunningly knotted rawhide-and-feather tokens that streetside performers tossed into appreciative crowds. At the back of the room was a tri-part shrine with a host of little jasper and malachite figurines meant to represent various southern deities. Dried karva flowers dusted with cinnamon lined the lacquered shelves of the shrine; an old Varkevian custom, to repel demons.

Marten, Talm and Lena homed straight in on the shrine. They moved it aside to reveal a vault set into the stone of the wall, warded tight as could be. As they settled in for another session of chanting, I said, "I'm gonna go peek outside, see if any of the kids around have noticed anything useful."

Marten flapped a hand at me without taking his eyes from the vault. "Don't go far."

"I'll stay in shouting distance." I left the door open wide. The stair was empty of people, kids or otherwise. But two doors onward, the stair turned left to end at the crumbling line of the warren's roof. I could run take a quick look, see if anyone was up there gaping at the approaching storm.

It was coming on fast. With noon not more than an hour off, the sun should be blazing straight down into the depths of the warren. Instead, the strip of sky above was hazed orange with windblown sand, the sun a pallid disc threatened by spreading fingers of cloud. Distant mutters of thunder warned of the show to come.

I scrambled up the stair—and froze, as a familiar sharp-chinned coppery face peeked over the roof's edge. Pello's dark eyes locked with mine and widened.

"Marten! He's here!" I shouted, and vaulted up the remaining stairs.

Pello was already running for the roof's far side. He didn't stop at the edge. He jumped off with all the confidence of a Tainter who knows he can fly.

My heart in my throat, I skidded to a stop at the edge and peered over. Ten stories below, Pello slid off the end of a hemp line anchored to a bar jutting out a handspan below the roof's edge. I reached for the line, only to jerk my hand back as wards flared to life on the bar. Damn him, he must've set this as an escape route long before.

Pello dodged a gang of gaping ore-haulers and cut left into an alley. I glanced over my shoulder. Marten was just pulling himself onto the roof, Talm and Lena behind.

"Break the wards and climb down the rope to the street—I'll stay high, try to scout his route!" I backed a few steps, then sprinted forward and hurled myself over the street to the opposite roof. I caught the roof's edge, nearly lost my grip from the shock of my body hitting the wall, but got a foot high enough to hook my heel and lever myself up. I pelted across pitted stone toward the canyon of the alley.

I reached it just in time to see Pello duck into the maze of slit-thin passageways that wound between a huddle of supply warehouses. I jumped again, this time for a scarred iron balcony strung with devil-ward charms. A skittering traverse across ledges and windows led me to a roof with a hawk's-eye view of the warehouses. I glimpsed Pello again, darting alongside a snaking line of ore carts, wending his way eastward. Only one exit from the maze that way—a gated alley that dumped out into Acaltar's market district.

The boil of thunderheads was nearly on us. Lightning stabbed the westernmost city towers, thunder trembling the air. Gusts of wind flung sand into my eyes and mouth. I backed and spotted the Alathians running down the alley toward the warehouses, long-legged Talm outpacing Marten and Lena.

I whistled, shrill and sharp, and yelled to him over the wind, "Pello's heading for Acaltar's markets! I'll cut over the roofs to get ahead of him. Circle around the smelters' yards and meet me at Zhivonis Street—hurry!"

Talm raised a fist in acknowledgement. I scrambled straight onward over the warehouse roofs, stabbing fingers and toes in crevices, vaulting across gaps and teetering along ledges. Wind yanked at me, whiptail lizards skittering from my questing fingers. When I reached the mouth of the alley that fed into Zhivonis Street, I half-climbed, half-slid down the wall to brace myself beneath a balcony.

Pello rounded the alley's far corner, no longer at a dead run, but at the steady, mile-eating lope that runner boys used when they had to cross the city. No sign of the Alathians beyond the Zhivonis Street gate. I'd have to slow Pello down and pray he wasn't carrying anything too nasty. I slid my boneshatter charm free of my belt, measuring distance as he loped closer. When he crossed under me, I dropped.

Some instinct made him glance up. He dodged aside so I didn't land straight on him, only caught him a glancing blow. We both fell sprawling. I lashed out with my charm, connected with his left arm and heard a muffled snap like a branch under snow. He cursed and twisted as fast as an adder. The sharp-edged gold crescent of a dragonclaw charm glittered in his right hand. I threw myself backward just in time to avoid a killing touch to the chest; instead, the charm passed over my left forearm, opening a gash from wrist to elbow.

Pello was already running back into the alley. Beyond the gate, Talm skidded into sight. I yelled for him to follow and took off after Pello, blood dripping from my arm to leave a trail on the stone.

❈

(Kiran)

Wind tore at Kiran's hair, the air sharp with the scent of lightning. From his stance on a balcony at the summit of Reytani's tallest tower, the black clouds looked low enough to touch. Shifting veils of wind-borne sand masked the terraced roofs of the lower city far below. Chaotic energies seethed in the aether, shocks of wild power rippling outward with each lightning strike.

Throughout the city, the fiery sea of the confluence surged and heaved, in turmoil far different from its usual flow. The tower's wards were already flaring and sparking, bare moments away from triggering fully.

Be ready, Ruslan said in Kiran's mind, the words terse and strained from the effort he exerted in raising power. Kiran sent wordless assent, and caught the echo of Mikail's from the tower's eastern side. They had decided to split their vigil; when Ruslan commanded it, Kiran would seek the sign of their enemy in the western half of the confluence, Mikail the eastern.

Kiran's grip tightened on the balcony's edge. Let it be Mikail who sighted their enemy! Then when Ruslan struck, it would not be Kiran who consigned scores of *nathahlen* to their deaths. Ruslan had said he would strike regardless of their enemy's location, even if it were the Aiyalen Spire—or the tower upon which Kiran and Mikail stood. *I warned Sechaveh to take shelter, and you and Mikail are* akheli—*you can survive even a strike of this magnitude.*

The *nathahlen* deaths were necessary. Kiran knew it, and yet his fingers were icy on the balcony's stone, his chest so tight he could barely breathe.

Sibilant whispers raked along his barriers. Kiran reached for Ruslan through the mark-bond. *Ruslan! He comes.*

Ruslan pressed through the link, his mind flooding into Kiran's. Kiran felt the flare of channels, sensed the deliriously sweet, seductive pull of power straining against its confinement.

The confluence convulsed as if some great beast thrashed in its depths. Kiran focused on the shuddering swell of currents. Deep in the heart of the lower city, the dark pinprick of the vortex appeared—

Strike! he thought as one with Ruslan, and magefire exploded free. Yet the moment it did, the vortex vanished. Horror sent Kiran to his knees.

"Call the power back!" he screamed. But he knew it was too late.

✳

(Dev)

I pounded down the alley after Pello. He ran as fast as a roundtail released from a snare, vaulting over stacks of adobe and scrap metal without pause.

The ground jerked sideways beneath my feet. I sprawled forward and cracked my chin on stone. Pello fell too, in a knot of limbs. Quake wards blazed to life above us, even as lightning stabbed down from the black bank of cloud above.

A concussion of sound slammed my ears, far louder than any thunder should be, and the entire sky glared crimson. A tornado of scarlet fire slashed past overhead.

Shock stopped me mid-scramble. Khalmet's bloodsoaked hand, what was that?

A second deafening concussion, and a vast, hot wind blasted down the alley, catapulting me backward into a pile of adobe bricks. I gasped and sucked in air that felt thick as heated oil. Cracks ripped open in the alley's stone. I twisted to look up, and my blood froze. The wall was crumbling, a cascade of rubble pouring off the rooftop ten stories above.

A good fifty feet separated me and Pello. Could Talm stop enough rubble to save us both? If not, it wouldn't be me he chose to save. Pello was our only lead. I sprang forward through a hail of stone fragments, desperate to close the distance.

Pello was on his knees, his injured arm dangling limp. He shouted and dug at something in his belt. I lost my footing on juddering ground, hit the alley floor and rolled. Stone blocks large as wagons ricocheted down toward us. Talm stood at the Zhivonis Street gate, his face impassive and his hands loose at his sides.

Why wasn't he casting? Oh shit, if he was the traitor—

An impact crushed me into darkness.

✳

(Kiran)

Kiran stared down at the lower city in sick, stunned horror. Fat plumes of smoke rose from a charred crater a half-mile wide, scattered fires burning red amid fragmented, jumbled stone. Kiran had felt Ruslan fight to contain the magefire as tightly as possible in the final instants, yet the strike left much of Julisi district a blackened ruin. Now Kiran's mark-bond was still and silent; after a final burst of disbelieving fury, Ruslan had abruptly withdrawn from Kiran's mind.

Lightning still lanced between clouds. Beneath crashes of thunder, an eerie chorus of screams and wails echoed from the lower city. How many *nathahlen* lay dead or dying beneath the shattered remains of buildings? Above the rubble, a mist of dark energies swirled, born of pain and death. Men, women, children, all crushed into bloodied pulp...

Kiran's stomach heaved. He bent and vomited; once, twice, until all that came up was sour strings of bile. He swiped a shaking hand across his mouth, and winced away from another glaring bolt of lightning. The flashes were too bright, the slowly settling currents of the confluence abrading his inner senses raw. He threw an arm over his eyes and struggled to reinforce his barriers.

"Kiran?" Hurried footsteps, and then Mikail's hands were on him, holding him upright.

"The power in Ruslan's strike...I think my *ikilhia* isn't yet recovered, from...from when he freed me of the Alathians' spellwork." Though that didn't explain the cold horror Kiran felt looking at the smoking ruin of Julisi. Before the strike, he'd assumed his dismay a remnant of Alathian alteration that he could overcome. But this ran so deep it felt rooted in his very soul.

Mikail put a hand to Kiran's forehead. His breath hissed through his teeth. "Your *ikilhia*'s a mess. We should have thought to give you damping charms. Here, let me..." A cool wash of green layered itself over Kiran's barriers, and the grating rasp of the confluence faded.

Yet the sickness within didn't ease. He could have accepted the deaths if they'd happened for good reason. But this…Kiran clutched at Mikail's arm. "We failed. So much destruction, and for nothing! How do you bear it?"

"You're right, it's maddening." Mikail scowled out at the storm. "I saw it all through Ruslan's eyes. I thought we had our enemy! How did he know to dodge the strike?"

Kiran stared at Mikail. Did his mage-brother share none of his horror?

"Are you still feeling ill?" Mikail's scowl faded into concern. "Here, come out of the wind." He tugged Kiran off the balcony, back into the spare stone antechamber at the top of the tower stairs.

Kiran fumbled for the stair rail. "We should go to the lower city. We could seek traces there, and…do what we can, to help." Ruslan had taught them nothing of healing magic. But they could seek survivors, extinguish fires, clear rubble…

Mikail checked. He gripped Kiran's shoulders, his gray eyes boring into Kiran's. "You're upset over the dead *nathahlen*."

"How can you not be?" Kiran slumped in Mikail's hold. "They're not mere animals, Mikail. They may lack mage talent, but they love and suffer just as we do."

"Perhaps," Mikail said. "But they murder, betray, and enslave each other, too. Don't think them innocents, Kiran. In helping Ruslan cast, you fight not only for your own survival, but mine, and his, and Lizaveta's. Do you imagine any *nathahlen* would hesitate in your place, if the choice were between saving the family he loves or sparing the lives of strangers?"

Put that way, the weight on Kiran's heart eased a little. "I suppose not. Yet every time I look at the rubble, I feel so…so sick, inside."

"No wonder, with your *ikilhia* so disordered," Mikail said. "You shouldn't drop your barriers, but if you allow me within them, I can help you further." He touched his belt knife, his head cocked in inquiry.

Shelter from the roil of guilt and horror, a chance at enough peace he could think again? Kiran wanted it, badly—and yet, he hesitated. Taking Mikail's offer of solace felt wrong, like a betrayal of the massacred *nathahlen*…but surely that was foolishness.

Kiran drew his own belt knife and cut a swift line down his palm, even as Mikail did the same. He clasped Mikail's bloodied hand. Mikail's mind flowed into his, a cool, green river of strength. Mikail reached for Kiran's *ikilhia*—and paused, at Kiran's instinctive, violent recoil.

Easy, easy, brother. Don't fight me…

Dimly, Kiran was aware of his breath coming in harsh gasps, his heart racing. Slowly, reluctantly, he released his innermost defenses, like relaxing a clenched fist.

Mikail slipped through. Tendrils of power wound through Kiran's *ikilhia*, bolstering it into a far smoother, steadier flame. *Now. Focus as you do when we cast together…*

Kiran shut his eyes and slowed his breath, counting each inhalation, striving to block out all emotion. Mikail helped him, his quiet strength allowing Kiran to bury remorse and horror deep, leaving only calm, clear focus.

There, you see? Mikail withdrew and said aloud, "Better?"

"Yes." The relief of it was enough to weaken Kiran's legs. He sank onto a step. Though his mind was calm, the pulse of his *ikilhia* remained dismayingly erratic despite Mikail's infusion of strength. Why was it taking so long to heal from the damage Ruslan had been forced to inflict? Ruslan had implied his recovery would go far faster.

Mikail said, "You spoke of seeking traces, but even if we found the exact spot where our enemy had appeared, I'm not sure it would profit us. We've had no success reading traces anywhere else."

It was so much easier to think, now the storm of emotion had subsided. How *had* their enemy so readily avoided the strike? Kiran summoned the memory.

Again he felt Ruslan release the magefire, saw the vortex vanish. Just as their enemy had vanished before Kiran's second strike in the dead mage's workroom…Kiran straightened.

"Mikail. What if our enemy can somehow detect channeled magic before it's cast? When I first struck and injured him after his attack on you, I cast with power pulled straight from a charm. But when I struck again, with channeled power funneled to me by Ruslan, our attacker vanished before the strike reached him. I thought he decided to retreat after my first strike, and I simply didn't cast the second one fast enough. But now…I think he felt Ruslan release the containment."

"How?" Mikail asked. "Today, he was half the city away, and Ruslan used shielding wards."

"I don't know," Kiran said. "But I think we need to find a way to strike at him without the use of the confluence. Either that, or distract him so thoroughly he doesn't feel a channeled strike coming." Thanks to Mikail's help, he could speak of a second magefire strike and feel only a faint twitch of unease.

Mikail grimaced. "I can't believe it's so hard to kill one *nathahlen*."

Kiran said, "If he can sense channeled spellwork better than even an *akheli* could manage, Ruslan must be wrong about him being untalented."

As if summoned by the mention of his name, Ruslan spoke in terse command through the mark-bond. *Sechaveh has summoned us. Join me at Kelante Tower.*

Mikail muttered, "This should be interesting."

Kiran suspected "interesting" was far too optimistic a word. Sechaveh would be furious, and Ruslan in no mood to tolerate chastisement by any *nathahlen*, even one with Sechaveh's ability to forbid him the confluence. They'd be lucky if they made it through the meeting with the tower still standing.

※

(Dev)

Somewhere, something was dripping. Plink, plink, plink, like icemelt in a crevasse. I felt chilled, my limbs numb and heavy—except my left arm, which burned with sullen fire. I opened my eyes to absolute blackness. Grit coated my tongue, my mouth so dry I couldn't swallow, and my head ached something fierce. I coughed and immediately regretted it as my ribs screamed.

"Well. It would seem outriders truly are favored of Khalmet."

Pello. He sounded terrible, his voice cracked and hoarse. I tried to roll, and managed only a scuffling twitch. Stone pressed down on my torso, tight enough to make breathing difficult. I wanted to thrash, to fight, get it *off*—instead, I slowed my panicked breathing, forced myself to lie still and take stock. My injured left arm was pinned, immobile, but my right arm could move. I wriggled it up and shoved against the weight on my chest. I succeeded only in showering grit into my eyes.

"Can you move at all?" My voice didn't sound much better than Pello's.

He laughed thickly. "No."

Remembering that cascade of rubble, I felt cold all over again. "How are we not crushed?"

"I sparked a barrier charm. Wasn't strong enough to hold off the falling stone entirely, but it left a little space. Of course, things have been…settling, since." He fell silent, his breathing strained.

Was the weight on my chest growing heavier? Visions of rock inexorably crushing me into paste had me panting all over again, panic creeping upward. *No.* Focus.

"How long, since…?"

"Some hours. Though…time stretches, in darkness."

Hours, and nobody had cast to get us out. I remembered Talm watching the rocks rain down on us without lifting a hand. I'd warned Cara we couldn't rule him out as a traitor, but still…I'd swear his love for Marten was real. What hatred did he carry that outweighed it?

Didn't matter. If the lying bastard had told Marten we were dead, maybe even cast one of those veiling spells to make sure nobody could easily seek us….shit. I still wore the signaling charm on my left wrist, but with my arm trapped I had no way to tap out the damn pattern.

I said to Pello, "If you work for the bastard responsible for these quakes, I'm guessing he's got better things to do than dig you out."

Pello laughed again, this time with a wild, hard edge. "I have two masters, and neither will save me. I knew the moment I saw you on that stair that I'd outlived my usefulness and death was coming for me."

"Who are your masters?" I might not survive to use the information, but so long as Pello kept talking, I didn't have to think about the pressure on my chest, the weight of rubble slowly sinking down.

"You guessed one," Pello said. "The Shaikar-spawn who seeks to destroy the city. But it was your Lieutenant Talmaddis who gave me over to him and told him how to leash me."

Surprise sent my voice high. "Talmaddis is working directly with the mage-killer?" I'd assumed he and any co-conspirators were simply hoping to take advantage of the situation. Impede Marten's investigation enough so he'd fail to stop the killer from destroying both confluence and city, and leave Alathia free of the so-called plague den on its border.

"For at least these last few months. Perhaps longer," Pello said. "Talmaddis hunted me down before I could cross the Alathian border. He concealed me from the others in his Watch, telling me he had a friend with a use for a Ninavel shadow man. I went along with him, thinking if I could only reach Ninavel again, I'd soon gain my freedom. The more fool, me."

The echo of my own experience brought a stab of uncomfortable sympathy. "What of the other Alathians at the embassy? Are any of them involved?"

"Not that I've seen," Pello said. "But that proves little. Talmaddis may well have partners in this madness—whether willing, or coerced as I was."

I thought again of the darkness in Lena's eyes. If she was working with Talm, might it be unwillingly? But I didn't buy for a minute that Pello had been forced into this.

"Coerced? Right," I sneered. "How much coin did you get to betray Sechaveh?"

Pello said, "Talmaddis knew coin wouldn't guarantee loyalty. He searched my mind, again and again until he broke through the veils Sechaveh's mages had set in me, and he found the collar to leash me. I have…a son. A child of nine years. His mother is long dead—she, too, played shadow games. I sent my son years ago to a distant cousin in Prosul Varkevia, thinking that would protect him. Talmaddis told the mage-killer of this when he handed me over."

I had to remember how readily he lied. "The killer threatened a kid who lives way down in southern Varkevia, and you rolled right over?"

"Says the man who'd crawl through magefire for a child that isn't even his," Pello said, with a cracked chuckle. "He did more than threaten. He can travel like demons in the tales, appearing in the blink of any eye wherever he chooses… though I learned he can only stay a short time before he must return to the source of his power. He went to Prosul Varkevia and kidnapped my son, even now holds him prisoner. To prove his power, he killed my cousin. And when he caught me seeking ways to counter his magic, he killed my closest friend."

"Who the hell *is* this murdering bastard?" I demanded.

"I wish I had his name, so I might curse his soul properly…" Pello coughed, harsh and dry. My own throat burned. Gods, what I wouldn't give for some water.

"I know you," I said. "All you'd need is five sentences from him to learn far more than his name." *Keep talking*, I willed him.

Pello said, "I saw him only twice, and he wore a *gabeshal* robe, only his eyes showing. But I know this: the robe is not mere disguise. He is Kaithan-born, though his accent is so faded I think it years since he last lived in the tribelands. He once lived in Ninavel, though he does not now. And how he hates the city! But he would not tell me what spawned that hate, no matter how I pricked him. I did not have much chance. After our first meeting, he contacted me only by message charm…except when he found I'd defied him. Then he came, and made me watch Nayyis die."

Khalmet's bloodsoaked hand. The stone seemed to press all the harder on my chest. "What did he need you for?"

"I scouted wards, reported the movements of certain mages…but my main task was to discover when and where Tainters would be working jobs."

"So he can snatch them," I said. "Why does he want the kids?"

Pello spat and said, huskier than ever, "He uses the children somehow to fuel his magic…I never saw what he does. But they do not survive it. I saw a room of bones, so small and white, clean of flesh as if it was burned away in magefire…"

Bile soured my throat. "How could you keep handing kids over?"

"You sound so horrified, so righteous," Pello said. "I have done worse in Sechaveh's service, and for less reason. You have the steel in you to do the same. Look at the choices you've made for young Melly's sake."

I flinched, remembering handing Kiran drugged and helpless to Gerran; of how even now I worked for Marten, despite all his betrayals. "This source of power you say the killer's got to return to…where is it?"

Pello groaned. "Ah, how I struggled to find out! He took me there to show me my son and my murdered cousin, but we traveled in demon-fashion, the journey done in an eyeblink. I think it is not in the city. The air was chill, as it is in the high mountains or the far north. I saw no windows, and the rooms were of rough stone, so rough I thought them hollowed by magic from natural rock, not built. The rock itself was far darker than any stone I've seen in Ninavel, though streaked with veins of rose quartz. I searched scholars' records and explorers' journals for locations where such rock might be found…but learned to my sorrow there are far too many possibilities, both in the Whitefires and elsewhere." He broke into more hitching, strained coughs.

There had to be some better use a mage could make of his information. "If we can get free and contact Captain Martennan…maybe Talmaddis isn't the only Alathian working with the killer, but I'm dead sure Marten's not part of this. If you share all you know, he can find this bastard's den and save your son."

"I fear my son's life is already forfeit," Pello said. "This…this is what comes of attachment. I knew it, and yet I could not burn it out of myself…and now, look. My son is dead regardless, and I, too, will feel Shaikar's touch…"

The slow, almost dreamy sound of his words alarmed me. "How badly are you hurt?"

"Badly enough. I have not an outrider's luck."

The maddeningly steady plinking took on a sinister new aspect. "You're bleeding out? I've a charm that might work to signal—"

"If you signal the Alathians, we are both dead men." Pello's voice strengthened. "The only thing saving you now is the shrouding charm I wear, strong enough to cover us both. Talmaddis cannot sense if we live. And so, he will tell the rest that we lie dead, all the while watching for any signal from you that might force him to ensure it. He knows if he waits long enough, we die in truth without him risking a single spell to accomplish it."

"It wasn't the Alathians I was going to signal." The charm Kiran had modified for me circled my right wrist. I didn't know if the charm would work if I sparked it, not him. But hell, I had to try.

"Talmaddis may feel the magic anyway."

"I have to risk it." I lifted my right arm, scraped my wrist against stone until blood ran slick over Kiran's charm. "*Ashantya*," I whispered, and concentrated with everything within me.

CHAPTER TWENTY

(Kiran)

"Tell me why I should not bar you from the confluence here and now, Ruslan!" Sechaveh stabbed a finger down at the warded sea of blue-violet flame before his great stone chair. "When you said I should seek shelter, you said nothing of blasting an entire district into ash! Ninavel's largest smelting houses destroyed, my workforce on the verge of rioting, the mines' production stalled...and you say my enemy is still at large? I say you have done far more to ruin my city than he has yet managed!"

Kiran hid a wince. He and Mikail waited by the audience chamber windows, well clear of Ruslan. Their master faced Sechaveh and Captain Martennan over the confluence charm's obsidian rings, his arms crossed tight. Lizaveta stood at his side, elegant and imperious. Ruslan's face was as severe and still as a statue's, but his hazel eyes burned.

He said, "I have caused no damage that cannot be repaired. Let the merchant houses flee, let the mines go fallow for lack of workers...the merchants will come crawling back sniffing after profit soon enough, and your coffers will once more overflow."

Lizaveta added in a tone of quiet reason, "Even a failed strike bought us more time, by driving away our enemy before he could deepen the confluence's instability."

Captain Martennan's drawling voice echoed off the marble walls. "Time bought at far too high a price! Lord Sechaveh, not only did Ruslan's ill-considered strike cost me one of my own people, a man whose efforts have proved invaluable to this investigation—but he destroyed our best lead! The spy

Pello could well have led us to the killer. Thanks to Ruslan, that chance is gone."

Ruslan glared at Martennan. "Your pursuit of the spy was a thin gamble at best. You yourself admit you do not know if he worked for the killer. As for your man..." The fire in his eyes brightened, turned vindictive. "You refer merely to your hired informant, do you not? He was Arkennlander, and *nathahlen*—hardly one of your own people. Hire another of the lower city's rabble if you choose to seek information there; I see no reason for sorrow."

Martennan's mouth twisted. Unaccountably, he glanced at Kiran. Kiran kept his face stolidly blank. Martennan must know of Dev's attempt to turn him against Ruslan. Did he hope the news of Dev's death would leave Kiran newly desperate for answers about his past, making him all the more vulnerable to coercion? If so, Kiran would show him how wrong he was.

Kiran only wished he could rejoice in Dev's death the way Ruslan so clearly did. Dev had betrayed him, tried to suborn him, and Kiran had wanted revenge. Yet between the tension in the audience chamber and his lingering dismay over the failed strike, he couldn't muster even a glimmer of satisfaction.

"I see plenty of reason for sorrow in your failure, Ruslan." Sechaveh's yellow eyes were lambent with anger. "We cannot afford any more such mistakes. I should ensure you cannot cast a channeled spell again without my approval."

Ruslan's *ikilhia* flared, power rippling out to stain the aether around him. Kiran caught Mikail's eye, saw his mage-brother's worry, twin to his own. Ruslan wouldn't be so foolish as to cast directly against Sechaveh or Martennan in violation of his vows, but his temper might drive him to some other casting nearly as ruinous in effect.

Lizaveta set her fingers lightly on Ruslan's wrist. Her beautiful face remained grave, giving no hint of what might be passing between them, but the power pulsing from Ruslan's *ikilhia* subsided.

He said sharply to Sechaveh, "You cannot *afford* to hobble me, or waste time in futile recrimination. Save your anger for our enemy! A failure still gives us information, and we must use it to plan our next attack..." He launched into an explanation of Kiran's theory about their enemy's sensitivity to channeled spellwork.

Kiran let out a relieved breath and glanced away. The view from the chamber windows remained ominous. The morning's massive thunderstorm had moved out eastward, leaving behind an eerily russet sky, the afternoon light dim and strange. Smoke still curled up from the charred remains of Julisi district. Beyond the city walls, pale dust vortices taller than the city spires whipped across the alkali flats. Lightning flickered over the Bolthole

Mountains from clouds as black as obsidian. The confluence twisted in sullen, unsettled spirals, the aether still rippling with dissonant energies.

A whisper teased at Kiran's senses. He stiffened. Was their enemy returning so soon? But no, the whisper was deep within his barriers, not outside them, and so faint he could barely discern it. Puzzled, he concentrated.

Kiran. Kiran! Mother of maidens, let this work, let him hear me...

Dev? Shock stopped Kiran's breath. Before he could think, he sent, *The Alathians claimed you were dead!*

A thin echo of stunned relief came. *Kiran! Oh, thank Khalmet...I'm trapped under rubble, and not alone—with me is a shadow man who knows much of the killer. You've got to get us free! But come alone, and don't tell anybody else we survived...One of the Alathians is working with the mage-killer.*

Kiran's heart pounded. Information on the killer within reach, and the chance to condemn one or more of the Alathians—the news was almost too good to be true. He had to be wary. *Come alone...*this could be some new scheme of the Alathians. Or what if Dev were the traitor? Mikail had said Dev sought only his own profit—such a man could easily switch sides. Dev might think to lure Kiran out alone so the killer could try some new scheme to strike an *akheli* down.

He said to Dev, *What proof do I have this isn't more of your lies? Mikail told me the truth you tried to hide. You betrayed me into Alathian hands. It's thanks to you they bound me so deeply Ruslan could not free me without damage.*

Mikail said what? Abject horror flooded through the link. *Oh gods, Kiran! You told him what you learned from Bren? No, no, oh mother of maidens, Melly...*

Whatever Dev's other lies, his concern for the child was all too real. The force of his panic threatened to shatter the link. Kiran snatched after the connection, shored it up with power from his own *ikilhia. She is safe from Ruslan's anger. Neither he nor Mikail know of our meeting. And I...I am more direct than Ruslan. The revenge I take for your betrayal will be on you, not on a child who did nothing to harm me.*

Dev's panic eased, though dismay continued to bleed through the link. *I didn't betray you! But gods, we can argue about it later. Doesn't matter what you think of me—just get me and Pello out, and we'll give you the information we hold.*

Kiran hesitated, his eyes on Captain Martennan, who was busy arguing with Ruslan and Lizaveta over means and methods of attack. *You say one of the Alathians is a traitor. Who?* How he hoped Dev spoke truth! Even if only one Alathian were involved, he could use the traitor to implicate them all.

Dev said, *Get me out, and I'll tell you.*

Tell me, and you'll have your rescue, Kiran countered.

Dry amusement crept through the link. *If you believe I'm such a liar, how do you know my answer would be true? Rescue us, and you can put us both under truth spell, learn all we know of traitor and killer. But…one warning. Pello's hurt, and badly. I'll get what I can from him in case he doesn't survive long enough for a truth spell. But the sooner you can reach us, the better.*

Dismay pierced Kiran's eagerness. He could go extract Dev and Pello right away, if only he told Ruslan. But how could he explain his knowledge of their survival? If Ruslan found out Dev had reached him via a linking charm, he'd search Kiran's mind until he discovered everything else.

Even if Kiran delayed, what chance did he have of maintaining secrecy? Ever since he'd confessed his clandestine excursion to Mikail, his mage-brother had rarely left Kiran's side. Coming up with an excuse so clever it allowed Kiran to travel alone and unquestioned to the lower city felt utterly impossible.

Besides…this could still be a trap. He couldn't let his desire to spare Mikail suffering blind him. And if Dev truly held vital information…how could Kiran delay, with so many lives hanging in the balance?

Reluctant conviction grew in him. This was too important. Kiran dreaded the price Mikail and even the *nathahlen* child would pay, but he had to set aside his fear and speak to Ruslan.

The mental link was fading, the power in Dev's charm nearly used up. Kiran poured more of his own *ikilhia* into the contact, and hoped none of his nervousness flowed with it.

I will come as soon as I can, he told Dev. He couldn't let Dev realize his intent. In Dev's place, Kiran could well believe fury and desperation might drive him to take the only revenge against Ruslan he could—killing both Pello and himself, to deprive Ruslan of the information he sought.

Thank Khalmet. The depth of Dev's relief made Kiran flinch. *I'll question Pello as best I can.* And softer, a mere wisp of a thought, bleak as winter: *He was right about me.*

Kiran wanted to ask what Dev meant. But even with the assist from Kiran's *ikilhia*, the link between them trembled on the edge of dissolution. *Where are you?* It would save more time if Ruslan didn't have to cast to discover Dev's exact location.

*Just off Zhivonis Street, in a gated alley leading to the smelters' yards…*the thought trailed off, as the link shivered and slipped apart into nothingness.

Ruslan was still arguing with Martennan. Kiran's chest tightened, sweat cold on his palms. A terrible time to confess disobedience, with Ruslan already angry. But he couldn't afford to take the coward's path.

Kiran gathered his courage and reached through the mark-bond. *Ruslan.*

I must speak with you. It's too important to wait.

Ruslan glanced his way, surprise in the arch of his chestnut brows. *What troubles you?*

The Alathians' guide and the spy Pello still live, buried in rubble. Dev claims they hold not only information on the killer, but on a traitor among the Alathians. Kiran called forth his memory of Dev's initial startling claim and offered it to Ruslan.

Ruslan halted his argument mid-sentence. For an instant he stood frozen, his expression unreadable. Kiran braced himself, fearing Ruslan would tear through the rest of his memories on the spot.

Sechaveh, Martennan, and Lizaveta were all peering at Ruslan with varying degrees of wary puzzlement. Ruslan turned to Sechaveh.

"Forgive me," he said tightly. "I have received word of a matter related to the confluence that requires my immediate attention. I must withdraw and take Kiran to aid me. Lizaveta and Mikail will remain and continue the discussion in my absence."

Without waiting for an answer, he strode for the door. Kiran met Mikail's mystified gaze. "I'm sorry," he whispered.

"Kiran?" The skin around Mikail's gray eyes creased with worry.

Kiran tore his gaze from his mage-brother and hurried after his master. Ruslan swept past Sechaveh's guardsmen and down a flight of stairs to an ornately furnished waiting room, full of silk-cushioned chairs and brightly patterned rugs of lambs' wool. Kiran followed him inside on leaden feet. Ruslan shut the door and sparked the wards, then cast a silencing spell.

He turned to Kiran. "Explain."

"Ruslan…" Kiran sank to his knees. He bowed his head and extended his arms, crossed at the wrist. He'd seen Ruslan do the same in apology to Lizaveta, once.

Through lips that felt numb, he said, "I was confused, and desperate, and…I disobeyed you. But out of that disobedience, we might gain much. I will show you, willingly and without reservation, and let you judge."

He released his barriers. Ruslan's mind lanced into his with a force that wrenched a gasp from his throat. But Kiran threw open the gates to his innermost self, held himself unresisting as Ruslan scoured his memories. When Ruslan reached Kiran's clandestine visit to Dev, fire seared Kiran so deeply he couldn't hold back choked whimpers. Even then, he didn't fight. He endured as the fire ate deeper yet, exposing every last thought and feeling he'd had during his conversations with Dev and Mikail.

At last, the fire retreated to prowl around the edges of Kiran's mind. Kiran found himself collapsed over his knees, breathing in great, tearing gasps, his forehead resting on the sweat-dampened rug. Ruslan's hand settled on his neck.

"Ah, Kiran," his master said. "You test me so. What am I to do with you? I thought your love for Mikail enough to keep you from foolishness. Yet even that did not suffice."

"I know you must punish me," Kiran said, his voice shaking. "But, Ruslan... can you not stay your hand until we've discovered what information the two *nathahlen* hold?"

Ruslan gripped his collar, hauled him back up to his knees. "Yes," he said. "You are not a child, to forget the cause if punishment is not immediate. And I am not a fool to ignore this chance. Besides..." Ruslan's fingers twined in Kiran's hair. He tugged Kiran's head back until Kiran's throat was bared in a tight, strained arch. "A delay will give me time to think on appropriate measures of correction."

The cold promise in his eyes shriveled Kiran's soul. Ruslan saw his fear and smiled, dark and satisfied. He slid his fingers along Kiran's throat, the pressure just short of pain.

"Punishment will come, *akhelysh*. But I know part of the fault is mine. It is as Mikail told you: I was ashamed of my failure to protect you from the Alathians, and took refuge in a lie, hoping it would spare us both further pain. Let that be a lesson: weakness born of love is still weakness, and should never be indulged."

He pulled Kiran to his feet. "Now. Let us go seek these *nathahlen*. I am not sorry the guide survived. Now I can watch his face when the child dies."

Kiran looked aside. He'd known the girl's life would be forfeit, and yet the idea still sickened him. "I want revenge too, but...shouldn't we take care not to act in haste? If Dev believes the child beyond help, he may kill himself and the spy to spite you, and we can't cast to force him to our will."

Ruslan chuckled. "Never fear, *akhelysh*. I will not be...hasty, as you say. With a little help from you, we can ensure we learn all he knows. And then...then, we can delight in revenge."

❋

(Dev)

I lay in darkness, listening to that terrible, continuing drip of blood. Pello's responses to my questions had grown increasingly erratic, his speech slowing. Before he fell entirely silent, he'd babbled scattered phrases of Varkevian, the words freighted with anguish. I'd tried to memorize the sound of them. My knowledge of Varkevian was limited to curses learned from convoy men. Did he speak of his son, or the killer, or something else entirely? I had no idea.

Now he wouldn't respond, no matter how sharply I spoke. For a while, I'd heard his breathing, shallow and rapid. But that had slowed too, until I was no longer sure if the faint rasp beneath the slow trickling was real or imaginary.

Guilt gnawed at me. One thing to tell myself that Pello was no innocent, that Melly's life was worth far more than his. Another thing to listen to a man's life bleeding away, wondering if I could have saved him. If I'd thought faster, come up with some excuse Kiran could have given Ruslan, some bargain I could've made…

Too late now. The charm was cold and dead on my wrist, and all I could do was pray with increasing desperation that Kiran would show up. What if Pello took some vital piece of information to the grave with him? I'd gotten what I could, and Pello had said himself that Talm would know far more of use—assuming Talm could be forced to reveal it. Mages could fight truth spells…though if Ruslan interrogated Talm, I didn't doubt he could make Talm talk. Yet still, I worried.

I tried to think of Cara. How if I saw her again, I wouldn't be such a coward. If I could have that moment in the embassy back, both of us alone in a bedroom—I'd cast caution aside, beg her forgiveness for all my stupidity, and kiss her so deep the world would vanish around us.

But Jylla kept intruding, her black eyes sharp and pitying, spearing straight through to my soul: *The coldness and deceit she hates in me is in you, too. You just hide it better.*

A sudden, sharp grinding made me start. Rocks groaned, shifted. Stone lifted off my chest. The release of pressure triggered a spasm of coughing that left me curled in a ball, every muscle cramping. Red light spilled over me. I squinted through watering eyes. Kiran stood in the crack left where two great blocks had shuddered apart. His teeth were bared in a grimace of effort, and a faceted crystal glowed like a burning coal in his hand.

He said, "The *ikilhia* in the crystal will not last long. Can you walk?"

"Yeah." My muscles still burned like they'd been dipped in acid, but I felt no sharp, stabbing pain of broken bones. The long gash on my arm had completely crusted over. "Is Pello…?" I twisted to look, and groaned.

Pello lay in a black lake of blood on a jagged-edged hunk of scrap metal. His right leg was crushed flat under a stone block, and an iron bar protruded from his gut. His chest was still, his eyes closed, his skin ashen. The knotted silver spiral of a pains-ease charm lay where it had fallen from one hand.

I scrabbled forward to reach for his neck. Kiran said, "I sense no trace of *ikilhia* in him. I hope you questioned him as you said."

He sounded so gods-damned cold about it. "He's veiled," I snapped. "Of course you can't sense anything." I felt for Pello's pulse. Nothing, no matter how hard I pressed. I scrubbed a hand over my eyes. Then, ignoring the blood, I made a hasty search of his clothes. In addition to the dragonclaw, barrier, and pains-ease charms, I found the ring to my old painbender charm, and a charm marked with runes reminiscent of a hide-me—likely the charm containing the veiling spell. Around his neck was a copper chain with a little crescent moon of malachite. I pocketed that too, feeling like a vulture. But if we found the killer and by some miracle Pello's son yet lived, maybe I could give him something of his father.

"Leave him, and come," Kiran said. "Now." His voice quivered with strain. Was it my imagination, or had the crystal's glow faded some already? I staggered after him as rocks groaned apart to admit us. When we emerged into cool night air, the stars a vivid spray high above the jagged outlines of ruined buildings, I had to stop. I bent and braced my hands on my knees. My eyes burned with grit and regret.

"Don't suppose you have any water," I croaked to Kiran.

"No." Something in his tone jerked my head up.

Red magelight flared beyond him in the darkness of the alley, revealing Ruslan. Melly stood before him, Ruslan's hands resting on her small shoulders. Her amber eyes were wide in silent appeal, fear printed on her heart-shaped face. Her red hair was loose in a tangled cloud, and a silver torc set with blood-dark rubies and etched with jagged sigils circled her throat.

Every muscle in my body locked. "*No!*"

Ruslan smiled at me in pure, malicious anticipation. Kiran was watching me, his face pale and set. He'd known Ruslan was here. I snarled at him, "You lying bastard! You said she was safe!"

A muscle jumped in his jaw, but he didn't reply.

Fear and despair stormed through me, my body trembling. Thinking felt like trying to walk a ridge in a howling wind. Ruslan couldn't cast against me. But if I attacked him, he'd hurt Melly. She could try and fight him with the Taint...but that torc around her neck must be some blood magic version of a painbender charm. Using the Taint was far easier than casting magic, but it still needed concentration. I'd learned long ago just how impossible it was to lift or shove or fly in the midst of pain so bad you couldn't breathe. Besides, even if she dumped an entire pile of rubble on Ruslan's head, it wouldn't do much more than piss him off.

"Dev?" Melly's voice was thin. "He says he won't hurt me if you obey him." I could tell she knew better than to believe it. She'd always been clever. But the confusion lurking in her eyes tore at my heart. She knew me only as Liana's friend, a friend who treated her and all Red Dal's Tainters with equal, casual affection. She had no idea why a blood mage had singled her out, or why I'd care.

"It'll be okay, kid." Because that was the lie you had to tell, even when we both knew it wasn't true.

Ruslan's smile widened. Kiran said to him, "The spy is dead." It sounded like a warning.

"A pity." Ruslan considered me. "After your previous defiance, I should tear the child's heart from her chest. Yet you are the least of my enemies. I will stay my hand from the girl and seek a different path for revenge if you cooperate in my hunt for more important prey."

Did he really think me so dumb as to believe he'd leave Melly alone? Still, I'd buy what time I could. "I'll cooperate."

"Then move not a muscle." Ruslan glanced at Kiran. "Hold the child. I will search his memories and learn what he knows of traitor and killer."

The minute Ruslan had what he wanted, Melly would die screaming. I had to think, had to stop him—

I blurted out, "Try it, and you break your vow. After my last little chat with Kiran, the Alathians cast a binding on me. They didn't want him digging their secrets out of my head. The minute you start mucking about in my memories, their spell will kill me, and your vow is broken. So don't even think about getting grabby." A total lie, but one I hoped Ruslan would find plausible. Especially if he could sense the killer's binding in me.

Ruslan's lips drew back from his teeth in a brief, silent snarl. One hand slid to the torc on Melly's throat. "Speak, then, and quickly. Who is the traitor?"

"Wait," Kiran said abruptly. "Ruslan, how can we be certain his answers are true? A truth spell will harm him if he resists, and break your vow. But if we take him before Sechaveh to question him, either Lizaveta or one of Sechaveh's mages can cast in our stead, and we can be sure of the information we gain. Also…if we take him straight to Kelante Tower, it may help mollify Sechaveh over our failed strike."

I blinked, remembering the tornado of fire howling past. The destruction around us was *Ruslan's* doing? I'd assumed the fire some new magic of the killer's. If Ruslan would just listen to Kiran, take me before Sechaveh—I couldn't ask for a better opportunity.

I said to Ruslan, "Leave Melly alone, and I'll gladly spill my guts to

Sechaveh. You want revenge on Martennan, right? So do I—you know why." I didn't look at Kiran. I wasn't such a fool as to try and counter the lies he'd swallowed, not with Melly right there in Ruslan's hands. "The traitor is someone Martennan cares for. Exposing this treachery will hurt him, more deeply than any casting of yours could do. So ask yourself…which of us do you hate more?"

Ruslan fingered Melly's torc, his eyes cold with calculation. She shuddered under his touch. Her breath quickened, her gaze flicking from me to Kiran, and her hands fisted.

She was nerving herself up to use the Taint. I caught her eye, willed her, *Don't*. She'd only provoke Ruslan into hurting her. If I could just get to Sechaveh, that was her best chance. I prayed, a silent, desperate litany.

"You are right, *akhelysh*," Ruslan said to Kiran. "We should be cautious. I will seek Sechaveh's aid in the questioning. But before we take him to Kelante…" He looked at me, and my stomach seized at the renewed malice in his eyes. "Caution also indicates we remind him of the consequences of any attempts at escape."

He didn't chant like the Alathians did to cast, didn't so much as twitch a finger. But Melly wailed, high and shrill, and clawed at her temples.

"It hurts, stop, *please*—" Stone shards rattled on the ground around her, skittered away to ricochet off the alley walls. She was shoving them blindly, unable to focus well enough through the pain to muster a proper blow at her tormentor. She fell to her knees, screaming.

The agony in her cries cut me deeper than any blade. Ruslan watched me with hungry delight. I snarled at him, "You've made your point. Keep it up, and I'll tell far more truth than you'd like." I cut my eyes at Kiran, who was staring at Melly, his face gone chalk-white. Not that I thought Kiran would believe me straight off if I started yelling about him and Alisa, but it'd sure as hell trigger his curiosity.

Ruslan's eyes narrowed. Melly slumped, her shrieks dying into gulping sobs. I hurried forward and gathered her into my arms. She clutched at me and pressed her tear-streaked face into my shoulder, her thin body shaking.

Kiran watched us, his face still bloodless, one hand pressed to the spot where Ruslan's sigil lay beneath his shirt. I hoped Melly's cries haunted his dreams so badly he never slept again.

"We go to Kelante Tower," Ruslan said. "Now. Carry the child if she cannot walk. If she dares again to use the Taint, she'll reap far more than a taste of pain."

I helped Melly to her feet, muttering, "Just hang on, kid. I'll get you free of this." But it was a promise I was terrified I couldn't keep.

CHAPTER TWENTY-ONE

(Dev)

"Think they'd give us some water?" Melly whispered, eyeing the guardsmen around us. They were Sechaveh's men, his scorpion crest prominent on their shirts and the ends of their gold sashes. Melly and I had been herded into a waiting room near the top of Kelante Tower while Ruslan spoke privately with Sechaveh. It wasn't the guardsmen we had to fear; it was Ruslan's partner Lizaveta, who lounged on a divan near the door, her eyes never leaving us.

This was the first I'd seen of her. She looked as beautiful and deadly as a demon from a tale. Jeweled pins studded her rippling sheet of black hair, her long-lashed eyes wide and dark in the perfect brown oval of her face. Crimson and black sigils patterned her indigo gown, and a barbed knife as long as my forearm hung from a black sash belted around her waist. The guards wouldn't get within five feet of her, or raise their eyes from her sandaled feet when she spoke.

"I'll ask," I told Melly. She was looking white around the mouth, her cheeks blotchy with dried tears and exhaustion. She'd refused my help on the long walk up to Kelante Tower, doggedly insisting she was fine. I'd let her regain a little pride, though I'd heard how her voice trembled. Until tonight she'd been boss Tainter in Red Dal's gang, cocky and brash as only a Tainter at the height of her power could be. But Ruslan was enough to make grown men cower, let alone a kid who'd just turned twelve.

I raised my voice. "Hey. The kid's feeling sick—she needs water, unless you want her throwing up on your fine carpet."

The head guardsman shifted his weight and glanced at Lizaveta. Her lush red lips curved in a smile that held the same cruelty as Ruslan's. "Perhaps after your testimony," she said. "It will encourage you to speak faster."

She wouldn't be giving Melly any water after my testimony. She'd be helping Ruslan carve Melly into shreds, and she'd wear that demon's smile the whole time. Unless I could convince Sechaveh to stop them. Nerves set my stomach jumping.

I put an arm around Melly's shoulders. "Here, sit down." She let me steer her over to a cushioned chair. I dragged a second chair over and sank into it. Every muscle ached. Bruises blackened my skin, the gash on my left arm still a crusted mess of blood and grime.

Melly perched gingerly on the edge of a cushion. She touched the torc around her neck, then jerked her hand down, grimacing. She leaned toward me and whispered, "Hurts when I touch the charm, and I don't know where to strike to shatter it. Do you?"

The kid had guts, just like her father. I eyed the jagged sigils on her torc. Red Dal taught his Tainters how to read ward patterns and identify the spots where physical damage would disrupt their magic without causing a deadly flare-out of magefire. We'd learned how to safely break the common sorts of charms, too; but blood magic wasn't common.

"I don't know the sigils," I whispered back. "Blood magic might mean the charm's too strong to shatter. It's sure as hell not safe to try. I'll get you out of this, Melly."

She gave me a look that said she wasn't at all certain I could pull that off. "Dev...why did the blood mage take me?"

I drew my hands over my face, wearily. I didn't want to have to explain the entire mess, but she deserved an answer. "Because...because I was friends with your father. He was an outrider, like me. He got killed on a convoy trip some years back, but when he was dying, he asked me to watch out for you, in his stead. I promised him I would—vowed it in Suliyya's name." Yeah, and what a disaster I'd made of that vow. All I'd ever done was drag her deeper into danger.

Melly said, "My father? But...why would he care? He didn't want me. If Red Dal hadn't taken me in when my mother died, I'd be dead too."

Red Dal told all his kids that. *Nobody wanted you but me. I saved you, because I saw you were special.* For most Tainters it was even the truth. The gods knew no family had come looking for me when I Changed, and my price had been cheap.

"Your father did want you," I said. "But he and your mother didn't get along." That was one way of putting it, given that Melly's mother had conceived her specifically to blackmail Sethan. "Then when she died, you were only a toddler. He had to work in the mountains, and couldn't afford to pay someone to care for you. So he gave you to Red Dal, thinking that after you Changed, you'd be old enough to travel the Whitefires with him." No need to tell her what a naïve idiot Sethan had been.

"He never came to see me," Melly said, scowling. "Not like you."

"Red Dal wouldn't let him." I'd heard from Liana that Sethan had tried once, not long after Melly came to the den. Red Dal had warned him: come again, and you'll be dead before sunset. No handler wanted his Tainters to have divided loyalties. Red Dal had tolerated my sporadic visits to the den after Sethan was dead, but only because I'd long been friends with Liana. I'd always taken care never to single Melly out, or breathe a word of my connection to her.

"Your father loved you," I told Melly. "A lot."

"I don't care," Melly said. "Red Dal's my father now." And then, in a choked whisper, "I want to go home."

New pain seized me. I couldn't bear to tell her that even if I saved her from Ruslan, she'd never return to Red Dal's den. "I know."

The door opened. Ruslan strode in, Mikail and Kiran at his heels. Melly and I both tensed.

Ruslan said, "Sechaveh is ready to question him." Behind him, Kiran's face was as blank as Mikail's; but unlike Mikail, he wouldn't meet my gaze.

Lizaveta rose from the divan. "Shall I cast to ensure he speaks truth, brother?" Her slim fingers caressed her dagger, anticipation gleaming in her eyes.

Oh, gods. I gripped the chair arms to stop myself from bolting.

"No," Ruslan said shortly. "Sechaveh insists his pet Seranthine should perform the spell."

If I'd been standing, I probably would've toppled over from relief. As it was, I relaxed my death grip on the chair and sent up a swift litany of thanks to Khalmet. I hoped I could take Sechaveh's insistence as a sign he remained deeply pissed at Ruslan. I'd need all the help I could get when the time came to try a bargain.

Lizaveta didn't take her hand from the knife. "Then I'll keep watch on the child for you while you attend the questioning."

My relief vanished. Keep watch…mother of maidens, let that be all she did! But I had little enough leverage here. She wouldn't kill Melly, not until Ruslan was certain he'd squeezed every last bit of information from me. I had to cling to that.

Ruslan nodded. "Mikail, Kiran, you will return to the house and work on the spells we discussed."

"Yes, Ruslan." Kiran said it in perfect unison with Mikail. He hadn't once looked at me, but I knew the true reason Ruslan was sending him from the tower. He didn't want Kiran anywhere near me while I spoke under truth spell.

Ruslan pointed at me. "Bring him." The guards moved in.

I stood and said to Melly, "I'll come back as soon as I can."

Her fingers locked white on a cushion. But her spine straightened, and she ducked her chin in a nod. My heart hurt all over again; I'd seen that same determined courage a thousand times in Sethan.

The guards herded me after Ruslan, out the door and up a flight of carpeted stairs to the audience chamber. Inside, Sechaveh sat slouched in his stone chair, his lizard's eyes hooded, his ringed fingers steepled before his chest. Just like the first time I'd seen him, he wore silken clothes in pale shades matching the room's stone, though this time his neckcloth was the color of dried blood—the color eastern Arkennlanders used for mourning. Magelights set in iron sconces shaped like rearing scorpions cast a cool silver glow over the chamber's marble floor. In the darkness beyond the windows, lightning still flickered over both the Whitefires and Boltholes. The blue fire within the obsidian rings before Sechaveh's chair leaped and coiled in a manner far more agitated than I remembered; another bad sign for the confluence, no doubt.

Edon shuffled out of the shadows, his manner as deceptively awkward as it'd been in Jadin Sovarias's house.

"Stand here," he ordered me, and pointed at a spot on the chamber floor that looked no different than any other. I obeyed, all too aware of Ruslan's basilisk gaze on me.

Edon unslung a soft-sided, funnel-tipped pouch from his back and poured sand from it in a circle around me. The sand was a strange dull green in color, like it had some other mineral mixed in. He poured a second circle beyond the first and embellished it with odd little swirls and loops.

Sechaveh watched in brooding silence, while Ruslan wore an expression of impatient contempt. A blood mage probably only needed a thought—or a dagger—to cast a truth spell. Sand mages like Edon were rumored to be only middling in power; though a middling mage was more than enough to ruin any untalented man's day.

I agreed with Ruslan on one thing: I wished Edon would hurry the fuck up. My gut was a mess of nerves, my blood buzzing in my ears. Gods only knew what Lizaveta was doing to Melly while I stood here. I ached to petition Sechaveh, but I had to prove my value to him first.

Finally, Edon finished drizzling sand on the floor. He knelt and laid a single sapphire within the swirls of the outer circle. An azure flicker raced over the sand. The innermost circle turned a vivid, startling cobalt, matching the flames in the confluence charm before Sechaveh's chair.

Edon said, "If he lies, the innermost circle will turn black, and the second layer of the spell will trigger to force the truth from him." He glanced at me. "It's not an experience you'll enjoy."

"I've no intention of lying," I said, with complete truth. Edon took up a stance to my left, his booted toes nearly touching the outermost line of sand. He shut his eyes and extended his hands.

I felt nothing, not even prickles over my skin. Ruslan contemplated the sand circles, frowning. He said to Sechaveh, "I wish to test the spellwork before you begin."

Sechaveh waved a hand. I repressed a grimace. Test the spellwork, my ass. Ruslan wanted to see me suffer, even if Edon's spell hopefully wasn't as vicious as Lizaveta's would've been. But I didn't protest. Better if Sechaveh was wholly certain of my answers.

Ruslan faced me and demanded, "Speak your name."

"Dev. Devan *na soliin*, if you want to get fancy."

The innermost circle stayed blue. Ruslan said, "Speak it again, and lie."

I eyed the sand around me and took a steadying breath. "My name is… Sethan ap—"

The circle turned jet black. A vise crushed my skull. Agony sent words boiling out of my throat. "Dev! My name is Dev, Devan *na soliin*—"

The sand regained its cobalt hue. Pain and pressure both vanished. I gasped for breath, running my fingers over my head to make sure it hadn't split open. Khalmet's bloodsoaked hand! The Alathians' truth spells were subtle, a slowly rising tide that couldn't be denied. This was about as subtle as a rockslide.

Ruslan said mildly, "The spellwork appears adequate."

"So it would seem." Sechaveh leaned forward to study me. "Devan *na soliin*. I hear you bring information that may help me end this threat to my city at last. I certainly hope so." He glanced at Ruslan, his yellow eyes gone hard. "After the catastrophic mistake Ninavel suffered today, I'm quite eager for better news."

Oh yeah, he was still pissed. Thank Khalmet. I said, "Even if what I know isn't enough for you to catch the bastard, it'll point you to someone who knows far more."

"Ah yes," Sechaveh said. "Ruslan told me you claim one of the Alathians is in league with my enemy. Speak now: who is the traitor?"

"Talmaddis," I said. "Martennan's second lieutenant."

When the sand circle around me stayed blue, Ruslan smiled, eager and predatory. Sechaveh's weathered face turned grim.

"I will want to hear your proof," he said. "But first, tell me what you know of my enemy."

I repeated everything Pello had said of the killer, down to the tiniest details of dress and mannerisms. How he had powers straight out of a demon tale, yet needed Tainters to fuel them, and had to return often to a source of some kind; of Pello's visit to that source, and his later attempts to discover its location. I added in Avakra-dan's tale of the killer's visit. When I got to the bit about him pouring blood on her contracts, Edon grunted as if I'd confirmed something for him.

Sechaveh put out a hand to halt me, and asked him, "This means something to you?"

Eyes still shut, Edon said, "The oldest tales of charm-making claim that mages first learned the practice from demons, who could bind malign magic into the blood of their victims. I also find it curious how closely Pello's report resembles the Kaithan legends of the origin of the Tainted...the legends speak of bargains made between untalented men and demons that allowed the men to take on the demons' power. The men soon sickened and died, but children conceived by them retained a shadow of the demons' talents..."

"A ridiculous tale." Ruslan gave Edon a look of withering contempt. "The Taint is merely the result of confluence forces affecting unborn *nathahlen* while their *ikilhia* is still coalescing. There are no such things as demons and devils; only the ignorant believe otherwise."

I wondered darkly if he was so adamant about it simply because he hated the idea of competition for the spot of Ninavel's worst nightmare, and smothered a half-hysterical urge to laugh.

Edon said, "How do you know? I do not mean to suggest the legends are true in every particular. But mysteries yet remain in the world...who is to say that non-human creatures do not exist who can confer their powers upon men? You are the one who insists our enemy bears no mage talent. How else do you explain his abilities?"

Ruslan made an irritated noise. "There is no need to resort to fanciful creatures. Any hireling mage can bind spells in blood for a *nathahlen* to use, crude and limited as the method is. As for the killer's apparent use of the Taint...we know the Alathians possess artifacts whose true use they do not understand; the Watch siphons power from them to fuel Alathia's wards, content in their ignorance. I think it far more likely that Talmaddis discovered that one of Alathia's treasures can be used in the manner of a charm, to give an untalented man an augmented version of a Tainted child's powers. Easy enough for Talmaddis to find a convenient catspaw when so many *nathahlen* resent mages, jealous of our power."

Sechaveh said, "Enough speculation. Our enemy's exact method is far less important than finding and destroying the source of his power. Attacking the source and not the person would solve the problem his ability to translocate poses, would it not?"

"Yes," Ruslan said thoughtfully. "Destroying the source is a far better strategy."

"Not even Pello could figure out where the bastard hides," I said. "You'll need Talmaddis for that."

Sechaveh said, "You are certain Talmaddis is a traitor—that Pello did not lie to you about his Alathian captor?"

"I have more proof than just Pello's word." I related the whole tale of Pello's snatch and handoff of me to Bren, and my growing suspicion afterward that the embassy harbored a traitor. I told of my chase after Pello, and how Talm had watched the rubble fall on us without trying to cast.

That wasn't even all the evidence I had. I'd had plenty of time to think under that rubble. To remember how Bren had died while Talm examined him—Talm had killed Bren right under Marten's nose, knowing Kiran would take the blame. How Talm had been so insistent ever since we got to Ninavel that Ruslan was the culprit, likely hoping to play on Stevan's prejudices. Hell, even the damn nightmare-inducing tea Kiran drank back in Tamanath had been his doing. He must've seen how terrified Kiran was of going, and thought if he augmented that fear a little, Kiran might refuse and deprive Marten of the leverage he needed to sway Ruslan.

I spilled it all, and watched Ruslan's triumph grow with every word I spoke.

"Are any of the other Alathians at the embassy involved?" Sechaveh asked.

"Pello thought not—he said he only ever dealt with Talmaddis, and that Talmaddis was always careful to keep his actions hidden from others in the Watch—but he wasn't certain. One thing I am certain of: Captain Martennan isn't working against you. He wants to stop the killer, save both Alathia's wards and Ninavel. Otherwise, he'd never have bothered to bring me and Kiran here."

I'd never imagined to hear myself defending Marten. But much as I hated him for his methods, I didn't doubt his goal…and the last thing I wanted was to leave the fate of the city solely in Ruslan's hands.

Ruslan said to Sechaveh, "We should arrest and interrogate all the Alathians, not just Talmaddis. Revoke your sanction! My vow binds me from casting, but Lizaveta can lead your mages in shattering the embassy's wards and capturing all within. She can break their minds and take every scrap of information they hold…if any of them know where the killer hides, I guarantee you, she will find out."

I flinched from an image of Lena, screaming and bloodied. I had to stop this.

I protested to Sechaveh, "If Lizaveta casts against the embassy, the Alathians will all fight her—and she might be powerful, but Martennan is as cunning as they come. It won't be quick or easy, no matter what Ruslan says. Even if she wins in the end, the fight would give Talmaddis a chance to run."

Ruslan's face darkened. I hurried on. "You want to be certain of capturing Talmaddis? Then call Martennan and his whole team here without any warning of what you intend. Make up some excuse to keep the other Alathians busy, keep your eye on Talmaddis, and get Martennan aside in a warded room. Let me talk to him, under truth spell if necessary; if we can convince him Talmaddis needs to be questioned, his orders will stop the others from trying to protect Talmaddis when you take him into custody. Then Talmaddis won't have a chance to escape—and you won't lose Martennan's help in the real fight: taking down this bastard who's trying to destroy everything you've built."

"An interesting proposition." Sechaveh studied me, his ringed fingers tapping in sequence on the chair's stone. "Pello said you were clever in his reports before Simon's death."

"Clever?" Ruslan made the word into a curse. "He merely seeks to preserve the lives of his foreign masters, putting their interests above yours."

"I don't give a fuck about the Alathians' interests." This was my chance, and I'd take it. "You think I work for them willingly? Martennan's just as much a viper as you, Ruslan. But he's a smart viper. If anybody can figure out how to take down the killer, *without* destroying all Ninavel in the process, it's him. This city is my home. My friends are here, everyone I love—I want them safe, and I want the bastard attacking Ninavel to burn."

The sand circling me stayed pure, cobalt blue. Sechaveh's head tilted, new interest dawning in his eyes. A thread of hope snaked through my heart.

I said, "Lord Sechaveh, Pello once told me you could use someone with my skills. His death left you short a good shadow man. I'd gladly work for you instead of the Alathians, in whatever capacity you want me. If you want to ensure my loyalty…Did Ruslan tell you how the Alathians coerced me into working for them? I wanted the chance to help a Ninavel-born child, the daughter of an old friend—the child Ruslan now holds, and intends to kill as revenge on me. Give your protection to the girl, and to my lover, the outrider Cara ap Denion—and I am your man."

Ruslan moved; checked himself. He snapped at Sechaveh, "Shadow men are no scarce resource in this city. This man deserves my revenge after all he has done to turn my apprentice against me."

Sechaveh said coolly, "Yet Kiran remains at your side. Is your control over him so weak that a single untalented man can break it?"

"Devan *na soliin* does not act alone, but as Martennan's tool." Ruslan fixed me with a direwolf's burning gaze. "Martennan yet plots to take Kiran from me. Tell me: what is his plan?"

I said with perfect truth, "I've no idea. I don't even think he has one. He's already had his use of Kiran in gaining Lord Sechaveh's sanction. He's said time and again the investigation is his top priority, the hell with everything else."

"But you admit you seek to goad Kiran to rebellion." Ruslan's hand had locked tight on the hilt of his belt knife. The murderous look in his eye was all too chilling a reminder that his vow only stopped him from casting against me, not slashing my thoat. I wanted to back away, but I knew better than to brave Edon's sand circles.

"All I want is to tell Kiran the truth, and let him make his own choice." Though after Kiran had handed Melly to Ruslan, I had to wonder: would that choice still be against blood magic?

"A truth skewed by your own ignorant prejudices." Ruslan turned to Sechaveh. The fire in his eyes faded, his expression shifting to one of sorrowful, proud entreaty. "You have raised sons. Would you allow a criminal to encourage a child of yours in foolish, youthful resentment of a necessary punishment? To entice him to reject his family, turn his back on a glorious talent, and take a path that leaves him easy prey to enemies?"

Sechaveh said, "I am not unsympathetic, Ruslan. But Kiran is your responsibility, not mine. Easy enough to find a clever shadow man; harder to find one whose loyalty can be assured."

My heart pounded, a prayer to Suliyya echoing in my ears: *please, please, please….*

Sechaveh said, "Here is my decision, Devan *na soliin*: I will take the child into my custody, and order Ruslan to stay his hand from her and your lover while I take your suggestion on how to handle the Alathians. If you can convince Martennan as you say, and Talmaddis is captured and interrogated without a fight—then I will give you the child, renew my order to Ruslan, and take you provisionally into my employ. If the killer is caught and my city's safety assured, I will consider your provisional period ended, and demand Ruslan swear a full blood oath not to harm the child and Cara ap Denion."

Thank the gods, I could work with that. I ignored the sudden uncomfortable memory of Pello shrugging off the murder of children with the claim he'd done worse on Sechaveh's orders. I'd worry about the future if I made it that far; for now, I snatched at the chance to keep Melly and Cara alive.

I told Sechaveh, "My loyalty is yours…so long as Ruslan's vow would also bind both his apprentices and his partner Lizaveta, and ensure they won't harm Melly or Cara by any means, physical or magical." I emphasized the "physical" part, keeping a wary eye on Ruslan's knife hand.

"I will not vow," Ruslan said flatly to Sechaveh. "If you bar me from the confluence in response…I am not an enemy you want, old friend."

Sechaveh held up a hand. "Wait, Ruslan. I would require you and Lizaveta to vow not to harm them—unless Devan na soliin should make further efforts to turn Kiran against you. In which case I would cast him out from my favor, and revoke all offers of protection."

I should've guessed I wouldn't get away with selling only myself. Kiran. Gods. Even after his betrayal tonight, guilt savaged me at the idea of leaving him with Ruslan. But then, maybe it was already too late. Maybe the Kiran who'd been my friend was gone forever, replaced by this new, coldly obedient version.

Ruslan was silent. Sechaveh said softly, "Come; would you deprive me of a useful tool in this battle we fight for our lives, all for a moment's fleeting satisfaction?"

At length, Ruslan said, "I would consider such a vow. Though I would ask the chance for a different revenge, in return. When Talmaddis is captured, I want Lizaveta to conduct the interrogation of him and any other Alathians he implicates."

Sechaveh smiled thinly. "I know her skill; I will grant your request, gladly. I warn you, though—if Lizaveta claims to find evidence implicating Alathians other than Talmaddis, I will want it corroborated by my own mages."

"Yes," Ruslan said, without hesitation. The savage anticipation in his eyes turned my stomach.

Sechaveh clapped his hands once and stood. "Summon Lizaveta, then. She can ward an interrogation chamber and prepare defenses against the

Alathians, in case Martennan balks. I will send a message to the embassy the moment she is ready. The sooner we have Talmaddis in hand, the better." He waved a hand at Edon. "Release him from the spell."

Edon knelt and removed the sapphire. The sand faded back into its old greenish color. I stepped out of the circles, gingerly.

"I want to see Melly," I said.

Sechaveh snapped his fingers at a guardsman. "Take him to the child. He may remain with her until the Alathians come." He surveyed me again, with proprietary satisfaction. "A good bargain, Devan *na soliin*. I regret the loss of Pello…I own few shadow men that are his equal. But you show some promise."

I nodded as steadily as I could, not wanting him to see how I flinched at his talk of ownership. I thought I'd left that behind me when Jylla and I killed Tavian. But Melly and Cara's lives were worth far more than my freedom.

❈

I paced between walls of blue-veined marble, ignoring the guards bracketing the warded door. They'd taken me from Melly's side only moments ago, saying the Alathians had come, and I was to wait here for Sechaveh and Martennan. The room was yet another of the tower's waiting chambers; this one was barren of furniture, though shelves cut into the marble held magelights cupped within bone sculptures carved to look like rose briars.

Thank Khalmet, I'd found Melly unharmed upon my return from the audience chamber. A silent servant had brought us food—bowls of delicately spiced meats, accompanied by cinnamon-glazed rasheil nuts and goblets of rosewater. The guards had even given me skin-seal and scouring charms, let me scrub the worst of the grime from myself and tend to my wounds. Melly had helped, with deft fingers. Liana made sure all her Tainters knew how to tend injuries, after difficult jobs.

Afterward, Melly had been droop-eyed and yawning fit to split her jaw. Dawn wasn't far away; at this hour, she was usually sleeping curled in a heap of her denmates. I was tired too, but nerves kept me as jittery as if I'd eaten a whole jar of Avakra-dan's beetles.

Especially now. I had to make Marten believe me. But I'd seen his love for Talm. Even if I spoke under truth spell, would he refuse to hand Talm over for interrogation?

Footsteps in the hallway outside, and voices. The wards flashed a brilliant blue, and the guards swung the door open.

Sechaveh strode in. Despite his seamed face and silver hair, he moved with the energy of a far younger man. He murmured to me, "Lizaveta and Edon have the Alathians in hand. Martennan comes now, with Ruslan."

Marten entered, talking over his shoulder. "I don't see why we could not—" He saw me and stopped dead.

"Dev?" He stared like he thought I might be an illusionist's charm-vision. "Talm said you were dead…"

"Strange, isn't it?" I said. Behind him, the guards shut the door, and Ruslan swept a hand over the wards. "Let me guess. Talm told you he'd seen me and Pello crushed to jelly, that he knew us dead despite Pello's veiling. He came up with some excuse why he hadn't saved us…maybe that he tried, but there was too much rubble to stop it all."

The dawning wariness in Marten's eyes told me I'd guessed right. I said, "Talm's betrayed you, Marten. He watched that rubble bury us without even trying a spell. Before Pello bled out from his injuries, he told me Talm had been working with the mage-killer for months now. It was Talm who caught Pello in Alathia and gave him over to the mage-killer to use."

"No." Marten's denial was sharp. "Talm would never betray his oaths to the Council. Pello lied to you."

"I'm not just accusing him on Pello's word," I said. "After Bren, and Avakra-dan, I suspected you had a traitor at the embassy. I just wasn't sure who it was…not until Talm stood there without lifting a hand while a wall collapsed on us."

Marten turned on Ruslan. "If this is some new scheme of yours against us, I warn you, I will not fall for it. You hold the child Melly's blood-mark. I know Dev would do anything, say anything, to protect her."

Sechaveh said, "Devan *na soliin* is not lying, Captain. He testified under truth spell—a spell cast by one of my own mages, I might add, and not Ruslan. The spell confirmed all he is telling you."

Marten shook his head. "Truth spells confirm only what a man believes to be true. If Ruslan altered his memories, replaced them with false ones—"

"I could not alter his memories without casting on him and breaking my vow," Ruslan said.

"Lizaveta, then!" Marten snapped. "She could cast, and you know it!"

For an instant, doubt assailed me. How *would* I know if Lizaveta had fucked with my head? No. If Ruslan had planned this, he'd have set me up to implicate all the Alathians, not just Talm.

That said, I knew how to be sure—and how I might convince Marten. I just wished the idea didn't make my skin crawl.

"Marten. You want to see if anyone's been in my head? Come look. See for yourself that I'm telling the truth."

"Mages of the Watch are forbidden from mind magic without the express permission of the Council," Marten said tightly.

Ruslan shifted, sudden fury flaring in his eyes. He'd just realized I'd lied about the Alathians' supposed binding. I allowed myself a small, humorless grin.

"Yeah, but Lena told me you can dodge that rule if someone willingly allows you into their mind. So…I'm inviting you, and I swear I say it of my own free will. I want the killer stopped, and you need to understand that Talm is the key to that."

Sechaveh said, "Let me be clear, Captain. We *will* interrogate Talmaddis. Your team is in the heart of my power, here in Kelante. You will not escape, and if you fight, you will lose. At which point I must imprison and interrogate you all. But young Devan has argued that you are a valuable asset in the fight against my true opponent. I have seen for myself you are a clever man, Captain. Use that cleverness now, and do not force me to treat you as an enemy."

Marten said to me, abrupt and clipped, "I would see your mind."

I offered him my wrist, and flinched when he took it. Smothering pressure in my head, an alien presence sliding through me—I wanted him out, *out*—

Forgive the discomfort, said Marten. *I don't have a blood mage's skill in this. But I must see…* Memory swallowed me. Rocks raining down, Pello shouting and snatching at his barrier charm, Talm watching impassively… then Pello's hoarse voice in the darkness, damning Talm further with every strained sentence.

Memory vanished, leaving me blinking. Marten took one staggering step back and splayed a hand against the wall. The look on his face was that of a man gutted.

Vicious triumph lit Ruslan's eyes. My mouth tasted of ashes. I'd wanted to see Marten suffer. Prayed for it, even. Yet now all I could think of was that terrible moment when I'd realized Jylla's betrayal. How I'd felt I couldn't get any air, my heart frozen mid-beat, the pain so sharp I'd expected to look down and see my chest slashed open.

Marten pulled himself together far more quickly than I had. He straightened, his face freezing into utterly blank formality. "I agree Talmaddis must be questioned," he said to Sechaveh. "But do not leap to condemn him until we have heard his answers. There may be another explanation for his actions."

How he must pray for it. *Tell me I'm hallucinating, that I'm lost in some taphtha vision,* I'd begged Jylla, before rage took hold. *Tell me the last ten years weren't a lie, that you didn't just knife me in the back like I was some mark who means nothing!*

Sechaveh said, "If Talmaddis cooperates, he will not be harmed until his guilt is proven. But I must be certain we learn the truth. Lizaveta will search his mind. I'm told that memories cannot be properly read without the mage under interrogation remaining conscious; she has the skill and power to keep him that way while she destroys his defenses."

"Lizaveta is far from impartial!" Marten stopped; took a breath, and lowered his voice. "What guarantee do you have that *she* will tell the truth of what she finds? Far more likely, she will claim all my team complicit, in service to Ruslan's desire for revenge."

Ruslan said smoothly, "Captain, if you fear Lizaveta's honesty…then all you need do is link minds with Talmaddis when she does, and observe as she casts. You will see all that she finds, even as she finds it."

What a sick, clever bastard. *You want to be certain we don't condemn the rest of your team without cause? Then you've got to experience your lover's pain while we rip his mind apart.*

Marten's face was gray. "Very well."

Sechaveh said, "You understand, we cannot risk giving Talmaddis warning. Lizaveta provided a charm that can send him unconscious and allow us to imprison him within her wards, but the charm must contact his skin before she triggers it. You can get close to him without suspicion. Take the charm, go call him out of the audience chamber, and touch him with it—she'll do the rest." He held out a thin disc of onyx chased with silver.

For long heartbeats, Marten didn't move. At last his hand rose to take the charm. "Give me the chance to speak with him before Lizaveta examines his mind, and I will do this."

"You may speak, but not privately," Sechaveh said.

"I understand." Marten glanced at me. "I wish Dev to be present when Talmaddis awakens, so I may see Talmaddis's reaction to Dev's survival."

His eyes said something different. *You were the one to accuse him. You face the result.*

I didn't relish the prospect. Not because of any sympathy for Talm—hell, he'd tried to kill me twice over—but because I didn't want to watch Ruslan rejoice in Marten's pain.

Damn it, it didn't matter if the taste of revenge wasn't to my liking. If Talm gave us the killer, I could stomach even Ruslan's triumph.

CHAPTER TWENTY-TWO

(Dev)

I shuffled after Edon and Ruslan into a magelit cell deep in Kelante Tower. Talm lay spreadeagled and unconscious on the rough stone floor. Manacles of sigil-marked silver bound his wrists and ankles, and freshly-laid ward lines coated every inch of the cell's walls. More lines were etched into the floor around Talm's body, but unlike the silver wards on the walls, these glowed the sullen red of banked coals. Marten and Lizaveta waited beside the glowing lines. Lizaveta had an air of calm anticipation; Marten's round face was armored and blank.

Already, I felt queasy. The whole scene reminded me horribly of Kiran in Simon's cave. Especially when Lizaveta knelt beside Talm, a bared blade in her hand. She'd pinned up her mass of black hair, but she still wore the same rich gown.

"I will release my charm's spell," she told Marten. "You may speak with him so long as he does not attempt to cast against his bonds or otherwise resist. If he does, I will not wait to begin breaking his inner defenses."

Marten nodded without a hint of emotion. After Talm's arrest, Stevan and Lena had willingly allowed Marten to search their memories. He'd proclaimed them free of guilt, unable to hide his relief. I'd been nearly as glad to hear it, hardly able to believe I hadn't fucked up after all in trusting Lena. Sechaveh wasn't yet convinced—he'd ordered Stevan and Lena held in a separate warded room until Talm's interrogation was complete, saying he wanted further corroboration of their innocence from Talm.

Sechaveh himself had declined to attend the questioning, sending Edon in his stead. He claimed pressing matters related to Julisi's destruction needed his attention. I suspected the old bastard was simply too cautious to enter a cell holding an enemy mage, even with Ruslan, Edon, and Lizaveta there to protect him.

I hovered as close to the cell door as I dared, not wanting to get anywhere near those glowing lines. Edon folded his arms and watched Lizaveta with dispassionate interest. Ruslan wore a small, eager smile, his gaze locked on Marten. I looked away, my nausea growing.

Lizaveta laid a hand on Talm's forehead. Talm jerked against the manacles, his eyes flying open. His gaze shied off Marten to land on me.

His olive skin went sallow. He slumped in his bonds and said in weary resignation, "I should have let you fall at the mine."

He wasn't even going to pretend innocence? Genuinely curious, I asked, "Why didn't you?"

"I didn't know then that Marten would be tasked with investigating in Ninavel, and seek your help. I've no quarrel with you, Dev—I'm sorry you got caught up in this."

He was looking at me as earnestly as Kiran might have. I snorted. "What a comfort, to know your attempts to kill me were nothing personal."

Marten's back had gone so rigid it hurt mine to see it. "Lieutenant Talmaddis, you are accused of—"

"I can guess what I'm accused of," Talm said. "Did Pello survive along with Dev?"

"Yes," Marten said. "He told us you captured him in Alathia and hid him from the Watch; that you have been working with our enemy."

Talm's gaze snagged on Lizaveta's knife, and his throat moved in a hard swallow. "Let me save you some time, Marten. What Pello told you is true. I've done all I can to aid Ninavel's enemy." Despite his measured tone, sweat sheened his brow.

Lizaveta smiled and traced a finger along her blade. Marten shut his eyes. His voice remained tightly controlled. "Why, Talmaddis? Were you coerced?"

I expected Talm to leap on that opening. Instead he laughed, a jagged, painful sound. "No. This was my choice. I saw the chance to gain everything you and I have worked for, and I couldn't pass it by. Don't you see? So long as Ninavel endures, with its confluence drawing unprincipled mages in droves and Sechaveh granting them free rein, the Council will never relax their policies. But with the confluence and Sechaveh destroyed, the Council will be freed to look beyond fear. Restrictions on magic eased, the conscription laws repealed, future generations of Alathia's mages given actual choice in their lives…think of it, Marten! Alathia can have the future we've fought so hard for."

So it wasn't hatred he carried. I'd seen men like him before, so devoted to some goal they didn't care what they sacrificed to achieve it. *Like you, with Melly,* an inner voice whispered, and I winced.

Marten's breathing was harsh. "A future bought at the cost of thousands of innocent lives."

"Twin gods' sake, Marten, have you *seen* this city? It devours the innocent. Destroying the confluence won't only help Alathia. Without it, there'll be no more savaging of the untalented by mages lacking in all accountability, no more abuse of Tainted children—I promise you, far more innocents will be saved than lost."

Ruslan made a disgusted, contemptuous noise. Lizaveta remained silent, turning her knife idly in her hands. Knowing their cruelty, I could see Talm's point. But easy for him to blithely talk of a confluence-free future. When the city dissolved into waterless anarchy, it wasn't his friends that'd die.

Just his lover. If Marten didn't leave, he'd burn with the confluence. No wonder Talm was talking so readily. He knew it was his last chance to convince Marten to turn his back on Ninavel and live. Question was, would Talm's logic sway Marten? If Marten were as cold-blooded as I thought him, he must be tempted. I peered at him, but couldn't read a damn thing off his face.

"This…calculus of innocents. Is this how the killer justifies his murders?" Marten asked.

"He has all the justification he needs," Talm said. "Do you remember how I told you of the first murders I saw a mage commit in Ninavel?"

Marten nodded. "A family, you said. Killed because the father jostled an air mage, too distracted by chasing after his youngest child to notice the man's sigils."

Memory darkened Talm's eyes. "The screams I heard that night in Reytani's hanging gardens still haunt me…I arrived too late to save the children and their mother, but I broke the spell in time to save the father's life. Not that he thanked me for it, at first."

Marten's puzzled frown shifted into sudden, startled realization. "The man you saved—you told me he was a Kaithan scholar…"

Lizaveta's hands stilled on her knife. Ruslan and Edon both leaned forward, their eyes gone sharp with interest. I leaned right along with them.

Talm said softly, "You see it now. Yes, he is Kaithan. A brilliant scholar of history and nature, who came to Ninavel hoping to exchange knowledge with those from other lands. Yet all for an instant's inattention, his wife and children drowned in their own blood."

If it were Cara and Melly murdered, I'd have burned for revenge as badly as this Kaithan. But I'd have stuck to revenge on the actual bastard that killed them, not set out to destroy an entire city.

"What is the Kaithan's name?" Marten asked.

Talm said, "That, I will not give you so easily. But Marten, admit it: in his place, you too would yearn for justice. Yet there is no justice to be had in Ninavel. I tried on his behalf, but the embassy is authorized to cast only in defense of our own people, and Ambassador Halassian told me Sechaveh would laugh off any complaint she made. I was heartsick, and the Kaithan…I feared despair would drive him to suicide. But his fury won out—he told me he would not rest until he discovered a way to abolish Ninavel's abuses of power. I promised him that if he did, I would provide what help I could. Truth be told, I did not expect him to succeed. Long years passed with no word. But this past winter I received a letter saying he'd found the solution at last. At first I didn't believe him, but then one night he appeared in my quarters as if by translocation. He took me deep into the desert and showed me the corpse of the mage who had slain his family, and then I believed in the power he'd gained."

"Power he gains by murdering Tainted children," Marten said, cold and level. "Did he tell you that?"

Talm's gaze dropped. "Not…at first. I regret the children. But they might well have died anyway, cast aside by their handlers after their Change. A few children dead before their time, to save hundreds of their unborn brethren from exploitation and abuse—I know you understand the necessity of sacrifice, Marten! Have I not seen you make similar choices?"

Like the choice he'd made with Kiran. Marten's face was bloodless. "Not with innocents. Never that. What magic does the Kaithan cast that requires children's lives?"

Talm shook his head. "I've been careful not to learn his secrets, so I could not betray them. I knew that this day would come, if I did not die with the confluence. If not here in Ninavel, then at the Council's hands, during this year's renewal of my oaths."

Kiran had told me how the Council examined the minds of Alathia's mages once each year to weed out and punish any who broke their laws. I would've thought Talm would run before then, whether or not Ninavel fell.

Echoing my thought, Marten asked, "You did not intend to flee?"

Talm smiled, bright and painful. "No. I did this for Alathia; I am not ashamed of my choice. And…I wanted as much time with you as I could, before the end.

Though I hoped I would burn with the confluence and spare you this."

"You wish to *spare* me, while children die to fuel your plans!" Marten's control cracked. Fury and anguish warred on his face. "Talmaddis, you—" He stopped, and I could see his desperate struggle to rebuild his armor. "You are not the man I loved. You never were."

I knew his pain. The worst part of Jylla's betrayal had been the way it poisoned every single moment of my ten years with her. If she'd died like Sethan, then once past my initial grief I could've treasured the good times we'd had. Instead, even the happiest of memories got twisted into something gut-wrenching and dark.

"Marten..." The name escaped Talm like it'd been ripped from him.

Lizaveta held her blade before his eyes, stroked her free hand through his curls. "Tell us where the Kaithan hides," she said, sweetly coaxing. "Tell us that, and I will spare your lover the taste of your agony. You realize that when I cast, I will tear your mind apart, but I will not kill you, oh no...I'll burn out your will, destroy your magic, and he'll feel every last instant of your soul shredding away."

Talm groaned. "I cannot tell you. I made certain of it. But I know this: the least use of magic near the source of his power, and he will know, and come to strike you down. Even you blood mages cannot stop him."

His hazel eyes fixed on Marten again, desperate and imploring. "Marten, *listen*. The confluence will be destroyed. You cannot prevent it. But you need not die with it! Leave Ninavel and return to Alathia with Ambassador Halassian. The Council will not fault you for that. The Watch needs you, Alathia needs you—in the aftermath of the border wards failing, they'll need your strength more than ever. Don't abandon the country you love, no matter how angry you are at me."

Marten knelt beside Talm, his face once more an icy mask. "I will not listen. You are a traitor to your oaths, a murderer whose life is forfeit under Alathia's law. But first, Lizaveta will discover what you know and I will use it. I will save this city, or I will die with it. And if I die, Talmaddis...I die cursing your name as liar and betrayer."

Talm shut his eyes. Slow tears leaked from the corners. "My love for you was never a lie."

Marten looked at Lizaveta. "I'm through talking."

"You're certain?" she said, her eyes glinting. "You don't wish to exchange a few more sweet lovers' words? When I finish with him, he'll lack the capacity to ever speak again."

"*Cast,*" Marten spat at her. He clamped Talm's manacled wrist in one hand.

Lizaveta sliced open Talm's shirt and cut a sigil into his chest with swift precision. Blood slicked Talm's skin, his breath quickening into rapid, panicked pants. Lizaveta cut a matching sigil into her own palm. She reached for Talm's chest.

He tensed. "Marten. Marten, forgive me—"

Her bloodied hand touched his wound, and he arched in his bonds, his teeth bared. Marten jerked as if stabbed. In the corner, Ruslan laughed.

I turned aside to stare grimly at the wards on the wall, wishing I could block my ears. The more so when Talm started screaming, wild and agonized. I thought of how he'd nearly killed me, how Pello had died despairing in darkness, of children's bones piled high. None of it helped. I bit the inside of my cheek bloody, desperate not to give Ruslan the satisfaction of seeing me cringe.

Talm's howls went on, and on, until his voice was little more than a hoarse, ruined whisper. I set my teeth and endured, though I felt like screaming myself, or bashing my head against the wall until I blacked out. What must Marten be feeling? He deserved it, every minute, for what he'd done to Kiran. But this...oh mother of maidens, let it be over!

Long after I thought I'd go mad, Talm's cries died into silence. I heard the rustle of Lizaveta's gown.

"I have all he knows," she said, sounding tired but satisfied. "Unfortunately, his claim was true: he does not know the location of our enemy's source of power. Yet I found a signpost to point the way...at our enemy's request, Talmaddis provided him with a treatise that described the strengths and locations of all the minor confluence points in the Whitefire Mountains. Whatever our enemy's method of magic, I suspect it requires a confluence as fuel. Not many confluences in the Whitefires are strong enough to allow significant magic; if we compare confluence locations with areas matching the rock the spy described, we might narrow the options considerably."

"An excellent thought," said Edon. He hadn't moved from his stance by the door, his narrow face as calm as if Talm's screams meant no more to him than bird calls.

I risked turning around. Talm lay slack in his bonds. His blood-smeared chest rose and fell in slow breaths, but his hazel eyes were perfectly, terribly empty.

Marten still knelt at Talm's side. He'd released Talm's wrist; his hands lay flat and rigid on his thighs. His face was dead of expression, but his eyes... gods. I looked away quickly. Only to see Ruslan release a satiated sigh, his gaze lingering on Marten, pleasure still softening his mouth.

My stomach convulsed. I locked my teeth and choked back vomit.

Ruslan said, "Tell me this, Liza. What is my enemy's name?"

"Talmaddis knew him as Vidai zha-Dakhar," Lizaveta said.

"Vidai." Ruslan rolled the name in his mouth. "It means 'hawk-souled' in Kaithan, does it not? Appropriate. But even the swiftest hawk can be taken."

He looked to Edon. "Tell Lord Sechaveh I wish to confer with Lizaveta on what we have learned before meeting with him to discuss potential strategies. Captain Martennan doubtless wishes the chance to share his lover's treachery with his own people and formulate his own suggestions. I expect much, from such a clever man."

Marten didn't respond to the jab, didn't so much as glance Ruslan's way. Worry pierced me. Had this broken him? Would he give up, abandon Ninavel as Talm had begged him to do?

"Is the innocence of the other Alathians proven?" Edon asked Lizaveta.

Marten answered first. "Yes." The word came out as dead as his expression. He stood, moving as if every muscle pained him. "Talmaddis worked alone. I want my team freed. Now."

At least he was talking. But his eyes were still windows on Shaikar's innermost hell.

Edon glanced at Lizaveta, who twisted a hand in dismissive assent.

Ruslan said, "Talmaddis is yours as well, Captain. To kill or to keep, whichever pleases you more." He sketched a sigil in the air, and Talm's manacles melted away. Talm didn't move. He stared into space, vacant and mindless as an illusionist's puppet.

Edon said, "Leaving him alive for the moment would be preferable. If we cannot determine how to strike at this Vidai zha-Dakhar's source of power, perhaps we can use Talmaddis to lure him into a trap."

"I will take Talmaddis to the embassy," Marten said, still in that horribly flat voice. He bent and put a hand on Talm's shoulder. Talm climbed to his feet, his motions slow and uncoordinated. Seeing him move made his empty eyes all the more chilling.

"We release Devan *na soliin* to your custody as well." Edon's dark eyes met mine, and I read the command in them. *Start earning your keep, shadow man.*

Marten likely knew I was Sechaveh's now. But he didn't protest, only nodded.

I said to Edon, "Melly comes with me." Sechaveh had promised, damn it.

"I will bring her and the Alathians." Edon released the wards on the door and slipped out.

Lizaveta followed. Ruslan paused by my side. "A pity Lizaveta had to break

Talmaddis's mind so quickly. There is an artistry to pain. To bringing a soul again and again to the brink of madness, while forbidding it to slide over. So by all means…speak to Kiran again. Try to turn him from me. I will delight in proving that artistry for you. Or perhaps…" He smiled, wide and white. "Perhaps I'll have Kiran prove it for me."

Almost, I could believe Talm had the right of it: destroying men like this was worth any price. "Maybe you'll all burn, and leave me laughing," I snapped. He still didn't know I was bound to the confluence and would burn with him.

Ruslan smiled wider yet, and flicked a hand at the empty shell that'd once been Talm. "Not after what you've given me." With that, he left; a good thing, because otherwise I might have spit in his face. I watched the door shut behind him, a cold, hard part of me wondering: was I on the right side in this fight?

✳

(Kiran)

Kiran peered at a map of the Whitefire range. The topographical information was nearly lost under cramped notations indicating the depth and strength of the currents radiating out from Ninavel's great confluence. In much of the mountains, the currents flowed so deep under magically inert rock as to make casting with them impossible. But in scattered spots, the currents converged and rose toward the surface to create small reservoirs of magic.

Just prior to dawn, Ruslan had contacted Kiran and Mikail from Kelante Tower. Through the mark-bond had come a brief summary of information gained from Dev and Talmaddis, and the order for Kiran and Mikail to find locations in the Whitefires that matched it.

Ruslan had also said, with a vast, delighted satisfaction, *Work quickly, akhelyshen, and when I return I will grant you a taste of the delight I had in my revenge.* He hadn't specified if that revenge included more than Talmaddis. The omission left Kiran desperately uneasy, the memory of the child's screams tearing at his heart. He had thought he wanted Dev to suffer for his betrayal, but seeing Dev's anguish hadn't felt the least bit satisfying. Kiran had felt only a hollow, horrible nausea that had thrown him into uncertainty all over again.

Perhaps if Dev had been the one hurt, Kiran could have shared in Ruslan's triumph. But savaging a child who'd done nothing to harm him…his gut insisted it was wrong. Why couldn't Ruslan see that revenge should only be visited upon those who deserved it? Perhaps if Kiran could find the right words to explain, he might convince Ruslan of what seemed so obvious.

Kiran sighed. First he'd need to convince Ruslan that *nathahlen* lives held worth, and that would be no easy battle. He'd given Dev the best chance he could to save the girl. He hoped Dev had been clever enough to use it.

Early morning sun painted the workroom's flagstones a rich, buttery gold. Black clouds crouched in a sullen phalanx over the Whitefires, but the storms wouldn't spread eastward for some hours yet. Ruslan had said the confluence wouldn't reach their enemy's desired alignment again until evening, though he'd also warned that the confluence's instability was increasing faster than anticipated. Two, perhaps three more upheavals, and the containing forces would skew too far to hold the magic in check.

They had to find the source. Kiran squinted at the map again. "What about this one?" He tapped a small valley on the western slope of the Whitefires, not far from the deep gorge that marked the Alathian border. "The valley might be too low to feel cold in midsummer like the spy said, but the confluence of currents is strong enough for decent casting."

Mikail leaned past opened scholars' texts and scribbled notepapers to eye the map. "No. The rock's wrong; that valley's got white granite."

"How do you know?" Kiran asked, surprised. Mikail had spoken without consulting any of his own maps, shaded in a rainbow of chalked colors to indicate rock types and elevations.

Mikail looked down at the chalk in his hands. "I've been there. So have you. That valley is where Simon Levanian died. And where Dev betrayed you."

Kiran stared at the innocuous lines on the map. His memory of the valley was gone with all the others. He couldn't picture a single moment of the time he'd spent in the Whitefires. His regret and anger over the loss still had the power to steal his breath; though now, guilt for the price his mage-brother would pay over his own ill-considered search for answers swamped him.

"Mikail...I'm sorry I didn't tell you I'd spoken to Dev. If you think of any way I can stop Ruslan punishing you along with me—I'll do anything, to spare you."

"I heard you the first hundred times you said it." Mikail slapped his chalk down on the table. "Little brother, I'm not sorry you told Ruslan. That was the right choice on your part, finally. But I would believe in your passionate desire to spare me if you had thought of me *before* you disobeyed, not after."

Kiran winced. "I did think of you beforehand! I only sought to know my past because I was so terrified I'd fail Ruslan, and he'd hurt you."

"So instead of asking my help, you lied to me and ran straight to an enemy."

That wasn't at all fair. "I *asked* you for answers. You wouldn't give them. I didn't know when I sought out Dev about his…history with us! If you and Ruslan had told me of it—if you hadn't lied to me in the first place, I'd never have needed to speak to him!"

"Yet when I gave you truth, still, you lied." The chill anger in Mikail's eyes made Kiran feel small, and ashamed—and desperately afraid that the rift he'd opened between himself and his mage-brother might not heal.

"I'm sorry," he told Mikail. "I just…you were so upset already. I didn't want to hurt you more." How ridiculous that sounded, given the agony Mikail would now endure for Kiran's sake. A choked, despairing laugh escaped Kiran. "I'm an idiot, I know."

"An idiot for a mage-brother, I can tolerate. But a liar…how can we cast together without trust between us?" The pain in Mikail's voice was worse than his anger.

"I won't lie to you again! I—"

The workroom door opened. Kiran hastily shut his mouth as Ruslan and Lizaveta entered. Ruslan's head was high, his stride brimming with buoyant energy. Weariness shadowed Lizaveta's smooth features, but the smile she bestowed on Kiran and Mikail was as bright as the rising sun.

"A good day, *akhelyshen*," Ruslan said. "We have our quarry's scent at last… and, ah! How wonderful it is, to see an enemy's pain."

Memory welled through the mark-bond: Talmaddis screaming and straining against his bonds as violet fire devoured his *ikilhia*; and Martennan watching, his own *ikilhia* bruised and guttering, pain leaking from it in waves. Ruslan's savage joy and satisfaction overlaid the images, deeply enough to leave Kiran breathless.

Even so, Talmaddis's agony was hard to watch at first. Kiran couldn't help but imagine the horror he'd feel in the man's place as his soul burned away. But Talmaddis had tried to ensure the deaths not only of Kiran's mage-family, but all Ninavel's mages. Martennan, too, deserved this revenge. According to Mikail, he'd been instrumental in the Alathian Council's attempt to cripple and chain Kiran.

Kiran's initial empathy faded, replaced by swelling triumph. Ruslan was right; it felt *good* to see the Alathians suffer, knowing the harm they'd caused. Mikail too wore a fierce grin, the anger gone from his eyes.

"Thank you," Kiran said to Ruslan, and meant it. "Though…what of Dev? Did you take revenge on him, also?" He tried to ask it with cool dispassion, and not betray how he hoped for the child's survival.

Ruslan's smile dimmed a fraction. "Sechaveh decided he had use for the guide, and wanted the child so he might ensure loyalty. I gave them over as a favor. I know this *nathahlen*; greed will tempt him from Sechaveh's service in the end, and I will take my revenge then."

Now Kiran could truly rejoice in the outcome. He smiled at Ruslan, a brighter, easier smile than any he'd managed since awakening with his memories lost.

Ruslan's eyes warmed. Looking more pleased than ever, he ushered Lizaveta to a cushioned stool at the table's head. "Sit, Lizenka…I know how tired you are, after casting with such skill for so long."

Lizaveta sank onto the stool. She sighed in pleasure as Ruslan gently kneaded her shoulders. "Talmaddis provided more challenge than I expected. Alathians are usually so weak when they cast alone…but he fought without care for his *ikilhia*, hoping to burn its fire out and escape into death before I could master him. Luckily, I am not so easily defeated."

Thinking of Lizaveta's subtlety and strength, Kiran could well believe it. Almost, he pitied Talmaddis, who must have known he didn't stand a chance against her.

"None can match you," Ruslan agreed, and chuckled. "So many fools in this city flinch from me, when it is you they should truly fear."

Lizaveta reached a slim hand up to tug Ruslan's long tail of hair. "Enough, flatterer. I'm eager to hear the fruits of my labor." She looked at Kiran and Mikail. "What news of Vidai's source?"

"We have three possibilities so far." Kiran held up his map. "Two confluences in valleys in the far north of the Whitefires, and one amid these peaks in the southwest."

Ruslan worked his thumbs into Lizaveta's neck muscles, earning more pleased, heavy sighs from her. "Lizaveta learned from Talmaddis that our enemy is indeed *nathahlen*—a Kaithan tribesman, Vidai zha-Dakhar by name—but he hired a bone mage to create wards for him, wards which Talmaddis believed were meant to conceal and protect some charm or artifact that provides Vidai's power. Vidai was clever; he killed the bone mage afterward, and Talmaddis knew no details of the wards. Without any knowledge of their construction, we cannot be certain of casting a spell here in Ninavel capable of breaking them. But if we can determine which of these confluence points holds Vidai's source, we can translocate there, observe the wards directly, and cast a channeled spell using that same confluence point to break the wards and take whatever they protect."

Mikail said, "We would have to be very certain of our choice. No confluence in the Whitefires is powerful enough to fuel a return translocation. Not for the spells we know, anyway…?" He glanced at Ruslan, brows raised in question; Ruslan nodded.

Kiran grimaced, imagining the consequences of an incorrect guess. The confluence points he and Mikail had identified were so widely scattered that travel between them by ordinary means would take weeks. They'd never make it to another confluence point or back to Ninavel before Vidai managed to destroy Ninavel's confluence and kill them all.

Lizaveta leaned back against Ruslan's chest, even as he wrapped his arms around her. Watching their ease with each other, the depth of their respect and affection, Kiran yearned all the more to repair his bond with Mikail.

"Careful, Rushenka," Lizaveta said. "Talmaddis was certain that any casting in the vicinity of Vidai's source would draw his attention—and translocation requires so much power we cannot hope to shield all the ripples. If Vidai senses our arrival and attacks, he might easily savage our bodies enough that we will be too weak from healing them to cast channeled magic."

"I will think on a solution to that," Ruslan said. "But first, we must find Vidai's source. If we cast scry-visions of each potential confluence, perhaps we can discover some sign of his presence. Kiran, Mikail: I wish you to cast one such scry-spell, even as Lizaveta and I scry a second location."

Kiran's heart jolted. To cast a spell capable of scrying such a distant location in detail, he and Mikail would need a fully channeled spell. One powered by the freshly taken life of a *nathahlen*, not the dimmed energies stored in *zhivnoi* crystals.

Reluctance welled up, but he stamped it down. This death would be for good purpose, unlike those caused by Ruslan's failed strike.

"Do you wish me to cast as channeler or as focus?" Kiran wasn't certain which answer he wanted to hear. If he channeled, then he would not have to kill. But if he cast as the focus…a sudden memory of the intoxicating, soul-wrenching joy he'd felt with Ruslan in casting the *altavish* spell swept him.

Ruslan smiled at him knowingly over Lizaveta's shoulder. "You wish to focus, *akhelysh*. Do you not?" The memory of joy strengthened, reinforced by Ruslan through the mark-bond until the craving to taste it again left Kiran shaking. Distantly, he heard Ruslan's voice. "I will help you throw off the last of your chains, Kiran. Shall I find you a criminal to kill? A *nathahlen* so brutish you need not feel the least shred of empathy?"

"Yes." The word burst from Kiran, propelled by the siren call in his blood. He could take a life if it belonged to a criminal and not a child like Melly.

He didn't need to torture the *nathahlen* to stoke his *ikilhia* higher; a scry-spell did not require so much power. A swift thrust of the knife, and the deed would be done. He would cast, and prove once and for all that he was *akheli*, whole and uncrippled.

Ruslan left Lizaveta's side to embrace Kiran. "Good," he murmured. "Cast for me without hesitation as we fight our enemy, and I will consider sparing Mikail from punishment."

New relief dizzied Kiran. "I will cast for you."

Ruslan wound a hand in Kiran's hair, his breath hot on Kiran's neck. Blood afire, Kiran sought Ruslan's mouth, felt Ruslan's hands lock hard on his arms. Lizaveta was watching them, her eyes bright and her lips parted.

Mikail coughed and shifted on his stool. "Ruslan...I, too, want Kiran to cast. But...you didn't see how disordered his *ikilhia* was after your strike. Are you sure he's recovered enough to handle casting channeled magic?"

Ruslan drew back, frowning. Lizaveta said, "Truly, his *ikilhia* showed signs of disruption? I would have thought his healing accomplished by now."

Kiran couldn't help wondering if Mikail had a deeper reason for his reluctance. Did he believe their bond so frayed it would endanger them in casting? But Lizaveta's words brought his own concern over the slowness of his healing flooding back.

He said to Ruslan, "I felt no pain when you struck, but afterward—it's as Mikail says. My *ikilhia* remained disturbed despite his help, and I felt...off, somehow, for hours after. Perhaps damping charms would've prevented it, but how long must I rely on such crutches?"

Ruslan's head tilted, his frown growing deeper. "Liza is right, you should not need such assistance any longer." He laid a hand on Kiran's forehead. Gentle fire slid through Kiran's mind.

After a moment, Ruslan said slowly, "Your *ikilhia* feels a touch unbalanced, but not so much it should prevent you from casting. Perhaps the strain of holding your barriers against the confluence's upheavals has slowed your recovery. Still... we can be cautious. Kiran, I'll give you *voshanoi* charms to wear while you cast. Mikail—if you wish, I will redesign the scry-spell pattern to allow you as the channeler to safely divert power if you sense Kiran's focus failing."

Mikail looked relieved. "That would be good."

At least Mikail was willing to cast with him. Yet new worry plucked at Kiran. If his focus failed while casting with forces as powerful as those of the confluence, Ruslan's redesign might save his and Mikail's lives, but serious injury would be inescapable. What if he left Mikail's mind damaged as badly as his own—or worse? A horrifying prospect at the best of times, but doubly so now, when so many lives depended on their casting.

Ruslan patted his shoulder. "Do not look so dismayed, *akhelysh*. I will check you more deeply once you and Mikail have prepared the spell. If I am not certain of your health, I will not allow you to cast."

Kiran nodded—and jerked to his feet, as harsh whispers filled his inner ear. "Ruslan! Our enemy returns."

"What?" Ruslan's voice was sharp with surprise. "The confluence is not in alignment yet!"

"Vidai must have another purpose," Lizaveta said, tight and worried.

"Quickly, then—up to my workroom. We'll look for him in the confluence; perhaps we can determine his intent." Ruslan hurried for the door.

Kiran ran after Mikail, even as the phantom whispers swelled until he couldn't hear his own swift footsteps. Images of bloodied, eyeless corpses swam before his eyes. Whatever Vidai's ultimate intention, he surely brought more death to Ninavel.

CHAPTER TWENTY-THREE

(Dev)

The embassy door burst open before I could touch the copper plaque amidst the wards. Cara shoved past Ambassador Halassian to reach me. I caught her in my arms and kissed her; a fierce, passionate kiss that left us both gasping.

I said into her neck, "I vowed never to miss another chance for that." My hands couldn't stop tracing the lines of her body, as if to make sure she was real.

Her laugh was ragged. "A good vow. Ever since the Ambassador told me Talm lied about your death, I've worried that I'm dreaming—that I'll wake to find you're still dead, buried in that rubble…"

I held her tighter, thinking of all those streetside in Julisi who hadn't been so lucky. I didn't know so many folk there as in Acaltar, but I knew enough to dread hearing the tally of the dead. The scent of smoke was still strong in the warm morning air, the sky above the city's towers the hue of tarnished brass.

"Today's been as much nightmare as dream. But one part's pure good news." I beckoned Melly into the embassy's tiled foyer. Halassian stood holding the door open, grimly watching Marten lead Talm up the sunlit causeway, Lena and Stevan at his side. I'd hurried ahead of them with Melly. Partly out of eagerness to see Cara, but also because Talm's empty-eyed shamble left me shuddering, as did Marten's dark, strained silence. He'd spoken only in curt orders to Stevan and Lena, brushing off their initial exclamations of horror upon entering the interrogation room. Stevan had promptly retreated into soldier-stiff formality. Lena had armored herself in controlled calm, but a terrible, stricken sorrow lurked in her eyes.

I turned my back on the causeway. I wanted to rejoice in my one victory while I could. "Cara, meet Melly ap Sethan."

"Oh, Dev. She looks just like him…" Cara reached to touch Melly's tangled hair. Melly backed a step, her jaw set. Ruslan's torc was gone from her throat, but I knew it'd take a lot longer than the short walk from Kelante Tower to erase the memory of his touch.

"I'm sorry," Cara said to Melly. "It's just…it's wonderful to meet you at last. Your father was a good friend of mine." A brief, wistful flash of memory touched her eyes.

A frown darkened Melly's face. "When can I go home?"

I still hadn't told her. I didn't look forward to the battle I'd have in convincing her that Red Dal wasn't the merry, loving father-figure she thought him. Tainted as she was, if I handled it wrong she'd simply dive out a window and swoop back to his den.

"I know how much you want to," I said. "But you're not safe from Ruslan at the den. I told you of this killer we're hunting. You need to stay behind the embassy's wards until we've caught him. Then Ruslan will vow not to hurt you, and you'll be safe." By which point I hoped I'd have found the words to counter Red Dal's lies.

Jylla approached from the hallway, grinning at me, her small feet bare and her black hair loose to her waist. "Here's to dodging Khalmet's bony hand."

It was what we'd always said to each other after a narrow escape on a job. Cara's arm warm around my shoulders blunted the stab of memory. I didn't give Jylla our old response: *May our feet stay swift.* Instead I said, easy as I could manage, "You know what they say. Khalmet loves an outrider."

Jylla's eyes flickered. She dipped her chin in wry acknowledgement and surveyed Melly. "Mother of maidens, and I thought Sethan was pretty. But who needs looks when you're Tainted? Bet you've got a good strong dose of it."

Pride sparked in Melly's amber eyes. "I can lift half again my weight."

"Can you?" Jylla's smile widened.

Damn. I eyed Jylla's petite curves. Melly could lift her down from the embassy windows, easy. "Don't get any ideas, Jylla. You're not safe outside the wards either. Ruslan's itching for a new way to hurt me, and in his eyes, torturing you to death would do just fine."

"How sweet to know you care," Jylla said. "You can't blame me for wanting to make a new bargain. Seeing how you found the traitor all by yourself." She looked out at Talm, shuffling toward the embassy with Marten's hand tight on his shoulder. Her mouth hardened. "I see they mindburned him. Good."

Screams echoed in my memory. "There wasn't anything good about it."

Marten and the rest reached the door, and Halassian urged them inside. Cara made a low, aghast noise as Marten led Talm past us. Jylla only watched, her eyes opaque.

"Dev, if you'll join us in the receiving room," Halassian said. "I want to hear your version of events along with Marten's report."

"I'll talk, yeah." Minus the part where I'd sold myself to Sechaveh, anyway, unless she forced it out of me with a truth spell. "But Marten…do you have to ask him for a report right away?" I could well imagine how every word would twist the knife deeper.

"I wish it wasn't necessary," Halassian said. "But with the confluence's instability growing worse by the hour, I can't delay." She turned to Melly. "You look exhausted, child. Why don't you go with Cara? She can help you clean up and find you a bed."

Melly sidled closer to me. "I'd rather stay with Dev."

I gave her my best reassuring look. "Don't worry, kid, I'm not going anywhere. My room's got two beds—if you want, you can sleep there." Much as I was dying for some privacy with Cara, I'd gladly find it elsewhere in favor of helping Melly feel at ease. In the den, she wouldn't ever have slept alone in a room.

"I'll come with you." Jylla's smile at Melly was as warm as one of Red Dal's. "I used to be a Tainter, like Dev. He and I didn't meet 'til our Change, but we shared all our best stories, after. I'll wager I've got some good ones about his Tainted days you haven't heard."

A shy, answering grin crept over Melly's face. "Okay."

Oh, great. I caught Jylla's eye. *Don't you try anything.*

She flashed me a look of wounded, perfect innocence. "This way, kid." She led Melly off.

I caught Cara's arm and whispered, "*Watch* her."

"Don't worry." Cara hugged me again and said in my ear, "I'm looking forward to hearing those Tainter stories myself."

"Outrider stories are better." I watched her hurry after Jylla, and turned to Halassian, my smile dying. "Can you change your warding spells so they'll stop someone from climbing out a window?"

Halassian gave a short, amused grunt. "After seeing that gleam in your friend Jylla's eye, I understand your concern. Adjusting the wards won't take long; go ahead to the receiving room, and I'll take care of it and join you there."

I nodded, relieved. At least then Melly would have to break the wards before flying out or lifting Jylla down, and that'd bring the Alathians running.

Halassian braced her hands on the ward lines beside the door and started chanting. I headed down the hall toward the receiving room. My steps slowed as I reached the entrance.

Talm sat slack-limbed in a chair beside the arched window. Jenoviann knelt before him, her bony hands gripping his and her rings glowing. Kessaravil squatted at her side, broad and stolid as a boulder.

A few feet away, Marten stood staring out the window. From the glacial distance in his eyes, the entire crest of the Whitefires could've been exploding in magefire and he wouldn't notice.

Jenoviann raised her head and said to him, halting and dismayed, "His memories remain, but the rest...I didn't know a man could live, with so much destroyed."

Marten didn't give any sign he'd heard. Stevan and Lena were huddled by the room's south wall, talking in low voices. Lena wore a strained, urgent expression. Stevan looked mutinous. I edged forward until I could hear them properly.

"...talk to him, Stevan! You endured similar pain when you lost Vinalyn. There must be something you can do to help him."

Stevan said in a fierce, furious whisper, "Don't you think I would, if help were possible? There is no remedy for this, Lena. After Vinalyn's mind crumbled, it was days before I could speak without shouting, months before I felt anything but rage. Nothing people did or said brought comfort; most of it only hurt me more. Even now, I—"

He broke off, glaring, as I stepped up to them. "Stevan's right," I said to Lena. "Mere words won't help. Only one thing does: focusing on a task so difficult you haven't time to think about your hurt." The gods knew helping Kiran cross the Whitefires had kept me too busy to agonize over Jylla. "Get Marten focused again on catching this Vidai zha-Dakhar, and that's the best help he can have."

Stevan gave a surprised, grudging nod. "That's so," he said. "After Vinalyn, it was my work that kept me from despair." He eyed me, and his face darkened further. "Though Marten's state is as much your fault as Talmaddis's. If you had called upon our help and not Ruslan's, we could have handled the interrogation properly. Marten wouldn't have been subjected to this...savagery."

I locked my hands together so I wouldn't punch him. "Hasn't it occurred to you Talm was waiting for that? If I'd signaled you, I'd be dead now. I tried to get Kiran to come without Ruslan. It's not my fault Mikail told him a pack of lies that's got him all twisted around." But guilt wormed through me. If Kiran had come alone, I still would've tried for a bargain with Ruslan in exchange for Melly, rather than going to Marten or Halassian.

"What lies did Mikail tell?" The voice was Marten's.

I turned, startled. He'd come right up behind us. His body remained as stiff as stone, but a glimmer of the old, sharp intelligence lurked in his eyes. Lena and Stevan exchanged a relieved glance.

"You didn't see when you were in my mind?" I asked Marten.

He looked away. "No. I did not...pursue your memory that far."

I remembered him staggering back from me in stunned anguish. "Right. Well. Mikail's a clever bastard..." I repeated what Kiran had said of the Alathians binding him, and my betrayal. "It's so close to the truth, it'll be hard to counter." After all, the Council *had* bound Kiran; hell, I'd even betrayed him, just not to the Alathians.

Marten was silent. At last he said, "I think you are the only one capable of showing Kiran the truth. When the time comes, you must convince him to look at your memories."

It was my turn to look away. I didn't even challenge him on that mealy-mouthed "when the time comes." If my memories were Kiran's only hope of learning the truth, he was fucked. I couldn't sacrifice Melly and Cara for his sake.

Halassian hurried in. "The wards are as strong as I can make them," she announced. She studied Marten and blew out a sharp, relieved breath. "Back among the living, are you? Good. Dev, if you'll start from the beginning..."

I ran through an account of my experiences since I'd woken under rubble, my only omission the full extent of my deal with Sechaveh. I even gave a quick, spare recounting of Talm's interrogation, as dry and clinical as I could make it, hoping I might spare Marten the need.

Marten's face closed up again as I spoke. The other Alathians listened in stolid silence, though I heard Lena's breath catch several times.

At the end, Halassian shook her head, looking weary and old. "I remember Talmaddis's outrage over that murdered family. But his outrage wasn't unusual. Every mage stationed at this embassy goes through it. The first time you see a man killed on a whim and watch the mage responsible walk away without a care...it's a terrible thing. Some can't handle their anger, and I send them home. But Talmaddis seemed to settle...I had no complaint of him over the next few years. I was sorry to see him go when he requested a transfer—"

The floor trembled, a swift, sharp shudder. The air beside Talm's chair shimmered, and a man appeared. Long sand-colored robes, amber eyes glaring from a slit in a headwrap, the whole of his body oddly blurred, as if seen through heat haze...Vidai zha-Dakhar. Fuck!

I stumbled backward, even as Jenoviann shrieked, echoed by Kessaravil. Their chests ripped open, blood gouting over Talm. Marten and Lena shouted as one and raised their hands. The air between Vidai and us blazed into a wall of flame.

Stevan shoved me backward. "Run!"

I ran, but not for the embassy door. Instead, I skirted the magefire and sprinted for the archway that led to the sleeping chambers. The wards—Shaikar take me for asking Halassian to alter them! Melly, Cara, and Jylla were trapped.

Wild, harsh chanting behind me, a crackling roar as of fire leaping high, and a rumbling crash. The floor still quivered beneath my feet, but not enough to impede balance. I kicked open the door to the room I'd shared with Cara. Jylla and Melly knelt on the bed, peering at the window's wards. Cara stood in front of them, grim and determined, a knife in one hand and a boneshatter charm in the other.

"The hold-fast line," Jylla snapped at Melly. "You've got to break it—"

"I know!" Melly's voice was high with fear. "I'm looking for it!"

I raced past Cara and vaulted onto the bed. I'd found the breakpoints in the wards the first night I'd stayed here. Old habits died hard. "You'll have to shatter three lines! This one first, then these."

Melly's small face tightened with concentration. The air over the first ward line blurred. A gouge appeared in the silver, glittering shards spraying onto the bed.

"Hit it again!" She'd have to make a complete break in the ward line, or the damaged ward would still trigger—and if it triggered while damaged, the magic might flare out in enough magefire to burn us all to a crisp.

"Stand away and I'll release the wards!" Ambassador Halassian panted into the room. Her sleeves were singed black, a burn oozing on one cheek. As Melly, Jylla and I scrambled back from the window, she said, "I told Marten I'd see you safe—he collapsed the archway behind me, but we can't count on that stopping Vidai." She reached for the ward lines.

I ran to the opposite bed. If I could block the door, that might gain us more time. I dragged the ironwood bedframe away from the wall.

"Dev—behind you!" Horror colored Cara's voice.

I whirled to see Vidai in the doorway. Halassian sang out in a keening yell. Fire sheeted over the door, but Vidai vanished, only to reappear not a foot from my side.

If he killed with the Taint, a physical barrier could block a blow where magic couldn't—and blows could be dodged, if a man moved quick enough. I dove over the bed, dropped flat on the far side, and kicked the bedframe toward him. Suliyya grant Halassian could finish with the wards!

Cara shouted. Her knife whizzed through the air toward Vidai, only to jerk aside and clatter against the wall. I rolled, heard Halassian shriek something, a shriek that suddenly cut off.

A warm, wet spray drenched me. I yelled in frightened reflex and twisted aside. Halassian's body thudded down next to me. Her throat was torn open so deeply I saw the white of her spine.

Vidai vaulted over the bed. His eyes fixed on me, and I saw the promise of my death in that furious amber gaze. I scrambled up, skidding in blood, and launched myself straight for him. If I could distract him that much longer, let the others get clear—

"No!" Melly screamed. Inches away from my chest, the air blurred. A thunderclap echoed through the room. I bounced off an invisible barrier and fell backward with my head ringing and the copper taste of blood in my mouth.

She'd blocked his strike! I leapt up again, even as the bed jerked into the air to fly at Vidai.

The bed shattered into a hail of ironwood splinters and cloth scraps. Vidai stood beyond, turning to keep Melly in sight as she darted through the air.

"I can feel you strike," she shouted. "Old man, so slow…you won't touch them!"

Jylla was creeping for the door, crouched low. Cara slid along the wall toward her fallen knife. If Vidai really was untalented—I saw no warding charms on his wrists. A blade might do for him where magic couldn't, if he was too busy to see it coming. I snatched up a handful of ironwood bits.

Vidai tossed something small and metal into the air. A searing flash blinded me. Melly cried out, and I heard a heavy thump. Mother of maidens, no! I scrubbed frantically at my eyes, but the world remained a glaring sea of white. A grating footstep, in front of me—I threw the ironwood shards and ducked sideways.

A sudden shove sent me flying. I landed on something horribly soft and wet. I rolled and scrabbled upright, blinking furiously. Through a bright, watery haze, I saw Vidai crouched over Melly's limp form. No blood marred her clothes, but the right side of her face was red and swollen, as if from a blow. Oh gods, this must be how he snatched Tainters. The flash-charm, so they couldn't see to strike at him, then he swatted them down—

Shouts, from the doorway: Marten, Lena, and Stevan, rock dust coating their faces, their uniforms blackened and bloodied. Magefire boiled in the air before them, lanced out toward Vidai. I lunged for Melly.

Too late. Vidai shimmered and vanished, taking her with him.

A wordless, agonized howl burst from me. With Ruslan, I'd had a chance, but this…Vidai would kill her to fuel his magic, and I hadn't a prayer of stopping him. I couldn't see, couldn't think, the horror of it too strong—

Marten gripped my shoulders. I struck at his hands. "You bastard! If you hadn't been so fucking quick to strike, I could've grabbed her, saved her!"

"Dev!" He shook me, hard. "Ruslan holds Melly's blood-mark! He can cast to find her."

If only that were true! "Vidai will kill her before Ruslan can cast! Talm knew about the blood-mark, Vidai will too—"

"No." Marten's fingers dug into my shoulders. "I saw in Talmaddis's mind—he didn't speak of Melly to Vidai. More, he knew—however Vidai uses Tainted children, the effects last some time, his power fading slowly until he must take another. Vidai would have wanted his power fresh for this fight. He must have killed another child recently. He won't kill Melly right away, won't want to waste her power. He'll keep her until he needs to fuel his magic again."

Desperate hope took hold, painful in its force. I clawed at Marten's arms. "You've got to tell Ruslan! He's got to cast, now!"

"Dev." The tight dismay in Cara's voice cut through my panic. "Get over here."

I turned, and new horror darkened my vision. Jylla lay sprawled in a widening pool of blood. Cara, Lena, and Stevan knelt beside her. Cara held a wadded sheet pressed to Jylla's chest and stomach. Already, the silk was wholly scarlet. Lena and Stevan each had one hand on Jylla's shoulders. Their free hands were linked in the air over her brow, and their mouths moved in silent unison.

I dropped to my knees in front of her. Her eyes were open, aware; her face drawn with pain.

I said numbly, "But…when? You were almost at the door…"

Jylla said in a hoarse whisper, "You were blind from his flash-charm. Stumbled right toward him, you idiot. He was about to…I thought I could push you away and dodge in time."

Blood darkened her tongue, her teeth. "You saved me?" I felt as stunned as if I'd been kicked in the head. Why had she done it? She didn't love me. Didn't love anyone.

She tried to speak; choked and groaned, more blood welling red from her mouth. "Damn you, Dev. You're the…one that went soft, yet I pay…the price…"

"Don't. Don't talk, Jylla. Just…fight, and let them help you." I glanced back at Marten, knowing he'd read the desperate question in my eyes. He shook his head slightly, his mouth tight.

Jylla saw it. She bared reddened teeth at him. "Fucking mages, so useless…" She heaved against Lena and Stevan's hands, grabbed for me. I took her hand and let her pull me close. Her fingers were icy, her breathing thick.

"Tell them to make that bastard…burn. Die in agony. And then, you… save yourself. Fuck the rest. I'll…see you, in Shaikar's hells…"

"Jylla, *no*." Memory drowned me: waking the first night after my Change, my ankle shackled to a wall and bruises layering every inch of my body, to find a skinny, hard-eyed girl crouched at my side, offering me water. I'd refused; she'd forced it down my throat anyway. *You think you don't want to live. You're wrong.*

"You saved me," I repeated, in a broken whisper. "Don't you die, Jylla."

Her eyes slid shut, her hand going limp in mine. I snarled over my shoulder at Marten, "Don't just stand there—*cast*! When I was dying, you bastards healed me! What, is she not useful enough to you?"

Marten said, "Your injuries weren't so severe as hers. I'm sorry, Dev. Lena and Stevan gained her these last few moments, but…"

"Try harder!" I yelled at Lena and Stevan, who were still chanting silently. Cara's hands tightened on the wadded sheet. Her eyes were wet, locked on my face.

Jylla's breath hitched, slowed…stopped.

Lena sat back and said in a slow, weary voice, "We took as much of her pain as we could, but we couldn't keep her soulfire burning."

I howled again, in fury and anguish, and pulled Jylla to me. I'd wanted her to pay, just like I'd wanted Marten to pay, and Shaikar himself had granted my prayers. He must be laughing in his hells, and I knew just what it would sound like: Ruslan's cruel, delighted chuckle.

I wouldn't let Shaikar have Melly. Still cradling Jylla's bloodied body, I turned to Marten. "Get Ruslan. Now."

Marten opened his hand and showed me the message charm glinting in it. "I already have. He was on his way here—he said he saw Vidai's location in the confluence, and knew us under attack. I think he was…a trifle disappointed, to hear any of us survived. But he is eager to cast the seeking spell. He says he will cast here, that our dead will give him all the power he needs." His voice broke on the last words, his eyes going to Halassian's body.

"Are we the only survivors?" Cara asked.

Lena answered, grief weighting her voice. "Yes. Vidai caught the others by surprise. He even killed Talmaddis…though with a knife to the heart, not his magic."

A kind, quick death for a friend. Not like the death he'd given Jylla. What kind of death waited for Melly? I thought of Pello's room of bones, and barely restrained myself from shouting at Marten to contact Ruslan again, make him *hurry*.

Stevan shoved to his feet. "You say Ruslan knew we were under attack, Marten? Vidai must have come here to take revenge for Talmaddis—but ask yourself, how did he know to come? Ruslan could have ordered Sechaveh's guards to spread the news of Talmaddis's mindburning. Vidai would know we are far easier targets than blood mages."

Easier targets. I looked down at Jylla's ashen face, at the gaping slashes still wet with blood. Hate swallowed me; for Ruslan, for Vidai, for myself, for everything that had led to this.

"I think it more likely that Vidai set watch on the embassy, and employs more shadow men than Pello." Marten's voice was strained. "I should have left Talmaddis at Kelante Tower. I was...too distracted to think properly, I..." He pressed his hands to his face.

Lena reached for him. "Marten. This is not your fault."

Marten stepped back from her. He dropped his hands, his face once again tightly shuttered. "Fault is not important. Finding Vidai is. Come; we must prepare for Ruslan. If Vidai does have eyes watching this embassy, I want our wards strong enough that no hint of Ruslan's spellwork will leak through to provide warning of our intent."

He was right. My hate didn't matter. Nothing did but getting Melly back.

✳

"Well?" I demanded. "Where is she?"

Ruslan ignored me, standing up from the ashy remnants of the blood he'd painted in a web over the receiving room's floor. In front of the arched window, Mikail lowered his hands, his eyes still remote with concentration. Ruslan glanced past him at Kiran, who was leaning against a patch of wall that was scorched but clean of bloodstains. Kiran had his arms crossed tight, fat bands of silver glittering with jewels and sigils covering his wrists. His pallid face was coldly imperious, as if it didn't bother him a whit to watch Ruslan cast with the blood of people he knew.

Thinking of Jylla's corpse wrapped in a prayer shroud and stacked with all the rest, waiting to be burned with flashfire charms, I felt sick with rage. Ruslan had fucking better have found Melly.

Beside me, Cara and the Alathians looked equally desperate for news. Marten echoed my question, his voice sharp with impatience. "Ruslan! Did you find the child?"

Ruslan turned away from Kiran. "Yes. We know Vidai's source; we have him now."

He lifted a hand. A mist of colors coalesced in the air, clarifying into a map of the Whitefires that looked straight out of some scholar's text. One spot glowed brighter than the rest: a tight cluster of peaks far to the southwest.

A cluster of peaks that every outrider knew, though few made the long trek to admire the savagery of its spires. Shit, of course—Pello had talked of rooms hollowed from rock, and the tiny basin within the ring of peaks had caves.

"The Cirque of the Knives," I said. "Good thing you mages can translocate."

"I take it the terrain is difficult," Marten said.

Cara snorted. "Picture a bunch of knife blades crammed together, standing on end. Reaching the cirque's mouth from the canyon below requires a five-pitch climb up a water-slick cliff, and nobody's yet stood on any of the cirque's summits. The rock faces are too sheer, without enough cracks for pitons. Like Dev says, you'll want to spell your way there."

"Translocating directly into the cirque will not be possible," Ruslan said, aiming the comment at Mikail and Kiran rather than the rest of us. "Vidai's wards encompass the entire floor of the basin, and I sensed more sentinel spells layered over the canyon leading up to it. We might translocate to the valley behind the cirque's headwall…with such a significant barrier of magically inert rock between us and his wards, Vidai might not feel our arrival. Especially if Lizaveta remained behind to cast a full shielding of our spell."

Kiran straightened off the wall, frowning. "But…the confluence in that cirque is deep yet terribly small in area. Channeled spellwork won't be possible outside the heart of the basin. We must reach the confluence to break Vidai's wards and take the source of his power—but how, if he's warded the approach?"

In my mind's eye, I saw the frozen couloirs lining the cirque's forbidding ring of peaks—and remembered Sethan sprawled beside a convoy campfire, telling me, *When I was young and even crazier than you, I once nearly made the Cirque's ridgeline by ice-climbing a couloir on the back side…*

"By climbing over the cirque headwall, of course," I said. "I'm guessing Vidai didn't think to ward that."

For the first time ever, Ruslan's glance at me held real interest rather than hatred or contempt. "An excellent solution," he agreed. "If the guide climbs first and sets us ropes, we need not risk using magic to ascend. Lizaveta can send us a storm for cover…"

"A storm!" Cara repeated, incredulous. She smacked my shoulder. "Don't be an idiot, Dev. Even in perfect weather, those peaks can't be climbed."

"Not the peaks! One of the couloirs between them. We only need to make the ridgeline and then rappel or glissade down. A storm's a little much, yeah, but if Lizaveta could whip up some simple low-lying cloud to fill the cirque and stop Vidai spotting us by ordinary means, I can make this work." I wasn't half the ice climber Sethan had been, but with Melly's life in the balance, I'd get up a couloir if I had to use my teeth to do it.

Mikail said to Ruslan, "Assuming we reach the floor of the cirque, the basin is so small in area that Vidai can't help but notice us laying channels in preparation to cast, even with fog for cover. How can we stop him attacking us?"

I remembered Melly shouting at Vidai *I can feel your strike*; saw the tangled lines of Kiran's Taint charm diagram, heard Lena saying, *You couldn't possibly use that charm safely without an entire group of mages casting continuously to heal you …*

I laughed, high and wild, realizing with searing clarity how I might ensure the blood mages sent Vidai screaming into Shaikar's hells. "Oh, I can hold off Vidai for you," I announced to Ruslan. "I just need a little help from you and the Alathians."

❋

(Kiran)

Kiran hurried in Ruslan's wake toward their home in Reytani district, Mikail silent and scowling at his side. The upper city's causeways were crowded despite the day's growing heat. Sweating, wild-eyed *nathahlen* shoved past each other to join shouting throngs around anyone spotted wearing Sechaveh's scorpion crest. Wagons laden with supplies and bristling with guardsmen forged downward toward the Whitefire Gate, as the wealthier members of the great merchant houses attempted to flee the city. But even amid the commotion, the sight of Ruslan's sigils cleared a path through the crowd like a knife parting flesh.

As they crossed the Moonstone Bridge, *nathahlen* shrank back from them in a crush so tight Kiran feared some might topple to their deaths over the bridge's waist-high opaline walls.

Surveying the cringing *nathahlen*, Mikail broke his silence. "Ruslan, I know we need Dev, but why did you agree to his lover's demands?"

Kiran understood Mikail's confusion. Dev's outrider lover Cara had insisted she must accompany them to the cirque, claiming not only that Dev would require a belay partner, but that she was the better ice climber of the two. But she'd also said to Ruslan, *I heard you gave a blood vow not to cast against Dev and the Alathians. I want that same vow for me and Melly before I go—and without any extra conditions.*

Kiran still didn't know what she meant by "extra conditions." But he'd been certain Ruslan would refuse her; he'd seen the depth of Ruslan's desire for revenge on Dev, and everything he knew of his master said he'd never bow to demands from *nathahlen*.

Yet Ruslan had agreed to vow before Sechaveh, to Mikail and Kiran's combined shock. Kiran's surprise had quickly faded into relief. Mikail's had changed to something far darker.

Ruslan didn't slow his pace. Sweeping past a line of wagons emblazoned with the crest of Suns-eye House, he said over his shoulder to Mikail, "The vow says only that we may not cast. It does not prevent physical harm, and does not bind Lizaveta. Once our enemy is destroyed…the mountains are so dangerous."

"I see." Mikail's scowl eased. Kiran glanced up at the distant spike of Kelante Tower, understanding as well. Sechaveh had claimed Dev for his own, but Ruslan intended to seize the chance to kill Dev either by blade or some result of Lizaveta's casting while he was far from Sechaveh's eye. Dev, Cara, the child…none would return to Ninavel, and Ruslan would claim their deaths an unfortunate accident. Sechaveh would probably guess the truth, but in the aftermath of Ruslan saving city and confluence, he wouldn't press the issue.

Kiran kept his face averted, hoping Mikail wouldn't see how the idea bothered him. He'd already repaid Dev for his treachery. One betrayal for another…Kiran didn't see the need for further suffering, particularly if it involved Cara and the child.

If they succeeded in destroying Vidai, in the aftermath Kiran might successfully convince Ruslan that Dev might yet be of some future use. When elated by victory, Ruslan was expansively generous in mood. He might yield to suggestion…

Or perhaps Kiran should try harder to confine his concern to the survival of his mage-family and the city as a whole, and stop worrying over the fate of three *nathahlen* he barely knew.

A mounted Suns-eye guard captain struggled to back his horse from their path; the animal snorted and balked, its eyes rolling. Ruslan slashed a hand through the air in annoyance. The animal shrieked and collapsed on the paving stones, half-crushing its unfortunate rider. A young, hawk-nosed Sulanian from the guardsman's troop made as if to spring off his wagon to help, but his fellows held him back, hissing warnings.

Ruslan stepped over the horse's limp legs, ignoring the groans of the injured guard captain. "I had another reason for agreement," he said. "We dare not waste time in foolish quibbling. Lizaveta contacted me with grave news: the confluence's containing forces have reached the breaking point. One more upheaval with the currents in the correct alignment—which will come near noon tomorrow—and they will rupture."

Kiran stumbled, new horror distracting him from the guardsman's plight. Noon tomorrow! A shadow seemed to pass over the city's spires, the unsettled roil of the confluence growing all the more ominous. Kiran imagined the moment of failure: a firestorm of power exploding through the Painted Valley, devouring every mage in its path, racing down linkages of blood oath and mark-bond to burn through all his own protections. One final instant of shattering agony, and he, Mikail, Ruslan, and Lizaveta would be nothing but ash in the aether, the city's *nathahlen* tearing each other apart in futile attempts to survive.

"Can we reach Vidai in time?" Kiran feared to hear the answer. They had so much work to do! Channels to lay for both translocation spell and weather magic, not to mention the Taint charm for Dev...Ruslan had said he could readily analyze and complete Kiran's original diagram, but still, the time needed to create the charm would be measured in hours, not moments. Once in the Whitefires, even more time would be needed to reach the cirque's interior and set their plan in motion.

"We must," Ruslan said. "If the guide does not keep his promises, I will ensure he burns with us." He slowed his stride and caught Kiran's arm, peering at the *voshanoi* charms on Kiran's wrist. "And you, Kiran...you are equal to your tasks, yes? The charms appeared to shield you adequately when Mikail and I cast the seeking spell."

Kiran had felt somewhat dizzy and unsettled in the embassy despite the *voshanoi* charms, but nothing like the queasiness and disorientation he'd endured in the aftermath of Ruslan's failed strike. Of course, the seeking spell's magic had been far less in magnitude...but, no. He was fine.

And he was ready to cast. To prove it, he steeled himself not to look back at the pinned guard captain. What did it matter how bad his injuries were?

"I'm ready to fight," Kiran assured Ruslan, and was rewarded with a warm surge of approval through the mark-bond. Mikail, too, grinned at him; a sight that did much to lift Kiran's heart.

"Wait and see, little brother," Mikail said. "When we defeat this Vidai, then you'll truly understand the joy of revenge."

✻

(Dev)

"You realize Ruslan means to kill us," I said to Cara. We sat in one of the embassy's storage rooms. Chests of spellcasting supplies and clothes had been shoved aside to leave space for a veritable mountain of climbing gear. Ropes, pitons, boot spikes, long hollow metal tubes that we'd twist into the couloir's ice instead of hammering pitons for protection, the specialized, smaller ice axes that Samis had developed a few years back for climbing icefalls instead of snowfields, down-filled gloves and woolen trousers…right now it looked like we'd never fit the lot into the empty packs sitting by the door.

Cara looked up from knotting a set of ascension cords. "I figured, when he agreed so easily. But I think he won't try anything until after Vidai's dead. If his vows stop him casting against us…well, that levels the field, some. Besides, Marten said he'd protect us."

"And you believed him?" Marten had been all cool assurance, claiming the Alathians' magic could easily counter Lizaveta's spellwork if she cast against us. He'd been so smoothly confident, in fact, it'd raised all my hackles. He was hiding something.

Cara said, "I didn't get the chance to tell you before, but…Jylla found something. When Talm told us you were dead, she didn't yell like I did, or weep—but gods, Dev, I've never seen anyone so furious. She told me she'd see the traitor dead if she had to summon a demon herself to do it. She had me keep Halassian busy while she sniffed out the embassy vault—don't ask me how, but she broke in and searched it. She found a list of herbs that Jenoviann had ordered from highside suppliers, supposedly on Marten's orders; most of the herbs were ordinary things, but some were very rare, and very nasty—Jylla said they're only used in poisons."

Jylla would know, given how she'd poisoned Naidar's original lover so she could take the woman's place. Pain twisted through me; I stared grimly at a piton in my hands. "What's this got to do with Marten protecting us?"

"Jylla thought the list might implicate Jenoviann, but now…what if Marten really does have some plan against Ruslan?"

"What, you think Marten means to poison him? Hard to believe that'd work on a blood mage." I'd seen herbs like hennanwort and yeleran affect Kiran, but Kiran had also told me a blood mage couldn't be killed by physical means.

Cara shrugged. "I don't know. But I'd wager Marten's got something in mind, and Khalmet knows he's clever enough to pull it off."

Maybe. But the Cirque of the Knives was only some thirty miles from the Alathian border. If we won out over Vidai, Marten could just as easily make a run for safety and leave me, Cara, and Melly to Ruslan as a distraction.

"You should've asked Ruslan to vow the oath I asked Sechaveh for, where he can't hurt you and Melly at all." I wished she hadn't asked at all. That she'd stay safely behind, out of Vidai's reach. But she was right: there was no way I could climb a difficult couloir without a partner. More, I wouldn't make my old mistake. I wouldn't shut Cara out, turn her aside, treat her like she wasn't smart enough to weigh risks for herself. She'd made her decision, and I would accept it, even when my heart screamed I shouldn't.

"You mean, the vow where Ruslan can boil our blood the minute you speak to Kiran?" Cara jerked her knots tight. "No. This way both frees you from playing Sechaveh's bond-slave and ensures we've all got a chance."

I couldn't deny I'd be glad to dodge Sechaveh's employ. But still…I shook my head. "You saw Kiran today, hopping to Ruslan's orders without even blinking. He gave Melly over to Ruslan, watched him hurt her and never said a word of protest." I tossed my piton into a pile of others, hard enough to set them all ringing. "Ruslan wouldn't have agreed to vow for you if he wasn't dead certain of Kiran's loyalty now. Maybe he fucked with Kiran's mind again. Or maybe Mikail was right, and I don't know Kiran as well as I thought. Either way, I'm not sure he can be helped."

"You said Kiran was the one to suggest Ruslan bring you to Sechaveh." Cara began coiling a rope. "Maybe he tried to help you the only way he could."

I snorted. "Have you seen the way Kiran looks at me now? He's swallowed Mikail's lies, hates me as his enemy. Hell, he'll probably be the one to knife me the instant Vidai's dead."

"Don't give up yet, that's all I'm saying."

Sudden, helpless anger drove me to my feet. "I'm not! I just…I can't think about it now, Cara." Ever since the attack, a constant round of images repeated behind my eyes. Vidai crouched over an unconscious Melly, her face swollen from his blow; Jylla's body heavy in my arms, her lifeblood dark on my hands…

"Dev." Cara stood. "I'm afraid for Melly too." I could see it in her eyes, the fear, the dark mirror of my own anguish. She laid a tentative hand on my shoulder. When I didn't pull away, she drew me close, whispered, "We'll save her."

She said it like she believed it. I wanted to believe it too, wanted to share her hope, her steadfast courage—I clutched at her like a drowning man and sought her mouth. Not tenderly, but in rough, near savage urgency, desperate to block out the blood and death in my head.

She met my ferocity, doubled it, her mouth hard on mine, her fingers raking down my back. I shoved her against the wall, even as her hands tore at my clothing.

Our coupling in Kost had been passionate rather than gentle, but there'd been laughter, even joy. This was different, darker, shadowed by grief and fear, both of us panting and silent, gripping each other hard enough to bruise. Afterward, I dropped my forehead against her shoulder, my face wet with tears and sweat.

She cupped the back of my head, her breathing still ragged. A raw, ugly sound escaped me. "Shhh," she said, her voice gentle as her hands hadn't been. "It'll be all right, Dev."

The lie you had to tell. But just like Melly, I knew better.

CHAPTER TWENTY-FOUR

(Dev)

Blood magic might allow a translocation spell to be cast with just two mages instead of fifty, but the aftereffects were far worse. I spent long moments curled in a retching ball, my mind a dizzy, roaring blank. Gradually, I became aware that the air was cold on my face, the ground beneath me hummocked tundra instead of polished marble.

When the world finally steadied enough I didn't feel like I was about to slide off a cliff, I shoved up to my knees—and stopped, transfixed.

Mountains surrounded me, tall and jagged and beautiful in the twilight before dawn. Snow lined their couloirs and lay in great patches on the north-facing slopes. Beyond the shallow tarn at the valley's head, a barren expanse of jumbled boulders lapped up against soaring rock faces so sheer I couldn't make out a single ledge. High above, the peaks constricted into improbably slender spires, dark as obsidian against a sky of palest violet. Four of the Cirque's seven Knives were visible from this vantage: Cloudbreaker, Stormmaker, Magelance, The Scythe of Night…the very names were the stuff of legend among outriders.

For one blessedly sweet instant, the sight swept away the black weight within. Khalmet's hand, but I'd missed this! The chill, clean taste of the air, the wild grandeur of the peaks, all of it eased my heart in a way nothing and no one else could.

Beside me, Cara climbed to her feet and surveyed the valley. She let out a long, slow breath, her shoulders relaxing. Her face was indistinct in the low light, but I knew what it'd show: the reflection of my own brief instant of joy.

All around us, the mages were still huddled in tight, miserable knots. Even Ruslan looked unsteady, braced on his knees with a bloody knife gripped in his hands.

He'd killed a man to send us here. Something Marten and Stevan had argued over; I'd thought Stevan would refuse to come. *I will not condone blood magic!* he'd shouted at Marten. *You break Alathia's laws by agreeing to this!*

Marten had said grimly, *Lord Sechaveh promised me the victim will be a sentenced criminal; and once in the Whitefires, Ruslan will use stored energies to fuel his spells. If the Council disagrees with my choice to condone one criminal's death in exchange for saving thousands of lives, I will accept the consequences.*

Was that not Talmaddis's logic? Stevan had demanded. I'd seen the knife thrust strike home. But Marten had straightened and said with icy, implacable authority, *You are under my command, Arcanist Stevannes. You will not refuse my orders.*

Stevan had obeyed, though he hadn't spoken a word to Marten since. Even now, as Marten and Lena helped each other to their feet, he staggered upright with his back to them.

Asshole or not, at least he had principles. Mine weren't so solid. I felt only a twinge of guilt for the translocation casting, a twinge easily pushed aside by thinking of Melly in Vidai's hands. When I thought of the newly-created Taint charm tucked in a warded box in Ruslan's pack, I felt only a fierce, soul-deep hunger. That might disturb me if I considered it too long, but I didn't plan on doing any considering. Not until Melly was safe.

Beyond Stevan, Kiran was still bent over his knees, breathing in harsh gasps with his hands pressed to his eyes. He hadn't so much as flinched when Ruslan sliced the criminal's throat—and damn it, his lack of reaction did disturb me, deeply enough I couldn't shut it out.

"Kiran?" Mikail scooted over to him and laid a hand on his back.

Marten turned to watch them. I couldn't read his expression, but his stance had an odd tension. Maybe it was guilt. If Kiran ended as Ruslan's obedient tool, Marten had to know it was his fault. After seeing the raw depth of Marten's pain over Talm's betrayal, I no longer thought him wholly cold-blooded.

Kiran uncoiled from his cramped hunch. He muttered something to Mikail and lowered his hands. The charms covering his wrists still glimmered blue with slowly dying magefire. He looked up at the peaks, and his mouth fell open. The fading light of his charms showed him gaping around at the valley with every bit of the wonder and delight I remembered from our convoy trip.

"Look at him," Cara said softly. "The Kiran we knew—he's still in there, Dev."

"Maybe." I turned aside, unable to stand the reminder of a friend I thought gone. Maybe I only wanted to believe him beyond help so I could take the easy way out.

Shaikar take me, I had to stop thinking about Kiran! Saving Melly would be hard enough; I couldn't afford distraction.

I strode over to the bulging packs piled in a heap on the tundra. Climbing supplies, crystals and warded flasks of quicksilver for the blood mages' channeled spell, charms, food—none of the packs were light, and we'd all wear one, even Ruslan. The mages weren't likely to enjoy the steep climb up the boulder-strewn slope to the couloir's base, but they'd manage.

Behind the packs sat several fat, warded storage barrels. They held more food and supplies meant for the long walk out to the nearest settlement—if we survived and returned to make the trek.

I heaved a pack over to Marten. Like the others, he wore sturdy outrider leathers over a woolen shirt and trousers. No sigil-marked silk or uniforms here.

Marten eyed the pack, then the valley's massive headwall. "Where do we go?"

"The couloir we'll climb lies between Cloudbreaker and Stormmaker." I pointed to a narrow slot between two of the Cirque's tapered spires. From Sethan's description, that couloir was the one he'd almost succeeded in climbing.

According to Ruslan, we had seven hours at most before Vidai killed Melly and destroyed Ninavel. Climbing the couloir would eat up much of that time, though I had another, earlier deadline to consider.

"I want to reach the ridge in time to scope the descent before Lizaveta's clouds move in," I told Marten. Ruslan had said the spellcast cloud bank should arrive by mid-morning—though he'd warned us Lizaveta's lack of a partner as she cast to guide the clouds meant precision in timing was impossible.

Marten hefted his pack onto his shoulders, wincing at the weight. "We're recovered enough to walk. That said, I have a whole new sympathy for pack mules. Do you truly do this for fun?"

A grin stretched my face, the first one I'd managed since Vidai's attack. "You haven't seen the fun part yet."

✳

The trudge up to the couloir seemed to take an eternity. This high in elevation, the air was thin enough to leave me and Cara gasping. The mages panted and wheezed like forge bellows, even moving at a pace so slow it left me twitching with frustrated urgency.

Yet to my relief, we reached the couloir's base before the sun rose above the eastern peaks. Streamers of high, thin cloud glowed carmine, the sweeping cliffs above us so vast I felt no larger than a sand flea toiling up a dune. The couloir itself was a crooked slit choked with ice that looked gray and featureless in the shadowed defile. The ice was steep enough I couldn't see the couloir's upper reaches; Cara and I had scouted them with a spyglass on the approach. The windblown cornice choking the top of the couloir had a ferocious overhang. That very overhang had defeated Sethan on his long-ago attempt, but I thought we could skirt the cornice by veering left onto the mixed ice and rock of the couloir's side wall. Tricky, terribly risky climbing, but Cara had agreed it was our best chance.

She and I unpacked and sorted gear with rapid, practiced efficiency. The mages collapsed by their packs in obvious relief. Even Ruslan sat with his head bowed, his chest still heaving in rapid breaths.

"You intend to climb *that*?"

I looked up from strapping on boot spikes to see Kiran gawking up at the couloir. Between his flabbergasted amazement and the softness of his words, he probably wasn't even aware he'd spoken aloud.

Ruslan was sitting far enough away he might not have heard Kiran speak under the clanking of Cara racking pitons. I kept my answer equally quiet.

"Looks fun, doesn't it?" Though in truth I far preferred climbing rock. Ice was finicky, and unstable, and you had to climb it so damn slowly. Cara enjoyed the patient, careful precision needed. I missed the freedom of movement rock afforded. But I'd climb even a poisoned slagheap if it let me reach Melly.

Kiran glanced at me, half-wary, half-puzzled. "Fun."

"Shame we haven't the time to let you try it," I said. "You weren't bad, on rock." A calculated risk. But hell, Ruslan already meant to kill me and Cara. I hadn't much left to lose.

The puzzlement on his face grew deeper yet. He studied me like I was some spell pattern that he was determined to unravel. The intensity of his gaze made my skin itch with hope and guilt combined. Maybe he wasn't so far gone. Maybe...

Kiran sucked in a breath as if to speak. But then he shook his head, and the puzzlement vanished from his face to leave it as blank as the cliffs above. He retreated from me without a word to sit beside Mikail.

Mikail lifted his head and looked straight at me. One corner of his mouth ticked upward in a tiny, triumphant smile that said, *You see? He's ours, now.*

I returned to strapping on boot spikes as if I couldn't care less. I shouldn't care, not after Kiran had let Ruslan hurt Melly, not with her still in such danger. But damn it, I did.

Kiran didn't look at me again. He took out one of the dense little nutcakes we'd brought as food and started chewing. Yet his gaze kept drifting back up the couloir.

So did mine, and not just to scout the ice as the sky slowly brightened. Melly was somewhere beyond this ridge. Hurt and afraid, maybe even despairing, thinking no one would come.

I belted on my harness and stomped over to Ruslan. "I want the Taint charm."

Speaking with the labored patience of a man forced to deal with a moron, Ruslan said, "The Taint uses confluence power, and this rock is inert. The charm cannot help you in the climb; it will do you no good until we reach the basin floor."

"Maybe not, but I want it waiting on my wrist when we do, not buried in your pack. What if Vidai sniffs us out before you're ready?" I didn't want any chance he'd stop me reaching Melly.

Sardonic amusement lit Ruslan's eyes. "How deeply you *nathahlen* yearn for the merest scraps of power." He dug in his pack and produced a thick silver bracelet crowded with sigils and set with emeralds.

I couldn't help leaning forward, my eyes locked on the charm. A little, knowing smile played about Ruslan's mouth. "Take it. The trigger word is *vishakhta*."

I forced myself to reach casually for the charm, not snatch it from his hand.

Watching me, Marten said sharply, "Once we reach the basin, don't spark it without cause, Dev. If you damage your organs before we cast, we risk losing this fight."

I'd asked Ruslan in Ninavel if he could make it so the charm didn't fuck me up so quickly. He'd smiled that sandcat's smile of his and said, *No. The charm works because of the damage caused; it is not a mere side effect.* I wasn't sure I believed him, but there wasn't much I could do about it. Instead, I had to depend on the Alathians. Stevan had said that with all three of them casting to heal me from the instant I triggered the charm, I might avoid mortal injury.

"I won't spark it," I promised Marten. But oh, how I longed to, even knowing the cost. I clasped the band onto my wrist and returned to help Cara uncoil ropes. Impatience buzzed in my blood, but I had to shut everything out but ice and rock. Otherwise, I'd never save Melly.

❋

Tink! Tink! I tapped the curved blade of one hand axe against fluted ice, searching for a good placement. My calves were on the edge of cramping after hours of standing on the front points of my boot spikes. Blood was stiff on my sleeve; I'd fallen, earlier, and sliced myself with an axe blade when the rope snapped taut and slammed me into the ice. Thank Khalmet, both rope and anchor had held, and I hadn't knocked Cara off her stance at the belay point. Both of us had countless cuts on our faces from falling ice shards, and numb, raw fingers from wiggling pitons into cracks on the couloir's sidewall to set up haul rope stations.

The mages were inching up the haul ropes behind us, strung out along the couloir like knots in a rawhide braid. We'd showed them how to ascend using short lengths of cord tied in slipknots around the rope and attached to harness and boots. Weight the harness cord, and the knot locked tight on the rope to hold a man's weight. Slide the boot cord knots higher on the rope, stand to release the harness cord knot and slide it high, sit, slide the boot cord knots, stand, repeat. Arduous and slow, but doable for even the least experienced of climbers.

The couloir's cornice loomed over me, a frozen wave whose underside bristled with dagger-sharp icicles thick as my leg. Nobody could climb over that monster; I couldn't believe Sethan had even tried. Time to bail to the side wall, though that had its own dangers. The ice there was thin and brittle, fading out entirely in sections to leave bare rock. No chance of placing protection, and the rock was likely to be just as brittle as the ice.

Cara had led all the previous difficult pitches, but she hadn't argued when I took the rope for this final stretch. She might be better at ice, but rock was my specialty. If there was a way up those barren patches of stone, I'd find it, even encumbered by clumsy hand axes.

Thirty feet later, I cursed my former confidence. Spreadeagled on the couloir's side, the front points of my boot spikes barely holding in a thin slick of ice, frost-scarred granite breaking away every time I tried to hook an axe blade…fuck! I hadn't been able to set any ice screws or pitons. If I came off now, I'd fall all the way past the belay point. Such a long fall would snap the hemp rope in a heartbeat, and if the mages cast to save me, they'd bring Vidai down on us all. The Taint charm was cold and dead on my wrist. Damn it, if only I was closer to the confluence, I'd spark it, hell with the consequences…

The ice cracked away under the spikes of my left boot, leaving me clawing for a foothold. The right foot was going to go too, I could feel it, and I still couldn't find an axe placement overhead—

I let the axe drop to dangle from the leash cord knotted tight around my wrist. Ripped my glove off with my teeth, and stretched again, searching with fingers instead of axe blade—

My fingertips locked over a lace-thin flake of rock, just as the ice beneath my right boot gave way. I hauled up in desperation, my boot spikes scraping sparks from the rock, and stabbed my remaining axe higher, knowing I was a mere heartbeat away from dooming us all.

Chunk! A solid placement, right in the heart of an ice patch. I scrabbled again with my feet, got one boot spike into a divot in the stone. The world narrowed to fingers, axe blade, and boot spikes, my entire being focused on tiny shifts of balance as I inched up lichen-smeared stone and rime ice.

After an eternity, my head poked over the crenellated, razor-edged ridgetop. My vision expanded outward in a rush. The Cirque's seven Knives pierced the sky all around, the dark rock of their sheer-sided summits in sharp contrast to the snowfields lining their sides. Cradled in the deep bowl at the base of the peaks was an oval lake, the water a startling chalky blue in color. No sign of human presence showed on the tundra and rock of its far shore, but Marten had warned me Vidai's wards included elements of veiling. The bastard could be doing cartwheels in plain view and I wouldn't see him.

As my ferocity of focus faded, triumph rose to replace it. Mother of maidens, what a climb! But I couldn't savor the moment. The sky above was gray with cloud, and fat fingers of drifting fog were already creeping up the valley. I shoved my freezing hand back in its wool glove—I'd carried the damn glove in my teeth the whole rest of the pitch—and peered down into the cirque, picking out landmarks in the sweep of snow and stone. We'd have to traverse along the ridge for a hundred feet, then rappel down a sheer cliff before we could reach a snowfield safe to slide down. Hopefully the mages remembered Cara's hurried lesson on how to stop an uncontrolled tumble with an ice axe.

I ducked back below the ridgetop and pounded pitons into cracks to make a belay station, muffling the blows of my hammer with a folded strip of wool. Once ready, I didn't dare shout to Cara, knowing how well sound carried in the mountains; instead, I gave three sharp tugs on the rope: *Climb when ready.*

Soon enough I felt the rope jerk twice: she was on her way. As I took in rope inch by inch, the clouds lowered and thickened, streaming between the Cirque's peaks in silent waterfalls. By the time Cara herself grunted up to my belay stance, the world beyond the ridge had become a misty gray void.

"Khalmet's bony hand," she said, swiping sweat from her brow. "I've no idea how you led that without falling." As the second climber, she'd had the opportunity to sit and rest on the rope, even use it as an aid in her climb.

"It was a near thing," I admitted.

She spared a moment to brush my cheek with her gloved hand. "I owe Khalmet a serious offering, then."

I longed to return the caress, but my hands were full of rope. "A summit's only as good as the partner you climb with—and no outrider could ask for a better partner."

Her smile was both beautiful and weary. "We haven't reached the summit yet."

Didn't I know it. Four hours gone already, at least two more to reach the basin...we'd be cutting it close. "I'll go set the rappel. Protecting the traverse for the mages would take too long—tell them to just straddle the ridge and scoot their way over to me."

Cara chuckled. "Good thing the cloud'll keep them from seeing how far the drop is." Visibility was so low I could barely see the rappel point through drifting veils of mist.

I untied from the pitons and snatched up our spare coil of rope—only to freeze, as a low, ominous rumble echoed out of the cloud surrounding us.

"Was that thunder?" Cara demanded.

"If it was, I'm going to kick Ruslan back down the couloir." *Just cloud,* I'd told him in Ninavel. *No storm—lightning loves a climber on a ridge, and we're not all blood mages to survive a strike.*

"Maybe it was a fluke." But the worry on her face matched mine. We'd be stuck on the ridgetop a good hour before we got all the mages down the rappel. Worse, lightning liked metal, and between ice axes and pitons, we were carrying enough to provision an army.

"Tell the mages not to dawdle." Nothing for it but to move as fast as we dared, and pray I hadn't used up all Khalmet's favor ascending the couloir.

※

(Kiran)

Kiran scooted along the ridge toward Dev, trying not to think about the void yawning on either side or the ever-louder growls of thunder. Straddling the sharp rock of the ridgetop was uncomfortable and made movement awkward, but at least it felt a thousand times safer than trying to walk the knife-edge. At the rappel point, Stevannes was easing off the ridge under Dev's supervision, the rope wound tight around his lean body. Ruslan and the other two Alathians had already descended the rappel rope, disappearing into cloud. Mikail was moving along the ridge behind Kiran, trailed by Cara.

A shatteringly loud thunderclap nearly toppled Kiran off the ridge. He gripped the stone all the tighter, his thighs spasming with the effort.

What the fuck is this thunder? Cara had demanded of Ruslan when Kiran's master first reached the ridgetop. *Didn't Dev say no storms?*

Ruslan had snapped, *The interaction of spellcast weather with natural systems is impossible to fully predict.* But Kiran knew the truth: Ruslan and Lizaveta had made their best guess as to the energetic effects of Vidai's wards when they designed the weather magic, but that guess had been wrong.

Kiran tried to scoot faster. His ears were still ringing from the thunder. Wait, no…that high-pitched whine wasn't his ears. It was coming from the blade of the ice axe strapped to his pack.

"Oh, shit." The dismay in Dev's voice yanked Kiran's head up. Fifteen feet ahead at the rappel station, Dev was staring at the pitons jammed into cracks in the ridgetop. An eerie blue glow played over the pitons' metal, softer than magefire.

Dev leaned down and snapped at Stevannes, "Move faster!" Stevannes began a harsh reply that died when he saw Dev's face. He loosened his grip on the rappel rope, letting it slide faster around his body to increase the speed of his descent, and vanished into fog.

Beyond his barriers, Kiran felt whispers of wild energy growing, and understood. Lightning was going to strike. Here, and soon. The ringing of his ice axe increased to a buzz that shivered his teeth.

The rock was too sheer; the rappel rope was the only way off the ridge. Unless they cast—but then Vidai would come, and they were still too far from the confluence for Dev's charm to work properly. But if lightning struck, Dev might well die—either from the strike itself, or in a reflexive power draw by an injured Mikail or Kiran—and leave them with no chance of protection from Vidai.

The hairs on Kiran's arms were standing up, the nape of his neck tingling. They'd never make it down the rope in time. Kiran twisted to call to Mikail, "We have to divert the strike!" If they timed the casting just right, perhaps the magic could be hidden beneath the natural power of the lightning.

Mikail halted his frantic scrabble along the ridge, looking torn. Kiran drew in a breath, ready to release his barriers—

"Don't cast!" Cara bounded along the ridgetop's knife-edge as lightly as if it were a city street. "Give me your axes." She sliced Mikail's axe free, jumped over him and darted to Kiran. A sharp tug, and Kiran's axe was gone as well.

Dev was pulling up the rappel rope; Stevannes must have finished his descent. Cara dumped the axes in front of him.

"Lower these down. Yours too. And stay here!" She darted past Dev, her own axe still in her hand, the metal crawling with blue light. Beyond, the ridge rose toward a crooked pillar of rock half obscured by cloud. Cara scrambled up the pillar's side and stabbed the haft of her ice axe into a crevice at the summit, leaving the axe poking skyward. Cara yanked her smaller hand axes from her pack and stood them upright beside the first.

Energies shifted in the aether. The glow faded on the rappel station's pitons, even as it brightened on the ice axes above. Abruptly, Kiran understood. Cara meant to draw the lightning away from them to the pillar.

"Cara, *hurry*." Dev's face was as pale as the mist. He tied the remaining axes in a tight bundle at the end of the rappel rope and cast the rope back down.

Cara turned, jumped for a lower rock—

A concussion of sound and light hammered Kiran. Slowly, he became aware he was face-down on the ridge, clinging to it like a limpet, stone sharp against his chest and cheek. He raised his head.

Cara's ice axes still stood silhouetted on the pillar's summit, their metal smoking and blackened. Dev was straightening up off the ridge, looking as dazed as Kiran felt. But the ridge beyond Dev was empty.

Kiran stared, horrified. He imagined lightning lancing down to smite the axes, the concussion blasting Cara from the ridge, her body tumbling through a thousand feet of air to the talus far below...

Dev blinked, focused on Kiran. Dread swept his face. "Cara..." he whispered, and turned. "*Cara!*" He yanked at the knot of the sling binding him to the pitons.

Kiran twisted around, terrified to see the ridge behind him empty as well. But Mikail still straddled the stone, looking shaky and wild about the eyes.

Dev abandoned the rappel station to race along the ridge, still calling Cara's name.

Behind Kiran, Mikail called, "She's gone, you fool! Get back here and help us off this ridge before lightning strikes again!"

Mikail was wrong about Cara. Straining his senses, Kiran could feel the dim flicker of her *ikilhia*, some twenty feet below the ridgetop—she must have caught herself as she fell, in some miracle of climbing skill. But her *ikilhia* was erratic, laced by fear and pain; she was hurt.

He scrabbled forward along the ridge. "Dev! She's alive, down there!" He pointed into the fog obscuring the Cirque's back side.

Mikail clamped his shoulder and whispered in his ear, "What are you doing? Let him think her dead—we don't need her anymore."

Mikail hadn't been mistaken about Cara; he'd lied. Anger shot through Kiran. He snapped back at Mikail, "How well do you think he would fight for us, stunned by grief? I don't care how much you hate him, we need him whole!"

Dev jerked sling cords from his harness and started knotting them together, a terrible mix of hope and fear on his face. "Cara, can you hear me?"

A hoarse, strained whisper floated out of the cloud, barely audible. "Dev… hurry, can't hold much longer…"

Dev straddled the ridge, looped a sling over his body, and tossed the remainder of his makeshift rope down where Kiran indicated. "Brace me," he ordered Kiran, and called to Cara, "Can you grab on?"

Cara didn't reply, but the slings snapped taut, driving a grunt from Dev as the cord dug into his waist. Kiran locked his arms around Dev to anchor him. Dev hauled on the slings, muscles straining, his teeth bared. A peal of thunder assaulted Kiran's ears. He gripped Dev all the tighter, terrified lightning would strike them again.

Slowly, Cara emerged out of the fog, dangling from one hand locked on the lowermost sling. Her other arm hung limp at her side, blood dark on her shoulder, bruises blossoming over her throat and collarbones. Her upturned face was pale but fierce with determination.

Dev heaved her back onto the ridge—and clasped her to him with desperate force. "Gods, Cara. I thought Shaikar had taken you."

"So did I." Her voice was a husky, damaged croak. "Got the wind knocked out of me, couldn't yell, my grip was slipping…" Her good arm tightened around Dev. "No better partner," she whispered.

Love and relief were so vivid on Dev's face that Kiran had to look aside, seized by renewed conviction that it was wrong for Ruslan to take further revenge. Talking with Dev at the couloir, he'd been startled anew by Dev's lack of vitriol toward him. After the danger Kiran had brought to Melly, he had expected Dev to abandon all pretense of friendship. Yet even now, Dev didn't respond to him like an enemy.

Dev twisted to look at Kiran. "Thanks," he said, his voice almost as rough as Cara's. "Now let's get the fuck off this ridge."

Kiran gladly wriggled backward to the rappel station. Mikail was already there, his gray eyes hard as he watched Dev help Cara along the ridge.

"She'll slow us down," he muttered to Kiran. "If we don't reach Vidai in time, our deaths are on your head."

"We'll make it," Kiran said, and hoped desperately it was true.

✳

Kiran crept over the tundra, trying to keep his steps noiseless. Fog surrounded him, so thick he could barely make out the other members of the group, let alone the insanely steep snow slope he'd just slid down, sitting on his rear like a child playing on a sand dune.

Despite everything, he'd found the descent oddly thrilling. The rush of speed had been intoxicating, snow spraying in his face and crusting his clothes, his eyes watering so strongly from the wind of his descent he could barely see...not that there was anything to see in the cloud. But Kiran remembered the view of the mountains at sunrise as he'd puffed his way up a haul rope: summits glowing pink, the shadowed couloirs a deep, mysterious blue, the panorama of spires and ridges a phantasmal vision straight out of the most incredible of explorer's tales. The pain of his lost memories was all the more acute now he'd glimpsed what wonders they might have contained.

When he'd leaped to his feet after finally sliding to a stop in the snow, he'd been grinning so wide his cheeks hurt. Martennan's solemn young first lieutenant had stared at him, pain so sharp in her eyes that Kiran wondered if he reminded her of one of her murdered friends.

Now the Alathians strode with military precision at Dev's side. They'd left a wan but determined Cara with the spare gear at the base of the snow slope; though the Alathians had hastily bound her wounds, they hadn't dared cast any healing spells.

Better for me to stay clear of the fight; you've got enough people to protect as it is, Cara had told Dev. *You go keep Vidai busy, and I'll scout those caves at the base of the Scythe. If he's got Melly stashed somewhere, maybe I can find her.*

Dev had protested, wanting her to stay put and rest, but she wouldn't hear of it. *I'll stay clear of sigils and wards, I promise. But I'll be damned if I'm going to sit on my ass.*

Kiran hoped she would stay safe. Vidai's wards burned in his head, a fiery barrier mere feet away. He could feel the cirque's confluence beyond, a mere eddy compared to Ninavel's blazing ocean, but brilliant in its beauty nonetheless.

Ruslan's dark shape halted beside a boulder looming out of the mist. He beckoned Kiran and Mikail forward. Silent words came through the mark-bond.

Here lies one of the anchors for Vidai's outer wards. Do you feel the second pattern within?

Kiran nodded. Deep within the area protected by the outer wards, a strange, chaotic swirl of energies lurked, ominously strong.

The outer wards can be shattered by a simple raw casting, but the inner pattern will require a channeled spell to break. A channel diagram flashed into Kiran's mind, a knotted maze of lines. *Once through the outer wards, Mikail and I will prepare the channels and cast. Vidai is certain to attack us; your task is to assist the guide in holding him off.*

Kiran glanced at Dev, who was edging from foot to foot, his fingers tracing the sigils on the Taint charm. At least Kiran need not worry that an instinctive power draw on his part would mean death for Dev. The confluence here was tame enough to touch directly. He could safely pull power from it to heal even the worst of physical injuries, though the healing would leave his *ikilhia* weakened and disordered.

Or rather, more disordered. Kiran knew the reason Ruslan had not asked him to channel was the continued instability of his *ikilhia*. Even now, standing next to a source of magic as powerful as Vidai's wards left him feeling queasy despite his *voshanoi* charms. But raw casting did not require much control; Kiran was confident he could strike at Vidai no matter how sick he felt.

Ruslan continued, *Once the inner wards are shattered, I will claim whatever artifact they protect. Your task then is to assist Mikail in ensuring neither Vidai nor the Alathians interfere. We must not allow the Alathians to take possession of a source of such power, lest they use it against us.*

Kiran's nervousness rose higher yet. He could well believe the Alathians would snatch at the chance to destroy them before Ruslan could take revenge.

I will break the outer wards for you, he told Ruslan. *Then you and Mikail can conserve your strength.* They would need it. Pouring channels with quicksilver was far faster than laying out rods of true silver, but the channels would be terribly dangerous to control.

Ruslan took Kiran's shoulder. Assent flowed through the mark-bond, a wordless expression of pride and confidence in Kiran. Kiran touched Ruslan's hand; remembered Lizaveta winding her hands in Ruslan's hair, pressing her cheek to his and saying in a choked voice, *Come back to me, brother.* A pang squeezed his heart, thinking of his own mage-brother. He met Mikail's eyes and willed him, *Stay safe.*

Mikail's *ikilhia* brushed against his outer barriers, a gentle touch carrying with it the memory of hundreds of childhood days spent casting together in sunlit workrooms. Kiran gave him a swift, warm smile in return, raised a hand to the boulder, and looked to Dev.

"Ready?"

Dev crowded forward. "Hell yes." He glanced back at the Alathains. "Assuming you are."

Martennan nodded and said softly, "The moment Kiran breaks the wards, spark your charm."

Kiran dropped his barriers. Fire sheeted over his inner vision, the wards resolving into a labyrinth of carefully balanced energies. He threaded his senses through the wards' perimeter. Confluence currents swirled beyond, beautiful and seductive, the power his for the taking. He drew in a great draught, fashioned it into a blazing lance of power, and hammered the lance straight into the heart of the wards.

The maze cracked, energies bursting wild out of their pathways. He caught the magic, tore power out of the wards in a great rush, funneling it back down into the confluence. Dimly, he was aware of the boulder crackling and sparking before him. And beyond, a startled, furious shout.

Dev yelled in answer, "*Vishakhta!*" Magic sparked to life, sickly green spirals springing from the charm on his wrist to pierce his *ikilhia*. Dev shouted again, a fierce, wordless cry of joy. The Alathians chanted, a cool blue wash of magic spreading from them to layer Dev's body.

The wards' invisible barrier vanished. A hot, dry wind blasted past Kiran, sweeping away the fog sheltering them. "Go!" he shouted, and Dev raced forward.

CHAPTER TWENTY-FIVE

(Dev)

I pounded past the boulder, its ward lines dark and empty of magic. The void in my mind sang with life once more, the thrill of it so sharp it wiped away all fear.

The air was clear of fog for the whole breadth of the cirque's basin, though clouds still sat low overhead, hiding the peaks. Fifty feet away on the lakeshore, glowing ward lines spiraled around a ring of slender pillars. The pillars were twice a man's height, formed of stacked, pallid bones carved with sigils that flickered with indigo fire. The space bounded by the pillars contained a strange, smooth bubble of darkness. Hints of indigo chased over its surface like colors in a soap slick, but beneath them lay only dead, lightless black.

Standing with one foot over the outermost ward line was Vidai zha-Dakhar. He wore his *gabeshal* robe, but his head was uncovered. He looked younger than I'd imagined, and sick, like a victim of wasting fever. His cheeks were sunken, his skin mottled and gray, his amber eyes fever-bright.

Melly lay limply unconscious in his arms, the barbed copper band of a sleep-fast charm circling her brow.

I didn't waste time yelling at Vidai to stop. I just *reached*, with that gloriously resurrected part of my mind, and snatched Melly from his arms.

A deep, vicious cramp stabbed my gut. Just as abruptly, it eased. A good thing, because Vidai struck. I felt the blow coming, like seeing wind ripples racing over a lake. I released Melly—she fell in a boneless sprawl on the stone, some ten feet from me—and *shoved* against his strike.

A sharp crack echoed through the cirque. Vidai's hollow-cheeked face twisted in frustration. I leapt into the air. If he'd never been a Tainter, he wouldn't be used to thinking like a falcon.

He struck again, this time at the mages behind me. I blocked it, barely—he might look sick, but fuck, he was strong!—and darted downward to kick at his head.

He ducked, ripped a knife free from his belt and slashed at me. I darted backward, *shoved*. He staggered back, almost landed on a glowing ward line, but jumped just in time, soaring high.

A crackling tornado of magefire shot past me. Vidai dodged it, releasing an angry shout. I glanced back. Kiran stood before the pillars, his hands raised and his teeth bared. Azure fire danced on his fingers and crawled over the charms on his wrists. Behind him, Ruslan and Mikail yanked flasks from Mikail's pack and poured quicksilver into tangled lines with swift precision. The Alathians crouched behind a boulder in a tight huddle, chanting with their eyes fixed on me.

I swooped after Vidai and struck again. He vanished; the pillars flared, blindingly bright. I soared over them, my heart in my throat, scanning snow and stone. Where was he, where—

The flare of light subsided. Vidai reappeared above the Alathians. Again, that warning ripple brushed against my mind. I shoved, but too slow, damn it, couldn't stop it all—

Stevan slammed forward into the boulder, blood spraying from gashes on his back. He cried out as he hit and collapsed to the ground. Marten and Lena didn't move, didn't falter in their chant. Yet dull pain took root in my gut.

Kiran whirled and slashed a hand. Another bolt of magefire exploded toward Vidai even as I *shoved*. Vidai jinked aside and vanished again. I darted through the air, straining my mind for the least hint of his Taint. Pain sank its teeth deeper into me, and I prayed Ruslan and Mikail would hurry.

✳

(Kiran)

Magic danced in Kiran's blood, blurred his vision, the touch of it so sweet it hovered on the edge of pain. He kept the sensation at bay and spun in a slow circle, searching for Vidai.

Dev shouted in warning. Kiran looked up, saw a rain of boulders catapulting out of the cloud hiding the slopes above. Some of the boulders jerked aside to drop harmlessly into the lake, and Kiran sent magefire boiling through the air to vaporize more, but it wasn't enough. Ruslan and Mikail dodged aside as one boulder crashed onto their quicksilver pattern.

Kiran shattered the boulder into smoking shards, but too late—the pattern was marred. What if they didn't have enough quicksilver to rebuild the disrupted channels?

A crack echoed in Kiran's ears, loud enough to deafen. A blow knocked him down onto hands and knees. Pain lanced his back; he reached and felt the hilt of a knife jutting from just below his ribs.

He ripped the knife free of his body and threw the gates of his *ikilhia* wide. Confluence energy seared through him, healing his flesh and burning away pain. Kiran's vision doubled, dizziness making him stagger. He twisted and cast another bolt of magefire at Vidai; but his control was weak, the fire threatening to escape its bonds and burn through the entire basin.

He risked a glance back. Mikail was bent over the marred area of the quicksilver pattern, a bloodied knife clutched in his hand, a long wound red on his arm. Ruslan dug fingers into Mikail's wound and painted blood in a line on the granite.

A solution, but a terrifying one. A channeler's blood could be used to complete a pattern, but it made the danger in casting extreme.

Vidai appeared again over Mikail—and Dev slammed into him, the two of them tumbling over and over in the air, clawing at each other. Claps of thunder boomed through the cirque. Dev shouted again, a hoarse, pained yell.

Kiran didn't dare try another magefire strike, fearing to burn Dev along with Vidai. Instead, he reached for the clouds above, yanked a veil of mist to coil around Dev and Vidai's struggling figures. If Vidai couldn't see Mikail and Ruslan below, perhaps he couldn't strike at them.

Mikail sheathed his knife and backed to stand beside the outermost channel line. The pattern was completed, quicksilver bridged by Mikail's blood—yet it seemed somehow altered from the one Ruslan had shown Kiran. That diagram had contained multiple anchor points, but this pattern looked to have only one. And why hadn't they taken any *zhivnoi* crystals from Mikail's pack? Mikail had his eyes shut, his hands outstretched, ready to channel.

Ruslan raced past Kiran to where Melly lay unconscious on the stone. He dropped to his knees and raised his silver knife.

Understanding hit, a stab to Kiran's gut sharp as Vidai's had been. Ruslan did not need the crystals. Not with Melly's life to fuel his casting. If her death came by his blade and not the spell itself, it would not break his vow.

A wordless cry of denial burst from Kiran. Ruslan slashed the knife down.

"*No!*" Dev's scream was wild with anguished fury. Ruslan's knife jerked to a halt mere inches above Melly's chest. High in the air, Dev and Vidai had burst free of Kiran's mist veil. Dev still grappled with Vidai, but his movements had slowed, his face twisted with effort.

Ruslan's arms quivered, straining to push the knife down. The knife didn't move. He hissed a curse.

Fear gripped Kiran. Ruslan had made a terrible mistake in choosing this revenge. Dev would fail against Vidai, sacrifice them all and Ninavel with them before he let Melly die.

But Ruslan had to cast. If he didn't, if they failed—hundreds of mages would die, the city would fall—

The desperate whirl of Kiran's thoughts halted, as his gaze lit upon Stevannes.

He lay sprawled not five feet away from Kiran. Blood leaked from his ears and nose, but he still lived; his eyes were slitted open, his mouth moving in silent syllables. A thin thread of magic twisted out from his *ikilhia* to join the rippling wash flowing from Martennan and Lena. No defensive wardings protected Stevannes's body; he must have released them all in his effort to continue casting healing magic on Dev.

The Alathians deserved death, as the child did not. If Kiran took Stevannes's life and channeled it through the mark-bond to Ruslan, then Ruslan could cast.

Kiran snatched up Vidai's knife, still red with his own blood. He threw himself to his knees before Stevannes. Another thunderclap assaulted his ears; Ruslan's knife descended another inch toward Melly, halted again.

Stevannes's eyes focused on him, hazed with pain. As Kiran aimed the blade, a smile terrible in its bitterness stretched his mouth. "Do it," he said, his voice thick. "Show Marten I was right about you."

The knife felt as heavy as an iron spar in Kiran's hand. Deep inside, a familiar, forgotten voice screamed, in frantic, agonized pleas that bound his arm as tightly as any spell.

"*Do it!*" Stevannes spat at Kiran. "Better me than the child!"

Kiran buried the screaming voice deep. He reached for Ruslan through the mark-bond, made of himself a perfect, open conduit…and drove the knife home.

※

(Dev)

I clutched Vidai close, both of us struggling, striking at each other with hands and knees as well as Taint. My gut was a mass of agony, my hold weakening. If he struck at the mages again I couldn't block him, not and hold Ruslan too—but I couldn't let Ruslan kill Melly, *couldn't*—

Vidai screamed, fear and fury in the cry. He thrashed free of me in one convulsive move. I rolled mid-air, saw the quicksilver pattern burst to life, lines shining bright as the sun.

Yet I still held Ruslan's knife hand—how could Ruslan cast?

Another shout, this one horrified. Marten reached toward Stevan, shock harrowing his face.

Stevan, who had a knife hilt protruding from under his ribs, blood welling dark around the blade. Kiran gripped the hilt, his head thrown back, his expression that of a man drowning in ecstasy.

The wards on the pillars ignited, flames running over the bones. Arcs leapt from the pillars to the bubble of darkness within. The bubble bulged, like a beast within was about to claw its way out. I abandoned Vidai and reached for Melly instead, sent her rolling away from Ruslan's knife to end at Marten's feet.

The world exploded in light. A hammer blow slammed me to the ground. Fire roared over me, close enough to leave my skin smarting and my hair singed. Black spots bloomed in my vision, but I held onto consciousness with desperate determination.

The light and heat faded. I scrabbled up to a crouch. My gut burned, though only a faint flicker of the Taint remained in my head. The bone pillars had collapsed into blackened shards. The black bubble was gone, but the air within the pillars still seemed strangely dark, details difficult to make out. The way Ruslan had talked in Ninavel, I'd expected to see some bizarre charm glittering on the stone. But the shadowed shape revealed by the vanished bubble was far larger than any charm, and it didn't look at all metallic. It almost looked like the crouched figure of a man.

Scant feet away from me, Vidai groaned and raised his head. He pleaded, "Lord of the fire, my work is not yet done! The lives I've given you, *please*— the children's deaths cannot be for naught! *Kavazh-adekh ammet tajik…*"

The shadowed figure laughed; a sweet, piercing sound. Words came, welling up in my mind through the place the Taint lived. *There is no mercy in fire.*

Vidai's body tore apart in a silent spray of blood. I jerked backward, stunned. Vidai was dead at last, just as Jylla had wanted—but mother of maidens, what had killed him?

Magelight sparked behind me, grew bright, chasing away the last vestiges of darkness between the pillars. Ruslan said, calmly arrogant, "Who steals my rightful revenge?"

The man—no, *demon*—before me laughed again. He was beautiful, just like the tales of the Ghorshaba—but it was a deadly, predatory beauty, sharp and cold as an icefall. And when I looked close, it was all wrong, not human. His black hair hung to his waist in what looked like countless slender braids—but the braids moved, slow and subtle, sliding over each other like snakes. His skin was the stark bluish-white of moonlit ice; but the blue tint came from a tracery of scales. He was naked, but despite the masculine proportions of his body, his groin was smoothly sexless. And his eyes—his eyes were pits of blue flame.

The demon spoke aloud, the words sibilant and oddly inflected. "Who speaks so boldly to a child of fire?" His tongue flicked out, silver and triply forked. "Ahhh…I taste you, *akheli*. Greedy creatures, scratching about our hearthfire like rats seeking crumbs…though I see you are bold indeed."

He prowled toward Kiran. Kiran jerked the knife from Stevan's chest and held it before him like a shield, magefire dancing on the blade. He looked unsteady, almost drunk, spots of febrile color high on his cheeks. He'd *killed* Stevan. Killed a helpless, injured man…but he'd saved Melly in doing it. I felt no horror, no relief, only the numbness of shock.

Marten and Lena moved protectively in front of Melly as the demon passed them, their ringed hands raised and their eyes wary. The demon didn't look their way. He stepped over Stevan's body without glancing down and circled Kiran, his tongue tasting the air.

He said to Ruslan, "You stole and bound a temple child, one molded in our image? Even for one as weak and poisoned as this, your life belongs to the red-horned hunters. A pity…your blood holds enough fire to taste sweet."

Molded in our image…and I could see it. The black hair, the icy pale skin, the blue eyes, the sharp lines of Kiran's cheekbones…all a shadow of the demon's inhuman beauty. Kiran was staring at the demon, his hands white on the knife.

"I fear no hunters." If Ruslan was rattled by facing a creature he'd insisted didn't exist, he hid it well.

The demon smiled, revealing ranks of disturbingly red, pointed teeth. "You will," he said. "Did you think the temple's worship false?"

Something in Ruslan's expression suggested he'd thought exactly that. But he said only, "Yours was the power Vidai zha-Dakhar borrowed. Did you give it freely?"

I knew what he was really asking. *Were you a prisoner who might be grateful for release? Or did you share Vidai's goal, making you an enemy we must destroy?*

But how did you destroy a demon? In the tales, only Shaikar himself had the power to unmake them.

"We bargained, he and I," the demon said. "He provided me an ancient treasure, long lost from the halls of flame. In return, I gave him his wish: to touch the fire within me, wield it as I do…though only so long as he could hold me." The demon glanced at Vidai's remains and made a noise like water sizzling off a sun-heated rock. "He was so low a creature, the gap between us was too far without a bridge to span it." The demon glanced at Melly, then turned his gaze on me. "Some of you rats born on our threshold have souls scarred by our fire, enough that I can touch you, use your lives as timbers."

Claws pierced the Tainted spot in my head and ripped through my mind. I screamed, clutching my head, the world lost in a red haze—

"The charm!" Lena shouted. "Take it off, Dev!"

I choked out the trigger word and yanked the band from my wrist. The pain in my head faded, though my gut still felt packed with razor-edged shards.

Ruslan hadn't taken his gaze from the demon. "You call the Well of the World your hearthfire. Did you know Vidai meant to destroy it?"

The demon's head cocked. "Destroy? If a dam fails, is the water destroyed? We care not for how our fire flows." He made the sizzling noise again. "If you seek favor, you will not find it, *akheli*. Your life is forfeit, and nothing you do will turn the hunters aside from your scent. But after long confinement, I am eager to taste sweeter lives than those of rat-children."

Ruslan pointed at Marten and Lena. "Take them and be welcome."

They drew breath to chant, light sparking on their rings. I jammed the charm back on my wrist with the trigger word crowding my mouth. But the demon shook his head.

"Not first. Brighter blood than theirs was woven in the spell that freed me…" He blurred forward toward Mikail. Mikail leaped away, magefire blazing from his hands to strike the demon. The demon only shivered, as if caught in a cold rain, and pounced on him. Mikail cried out, wounds gaping open on his body; green fire limned his skin, and the wounds closed just as swiftly, only to rip open again.

Ruslan leaped forward, horror and fury combined on his face. Magefire lashed at the demon; the demon laughed. "It was we who taught the *akheli* to savor pain." His tongue darted to touch the blood pouring from Mikail's wounds.

Mikail gasped, his body slumping. Ruslan lunged for the demon, hands outstretched as if to tear him from Mikail bare-handed.

Kiran shouted a string of sibilant, guttural words.

The demon stilled. He dropped Mikail, who collapsed in a boneless heap, and turned to Kiran. Ruslan turned also, surprise writ large on his face.

Kiran repeated the words, stumbling over them this time. His eyes were glassy and huge, his body shaking.

"Do you say so?" The demon made a chuffing sound. "You have blood-right; they are yours to kill."

"Then leave," Kiran said. "Return to your fire, and do not touch us or Ninavel again."

The demon smiled his red, fanged grin. "I'll yield, child. But only so long as you live…and I think that is not long. Soon enough, their blood is mine."

He vanished.

For a moment, nobody moved. Then Mikail stirred, groaning. His wounds shimmered and closed. Ruslan shut his eyes in relief. For once, I shared it. If the demon came back before we could get the fuck out of here, better if he had someone with tastier blood than mine to draw his attention. But what had the demon meant about Kiran not living long? Was that only in comparison to demonkind?

I jumped in surprise when Kiran spoke again. He said in the thin, wavering voice of a child, "Ruslan…I remember the temple, I…"

Ruslan hurried toward him; halted. He reached for Kiran, slow and cautious as a man seeking to gentle a skittish horse. "You need not remember it, Kiran. You are safe now."

"My barriers," Kiran said. "I can't rebuild them. It hurts, Ruslan, it *hurts*—" He keened and toppled over, his back arching into a taut, straining bow.

Ruslan caught him, sank to his knees on the stone. Kiran convulsed in his arms, his eyes rolled up to the whites, his heels drumming on the ground.

"Kiran!" Never before had I seen Ruslan afraid. I stood frozen, at a total loss. What was wrong with Kiran?

"*Marten.*" The sharpness of Lena's tone made me turn. Marten was staring at Kiran with an expression that left my chest hollow. There was no surprise in it. Only a silent, grim struggle, as if he weighed some terrible decision.

Lena had seen it too. She caught his arm. "What do you know?"

Marten met her eyes. After a heartbeat, hers widened. The blood drained from her face to leave it sallow. "Give him the drug, Marten! He thought Stevan his enemy—" Lena stopped, swiped a hand over her eyes. Her voice tightened. "The demon. You heard what he said. If Kiran dies, and he returns…"

"Yes." The struggle on Marten's face eased. He drew a vial of black liquid from a pocket.

Lena snatched it from him and raced to Kiran's side. Ruslan caught her hand, glaring at the vial. "What is that?"

"It will stop the convulsions." Lena tore her hand free. "Hold him while I get his mouth open."

Ruslan's glare didn't lessen, but he obeyed. Lena pressed her fingers deep into Kiran's jaw, his neck; the muscles slackened and his teeth parted. She dumped the vial's contents into Kiran's mouth and stroked his throat to force a swallow.

Kiran arched backward so hard I heard his spine crack. Ruslan snapped, "You said it would—"

Kiran slumped with a long, wavering sigh. His eyes fluttered open, but they were unfocused, the pupils blown wide. Ruslan pressed his hands to Kiran's temples. For an instant he held the pose; then his head jerked up.

"*What have you done?*" he shouted at Marten.

A bleak smile touched Marten's mouth. "Did you think I would simply hand you Kiran without taking precautions first? We have not your skill with bindings, Ruslan…but we know far more of the body's functioning than you have ever bothered to learn. There is a certain balance of humors in adult mages that allows them to withstand the energies of confluence magic. Distort that balance enough—as happens when a body has built a dependency on a certain drug, and that drug is withdrawn—and spellcasting itself will push body and soulfire further and further out of balance, until any touch of magic brings death even a blood mage cannot escape. Unless more of the drug is given…and we hold the only knowledge of its formulation."

Horror leached through me. Marten's plan hadn't been to poison Ruslan, but Kiran? Turn him into an addict, chain him with a drug that ensured he'd die if he tried to slip his bonds? The Alathians must have drugged Kiran's food during those long weeks in Tamanath…but Lena hadn't known of it. Talm couldn't have either, or else Lizaveta would have seen it in his mind.

Of course Talm and Lena hadn't. Marten must not have wanted any of the mages who regularly guarded Kiran to know, in case they let something slip. Because long before the trip to Ninavel, the Council had wanted a way to kill Kiran—and that didn't exactly match with all Marten's promises to him of sanctuary and acceptance.

Ruslan looked ready to tear Marten's throat out with his teeth. "You will tell me of this drug."

"No," Marten said simply. "You cannot cast against us, cannot take the knowledge from my mind. I do not even have any of the drug here. Lena gave Kiran enough of a similar substance to keep him alive for a few hours yet; but any spellcasting will hasten his death. If you wish Kiran to live, you must let me take him back to Alathia."

"Alathia!" I blurted. "You'll never make it to Alathia in only a few hours, Marten!" Thirty miles from the cirque to the border…that meant at least three days' travel over terrain as rough as that of the cirque's surroundings.

Marten said, "The Watch waits just outside our wards. For a distance this close, I need only mark an anchor point and signal them"—he slid a message charm from his pocket, held it up—"and they can cast a translocation spell to bring any who stand in the anchor point's sigils to them. Once we cross inside the wards, they will give Kiran another dose of the drug. If that comes soon enough after the translocation, he may survive. But if he remains here, his death is certain. The choice is yours, Ruslan."

He may survive… Marten wasn't sure Kiran should live. Did he know why Kiran had killed Stevan, or had he been too busy casting to see Ruslan's attempt on Melly? But gods, his so-called precautions…he'd planned all along that if Kiran slid too far into blood magic, he'd simply stand back and let him die. The bastard! So much for that talk of *I will not abandon you.*

Ruslan didn't move, his body rigid. I couldn't breathe. What would he do? Would he let Kiran go, knowing he couldn't cast against Alathia to get him back? Or would he rather see Kiran dead than let Marten win?

Mikail spoke, hoarse and strained. "Ruslan."

Ruslan turned to hold Mikail's gaze. I couldn't read in their expressions what they said to each other. But Ruslan's fingers dug hard into Kiran's shirt, over Kiran's heart. He looked up at Marten, his hazel eyes bleak and furious.

"Take him. But my knife will find you even if my spells do not, Martennan. We *akheli* live long…and we do not forget. You have sealed your country's ruin."

Marten's grip tightened on the message charm. He said to Lena, "Go find Cara. I'll scribe the sigils."

So he meant to take us all to safety, not just Kiran. I hadn't been sure. The clouds above were clearing, patches of blue sky showing through. Across the tundra and talus, the caves at the base of the Scythe of Night were visible, dark holes dotting the lower cliffs.

"Wait," I said to Lena. "While you're looking for Cara, can you check if there are any other people in the caves? Other kids?" Like Pello's son.

"I will cast a seeking spell." Lena hurried away from the lake toward the caves.

Ruslan stood, but Kiran twisted to clutch at him. "Ruslan…" Fear glazed his eyes, his face as white as the demon's. "No, please! They'll bind me, change me…"

Oh, gods. He still believed Mikail's lies, thought himself given up to suffer at the hands of enemies.

Pain spread over Ruslan's face. He knelt again and clasped Kiran to him, whispered in his ear. Kiran's panicked breathing slowed—only to speed again, as Ruslan murmured something else.

"No!" Kiran sounded more terrified than ever. "Ruslan, *no*, you must not—"

Ruslan touched Kiran's brow. Kiran's eyes rolled up, his body relaxing into unconsciousness.

Fuck. What had Ruslan done to him? Marten was watching them with grim intensity. Would he give Kiran the drug if we made it through the border? Or did he think Kiran beyond saving, as Stevan had?

I glanced at Stevan's body. His eyes were open and staring, his mouth drawn in a rictus. Blood was crusted on the wound left by Kiran's knife.

Was Stevan right? This business of temples, and blood-right…was there some deeper link between Kiran and demonkind than that shadow of physical resemblance?

I didn't know. And damn, my gut hurt. I staggered over to Melly, lifted her off the stone. "Marten. Can you break this sleep-fast charm and wake her up?"

He said shortly, "Leave her sleeping. Our healers will look at her after we cross the border. And you. Your injuries will only worsen without treatment."

In other words, *don't even think about running off after the spell's cast.*

I hadn't planned on it. "Marten…did you see what happened with Melly? Or were you too busy casting?"

He said, "I saw, but I am not yet certain of Kiran's reasons. If I bring him to the Council as he is now…"

He didn't continue, but I heard what he wasn't saying. They'd sentence Kiran to death in a heartbeat. A sentence they could now carry out with terrible ease.

I lowered my voice even further. "Just now, did…did Ruslan mess with his head again?"

"I felt no casting," Marten said. "Do you remember what I told you about showing Kiran the truth?"

"Yeah." Though even if Kiran agreed to look at my memories, and believed them… "Would that be enough?" I wasn't so sure the Council would care.

Marten said, "No. There is more you must convince him to do. We'll speak of it in Alathia." With that, he turned away.

Well, that was disturbingly vague. But I was too tired and sore to care. I settled against a boulder and cradled Melly to me, stroked her hair off her bruised face. For a time, I didn't think of anything else but her slow, steady breathing.

"Dev!" I looked up to see Cara kneeling before me, concern in her eyes. Her injured arm was bound in a sling, but her lacerations had closed, her bruises faded. Lena must've given her charms or cast some healing spellwork. I gave Cara a wan smile.

"We kept Vidai busy, all right," I said.

Her laugh came out more like a sob. "So I hear. And look who I found."

She moved aside. Behind her was a scrap of a boy with hard, wary eyes. He had Pello's wild mop of curls, though his face was round, his skin Sulanian-dark. His clothes were ragged, and one ankle was bruised and raw.

Maybe Vidai hadn't wanted to kill yet another child. I remembered Pello gasping out those anguished phrases of Varkevian, and my heart twisted within me. Likely the boy had never known his father. Just as Melly hadn't known Sethan; and now, they never would.

"I've something for you," I said to the boy. "It's from your father. He was...a brave man." The crescent moon necklace hung around my own neck. I slipped it off and handed it to him.

He didn't speak, but one fist closed tight on the little moon of malachite.

"We're ready," Marten said. I levered myself to my feet, groaning as pain spiked through my stomach. Melly felt as heavy as ten coal sacks, but I shrugged off Lena's offer to carry her. Stupid, maybe. But I couldn't let her go.

Lena herded us into a ring of sigils scribed on a granite slab, well away from the scorched and darkened lines of Ruslan's quicksilver pattern. Kiran lay huddled at Marten's feet. Stevan's body lay in the ring also, wrapped in a leather coat I recognized as Cara's.

Beyond the ring, Ruslan stood framed by the Cirque's sky-piercing Knives, watching us with glittering eyes. Mikail sat by his side with his head hanging low. New anger burned in me. We'd saved Ninavel, but I didn't feel a damn bit of triumph in it. Life would go on, streetside—my friends would laugh and dance in the night markets, safe from riots and from dying of thirst—but Ruslan and those like him would go right on killing as they pleased. The bastard hadn't suffered so much as a hangnail in this, while so many others paid with their lives.

I understood now the desperate outrage that had driven Talm and Vidai. There had to be a way to change things in Ninavel. One that didn't involve killing kids or destroying the city outright.

Marten and Lena started singing. The sigils around us lit. Kiran stirred at Marten's feet, moaning. Before light rose to swallow us, I saw Ruslan stride forward, his gaze locked on Kiran. His mouth moved in one silent word.

Remember.

CHAPTER TWENTY-SIX

(Kiran)

"**K**iran? Can you hear me?"

The voice was female and concerned, but it didn't sound like Lizaveta's. Kiran opened his eyes, confused.

He lay on a cot in a one-room wooden cabin, the rough-hewn planks of walls and floor covered in freshly laid ward lines. Dusty gold shafts of sunlight slanted through pine branches outside the cabin's single small window.

A young woman leaned over him, studying him with grave intensity. Circles showed dark beneath her eyes, and lines of stress and sorrow marked her freckled face. Kiran's gaze skipped downward to land on her uniform.

Alathian. Kiran thrashed upright on the cot, his heart racing. He sought power to reinforce his barriers—and cried out, his hands flying up to his temples, as agony seared through his head.

"Don't," the woman said, anxious. "Kiran, you must not try any spellwork. Your soulfire is not yet recovered from our translocation. If you let me, I can ease the pain…" She reached for his forehead.

"No!" Kiran flinched back. He knew her now: Lena, Martennan's first lieutenant. Did she mean to bind him? Had they done so already? His head hurt, he couldn't think—

Lena drew her hand back. "My apologies…I know you believe us your enemies." She sighed and pushed aside a lock of dark hair that had straggled free of her braids. "Do you remember what happened when we fought Vidai?"

Fragmented flashes tumbled through Kiran's mind. He took a deep breath and focused inward. His barriers were terrifyingly thin, his *ikilhia* guttering lower than he'd ever felt it. But raw as his mind was, he sensed no foreign bindings, only the same gaping holes in his older memories. As for more recent events…he remembered fighting, remembered…

The knife sinking deep to pierce Stevannes's heart, ikilhia *bursting free in a flood so intoxicating Kiran thought his own heart might fail from the pleasure of it—*

"I…helped Ruslan cast," he said, the words thick on his tongue.

Lena's breath faltered, grief darkening her eyes. "You took Stevan's life."

Pain colored her voice, though he didn't hear anger. But she must be angry; he'd killed one of her friends. Had she and Stevannes been as close as he and Mikail? He couldn't imagine the chasm in his heart if Mikail died. Guilt shot through him, fracturing the memory of that terrible, wondrous ecstasy.

He shouldn't feel guilt. Stevannes had been his enemy. Besides, if he hadn't killed Stevannes… "We all would have died, and Ninavel with us, if I had not," he said to Lena.

Her eyes searched his face. He didn't know what she was looking for. After a short silence, she said, "Do you recall what happened afterward?"

Everything after was hazy and muddled, like a fever-dream. He remembered trembling, feeling sick and strange, as something prowled around him, watching him with eyes that dragged at him like claws.

The demon. It had spoken of temples, and scarred souls, and attacked Mikail…and out of Kiran's horror and desperation, a fissure had cracked open in the wall at the core of his memories. He'd said—

His mind recoiled in a rejection so violent it nearly shattered his hold on consciousness. He hastily blinked away the darkness that threatened his vision.

"I don't remember." He didn't. Wouldn't. The wall was solid. The demon had left, and Mikail had survived—that was all he needed to recall while he remained in Alathian hands.

"You don't know why we brought you here?" Lena looked anxious again.

Here. Kiran glanced around the cabin. The wooden walls…and beyond his fragile barriers and the sharp, forbidding mutter of the wards, the aether was dead of magical energies. Another flash came, of Ruslan shouting at Martennan, something about a drug…

Alathia. He was in Alathia, trapped behind their border wards, where Ruslan could not reach him. A new memory broke over him, a brief instant of clarity as bitingly sharp as mountain air: Ruslan holding him close, whispering, *I once burned a confluence to claim you for my own. I would not let Martennan take you from me, except that I have seen your soul today. You are* akheli*, and you will break your bonds and come back to us. I promise you, the Alathians will pay in blood for daring to touch you. If a* nathahlen *can bargain with a demon, think what better alliance an* akheli *can make!*

Ruslan must not bargain with those…those creatures! Cold, unreasoning horror left Kiran reeling. He scrambled off the cot, only to fall back with a strangled cry as the wards' magic lashed across his mind.

Lena made a low, dismayed noise. "Kiran, please. You need to take care."

Kiran gripped his knees to hide the shaking of his hands. "You must let me go. Now! Or Ruslan will take Vidai's path. You saw what an untalented man could do with a demon's power. Imagine Ruslan turning that against your country!"

No surprise showed on Lena's face, only solemn, worried intensity. "He will do it anyway. Even if we released you. His pride and arrogance will allow no less, after Marten outmaneuvered him."

"Free me, and I will convince Ruslan not to deal with demons." Kiran had to convince him. *Otherwise,* the fear whispered, *he will bring destruction on himself and all you love along with those you hate, and innocents will die in numbers Vidai never dreamed.* If Kiran returned and enlisted Lizaveta and Mikail to help cool Ruslan's temper and recall him to caution, Ruslan would yield. Ruslan would not abandon the idea of revenge entirely, but he would take a more temperate course.

Lena said, "I fear he would instead convince you. Just as he convinced we are your enemies. The mark-bond gives him too much power over you, Kiran. You can't hope to deal with him as an equal."

Of course he wasn't Ruslan's equal, inexperienced and damaged as he was. Kiran changed tactics. "What does it profit you to keep me?" he demanded. "If you kill me to spite him, you will only goad him further. Or do you mean to bind me again in some ill-considered attempt to use me against him?" Whatever the Alathians' intent, Kiran had to escape them. Yet right now he felt so weak he doubted he could make it across the room, let alone break the wards that imprisoned him.

"Marten brought you here to *help* you." For the barest instant, Lena displayed a dark, strained desperation equal to his own. "There is someone you must speak with." She unbarred the cabin door.

Dev edged through. He looked as weary as Lena, his wiry shoulders slumped and his face shadowed, but his green eyes remained sharp as ever. When he crossed the wards on the cabin floor, the lines stayed dark and inert. The wards were keyed directly to Kiran, then; an important fact to know.

"Kiran." Dev crouched beside Kiran's cot and said to Lena, "Give us a minute, huh?"

"I'll be right outside," she said.

Kiran suspected that was a warning more than an assurance. He eyed Dev warily as the door shut behind Lena. Ruslan had said Dev was Sechaveh's man, but Kiran feared the Alathians held Melly now. If so, Dev would do their bidding without hesitation.

Dev heaved a sigh. "Couldn't tell you this with an Alathian in the room. It's disturbing enough to hear myself say it. But...thanks. For, uh...making sure Ruslan didn't cast using Melly."

"She didn't deserve to die." The words escaped Kiran before he thought.

"No," Dev said. "Do you wonder where you got that idea? I think you know it didn't come from Ruslan."

Kiran shifted on the cot, uneasy. The conviction was as strong in him as his certainty that disaster would result from Ruslan seeking out demons... yet if he were honest, he didn't fully understand the grounds for either belief. "The Alathians bound me. Some effects still remain."

"They did bind you," Dev agreed. "But not like that. They bound your magic, that's all. They didn't fuck with your head. That's Ruslan's specialty."

Ruslan had destroyed Kiran's memories, but not with malicious intent. Or so Mikail insisted, and Kiran believed his mage-brother. How could he not, when he knew the depth of Mikail's love for him? And despite Ruslan's high-handed ways and harsh punishments, Kiran knew Ruslan loved him just as fiercely. *I once burned a confluence to claim you for my own...*

He crossed his arms and gave Dev a cold stare. "Ruslan loves me, while the Alathians tried to cripple me. It seems clear enough whose account I should believe."

Dev rubbed at the spot between his eyebrows. "We could argue about this all night," he said. "But you know, there's an easier way. I told you if I got Melly safe I'd let you see my memories. All of them."

A thread of curiosity surfaced; Kiran buried it. He needed to escape, not let the Alathians lure him into relaxing his guard. "I don't need to see your memories."

"You're afraid," Dev said. "You don't want to think Ruslan and Mikail lied to you. Because yeah, there are few things worse than finding out someone you love betrayed you. But tying on a blindfold doesn't change the truth. It only makes you more likely to walk off a cliff."

The air in the cabin felt suddenly stifling, the wards' mutter scraping all the harder against his injured mind. Kiran shook his head. Dev was wrong about Ruslan and Mikail. This was all some Alathian trick. "Who says your memories are the truth?"

Dev cast his eyes to the ceiling. "Not this again," he muttered. "Listen. I don't trust the Alathians either. For reasons you'll see, if you look in my head. So by all means, if you find somebody's messed with my mind, I'd love to know."

Kiran was silent. He shouldn't do this. Shouldn't be tempted. On the other hand, when he found evidence of tampering, as he surely would…he might use it to convince Dev to help him escape.

A crooked grin twisted Dev's mouth. "At the very least, you'll get to see where you traveled in the mountains."

Kiran remembered Dev saying, *You weren't bad, on rock.* Hesitation crystallized into decision.

"Do you have a knife?" he asked Dev.

"A knife." Dev looked wary now.

Kiran smiled, not kindly. "If you want me to look in your mind, it will be on my terms." Blood contact would make the search far easier, a boon with his *ikilhia* so weak—and it would allow him to cast any manner of binding he chose upon Dev. Assuming he could manage a casting in his current condition. Or that the Alathians wouldn't notice it if he did.

He thought Dev might bolt. Instead, Dev studied him, long and hard. At last he muttered a curse and pulled a thin blade from a slit in his belt. "You'd better not suck the life out of me."

"I don't need a knife for that." Kiran meant it as a warning, in case the Alathians intended to play some harsher game than merely confusing him with false memories. But when Dev flinched, guilt returned to plague him. The Alathians might easily have altered Dev's mind without his consent, making him as much their prisoner as Kiran.

If so, Kiran wouldn't try to bind Dev. He'd free them both. He softened his tone. "If this is no trick, you need not fear I will harm you."

"It's not a trick." Dev handed Kiran the blade.

"Give me your hand," Kiran said.

Dev extended it gingerly, as if he was afraid Kiran might burn it off. Kiran sliced a swift line down Dev's palm, then a matching one in his own.

Dev breathed like a man running, but he didn't pull his hand back. Kiran clasped it and slid through the blood contact deep into Dev's mind.

Strange, to explore a mind so defenseless, lacking any of the myriad wardings that layered a mage's inner self. To Kiran's surprise, Dev's memories shone in a thick, tightly woven web, with no sign of holes, discolorations, or other evidence of tampering. But right at the heart of Dev's mind, a raw, recent wound lurked, ugly and dark. Strange threads of energy trailed downward from it to meet a binding anchored deep within Dev's body. Kiran touched the threads, felt Dev gasp and jerk.

The Alathians bound you, he said to Dev.

Negation came from Dev. *It wasn't the Alathians, it was Vidai. He stole a blood-mark of mine along with a bunch of others, and used the demon's power to bind us all to the confluence so we'd die if it burned. The Alathians said that's all the binding does.* Beneath Dev's veneer of confidence lurked a hint of fear, growing stronger. *Were they wrong?*

Kiran focused more tightly, ignoring warning twinges of pain. Both binding and wound gave off a chill dissonance all too reminiscent of the demon's strange aura. The sensation was far different than the subtle shimmer of Alathian spellwork. The binding did appear to affect only Dev's body, but those odd threads trailing from the wound in his mind…

If the Alathians claimed it was safe to leave you bound, they lied, Kiran said. He could offer to break the binding in exchange for Dev's cooperation, but he wasn't sure he could break the spell without harming or even killing Dev. Not something he was willing to risk, not when he needed Dev's help to escape. He shut out the heightened pulse of Dev's worry, and turned his attention to Dev's memories.

The Alathians must be cleverer than Kiran had thought. No sign of alteration showed, no matter how closely he focused. He would have to examine the memories individually to find the proof he needed.

He sought the image he'd seen in Bren's mind: himself, watching as Bren hired Dev to guide him. There, a matching image…he sank into a shining strand of the past.

✳

(Dev)

Kiran yanked his hand from mine. I blinked, dazed, still half-drowned in memories. I'd relived every instant of the past few months, all the way from my first meeting with Kiran until this cabin, again and again until I wasn't sure any longer what was past and what was present. How long had he spent rummaging around in my head? It was still day outside the window, though the light leaking through the pine branches had gained a rusty quality that spoke of approaching sunset. Only an hour or so had passed, then, and not the eternity it had seemed.

Kiran was staring into space, his profile unreadable. He was gripping the cot edges as tightly as if he feared it might vanish from beneath him.

"Kiran?"

He bent his head, his black hair sliding over his shoulders to block his face. "Your memories—I thought I would see signs of tampering, but..."

"You didn't."

"No."

I said cautiously, "So...you believe me, then."

He turned his head, and my breath caught at the lost, wild look in his eyes. "I don't know! I don't know what to believe. But it doesn't matter—I must return to Ruslan. If I don't, Ruslan will bargain as Vidai did, and the result will be the destruction of far more than a single city."

He said the last part with utter certainty. I remembered Ruslan whispering in his ear, and Kiran's frantic pleading in response—fuck. "Ruslan told you he means to seek out a demon."

Kiran nodded. "I can talk him out of it if I'm allowed the chance. But I saw in your mind—the Alathians intend to kill me. They will withhold their drug and let me die. Martennan would have done it in the cirque if not for the demon's threat."

His voice cracked on the word "demon." I winced, remembering my speculation about the link between Kiran and demonkind, knowing he'd seen it. Seen everything—including my own uncertainty over whether he had gone too far to be saved.

"You must help me escape," Kiran said. "*Please.* If you don't, it's not just Alathia that will suffer. You, and Cara, and Melly...you're in just as much danger. After seeing your mind, I know all you've done on my behalf—I don't want you hurt."

He didn't believe what he'd seen in my memories, not all the way. Not if he was talking about going back to Ruslan. "Since you've seen my mind, you know I'll help you run to Shaikar himself before I help you become Ruslan's mind-fucked slave."

His teeth showed in a brief, frustrated grimace. "I must go back to him. It's the only way."

"No," I said. "It isn't. Ruslan needs to be stopped, yeah. But you're fooling yourself if you think mere words would do it."

Kiran laughed, sharp and wild. "You cannot kill him. You saw what it took to destroy Simon."

"It took you," I said.

Kiran looked away. "Simon killed himself; I was only the catalyst. Ruslan is far too clever to make a similar mistake."

"You know his temper," I said. "Drive him wild enough, and he'll break his blood vow and burn to ash. Or are you saying you don't *want* to kill him?"

Kiran didn't answer. My hands itched to shake him. "For fuck's sake, Kiran! He murdered your lover, burned away your memories—you *know* I'm not lying in this!"

Kiran turned back to me. His face was stark and bloodless, his jaw tight. "I know you believe it. But after all that's happened, you can't blame me for being cautious over what I take as truth. I didn't see any signs of alteration in you, but that might mean only that I lack the skill to find them."

He was reaching, and he had to know it. I choked back sharp words, remembering my shock after Red Dal had sold me off, my countless desperate rationalizations: Red Dal had been forced into the sale, he'd come back for me, his affection wasn't a lie…Jylla hadn't tried to talk me out of it. She'd only listened, and let me figure out the truth for myself as the black days wore on and my anger grew.

Instead of pushing Kiran harder, I said, "You told me Vidai's binding wasn't safe. Could you get rid of the damn thing?" The mages of the Watch had hemmed and hawed when I asked, claiming the binding would need to be examined first by specialists at the Arcanum.

"Perhaps," Kiran said. "But—"

A knock cut through his answer. The cabin door creaked open to admit Marten, and Kiran fell silent. He hunched in on himself and watched Marten like a man trapped in a sandcat's den.

Marten said to me, "Did he see your memories?"

I nodded. "Marten, he says Ruslan means to—"

"Forge an alliance with demonkind, yes, Lena told me. I feared that might be Ruslan's intent." Marten drew his hands over his face. "Quite an unpleasant prospect. Though given the demon's talk of Ruslan's life being forfeit, Ruslan may not find alliance as easy as he might hope."

"You can't count on that," Kiran protested. "You must free me!"

"No." Marten's voice hardened. "I will not have you go back to him. Not as you are."

Kiran tensed on the cot. "Not as I am?"

Marten looked weary. "A poor choice of words. Kiran…this unfortunate situation you are in is my doing, and I know it. All I ask now is for you to let me help you out of it."

Kiran said, "Help me? If I believe Dev's memories...you lied to me. Betrayed me, used me, addicted me to a drug so you might kill me...what *help* can I expect from you now?"

I'd once wanted him to be more wary of Marten, but this new hard-eyed Kiran was painful to see.

"I suggested the drug to the Council, it's true," Marten said. "Not to kill you, Kiran. I hoped the drug would serve as a replacement for their binding on your magic. I knew how you longed to cast again, and I thought I could give that to you."

I couldn't keep silent. "Maybe you should've thought to *ask* him which he preferred before dosing him, Marten." Not that I believed Marten's motives had been anywhere near so innocent as he claimed. But saying so directly wouldn't help a damn thing.

Marten said, "I would have asked, had the Council allowed it. But the past is done. Now I have something better to offer you, Kiran: your lost memories. At your trial, you allowed us within your mind, and I was one of those who cast. I saw your memories, lived them as my own. If you let me within your mind again, I can give you all I saw."

One of Kiran's hands went up in a warding gesture. "No. You'll bind me."

Marten sighed. "Not yet, though if you wish to live, you'll have to accept another binding on your power. But before then...if you don't take these memories back, I can't hope to sway the Council to spare you."

"The Council would be fools to kill him!" I protested. "If you want to beat Ruslan, you need Kiran's help. Not to mention whatever he knows about demons..."

Kiran jerked as if I'd struck him. "I know nothing of them!"

That was so patently a lie it left me tongue-tied in surprise. Marten said gently to Kiran, "You mean you remember nothing of them. I saw the wall in your mind. We could not breach it at your trial, but now...the imbalance you currently suffer has weakened more than just your soulfire. Not such a bad thing, perhaps...as Dev says, we may need those memories."

Kiran edged backward on the cot, eyeing Marten with redoubled wariness. "Free me, and I will do my best to stop Ruslan from destroying you and your country. Kill me, and you forfeit all hope of advantage. Those are your only options, Martennan. I will not let you into my mind."

Frustration flickered over Marten's face. "Kiran. Think. What have you to lose?"

Kiran smiled, painful and terrible. "My self. Such as it is. You, Ruslan, even this temple the demon spoke of—you all want to mold me into some shape that pleases you. I want to make my own choices."

I remembered saying to Ruslan, *All I want is to let him make his own choice.* I'd meant it at the time…but even then, I worried he wouldn't choose against Ruslan. Now that I'd watched him kill a man, seen the bliss on his face afterward—I wasn't at all sure of it.

He'd saved Melly from Ruslan, and Ninavel from Vidai, and he wanted to stop Ruslan from killing us now. He hadn't yet changed out of all recognition from the Kiran I knew.

Marten said, "If you've seen Dev's memories, you know of your lover Alisa. Will you choose to destroy her in truth? She lived still in your memories. If you leave her forgotten, you erase her as if she never existed. I saw her, Kiran: she never tried to alter you or possess you. She only loved you, in a way you had never seen, hadn't any idea was possible. Even Ruslan could not eradicate all the traces of that love in you. She gave you such a great gift… would you turn your back on her now? Let her vanish into the darkness of time unremembered and unloved?"

Kiran went white, breathing as if each inhalation hurt him. "Then let me into *your* mind, Martennan. Show me your memories."

Marten shook his head. "If I did that, the Council would demand your death, and perhaps mine as well. I bear too many of my country's secrets."

Kiran gave a strangled laugh. "Dev is right to fear your clever tongue. Yet I can see the truth you wish to hide—you don't care what I remember of Alisa. You only want to take what you think I know about these demons. You'll tear my mind apart in your search, and afterward…what need have you for me? You'll kill me just as you wanted to do in the mountains."

"I don't wish to harm you!" Marten's voice rose. "I only want to return what Ruslan stole from you."

Yeah, even I didn't buy that one. Maybe Marten wouldn't spellcast against Kiran, but he sure as hell wanted to sift through Kiran's head so he could decide how best to use him.

"You try to bind me with words even now," Kiran said. "*No.*"

"You—!" Marten pinched the bridge of his nose and turned to me. "A word, outside."

I followed him out the door into the trampled forest clearing beyond. Cinnabar trees towered over a scattering of squat cabins. The sun was setting, the scraps of western sky visible between thick-needled cinnabar branches a molten orange. Two unfamiliar mages stood some ten feet away, staring at Kiran's cabin with fierce, intent eyes. Guards, watching for any hint of spellwork on Kiran's part.

The camp wasn't even a mile inside the border, though we were too far for me to hear the rush of the Elenn River that marked it. The translocation spell had left us kneeling amid ferns and fiddleneck flowers on the riverbank, surrounded by a horde of stern, uniformed mages.

Kiran had been screaming and convulsing at Marten's feet. They'd slapped an amulet on him—one I recognized, to my great surprise: it was his old magic-blocking one. That calmed him some, though the convulsions continued as they carried him through the border. I hadn't seen him again until now, being stuck on my own cot while mages poked and prodded me with an anxious Cara looking on. They'd already cast to heal her arm, leaving her hale except for fading shadows of bruises. The mages had chanted over me until I thought I'd go crazy, and made me drink a whole host of rancid-tasting liquids. At least now my gut no longer hurt every time I moved. Afterward, they'd moved on to checking over Melly; I'd wanted to stay, but Marten had insisted I go to Kiran.

Melly. Hell. If Kiran's warning about Ruslan was true, she wasn't safe here—wouldn't be safe anywhere. Wards wouldn't stop a demon. *Damn* Ruslan!

Marten led me past the guard mages to the edge of the clearing. In the shadow of a massive cinnabar pine, he stopped and faced me. "You must convince Kiran to allow me within his mind."

"I don't know if I can," I said, honestly. "You saw him in there. He's stubborn when he's decided on something." My memories weren't helping, full as they were of hate and distrust of Marten.

"You *must*." Marten said it like he thought I was the one holding out. I glared at him.

"I know the stakes here. But damn it, Marten, you can't just sit back and count on me to clean up your mess. You're the one who fucked him over; it's no wonder he'd rather die than let you in his head."

"Marten!" Lena hurried across the clearing toward us. She had the jeweled band of a message charm clamped in one hand, and she looked so worried it set all my nerves jumping. "The Council has already considered your report—they want you to contact them for new orders."

Marten's face sagged in dismay. "So soon…I'd hoped Councilor Varellian could gain me more time." He took the message charm with slow, heavy reluctance.

New orders…about Kiran? The Council couldn't be so stupid as to sentence him to death. Right?

Marten slid the charm into his wrist, and his eyes took on the familiar distance of spellcasting. I turned to Lena, words spilling out in protest.

"The Council can't kill Kiran! You need what he knows, and he's already chained as tight as you could want, thanks to your Shaikar-cursed drug!"

Lena said, low and reluctant, "You assume too much. If the Council decides Kiran is too dangerous to trust, there are ways to take his knowledge that will not require his cooperation…or his survival. If the drug is withheld, before he dies he will grow too weak to fight our casting."

I went cold, all the way through. "Khalmet's bloodsoaked hand! You call yourselves better than Ruslan?"

Pain flared in Lena's eyes. "I don't want Kiran dead. Neither does Marten! But Stevan's death is not something the Council will easily forgive. Especially Councilor Niskenntal…Stevan was his sister's son."

"Fuck," I said, with feeling. I remembered Niskenntal from my testimony at Kiran's trial. The skinny, sour-faced asshole had argued I should be burned alive, and all I'd done was smuggle a few charms.

The sky between the cinnabar branches had gone blood-red. I prayed it wasn't an omen. "If the Council decides against Kiran, how long before the withdrawal kills him?" How long would I have to try and get him free?

Lena let out a shuddering breath and braced a hand on the cinnabar pine's trunk, her eyes locked on Marten and the message charm. "We gave Kiran a dose of the drug immediately after we crossed the border, but his soulfire remains terribly unbalanced. Even though there is no confluence here, without further doses his deterioration will be rapid. I am no healer, but…he might survive a few days. Far less, if he attempts to cast or if any powerful spells are cast by others in his vicinity."

"You mean, spells like the Watch would cast trying to rip knowledge from his mind."

"Yes." Lena's fingers dug white into cinnabar bark.

Marten shifted, his shoulders slumping. He took off the message charm, and I didn't need to see the bleak defeat in his eyes to know the news wasn't good.

"What orders, Marten?" Lena looked like she was praying to Alathia's twin gods.

"We are forbidden from giving Kiran any more of the drug," Marten said, his voice brittle. "We are to wait until he weakens, and then…take what we can."

Lena shut her eyes. I grabbed Marten, heedless of his magic. "Don't you dare kill Kiran! You said it yourself: this is *your* doing. If you hadn't given him to Ruslan—"

Marten pulled free. "I did not force Kiran to kill Stevan. That was his choice."

"Damn it, Marten! You need Kiran alive, with his mind intact. Not just for what he knows about demons—if you want Ruslan to burn before he destroys all Alathia, I'm telling you, Kiran is the only one who can make that happen."

"Don't you think I argued as much?" Real anguish lay in Marten's voice. "I must see Kiran's mind. If I can prove he killed Stevan to spare Melly, to save Ninavel—that is my best hope of appealing the Council's decision."

Yet he didn't sound at all confident he could do it. I glanced at the guards and lowered my voice to a hiss. "If you had any guts, you'd give Kiran that magic-blocking amulet back and a supply of the drug, take him across the border and let him go free." From what Kiran had said of the amulet, it'd work just fine to block his mark-bond if Ruslan wasn't actively looking for him. And Ruslan wouldn't look, thinking he already knew where Kiran was: captive in Alathia.

"It is not a matter of courage," Marten said tightly. "It is a matter of duty. I cannot break my oaths. Or I am no better than Talmaddis."

"You aren't," I snapped. "Stevan was right: you're happy to slither around Alathia's laws when it profits you. You let Ruslan kill a man for a translocation spell without a single protest. Now Kiran's killed a man for far greater reason, and you'll throw him into Shaikar's hells! But hey, you've killed half your team already, right? What's one more?"

Marten's control slipped. He raised a hand, grief and anger dark in his face, and I didn't know if he meant to hit me or cast against me.

Lena caught his arm. "*Marten.*" She looked at me. "Go back to the healers' cabin. They should have woken Melly by now. She'll want to see you. I will speak again with Kiran; he must see that yielding to Marten is his only hope, now."

She didn't look any more certain than Marten that yielding would save Kiran's life. I snarled, "Think on this, both of you: if Kiran dies, you condemn your whole fucking country with him."

I turned my back on them and stomped past the guards, wishing with every footfall that I was kicking Marten in the gut. I'd known I couldn't trust him to help Kiran. Yet each new time he proved it brought just as much rage as the first.

Why couldn't he see that Kiran was the key to stopping Ruslan? Shaikar take Marten! If he wouldn't free Kiran, I'd have to. Though even if I stole both amulet and drug under the noses of a camp full of mages, I didn't know how to get him past the border. From the peaks I'd glimpsed to the east above the cinnabar trees, we were in the middle of nowhere in southern Alathia, at least fifty miles from the nearest border gate at Loras. Alathian mages could walk through their border wards wherever they damn well pleased, but nobody else could.

As I approached the cabin the Watch had turned into a makeshift infirmary, I heard a child sobbing, in wild, gulping wails like her heart had shattered.

Melly! I sprinted the last distance and flung open the door.

She was curled in a ball on a cot beneath an open window, her body shaking with the force of her crying. Pello's son Janek stood staring down at her, his dark eyes wide. Cara knelt at Melly's side, a hand on her back, glaring at a group of uniformed Alathian mages. Some of the mages looked anxious, others irritated.

"Get Dev," Cara said. "She needs—" She saw me, and relief brightened her face. "Thank Khalmet, you're here."

"What's wrong?" I demanded.

"There is nothing wrong with her," said the oldest mage, a fat man with graying hair. He added in a tone of annoyed impatience, "She is merely overwrought."

Cara said, "It's her Taint, Dev. She says she can't feel it anymore."

The Change, already? No—*the Taint uses confluence energy,* Kiran had said, and there was no confluence here. The heart of her mind would be as dead as mine. Something she'd never before experienced, growing up in Ninavel. Worst of all, it would stay dead. Her true Change might still be days or even weeks off, but she would hit it long before she ever saw another confluence.

I hurried to Melly's cot and pulled her into my arms. She clawed at me and sobbed out a string of words so broken I couldn't understand them.

I didn't need to. I knew what she felt: that terrible emptiness like your soul had been torn away, the world turned to ashes and shadows. "It isn't fair," I whispered in her ear. "When it goes, it rips the life out of you. I won't lie, Melly…it hurts, and it's going to hurt, for a long time. But there are other joys in this world, and you'll find them." I thought of Jylla crouched at my side telling me I wanted to live, and felt my eyes grow hot and wet.

Melly kept crying, but her sobs were quieter, her grip not so desperate. I held her as the light through the window slowly failed, my own tears of regret leaking into her hair.

CHAPTER TWENTY-SEVEN

(Dev)

Someone gripped my arm. I started upright, a shout trapped in my throat.

"Shhh." Lena stood over me holding a dimly glowing magelight, Cara at her shoulder. Both cabin and window were dark. Melly lay curled on the cot before me, Janek on another next to her. I'd only meant to rest a moment while Cara went to ask the mages for some food for us, and then start hashing over plans to get Kiran free. But from the pitch darkness outside, I'd been asleep for hours.

Lena took her hand from my arm, and my voice unlocked. New worry shot through me at the determined urgency on her and Cara's faces. "What's going on?" I whispered. "Has Kiran let Marten—"

"No. Wait until I cast." Lena drew me away from Melly's cot, Cara crowding close behind her, and chanted a phrase. The cheeping whirr of nightbugs outside and the soft sounds of Melly and Janek's breathing hushed into silence.

Lena said to me, "If I did what you asked of Marten—if I gave Kiran the amulet and the drug, and passed him through the border—would you go with him?"

I stared at her, wondering if this was some crazy dream. "You would free Kiran?" Helping me with Red Dal in Ninavel had been one thing, but I'd never imagined to see Lena break ranks with Marten to this extent.

Lena said, "You may be right that Kiran is Alathia's best hope. But even if Kiran relents and allows Marten to search his mind, I do not think the

Council will change their decision. Councilor Niskenntal has argued too well that Kiran's mark-bond makes him a risk Alathia cannot afford. Marten knows the chances are extremely slim, but…I think he is so desperate to believe he can save Kiran, that he is letting that desperation blind him."

She took a deep breath, her ringed hands lacing tightly together. "When Marten gave Kiran to Ruslan, you said that I had a choice, and yet I did nothing. This time…this time I will not stand by again. Not when holding to my oaths might mean my country's destruction. But I do have two conditions. One is that you must go with him."

Go with Kiran. The implications of that simple statement unfolded like a deadly, razor-edged flower. Go take on Ruslan without the Watch's help… but that wasn't all. I knew what she was really asking of me.

"You want me to stop Kiran going back to Ruslan and blood magic."

"Yes." Pain lurked in the word. "Kiran might think returning to Ruslan is the best way to prevent disaster, but you know how terrible an error his return would be."

"Hell yes, I know it. But what makes you think I can make him understand?" I sure hadn't had much success earlier.

Lena said, "He's seen your memories. He knows all you have done for him, and what you've sacrificed. He'll listen to you, reluctant though he may be at first, and he won't want to expose you to Ruslan's anger. My other condition is for him, and it will help in this…but Marten was right. You are the only one who can guide him to save not only Alathia, but himself. The Kiran I knew in Tamanath—I can't bear to think of him lost forever."

She talked like I could somehow snap my fingers and make Kiran into that person again. I thought she was as blind as Marten; you couldn't reverse time. Not by erasing memories, not even by stuffing them back in Kiran's head the way Marten wanted. The choices Kiran had made in Ninavel had changed him, and he'd never be the same as he was beforehand. But I wouldn't challenge Lena on it. I'd keep my mouth shut and play along if it meant Kiran's survival.

Yet there was another problem, one I quailed to consider. I looked between Cara and Melly, who was frowning in her sleep, her hands knotted in her blanket and her cheeks still puffy from crying.

"Gods, Cara, what do I do? I can't leave Melly here—Khalmet only knows what the Alathians would do. But to take her along while we go against Ruslan…I can't risk her like that."

Cara said quietly, "You don't have to. Lena's agreed to take us all through the border: Kiran, you, me, Melly, even Janek. You'll go with Kiran, and I'll take Melly and Janek up north to the Tarnspike Mountains. I've got family there who'll take them in and treat them right."

The Tarnspike Mountains were way up near the northern border of Arkennland, a good three months' journey away. I wanted to argue, but damn it, I couldn't. I'd gone through all this to get Melly safe. She wouldn't be wholly safe in the Tarnspikes, not until we ensured no demon would come hunting, but she'd be a lot better off than at my side.

But to leave Melly—to leave *Cara*—loss set my heart aching. I'd thought Melly my one victory, and I'd longed so badly for the chance to savor it with Cara at my side.

Cara took my shoulders and bent her head against mine. "I don't want to part from you either. The minute I've got Melly and Janek settled, I promise you, it doesn't matter where you are—I'll ride so fast to reach you that you'll swear I had wings. I'll help you take down Ruslan...assuming you and Kiran haven't already tricked him into breaking his vows."

She sounded a hell of a lot more confident than I felt. I held her tight, wishing I could burn the feel of her so deeply into my memory that her touch would never leave me.

"Will you at least start the mountain crossing with us?" That way we could have a few last precious days together before she took the kids north.

She took my face in her hands, her thumbs tracing my cheekbones. "You think I'd give up even one instant with you?"

The lump in my throat felt as big as a boulder. My heart cried that a few days wasn't nearly enough time. Reason said it would have to be.

Reluctantly, I drew back and said to Lena, "I'm guessing the Watch will hunt us. Got any ideas on how to evade them? With two kids in tow, we won't be able to move fast."

Lena said, "Since you aren't mages, your soulfire is dim enough that Kiran's amulet can conceal all of you from seeking spells if you remain close to him. More, I believe Marten will do all he can to prevent any sustained search for you. I think some part of him is hoping for Kiran's escape. Otherwise he wouldn't have suggested the Watch use Kiran's amulet to help lessen the effects of the drug withdrawal."

Cara made a startled noise. "Wait. What about you—aren't you coming? Dev will need your help."

"Now there's an understatement," I said. "We could sure use a mage who can actually spellcast. Kiran can't cast once across the border, or Ruslan will know where he is." Kiran had told me the amulet could only hide him from Ruslan so long as he used no magic.

Lena shook her head. "If I came with you, the Watch would not relent in their hunt until I was captured. The Council can't risk an officer of the Watch turning renegade; we know far too much of Alathia's defenses. If I stay, Marten has a far better chance of convincing the Council to abandon the search."

I said, "But...if you stay, won't the Council find out you were the one to sneak us across the border?" Suliyya grant she wasn't planning on marching straight to her own mindburning like Talm had intended to do.

Lena said, "You needn't fear for me. If Kiran agrees to my condition, I will be safe enough."

"What condition?" I asked.

"It has two parts. First, he must let me give him what I can of his old memories."

"How? You weren't one of those who cast at his trial." She'd played watchdog over me the whole time.

She said, "I asked Marten to share with me the memories he thought most important, in case I could get Kiran to agree to accept them from me rather than him."

"He wasn't suspicious at all?" Marten was far too smart not to wonder.

"Perhaps he was," Lena said, with a faint, wry smile. "But I think it is like the amulet. He puts the conditions in place and hopes, while observing the letter of his duty."

"So he'll let you be the one to get mindburned if something goes wrong." Khalmet's hand, what a bastard!

"Marten is already under far too much scrutiny," Lena said. "Niskenntal is calling for him to be stripped of his captaincy and to undergo a criminal trial. He claims Marten violated his oaths in saving Kiran, that Marten put his personal desires over Alathia's safety. Niskenntal is not Marten's only enemy; Marten has a difficult enough battle ahead of him. While I...I have more freedom to act."

Freedom. Far as I could tell, nobody had any of that in Alathia. "Don't risk it, Lena. Come with us—you don't have to stay here. So the Watch will hunt us...we'll figure something out."

"That's not my only reason," she said. "I must do what I think will help my country most. Kiran may be Alathia's best hope, but he is not our only hope. Marten and I have other ideas on how to counter Ruslan, and Marten will need my help to set those plans in motion."

Cara said, "It won't help Alathia if you get mindburned. I still don't see how you'll avoid that."

Lena said, "Once through the border, Kiran must destroy my memory of this last day and leave me unconscious for the Watch to find. They will see the damage in my mind and the traces of blood magic, and assume Kiran forced me into helping him escape."

That was disturbing on so many levels I didn't even know where to start. To *ask* someone to fuck up your mind…Khalmet's bloodsoaked hand! I felt like fire ants were crawling over me just thinking about it.

Cara said, "Afterward, you won't know either, will you? You'll think Kiran proved himself every bit a blood mage, and you'll hate him for hurting you."

"Perhaps," Lena said. "Though again, Marten and I may suspect otherwise…but the Council will have no proof to condemn me." She looked at me. "Kiran will live, and I will have given both you and Alathia the best chance I can. The sacrifice is one I'm willing to make."

I wanted to protest Lena's decision; if nothing else, because the thought of facing Ruslan when Kiran couldn't cast to protect us was enough to turn my spine to ice. But I could see in Lena's face that Cara and I could argue 'til the Whitefires crumbled to dust and it wouldn't change her mind.

Lena said, "I'm going to Kiran now. Consider what supplies you will need; if he agrees, we leave soon."

"How will you get us out of the camp?" There had to be at least thirty mages here. Hard to imagine we'd be able to steal enough supplies for three adults and two kids and tiptoe off into the woods without a single one of them noticing.

Another faint smile touched Lena's mouth, though it didn't warm her eyes. "I will not. Kiran will."

✳

I paced between cots in the darkened cabin, trying to walk quietly so I wouldn't wake Janek. We'd left him sleeping; Melly, we'd woken, and told an abbreviated version of our plan. She'd only said dully, *Good. I don't want to stay here. They look at me like I'm some bug they'd rather squash.* Now she sat slumped on her cot, staring at something only she could see. Cara leaned against the window, peering out at the dim magelights held by the guards around Kiran's cabin.

"Any sign of Lena?" I asked. She'd been inside with Kiran for a good half hour now. I'd warned her he'd assume her offer of escape was a trick. She said if he balked at letting her into his head straight off, she would offer to prove her sincerity by first taking us to the border—but he had to let her give him his memories before she'd take us through.

"Not that I can see—wait." Cara sucked in a breath. "Dev. Come look."

I hurried to the window. The guards outside Kiran's cabin had their hands raised, their rings glowing. One of them shouted something. Mages poured out of nearby cabins in response, Marten among them.

"Oh, shit." The guards must've caught Lena out somehow. Khalmet's hand, what would we do now? Melly had turned to watch us, her small body gone tight. I moved for the door, not sure what I meant to do, but certain I couldn't just sit here and watch our plans fall to ruin.

Cara caught my shoulder. "Remember what Lena said."

Lena had made us promise not to leave the cabin until we saw Kiran leave his, no matter what. "You really think this is part of her plan?"

"I don't know, but I think you shouldn't go charging out there."

Reluctantly, I returned to the window. Melly slid up against my side to peer out. I gave her shoulders a reassuring squeeze, praying Cara's faith in Lena was warranted.

Lena emerged from Kiran's cabin. Marten stepped forward to meet her. My nerves settled a little at the calm assurance of her body language as they talked. After a moment, Marten called an order to the crowd of mages. Silent and purposeful, they formed a circle about Kiran's cabin. Lena and Marten backed to join them.

The mages started singing. Silver light flickered over the wards around Kiran's cabin door.

Abruptly, the song cut off. Magelights and rings alike went dark. Every mage in the circle collapsed to the ground, including Marten. Lena was the only one left standing.

I held my breath, waiting for cries of alarm, for magefire—but nothing happened. The camp stayed dark and silent.

The cabin door opened, and Kiran staggered out, weaving like a drunk. Lena caught him, helped him pick his way through the downed mages.

I said hastily to Melly, "Wake Janek. I need you to watch out for him in this, same as you did with the littlies in the den."

She nodded, and I was glad to see a spark of resolution in her eyes. Helping Janek might help her fight despair. As boss Tainter in Red Dal's den she had plenty of experience in cajoling younger kids through difficult situations.

I ran outside to meet Lena and Kiran. "How the hell did you pull that off?" I asked, pointing at the sprawled bodies.

Lena let Kiran slide to the ground. He was breathing through clenched teeth, pain in every line of his body. I didn't think he'd seen those memories yet. What I could see of his face was merely wary, not stunned or anguished.

Lena said, "I told Marten that the guards and I had caught Kiran breaking a ward and we needed to recast them to a far stronger level. All the Watch is needed for such a casting, and we link minds to complete it. When we began casting, I let Kiran into my mind, and he used my link to pull soulfire from every mage here, enough to send them unconscious."

She looked down at Kiran, who had curled in on himself, his hands pressed to his temples. "He needs another dose of the drug, right away. I'll get the drug and the amulet, and then break the wards for you on our supply stores."

I wanted to demand she bring the Taint charm along with the amulet. The Alathians had taken it from me at the border, back when I'd been too dizzy and nauseated from their translocation spell to put up much of a protest. I knew I couldn't wear the charm for more than bare instants without serious damage, but I hated to give up a weapon...or the pure, delirious joy of feeling the Taint once more.

Then again, Ruslan had made the charm. If I took it back into Arkennland, would he know? I wouldn't put it past him to have put some kind of find-me spell in the damn thing.

Well. If Kiran could give up blood magic, I could give up this. "How long before the mages wake?"

Kiran answered, his voice strained. "A few hours at most. We should hurry."

Thank Khalmet, the Alathians were as meticulous about the organization of their stores as they were in everything else. They didn't have ropes or mountain gear, but they had food, charms, blankets, and warm clothing, and that was enough. Cara and I shoved as much as we could into packs and rigged up a sling from a sliced-up carriage harness so we could carry Janek. His short legs would never keep our pace. Melly had him well in hand. As she moved about helping us pack, he stuck so close to her side you couldn't have fit a piton between them.

By the time we finished, Kiran had recovered enough to help us too. Lena had given him the amulet already; I could see the lump of it beneath his shirt. When we started off into the darkness beneath the cinnabar pines, I flashed him a grin and said, "Just like old times. Nothing like a death march in the dark."

He looked away, his shoulders hunching, and I sighed. Just like old times, indeed. It had been hard enough for us to trust each other then.

The forest was open, the only undergrowth between the pine trunks a mix of ferns and furry-leafed silverweed. Lena's magelight made the night travel easy. I carried Janek in the sling, and Melly matched our pace without complaint. But she was silent, never once looking up from her feet, and I knew how deep her pain still ran.

Soon enough we heard the river. When the rush of the water grew loud, Lena stopped next to a dead cinnabar pine. Moonlight filtered down through the gap in the canopy, bright enough the ferns cast soft shadows.

"The border is here." She waved a hand at the air behind her. I couldn't see anything different about it, but Kiran was squinting like a man staring into the sun.

Lena turned to him. "I've proved my good faith in taking you here. Before I take you across and give you a supply of the drug, you must fulfill the first part of our agreement."

Kiran was still for so long I feared he would refuse. Yet in the end, he reached for the knife at his belt. She put her hand over his.

"I don't need blood contact. Not if you release your barriers." Lena glanced at us. "This will take a moment. Rest while you can."

Janek was asleep in the carry-sling, his body warm against my back. I eased myself down into the ferns, my heart thudding. I knew one memory Marten would have been sure to pick, and I didn't envy Kiran one bit for having to relive it.

※

(Kiran)

Lena took Kiran's hands in hers. A gentle touch ghosted over his barriers like a soft knock against a door.

Every instinct in him screamed against lowering them. A panicked voice yammered within, insisting this could still be a ruse on the part of Martennan. *They bound you, hurt you, and they will do it again…*

But the border waited beyond, a deep, soundless thrum of magic he hadn't the power to break on his own. Dev, Cara, and Melly watched him, silent and waiting. If Dev's memories were true, he owed them the chance at freedom.

If Dev's memories were true…the pain in his head was nothing to the pain in his heart. Ruslan, Lizaveta, Mikail…they were his *family*. To think they had hurt him so terribly, when he'd been so certain of their love…how could it be true? And Alisa, who'd supposedly been his lover and died at Ruslan's hands…he'd seen his own grief and anger and guilt through Dev's eyes, but it felt no more real than a scry-vision. Had he really fallen in love with a *nathahlen* despite all Ruslan's warnings? He found it impossible to fathom. He remembered nothing of her, didn't even know what she looked like.

Doubtless he was about to find out. Slowly, nervously, Kiran dropped his barriers. Lena slid into his mind, her cool, quiet presence reminding him of Mikail's. She reached for the damaged web of his memories.

I can fill only a few of these voids for you...but I hope it is enough.

A shining set of memories rolled over him, bright and beautiful and full of joy. A slender Arkennlander girl, her amber eyes alive with curiosity, her smile dazzling in its radiance...Alisa. Laughing with him, sharing her favorite volumes of adventure tales, talking with wistful eagerness of the lands she hoped to explore; and all the while, he'd been so *happy*, so amazed by her eager intelligence, so captivated by the world seen through her eyes: a place where love did not have to coexist with cruelty, where every life held value. Later, he'd reveled in the softness of her lips, the gentle coaxing of her hands, her eyes dark with pleasure as they savored each others' bodies in a sweet, stolen moment...

He wanted more, *more*, but he felt Lena's regret. *I am sorry, Kiran. I have only this last one.*

A new memory welled up. He was standing before Ruslan's workroom, the *akhelashva* ritual about to begin—

He knew what this memory would be. In Dev's mind, he'd seen himself standing amid the charred remains of Simon's spellwork, white-faced and stricken, shouting at Ruslan: *You stole not only her life from her, but her pain, her tears, her blood...*

He tried to recoil, to tear free. *No*, he begged Lena. *I don't want to see this. I don't want to know this—*

But her magic bore down on him, and he was too weak to stop her. The memory swallowed him, horrible and inexorable. Alisa, screaming agonized pleas he was helpless to answer, rage and horror beating behind his eyes as Ruslan mutilated her flesh—

He wrenched free of Lena and stumbled aside, gagging. Tears were wet on his face, his mind a black, confused whirl of images. Ruslan, cutting out Alisa's eye—his own knife stabbing deep into Stevannes's heart—

Kiran fell to his knees, shuddering. He wanted desperately to deny the memory of Alisa's death, to believe it was false, some Alathian trick...but he couldn't. He'd sensed not one false note in the thoughts of his past self. That was *him*. He'd watched her die...and then he'd forgotten her, let Ruslan seduce him into betraying everything she believed in. Even now, his soul hungered to cast again, to taste once more that delirious, unleashed flood of magic...he covered his face, a hoarse, anguished cry escaping him.

"Kiran." Lena laid gentle hands on his back. "It's in the past. You cannot change it. But you can change yourself."

Deep in his mind, a soft, insistent voice whispered, *Remember.* Something rose from the depths, pushing toward his consciousness—

No. With force born of terror and instinct, he shoved it back. He wanted no more revelations, no more horrors. He shook off Lena's hands and staggered to his feet. "You want me to forswear blood magic, yet you want me to burn out your memory. To…to hurt you, as Ruslan did me. How can you ask it of me, after this?"

Dev, Cara, and the children were watching him with wide, worried eyes. Lena said, "I do not ask it lightly. I'm sorry, Kiran. But come…spark your amulet, and I'll take you through the border."

He drew out the jeweled disc on its chain. The pattern within was intact, ready to be kindled and fueled with his own *ikilhia*. He sent a burst of power into the charm. It flared blue, spitting sparks, reacting against the magic of the border wards. He'd have to move away quickly once on the border's far side, lest the pattern be damaged to the point of failure.

Thinking of practicalities, he could block out the morass of confusion and pain that threatened to swallow him. One step at a time; he dared not think beyond that.

Lena took Kiran's hands again. Her magic washed over him, shrouding him in a shimmering wash of green. She backed, drawing him with her. The immense wall of power parted around them without even a flicker as she led him through. He hastily retreated from the border until the amulet cooled against his skin, its energies flowing smoothly again.

Lena brought the others to him, one by one. Dev said to Cara, "Take the kids and start; I'll follow with Kiran when we're done here."

He must not want Melly and Janek to watch Kiran hurt Lena. Just imagining it made Kiran cringe.

Lena handed him a warded silver flask and a folded piece of paper. "Here is all we had of the drug at the camp. Swallow one capful a day, and it should be enough to last you six weeks if you stay clear of confluences and spellcasting. I fear only Marten knows the drug's exact formulation, but I wrote down what information I could. I suggest you go to Prosul Akheba—the scholars there know enough of herbal and healing lore they may be able to safely wean you from the drug."

Prosul Akheba was just over the Varkevian border, in the red-rock desert beyond the southern end of the Whitefires. To travel so far south would eat up a frighteningly large chunk of time, but Kiran knew he had little choice.

Six weeks' supply of the drug wasn't enough to ensure success against Ruslan.

Kiran still couldn't believe he hadn't realized something was wrong in Ninavel. The sickness he'd felt after spellcasting, that had gotten worse with time instead of better—but he'd been so focused on his struggle to accept blood magic that he'd never thought to look for a physical cause for his discomfort.

He felt sick now, but it wasn't from the drug. Cara and the children had gone. Lena's face was calm, but he could see her *ikilhia* flickering. She was afraid.

"Don't," he said. "Don't ask this of me. Come with us."

Dev nodded. "It's not too late. We've enough supplies we could manage with you along."

Lena said, "No. This is my choice." She put her hands on Kiran's shoulders. "Not all gifts are pleasant, but this is a gift you give me, nonetheless." She leaned close and kissed his mouth before he could react, her lips butterfly-soft. "Twin gods preserve you, Kiran. I hope you find peace."

Kiran didn't think he'd ever find peace again, but he nodded tightly.

She released her defenses, leaving her mind wide open. *Do it.*

The echo of Stevannes's words stabbed him to the quick. Yet while he could feel Lena's fear, he also felt her determination, hard as spelled iron. He eased into her mind, cautious, reluctant. She did not flinch. He sought her memories, found them unguarded.

She'd asked him to destroy everything since they'd translocated from the cirque. He slid backward through her memory, searching for the translocation—and found a memory of Marten, sitting on a cot with his face buried in his hands, utter defeat in the slump of his shoulders.

I succeeded in our mission, Lena. Yet in every other way, I have failed. Alathia is in far worse danger now...and Niskenntal is right. If I had said nothing in the cirque and let Kiran die, Ruslan might never have realized the reason, and Alathia would remain safe. But I couldn't bear to let Kiran die, not when I was the one to cast him into darkness. I thought I could save him, as I couldn't save Reshannis...but now my oaths bind me, just as they did then, and I must watch Kiran's soulfire burn to ash.

Lena had said, *You chose rightly in the cirque. If we build our country's safety on the blood of sacrifices, how are we any different than mages like Ruslan?*

Marten had given a pained laugh. *I think we are not. Stevan's blood is already spilled...he would curse me for my choice, and I'm not sure he is wrong. But it is Talmaddis that I see when I close my eyes...he tells me that if only I hadn't been so blind, I could have turned him from his path in time to save them all. Talmaddis…How is it that I hate him for his deceit, and yet I miss him more than my own breath?*

Lena had said nothing, only wrapped her arms around Marten, her heart full of regret and concern and a deep, abiding friendship. He had returned her grip, desperate as if he clutched a lifeline. *I only thank the gods you survived, Lena. If I had lost you with all the others, I don't think I could bear it. Though if you choose to leave my Watch for another…I will understand. I think it better if you do…Niskenntal intends to destroy me over this, and I don't want to see you burned in the spillover.*

Lena had replied, *I will not leave, Marten. Do you think the bond of our friendship is so easily broken? I will stand by you in this fight, both against Ruslan and enemies closer to home. More than that…you need not shoulder your grief alone. I didn't love Talmaddis as you did, but I miss him too.*

That was the truth of her decision. She loved her country, yes; but she would not abandon her friend in his time of need. No more than Dev had abandoned Kiran.

A loyalty that still humbled Kiran, even as it lightened a little of the black chasm in his heart. He could only hope that one day he might repay it.

Kiran focused, readied himself. He couldn't cast to take Lena's pain, not without alerting Ruslan. *I'm sorry,* he told Lena. *This will hurt.*

I know. Acceptance radiated from her mind, stronger than her fear.

He took a piece of his own *ikilhia* and stoked it until it was a searingly bright coal. He touched the coal to Lena's memories.

A piece of her mind seared away; she screamed in agony, arching backward. Quickly, he siphoned power from her *ikilhia*, enough so she slumped unconscious in his arms.

"Is it done?" Dev's voice was tight.

"Yes." Kiran laid her gently on moonlit pine needles. "Forgive me," he whispered to her. He didn't know if he'd ever see her again. Perhaps…perhaps in some distant future they might meet in the peace she'd wished upon him.

Dev crouched at Lena's other side. He traced her cheek, drew his hand back. "She'll be all right?"

Kiran nodded, though it felt like a lie. If he didn't stop Ruslan, no Alathian would be all right. Nor would Dev, Cara, and Melly.

Dev stood and said shortly, "We should get moving."

Kiran followed, clinging to determination. Lena had wanted him to live. He would make certain she didn't regret her choice.

✳

(Dev)

I waded through knee-deep wildflowers, a quartet of empty waterskins dangling from my hands. The sun was rising, golden light spreading down the pale cliffs rearing high over the meadow. The wildflowers' riot of color ended in a lake whose water was so still as to be a perfect mirror for the fanged, snow-streaked peaks circling it. The sky above was a deep, pure blue, the air chill but holding the promise of warmth to come.

Kiran stood on a slanting mica-flecked boulder at lake's edge, looking out over the water. He was huddled into his overjacket, his arms crossed tight over his chest. I knelt beside his boulder and started filling the waterskins. Hushed voices broke the meadow's silence. Back at our campsite beneath a gaggle of stunted little pines, Cara was helping Melly and Janek pack up their sleeping blankets.

We hadn't yet hashed out this business of Ruslan and demons, what with Kiran needing all his breath and energy just to keep up. The drug might've saved his life, but he was still weak, slower even than the kids. We'd pressed hard for two days, snatching only brief moments of rest as we climbed ever higher into the mountains. By the time we reached timberline, Kiran was stumbling and glassy-eyed with exhaustion. Cara and I had judged it best to catch up on sleep before pushing on into terrain where a stumble from tiredness could mean a fall that would kill.

"You feel any more spellwork seeking us?" I asked Kiran.

"None strong enough to pierce the amulet's warding." His voice sounded husky, and when he turned to me, his eyes were wet. He twitched a hand at the lake and its backdrop of soaring mountains. "I wish Alisa could have seen this."

It was as much an admission as an expression of regret. If he'd accepted that Alisa was real..."You believe us, then? You won't go running off to Ruslan the moment my back's turned?" Cara and I had been worried enough about it that we'd slept in shifts to keep a constant eye on him.

"No." Kiran hugged himself all the tighter. "You, Lena, Cara—all of you have such faith in me. But...Ruslan is so strong. I know I must stop him, but I keep fearing...what if I can't?"

"You can," I said. "Know why? Because you won't be taking him on alone. Ruslan's scary as shit, I'll give you that. But I'm telling you: together, we'll find a way to send him to Shaikar's hells, no matter how strong his magic." Standing in the heart of the Whitefires' wild beauty, I believed anything was possible.

Hell, look at Melly…these last months I'd despaired about a thousand times over that I'd never save her, and yet here she was, alive and whole.

Kiran slanted me a glance, and a little of the tension eased from his body. "I hope you're right," he said softly. "Regardless…I thank you. It does help, to know I'm not alone."

I'd learned that lesson thanks to Cara. Thinking of our coming parting, my throat tightened. I took a deep breath of crisp mountain air and put aside sadness. Cara was here now, and so was Melly; I'd make the most of the time we had left. I stood with Kiran, watching sunlight spill down stone, and let the new day fill my heart with hope.

ACKNOWLEDGEMENTS

Thanks to the long-suffering members of my critique group: Carol Berg, Curt Craddock, Catherine Montrose, Susan Smith, and Brian Tobias. They waded through massive chunks of horrifically rough draft without a single word of complaint over the work involved, all while providing their usual stellar critique. I still can't believe how lucky I am to have critique partners with such keen eyes for flaws and such patience for dispensing advice to an excitable newbie author. Susan in particular deserves more thanks than I could possibly express for providing critiques of re-written chapters on super-short notice and listening so readily to all my worries and woes.

Similarly, thanks once again to Teresa Frohock, who sprang to my aid whenever I needed it and has been a font of friendship and support. Thanks also to Jeanne Atwell, not only for her steadfast friendship but her excellent reading recommendations. And thanks to fellow moms Maria Mitchell and Karen Hodgekinson-Price for their generous offers to watch my son when I lacked other childcare; without them, I might never have finished this book.

Enormous thanks to my hardworking agent, Becca Stumpf, who helped me weather many a crisis with her usual mix of patience, creativity, and enthusiasm. And it takes a lot of work to turn a manuscript into a book: thanks to Jeremy Lassen, Ross Lockhart, Liz Upson, Tomra Palmer, Amy Popovich, and the rest of the Night Shade gang for all their efforts behind the scenes. Special thanks to Dave Palumbo, for his stunning art and his patience and responsiveness to requests.

Thanks to everyone out there who read and enjoyed The Whitefire Crossing, especially those who sent emails to tell me how much you loved the book. It's truly amazing how an email like that can brighten even the darkest of days.

My undying gratitude and love to my husband Robert, who continues to hang in there no matter how crazy our lives get. Life is truly sweeter when shared with a partner, and there's none better than you.

Night Shade Books is an Independent Publisher of Quality Science-Fiction, Fantasy and Horror

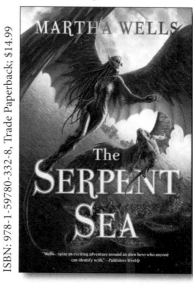

Night Shade Books is an Independent Publisher of Quality Science-Fiction, Fantasy and Horror

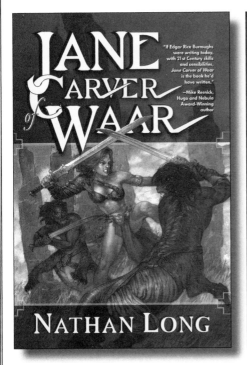
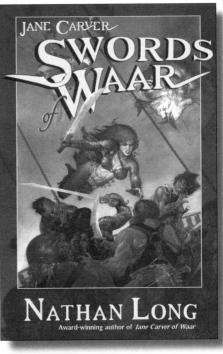

ABOUT THE AUTHOR

Courtney Schafer was born in Georgia, raised in Virginia, and spent her childhood dreaming of adventures in the jagged mountains and sweeping deserts of her favorite fantasy novels. She escaped the East Coast by attending Caltech for college, where she obtained a B.S. in electrical engineering, and also learned how to rock climb, backpack, ski, scuba dive, and stack her massive book collection so it wouldn't crush anyone in an earthquake. After college she moved to the climber's paradise of Boulder, Colorado, and somehow managed to get a masters degree in electrical engineering from the University of Colorado in between racking up ski days and peak climbs.

She now works in the aerospace industry and is married to an Australian scientist who shares her love for speculative fiction and mountain climbing. She's had to slow down a little on the adrenaline sports since the birth of her son, but only until he's old enough to join in. She writes every spare moment she's not working or adventuring with her family.

Visit her online at www.courtneyschafer.com.